Praise for Orcs:

'Wall to wall action . . . gritty and fast-paced'   David Gemmell

'High fantasy for readers who like their heroes ugly'
                                        Jon Courtenay Grimwood

'Fast, dirty, very funny, often surreal'   *Guardian*

'Buy now or beg for mercy later'   Tad Williams

'Excellent fantasy with a twist'   *SFX*

Also by Stan Nicholls from Gollancz:

Orcs: The Omnibus Edition

ORCS
BAD BLOOD

OMNIBUS

Weapons of Magical Destruction
Army of Shadows
Inferno

First published in Great Britain in 2013 by
Gollancz
An imprint of the Orion Publishing Group
Orion House, 5 Upper St Martin's Lane,
London WC2H 9EA
An Hachette UK Company

3 5 7 9 10 8 6 4 2

A CIP catalogue record for this book
is available from the British Library

ISBN 978 0 575 09282 2

Typeset at The Spartan Press Ltd,
Lymington, Hants

Printed and bound by CPI Group (UK) Ltd,
Croydon, CR0 4YY

The Orion Publishing Group's policy is to use papers
that are natural, renewable and recyclable products and
made from wood grown in sustainable forests. The logging
and manufacturing processes are expected to conform to
the environmental regulations of the country of origin.

www.stannicholls.com
www.orionbooks.co.uk
www.gollancz.co.uk

Contents

ORCS

BAD BLOOD I

Weapons of Magical Destruction

In fondest memory of
David Gemmell, 1948–2006

How the Wolverines
won their Freedom

Maras-Dantia abounded with a diversity of lifeforms. There were
inevitable conflicts between these elder races, but mutual respect
and tolerance maintained the social fabric.

Until a new race arrived.

They called themselves humans, and braved unfriendly wastelands to enter Maras-Dantia from the far south. Small in number
at first, over the years they grew to a torrent. They claimed the land
as their own, renamed it Centrasia, and set about exploiting its
resources. Rivers were polluted, forests stripped and elder race
settlements destroyed. They showed contempt for the cultures they
encountered, demeaning and corrupting the native inhabitants.

But their greatest crime was to defile Maras-Dantia's magic.

Their greed and disregard for the natural order of things began
to drain away the land's vital energies, diminishing the magic elder
races depended upon. This in turn warped the climate. Before
long, an ice field was advancing from the north.

So it came to war between the elder races and the humans.

The conflict was far from clear cut. Both sides were disunited.
Old divisions within the elder races resurfaced, and some even
threw in their lot with the incomers. The humans themselves
suffered from a religious schism. Some were Followers of the
Manifold Path, commonly known as Manis, and observed pagan
ways. Others adhered to the precepts of Unity. Dubbed Unis, they
supported the newer sect of monotheism. There was as much
animosity between Unis and Manis as between elder races and
humans.

One of the only native races without magical powers, orcs made
up for the deficiency with their superior martial skills and a savage
lust for combat.

Stryke captained a thirty-strong orc warband called the Wolverines. His fellow officers were Sergeants Haskeer and Jup, the latter the band's only dwarf member, and Corporals Alfray and Coilla, the group's sole female. The balance of the command consisted of twenty-five common grunts. The Wolverines were part of a greater horde serving despotic Queen Jennesta, a powerful sorceress who supported the Mani cause. The offspring of human and nyadd parents, Jennesta's taste for sadism and sexual depravity were legendary.

Jennesta sent the band on a perilous mission to seize an ancient artefact from a Uni stronghold. The Wolverines gained the artefact, which proved to be a sealed message cylinder, along with a cache of an hallucinogenic drug called pellucid. But Stryke made the mistake of letting his band celebrate by sampling the drug. The following dawn, returning late to Jennesta and fearing her wrath, they were ambushed by kobold bandits who stole the artefact. Knowing they would pay a terrible price for their negligence, Stryke decided to pursue the raiders.

Assuming treachery by the Wolverines, Jennesta declared them outlaws and ordered their capture, dead or alive. She also established contact with her brood sisters, Adpar and Sanara, with whom she was linked telepathically. But bad blood between the siblings prevented Jennesta discovering if either knew the whereabouts of the band or the precious artefact.

During the search for the kobolds, Stryke began to experience lucid visions. They showed a world consisting solely of orcs, living in harmony with nature and in control of their own destiny. Orcs who knew nothing of humans or the other elder races.

He feared that he was going insane.

Locating the kobolds, the Wolverines exacted bloody revenge and regained the artefact. They also liberated an aged gremlin scholar called Mobbs, who thought the cylinder might contain something that had a direct bearing on the origin of the elder races. He believed the cylinder was connected with Vermegram and Tentarr Arngrim, two fabled figures from Maras-Dantia's past. Vermegram was a sorceress, and the nyadd mother of Jennesta, Adpar and Sanara. She was thought to have been slain by Arngrim, a human whose magical abilities equalled hers.

Mobbs' words brought out a latent spirit of rebellion in the band, and Stryke successfully argued that the cylinder be opened. Inside was an object fashioned from an unknown material, consisting of a central sphere with seven tiny radiating spikes of variable length. To the orcs it resembled a stylised star, similar to a hatchling's toy. Mobbs explained that it was an instrumentality, a totem of great magical power long considered mythical. When united with its four fellows it would reveal a profound truth about the elder races, a truth which the legends implied could set them free. At Stryke's urging, the Wolverines abandoned their allegiance to Jennesta and struck out to seek the other stars, reasoning that even a fruitless search was better than the servitude they knew.

Their quest first led them to Trinity, a Uni settlement ruled by fanatical preacher Kimball Hobrow, where an instrumentality was revered as an object of worship. Seizing it, the band narrowly escaped and made for Scratch, the trolls' subterranean homeland, where they hoped a further star might be located.

Impatient with her own minions, Jennesta employed the services of Micah Lekmann, Greever Aulay and Jabez Blaan. Ruthless human bounty hunters who specialised in tracking renegade orcs, they undertook to return with the Wolverines' heads.

The band's expedition to Scratch was successful, and a third star was secured. But Haskeer, seized by a strange derangement, made off with them. Coilla, giving chase, fell into the hands of the bounty hunters, who negotiated to sell her to goblin slave traders. Haskeer himself, convinced that the stars were communicating with him in some way, was captured by Kimball Hobrow's zealous followers, the custodians.

Having rescued Coilla and Haskeer, the band learned that an instrumentality could be in the possession of a centaur called Keppatawn and his clan in Drogan Forest.

Jennesta stepped up the hunt for the Wolverines, including more dragon patrols under the direction of her mistress of dragons, Glozellan. She also maintained telepathic contact with her brood sisters, Adpar and Sanara, queens of their own domains in different parts of Maras-Dantia. Adpar, ruler of the underwater nyadd realm, was making war against a neighbouring race, the merz. Jennesta offered her an alliance to help find the stars, promising to share their power. Not trusting her sister, Adpar refused. Enraged, Jennesta used sorcery to cast a harmful glamour on her sibling.

7

On their way to Drogan, the band several times encountered an enigmatic human called Serapheim, who warned them of approaching perils before disappearing, seemingly impossibly.

Entering Drogan forest, the band made contact with the centaur Keppatawn. A renowned armourer hampered by lameness, Keppatawn had a star which he stole from Adpar when he was a youth. But a spell cast by her left him crippled, and only the application of one of her tears could right him. Keppatawn declared that if the Wolverines brought him this bizarre trophy he would trade the star for it. Stryke agreed.

The orcs made their way to the nyadd's domain. Nyadds and merz were at war, and Adpar had slipped into a coma as a result of Jennesta's magical attack. Fighting their way to her private chambers, the Wolverines found the queen on her deathbed, abandoned by her courtiers. When the cause looked lost, she shed a single tear of self-pity, which Stryke caught in a phial. The tear healed Keppatawn's infirmity, and he gave up the instrumentality.

Stryke's visions continued, and intensified, and he became preoccupied by the notion that the stars were singing to him.

The final instrumentality was housed in a Mani settlement called Ruffetts View, where a fissure had opened in the earth and was expelling raw magical energy. Once there, the band became a rallying point for disaffected orcs, many of them deserters from Jennesta's horde. Learning that two armies, Jennesta's and Hobrow Kimball's, were heading towards Ruffetts View, Stryke reluctantly allowed the deserters to join him. A siege ensued, and in the chaos of its aftermath the Wolverines made off with the last star.

When connected, the five artefacts formed a device that magically transported the band to Ilex, an ice-bound region in the extreme north of Maras-Dantia. In a fantastical ice palace they discovered Sanara, who proved benevolent, unlike her tyrannical sisters. She was held captive by the Sluagh, a pitiless race of near immortal demons who had pursued the instrumentalities for centuries. Unable to defeat the Sluagh, the orcs were imprisoned by them.

Their saviour appeared in the form of the mysterious Serapheim, revealed as the legendary sorcerer Tentarr Arngrim, father of Jennesta, Sanara and Adpar. Through him Stryke learnt that

Maras-Dantia was never the orcs' world, or the natural world of any of the elder races. Arngrim's ex-lover turned enemy, the sorceress Vermegram, brought orcs into Maras-Dantia to create her personal slave army. But the magical portals she opened also swept in members of other races from their own dimensions. Ironically, Maras-Dantia was and always had been the home world of humans.

Stryke's visions were not insanity but glimpses of his race's home world, brought on by contact with the powerful energy generated by the instrumentalities.

Tentarr Arngrim, trying to make amends for what humans had done, created the instrumentalities as part of a plan to return the elder races to their home dimensions. But the scheme was dashed and the stars scattered.

The sorcerer helped the Wolverines escape, and they managed to take the instrumentalities back from the Sluagh. A portal was located in the ice palace's cellars, and the sorcerer guided the band to it. But as he prepared to send them to the orcs' dimension Jennesta arrived with her army. A magical battle with Arngrim and Sanara on one side and Jennesta on the other ended with Jennesta consigned to the portal's fearsome vortex. The sorcerer queen was either torn apart by its titanic energy or flung into a parallel dimension.

Jup, the dwarf member of the Wolverines, chose to stay in the world he knew rather than cross to his race's home dimension. He and Sanara went off in hope of escaping under cover of the anarchy that engulfed the ice palace. For his part, Tentarr Arngrim elected to stay in the crumbing fortress and hold the Sluagh at bay while the others got away. Thrusting the instrumentalities into Stryke's hands, he set the portal for the orcs' dimension.

And the Wolverines stepped into the vortex . . .

1

Bilkers were the second most dangerous species in Ceragan. They had teeth like knife blades and hides as tough as seasoned leather. The only thing greater than their fearsome strength was their aggression.

The bilker being stalked by two of *the* most dangerous of Ceragan's inhabitants reared on its massive hind legs. Its scabby head brushed the crest of a tree that a flick of its barbed tail would have been powerful enough to fell.

'Think we can take it alone?' Haskeer whispered.

Stryke nodded.

'Looks like a mob-handed job to me.'

'Not if we're smart.'

'*Shit's* smarter than a bilker.'

'You should be all right then.'

Haskeer shot him a mystified glance.

They were fine specimens of orc adulthood, with imposing shoulders, expansive chests and a muscular build. Their craggy faces bore proudly thrusting jaws, and there was flint in their eyes. Both had fading scars on their cheeks where the tattoos signifying their rank, the marks of enslavement, had been purged.

The bilker thudded down on to four legs. It gave a watery growl and resumed lumbering. Trampling shrubbery, grating bark from trees it rubbed against, it began moving along the bottom of the valley.

Stryke and Haskeer emerged from the undergrowth, spears in hand, and followed stealthily. They were downwind, catching the noxious odour the beast exuded.

The orcs and their prey meandered for some distance. Occasionally, the bilker stopped and clumsily turned its head, as if suspecting their presence, but the orcs took care to stay out of sight. The creature gazed back along its wake, sniffed the air, then trudged on.

Passing a small copse, the bilker waded a pebbly stream. On its far side was a broad rocky outcrop, dotted with caves. To carry on the pursuit, Stryke and Haskeer had to break cover. Keeping low, they dashed for the shelter of a lichen-covered boulder. They were within five paces of it when the bilker swung its head round.

The orcs froze, mesmerised by the beast's merciless, fist-size eyes.

Hunters and hunted stood transfixed for an age. Then a change came over the creature.

'*It's bilking!*' Haskeer yelled.

The colour of the animal's skin started to alter. It took on the hue and mottled appearance of the sandy granite wall behind it. All except its swaying tail, which aped the green and brown of an adjacent tree. With increasing rapidity the bilker was blending into the background.

'*Quick!*' Stryke shouted. '*Before we lose it!*'

They ran forward. Stryke lobbed his spear. It struck square in the creature's flank, drawing a thunderous bellow from the wounded beast.

Camouflage was a bilker's principal defence, but far from all it relied on. Its fighting capacity was just as effective. Turning head on, it charged, the spear jutting from its bloodied side. As it splashed back across the stream, its cloaking ability, triggered by self-preservation and working overtime, continued to mirror the terrain. But with concealment giving way to attack, it functioned chaotically. The bilker's upper body still imitated the rock-face, while its bottom half mimicked the water. Charge gathering pace, its hide shimmering bizarrely, the creature's lower quarters seemed almost transparent.

Stryke and Haskeer stood their ground. Haskeer had held on to his spear, preferring to use it as a close range weapon. Stryke drew his sword.

They stayed put until the last possible second. When the bilker got close enough for them to feel a gust of its rank breath they dived clear; Haskeer to the left, Stryke to the right. Immediately they commenced harrying the animal from either side. Haskeer repeatedly thrust his spear, puncturing flesh. Stryke slashed with the blade, his strokes deep and wide.

Roaring, the bilker lashed out at them, spinning from one to the other, its great jaws snapping loudly. It raked the air with its claws, coming perilously close to shredding orc heads. And it brought its tail into play.

Haskeer felt the brunt. Whipping round shockingly fast, the tail struck him a glancing but potent blow. It knocked him flat and almost senseless, and parted him from his spear. The bilker moved in to finish the chore.

Stryke darted in and scooped up the spear. With a heave he drove it into one of the animal's hind legs. That proved enough of a distraction for Haskeer to be forgotten. The bilker turned about, its drooling jaws wide open, looking to tear its antagonist apart. Stryke had hastily sheathed his sword before reaching for the spear. Now he groped for it.

A throwing knife zinged into the side of the bilker's snout and the beast recoiled. It was enough of a sting to hinder the advance on Stryke. Haskeer was on his knees, plucking another knife. Stryke wrenched his sword free. The bilker came at him again. He saw inky black orbs floating in jaundice-yellow.

Stryke plunged his blade into the beast's eye. There was an eruption of viscous liquid and an unholy stink. The bilker mouthed a piercing shriek and pulled back, writhing in agony.

Haskeer and Stryke moved in and set to hacking at the animal's neck. They struck alternately, as though hewing the sturdy trunk of a fallen oak. The bilker thrashed and howled, its hide trans-muting through a succession of colours and patterns. One moment it faked the blueness of the summer sky, the next it copied the grass and earth of its deathbed. It briefly wore the image of Stryke and Haskeer as they laboured to stifle its life with their blades.

Just before they parted its head it settled for a coat of crimson.

Stryke and Haskeer backed off, panting. The bilker twitched, blood pumping from the stump of its neck.

The orcs slumped on a downed tree trunk and regarded their kill. They breathed the pure air of victory, and relished the way life seemed brighter, more immediate, after a kill.

They sat silently for some time before Stryke became fully alert to where they were. A stone's throw away stood the gaping mouth of the largest cave. Not for the first time he reflected on how often he was drawn to the spot.

Haskeer noticed too, and looked uncomfortable. 'This place gives me the creeps,' he confessed.

'I thought nothing spooked you.'

'Tell anybody and I'll tear your lungs out. But don't you feel it? Like a foul taste. Or the smell of carrion. And I don't mean the bilker.'

'Yet we still come here.'

'*You* do.'

'It reminds me of the Wolverine's last mission.'

'All it reminds me of is the way we arrived. I'd like to forget that.'

'Granted it was . . . troubling.' Stryke flashed the memory of their crossing, as he thought of it, and suppressed a shudder.

Haskeer's eyes were fixed on the cave's black maw. 'I know we came to this land through there. I don't understand how.'

'Nor me. Except for what Serapheim said about it being like doors. Not to billets, but worlds.'

'How can that be?'

'That's a question for his sort, for sorcerers.'

'*Magic.*' From Haskeer, it was an expression of contempt. He all but spat the word.

'It got us here. That's all the proof we need.' Stryke indicated their surroundings with a sweep of his hand. 'Unless all this is a dream. Or the realm of death.'

'You don't think . . . ?'

'No,' He reached down and yanked a fistful of grass. Grinding it in his palm, he blew the chaff from his stained fingers. 'This is real enough, isn't it?'

'Well, I don't like not knowing. It makes me . . . uneasy.'

'How we came here is a mystery beyond an orc's grasp. Accept it.'

Haskeer seemed less than pleased with that. 'How do we know that thing's safe? What's to stop it happening again?'

'It'd need the stars to work. Like a key. It was the *stars* that did it, not this place.'

'You should have destroyed 'em.'

'I'm not sure we could. But they're kept safe, you know that.'

Haskeer grunted sceptically and continued staring at the cave mouth.

They sat like that for a while, neither speaking.

It was quiet, save for the rustling of small animals and the faint chirruping of insects. Flocks of birds flapped lazily overhead as they made for their nesting grounds. With the sun going down, the evening was growing cooler, though that didn't stop a cloud of flies gathering over the bilker.

Haskeer sat up. 'Stryke.'

'What?'

'Do you see . . . ?' He pointed at the cave.

'I can't see anything.'

'*Look.*'

'It's just your fancy. There's noth—' A movement caught Stryke's eye. He strained to make out what it was.

There were tiny pinpoints of light inside the cave. They swirled and flickered, and seemed to be getting brighter and more numerous.

The orcs got to their feet.

'Feel that?' Stryke said.

The ground was shaking.

'Earthquake?' Haskeer wondered.

The vibrations became stronger as a series of tremors rippled the earth, and their source was the cave. In its interior the specks of luminosity had coalesced into a glowing multicoloured haze that throbbed in unison.

Then there was an intense blast of light. A powerful gust of blistering wind roared from the cave. Stryke and Haskeer turned their faces from it.

The light died. The trembling ceased.

A shroud of silence descended. No birds sang. The insects quietened.

Something stirred inside the cave.

A figure emerged. It walked stiffly, moving their way.

'I *told* you, Stryke!' Haskeer bellowed.

They drew their blades.

The figure was near enough to reveal itself. They saw what it was, and the recognition hit them like a kick in the teeth.

The creature was quite young, insofar as it was possible to tell with that particular race. Its hair was a shock of red, and its features were flecked with disgusting auburn spots. It was dressed for genteel work, certainly not for combat. No weapon could be seen.

Cautiously, they edged forward, swords raised.

'Careful,' Haskeer cautioned, 'might be more.'

The figure came on. It didn't so much walk as lurch, and it gaped at them. With an effort, it raised an arm. But then it staggered, legs buckling, and fell. The ground was uneven, and it rolled a way before finally coming to rest.

Warily, Haskeer and Stryke approached.

Stryke lightly toed the body. Getting no response, he booted it a couple of times. It lay still. He crouched and felt for a pulse in the creature's neck. There was nothing.

Haskeer tore his attention away from the cave. He was agitated. 'What's this thing doing here?' he wanted to know. 'And what killed it?'

'Nothing obvious I can see,' Stryke reported, examining the corpse. 'Here, give me a hand.'

Haskeer knelt beside him and they turned the body over.

'There's your answer,' Stryke said.

The human had a knife in its back.

2

They ventured into the cave to make sure there were no more humans lying in wait.

There was a lingering smell of something like sulphur in the surprisingly large, high-roofed interior. But the gloom proved empty.

They went back to the body.

Stryke stooped, took hold of the dagger and tugged it from the corpse's back. He wiped the blood on the dead man's coat. The blade had a slight curve, and its silver hilt was engraved with symbols he didn't recognise. He thrust it into the ground.

They turned the body over again. The colour was draining from its face, making the ginger hair and freckles all the more striking.

The human wore an amulet on a thin chain about its neck. It bore symbols different to the ones on the dagger, but they were unfamiliar too. There was nothing in the pockets of the corpse's jacket or breeches. Nor did it have a weapon of any kind.

'Not exactly kitted out for a journey,' Haskeer remarked.

'And no stars.'

'So much for them being a key.'

'Wait.'

Stryke pulled off one of the man's boots. Holding it by the heel, he shook it, then tossed it aside. When he did the same with the other boot, something fell out. It was the size of a duck's egg and wrapped in dark green cloth.

The object bounced and landed nearest Haskeer. He made to reach for it, but checked himself. 'What if—?'

'He doesn't look too dangerous,' Stryke said, nodding at the corpse. 'Same probably goes for whatever's in his boot.'

'You never know with his kind,' Haskeer replied darkly.

'Well, we have to find out some time.' Stryke scooped the thing up.

Once the cloth was unwound, instead of some smaller version of the stars, as they half expected, they found a gemstone. Whether it was precious, or deceiving glass, they couldn't say. It covered an orc's palm, and it was weighty. One side was flat, the other multifaceted, and at first they thought it was black. Looking closer, they saw that the gem was the colour of darkest red wine.

'Have a care,' Haskeer warned.

'Seems harmless enough.' Stryke ran his fingers across its shiny surface. 'I wonder if— *Shit!*' He tossed the gem away.

'What is it? What happened?'

'Hot!' Stryke complained, blowing on his hand and waving it around. '*Damn* hot.'

The gemstone lay on the grass. It appeared redder than before.

'It's doing something, Stryke!' Haskeer had his sword out again. Stryke forgot his pain and stared.

The gem had a glow about it. Suddenly, silently, it sent up a beam, not so much of light as something resembling smoke. Disciplined smoke, pale as snow, that flowed in a perfectly straight column, untroubled by the evening breeze. At the top of the column, taller than the orcs, the creamy smoke formed a large oval shape. It swirled and shimmered.

'It's a hex!' Haskeer yelled, and would have dashed the gem with his blade.

'*No!*' Stryke protested. 'Wait! *Look.*'

The pillar of smoke issuing from the gem had changed colour from white to blue. As they watched, the blue gave way to red, and the red to gold. Every few seconds the hue changed, so that the column hosted all colours in rapid succession. In turn these bled into the egg-shaped cloud suspended above their heads, giving it a rich vibrancy.

Haskeer and Stryke were mesmerised by it.

The coloured haze took on the appearance of solidity, as though it were a canvas hanging in the air. A canvas upon which a deranged artist had hurled pots of paint. But order soon swept away the chaos, and a distinct feature came into focus.

A human face.

It belonged to a male. He had shoulder-length auburn hair, and a beard, trimmed short. His eyes were blue, his nose hawkish, and his well shaped mouth was almost feminine.

'It's him!' Haskeer exclaimed. 'Serapheim!'

Stryke needed no confirmation. He, too, instantly recognised Tentarr Arngrim.

The sorcerer was of indefinite age to an orc's eye, but they knew him to be much older than he appeared. And no matter how alien a race humanity might be, the man's presence and authority were obvious to them, even filtered through an enchanted gem.

'*Greetings, orcs.*' Arngrim spoke as clearly as if he stood before them.

'You're supposed to be dead!' Haskeer shouted.

'I don't think he can hear you. This isn't . . . now.'

'What?'

'His likeness has been poured into that gemstone somehow.'

'You mean he *is* dead?'

'Just *listen.*'

'*Don't be afraid,*' the wizard's image went on. '*I realise how foolish a thing that is to say to a race as courageous as yours. But be assured that I mean you no harm.*'

Haskeer looked far from comforted. They kept their swords raised.

'*I'm speaking to you now because the stone was designed to be activated once it detected the presence of Stryke.*' Arngrim smiled, adding mellifluously, '*I hope this is so, and that you can hear my words, Captain of the Wolverines. I can't see or hear you, as should already have been explained by Parnol, the emissary who delivered this message. He's a trusted acolyte. And don't be deceived by his youth. He's wise beyond his years, and brave, as you'll find.*' The sorcerer smiled again. '*Forgive me if this embarrasses you, Parnol; I know how you dislike a fuss.*'

Stryke and Haskeer glanced at the messenger's body.

'*Parnol's role, as I expect he's already told you, was not only to bring you the gem, but to act as your guide, should you agree to my proposal.*'

'Guide?' Haskeer said.

'*What Parnol wouldn't have told you is the nature of the task,*' the sorcerer continued. '*I judged it best to present that myself.*' He paused, as though collecting his thoughts. '*You believed me to be dead, perhaps. The circumstances in which we parted must certainly have led you to that conclusion. But I had the good fortune, and the necessary skills, to survive the destruction of the palace at Ilex. My story isn't important at the moment, however. Of much more significance is the reason I've sought you out, and the point of this message.'*

''Bout time,' Haskeer grumbled.

'Ssshh!'

'On the principle that a picture outweighs a torrent of words, consider this.'

Arngrim vanished. He was replaced by a kaleidoscope of images. Scenes of orcs being whipped, hanged, burnt alive or cut down by cavalry. Orcs fleeing, their lodges plundered and their livestock scattered. Orcs herded like animals, to internment or slaughter. Orcs humiliated, mocked, beaten, put to the sword.

In every case, their tormentors were human.

'I feel shame for my race,' said Arngrim, his voice accompanying the imagery. *'Too often we act like beasts. What you see is happening now. These outrages are taking place in a world similar to yours. But a world less fortunate, where orcs are dominated by cruel oppressors and have had their freedom stolen, as yours was.'*

'Orcs fucked over by humans,' Haskeer muttered. 'What's new?'

'You can aid your fellow creatures,' the sorcerer told them. *'I'm not saying it would be easy, but your martial skills, your valour, might even help bring about their liberation.'*

Haskeer grunted charily. Stryke shot him a glare.

'Why would you want to undertake such a mission? Well, if the plight of your orc comrades isn't enough, look upon something else you know.'

The scenes of persecution and destruction faded. They were replaced by a female form, not entirely human, nor totally of any other race. Her eyes were somewhat oblique and unusually long-lashed, and they had dark, immeasurable depths. Her aquiline nose and shapely mouth were set in a face a little too flat and broad, framed by waist-length hair the colour of squid's ink. Most striking was the texture of her skin, which had a faint glistening of green and silver, giving the impression that she was covered in minute scales. She was beautiful, but her allure was just this side of freakishness.

'Jennesta,' the wizard supplied unnecessarily.

The sight of her chilled Stryke and Haskeer's spines.

'Yes, she survived the portal. I don't know how. And even though she's my own offspring, my bitterest regret is that she lived.' Jennesta was shown riding a black chariot at the head of a triumphant parade; addressing a frenzied crowd from the balcony of a palace; presiding at a mass execution. 'Let me be blunt. Her continued existence is a bigger problem than the fate of your kin, no matter how dire their situation. Because if left unchecked, she'll enslave more, of your kind and mine. Alone, I'm unable to defeat Jennesta. But it could be within your power, perhaps, to stop her, and to gain your revenge. If you choose that path, Parnol will thoroughly brief you. But he'll need the instrumentalities you possess if he's to be your guide. His journey to your world was one-way. I trust you still have them, else the enterprise is doomed before it's begun.' Arngrim smiled again. 'Somehow, I think you do.'

'Know-all,' Haskeer mumbled.

A fresh image emerged: five perfect spheres of different colours, each the size of a newborn's fist. They were fashioned from an unknown material. All had projecting spikes of variable lengths, and no two spheres had the same number. 'The instrumentalities, or stars, as you choose to call them, have remarkable powers. Greater even than I was aware of when I created them. Though perhaps I should have known, given how bringing them into being drained me of so much. It was the kind of achievement sorcerers have only once in a lifetime. I could never construct another set. But note. Although rare, the instrumentalities are by no means unique.'

'Does he mean there's more of 'em?' Haskeer whispered.

'Must be. How do you think he got here?' Stryke jabbed a thumb at the corpse.

'Parnol would use the stars you hold to navigate the portals,' Arngrim explained. 'For instance, to reach the place you last left, Maras-Dantia, they would have to be manipulated like this.' As he spoke, the spheres came together in a way that seemed implausible, if not actually impossible, and formed a single, interlocked entity. 'To travel to the land I showed you requires this configuration.' The stars executed another improbable manoeuvre, ending again in one piece. 'And to return to where you now are . . .' They shifted and locked together in a different but still perfect combination. 'Attempting to use the instrumentalities without having first set them causes them to act randomly, and that can be very dangerous. But

you've no need to worry about how they operate. That's Parnol's job.'
His voice took on a graver tone. *'Your duty is to guard them as you would your own lives. Apart from being your only way home, they must never fall into the wrong hands. I urge you to accept the task I've outlined, Wolverines. For the sake of your kind, and for the greater purpose.'*

The light went out of the enchantment. Instantly, the column of smoke was sucked back into the gemstone. Evening shadows returned, and the quiet.

'I'll be fucked,' Haskeer said.

'You put it like a poet.'

'Greetings, orcs.'

They swung back to the gem, blades ready. It was glowing again.

'Don't be afraid, I realise how foolish . . .'

The stone began fizzling. It throbbed with a grey luminescence.

'. . . a thing that is to say to a race as courageous . . .'

A greenish vapour was streaming from the gem. It crackled and spat.

'. . . as yours. But be assured—'

There was a loud report. Fragments of gemstone shot in all directions.

Stryke went over and prodded the smouldering remains with his sword tip. The dying embers gave off a fetid odour.

They stood in silence for a while, then Haskeer said, 'What the hell do you make of all that?'

'It could be what we need.'

'What?'

'Do you ever feel . . . ?'

'Feel *what*?'

'Don't get me wrong; finding Thirzarr, coming here, having the hatchlings . . . they're the best things that ever happened to me. But . . .'

'Spit it out, Stryke, for fuck's sake.'

'This place has everything we hoped for. Good hunting and feasting, comradeship, tourneys, our own lodges. Yet, now and again, don't you get a little . . . bored?'

Haskeer stared at him. 'I thought I was the only one.'

'You feel that way?'

'Yeah. Don't know why. Like you say, life's good here.'

'Maybe that's it.'

Perplexity creased Haskeer's brow. 'Whadya mean?'

'Where's the danger? Where's the *enemy*? I know we skirmish with other clans sometimes, but that's not the same. What we're missing is a . . . purpose.'

Haskeer glanced at the fragments of the gemstone. 'You're not taking this seriously, Stryke?'

'Wouldn't it be good to have a mission?'

'Well, yeah. But—'

'What better than to whet our blades again, and to help some fellow orcs? *And* have the chance to pay back that bitch Jennesta.'

'It's crazy. Ask yourself: why's the sorcerer taking our side? Why not his own kind? If we learnt one thing, it's don't trust humans.'

'He helped us before.'

'When it suited him. I reckon there's more to this.'

'Could be.'

'Anyway, this is all so much jaw flapping.' He nodded at Parnol. 'He ain't gonna be doing no guiding.'

'Maybe we don't need him.'

'Oh, come on, Stryke. You couldn't follow all that fucking around with the stars Serapheim showed us . . . could you?'

'The movements that get us back here; I'm trying to keep them in my head.'

Haskeer looked impressed. 'What about the others?'

'Er . . . no.'

'Not much good then, is it? He said it was dangerous if—'

'I know what he said. But something's been nagging at me.'

He went over to the dead body. Kneeling, he removed the amulet the man was wearing. Haskeer peered over Stryke's shoulder as he examined it.

The engravings etched into its surface were small, and they strained to make them out. They consisted of rows of symbols in groups of five. The symbols were circles with lines protruding at various angles. Stryke studied it for what seemed like a long time.

'That's it,' he finally announced.

'What?'

'See that third lot of figures? It's the same as the way the stars have to be moved to get back here.'

Haskeer did nothing to hide his incomprehension. 'Is it?'

'Looks that way. All these markings are different, and there's a lot more than the three Serapheim showed us.'

'You mean . . . that tells you how to use the stars?'

'Yes. The messenger must have had it to help him remember. Like a map. I reckon this first line is how to get to Maras-Dantia, and the second gets you to that world with the orcs. The rest . . . who knows?'

'That's pretty smart, Stryke,' Haskeer stated admiringly.

Stryke put the amulet around his neck. 'Don't get too excited; I could be wrong. But I've often wondered why Arngrim gave me the stars. Perhaps we know now.'

'Think he planned this? From the start?'

'Could be he was mindful of future trouble.'

'And counting on us to deal with it.'

'Who knows? Humans are two-faced.'

'That's no lie.'

Stryke adopted a pensive expression. 'There was something about the things he showed us. Did you notice? Not once were those orcs fighting back.'

It hadn't occurred to Haskeer before. 'They weren't, were they?'

'And when did our kind ever turn a cheek?'

'What's *wrong* with 'em?'

All Stryke could do was shrug.

Haskeer pointed at the corpse. 'And who killed him?'

'I don't know. But I've a mind to find out. You game?'

Haskeer thought about it. 'Yeah. If there's a fight in it.'

3

The summer afternoon had softened into early evening, the quality of the light mellowing from golden to carroty. A gentle breeze brought the sweet perfume of lushness. Tender birdsong could be heard.

Eight or nine lodges stood together, along with a corral and a couple of barns.

The settlement occupied the crest of a low hill. In all directions, the outlook was verdant. There were luxuriant pastures and dense forests, and the silver thread of a distant river marbling the emerald.

In one particular lodge, a female was diverting her offspring.

'In those days,' she told them, 'a blight afflicted the land. It was a walking pestilence. A puny race of disgusting appearance, with yielding, pallid flesh and the nature of a glutton. An insatiable host that gloried in destruction. It tore the guts from the earth, plundered its resources and poisoned its waters. It spread disease and stirred up trouble. It threw away the magic.'

Her offspring were rapt.

'It felt contempt for other races, and revelled in their slaughter. But its hatred wasn't directed solely at those who were different. It fought its own kind, too. There was warfare between their tribes. They killed when there was no good purpose to it, and all the other races were fearful of them.' She eyed the siblings. 'Except one. Unlike the pestilence, they didn't murder for pleasure, or wreak havoc for the sake of it. They didn't lack nobility or honour, and weren't hideous to look at. They were handsome and brave. They were—'

'Orcs!' the hatchlings chorused.

Thirzarr grinned. 'You pair are too smart for me.'

'We're *always* heroes in the stories,' Corb reminded her.

24

She tossed them each a chunk of raw meat. They gobbled the treats with relish, red juice trickling down their chins.

'Are there any of those human monsters around here?' Janch asked as he chewed.

'No,' Thirzarr told him, 'not in the whole of Ceragan.'

He looked disappointed. 'Pity. I'd like to *kill* some.'

'No, *I* would,' Corb announced, brandishing the wooden sword his sire had made for him.

'Of course you would, my little wolf. Now give me that.' Thirzarr held out her hand and he reluctantly surrendered the weapon. 'It's time you two slept.'

'*Ah, no!*' they protested.

'Finish the story!' Corb insisted.

'Tell us about Jennesta again!' Janch piped up.

'*Yes!*' his brother echoed, bouncing. 'Tell us about the witch!'

'It's *late*.'

'*The witch! The witch!*'

'All right, all right. Calm down.' She leaned over their couches and tucked them in, then perched herself. 'You've got to go to sleep straight after this, all right?'

They nodded, saucer-eyed, blankets to their chins.

'Jennesta wasn't a witch, exactly,' Thirzarr told them. 'She was a sorceress. A magician born of magicians, she commanded great powers. Powers made stronger by her cruelty, which fed her magic. She was part human, part nyadd, which accounted for her strange appearance. And no doubt the human part explained her cruelty. Jennesta called herself a queen, but her title and realm was gained through deceit and brutality. Under her rule, fear held the whip hand. She meddled in the affairs of humans, supporting them one moment, battling them the next, as her self-interest dictated. She waged needless wars and relished sadism. She sowed conflict that steeped the land in blood and fire.'

'*I'm back!*'

'Dad!' Corb and Janch cried. They sat bolt upright and tossed aside their blankets.

Thirzarr turned to the figure who'd silently entered. She sighed. 'I'm trying to get them to *sleep*, Stryke. Oh, Haskeer. Didn't see you there.'

The males sidled in. 'Sorry,' Stryke mouthed.

Too late. The brood were up. They rushed to their father and clamped themselves to his legs, clamouring for attention.

'Steady now. And what about Haskeer? Nothing to say to him?'

' 'lo, Uncle Haskeer.'

'I think he's got something for you,' Stryke added.

They instantly transferred their affections and stampeded in Haskeer's direction. He grabbed the hatchlings by their scruffs, one in each massive fist, and hoisted them, giggling.

'What've you got us? What've you got us?'

'Let's see, shall we?' He returned them to the compacted earth floor.

Haskeer reached into his jerkin and hauled out two slim cloth bundles. Before handing them over, he looked to Thirzarr. She nodded.

The brothers tore at the wrapping, then gasped in delight. They found beautifully crafted hatchets. The weapons were scaled-down for small hands, with polished, razor-keen cutting edges and carved wooden grips.

'You shouldn't have, Haskeer,' Thirzarr said. 'Boys, what do you say?'

'Thank you, Uncle Haskeer!' Beaming, they began to slash the air.

'Well, it should be their blooding soon,' Haskeer reckoned. 'They're . . . how old now?'

'Corb's four, Janch's three,' Stryke supplied.

'And a half!' Janch corrected indignantly.

Haskeer nodded. 'High time they killed something, then.'

'They will,' Thirzarr assured him. 'Thanks, Haskeer, we appreciate the gifts; but if you don't mind . . .'

'I need to talk to you,' Stryke said.

'Not now,' Thirzarr told him.

'It's important.'

'I'm trying to get these two settled.'

'Would a bit longer hurt? I have to tell you about—'

'*Not now.* You went for meat. Where is it?'

Given the hint of menace in her voice, Stryke knew better than to argue. He and Haskeer allowed themselves to be pushed out of the door.

When it slammed behind them, Stryke said, 'I'll tell her what happened when she's cooled down.'

'You know, Stryke, I could almost believe you're afraid of that mate of yours.'

'Aren't you?'

Haskeer changed the subject. 'So what do we do now?'

'We find our mistress of strategy.'

4

A bucketful of water consists of billions of minute droplets. Rivers and oceans have untold trillions.

No number could be applied to the sea of parallel realities.

Its constituent parts were infinite. They decorated the void in dense, shimmering clouds, each particle a world. In the impossible event of a spectator being present, these tiny grains would appear identical.

But a particular globule, looking like all the others, shining no more or less brightly, differed in one very important respect.

It was dying.

The imaginary observer, peering closer, would make out a world in flux. A bubble of acrid waters and fouled air.

Its surface was one of extremes. Much was still blue-green, but tendrils of aridity patterned the globe. White masses were spreading from the poles, like cream trickling down a pudding, and the atmosphere was tinted by an unhealthy miasma.

There were four continents. The largest, once temperate, now included swathes of semi-tropical terrain. At its core a dustbowl had formed, and previously fertile land was drifting to desert.

A group of militia, fifty strong, made its way across the wilderness. In their midst, two men struggled to keep up on foot. Each was led by a horse to which they were roped. Their hands were tied.

The soldiers bore the crest of a tyrant on their russet tunics. The prisoners were civilians, their clothes stained with sweat and dust.

It was hot. With midday approaching it would get much hotter, but neither man had been allowed water. Their lips were cracked, and their mouths were so dry it was hard for them to speak. They laboured on blistered feet.

There was little between them in age. The slightly older of the two had the look of someone who enjoyed a soft life. His waist was beginning to thicken, and his reddening skin was pasty. He had quick, some would say shifty, blue eyes, and a bloodless slash of a mouth framed by a skinny goatee. His black hair showed a hint of grey and was thinning, revealing the start of a tonsure.

The younger of the pair was fitter and taller. His build was strapping. He had a full head of blond hair and he was clean-shaven, bar a couple of days' growth. His eyes were brown, and his flesh tone healthy. The filthy clothes he wore had been much cheaper to start with than his companion's.

The older man shot the younger a sour, anxious look. 'When are you going to do something?' he hissed.

'What do you expect *me* to do?'

'Show some respect, for a start.'

'What do you expect me to do, *sir*?'

'Your duties include my protection. So far you've made a complete—'

'*Keep it down!*' an officer barked. Several other riders directed hostile glances their way.

'. . . a complete cock-up of it,' the older man continued in a coarse whisper. 'You did precious little to stop us being captured, and now you're—'

'You got yourself into this,' the younger returned in an under-tone, 'not me.'

'*Us.* We're in it together, if you hadn't noticed.'

'So it's *you* when times are good and *us* when you're in the shit. As usual.'

'That insubordinate tongue of yours is going to get itself cut out.' His face was growing redder. 'Just you wait 'til I—'

'Until you what? Not exactly a free agent at the moment, are you?'

The older man wiped the back of a manicured hand across his forehead. 'You know what's going to happen when they get us to Hammrik, don't you?'

'I can guess what's going to happen to you.'

'What's good for the master's good for the servant.'

'That's as maybe.' He nodded at what was coming into view. 'We'll find out soon enough.'

The towers of a fortress could be seen, wavering in the heat haze like a mirage.

As they drew nearer they saw that it was constructed of a yellowish, sandy stone, not dissimilar to the colour the surrounding landscape was turning to. And it was massive, with walls that looked thick enough to resist an earthquake. Close to, the structure bore signs of conflict. Fresh pockmarks, nicks and cracks told of a recent onslaught.

A ramshackle township mushroomed at the fortress' base. A muddle of shacks and tents stood in its shadow, and lean-tos hugged the ramparts. People and livestock were everywhere. Water carriers, hawkers, nomads, farmers, mercenaries, prostitutes, robed priests, and plenty of soldiers. Mangy dogs ran loose. Hens scratched and piglets ate garbage. There was a sickly odour of sewage and incense.

The riders barged through the crowd, dragging their captives. They passed heckling street urchins, hard-eyed guardsmen and merchants leading strings of overloaded donkeys. People stared, and a few flung insults.

They went by vendors' stalls heaped with bread, goat's cheese, spices, meat and limp vegetables. Some offered wine, hogsheads of brandy or pails of beer. The prisoners turned particularly envious eyes on these wares. All they got was a half-hearted pelting with rotten fruit, each piece raising a little puff of dust when it struck their backs.

The fortress gates were suitably imposing, their surrounds frothing with epic statuary and heraldic symbols. But old and faded. Inside was a large inner courtyard. There was noise and bustle here too, though of an ordered, soldierly kind.

Greetings were exchanged. The prisoners were glared at or ignored. Everyone dismounted. Grooms came forward and led the horses to troughs, which was more than the captives were allowed. Left with their wrists bound, they sank exhausted to the warm paving slabs. Nobody rebuked them.

They slumped next to a small garden enclosed by a low wall. It dated from earlier, more verdant times, and had long dried out. The soil was like powder, and the pair of trees at its centre were desiccated and skeletal.

Most of the prisoners' escort dispersed. Four remained, eyeing them from a distance while they conferred with an officer.

The elder prisoner turned his face from them and whispered, 'Let's make a run for it.'

'Bad idea,' his companion judged. 'We've no allies here. That crowd wouldn't be a haven.'

'It's a better chance than waiting on our fate like cattle, isn't it?'

'Not unless you want an arrow in your back.' He indicated the battlements. Several archers were looking down at them.

'They aren't going to kill us. Hammrik would be furious if they denied him that pleasure.'

'But I doubt they're under orders not to wound. If you fancy a couple of bolts through your legs, go ahead. Master.'

The older man glowered at the fresh impertinence, then returned to sulking.

A minute later the guards were rousing them with cusses and kicks. He asked if there was any chance of a drink.

'Favours are my lord's privilege, not mine,' the highest-ranking replied, jerking them to their feet.

The brief rest had made their aches more noticeable now they were moving again. They were stiff, and their muscles were knotted. But their captors treated them no more gently for it. Stinging blows from leather riding crops hurried along their progress.

They were driven to a set of double doors opening into the castle proper. The interior was gloomy to their dazzled eyes, and it was cooler, which was a mercy.

Like many fortresses that had been added to and built on over the years, there was a warren of passages, corridors and stairways to be negotiated. They passed through checkpoints and locked doors, but saw few windows, save arrow slits.

Finally they arrived at a sizeable hall. It was wood panelled and high-ceilinged, and its drapes were drawn to keep out the heat. Light came from oil lamps and candles, and the air was stuffy. High up, where the panelling ended and a stone wall began, there had been coats of arms. But they were freshly defaced, their features smashed, revealing whiter granite beneath.

The guards in attendance wore the livery of a personal bodyguard. A handful of civilian officials were also present.

There was no furniture except an oak throne on a dais at one end of the room. It, too, had been vandalised; someone had hacked away the device on its tall backrest. The prisoners were made to stand in front of it.

A minute passed, glacially. They exchanged bleak glances.

Behind the throne was a cleverly concealed door, set flush to the panelling. It opened, and someone entered.

Rulers come in a variety of guises. Those who inherit leadership can be unprepossessing. Those who seize it often have the appearance of brutish warriors. Kantor Hammrik looked like a clerk. Which was appropriate for someone who had effectively bought a kingdom. Bought in the sense of financing the bloody overthrow and regicide of an existing monarch.

Hammrik resembled a quill-pusher because, in a way, that's what he was. Early on in his illicit career he realised the efficacy of the equation between money and power. Learned it, and took it to what passed for his heart. He grew adept at using his ill-gotten riches to manipulate the greed of men without scruples, and rose on a tide of other people's blood, bought and paid for.

His build was more suited to running from a fight than engaging in one; what some called wiry framed. Any muscularity he had was restricted to his brains. He responded to hair loss by having his head completely shaved, which stressed the angularity of his skull. His raw-boned, beardless face was dominated by acute grey eyes. But woe to anybody who took him for a book-keeper.

As Hammrik swept in, the prisoners were forced to their knees. Everyone bowed.

'Ah, Micalor Standeven,' the usurper uttered as he perched on his stolen throne. 'I was beginning to think I'd never have the pleasure of your company again.'

The elder prisoner looked up. 'How delightful to see you, Kantor.' He went for casual bonhomie.

Hammrik gave him a stony, threatening look.

'That is,' Standeven hastily corrected, 'greetings, my liege. And may I take this opportunity to congratulate you on your elevation to—'

Hammrik waved him to silence. 'Let's take the fawning as read, shall we?' His gaze fell upon Standeven's companion. 'I see you've got your lapdog with you, as usual.'

'Yes, er, sire. He's—'

'He can speak for himself. What's your name?'

'Pepperdyne, sir,' the younger prisoner replied. 'Jode Pepperdyne.'

'You're bonded to him?'

Pepperdyne nodded.

'Then you're equally liable.'

'If this is a misunderstanding about money,' Standeven said, as though it had just occurred to him, 'I'm sure we can settle such a trifling matter cordially.'

'Trifling?' Hammrik repeated ominously.

'Well, yes. For a man of your newly acquired status it must be a mere—'

'Shut up.' Hammrik beckoned to a studious-looking old functionary standing to one side. 'How much?'

The old man was carrying a dog-eared ledger. Wetting a thumb, he began flipping pages.

'A round figure will do,' Hammrik told him.

'Certainly, sire.' He found the entry and squinted. 'Let's see. With interest, call it . . . forty thousand.'

'Is it *that* much?' Standeven exclaimed in mock surprise. 'Well, well. Still, I'm a little puzzled as to why you should call us in over this. I can understand it might have been necessary when you were a money len—when you were providing pecuniary services. But surely, sire, you don't need it now?'

'Look around you. This hardly resembles a thriving kingdom, does it? Overthrowing Wyvell was a costly business, and though his followers were beaten, they're not entirely crushed yet. It all takes money.'

'Of course.'

'A debt is a debt, and yours is overdue.'

'Absolutely. It's a matter of honour.'

'So what are you going to do about it?'

Standeven stared at him. 'Do you think I might have something to drink? We were out in that sun for an awfully long time, you see, and . . .'

Hammrik raised a hand, then called for water. A young flunkey brought him a hide pouch. Hammrik rose and stepped down to the kneeling Standeven. But he didn't give him the pouch. Instead, he tilted it, so that a single drop splashed into Standeven's out-stretched palm. Frowning, the prisoner licked up the moisture with his parched tongue.

'One drop,' Hammrik said. 'How long do you think it'd take to feed you say, forty thousand?'

Standeven was baffled, and said nothing.

'Probably no time at all,' Hammrik decided, 'if you had it all in one go. In a tankard, for instance.'

'Kantor . . . I mean, sire, I—'

'But suppose you had it one drop at a time, like just now. How long would that take? Days? Weeks?' Hammrik held the water pouch at arm's length, as though studying it. 'This stuff's going to be precious here soon, given the way this land's going. The way the whole world's going. I can see water being as valuable as . . . blood.'

Standeven shifted uncomfortably. Pepperdyne betrayed no emotion.

'That's the deal,' Hammrik continued. 'Repay me in coin or I'll take it in blood. Forty thousand drops, one at a time.' He leaned closer to Standeven's face. 'I don't mean that as any kind of figure of speech.'

'I can pay!' Standeven protested.

'Does he have the money?' Hammrik addressed the question to Pepperdyne.

'No.'

'You're asking a *slave* about my financial arrangements?' Standeven complained. 'What would he know?'

'He's smarter than you. Or maybe not, seeing as he hasn't yet cut your throat while you were sleeping. But at least he didn't insult me with a lie. That earns him a quicker death than yours.'

'You can have him.'

'What?'

'To settle the debt. He's strong and hard working, and—'

Hammrik laughed. 'And I thought *I* was a bastard. He's not worth a fraction of what you owe me. Why would I want another mouth to feed?'

'I can pay you, Hammrik. I just need a little time to get together the—'

'I've wasted enough time as it is. I've no alternative but to have you both executed. *Guards!*'

Men came forward and took hold of the prisoners.

'There's no need for this,' Standeven pleaded. 'We can work it out!'

Hammrik was walking away.

'Suppose we could get you something more valuable than money?' Pepperdyne called after him.

The upstart king halted and turned. 'What could you possibly have to interest me?'

'Something you've long wanted.'

'Go on.'

'Everybody knows about your search for the instrumentalities.'

A passionate glint lit Hammrik's eyes, though his words belied it. 'And many have lied about knowing where they're to be found.'

'We're different. We really could help you gain them.'

'How?'

'As it happens, my master wasn't being entirely untruthful when he said he could pay you. The plan was to locate them, sell them to the highest bidder and settle your debt from the proceeds. In fact, we were following their trail when your men picked us up.'

'Why didn't you mention this before?'

'Would *you* in our position, and run the risk of losing such a prize?'

Standeven had looked bewildered at this turn of events. Now he was nodding furiously. 'It's true. Like you, I've heard the stories, though I confess to being unclear about what the instrumentalities are supposed to actually do. But I've always thought that anyone who found them would make a fortune.'

'I've no interest in making money out of them,' Hammrik stated.

'You're not interested in their *value*?' Standeven was shocked.

'Not that kind of value. If they function as they're rumoured to, there's a chance me and my people can escape this stinking world.'

Pepperdyne and Standeven were puzzled at the remark, but thought it wise to keep quiet.

'So what makes you think you've a chance of finding them when everyone else has failed?' Hammrik asked.

'We've come across evidence,' Pepperdyne replied.

'What evidence?'

'You'll forgive us for not throwing away our only bargaining chip,' Standeven said.

'You're bluffing, the pair of you.'

'Can you afford to take that chance?'

'And what do you have to lose if we're lying?' Pepperdyne added.

Hammrik considered their words. 'What does finding the instrumentalities involve? What would I have to do?'

'With respect, sire,' Pepperdyne told him, 'not you, us.'

'Explain.'

'The information we have indicates that they're to be found upcountry.'

'How far upcountry?'

'All the way north, to the new lands.'

'Centrasia? From what I hear it's full of freaks and monsters.'

'They say there's magic there too, of a sort. But that makes it the logical place to find what we're seeking, doesn't it?'

'What can you do there that I couldn't achieve with an army?'

'Do you have one to spare? Besides, we have the contacts.'

'Why don't I just have you tortured to find out what you know?'

'Our contacts will only deal directly with us. If anybody else turns up they'll be long gone.'

A long moment of silence ensued as Hammrik weighed the options. At last he said, 'On balance, I don't believe you. But if there's a chance, I'd be a fool not to take it.'

It was all Standeven could do to suppress a loud sigh of relief.

'There'll be a time limit, naturally,' Hammrik: explained, 'and I'll be hand-picking your escort.'

'Escort?'

'Of *course*. You didn't think I'd let you two swan off by yourselves, did you?'

'No. No, of course not.'

'If you get the instrumentalities, the debt's cancelled. I'll even reward you on top. If this is a ruse you'll just be delaying your deaths with a brief reprieve in a land of horrors. You'll be brought back here and I'll kill you. Understood?'

They nodded.

Without further word, he walked away.

Standeven turned to his bondsman. 'What were you thinking of?' he whispered. 'We don't know where to find those things, or even if they exist.'

'You'd prefer it if they killed us? I had to come up with a story that bought us time.'

'And what happens when his thugs find out we were talking through our arses?'

'I don't know. We'll think of something.'

'It'd better be a damn good—'

'*Ssshh.*'

An officer approached, the same one who earlier refused them water.

'As you're in my master's good books,' he announced, 'at least for now, I thought you could use that drink.'

Standeven looked up expectantly.

To laughter from most of the other people in the room, the officer poured the contents of a canteen over Standeven's raised face.

He shook his head, like a dog leaving a river, scattering a million droplets of water.

5

Glass was an uncommon commodity. Orc artisans knew how to make it, but rarely bothered except for specific purposes, such as casements in certain places of worship and one or two of the chieftains' grand lodges. It was occasionally found in taverns.

As Stryke and Haskeer approached the inn they sought, they witnessed why glass was so infrequently used as a building material.

With a resounding crash, an orc was propelled through one of the windows. He bounced a couple of times before coming to rest in the shards.

The tavern's door was stout. But not so strong as to resist another flying body. The battered orc that crashed through it managed to stumble a couple of paces before collapsing.

There was uproar inside. A wild cacophony of shattered earthenware, breaking furniture and yelled curses.

Stryke said, 'This must be the place.'

They stepped through the splintered doorframe. An orc landed on his back in front of them. He came down heavily, shaking the floorboards.

Stryke nodded to him. 'Morning, Breggin.'

'Captain,' the orc groaned.

The interior of the inn was essentially a single, large room. There was a serving bench at one end and a storm in the middle. The storm's eye stood astride a table.

Coilla wielded an iron cooking pot. Clutching the handle, she swung at the heads of the half-dozen males struggling to reach her.

She was a handsome specimen of orc womanhood, with attractively mottled skin, dark, flashing eyes, barbed teeth and a muscular, warrior's physique. Most alluring of all, she fought like a demon with toothache.

As Stryke and Haskeer entered, she delivered a well-aimed kick to the jaw of an opponent who ducked too late. He met the floor as surely as a dropped sack of offal. The others tried to catch her legs and topple her, but she skipped away with ease. They started rocking the table.

'Should we help?' Haskeer wondered.

'I don't think we could beat her,' Stryke replied dryly.

Chiming like a bell, Coilla's cooking pot caught one of her antagonists square to the side of his head. Knocked senseless, he tumbled floorward.

Haskeer spotted a half full tankard of ale. He lifted it and started drinking. Stryke leaned against the counter, arms folded, watching the brawl.

The four remaining males finally upended the table. Coilla leapt clear, feet-first into someone's chest. He spiralled out of play. Quickly righting herself, she swiped at the next in line, flattening his nose with her pot. Driven backwards, he came to grief in a tangle of chairs.

The two still upright rushed her in unison. One was dispatched by the simple expedient of running into her raised elbow. It connected with the bridge of his nose, sending him downhill and comatose. She dodged the clutches of the last orc standing and pounded his features with the fist of her free hand, rendering him insentient.

Coilla briefly savoured the scene then, tossing the cooking pot aside, gave Stryke and Haskeer a cheery greeting.

'What was that about?' Haskeer asked. He thumped down the empty tankard and belched.

'It started as a fight *over* me, then kind of developed into one *with* me.' She shrugged. 'The usual.'

'Keep up these courting rituals and you'll run out of suitors,' Stryke commented.

'Cosy up to *that* lot? You must be joking. Anybody who can't knock me down doesn't deserve consideration. So, what are you two doing here?'

'We've news,' Stryke told her. 'Let's go outside.'

It was the beginning of a glorious day. The sun was up, bathing the land in balmy warmth. Birds were on the wing and bees droned.

They went and sat on a little hillock. Stryke explained what had happened, with Haskeer adding unhelpful interruptions. They showed her the amulet.

'But Jennesta's dead, surely?' she said. 'We saw her pulled apart by that vortex thing.'

'Maybe she can't be killed that easily,' Haskeer contributed. 'The sort of powers that bitch had, I'm thinking she can't be killed *at all*.'

'I'd bet on cold steel through the heart revoking her sorcery,' Stryke replied.

'You reckon she's got one?'

'We don't know how she survived, but it seems she did, and she's making orcs suffer. What are we going to do about it?'

'If we leave this land, you know what we're likely going to,' Coilla reminded him. 'Prejudice about us, and hatred and bigotry. Sure you want to go through all that shit again?'

'We've rode out worse than words.'

'It's not words that worry me. And don't count on too many allies wherever we fetch up.'

'I'm not saying there isn't going to be hardship, sweat and violence.'

'Just like old times, eh?'

'So where do you stand, Coilla? Are you saying no?'

She grinned. 'Hell, I'm not. This is a good place, but it can get kind of dull after a while. I've been itching for a real fight. I'm tired of lightweight scuffles.'

A wheezing orc staggered out of the tavern, gobbing teeth.

'You're game, then?'

'Sure.'

'So what next?' Haskeer asked.

'We round up the rest of the band and put it to 'em,' Stryke decided.

Haskeer wrinkled his craggy brow. 'Strange to think of the Wolverines re-formed.'

'If they want re-forming,' Coilla said.

Nep and Gleadeg were easily found; they lay insensible in the tavern, alongside Breggin. Zoda and Prooq were fishing with spears a little way upriver. Reafdaw was helping build a longhouse as part of a service to the community edict imposed by local elders, following an affray. Eldo, Bhose, Liffin and Jad were with a recently returned hunting party. Calthmon was discovered drunk on the steps of a hostelry and required dunking in a nearby rain butt. Orbon and Seafe, like Stryke, had mated, and were at their lodges, coddling offspring. Vobe, Gant, Finje and Noskaa were traced to a regional tourney they were competing in. Toche and Hystykk turned up in a felons' compound, the result of a little horseplay involving riot and arson, and had to be bailed.

Stryke explained the mystery of the human who came through the portal, and outlined Serapheim's message. There was some discussion, but a surprising degree of unanimity, despite Coilla's doubts. Much as they relished their hard-won freedom, all felt jaded and welcomed the prospect of a mission.

By late afternoon, Stryke was ready to begin a new search. Recruits were needed to replace those lost in the Wolverines' previous battles and bring the warband up to strength. He set about tracing a half dozen likely prospects he'd had his eye on.

Word got around that something was afoot. That evening, a curious crowd gathered at the clearing where Stryke mustered his troop.

Several of the Wolverines' mates were there, too. Thifzarr came, wearing the flaming crimson headdress Stryke first saw in his visions of this place. They stood away from the others.

'And you're sure you don't mind?' Stryke repeated.

'Would it matter if I did? Don't look doleful, you know you're desperate to go.'

'Don't put it that way. I'll be back. It's just—'

She stilled his lips with a coarse finger. 'I know. You don't have to explain an orc's instincts to me. I'm only sorry I'm not going with you.'

He brightened, relieved at her reaction. 'That would have been good. We've never had the joy of fighting side by side. I've always felt it's something missing from our union.'

'Me, too. Couples should spill blood together.'

'We will,' he promised.

'Be careful,' she said, suddenly serious. 'Stupid thing to say. But I'd like to think the kids' father's going to be around as they grow. Don't take risks, Stryke.'

'I won't,' he lied. He looked round. Haskeer had got the Wolverines into a semblance of order. To one side, another, smaller group shuffled their feet and looked slightly self-conscious. 'I need to get started.'

She nodded, and he went to his band.

'Heads up!' Haskeer bellowed.

The company straightened their backs.

'I'm glad you all volunteered,' Stryke told them. 'We always worked well together, and we can do it again.' His tone hardened. 'But let's get one thing straight. This is a well-ordered fighting unit. Or it used to be. We've all back-slid a bit while we've been here. Got soft, some of us. Sign on for this mission and you'll be subject to military discipline, just like before. I'm in charge, and there'll be a chain of command.' He shot a sideways glance at Haskeer. 'Anybody got a problem with that?'

Nobody had.

'At a time like this we remember fallen comrades,' he went on. 'Kestix, Meklun, Darig, Slettal, Wrelbyd, Talag. They all died serving this band, and we should never forget it.' He paused. 'That means we don't have our full quota. So I'm bringing in replacements.' He waved forward the recruits, and counted them off. 'This is Ignar, Keick, Harlgo, Chuss, Yunst and Pirrak. I expect you to make them welcome. Show them our routines and get them used to our ways. They're good fighters, but not combat trained. Though they will be by the time we've finished with them.'

There was laughter. In the case of the recruits, somewhat nervous.

'Somebody else we lost can never be replaced,' Stryke continued. 'We all respected Alfray.' Heads were nodding agreement. 'He was more than the band's medic and a veteran fighter; he was a link in the chain binding us to our kind's past. We can't replace him, but we need another corporal alongside Coilla here, so we'll fill the void he left as best we can.' He beckoned. Someone came out of the crowd.

He was an orc of advanced years, though still in his prime and looking fit. But the light in his astute eyes owed more to autumn than summer, and of all the fighters present he was easily the oldest. He approached with assurance.

'Meet Dallog,' Stryke said.

The older orc lightly nodded to them; a small gesture but amiable enough.

'Some of you might know him already, particularly if you've needed a broken bone put right.' There was another ripple of laughter. 'He has talent as a healer. He's steady and he's smart, and I'm making him a corporal. And he's got an important duty.' Stryke raised a hand.

A youngster trotted towards them. He carried a spiked lance with a furled pennant, which he passed to Dallog. At Stryke's signal, Dallog opened it, revealing the band's standard. He held the pole aloft and the ensign fluttered in the evening breeze. The Wolverines cheered. Except for Haskeer, who wore a dour expression.

'The standard's in your charge,' Stryke said. 'Guard it well.'

'With my life,' Dallog promised. He went to join the ranks.

'We've plenty to do tonight,' Stryke reminded them all, 'so go about your tasks. *Dismissed!*' As they moved off, he called, 'Get to know the new ones! They're Wolverines now!'

Haskeer arrived at his side. 'It's not true,' he complained.

'What isn't?'

'What you just said about the new intake being Wolverines. They have to earn it.'

'We all started from scratch.'

'We were already battle-hardened when we joined. Not like these . . . *civilians*.'

'That's the point. We need to get the band in shape fast, which means making them feel a part of it from the outset.' He regarded his sergeant. 'Is that all you're in a foul mood about?'

Haskeer said nothing. But his gaze flicked to Dallog as he went off with the standard.

'Ah,' Stryke said, 'that's your beef, is it?'

'He's no Alfray.'

'Nobody said he was.'

'So why do we need him?'

'Chain of command, remember? We have to have another corporal, and a band healer. I reckon Dallog fits the bill.'

'Well, I don't like it.'

'Too bad. You just heard me say I'm in charge. If that's not to your liking either—'

'Oh, shit.'

Stryke balled his fists. 'You want to make an issue of this, Sergeant?'

'No. What I meant was, look who's coming.'

The youth walking their way was barely on nodding terms with adulthood. He dressed extravagantly for an orc. His jerkin consisted of strips of different coloured material, and his breeches were lilac. He wore gaudy boots. Looped about his neck was a stringed instrument. It had a long fingerboard and a body the shape of a sliced strawberry. He cradled it as tenderly as a babe.

'Oh, shit,' Stryke said. 'Be tactful. Remember who he is.'

Haskeer gave a weary grunt.

'Stryke! Haskeer!' the youth greeted. 'I've been looking for you.'

'Wheam,' Stryke replied.

'What do you want?' Haskeer demanded, stony-faced.

'You're about to set out on a great adventure,' Wheam enthused, 'and it should be celebrated.'

'Maybe they'll be time for feasting when we get back,' Stryke responded. 'But at the moment—'

'No, no, I mean celebrated in *verse*.'

'We couldn't put you to the trouble.'

'This is history in the making; it *must* be recorded. Anyway, I've already started an epic ballad about this mission. It's work in progress, of course, but—'

'Well, if it's not finished . . .'

'How can it be? You haven't started yet, have you?'

'True.'

'So I thought I'd let you hear the opening, as a kind of inspiration.'

'Must you? I mean, must you *now*?'

'It won't take long. There's only about forty verses so far.'

'We're very busy just now and—'

Wheam began discordant plucking. He cleared his throat loudly and proceeded to sing off key.

'*On battle's eve the Wolverines*
Whet their blades and readied their spleens . . .

44

It's hard to get anything to rhyme with Wolverines, but I'm working on it.

Their Captain bold he seized his chance
To take up dagger, sword and lance
And spitting in the face of fate
He marched his band to the magic gate . . .'

'Gods,' Haskeer muttered.

'With swelling breasts and hearts so true
They smote the foe for me and you . . .'

Coilla arrived, pulling a face behind the minstrel's back. She saw the expressions of appeal Stryke and Haskeer wore, and took pity.

'Upon the field of slaughter red
His gallant crew he bravely led
And taking up his cleaver keen . . .'

'Excuse me.'
'He hacked his way to—'
Coilla prodded Wheam's shoulder-blade with a bony finger.
'Ouch!'
'Sorry,' she smiled, 'but I have to talk to my superior officers. You know; operational matters.'
'But I've barely got going.'
'Yes,' Stryke intervened, 'and it's a pity. We'll just have to hear the rest some other time.'
'When?' Wheam asked.
'Later.'
Stryke and Haskeer grasped the protesting balladeer's elbows and impelled him towards the crowd.
Rejoining Coilla, Stryke breathed a sigh. 'Thanks. We owe you one.'
'At least we won't be seeing him again for a while.'
'Never would be too soon,' Haskeer suggested.
'Did you want something, Coilla, or was this just a rescue?' Stryke said.

'Actually, I was wondering how things were going with the stars.'

'We had them hidden in five locations, as you know. I've got four of them back. The fifth—' There was a commotion at the edge of the crowd. 'Matter of fact, this should be it now.'

A massively built individual appeared, a retinue in his wake. He was elderly but still fearsome. At his throat he wore an emblem of valour; a necklace of snow leopards' teeth, numbering at least a dozen. He was battle-scarred and proud.

'Hard to think he could have sired such a fop,' Coilla remarked.

'Best keep that opinion to yourself,' Stryke advised.

The chieftain and his entourage swept in.

Stryke welcomed him with, 'Good of you to come, Quoll.'

Quoll snorted. 'You left me little choice.'

'Sorry for the short notice. We have to move quickly.'

'You're leaving soon?'

'First light.'

'And you've everything you need?'

'All except the item in your safekeeping. Do you have it?'

'Of course. But I've been thinking.'

'With respect, Chief, what's there to think about?'

'My thought is that you could render me a service.'

'We're always happy to help,' Stryke replied warily, 'if it's in our power.'

'This is well within your gift, Captain.'

'And providing it doesn't put our mission at risk.'

'There's no reason it should. You know my son?'

Stryke felt a cold apprehension. 'Wheam? He was just here.'

'Spouting nonsense, no doubt.'

'You said it,' Haskeer remarked.

Stryke shot him a poisonous look. 'What about Wheam, Chief?'

'I want him to go with you.'

'*No way!*' Haskeer exclaimed.

'Who's in charge here?' Quoll asked. 'You or your sergeant?'

'I am,' Stryke confirmed. 'Shut it, Haskeer. Let's get this straight, Quoll; you want your son on this mission?'

'That's right.'

'Why?'

'Look at him.' He pointed at Wheam, who was strumming his lute for a group of disinterested bystanders. 'I spawned a popinjay. A fool.'

'What's that to do with us?'

'I want the tomfoolery knocked out of him. He needs toughening.'

'We've no room for amateurs. The Wolverines are a disciplined fighting unit.'

'That's just what he needs: discipline. You're taking other unproven recruits, why not Wheam?'

'They've shown combat skills. I don't see that in your son.'

'Then it's time he learnt some.'

'Why us? There must be another way of cutting his teeth.'

'None as good as an actual mission where his survival's at stake.'

'And ours. We've got six tyros as it is, without carrying somebody untrained and unsuited. It puts the whole band in peril.'

'Much as I hate to say this, Stryke, you and your band have had things pretty much your own way since you came here. Isn't it about time you did something to repay our hospitality?'

'Much as *I* hate to say it, you don't own this land, Quoll. You're a clan chief, and we respect that, but you're not the only one in Ceragan.'

'I'm the only one in these parts, and I want Wheam signed on for this mission.'

'And if we refuse?'

'If you were to do that, I'm afraid there might be some delay . . . some *lengthy* delay in finding the artefact I'm holding for you.'

Stryke sighed. 'I see.'

'That's blackmail!' Coilla erupted.

Quoll glowered. 'I'll pretend you didn't say that.'

'Pretend what you like, it's still what you're doing!'

'That's enough, Corporal,' Stryke told her.

'But he can't—'

'*That's enough!*' He turned to Quoll. 'All right. We'll take him.'

The chieftain smiled. 'Good.' He snapped his fingers.

One of his followers came forward holding a small wooden chest. Quoll opened it and took out the remaining instrumentality. 'I confess I'm glad to see the back of this. I've not been happy having such a powerful totem in my lodge.'

As Coilla and Haskeer silently fumed, he handed it to Stryke, who slipped it into his belt pouch.

'I'll have Wheam report to you this evening,' Quoll said. He started to leave, then stopped and added, 'And Stryke, if anything happens to him, don't bother coming back.'

The chieftain strode off, trailed by his helpers.

'Oh, that's just great, isn't it?' Haskeer moaned. 'Now we're fucking babysitters.'

'Calm down,' Stryke advised.

'Haskeer's right,' Coilla reckoned. 'The last thing we need is a hanger-on.'

'What else could I do?'

'Refused, of course!'

'And never see the star again?'

'We could have taken it.'

'Not a smart move, Coilla. This is our home now.'

'It won't be if that idiot gets himself killed,' Haskeer put in.

'There's no point arguing about it. We're stuck with him. Let's just try to make the best of it, shall we? We'll put him on fatigues or something, and have one of the older hands keep an eye on him.'

'It doesn't bode well,' Haskeer grumbled, 'having a clown on the team.'

'I'm not going to apologise for it. But there's something I should say sorry to you about, Coilla.'

'What's that?'

'By rights I should have promoted you, to fill the vacancy for a sergeant. You could do the job, and you certainly deserve it.'

'Thanks, Stryke, but I don't mind. Really. To hell with that much responsibility. I like the level I've reached.'

'Well, I said the band needed two corporals, which didn't go down well with everybody.' He glanced at Haskeer. 'But it needs two sergeants, too.'

'Who *are* you thinking of promoting then?'

'I'm not.'

'Come again?'

'My idea's to reform the band as completely as we can.'

'Yeah, well, that would mean having Jup, and he's . . . Oh.'

'Right. We're going back to Maras-Dantia.'

48

6

'They're dangerous,' Coilla whispered. 'Remember what they did to Haskeer. Hell, remember what they did to *you*.'

Stryke was staring at the instrumentalities. He had them laid out on a bench in a kind of order: two spikes, four spikes, five, seven and nine. Grey, blue, green, yellow, red. He found them fascinating.

'*Stryke*,' Coilla hissed.

'It's all right, I'm just looking. Nothing sinister's going on.'

'You know what they can do, Stryke. Or at least a *part* of what they can do. And it's not all good.'

'They're just a tool.'

'Yeah?'

'Long as you don't get too involved with them.'

'My point exactly.'

'Why are we whispering?'

'It's them.' She nodded at the stars. 'When they're all together like this, they make you want to.'

'I wonder what they're made of?'

'Damned if I've ever been able to figure it out.'

'Wish I had a blade forged from it.'

'Don't get too interested. We've got enough problems brewing in the band without you going AWOL from your senses.'

'Thanks for putting it so delicately.'

'I mean it, Stryke. If those things start singing at you again—'

'They won't.'

'You'll be carrying them. *Exposed* to them, all the time. It could affect you.'

'I've been thinking about that. Once we get to Maras-Dantia, would you carry one? Maybe breaking them up will dampen their influence.'

49

'I'm flattered. You've never been keen on parting with them in the past.'

'And look what happened. Will you do it? I would have asked Haskeer, but he's such a crazy bastard.'

'Rather than burden the helpless female, you mean? Don't go spoiling it, Stryke.'

He smiled. 'I'm no human. I could never think of you as helpless.'

'Course I'll do it. But what if it doesn't work? Will you share them between more of us?'

'I don't want to up the risk of any being lost. So . . . I don't know.'

'Great. Something else for us to worry about.'

'We'll face that if and when. It's near time. We should be getting ready.'

They slipped into thick over-breeches and lined boots, then donned fur jerkins. Before she put hers on, Coilla laced a sheath of throwing knives to each arm.

'Seems weird doing this in a heat wave,' she remarked.

'Maras-Dantia's going to be a damn sight cooler than here, that's for sure.' He collected the instrumentalities and put them in his belt pouch.

They buckled on swords, daggers and hatchets.

'Don't forget your gloves,' Stryke said.

'Got 'em.'

'All right, let's go.'

Outside, by the mouth of the cave where they first arrived in Ceragan, the band waited, sweating in their furs. Haskeer was keeping them in order, when he wasn't shooting disgusted glances at Wheam, who'd insisted on bringing his lute.

Quoll and his usual entourage were at the forefront of the crowd of spectators. Thirzarr was there too, along with the hatchlings. Stryke went to them.

Before he could speak, Thirzarr mouthed, 'We've already made our goodbyes. Let's not stretch it out, for their sakes.' She indicated Corb and Janch.

Stryke knelt. 'I'm counting on you to look after your mother. All right?'

They nodded solemnly.

'And be good while I'm away.'

'We will,' Corb promised.

'Kill the witch!' Janch squeaked.

His brother bobbed in gleeful agreement and they waved their miniature cleavers about.

Stryke grinned. 'We'll do our best.'

He took one last look at his brood and turned away.

'Fare well,' Quoll said as he passed him.

Stryke gave a faint tilt of his head, but didn't speak.

At the cave's entrance, he faced the band.

'Conditions were bad in Maras-Dantia when we were last there,' he said. 'They're going to be much worse now. Expect extreme hostility, and not just from the weather. This particularly applies to you new recruits, so stick by the buddy you've been assigned. As I'm assuming we'll fetch up in Illex, in the far north, we can't take horses; they couldn't handle the conditions. Be prepared for a long, hard march south.' He weighed his next words carefully. 'Last time, we had to face the Sluagh.' He bet more than a few of the band suppressed a shudder remembering the repellent demon race. 'I don't know if we'll run into them this time. But we beat 'em once, and we can do it again if we have to. Are we all set, Sergeant?'

'Ready and eager,' Haskeer replied.

'If anybody's having second thoughts about this mission, this is your last chance to pull out. They'll be no dishonour in it.' He stared pointedly at Wheam. No one said anything. 'Any questions?'

Wheam raised a hand.

'Yes?'

'Going through this . . . portal thing. Will it hurt?'

'Not as much as my boot up your arse,' Haskeer assured him.

Laughter eased the band's tension a little.

Stryke checked that the crowd was held well back, then nodded. Haskeer barked an order. Brands were lit, and jerkins fastened.

A rhythmic pounding started up. The onlookers were beating their spears against their shields in a traditional farewell for orcs off to war. There was some shouted encouragement, and a few cheers.

Stryke led his band into the cave.

It was cool and echoing inside.

Coilla caught up with Wheam. 'Going through's unsettling,' she explained. 'Just remember we're all doing it together.'

He looked pale. 'Thanks,' he said, and walked on.

Stryke overheard. '*Unsettling?*'

'I couldn't say terrifying, could I? He's just a kid.'

They reached the centre of the cave, and Stryke had them all gather round. He studied the amulet by the light of the brands. Next, he took out the stars and began manipulating them.

For a clammy moment, he thought he couldn't do it. There seemed no sense in the way they linked to each other. He started to fumble and grow confused.

Then four stars slotted together smoothly, in quick succession, and he could see exactly where the final one should go.

'Brace yourselves,' he warned, pushing it into place.

They fell, plunging down a shaft made of light.

Sinuous, pulsating, never ending. Beyond its translucent walls was blue velvet, smothered with stars.

They dropped ever faster. The starscape melted into a blur of rushing colours.

Transient images flashed by. Fleeting glimpses of perplexing otherwheres.

There were sounds. An inexplicable, discordant, thunderous cacophony.

It lasted an eternity.

Then a black abyss swallowed them.

Stryke opened his eyes.

He felt like he'd taken a beating, and his head throbbed murderously.

Getting to his knees, it took him a moment to focus on his surroundings. But he didn't see what he expected.

There was no snow or ice, though it was cold. The grim landscape seemed gripped by deepest winter. Trees were leafless. The grass was brown and patchy, and much of the foliage wasn't just dormant, but dead. Black clouds dominated the sky. It was in total contrast to the balmy climate they'd just left.

He climbed to his feet.

The rest of the band was scattered around him. Some were on

the ground, still dazed, and several were groaning. Others, recovering more quickly, were already standing.

'Everybody all right?' he called.

'Most of us,' Haskeer said. He scornfully jerked a thumb at Wheam, who was being sick against a rock, with Dallog in attendance.

Coilla and Haskeer went to Stryke. They looked shaken after the transference, but rode it well.

'This isn't Illex,' Haskeer pronounced.

'You don't say,' Stryke told him.

'But it *is* Maras-Dantia,' Coilla said. 'I recognise some of the landmarks. I reckon we're near the lip of the Great Plains, not far from Bevis.'

'You could be right,' Stryke agreed. 'Looks like the stars don't put us down in exactly the same place each time.' He realised he was still clutching them, and began dismantling.

'At least it cuts the amount of marching we'll have to do.'

'And with any luck we won't have to go to Illex next time we use them.' He was stuffing the instrumentalities into his belt pouch. 'But I'm sorry we didn't bring those horses.'

'It's not morning here,' Haskeer decided.

Coilla sighed. 'You're an expert in stating the obvious now, are you?'

It looked to be late afternoon, going on early evening.

'And the season's wrong,' Haskeer added.

'I'm not so sure about that,' Stryke said. 'This could be what passes for summer in Maras-Dantia these days.'

Coilla stared at the terrain. 'Things have got that bad?'

'It was heading that way when we left, so why not?'

Haskeer frowned. 'What'll we do? Camp 'til first light?'

'I say march on,' Coilla suggested. 'I mean, we only got up about two hours ago. It's not as though we need the rest.'

Stryke nodded. 'Makes sense. If we are where you think, Coilla, we need to bear south-west. It's still a hell of a march to Quatt, but not near as far as we reckoned on.'

'Maybe we can rustle up some transport on the way.'

'I'm counting on it. All right, let's get 'em organised. Haskeer, see how the new intake are faring; Coilla, secure the area. Get some lookouts posted.'

Coilla went to pick sentries. Haskeer walked over to Dallog and Wheam.

The band's banner thrust into the ground beside him, the aged corporal was offering the young recruit a drink from his canteen. Wheam took it with trembling hands.

'Why the idling?' Haskeer snapped.

'He was shaken by the crossing,' Dallog explained.

'He can speak for himself.' Haskeer turned his glare on Wheam. '*Well?*'

The youth flinched. 'Going through that . . . thing . . . really . . . unsettled me.'

'Oh, what a shame. Would you like your daddy?'

'You don't have to be so—'

'*This is no fucking picnic! We're in the field now! Get a grip!*'

'Go easy, Haskeer,' Dallog advised.

'The day I need *your* advice,' Haskeer thundered, 'is the day they can take me out and cut my throat. And it's *Sergeant* to you. *Both* of you.'

'I'm only doing my job, Sergeant.'

'You're nurse-maiding him.'

'Just cutting the boy some slack. He doesn't know the ropes.'

'You and him both. You've never been on a mission, and you don't know this band.'

'Maybe not. But I know orcs, Sergeant, and I know how to mend 'em.'

'Only been one Wolverine could do that, and you ain't him.'

'I'm sure Alfray was a—'

'You're not fit to use his name, Dallog. Nobody matches Alfray.'

'Pity you were so careless with him then.'

Haskeer's face darkened dangerously. 'What'd you say?'

'Things change. Live with it. Sergeant.'

Wheam gaped at them.

'Being old don't excuse you from a beating,' Haskeer growled, making fists.

'Whenever you want to try. But maybe this isn't a good time.'

'Now you're telling me what's what?'

'I meant we shouldn't brawl in front of the band.'

'Why not?' Haskeer said, moving in on him. 'Let 'em see me knock some respect into you.'

Somebody was shouting. Others took it up.

'Er, Sergeant . . .' Wheam pointed.

Haskeer stopped and turned.

A group of riders could be seen, moving their way across the sward. It was hard to gauge their number.

'We'll settle this later,' he promised Dallog.

'What's happening, Sergeant?' Wheam asked. 'Who are they?'

'I doubt they're a welcome party. Be ready to account for yourselves. And try not to shame the band by dying badly.' He left Wheam looking terrified.

By the time Haskeer reached Stryke and Coilla, the approaching riders were recognisable.

'Oh, good,' Haskeer muttered. 'My favourite race.'

'What do you think,' Coilla said, 'around sixty?'

'More or less,' Stryke replied. 'And they look ragtag; no uniforms.'

Dallog arrived, exchanging glowers with Haskeer as he passed. 'What *are* they, Captain?'

'Humans.'

'They're . . . freakish.'

'Yeah, not too pretty, are they?'

'And they're getting closer,' Coilla reminded them.

'Right,' Stryke said. 'We assume they're hostile.' He addressed Haskeer and Dallog. 'Get the band into a defensive formation at that table rock over there. And keep an eye on the new recruits. *Move!*'

They rushed off, barking orders.

'What about me?' Coilla asked.

'How many good archers we got?'

'Five or six, counting a couple of the tyros.'

'And you. Get yourselves on top of the rock. *Go!*'

The rocky outcropping Stryke had indicated was a slab the size of a cabin. It jutted out of the ground at an angle. But its highest point, tall as a tree, was flat.

Band members were drawing blades, and discarding their heavy furs, the better to fight.

Coilla steered her archers to the rock and they scrambled up. Stryke joined the rest of the Wolverines under the tapering overhang at its base.

The humans were galloping in at speed, and a clamour rose from them. Stryke was sure he heard them chanting the word *monsters*.

He slapped the rock above his head. 'We've got a good natural defence here,' he told the band, 'as long as we don't break ranks.' The veterans knew that well enough; he was thinking of the recruits. 'Let's see those shields!'

The old hands deployed theirs expertly, slipping the shields from backs to chests in a single, deft movement. The newbies fumbled. No more so than Wheam, who got himself in a tangle trying to swap his shield for his beloved lute.

'Like *this*,' Stryke instructed, extricating the youth. 'And hold your sword *that* way.'

Wheam nodded, grinning dourly and looking bemused. Stryke sighed.

A greater racket went up from the riders.

They charged.

Coilla's unit had arrows nocked and were stretching their bow-strings. Some preferred kneeling. She stood.

The leading humans were no more than a spear throw away, horses white-flecked and huffing vapour.

'*Hold fast!*' Haskeer bellowed.

Coilla waited until the last possible moment before yelling, '*Fire!*'

Half a dozen bolts winged towards the charging attackers. One of the leading riders took a hit to his chest. Unhorsed by the impact, he tumbled into the path of those following, bringing several down.

A handful of the humans had bows, and returned fire. But shooting from the saddle meant most of their shafts were wide.

The orcs' next volley found three targets. Arrows struck the thigh of one man and the shoulder of another. The third grazed a rider's temple. He fell, to be trampled.

Coilla's team kept on firing.

Within spitting distance of the rock the humans slowed and their charge turned into a confused milling. Shouts were exchanged, then they broke into two groups. The largest turned and began galloping around the outcrop, hoping for a breach. The rest advanced on the orcs at ground level.

Some of Stryke's cluster carried slingshots. As the humans

approached, they deployed them. The salvo of hard shot cracked a couple of skulls and fractured an arm or two. But there was no time for more than a few lobs before the raiders were at their line.

Their horses gave them the advantage of height, and flailing hooves could prove deadly. The snag was reach. To engage the orcs they had to lean and hack, making themselves vulnerable.

All was churning mounts and slashing blades at the base of the rock. Blows rained on the orcs' raised shields. They struck back, and fought to bring down the riders. A dagger to the calves was sufficient in some cases. In others, concerted efforts were needed to drag horsemen from their saddles. A grinding melee ensued.

Around a dozen raiders dismounted of their own accord, the better to engage in close quarters fighting.

One human singled out Stryke for particular attention. He was burly and battle-scarred, with an overlong, disorderly beard. Like his fellows, he wore mismatched, raggedy clothes. And he swung a double-headed axe.

Stryke dodged and felt the displaced air as the weapon skimmed past. Before it reached the end of its arc, he lunged, slashing with his blade. The human moved fast, pulling back in time to avoid contact. Then he attacked again, unleashing another murderous swing. Stryke dropped and kept his head.

The man fell to hammering at Stryke's shield, looking to dislodge it. Stryke weathered the battering, and at the first let sent back a series of blistering swipes. He failed to penetrate the human's guard. But it seemed that, for all his heftiness, his opponent was starting to slow under the effort of handling the axe. Stryke wasn't about to break the formation, regardless of that. He forced the man to come to him.

The human rushed in again, spitting fury. Another pass whistled by Stryke's skull, too close for comfort. Stryke powered forward, using his shield as a ram. There was a tussle, orc and human straining with all their strength against each other. At its height, Stryke sidestepped, wrenching the shield out of play. His balance spoilt, the man stumbled forward, losing his grip on the axe. It dangled on a thong at his wrist, and he scrabbled to bring it into play. Stryke was quicker. With a savage downward sweep, he lopped off the human's hand. The man howled, his wound pumping crimson, the axe in the dirt.

Stryke stilled his pain with a thrust to the heart.

As the axeman fell, a confederate barged in to take his place. Scowling, broken-toothed, he took on Stryke with knife and sword. Their pealing blades added to the melody of clashing steel.

The orcs' line still held. But the fights boiling at the base of the rock were making it indistinct.

Up above, Coilla's archers continued to take their shots where they could. Though as the struggle became fiercer, and friends and enemies began to mingle, their task was harder. Coilla judged the attackers to be as undisciplined and ill-assorted as the way they dressed. Not that it made them any less determined, and there was an unpredictability in disorder that could be more dangerous than facing a well-organised force.

Coilla switched to throwing-knives, which she felt she used with more expertise than a bow and were more precise in chaotic situations. Taking in the scene, she spotted two likely marks. Mounted on a white mare, a wild eyed, mop-haired human was laying about an orc with a broadsword. She got a bead on him and hurled a knife with force. It buried itself in his windpipe. He flew backwards, arms spread wide, and met the ground. As a bonus, his horse panicked and kicked out with its rear legs, downing a man on foot.

Her second target was also on foot. Bald and beardless, he was built like a stone slab privy. As Coilla watched, he broke into a run at the defensive line, a javelin outstretched. She drew back her arm and flung hard. Her aim was true, but the human made an unexpected move, swerving to avoid a fallen comrade. The blade pierced his side, near the waist, proving painful but not fatal. He bellowed, nearly tripping, and went to pull out the knife. She swiftly plucked another and threw again.

This time she put it where she first intended, in his chest.

Stryke wrenched his sword from a human's innards and let him drop. He glanced around. Bodies littered the ground, slowing the raiders' advance, but there were still plenty to deal with.

Further along the line, Wheam cringed under the onslaught of a human with a mace. The metal ball's continuous pounding was distorting the shape of his shield. Wheam simply clung on, white knuckled, making no attempt to hit back. It was left to the veterans on either side to lash out and deal with his tormentor.

Nearby, Dallog was giving a much better account of himself. The band's standard jutting from the ground behind him, he made good use of his sword and dagger. Slashing the face of an attacker, the ageing corporal followed through with a thrust to the man's guts.

Hollering at full volume, a human with a spear hurtled towards Stryke. Leaping aside, Stryke grabbed the shaft. There was a forceful, snarling battle for possession. Stryke broke the deadlock with a brutal head-butt. His adversary was knocked senseless, releasing his hold. Flipping the spear, Stryke drove it through the man's torso.

Beyond the siege at the outcrop's base, riders were still circling. Every so often, one of them loosed an arrow at Coilla's archers. None caused harm. But it was only a matter of time before somebody got lucky.

On top of the rock, Coilla stood shoulder to shoulder with new recruit Yunst, who was proving adept with a bow.

She pitched a knife. A human crashed headlong into the barren ground.

'Nice shot,' Yunst said.

'Keeping count of yours?' she asked.

'Not really.'

'I make us about even.'

'Can't have that.' He focused on a target and drew his bowstring taut. 'Let's see if I can—'

There was a fleshy *thump*. Coilla was splattered with blood. An arrow had gone through Yunst's neck. He collapsed into her, a dead weight, and she went down. The impact sent her tumbling to the nearby edge. She cried out, and went over.

It was a short drop, but Coilla fell awkwardly. The jolt of landing knocked the breath out of her and jangled her senses. Lying on her side, swathed in pain, she tried to gather her wits. She was aware of fighting all around. Shuffling feet and stamping hooves. Shouting and screaming. With a groan, she rolled on to her back, then lifted her head.

Something swam into view. A shape loomed over her. She blinked and cleared her vision. A leering horseman was bearing down, his iron-tipped spear aimed at her chest. Coilla struggled to get herself clear, while groping for her blade. It was fifty-fifty whether she'd suffer the spear piercing her flesh or the rearing mount shattering her ribs.

Then someone was there, putting themselves between her and the threat. She saw that it was Haskeer. He had hold of the horse's bridle with both hands as he ducked and weaved to avoid the probing spear. Orc and beast wrestled. Several times the strength of the shying horse lifted Haskeer's feet off the ground. The thrusts of the spear came near to running him through. Finally, he lost patience.

Letting go, he jerked back his fist and gave the horse a mighty punch. The stunned animal's front legs buckled and its head went down. Yelling, and parted from his spear, the rider was unseated. As he fell, several orcs rushed forward to finish him.

Stryke appeared. He and Haskeer jerked Coilla to her feet and half dragged her to the relative safety of the orcs' line.

'Anything broken?' Stryke said.

She shook her head. 'Don't think so.'

'What happened up there?'

'We lost a new one. Yunst.'

'Shit.'

'That's what we get for using amateurs,' Haskeer remarked.

'He was a good fighter,' Coilla informed him sternly. 'And don't hit horses, you bastard.'

'No, don't bother thanking me,' Haskeer came back acerbically. 'I only saved your life.'

'We've work to do,' Stryke rebuked.

They pitched into the attackers.

The human ranks were starting to thin. But fighting was still intense. Heartened by killing Yunst, the surviving raiders stepped up their assault, and the orcs' defences were sorely tested. The otherwise silent landscape continued to echo to the rattle of steel on steel and the shrieks of the dying.

Given his shaky resolve, only luck and his comrades had kept Wheam safe. Now good fortune was put to the test. While all about Wheam were occupied, a human dashed in and laid about him with zeal. Wheam adopted his usual tactic of hiding behind his shield and letting it soak up the blows. But his assailant was determined. Wielding his broadsword two-handed, he beat the shield relentlessly, striking sparks off its misshapen surface. Then a solid swipe dislodged it from Wheam's grasp.

Wearing a look of terror, Wheam faced his foe undefended bar his sword. He gave a couple of feeble swings that barely connected with the human's blade. The volley he got back almost pummelled the weapon out of his trembling hand. A further blow snapped his sword in two. He stood transfixed and at the mercy of his opponent.

An orc careered into the human. They fought, Wheam forgotten. For a moment it looked as though the Wolverine had the better of it. But in the struggle his back was turned to the enemy. A nearby human saw his chance and buried his blade in it. As the orc went down, both men hacked at him mercilessly.

'That's Liffin!' Coilla yelled. She made to move.

'*Hold fast!*' Stryke barked. Then added softly. 'There's nothing you can do.'

The pair of humans had little time to savour their kill. From the rock's peak, the archers repaid the blood debt. The man with the broadsword took three arrows, any one of them fatal. His comrade caught two. For good measure, several Wolverines ran forward to add their wrath with steel and spears.

There was no let to the band's fury. Any humans venturing close were slashed, flayed, mauled, cut down. Soon, their numbers and their resolve ebbed away. With over half their company lying dead or mortally wounded, the raiders retreated. They rode off, back towards the plain.

The Wolverines expelled a collective breath. Yunst and Liffin's corpses were retrieved. The band took to binding their injuries and wiping their blades.

'That's a *fucking* good start!' Haskeer raged. 'Two dead, and one of 'em Liffin!'

'We take losses,' Stryke told him evenly, 'it's part of the job. You know that.'

'At this rate we'll all be dead before we even *find* Jup! Not an hour gone and this happens!'

'Anger won't bring them back,' Coilla said.

Haskeer wasn't mollified. 'We should never have lost 'em! Or Liffin at any rate. I don't care about the tyro, but Liffin was an old hand. And he threw his life away for . . . *what*? That . . . little shit!'

'He died for the band. We look out for each other, remember?'

'There's some not worth looking out for. If I had my way—'

Wheam appeared, still clutching his broken sword. 'I wanted . . . I wanted to say I'm sorry about—'

'*You cowardly bastard!*' Haskeer shrieked. 'I could kill you for what you just did!'

'That's enough!' Stryke cautioned.

Sheepishly, Wheam tried again. 'I didn't mean—'

'Liffin was worth ten of you,' Haskeer thundered, 'you snivelling heap of crap!'

'Shut it, Haskeer!' Stryke ordered.

'I'll shut *him*!' He lunged at Wheam and slammed his palms against his chest, sending him sprawling. Then he went for a knife.

Stryke and Coilla grabbed him, pinning his arms.

'*I said that's enough!*' Stryke bellowed in his sergeant's ear. 'I'll have no insubordination in this band!'

'All right, all right.' Haskeer quit struggling and they loosened their hold. He shrugged them off.

'Any more of that and I'll break you back to private,' Stryke promised. 'Understand?'

Haskeer gave a grudging nod. 'But this ain't over,' he growled. He jabbed a finger in Wheam's direction. 'Just keep that freak away from me.'

7

They should have honoured tradition and disposed of their dead with flame. But they couldn't afford the attention fire might bring. So they buried Liffin and Yunst deep, their swords in their hands. Dallog proved adept at carving, and fashioned small markers bearing the symbols of Neaphetar and Wystendel, the orc gods of war and comradeship.

By the time that was done, and some of the humans' abandoned horses were tracked down, a good chunk of the day had gone. At last, with the watery sun high, the band set out for the dwarves' homeland.

There weren't enough mounts for everybody, even with doubling up, and a third of the band had to take turns walking. The sole exception was Haskeer, whose mood was so foul Stryke encouraged him to ride alone. And he saw to it that Wheam, paired with Dallog, was as far away from the sergeant as possible. None of it made for rapid progress.

Stryke and Coilla headed the party, sharing a ride, and tried to take a route offering fewest chances for ambush. The landscape was chill and miserable, and they saw no other living creature in four hours of travelling. No one was particularly talkative, and the convoy moved quietly.

Coilla broke the silence, albeit in an undertone. 'He was right, you know, Stryke.'

'Hmm?'

'Haskeer. Not the way he acted; what he said. We've not started well.'

'No.'

'I feel bad about Liffin. He was a brother in arms, and we've been through a lot with him. But I feel worse about Yunst somehow. What with it being his first time out, and depending on us to—'

'I know.'

'Don't think I'm blaming you.'

'I don't.'

'I blame myself, if anything. About Yunst, I mean. I led that detail. I should have looked after him.'

Stryke turned his head to glance at her. 'How do you think I feel?'

Silence returned for a while.

'Who do you think those humans were?' Coilla asked, steering the conversation into less murky waters.

'Just marauders, I reckon. They didn't have the look of Unis or Manis, nor the discipline.'

'If they're typical, Maras-Dantia's sunk even deeper into anarchy.'

'All the more reason I should do this,' Stryke said, reaching into his belt pouch. He brought something out and passed it to her. 'If you still want to take it.'

She held an instrumentality. The blue one, with four spikes. It felt strange in her hand, as though it was too heavy and too light at the same time. And it had another, deeper quality Coilla found even harder to understand.

'Course I want it,' she replied, pulling out of her reverie. She slipped the star into her own pouch.

'If it starts to trouble you, give it back.'

'What about getting the band to carry it in turns, a couple of hours each? Not all of them, of course, just the true Wolverines.'

'And what happens when Haskeer wants his turn? No, it just makes problems. But if you don't want it—'

'I said I did, didn't I?' Her hand instinctively went to the pouch, and she wondered how it was for him, carrying four of the things. She changed the subject again. 'How long to Quatt, do you think?'

'Couple of days at this rate.'

'Assuming that's where Jup's going to be.'

'Well, we're not going to find out tonight, that's for sure.'

The pewter moon was up, big and fat, tendrils of cloud swathing its face. Colder winds blew.

'Where do you want to strike camp?'

64

'You're our strategist. What looks like the most defensible spot?'

Coilla scanned the drab terrain. It was flat and mostly feature-less. 'Not much choice in these parts. Wait. What's that?' She pointed.

Well ahead of them, and not far off the trail they followed, there was a jumble of shapes.

'Can't tell,' he replied, straining to make them out. 'Curious?'

'Sure.'

'Then let's head that way.'

As they got nearer they saw that the shapes were ruins. A small settlement had once stood there, but now only shells of buildings remained, or just their foundations. Charred timbers indicated that fire played its part in the destruction. There were tumbledown fences and the hulk of an abandoned wagon. Sickly green lichen grew on the stonework. Weeds choked the paths.

Stryke ordered the band to dismount.

'Humans lived here,' Coilla said.

'Looks like it,' Stryke agreed.

'I wonder what destroyed the place?'

'Probably other humans. You know what they're like.'

'Yeah.'

'Let's get organised. I want sentries posted. See to it.'

She set off.

Stryke called to the nearest grunt. 'Finje! That could be a well. Over there, see? Go and check it.'

Haskeer arrived, face like granite.

'Have this place searched,' Stryke told him. 'We could do without any more little surprises.'

'Right,' his sergeant grunted morosely, turning to obey.

'And Haskeer.'

Haskeer looked back.

'What happened with Liffin and Yunst is done. Live with it. Your moods put the band off whack, and I won't have it. Save your temper for enemies.'

Haskeer nodded, curtly. Then he went off to scare up a search party.

'*Well's dry!*' Finje shouted. He demonstrated by upending a shabby bucket. Only dirt and gravel came out of it.

Coilla returned. 'How *are* we for water?'

'It's not a problem yet,' Stryke replied. 'But we could do with finding a clean source soon. Guards in place?'

'Done. But there's something you should see.'

'Lead the way.'

She took him to the largest and most intact of the ruins. Parts of three walls were still standing, and they could see that it once had peaked eaves. A pair of large, heavy doors lay in the debris. They showed signs of having been breached with force.

As they scanned the scene, Haskeer joined them.

'What's so special about this?' he asked.

'I reckon it's a place of worship,' Coilla explained.

'So?'

'Look over here.'

They followed her to a low dry stone wall. Parts had collapsed, and there was what was left of a gate. The wall enclosed about an acre of land. Very little grew in it beyond three or four gaunt trees. Dozens of stone slabs and wooden pointers jutted from the ground, many at skewed angles.

'You know what this is, don't you?' Stryke said.

'Yes. A burial ground.'

'Oh, great,' Haskeer muttered.

'Not afraid of a few dead humans, are you?'

He glared at her.

'But why is nothing growing in there?' she wanted to know. 'Look out here; they're weeds everywhere. Nature's reclaiming it. Why not there?'

'Maybe they did something to stop things growing,' Stryke suggested. 'Sowed it with salt, or—'

'Why?'

'Out of respect for their dead? Who knows with humans.'

'Too right,' Haskeer agreed. 'They're fucking crazy.'

Stryke thought this a little rich coming from Haskeer, but kept the observation to himself. 'This is as good a place as any to pass the night. The wall can serve as a windbreak. Get them to pitch camp, Haskeer. But no fires.'

'That won't make for much cheer.'

'Just do it.'

Haskeer strode away, looking unhappy.

Coilla watched him go. 'He's being his usual joyful self then.'

'That's not our only problem right now.'

'Wheam?'

'Wheam.'

'What you gonna do about it?'

'Give him some kind of job that keeps him out of our faces, and clear of Haskeer. Come on.'

Looking bemused at the bustle of activity going on around him, Wheam was standing by Dallog further along the wall. An uncomfortable expression came to his face when he saw Stryke approaching.

Before Stryke could speak, Wheam said, 'You're going to punish me, aren't you?'

'Because of Liffin?'

'Of course. But I was afraid and—'

'Nobody under my command gets punished for being afraid.'

'Oh.' Wheam was confounded.

'Only fools don't feel fear,' Stryke went on. 'It's what you do despite the fear that affects our survival. So you'll be trained in combat, and you'll practise what you're taught. Agreed?'

'Er, yes.'

'But we don't carry non-combatants; everybody's expected to fight. That's your part of the bargain. Understand?'

'Yes, sir, Captain.'

'All right. I'll work out a training rota for you. If you want to honour Liffin, you'll stick with it. Meantime you need to have a proper role. What special skills do you have?'

'I could be our official balladeer,' Wheam replied hopefully, holding up his lute.

'I meant something useful.' Stryke turned to his new corporal. 'Dallog, what are you doing?'

'I was about to check the wounded. Change dressings, that sort of thing.' He nodded to a small group of waiting orcs.

'Wheam can help. All right with you?'

'Fine. If today's anything to go by I could use an aide.'

Wheam looked apprehensive.

'We can't risk kindling any light for you,' Stryke said. 'Got enough to work by?'

'The moon's good enough.'

'Make a start then.'

67

Dallog got Wheam to move closer, then beckoned over the first in line. Pirrak, one of the new intake, stepped forward, a grubby dressing on his forearm.

'How's it been?' Dallog enquired.

'Bit sore,' Pirrak answered.

Dallog began unwinding the bandage. 'Did you know blood flows more copiously when the moon's full?' he remarked conversationally and to no one in particular.

'Course I did,' Coilla replied. 'I'm a female.'

'Ah. Yes.' There was just a hint of awkwardness in the corporal's response.

He carried on unravelling. As the layers of binding peeled away they grew more soiled, until finally the wound was exposed. Dallog absently draped the gory bandage over the graveyard wall.

'Hmm. Lot of congealed blood. Might need to sew this gash. See how the flaps of skin hang loose on either side, Wheam? And all this pus—'

There was a groan and a weighty thud.

'He's fainted,' Coilla said.

The queuing orcs burst out laughing. Pirrak laughed, though he winced at the same time.

'What kind of an orc *is* he?' Using her teeth, Coilla pulled the cork from her canteen and poured a stream of water over Wheam's ashen face.

'Go easy with that,' Stryke warned, 'we've none to waste.'

Wheam spluttered and wheezed, causing more hilarity among the onlookers.

'I'll take care of him,' Dallog sighed, kneeling to his new patient.

Stryke and Coilla left them to it.

'Perhaps medicine isn't Wheam's calling,' she commented dryly.

'I wonder what is.'

'He should have *some* kind of job.'

'Such as? I wouldn't trust him on sentry duty, or in a hunting party. He might cope with digging latrines and preparing rations, though I wouldn't put it past him to poison us.'

'I don't think that's what Quoll had in mind.'

'To hell with him. He should have raised his spawn right in the first place, rather than dumping him on us.'

'Maybe that training you promised will sort Wheam out.'

'Maybe.'

'It's bound to be a bit of a struggle fitting new members in, Stryke.'

He nodded. 'What do you think of Dallog?'

'I like him. He fought well today, and he's all right with the medic thing. I know he's not Alfray, but who is?'

'I wish everybody felt that way.'

Reaching the wrecked hay wagon, they perched themselves on the still intact shafts. They watched the band making camp and attending to chores. The breeze grew colder as evening shaded into full night.

Working his way through the wounded, Dallog continued to absent-mindedly deposit their bloodied bandages on the stone wall behind him. More than a dozen white strips had accumulated, fluttering in the wind. Unnoticed, a stronger gust whipped most of them away. They blew into the cemetery. One became entangled in the emaciated branches of a tree, another was caught by a wooden grave marker. The rest were scattered across the barren ground.

High above, the stars were sharp and hard, like diamonds.

'Funny to think we were born under these skies,' Coilla reflected. 'Do you ever feel homesick?'

'No.'

'Not even a twinge of longing?'

'It was a different land then. Humans ruined it.'

'That's true. But it still feels strange to be back here. Everything seems so long ago, and yet as near as yesterday. If that makes any sense.'

He smiled. 'I know what you mean.'

They passed time in silence, surveying the scene. The band went about the business of preparing to settle for the night. Weapons were cleaned and rations passed round. In the distance, sentries patrolled.

The few grunts waiting to be seen by Dallog had seated themselves on the graveyard wall. Wheam, still looking unsteady, had been sorting lengths of bandages for the corporal.

'I've finished,' he announced. 'What else can I do?'

'I'm busy here,' Dallog replied, intent on cleaning a lesion

Wheam couldn't look at. 'Use your initiative.' He thought better of that and looked around. 'Make yourself useful and pick up those dressings. Can't have infections spreading.'

'What do I use to—'

'Here.' Dallog thrust a small canvas shoulder bag at him, normally used to carry shot for catapults.

Wheam set about the task with minimal enthusiasm. Making a face, he collected the couple of bandages still clinging to the wall, lifting them with thumb and forefinger at arm's length. The watching orcs elbowed each other's ribs and snickered.

He peered into the graveyard and saw the other scattered strips. Clumsily, he negotiated the wall. Once inside, he bent, picked up the first bandage and stuffed it into the bag. Spotting the next, hanging on the wooden marker, he went to retrieve that. Slowly, he worked his way through the cemetery, gathering the grubby windings of cloth.

He stooped to a bandage lying across a grave. There was a sound. He froze, listening. Nothing. He reached for the bandage. As his fingers almost brushed it, the noise came again. Once more he paused, trying to work out what it might be. The sound had a kind of scuffling, scrabbling quality, as though something subterranean was burrowing. Wheam stared at the ground. The earth was bulging and shifting. He leaned closer.

The ground burst open. A bony hand shot out and grabbed his wrist. Wheam struggled against its iron grip. He opened his mouth to shout but nothing came.

The earth was erupting on every side, spewing writhing shapes.

Sitting on the wagon's shafts, Coilla and Stryke were savouring the night air and the quiet.

'Doesn't seem so bad now, does it?' Coilla said. 'With the moon up and the stillness, we could almost be back in Ceragan.'

'I wouldn't go *that* far.'

'So what would you be doing if you were there on a night like this?'

'If I was at home I'd—'

A piercing scream rent the air.

Coilla leapt up. 'What the fu—'

'Over there! The graveyard. *Come on!*'

They ran towards the cemetery wall. Others were dashing that way too.

There was another loud yell.

They arrived to see Wheam in the middle of the graveyard, bent over and apparently tugging at something like an oversized tree root. All around him, indistinct figures were hauling themselves out of the earth.

Coilla and Stryke moved closer, most of the band at their heels, and took in the scene. The graves were disgorging strange fruit. What looked like rotting melons or oversized, cracked eggs were pushing through the soil. It took them a moment to realise that they were heads.

Creatures rose, heaving from the loam with wriggling, undulating movements. As they emerged, their forms could be seen. They were human. Or had been. Their bodies were decayed. Some were merely putrid, with discoloured, rotting flesh. Others were near skeletal, scraps of skin and cloth hanging from their exposed bones.

They progressed fitfully, decomposing limbs jerking and quivering, and their eyes were afire with malicious hunger. The smell that accompanied them was obnoxious.

One of the creatures scooped up a gory bandage and crammed it into its mouth. Its dislocated jaw clicked loudly as it chewed on the sodden fabric.

A score of the animated dead had surfaced, with more appearing. The orcs watched, transfixed.

Haskeer arrived, panting. 'What the *fuck*?'

'That's what I said,' Coilla told him.

'Snap out of it, Wolverines!' Stryke yelled. 'Let's deal with this!'

Everyone drew swords and headed for the wall.

'I'm going for Wheam,' Coilla announced.

'Can't we forget the little bastard?' Haskeer pleaded.

Coilla ignored him.

As the band approached, the walking corpses stopped and turned their heads as one. Then they advanced on the orcs.

The creature hanging on to Wheam was out of its grave. It was far gone in corruption, with much of the flesh on its chest rotted away, revealing the ribcage and foul innards. Wheam struggled to escape its grasp. He pawed at his sword sheath with his free hand, trying to reach the weapon. The creature dragged him closer.

The Wolverines swept to the wall. Coilla leapt over it and ran into the graveyard. Stryke and Haskeer chose its broken gate. A pair of the monstrosities were shambling through, and it seemed to Stryke that they were starting to move faster and with more fluidity. He charged at the nearest. The creature lurched to one side, but not quick enough to avoid the attack. Stryke's sword met no resistance as it plunged into the fetid chest. The only effect was to make his target stagger slightly, and as he swiftly withdrew the blade a puff of rank dust was liberated.

Haskeer struck out with his sword, burying it deep in his foe's side. It hewed parchment flesh, and splintered bone, but hardly slowed the creature. Haskeer delivered a weighty slash across its belly. The contents spilled out, releasing an unspeakable stench. Entrails dangling, the abomination kept coming, arms outstretched, hands like talons.

More of the creatures stumbled out of the gate. Others dragged themselves over the squat wall. The orcs met them with steel and spear. But Stryke's sense that the brutes' speed and mobility was growing proved right. One of them, moving surprisingly fast, landed a powerful arm swipe to the side of a grunt's head, knocking him senseless. Ignoring menacing blades, another crashed into an orc and encircled him in a crushing bear-hug. The pair of them collapsed struggling.

Coilla did as much dodging as fighting to get to Wheam. The creatures were noticeably gaining rapidity, though still reacted slowly compared to the living. But that wasn't an issue when a hulking specimen blocked her path with arms spread wide. She skidded to a halt. The putrefying figure instantly lashed out, cuffing her hard in the face. Coilla went down.

She rolled and quickly regained her feet. Spitting a mouthful of blood, she went on the attack, sword extended. Her opponent strode forward into her driven blade. It entered a little above his heart, or where his heart should be, and exited through his back. The blade met no resistance. Nor did it do any harm. Coilla tugged it out and switched from point to edge.

Her hacking caused more damage, cleaving chunks of rotten flesh, but didn't halt the advance. Then she cursed herself for not seeing the obvious solution sooner. Leaping to one side, out of the creature's course, she stooped and swung her sword. It sliced through the creature's leg, and the limb was so desiccated that one blow was enough. Amputated just below the knee, the creature lost balance and crashed to the ground. Coilla left it thrashing about.

When she got to Wheam he was still trying to get away. And Coilla saw that his captor was female. She had straggly, once blonde hair, and a hint of almost vanished comeliness in her gaunt features. One hand remained clamped to Wheam's wrist. With the other she had hold of his jerkin front, and was drawing him to her.

The corpse jerked Wheam close to her blotchy face. Her mouth gaped open, revealing a pair of unusually long, yellow-stained incisors. Darting like a venomous snake, she buried the fangs in Wheam's neck.

Coilla rushed in, yelling and brandishing her sword. The female pulled back, blood trickling from the corners of her rancid lips. Wheam looked to be in a state of shock, his complexion ashen, a seeping wound at his jugular. Keeping hold of his wrist, the creature turned. There was a large cavity in her chest that exposed the ribcage and viscera. Wheam's blood dribbled from it.

Carving a downward arc with her blade, Coilla cut through the creature's arm. Wheam fell away, the withered hand still attached to his wrist. Fangs bared, her features hideously distorted, the female let out a guttural hiss.

Coilla swung her sword again and sliced off the creature's head. It bounced away into the darkness. The decapitated body stood swaying for a second, then fell, crumbling to a heap of arid skin, dust and bones.

'*Bloodsuckers!*' Coilla yelled.

They heard it at the wall. But Stryke and the others needed no warning. The undead they faced were also trying to target orc throats.

'What kills 'em?' Haskeer shouted, holding a ravenous corpse at bay with jabs from a spear.

'Beheading!' Stryke hollered, slashing at an opponent of his own.

'Right!' Haskeer yelled back. Discarding the spear, he brought out a hatchet to do the job.

'And fire!' Dallog added.

Having parted the head from his adversary's shoulders, Stryke barked an order. '*Use fire! Deploy your bows!*'

A handful of archers peeled off from the fighting. Some already had tar arrow tips, and quickly attached them. The rest used windings of cloth smeared with oil. Flints were struck.

The night air was filled with fiery streaks. Incendiary arrows smacked into the bloodsuckers, engulfing them in flame. Turned to fireballs, the creatures blundered about, wailing.

Dallog tackled the problem more directly. Producing a flask, he threw a copious amount of brandy over the nearest undead. An applied spark converted the corpse into a walking blaze.

Stryke was impressed. 'Good thinking!' He dug out his own flask and drenched another of the creatures. Aflame, it collided with a fellow, igniting it too.

Haskeer looked resentful at his captain's approval of Dallog's initiative.

'Come on, Haskeer!' Stryke snapped. 'What about yours?'

'My *brandy* ration?' His hand went to the flask at his belt, protectively.

'Haskeer!'

'All right, dammit.' He took the flask and ripped out the stopper. Then he had an idea of his own. Snatching a scrap of clothing from a decapitated bloodsucker, he crammed it into the flask's neck. He used the flames from a burning corpse to light it.

Bringing his arm well back, he lobbed the flask at a group of three undead. It exploded in their midst, showering them with burning liquid. They staggered and fell, aflame. There were cheers from the orcs.

A further ten minutes of beheading and incineration put paid to the last of the creatures.

Stryke called out, *'Is anybody down?'*

'Here!' Coilla yelled back.

The ran into the graveyard. Wheam was sitting on the ground, Coilla bending over him.

'What happened?' Stryke said.

'He got bitten.'

'Trust him,' Haskeer muttered. 'Stupid little bugger.'

'I'm all right,' Wheam told them.

Dallog knelt by him. 'You don't look it.'

'I'm . . . fine. Really. What . . . what were those things?'

'They were humans to start with,' Stryke explained.

'Is that what . . . humans are . . . like?'

'No,' Coilla replied. 'They're vile, but not usually this disgusting. Well, not quite.'

'So what—?'

'I think it's the magic,' Stryke offered. 'This land's steeped in it. Or it was until their sort came. Their greed and plunder let most of it bleed away. I reckon what's left went bad, got corrupted . . . I don't know; I'm no sorcerer.'

Coilla took up the notion. 'And when these humans died and were buried here the tainted magic brought them back like this?'

'Can you think of a better reason?'

'I don't know about that,' Dallog said, examining Wheam's neck, 'but I do know this wound needs binding.'

'It needs more than that,' Stryke replied.

'What do you mean?'

'We've run across vampyrs before. Not like these, but close enough. And they pass on the infection.'

Coilla was nodding. 'Stryke's right. If this isn't dealt with right now, Wheam's going to become like them.'

'What?' Wheam squeaked.

'The bloodlust's a contagion, and it's in that wound. It has to be purified.'

Dallog was rooting through his medical satchel. 'How?'

'Not with some herb or salve, that's for sure.'

'It needs the same thing that killed most of them,' Stryke added. 'Anybody got any brandy left?'

'I'm sure it'll be all right,' Wheam protested feebly.

'Here.' Coilla handed over her flask.

'Somebody get a flame going,' Stryke said. 'And hold on to him.'

Wheam's puny resistance didn't amount to anything and they got him pinned. Dallog poured brandy on the wound, which had Wheam yelping. With ill-concealed delight, Haskeer applied the flame.

Wheam shrieked.

He carried on doing it for a good half minute while they let the brandy burn itself out.

'He's fainted,' Dallog pronounced.

'Typical,' Haskeer sneered.

'Think it worked?' Stryke wondered.

Dallog surveyed the damage. 'Looks like it. But I suppose we'll know soon enough. I'll get him bound.'

Stryke and Coilla stood. On every side, corpses smouldered and crackled.

'So much for no fires,' she said.

8

A rough diamond lying among a fall of hailstones. A beetle moving unhurriedly across a table strewn with grapes. A wind-tossed lily petal caught up in a distant flock of doves. None are less real for being hard to see.

So it was in the limitless ocean of existence, where parallel worlds teemed in numbers beyond reckoning. There were anomalies, constructs that differed from the norm though superficially identical. They were rare to the point of improbability, but genuine enough.

One singularity of this kind was a radiant sphere created and maintained by the vigour of unimaginably potent magic. Within was a world whose entire resources and population were devoted to a single cause. This enterprise was carried out in secrecy, and its heart lay in their only city.

The city was as remarkable as the curious world fashioned to house it. Had an outsider been permitted to see it, not that any ever were, they would have been awed by its startling diversity. It embraced a myriad architectural styles. Crystal spires and squat enclosures, soaring arches and faceless blocks. Grand amphitheatres standing adjacent to lofty tree houses; groups of round huts overshadowed by multi-turreted citadels. The city was made of stone, glass, timber, quartz, seashells, congealed mud, iron, brick, marble, ebony, canvas, steel, and materials that resisted identification.

Many structures appeared incomprehensible, with no obvious practical or aesthetic function. Some melted into one another as though they had grown rather than been erected. A few appeared to disobey gravity, or continuously shifted, flowing into different shapes as they subtly remade themselves.

Highways and watercourses riddled the conglomeration. The

twisting roads, elevated at some points, or burrowing into subterranean labyrinths, defied logic, and only a percentage of the canals and conduits contained water. What ran in others was viscous and of varying colours, and in certain stretches could be taken for quicksilver.

The whole bewildering muddle seemed hardly to qualify as a metropolis at all, yet it had an eccentric kind of organic coherence. Given enough time, a visitor, of which there were none, would realise that the city was best understood as the coming together of numerous cultures. A glimpse of its inhabitants would confirm it.

At the centre of the city there was a particularly imposing cluster of buildings. They were topped by a tower made of something that looked like polished ebony. It had no windows, or need of them; those inside saw infinitely more than mere glass could show.

The hub of the tower was a large chamber near its apex. Had a stranger entered they would have seen that the walls seemed to be covered in hundreds of framed works of art, all of the same size and uniformly rectangular. Closer inspection would reveal that they weren't paintings or sketches, and far from still life. They moved.

The frames were like apertures, through which a perplexing variety of constantly changing landscapes could be glimpsed: deserts, forests, oceans, cities, villages, rivers, fields, hamlets, cliff faces, towns, marshes, jungles, lakes and other, unrecognisable terrains, bizarre and alien.

One wall consisted of a single enormous aperture, its surface faintly rippling as though covered by an oily, transparent film. The scene it displayed was less easy to grasp than the others. It was entirely black, except for five pinpoints of golden light, clustered together and glowing like hot embers.

There were beings of many races present, and they were engrossed by it.

The highest ranking was human. Entering late maturity, Karrell Revers had silvering, close-cropped hair and beard, though he remained vigorous and straight-backed. Astuteness glinted in his jade eyes.

'That's it,' he declared, pointing at the image. 'We've found them.'

'You're sure?' Pelli Madayar asked. She was a young female of the elf folk, dainty of form and with features so delicate she looked almost fragile. An appearance that belied both her stamina and the force of her will.

'You've not seen instrumentalities via the tracker before, Pelli,' Revers replied. 'Over the years, I have, though seldom. Believe me, we've found them.'

'And they've been activated.'

He nodded at the screen. 'As you can see.'

'Do we know who by?'

'Given where the artefacts are located, we can make an educated guess. I think they're with the one race not represented in the Gateway Corps.'

'Orcs?'

'I'd bet on it.'

'So you take this to be the set created by the sorcerer Arngrim.'

'Almost certainly. We're sure they were fashioned there,' he indicated the screen again, 'in the region known locally as Maras-Dantia, and that they passed through many hands before being seized by a band of renegade orcs.'

'And then they disappeared.'

'Several years ago, after we picked up their last flaring. Which indicated, of course, that they must have transported whoever possessed them to another habitation. Where that may have been, we have no idea. Tracking is an imprecise art, relying more than a little on luck. Wherever they were, the instrumentalities have lain dormant until now.'

'So we don't know it's the set Arngrim made.'

'Their provenance can be established. As you're aware, every assemblage of instrumentalities has a signature. Its own song. We can verify their origin once we've recovered them. That's not important. What is important is that a set has been activated, and the possible consequences of that are dire at the best of times. But to think they could be in the keeping of a race like the orcs—'

'We don't know that either. Perhaps they've passed to someone else.'

'Someone capable of taking them from orcs? Unlikely. And I can't see the orcs trading them once they realised what they were capable of.'

'Could they? See their potential, I mean. They don't have a reputation for being the brightest of races.'

'But we can credit them with a certain base cunning. Which seems to have served them well enough to employ the instrumentalities. Though to fully direct the artefacts requires magical ability, and we should be grateful that's something orcs don't have.'

'As do few of your race, Commander,' she gently reminded him.

'You're not suggesting they're capable of mastering sorcery?'

'Who's to say what rogue intellect nature might have thrown up? Or perhaps they have help from someone who already has the necessary skills.'

'So we have two alarming prospects. Instrumentalities in the hands of an ignorant race wedded to bloodletting, or somebody directing the orcs for purposes of their own. The ramifications of either are incalculable.'

'What do we do?'

'We fulfil the remit the Corps was established for; the duty our forebears have carried out over the centuries. We do what we were all born to, Pelli. Whatever it takes.'

'I understand.'

'This needs dealing with at the highest level. As my second-in-command, I'm entrusting you personally with the task of recovering the artefacts.'

She nodded.

Revers turned to face the rest of his team. Dwarfs, gnomes, brownies, centaurs, elves and representatives of half a dozen other races stared back at him. All were dressed in variants of the black garb he and Madayar wore, with a stylised field of stars motif on their chests.

'We have a crisis brewing,' Revers told them. 'Instrumentalities falling into unauthorised hands is such an uncommon event that, for some of you, this is the first time you would have experienced it. But you've been trained for such an eventuality, and I expect you to act in accordance with the highest standards of the Gateway Corps.' He looked to the screen and its five luminous points of light. Everyone followed his gaze. 'We take for granted the multiplicity of worlds. We don't know who first discovered their existence or the means to move between them. Some conjecture that it was an ancient, long-extinct race. Others among you credit your gods. We can speculate on that endlessly and never find an answer; any more than we will ever know the true origins of magic. But that doesn't matter. Our purpose is not to plumb the mystery but to bar irresponsible access to the portals.' He scanned their faces and saw resolve there. 'The Corps has never failed to recover known instrumentalities, or to punish those responsible for their misuse. This will be no exception. You all have your duties. Attend to them.'

The crowd dispersed.

He returned his attention to Madayar. 'We have to move quickly, before the artefacts are used again and we lose sight of them. Pick whoever you want for your squad and take any provisions you need.'

'Do I have discretion in how I deal with this?'

'Act in any way you see fit. And I know it's asking a lot of you, Pelli, but bear in mind it's vital that the existence of the Corps remains secret.'

'That won't be easy, particularly if we have to use force.'

'Try persuasion if you can. Though I've little faith in that approach working with orcs. They're beyond the pale. Remember, you serve a higher moral purpose. If it's necessary to exterminate any who stand in your way, so be it. You'll have weaponry superior to anything you're likely to run into in Maras-Dantia.'

'I hope it doesn't come to that. We elves like to think that few beings are beyond salvation. Surely even orcs are susceptible to reason?'

9

Stryke dragged his blade from the human's gizzard and let him drop. Spinning, he slashed the throat of another man-thing, unleashing a scarlet gush. Then he bowled into a third, thrashing at his sword with brutal, ringing blows.

To left and right, the Wolverines were joined in fierce hand-to-hand combat. Coilla and Haskeer dispatched two adversaries, she with a pair of daggers worked in harmony, he wielding a lacerating hatchet. Dallog impaled an opponent with the spar the band used to fly its standard. Underfoot, the withered sward was slick with blood.

It was dawn, and they fought in a makeshift campsite set in a hollow, screened from the trail by a thick copse. A covered wagon was parked, with over a score of horses tethered nearby. The same number of humans battled to defend it.

The conflict was intense but short-lived. With more than half of their strength downed, somebody on the human side yelled an order. They pulled back and fled.

'Let 'em go!' Stryke barked. 'They're leaving us what we want.'

Coilla glimpsed one of the retreating humans. It was a woman, and she had long, straw-blonde hair.

'See that?'

'What?' Haskeer said.

'Those humans riding off. One of them was a female. Young, barely adult.'

'So?'

'I think I've seen her before. Though I'm damned if I can remember where.'

'Humans all look the same to me.'

'That's true.' She shrugged. 'Don't suppose it's important.'

Stryke joined them. He was wiping the gore from his blade with a cloth. 'Well, that was a lucky meeting. For us.'

'Who do you think they were?' Coilla asked.

'Does it matter?'

'Notice how many of them were dressed alike? Could have been Unis.'

'So humans are still divided amongst themselves. Surprise. Let's get on with it, shall we? That wagon should have drinking water and victuals. And now there's enough horses for everybody. If we move ourselves we can reach Quatt today.'

For all that they were travelling south, and into supposedly milder climes, the terrain grew even more bleak. The trees were bereft of greenery, and a brook they passed ran yellow with filth.

'You sure we're on the right path?' Coilla asked.

Riding alongside, Stryke cast her a wry look. 'For the tenth time, yes.'

'Doesn't look much like the way I remember it, that's all.'

'This place's had four more years of being broken by humans. That takes a toll on the land. And they've spoilt the magic. Those bloodsuckers were one upshot of that.'

'At least Wheam seems to be on the mend.' She turned and looked back down the line to where Wheam and Dallog were riding abreast. The youth wore a miserable expression, as usual, and his neck was bound, but some of his natural olive-grey colour was back.

'What's this?' Stryke said.

Coilla returned her attention to the road. A small group of figures was approaching. Some rode a rickety wagon, most were walking.

Haskeer galloped to the front of the line. 'Trouble, Stryke?'

'I don't know. They don't seem too threatening.'

'Could be a trap.'

'*Stay alert!*' Stryke warned the column.

Coilla shaded her eyes and squinted at the newcomers. 'They're elves.'

'And a mangy looking lot,' Haskeer added.

The party consisted of no more than a dozen. Those on foot trudged wearily. The wagon carried three or four old-timers, along with a couple of youngsters. All appeared fatigued and ill-nourished. They didn't react to the orcs in any noticeable way, or slow their somnolent plodding.

Leading them was a male. He was mature, although it was always hard to determine exactly how old an elf might be. His once fine clothes were shabby and he bore grime from too many days on the road.

When he reached the orcs he raised a painfully thin hand and his entourage ground to a halt.

'We have nothing,' he declared by way of greeting.

'We've no need of anything from you,' Stryke replied.

'Does that include our lives? It's all we have left.' There was only fatalism in his voice.

'We don't harm those who show us no threat.' Stryke eyed their sorry state. 'You're a long way from home.'

'What's brought a noble race like the elves down to this state?' Coilla said.

'I could ask the same of orcs.'

'We're doing all right,' Haskeer informed him gruffly.

'Then you're rare among your kind,' the elf returned. 'No race prospers in this land anymore. Except one.'

'You mean humans,' Stryke said.

'Who else? They are in the ascendancy and the elder races are being pushed back to ever remoter enclaves. Soon, our kind will retreat into myth as far as humans are concerned.'

Stryke could have told him that this was the humans' world by birthright, let alone conquest. Instead he asked, 'Where are you headed?'

'Few havens remain, and all in distant parts. We decided on the far north.'

'That's a bleak region to choose.'

'It will be no more bitter than life here has become.'

'You can't be all that's left of the elf nation, surely?' Coilla remarked.

'No. Our numbers are greatly decreased, but not to this extent. We are merely the remnants of one clan.'

'And the rest of your race?'

'Those who aren't dead are enslaved or scattered. We seem destined to be a diaspora. If we survive at all.'

'Why run?' Haskeer growled. 'Stand up to 'em. Fight the human bastards.'

'We don't possess the superior combat skills of orcs, or have as strong a taste for bloodshed. Magic was our only real weapon. But that's so depleted as to be near useless. It's come to one thing only for us: the hope that we may continue to exist.'

'Is there any way we can aid you?' Stryke asked.

'You've spared our lives. That's aid enough in these troubled times. Now if you'll permit us to pass . . .'

Stryke brought out his water pouch and offered it to him. 'You can probably use this. And we can spare a little in the way of food.'

The elf hesitated for a moment, then took the pouch. He nodded his thanks. Then Stryke had a couple of the privates load some provisions on the wagon.

As the elves were about to depart, their leader paused. 'Let me repay your benevolence with a word of caution, though you should know what I'm about to say well enough. Maras-Dantia holds nothing but misery and peril, even for orcs. It's become a wheel that breaks the hardiest spirit. You'd be well advised to find yourselves a fastness and try to weather the storm, as we are.' Without waiting for an answer, he turned and left.

The Wolverines watched the little troupe make its way along the north-bound trail.

When they were out of earshot, Haskeer said, 'What do you think of that?'

'I'll tell you what I think,' Coilla replied. 'Why won't you males *ever* ask for directions?'

Riding hard, they arrived at Quatt three hours later.

What was a particularly verdant district now looked as if it had been in the grip of an endless winter. In common with every other part of the land they'd seen, the terrain had an exhausted, washed-out quality.

They looked down on the wooded heart of the dwarfs' homeland from the crest of a hill.

'I feel a bit uneasy,' Coilla admitted.

'Why?' Stryke said. 'Think they won't welcome us?'

'We're *orcs*, Stryke; when is anybody ever pleased to see us? But it's not that so much. I'm more worried they might have moved on, like those elves. Or that Jup's dead.'

'Or maybe the unfriendly ones have taken over down there,' Haskeer put in.

Stryke stared at him. 'Unfriendly?'

'The ones who sided with the humans for coin.'

Coilla rolled her eyes. 'Aah, not that again!'

'Dwarfs can't be trusted, you know that.'

'Jup could,' Stryke reminded him. 'And his tribe didn't go over.'

'I'm just—'

'You want to turn back?'

'No. I'm only saying—'

'*What?* What are you saying?'

'Fuck me, Stryke, I'm just saying what we all know. Dwarfs are treacherous. They're notorious for it.'

'Keep that opinion to yourself. The band's got enough problems without your beef. Now get yourself back in line, Sergeant.'

'We should be alert, that's all,' Haskeer grumbled as he wheeled and spurred his horse.

Stryke caught Coilla's expression. 'Was I too hard on him?'

'*Can* you be too hard on Haskeer? All right, maybe you were. A little.'

'Well, it takes a lot to get through his thick skull. And I'd rather parley with Jup's folk than brawl with them.'

'If Jup's still alive, do you reckon we'll be able to persuade him?'

'I don't know. He turned down the chance of leaving Maras-Dantia once before. We should be ready for a knock-back on this. But we're not going to find out sitting here. Come on.' He gestured for the band to follow.

Quatt nestled in a great valley, wide enough that its far side was barely visible through the misty air. The trees surrounding its core were sorry things compared to the fecundity the band remembered. But the foliage was still abundant enough to make a dense barrier.

They followed a snaking, overhung path that filtered the dreary day's mean light even further. The odour of the forest was far from summery; it's acrid smell of decay was more autumnal. There was no sound save the thud of their horses' hooves on mulch. They kept one hand on their sword hilts as they weaved their way to the interior.

Gloom gave over to watery daylight as they entered a sizeable clearing. At its centre was a large rock pool, fed by an underground spring, the sulphurous water gently bubbling. Garlands of withered flowers were heaped around it. Tracks branched off from the clearing in three different directions.

'Which way?' Coilla asked.

Stryke looked from one path to another. 'Hold on, I've lost my bearings.'

'Oh, good.'

'Long time since I was last here. It all looks different.'

'Should we send scouts out?'

'I'm not splitting the band. We'll find our way to the dwarfs together.'

'Er, I think they've found us, Stryke.'

Scores of stocky men poured into the clearing via the paths and through the undergrowth. They were armed with staffs and short-bladed swords, and outnumbered the Wolverines by at least four to one. Swiftly, they surrounded the orcs' column.

'*Steady!*' Stryke warned the band.

A burly dwarf stepped forward. 'Who are you?' he demanded, scowling. 'What are you doing in our forest?'

'We're here in peace,' Stryke told him. 'We mean you no hurt.'

'Since when did orcs go anywhere in peace?'

'We do when we're seeking an ally.'

'You've no allies here.' The dwarf pointed to the rock pool. 'This is a holy place. The presence of any but dwarfs offends our gods.'

'Live underwater, do they, these gods of yours?' Haskeer piped up.

The dwarf gave him a murderous look, and his companions tensed.

'*Haskeer,*' Stryke hissed ominously.

'The gods dwell in all parts of the forest,' the dwarf replied, swelling his barrel chest. 'They are in the trees, and in the spirit of the woodland animals. They inhabit the very soil itself.'

'Oh, right. Having a bath, are they?'

'*Haskeer!*' Stryke snapped. He turned to the dwarf. 'Ignore my subordinate. He's . . . ignorant of your ways.'

'Stupidity is no excuse for blasphemy.'

Haskeer glared. 'Who you calling—'

'*Shut up, Sergeant!*' Stryke bellowed. 'Look,' he told the dwarf, 'if you'd just let me explain—'

'You can have your hearing. We're not unreasonable in Quatt. But give up your weapons first.'

'That *is* unreasonable for an orc,' Coilla said.

'She's right,' Stryke agreed. 'We don't do that.'

'You want 'em, you take 'em,' Haskeer added.

'If you won't disarm,' the dwarf stated coldly, 'then you're hostile. I'm giving you one last chance to throw down your blades.'

Haskeer hawked noisily and spat, narrowly missing the dwarf's boots. 'You can kiss my scaly arse, sawn-off.'

Weapons raised, the dwarfs began advancing. The orcs drew their swords.

A figure elbowed through the crowd.

'Well fuck me slowly with a barbed pike.'

'Only if you insist,' Coilla said. She smiled. 'Hello, Jup.'

10

'So you have *control* of the instrumentalities?' Jup said.

'Some,' Stryke replied. 'Only because of this.' He brought out the amulet.

'Can I see it?'

Stryke looped the chain over his head and handed it to him.

Jup examined it, absently tugging at his beard. 'I've never come across anything quite like this script before.'

'Nor me. But it's what got us here.'

Jup gave the amulet back. 'What about the influence the stars have? You know, the way they . . . What's the word? The way they captivated you, and Haskeer. Doesn't that worry you?'

'What's life without a few risks?'

'You can't brush it off, Stryke.'

'No. Coilla's looking after one. I thought breaking them up might weaken their power.'

'*You*, loosening your grip?' He smiled. 'But no, it's a good idea.'

They glanced to where she was standing, further along the row of oak benches.

The tables were set out in tiers in an even larger clearing than the one they first entered. It held a village of thatched huts, storage sheds and livestock pens. Fires had been lit in several shallow pits, to keep the unseasonable chill at bay and to roast meat.

Hospitality had been extended to the orcs once Jup insisted they were honoured guests. But many of the dwarfs appeared grudging. Now most sat apart, eyeing the Wolverines suspiciously.

Haskeer came and plonked himself down next to Stryke and Jup.

'And how are you, you old bastard?' Jup said.

'Hungry.' He fidgeted. 'And these seats are too small.'

'They weren't made for a massive rear end like yours. Ah, how

89

I've missed that scowl. You know, I can't get used to you all without your tattoos of rank. Looks odd. How'd you get rid of them?'

'A sawbones back in Ceragan,' Stryke explained. 'He used some kind of vitriol. Stung like fury, took an age to heal.'

'Then itched like buggery for a month,' Haskeer added. 'Worth it though. Shows we're nobody's slaves.' He stared at the struck-through crescents high on Jup's cheeks that indicated his one-time status as sergeant. 'You should lose yours, too. Like me to cut 'em out for you?' He made to reach for his knife.

'Don't think I'll bother, thanks. They give me a certain distinction around here.'

'Really?' Stryke said. 'I'd have thought being in Jennesta's horde wasn't something to brag about.'

'Not everybody saw her as the evil bitch we knew and hated. And that's something else I can't get my head around: her surviving that . . . vortex thing.'

'Seems she did. If Serapheim's to be believed.'

'Big if.'

A dwarf arrived with tankards and deposited them on the bench without a word. Haskeer snatched one and gulped a long draught.

Stryke took a drink himself. 'Strange to think,' he reflected, lowering his tankard, 'that if it hadn't been for Jennesta we'd never have known about Ceragan. I wouldn't have met Thirzarr and sired young.'

'You have hatchlings?' Jup said.

'Two. Boys.'

'Things *have* changed.'

'And like I said, if Jennesta hadn't sent us after that first star—'

Haskeer slammed down his tankard. 'We don't owe her a fucking *thing*. Whatever we got was our due.'

Jup nodded. 'Much as I hate to agree with latrine breath here, that's how I see it, too. It seems a fair exchange for all the grief she doled out. Talking of Ceragan . . .' He looked about the clearing. 'I see some new faces, and the absence of others.'

'The two are linked,' Haskeer muttered darkly. He jabbed a thumb in the direction of Wheam and Dallog.

'Take no notice of him,' Coilla said, arriving to claim a seat.

'When did I ever?'

She lifted a tankard. 'Hmm. Potent stuff.'

'We pride ourselves on our brew.'

Coilla had another mouthful, then remarked in a lower tone, 'Your folk take their gods a bit seriously, don't they?'

'Some do. More so since things really started to fall apart. Religious zeal's got even stronger in Maras-Dantia while you were away, and not just among humans.'

'We met a bunch of elves on the way here. They reckoned humans are going to be the end of the elder races.'

'I might have argued against that once. I'm not so sure they're wrong now fanatics have the whip hand.'

Coilla snapped her fingers. 'Fanatics. Of course. It was *her*!'

'Who?'

'The female I saw when we took those humans' horses.'

'What about her?' Stryke said.

'I *thought* she looked familiar. It was Mercy Hobrow. That lunatic Kimball Hobrow's daughter. Grown up now, but still recognisable.'

Jup expelled a low whistle. 'You had a lucky escape then. She's as crazy as her old man, and she's carried on his work. Her group's a rallying point for Unis, and she's got an army of followers even bigger than her father's. They're a scourge in these parts.'

'And we've given her another grudge against us,' Stryke observed.

'You'd be well advised to steer clear of her in future.'

'We don't intend being here that long. But talking of fathers and daughters, Jup, I meant to ask; last we saw of you, you were getting Sanara out of the palace in Illex. What happened to her?'

'Good question. Jennesta's army was in chaos, and these helped us get through.' He pointed at his tattoos. 'Then we were days crossing the ice fields. The woman was tough, I can tell you that. When we got down to the plains . . . well, I didn't lose her, exactly. But she went. Don't ask me how. She was there one minute, gone the next.'

'Fucking magic-mongers,' Haskeer grumbled. 'Slippery as spilt guts.'

'Anyway,' Jup finished, 'I gave up looking for her and made my way here. Haven't seen her since.'

'Quite a family, eh?' Coilla said. 'Serapheim and his brood.'

Dwarfs were heading their way carrying wooden trenchers heaped with steaming meat.

Stryke nudged Haskeer. 'Looks like your belly's about to stop rumbling.'

'Sorry if it's less than a feast,' Jup stated apologetically. 'The forest doesn't bring the yield it once did, and game's scarce.'

Wheam and Dallog wandered over.

'Mind if we join you?' Dallog asked.

'If you must,' Haskeer grated.

Coilla shot him a hard look. 'Course. Park yourselves.'

Platters of spiced roast meat were set down on the table, along with baskets of warm bread. There were dishes of berries and nuts.

'You don't know how welcome this is after field rations,' Stryke said.

'Hmmph,' Wheam agreed, mouth full. 'Food good.'

'We're grateful,' Coilla put in, 'especially with hunting so poor.' She jabbed Haskeer's ribs with her elbow. *'Aren't* we?'

He glared at her and dragged a sleeve across his mouth. 'It's all right. Could be more of it.'

'Is this usual dwarf fare?' Dallog intervened diplomatically.

'More or less,' Jup replied. 'Though we'd prefer a greater quantity.' He aimed that at Haskeer, who stayed oblivious.

'Those of us from Ceragan have never seen dwarfs before,' Dallog said, 'so don't take my ignorance for a lack of courtesy.'

'No offence taken. I remember how I felt when I first saw an orc.'

'You didn't think we were as revolting as humans, did you?' Wheam piped up.

Jup smiled. 'Nowhere near. Though the storytellers would have us believe you ate the flesh of your own kind, among other things.'

'I'm a balladeer,' Wheam declared proudly.

'I noticed the lute.'

'That's putting it a bit grandly,' Stryke said. *'Hoping to be* would give a better account.'

'I can prove it,' Wheam protested. 'I could sing something.'

'Oh gods,' Haskeer groaned. He upended his empty tankard. 'More drink.'

'That we do have,' Jup told him, beckoning a female dwarf carrying a laden tray.

She was fair of form, as far as the orcs could judge. Her skin was smooth as ceramic, and her long auburn hair was woven in plaits. She was hale, and though powerfully built she moved with graceful ease, for a dwarf.

Putting down the tray, she leaned over and kissed Jup. The clinch was lingering.

'Now that's what I *call* service,' Coilla remarked.

The pair disentangled themselves.

'Sorry,' Jup said. 'This is Spurral.'

'Somebody . . . special?' Stryke asked.

'She's my cohort.' He saw they didn't grasp what he was saying. 'My other half. Perpetual companion, mate, partner. *Spouse.*'

'You were right,' Stryke said, 'things really have changed.'

Coilla smiled. 'Good on you both.'

Haskeer lowered his tankard. 'Hell, I never thought you'd let yourself be tied down, Jup. Hard luck.'

'You must be Coilla.' Spurral smiled at her. 'And you're Stryke.'

'Good guess.'

'Oh, I've heard a lot about you all.' The smile faded. 'And you just have to be Haskeer.'

Haskeer bobbed his tankard at her and downed more ale.

'Spurral and me have known each other since we were kids,' Jup explained. 'When I got back here it just seemed right that we made it kind of official.'

'So two proud dwarf families were joined,' Spurral added. 'Me being a Gorbulew and Jup a Pinchpot.'

Haskeer choked on his beer. 'You're right about that!' he spluttered.

'Pinchpot,' Jup repeated through grated teeth. '*Pinch*pot.'

Haskeer rocked with mirth. 'So you,' he pointed at a stony-faced Spurral, '. . . you stopped being a . . . Gorbulew and . . . became a pis—'

'*Haskeer,*' Jup growled ominously.

'Talk about learning something new every day,' Haskeer ploughed on, hugely amused and insensible to their sour expressions. 'You never told us you were a . . . *Pinchpot.*'

'I wonder why,' Spurral remarked dryly.

'That's enough, Haskeer,' Stryke cautioned, a note of menace in his voice.

'Come *on*. I know getting hitched can kill your sense of humour, but—'

'We're guests here. Be mindful of it.'

Haskeer sobered. 'Seems to me there was no point in our coming.'

'How's that again?' Jup said.

'Can't see you joining us, what with you having a mate and all. It was a wasted journey.'

Jup and Spurral exchanged glances.

'Not necessarily,' Jup said.

Coilla swept her arm to indicate the throng of dwarfs in the clearing. 'I thought you stayed here because of them.'

'Given the choice of spending your life with another race or your own, wouldn't *you*?'

'You could have been sent to the dwarfs' home world. Serapheim offered.'

'I wouldn't have known anybody there either.'

'So why the change of heart?'

'I never thought I'd say it, but I want to get away from here. The time's come.'

'You can see this land's dying,' Spurral said, 'and our folk along with it. Did you get a close look at our tribe? Almost all are old, lame or infirm.'

Jup shrugged. 'We don't want to leave, but—'

'We?' Stryke said.

'There's no way I'm going without Spurral.'

'That complicates things, Jup.'

'Why should it? Unless you've got a problem with dwarfs in the band.'

'You know it's not that. But we've no idea what we're going into, except it'll be dangerous.'

'I can look after myself,' Spurral protested. 'Or is it taking females along that you don't like?'

'In case you hadn't noticed,' Coilla told her, 'I'm a female myself. What's important is being able to fight.'

More than one pair of eyes flashed to Wheam.

'Spurral's a good fighter,' Jup replied. 'She's had to be.'

'You're not going to shift on this, are you?' Stryke said.

'Nope. It's both or neither.'

'I'm running this band just like I did in the old days, as a tight unit. Everybody in it takes orders.'

'We've no gripes with that.'

'Don't say you're going along with this, Stryke,' Haskeer complained.

'I make decisions about the band, not you.'

'Then don't make a bad one. We're carrying enough dead wood as it is, and—'

'Didn't Stryke just say you all obey orders?' Spurral interrupted. 'Doesn't sound like it to me.'

'Stay out of this.'

'This is *about* me!'

'Call her off, Jup,' Haskeer snarled.

'She can fight her own battles.'

'Yeah,' Spurral confirmed, squaring up to Haskeer. 'Want to put your fists where your mouth is?'

'I don't hit females.'

Coilla laughed. 'Since when?'

'*That's enough,*' Stryke decided. 'Haskeer, shut your mouth. Jup, Spurral; back off. Everybody, sit down.' They settled. 'That's better. I'll think about Spurral, Jup. All right?'

'That's all we're asking for.'

'So let it rest.'

'Yes. This should be a celebration. More drinks.' He reached for a jug and topped up their cups. 'And we have a little pellucid if anybody's—'

'Oh, no. Not after the last time. Mission first, pleasure later.'

Haskeer mumbled, 'Shit.'

'What about that song then?' Jup suggested. 'Wheam?'

Coilla rolled her eyes. 'Gods, must we?'

But Wheam had his lute in his hands. 'This might be a little rough. I'm still polishing it.' He began strumming.

'The Wolverines, that dauntless band,
Fought their way across the land
They beat a path through rain and mud
And left their rivals in pools of blood

'They met rank fiends in battles dire
And sent them to eternal fire
No demons grim or human waves
Could overcome the Wolverines' blades

'They came to where the dwarfs did dwell
And saw that they had not fared well
But still their welcome was quite fulsome
And hospitality was truly awesome.'

'Shall I kill him or will you?' Spurral asked Jup.

'Here's the chorus,' Wheam declared, upping the tempo of his discordant plucking.

'We are the Wolverines!
Marching to foil evil schemes!
Fleet of foot and strong of arm!
We—'

'Well, it's getting late,' Stryke announced loudly.

Wheam came to a grating halt. 'But I haven't—'

'Been a long day,' Coilla added, stretching.

'Sure has,' Jup agreed, 'and a big day tomorrow.'

Wheam's face dropped. 'You never let me fin—'

'Turn in or I'll break that fucking string box over your head,' Haskeer promised.

'Time we all hit the sack then,' Dallog said, taking Wheam's arm.

'We set off in the morning,' Stryke told them. 'Early.'

They dispersed to their various billets, with most of the privates making for a couple of long houses. Jup and Spurral led Stryke, Haskeer and Coilla to a pair of much smaller huts.

'Stryke,' Jup said, 'you and Haskeer are going to have to share this one.' He pushed open the door.

Striding in, Haskeer cracked his head on the top of the door frame. He let out a stream of curses.

Spurral covered her mouth to stifle her glee.

'Don't forget everything's dwarf scale,' Jup added.

'Thanks for reminding me,' Haskeer retorted. He looked

around the poky room and noticed the cots. 'That goes for the beds too, does it? These are only fit for hatchlings.'

'We'll sleep on the floor,' Stryke told him. 'And if you snore I'll kill you.'

'We'll leave you to it,' Jup said. 'You'll let us know about Spurral, Stryke?'

'In the morning.'

Coilla was taken to the adjoining hut.

Spurral ushered her in. 'You get this one all to yourself. Though the bed's no bigger.'

'I don't care. I could sleep on a rack of knives.'

They left her stripping blankets and tossing them on the floor.

Coilla was so tired she didn't even bother taking off her boots. As soon as she stretched out, she was asleep.

There was only the black velvet of oblivion. Mindless, timeless. All embracing.

The first frail light of dawn seeped in through the cracks around the door and window shutters.

She stirred.

Instantly, she knew she wasn't alone. A figure loomed over her. She tried to move.

The cold edge of a steel blade pressed against her flesh.

And an unmistakably human voice whispered, 'Don't make me cut your throat.'

11

'If you're going to do it, get it over with,' Coilla said, the blade tight against her throat.

'We don't want to hurt you.'

'We?'

'I'm not alone.'

Out of the corner of her eye she was aware of someone else skulking in the shadows.

'We're just trying to help you,' the human added.

'You've a funny way of showing it.' Coilla's fingers snaked towards her own knife.

'I didn't want you bawling the place down and bringing the others in here.' He grabbed her hand, then wrenched her knife from its sheath and tossed it aside. 'Or getting any bright ideas.'

'Who *are* you?'

'Long story.'

'Why would your kind help an orc?'

'Another long story.'

'Not much of a talker, are you?'

'There's no time. This place's about to be attacked. But you might be able to do something about it if you can get your forces mustered.'

'Why should I believe that?'

'We've seen what's massing out there. Take my word.'

'A human's word?'

'How could warning you be a trap? Look, if I take this knife away are you going to behave?'

Coilla nodded.

He removed the blade and backed off.

She lay still. 'At least let me see you.'

98

The human fumbled for a moment before sparks were struck and a candle lit.

As far as Coilla could tell with humans, he seemed in his prime. He certainly looked fit. His mass of hair was blonde, but he had none of the facial growth many of his race favoured.

He moved the candle. The circle of flickering light showed the other man's features. He was older, and had the build of someone used to sloth. There was grey in his thinning black hair and tightly trimmed beard. His pallid skin had a sheen of sweat, despite the early morning chill.

'You have names?' she said.

'I'm Jode Pepperdyne,' the younger man replied. 'This is my . . . This is Micalor Standeven. You?'

She got up. 'Coilla.'

The older man spoke. 'We're wasting time. A small army of religious fanatics are going to be here any minute.' He was noticeably more nervous than his companion.

'Unis?' Coilla asked.

'Does it matter?' Pepperdyne said. 'All you need know is that they're hell-bent on mayhem.'

'We're well guarded.'

'Really? We got in easily enough.'

'I don't understand why you'd side with us against your own.'

'They're nothing to do with us,' Standeven insisted.

'Let's just say we have mutual interests,' Pepperdyne offered. 'And we'll be mutually dead if you don't start mounting a defence *now*. Trust me.'

'That's asking a lot.'

'What have you got to lose? If we're lying, all you've done is put everybody on alert. If we're telling the truth, you've a chance to hold off the attack.'

'But decide now,' Standeven added. 'Because if your answer's no we can try getting out of here ourselves.'

'Will you do it, Coilla?' Pepperdyne said.

'I'll do it. But if this is a trick,' she vowed, 'you'll both pay.'

He smiled his gratitude. 'Do it quietly. We don't want to warn the raiders.'

'Oh *really*? I never would have thought of that.' She gave him a withering look, then headed for the door. 'You two stick by me. Many here would bring you down soon as look at you.'

She led them to the adjoining hut and barged straight in.

Haskeer still slept, snoring loudly. Stryke stood on the far side of the room, stropping a blade. He spun around.

Coilla held up her hands. *'Easy.'*

He glared at the humans. 'What the hell's this?'

'They're . . . friends. Or at least not hostile.'

'What?'

'Listen, Stryke. There might be an attack coming.'

'Says who?'

'They do.' She jabbed a thumb at Pepperdyne and Standeven. 'And I don't think we can risk ignoring them.'

'But—'

'If they're right, there's no time to waste, and— Can't you stop that fucking *noise?'*

'Huh? Oh, yeah.' He turned and gave his snoring sergeant a kick.

Haskeer leapt up, tangled in his blanket. 'Uhh? Fuck! *Humans!'* He whipped out a knife.

'Calm down,' Stryke told him. 'We know.'

'But what—?'

'There could be trouble.'

'Trouble?' Haskeer was still negotiating wakefulness.

'Yes. According to them.'

'According to *them?'* he replied, rubbing sleep from his eyes. 'They're nothing but lousy—'

'We appreciate you don't know who we are,' Pepperdyne said.

'We know *what* you are,' Haskeer rumbled.

'And you've no reason to trust us. But brush us off and you'll have a crowd of lunatics down on you.'

'Makes sense, Stryke,' Coilla said. 'We upset Mercy Hobrow and her Unis. If they tracked us here . . .'

Stryke looked from her to the humans. 'What's your interest in this?'

'You don't have time for our life stories,' Pepperdyne replied.

Several long seconds passed while Stryke studied their faces and thought things over. 'All right, we'll sound the alarm.' Haskeer started to object. Stryke waved him away. 'Better prepared than caught unawares.'

Haskeer gave a resigned sigh. 'So what do we do with them?' He nodded at the two men.

'Lock 'em up somewhere.'

Pepperdyne tensed. 'Nobody locks us away. We're part of this.'

'We can't have 'em running around armed,' Haskeer objected.

'I don't carry a weapon,' Standeven said. As proof, he held open his jerkin.

Haskeer was appalled. 'No weapon? Humans *are* crazy.'

'This one has a blade,' Coilla said.

'And if anybody wants it,' Pepperdyne came back defiantly, 'they'll have to take it.'

Coilla appreciated the sentiment. 'We can respect that.'

'But if this is some kind of ploy,' Stryke promised, 'being armed won't stop us taking it out of your hides. Now let's move.'

They left the hut. Stryke ordered the humans to wait, with Coilla keeping an eye on them. Then he and Haskeer set off stealthily to rouse the others, creeping from door to door. In their wake, orcs and dwarfs emerged, bearing arms and treading softly.

Tousle-haired, Jup and Spurral made their way across the clearing to Stryke.

Spurral looked indignant. 'What are *they* doing here?' she demanded, pointing at Coilla's charges.

'Warning us. They say. And before you ask, I haven't a clue who they are.'

'You *believe* them?'

'Best not to take chances.' He turned to Jup. 'Can your people get into a defensive pattern?'

'In their sleep. What are we facing?'

'Don't know. Or if. But could be big.'

'You've seen the state of our tribe. Not a lot of prime fighters.'

'You've got us.'

Jup nodded and moved off. Spurral glowered one last time at the pair of humans and went after him.

Haskeer arrived. 'The band's ready, Stryke. How do we deploy?'

'We need to be mobile. We'll split into five units, headed by me, you, Coilla, Jup and Dallog.'

'*Dallog?*'

'I'm not debating it. Get those squads sorted, and make sure you spread around the new recruits.'

He left Haskeer to it and jogged to where Coilla stood with the humans.

'I'm splitting the band into groups,' he told her. 'You're leading one. There'll be a hideaway for non-combatants. These two can go there.'

'Fine by me,' Standeven responded eagerly.

Pepperdyne gave him a contemptuous look. 'But not me.'

'You've no say in it.'

'I can fight, and you need every sword arm you can get.'

'Your place is at my side!' Standeven retorted.

His tone had Stryke and Coilla exchanging curious glances.

Pepperdyne ignored his master's petulance. 'I can be more use out here.'

'Do as you please,' Stryke decided. 'We've no time for squabbles.'

'You'd better stay with my unit,' Coilla said. 'Unless you want to be mistaken for an enemy.'

Pepperdyne nodded. 'Right.'

'Haskeer's forming the groups,' Stryke explained. 'Get over there, and take him with you.' He indicated Standeven. 'He can cower with the old ones and sucklings.' He thrust a finger in Pepperdyne's chest. 'And *you*. Make a wrong move, or get in our way, and you're dead.'

Practised at repelling intruders, the dwarfs were swift to take up positions. They occupied defensive trenches. Lookouts climbed tall trees. Archers were placed on the roofs of buildings. The five teams of orcs were stationed at strategic points across the clearing.

Those who couldn't fight, along with Standeven, took shelter in the sturdiest barn.

Wheam was assigned the job of guarding them. A meaningless role, given that if the enemy reached it, everything would already be lost.

The bout of furtive activity over, everyone settled in to wait. Nothing, not even birdsong, disturbed the early morning quiet.

Coilla's group sheltered behind a small cluster of bushes, ready to fire-fight where needed. Pepperdyne knelt beside her, his breeches moist with dew. Half a dozen privates under her command eyed him charily.

The minutes seemed unusually reluctant to pass.

'You'd better be right about this,' she whispered, scanning the tree-line.

'I am.'

'Sure? They're taking long enough showing themselves.'

'They'll come.' He twisted to face her. 'Do you know what you're going to be up against?'

'We've tangled with Unis before.'

'Lately?'

'Few years back.'

'Word in these parts is that they're even more ruthless now.'

'You're not from these parts then?'

He turned wary. 'Not really.'

'Then maybe you don't know about orcs.'

'These fanatics are *savage*. They're a death cult.'

She smiled. 'So are we.'

There was a shriek. Across the way, a dwarf plunged from the upper branches of a tree, his body peppered with arrows. Bolts winged through the greenery, slashing leafs and splintering bark; clearing the way for black-clad figures emerging from the forest.

Coilla snatched her sword. 'Time to show what you're made of, pink skin.'

Stryke's group was well away from Coilla's, and sharing one of the dwarfs' trenches. Jup's was stationed behind several hay wagons parked in the middle of the clearing. Dallog's had hidden themselves in and around an outlying barn. But it was Haskeer's group, concealed in undergrowth not far from the forest's edge, that took the first brunt.

The humans rolled in softly, like a wave on an ocean of pitch.

From their hiding places, defending archers loosed a hail of barbed shafts. A score of the raiders dropped. Then thirty or forty dwarfs broke cover and rushed forward to take issue, wielding short-bladed swords and staffs. That left Haskeer's troop with no option but to wade in.

The first few minutes of combat stretch time and overwhelm the senses. Movement, clamour and the stink of fear are all-pervasive. The only counter is bloodlust.

Haskeer plunged into the human deluge, cutting down two men in short order. The shield of a third took the full force of his broadsword. But its bearer was knocked off kilter. He yielded his guard and let in Haskeer's cleaving blade. Blood gushed and the man fell. Haskeer spun to face another.

The air was filled with the natter of quarrelling steel, bellowed curses and anguished screams. All around, Haskeer's unit fought to stem the tide of flesh, toiling like harvesters scything corn.

Though the dwarfs fought with passion, few races possessed the martial skills of orcs. So dwarfs were the first to fall.

One, his head split, collapsed across Haskeer's path. He stepped over the corpse to face its killer. Muscular, and of impressive girth, the human brandished a pair of axes that looked toy-like in his massive fists. And he moved with a swiftness that ignored his size.

Haskeer dropped, spurning a wild axe swing. Then dodged again when its partner came close to dismembering him. Lunging from all-fours, he scurried clear, turned and engaged for a second time. Slicing and ducking in equal measure, he searched for an opening. But the human handled his axes with practised agility, and appeared tireless. It was all Haskeer could do to keep clear.

Knowing that any one of the humans in the surrounding melee could elect to stab his back, he put on a spurt. Powering forward, he tried simply battering through. The human drove him off. Haskeer rallied and went in again. There was a moment of stasis, with fierce blows exchanged but no give on either side. Finally the man faltered and took a step in retreat. Haskeer upped the pace. He thrashed metal, his blade whipping a squall.

Then it was through, and cut deep. The man's arm was laid open crook to wrist.

Blood surged and he dropped an axe. Haskeer didn't loiter. A crisp flip of his blade had it homing in for another bite. He struck flesh again. The human cried out, an oblique wound reddening his chest. Grievous, but not fatal, though enough to let the other axe slip from his sweaty grasp. He staggered.

Haskeer rushed in, grabbed one of the axes and swung it solidly. The human's head bounced off into the melee. His body briefly stood, a crimson fountain, before buckling.

Nearby, Seafe was coming off second best in a scrap with a burly swordsman. Haskeer lobbed the axe. It struck the human square in his back. Arms flailing, he collapsed. Seafe gave his sergeant a thumbs-up and picked another foe.

Raiders were still coming out of the trees, and the struggle boiled on every side. Turning his sword on the next pallid human, Haskeer was beginning to think Quatt would be overrun.

A tight-knit group powered through the crowd. They travelled with purpose, hacking down any opposition. In minutes they reached Haskeer's team and joined the slaughter.

'Took your time!' Haskeer grumbled, batting at a human's probing spear.

'You're lucky we came!' Coilla retorted.

She whacked the sword from a Uni's hand and punctured his skull. His fellow took the edge of her blade across his belly. Coilla had enough wrath left over to run-through the next human in line.

She stood panting as two more Unis approached warily. Weighing up whether to spend her precious throwing knives on them, she noticed Pepperdyne.

The human moved among the enemy like a fish in limpid water. He was master of his blade and used it as a veteran would. Weaving and turning, he stayed clear of whistling steel with an almost contemptuous ease. When he struck, it was as quick as thought, and always to the true.

He killed two men in rapid succession. Neither so much as engaged him. As they fell he sought more flesh, wielding his sword with the skill of a surgeon. In seconds, his sinuous dance brought death to another black-clad human.

Haskeer saw it too. Then he tugged his blade from the spearman's guts and let him drop.

The attack was coming from all directions. There was no point on the clearing's boundary where there wasn't conflict. In places the line had broken and the defenders were falling back. Dwarfs were suffering casualties, and some lay dead, but so far, orc injuries were light. Stryke doubted that would last.

Using a sword and dagger combination, he reaped the flood of invaders. A twin thrust took down a pair as one. The swiftness of his blades caught three more in as many heartbeats. Still the enemy came.

Stryke found himself facing a studded mace. Its handler showed little finesse employing it, but his wild, two-handed swipes were no less dangerous for that. For a full minute Stryke managed nothing more than avoiding it. Then he got his opponent's measure. Holding back until the club was in full swing, he dived under the man's outstretched arms and pierced his torso. The Uni crumpled.

Stryke ran the back of a hand across his clammy brow and pushed on.

Despite all the resistance they met, humans were getting through to the settlement. Most stayed in groups, knots of belligerence fuelled by pious zeal, lashing out savagely at all in their reach. The defenders slowed them, but they were hard to stop.

Dallog's troupe, obeying orders by remaining at the barn, had seen no action. What happened next made up for that. A bunch of howling humans, twice their number, sped in to take issue. Half a dozen uneven duels broke out.

Standing to the fore, Dallog was set upon by a trio of enraged fanatics. Their frenzy and number worked to his benefit. Fury made for poor judgement, and fighting as a group had them getting in each other's way. He quickly profited. A scouring blow across the side of a Uni's head put him out of the picture.

The fallen man's companions were less easy to better. One jabbed at Dallog with a shortened spear, its tip wickedly barbed. The other contrived to circle him, for an attack from side or rear. They were working together. Lessening the odds had increased the threat, and the irony wasn't lost on Dallog.

Twisting away from the spear, he lashed out at the circling swordsman. Metal echoed as they pounded each other's broadswords. Deadlock ensued, and might have continued had not the spearman intervened. Losing patience, he rushed in, thrusting the weapon at Dallog, passion outwitting skill. His recklessness was a gift. Dallog spun, brought down his blade hard and knocked the spear from the Uni's hands. Without pause he followed through, delivering a fatal blow.

The swiftness of the kill threw the sword-bearer off his stroke. Before he recovered, Dallog got in close and nasty. He swiped, raking the Uni from armpit to waist. Then he put all he had into a high swing that buried his blade in the human's skull. The man plummeted, so much dead weight.

Dallog leaned on his gory sword, breathing heavily and hoping none of the grunts noticed his fatigue.

The Unis had torched the barn. Thick black smoke belched from its open doors. Flames scaled the wooden exterior and the roof steamed. A screaming human stumbled past, his clothes ablaze. Orcs and Unis fought without let. Havoc reigned.

Something caught Dallog's eye. Towering shapes were emerging from the tree-line. At first he couldn't make out what they were. As they entered the clearing he saw. Black-garbed horsemen, in their dozens.

'*Second wave!*' he bellowed '*Second wave!*'

12

Riders were charging across the field of battle, trampling defenders and cutting them down.

In the middle of the clearing, by a couple of hay wagons, Jup's group was oblivious, absorbed as they were in vicious hand-to-hand fighting.

Spurral was at Jup's side. They were armed with the dwarfs' traditional weapons; he with a leaden-headed staff, she with a short, curved sword and knife. And they were working the weapons hard.

Jup dodged a blow and gave the head of his attacker a resounding crack. Flipping over his staff, he thrust the weighted end into the midriff of another. He used the staff with speed and seasoned grace. Spurral was no less skilful with her blades. Crowded by a pair of Unis, she expertly slashed the face of one and knifed his companion.

Eldo fought alongside them. Fending off the attentions of a brute with a club, the grunt took a hit that dented his helm and had him reeling. Spurral quickly deflected the clubman's follow-through and ripped his belly. A grateful if dazed Eldo nodded gratitude, and Spurral earned further respect from the grunts looking on.

After a seeming lifetime of grinding conflict there was a brief hiatus. But no respite.

Chuss, one of the new recruits, pointed. *'Look!'*

They saw the riders.

Then two horsemen broke through the forward defences and galloped their way.

'Take cover!' Jup bellowed, waving his group towards the wagons.

He made Chuss and fellow newbie Ignar shelter under one of

them. The rest of the team clustered defensively. Jup and Spurral clambered to the top of the wagon nearest the approaching riders.

Seconds latter, the pair of horsemen arrived, brandishing cutlasses. Their mounts were steaming and foam-flecked.

One of the Unis made straight for Jup and Spurral. They battled to fend him off, but his mobility kept him frustratingly beyond reach. His companion, meanwhile, was leaning and slashing at the knot of orcs. Trying to avoid his horse's thrashing hooves, they jabbed and swiped at him.

The skirmish ground on, with neither side gaining the advantage. Then seasoned hand Gleadeg had an idea. He dug out a slingshot, quickly primed it and commenced swinging. The unleashed shot peppered the rider's face and chest. He cried out, lost his balance and crashed to the ground. His horse bolted. The orcs rushed in and pounded out his life.

Jup made to follow Gleadeg's example and use his own sling on the remaining horseman. But as he reached for it a keen hissing filled the air. A swarm of arrows thudded into the horseman, hurling him from his saddle.

When Jup and the others looked for their source, they saw a dozen or more dwarf archers on the longhouses' roofs. The Wolverines waved their thanks. They were ignored. The dwarfs were busy picking off more riders.

That wasn't the end of the Unis. They were still worming their way into the clearing, though there were fewer of them. Jup and his comrades took up their swords again.

Those near the perimeter had more than a couple of horsemen to contend with. Their burden was thinning the stream of incoming riders. Haskeer and Coilla's groups had faced a virtual cavalry charge. Dead and dying humans, dwarfs and horses were scattered across the forward combat zone. But the fighting went on.

Seizing a discarded lance, Haskeer impaled a charging Uni. The man was propelled from his horse, the spear lodged in his chest. Haskeer made do with his dependable blade to challenge the next interloper.

Coilla had spent her knives freely. Now there were just two left. She lobbed one at a rampaging horseman. It was aimed at his chest. He turned and the blade struck above his armpit, but the force was enough to spin him in his saddle. He lost control. The reins whipped free. A couple of orcs grabbed them and tugged hard, bringing down horse and rider. Spears and hatchets sealed his fate.

Pepperdyne battled on. He showed no loss of stamina, or lessening skill. His sword was a blur, slashing throats, puncturing lungs, severing limbs. He outfought or outwitted any who faced him.

For her part, Coilla was eyeing another rider. He was laying about a group of dwarfs with an axe. As she watched, he cracked open someone's skull, dropping him like a stone. Drawing her last knife, she took aim, reckoning on a clean kill this time.

She missed. The knife clipped the neck of the Uni's horse. Startled, the wounded animal bucked, throwing its rider. He fell heavily, but found his feet at once, buoyed with rage. Spotting Coilla, he battered his way towards her. She was bracing herself to meet him when a swinging blade came within a hair's-breadth of hacking her flesh. Unnoticed, another Uni had emerged from the scrum to challenge her.

Coilla spun to the new foe and their swords collided with a strident impact. They fell into a frenzied bout of swordplay. He was powerfully built, and what he lacked in finesse he made up for with might. They didn't so much fence as hammer at each other, and Coilla parried a series of jarring blows.

Then the human got lucky. She was slow in dodging a wild swipe. His blade skinned the knuckles of her sword hand, dashing the weapon from her grasp. It bounced beyond reach. Backing off, Coilla went for her dagger, the only weapon she had left. As she fumbled for it, the unhorsed Uni appeared.

The pair of glowering humans closed in on her. One had a broadsword, the other an axe. No way was her dagger a match for their reach. She could only twist and duck to avoid their aggression. But there was a limit to how long she could evade them. Rapidly, she lost ground. The humans came on for the kill.

'*Coilla!*'

Suddenly Pepperdyne was there. He tossed her a sword. Then he took on the second Uni, leaving the axeman to her.

She piled into him, intent on a reckoning. Bobbing to elude a swing from his axe, she went in fast and low, blade level. He swerved and half turned, hoping to sidestep her attack. Coilla's sword connected, but it glanced, skimming the side of his waist.

Far from a fatal wound, it was still a painful enough distraction. Sufficient for Coilla to spin and strike again.

This time, the blow was true. She buried a third of her blade in the Uni's midriff. Jerking the sword free, she arced it and swept down hard to brain him. The man sprawled, lifeless.

Breathing hard, Coilla looked to Pepperdyne. He had bettered his own opponent, and was stooping to deliver the killing stroke. As he rose from slashing the Uni's throat, she caught his eye. She nodded her thanks, puzzled that he should side with her against one of his own kind.

'Look at that!'

Haskeer was pointing to a rider near the tree-line. The figure was unmistakably female. Her long blonde hair flowed free, and she wore a metal breastplate that glinted in the feeble sunlight. She was mounted on a pure white horse that reared as, sword held high, she rallied her remaining followers.

'Mercy Hobrow,' Coilla spat.

'You were right,' Haskeer conceded.

'The bitch. Why don't you ever have a bow when you need one?'

As they watched, the woman wheeled her mount and headed into the trees.

The defenders at the vanguard, by the defensive trench, saw Hobrow too. Her supporters were retreating in her wake, the stragglers chased by angry dwarfs seeing them off with arrows and spears. All across the village clearing the last of the Unis were pulling back.

'More a last gasp than a second wave,' Stryke reckoned, looking on.

Breggin nodded.

'Not much more we can do here. Round up the unit.'

The private grunted and went off.

Stryke surveyed the carnage around him. The bodies of dozens of dwarfs were scattered about, and many more humans. They were outnumbered by the wounded, walking and prone, though he saw no orcs in the latter category. Or humans in either.

He made for the cluster of huts, his crew in tow.

The rest of the Wolverines were already gathering there.

'Anybody hurt?' Stryke called out.

'A few,' Dallog replied. 'Nothing too serious.'

'Coilla? You all right?'

'This?' She waved her bandaged hand dismissively. 'Just a sting.'

'She ain't the only one stinging,' Haskeer butted in.

'Meaning?' Stryke asked.

'Wheam.'

Stryke sighed. 'What about him?'

'Caught an arrow in his arse.' He jabbed a thumb.

A small group was arriving. Several grunts carried Wheam, face-down on a plank, a bolt protruding from his rear. Standeven followed sullenly.

Haskeer was gleeful. 'It gets better,' he went on. 'The arrow was one of our own.'

Wheam's makeshift stretcher was brusquely dumped on the ground. He groaned loudly.

'Get him sorted,' Stryke ordered.

Dallog knelt and began rummaging in his medical bag.

To one side, Coilla got Pepperdyne alone.

'Thanks,' she said.

He nodded.

'You fight well.'

The human smiled tightly.

'Where'd you pick up the skill?' she persisted.

He gave a cursory shrug. 'Here and there.'

'You're talking me to death again.'

This time his fleeting smile had a speck of warmth in it. 'It's a long story.'

'I want to hear it.'

'*Pepperdyne!*' Standeven was elbowing their way.

Pepperdyne's expression went back to pokerfaced.

'Your place is with me,' the older man asserted.

'I know.'

To Coilla, Pepperdyne's manner seemed almost subservient. 'What is it with you two?' she asked.

'*Coilla!*' Stryke beckoned her over.

She gave the pair of humans a last, hard look and left them to it.

Stryke was with Jup and Spurral, and they were obviously troubled.

'What's up?' Coilla said.

'Our people have paid a high price for this,' Spurral replied, indicating the detritus of battle.

'But they did well. Specially as you've so few veterans.'

'We've even less now,' Jup came back gloomily.

'There are casualties in a fight,' Stryke told him. 'You know that.'

'The Wolverines haven't come out of this nearly so badly.'

'We're born to combat, and we've got the skills. If we'd had losses we'd accept 'em.'

'Most dwarfs don't have the orcs' attitude to these things.'

'So I see,' Coilla said, nodding.

They followed her gaze to a group of villagers standing in the clearing. They were looking the Wolverines' way and whispering amongst themselves. Others were drifting over to swell their ranks.

'This could get nasty,' Stryke judged. 'Jup, what do you think?'

'They're angry. It'd be as well to tread lightly 'til this blows over.'

'Coilla?'

'I'm thinking of that old saying. You know, the one that goes, "Trust in the gods, but tie up your horse".'

Stryke eyed the growing crowd. 'I'll go along with that. We'll do nothing to goad them. But we stay alert.' He turned to Dallog. 'Get Wheam on his feet.'

'I'm not sure if he's—'

'He'll live. Just do it.'

Dallog shrugged and beckoned a couple of grunts. 'Give me a hand here,' he instructed. 'Hold him. *Tight*.'

He bent to his patient. Wheam began whimpering. Dallog swiftly plucked out the arrow, drawing a yell from the newbie. Then the corporal produced a flask of raw alcohol and sprinkled it liberally over the wound. Wheam howled. Dressing hastily applied, the grunts tersely hauled him to his feet, raising more yelps. Wheam was ashen. His grimace made him look like he'd sucked a bushel of lemons.

Giving off a disgruntled mutter, the throng of dwarfs had started to move towards the orcs. A number of them nursed wounds or hobbled. Many had their weapons drawn.

'To me!' Stryke ordered.

His band fell in beside him.

Out in front of the mob was a familiar face; the dwarf who harangued them in the glade when they first arrived in Quatt.

He marched up to the Wolverines, chest puffed, and holding aloft a short spear.

'Have you any idea what mayhem you've caused here?' he shouted.

'That was down to the Unis,' Stryke replied evenly.

'And look how many of our people paid for it!'

'The orcs fought at our side, Krake,' Jup reminded him. 'We wouldn't have won otherwise.'

'We wouldn't have had to fight at all if it weren't for them!'

There was a murmur of agreement from the crowd.

'That's not fair,' Jup returned. 'We should count ourselves lucky they stood with us.'

'Trust you to take their part. All you've done is bring us trouble.'

'Seems to me,' Stryke said, 'it was time you stood up to those humans.'

'You think we *haven't*?' Krake was red faced. 'What we don't do is go round provoking 'em!'

Again the mob backed him.

'You can't blame the orcs for that,' Jup reckoned. 'You know how crazy those Unis are. If it hadn't been the Wolverines it would have been something else.'

'Backing outsiders again,' the ringleader spat. 'You're too fond of these . . . *freaks*.'

'Who you calling a freak?' Haskeer demanded indignantly.

Krake glared at him. 'If the cap fits.'

'I wouldn't push it with our sergeant,' Coilla advised.

'Let's just be calm,' Jup appealed.

'Traitor!' Krake seethed.

'Don't you call my Jup a traitor,' Spurral waded in.

'Wotcha mean *freak*?' Haskeer repeated.

'It's what I'm looking at,' Krake told him. He waved his spear in Haskeer's face.

The crowd was cheering him on.

'I wouldn't do that,' Coilla warned.

'I don't take advice from grotesques,' Krake informed her, 'least of all a female.' He laughed derisively. Most of the crowd joined in.

Haskeer snatched his spear, upended it deftly and plunged it into the dwarf's foot.

There was a crimson geyser. Krake shrieked. He hobbled a couple of steps before falling into the arms of his fellows. The crowd let out a collective gasp.

'Oh, great,' Jup groaned.

The enraged mob surged forward, weapons raised, and the orcs primed themselves to meet them.

'I don't want you fighting our people, Stryke!' Spurral pleaded.

'No, we don't need this,' Jup added, one eye on his advancing countrymen.

'Pull back, Wolverines!' Stryke barked. '*All* of you!'

The band withdrew. Soon they were clustering in front of a large wooden hut.

'In here!' Stryke bellowed, kicking open the door.

Everyone piled through. Furniture was dragged over to barricade the entrance, and the lone window was blocked. Outside, the roar of the mob grew louder.

Coilla glowered at Haskeer. 'So much for not goading them!'

'The little shit asked for it. He was lucky I didn't— What are *they* doing here?' He thrust a finger at Pepperdyne and Standeven.

'They warned us, remember?'

'So what?'

'So there's not much we can do about it now, is there?'

'I could,' Haskeer replied menacingly.

Stryke stepped between them. 'You going to disobey another order?'

'I don't remember one about them.'

'There is now: *leave it*. I'm no happier with humans around than you are, but we've more pressing worries.'

A grunt jogged from the back of the building. 'That's the only door, chief. No other way out.'

Stryke looked up to the distant rafters. 'We couldn't reach the roof either.'

As soon as he said it, they heard the sound of movement overhead.

'But they can,' Coilla said.

There was a battering at the door. It shook in its hinges. Several grunts rushed forward and threw their weight against the barricade.

'Can't fight, can't run,' Haskeer grumbled. 'What do we do, Stryke?'

'We'll try smashing our way through that back wall and—'

'Can you smell something?' Spurral exclaimed.

The hammering had stopped.

'*Shit.*' Coilla pointed towards the door. Thick black smoke was seeping through the cracks. 'They've torched the place.'

Smoke was coming in through some of the wall planks too, and it began to billow up above, over the rafters.

'They want us so badly they'd burn one of their own buildings?' Stryke said.

'They're pretty pissed off,' Jup confirmed.

'*Now* what?' Haskeer wanted to know.

Stryke held out a hand. 'Coilla, the star. You've got it?'

'Course. I check the damn thing every ten breaths.' She dug it out and passed it to him.

He moved to a crude table and placed the instrumentality on it. Then he added the others from his belt pouch. He consulted the amulet about his neck then, brow taut with concentration, began slotting the stars together.

The smoke grew denser. Coughing broke out and eyes were stinging. Dallog was ripping up portions of cloth, dunking them in a water butt he'd found and passing them out to the grunts to cover their mouths with.

The ceiling was on fire. Sparks drifted and embers fell. The stink was acrid.

Still Stryke fiddled with the stars.

Everyone had gathered round him now, watching intently. Only Pepperdyne and Standeven, silent and forgotten, stood further back.

Stryke had just the final piece to fit in.

'I don't like this bit,' Wheam snivelled.

'Oh, *shut up*,' Haskeer chided.

Stryke began easing the last star into place.

'*Hold tight, everybody!*' Coilla yelled.

Pepperdyne grabbed Standeven's wrist, dragging him closer to the scrum.

There was an implosion of non-light.

And the bottom fell out of the world.

13

Only tender sounds disturbed the calm. A tinkling brook flowed down a mild rocky incline to join a lazy river. The distant baas of sheep mingled with the soothing drone of honeybees.

Green fields and softly undulating meadows extended from the banks of the river. Trees in full blossom dotted the landscape. Gentle hillocks marked the horizon, crowned with leafy copses. High above, languid birds flapped across a perfectly blue sky.

The day was still and warm. All was bucolic tranquillity.

There was a subtle change in the quality of the air. At a point just above the ground it wavered, like heat over stone on a summer afternoon. Soon, a spot of dull milky radiance appeared, and grew. It became a vortex, spinning frantically, and coloured pinpoints swirled in the mix. The whirlpool birthed a breeze, which swiftly built to a wind. Then a gale. Grass bowed under its force, and plants and trees.

It climaxed in a blinding white flash that rivalled the noontime sun.

The gaping maw of the churning radiance spewed out its load. A mass of shapes tumbled on to the sward.

Instantly, the wind vanished and the vortex snapped out of existence.

A sulphurous odour hung in the air.

Thirty and more figures were strewn along the riverbank. For some minutes none of them moved. Slowly, they began to rouse. A few groaned. Several vomited.

Stryke and Coilla were among the first to get to their feet.

'Gods, it's no easier the second time, is it?' Coilla said, shaking her muzzy head. She took in the scene. 'You brought us home? To Ceragan?'

'No. Though it looks a lot like it. I set the stars for the place Serapheim told us about.'

'This is supposed to be a land oppressed, is it? And there are orcs here?'

He scanned the landscape. 'Somewhere.'

'If we've wound up where we're supposed to.'

'That we'll find out.' Stryke realised he was still clutching the assemblage of stars. He plucked one free and offered it to her. It was green, with five spikes. 'Are you still willing to—?'

'Sure.' She took it. 'It's not the same one. The one I had was blue and it only had four—'

'Does it matter?' He was pulling the others apart and putting them in his pouch.

'No, course not. I'm being stupid. Still dazed from getting here Wherever *here* is.'

Jup and Spurral joined them. They were pale, and looked mildly shocked.

'That's a hell of a way to travel,' Jup said.

'Where *are* we?' Spurral asked.

'Don't know,' Stryke told her. 'But it's where our mission is.'

Haskeer had been haranguing the band. Now he strode over.

'Everybody all right?' Stryke wanted to know.

'More or less. No thanks to his lot.' He glowered at Jup.

'My people were out of order,' Jup conceded. 'But they felt they had cause.'

'*Cause?* That's one word for it.'

'What are you saying?'

'You dwarfs know which way the wind blows.'

'Meaning?'

'What happened back there, turning on us, you're well known for that.'

'Oh, that old song again.'

'And it's got a name.' Haskeer leaned and put his face close to Jup's. '*Treachery.*'

Jup made an effort to keep his temper in check. 'Some of my folk . . . *some* . . . escaped the poverty we've been pushed into by working as soldiers of fortune. You could say I did myself, when I joined Jennesta's horde. The same army you served in.'

'You had a choice. We didn't. *Pisspot*.' He drove his forefinger hard into the dwarf's chest.

'You want to settle this?' Jup flared, balling his fists.

'Jup, please!' Spurral begged. 'This is no time to—'

'Whenever you're ready,' Haskeer growled. He raised his own ham-like knuckles.

Stryke barged in and flung them apart. '*Cut it out!*' he roared. 'We're a disciplined band, not a rabble!'

'He started it,' Jup mumbled.

'That's *enough*! I won't have disorder, and I'll back that with a whipping if I have to!'

Unable to meet his gaze, Haskeer and Jup resumed glaring at each other.

'Just like old times, eh?' Coilla observed, breaking the impasse. 'Your memory's short, Haskeer. When did Jup ever let us down? And Spurral fought righteously today.'

'Well, that's fine, ain't it?' Haskeer replied with a hint of mockery. 'And now you've got another female to play with.'

'Yeah, we can press flowers together.'

Spurral stifled a grin.

'Waifs and strays,' Haskeer muttered disgustedly. 'Bloody circus.'

'*Haskeer*,' Stryke intoned menacingly.

'All right, all right. But what about them?' He pointed along the riverbank, to Pepperdyne and Standeven. 'If they're not dead-weight then I don't know—'

'The younger one helped me out of a tight fix,' Coilla reminded him.

'Ask yourself why,' Haskeer came back. 'What're they after?'

'You're right,' Stryke agreed. 'For once. I want some answers from those two before we move on.'

'About time.' Haskeer started to move.

'Not you, Sergeant. You posted guards? Sent out scouts? No. Do it. *Now*.'

Haskeer departed, grumbling.

'Is it always like this in the band?' Spurral asked.

'Just about,' Coilla replied.

'Particularly when Haskeer's got a wasp up his backside about something,' Jup added.

'I don't want to tackle those two mob-handed and make this look like a grilling,' Stryke decided. 'They're bound to clam up.'

'We could beat it out of 'em,' Jup suggested, half seriously.

'I will if I have to. But they get a chance to talk first. We owe them that much for the warning, and for aiding Coilla. So help out with the band, Jup. And stay away from Haskeer. Hear me?'

Jup nodded and left. Spurral went with him.

'What about me?' Coilla said.

'We'll see the humans together. You get on with them.'

'*Whoa.* I don't count humans as friends.'

He turned without answering and headed along the riverbank. She followed.

The band was recovering. Those who didn't have a chance earlier were cleaning the gore from their blades. Others were having wounds tended. Haskeer was working off his temper by barking orders.

They found the two men by the water's edge. Pepperdyne stood looking down at Standeven, who sat on the grass, clutching his knees to his chest. He was sweaty and trembling.

'What's the matter with him?' Stryke said.

'You might have noticed that getting here was quite a ride,' Pepperdyne replied.

'You seem all right.'

He shrugged. 'Where the hell are we?'

'We're asking the questions. Who are you?'

'Like I said. I'm Jode Pepperdyne and—'

'I mean *what* are you.'

'Merchants,' Standeven said, a little too quickly. He glanced up at them and shuddered. 'That was hellish. I never believed them. I never thought it was true.'

'What you talking about?'

'Those . . . objects that got us here.'

'So you knew about them? Before you came to us, I mean.'

The pair of humans exchanged the briefest of glances.

It was Pepperdyne who answered. 'There've been rumours about instrumentalities for as long as I can remember.'

'We knew no such stories,' Stryke said. 'Not until recently.'

'You hear all sorts of tales in our business. Including things outsiders aren't privy to.'

'You say you're merchants.'

'Yes,' Standeven replied. 'That is, I am. He's my aide.'

'He fights pretty well for a merchant's lackey,' Coilla remarked.

'His duties include guarding me. You attract the attention of brigands in our line of work.'

She addressed Pepperdyne directly. 'You didn't pick up your skills from traders.'

'I've been around,' he told her.

'Military service?'

'Some.'

'You Manis?' Stryke wanted to know.

Standeven looked surprised. 'What?'

'You tipped us off about them Unis.'

'No, we're not. Not all humans support religious factions. Besides, we're not from Centrasia. Things are different in our part of the world.'

Coilla bridled. 'It's called *Maras-Dantia*. Centrasia's the name foisted on us by you outsiders.'

Pepperdyne spoke for his flustered master. 'Sorry,' he offered.

'I don't get it,' Stryke said, frowning. 'You're not Manis, yet you helped us against other humans. Why?'

'You're after something, aren't you?' Coilla added.

'Yes,' Pepperdyne admitted.

Standeven looked shocked, and opened his mouth to speak.

Pepperdyne got in first. 'We need your help.'

Stryke stared hard at him. 'Explain.'

'We didn't warn you because those Unis were our enemies. We warned you because of someone who is. Your enemy and ours.'

'That's clear as mud.'

'The sorcerer queen,' Pepperdyne said. 'Jennesta.'

A cold chill took hold of Stryke's spine, and he knew Coilla felt the same way. 'What the hell are you talking about?'

'She owes us. And we heard she's in debt to you too, in a manner of speaking.'

'What do you know about Jennesta? Be plain, or this ends here and now. The hard way.' Stryke's expression left no doubt as to what he meant.

'My employer here lost a valuable consignment. It turned out to be her doing.'

'What was it?'

'Gems. Along with not a few good men. Including some of my master's kin.'

'This happened where?'

'On the edge of the wastelands. That's what we call it anyway. The wilderness separating the wider world from Cen— . . . from Maras-Dantia.'

'So you went to Maras-Dantia yourselves.'

'To seek recompense, yes.'

Coilla was sceptical. 'Just the two of you? And only one with the guts for a fight?' She glanced at Standeven.

'We weren't alone. We had a group of fighters with us. But when we got here . . . *there*, rather, we found the place in chaos. Unis ambushed us and most of our men were killed. Some of us were caught and held for a while. That's how we knew about the attack, and where we learnt your story.'

'The Unis told you about us?'

'Yes. Didn't you know the Wolverines are a legend in those parts? Anyway, we escaped and—'

'How?' Stryke said.

Pepperdyne shrugged glibly. 'Nothing very heroic. They were more interested in attacking you and the dwarfs. We were lightly guarded.'

'And you thought that by helping us . . .'

'We hoped you'd aid us in exacting revenge on Jennesta.'

'Jennesta's thought dead. Didn't the Unis tell you that?'

'They said she hadn't been seen for quite a while. That's not the same, is it? Unless you know different.'

Stryke and Coilla stayed tight-lipped.

'So you reckoned we'd be so grateful that we'd join your little mission,' Stryke summed up.

'Something like that.'

'And if gratitude wasn't enough?'

'A reward, maybe. If the gems were recovered, my master would be willing to share them with you.'

'We kill what we eat and take what we need. We've no use for riches.'

'Where does that leave us?' Standeven asked uneasily.

'Where you're not wanted.'

'What do you intend doing?' Pepperdyne said.

'I'll think on it,' Stryke replied. 'Stay out of the band's way. I'll deal with you later.'

He turned on his heel and strode away, Coilla in tow.

When they were out of earshot, she remarked wryly, 'So, how does it feel to be a legend?'

'Did you believe any of that?'

'I don't know. Maybe.'

'Sounded like horse shit to me.'

'Notice how the servant had more to say than the master? That's the most I've ever heard him say.'

'Perhaps he's the better liar. And I think it was a slip when they said they knew about the stars. We didn't ourselves until a few years ago.'

'There might be no mystery in that. We lived closed-off lives when we were in the horde. A lot was kept from us.'

'That didn't stop us picking up hearsay. I don't buy it. And why would Jennesta hijack shipments of jewels? She had whatever she wanted nearer to home.'

'I don't know; I wouldn't put anything past her. But, Stryke . . . I owe Pepperdyne. I might not be here if he hadn't—'

'I know. And they did warn us about the attack, whatever their motive. That's why I didn't just have their throats cut and be done with it.'

'Would you?'

'If I thought they were set on betrayal, sure I would.'

'But they *could* be telling the truth. What do we do about them?'

'Dump 'em as soon as we can.'

They came to where Dallog had planted the band's standard. It fluttered feebly in the light wind. The corporal was busying himself with the wounded, though he still seemed queasy after the transference.

Wheam looked a lot worse. He lay on his side, presumably to avoid putting weight on his earlier injury. Propped on one elbow, he stared into a wooden bowl he'd been filling.

Dallog rose when he saw Stryke and Coilla.

He indicated the landscape with a sweep of his hand and said, 'You know, this could be Ceragan.'

'We've done that,' Coilla informed him.

Pepperdyne and Standeven watched Coilla and Stryke go.

When they were far enough away, Standeven's expression hardened. 'What were you hoping to achieve with that bullshit you just fed them?'

'Only saving our lives, that's all. And giving them a reason for letting us stick around.'

'But shipments of gems? And this Jennesta woman, who we've only heard about in tall tales? You're digging us in deeper here.'

'They can't disprove any of it.'

'The thing about lies is that you have to build other lies to support them. Believe me, I know.'

'As you're such an expert on the subject it shouldn't be too hard for you to keep up, should it?'

'Tall tales need to be thought through. They have to be plausible. When we overheard those Unis planning the attack, when we hid there listening, we should have formulated a plan. A watertight lie.'

'We didn't have the time; we had to grab the opportunity. We knew these orcs were rumoured to have the instrumentalities. Now we're sure.'

'Oh, yes, we're sure now,' Standeven replied, the trauma of the crossing etched on his face. 'But what good does it do us?'

'Do you want those artefacts or not?'

'Do I need them now?'

Pepperdyne gave an exasperated sigh. 'You've been slavering at the prospect of getting your hands on them! If you've bent my ears once about their value, you've done it a hundred times.'

'Watch your tongue!' Standeven retorted, haughtily puffing himself up. 'Remember who's master here.'

'Or you'll do what? Circumstances have changed. It's about survival now.'

Standeven seethed, but didn't push the issue.

'I'll tell you why you need the instrumentalities,' Pepperdyne said. 'Kantor Hammrik. He'll never give up until he's found you, and they're the only thing you can barter with.'

'How could he find us here?'

'I intend getting back. Don't you? And it's my neck as well as yours.'

'I still don't think—'

'I can't fight our way out of this like I did with Hammrik's escort. It'd be insane to square up to an orc warband. We have to use stealth, and bide our time. Or do you have a better idea?'

If Standeven had an answer there was no chance to give it. A clamour broke out further along the riverbank, where most of the band was concentrated. Two of the scouts were back, and they had someone with them.

'Let's see what's happening,' Pepperdyne said.

Standeven held out a hand. Pepperdyne hoisted him to his feet.

As they approached, they saw that the scouts had brought back another orc. He looked mature, perhaps old, as far as the humans could tell. His garb consisted of a sleeveless lambskin jerkin, baggy cloth trews and stout leather ankle boots. He was nearly as tall as the wooden crook he carried, which he used to help him walk.

They took him to Stryke. The prisoner's anxious eyes darted from face to face as the band gathered round.

'We're not going to hurt you,' Stryke assured him. 'Understand?'

The shepherd nodded.

'What's your name?'

'Yelbra.' He spoke hesitantly.

'Are you alone out here?'

He nodded again.

'We didn't see anybody else,' one of the scouts confirmed.

'Where's the nearest town, Yelbra?' Stryke asked.

The shepherd ignored him. He was staring at Jup and Spurral. 'What are . . . *they*?' he exclaimed, pointing at them.

'You've not seen dwarfs before?'

He shook his head, much more vigorously than he'd nodded.

'They're with us. Don't worry about them, they won't harm you. The nearest town?'

'You don't know?' he said, his confusion mounting.

'We wouldn't have asked otherwise,' Haskeer rumbled.

'It's—' His attention had shifted again, and his eyes widened. He let out something between a gasp and a groan.

The cause of his alarm was Standeven and Pepperdyne, who were pushing their way through the crowd.

Visibly shaking, Yelbra sank to his arthritic knees and uttered, '*Masters.*' His manner was one of complete obeisance.

'What the *fuck's* going on?' Haskeer wanted to know.

The shepherd gazed up at him with something close to terror distorting his features. '*Get down,*' he hissed. 'Show respect!'

'To *them?*' Haskeer sneered. '*Humans?* They can kiss my scaly arse!'

Yelbra seemed profoundly shocked. His mouth hung open and all trace of colour left his face.

'Since when did orcs prostrate themselves in front of humans?' Coilla said.

The shepherd looked as though the question made no sense to him.

'Serapheim said humans had the upper hand here,' Stryke reflected. 'Seems he was right. Get up,' he told Yelbra.

He stayed where he was, eyes fixed on Pepperdyne and Standeven.

Stryke nodded at the scouts. They heaved the shepherd to a standing position. He clutched his crook as if it was all that kept him upright.

'I'm asking the questions,' Stryke reminded him in a harsher tone, 'not them. What's the name of this land?'

Still he remained under the spell of the humans, staring their way and trembling. He said nothing.

Stryke beckoned Pepperdyne. 'Here.'

The human hesitated for a second, then came forward.

'You ask him,' Stryke said.

'Me?'

'He's more in thrall of you two than us. Do it.'

A little awkwardly, Pepperdyne cleared his throat. 'Er, Yelbra. What's this land called?'

Even with his head bent to avoid Pepperdyne's gaze, it was apparent he was taken aback at them not knowing. 'If it pleases you, master; Acurial.'

'It does please me. But I'm not your master. Do you hear me?'

The shepherd shot him a glance suffused with bewilderment, and a hint of what might have been pity for someone self-evidently insane. 'Yes, mas— Yes, I hear you.'

'Good. What's the name of the nearest settlement?'

'Taress.'

'And there are orcs there?'

'Of course. Many.'

'Where is it? How far?'

'Due south. On foot, it can be reached by sundown.'

'Thank you, Yelbra.' Pepperdyne looked to Stryke, and was about to step back when the shepherd spoke again.

'Begging your pardon, my . . . Your pardon, but I'm at a loss to understand why you don't know these things. Is it a test?'

'No. We're . . . from a far country.'

'It must be *very* far from here.'

'More than you can guess,' Stryke put in. He waved Pepperdyne away. 'I meant what I said, Yelbra; we won't harm you. But I want your word that you'll tell nobody about seeing us. Or do you need to hear that from him, too?' He jabbed a thumb Pepperdyne's way.

'No one would believe me if I told this story. Anyway, I see few others out here. Tending sheep is a solitary business.'

'What kind of job is that for an orc?' Haskeer said with contempt.

Once more the question seemed irrelevant to the shepherd. In any event something else had caught his eye. 'You bear arms,' he whispered, as though noticing for the first time. There was wonder and fear in his voice.

'That's unusual in these parts?' Coilla asked.

'You are indeed from a distant land. It's forbidden by law.'

'We've spent enough time here,' Stryke decided, turning away from Yelbra.

Clear of the others he went into a huddle with his officers.

'We'll get ourselves over to this Taress,' he told them. 'And it looks like we'd do well to conceal our weapons.'

'Are we all going?' Coilla said. 'What about a base camp?'

'Not this time. If we have to use the stars again in a hurry I want us all together.'

Jup glanced over at the humans. 'How do we deal with them?'

'They'd better come along. From what we've just seen they might be the only way anyone's going to talk to us.'

'I don't like it,' Haskeer grumbled.

'Me neither. But we can be rid of them as soon as they stop being an asset. Now get the band organised for a march.'

As they scattered to their duties, the shepherd called out to them.

'What about me? I've my animals to tend to.'

'You can go,' Stryke shouted back.

'Yeah,' Coilla added. 'Get the flock out of here.'

14

In sharp contrast to the ruined land of Maras-Dantia, Acurial was fair.

Its jade-coloured fields and lush pastures washed against the rims of dense forests. The streams ran crystal clear. An abundance of wildlife roamed the woods, and smaller creatures burrowed in the undergrowth. Birds of many hues wheeled in the cloudless skies.

The river flowed southward, so the Wolverines marched beside it for several hours. When it curved to the west, they found a trail running in the direction they sought, and took that. They met no other travellers.

As the day lengthened the earlier warmth began to abate.

Stryke was at the head of the column, with Jup at his side.

The dwarf looked back at the band. 'They're starting to flag a bit. Can we spare time for a break? They haven't eaten properly since yesterday, and that was a world away.'

Stryke nodded. 'But we'll keep it short, and no fires. And we eat the rations we're carrying; I don't want anybody off hunting.'

The band left the trail and made for a stand of trees. Lookouts were posted, and hardtack and water was distributed.

When everyone had eaten their fill, Stryke allowed them a brief rest. Perched on fallen tree trunks, some of the band reflected on how Acurial differed from the world they recently left.

'Compared to this place,' Jup was saying, 'Maras-Dantia's completely bust. Failing harvests, barren livestock, fouled rivers; you know the score.'

'Yet there are humans in Acurial too,' Coilla replied, 'and they don't seem to have screwed things up here.'

More than one pair of stern eyes turned to Standeven and Pepperdyne.

'So far,' Jup amended. 'We don't know how long they've been here. It took them a generation or more to devastate Maras-Dantia, and maybe longer before the magic started to bleed away.'

'I wonder if magic works in this world,' Coilla mused.

'That hadn't occurred to me. But . . . why shouldn't it? Unless Maras-Dantia was special in some way, maybe all worlds have magic. Or at least the energy to make it work.'

'Find out,' Stryke suggested. 'Your skill could be useful to us.'

'All right.' Jup got to his feet and surveyed the area. 'I'll try over there.'

As everyone watched, he set off for a gully thirty or forty paces away. A small stream trickled along it, and it was shaded by a couple of mature trees. Jup took out a knife and squatted by the stream. He gouged a hole in the earth, and when he judged it deep enough, wormed his hand into it.

'What's he doing?' Wheam asked.

'Magic shows itself in different ways for different races,' Stryke explained. 'With dwarfs, it's farsight.'

Wheam was puzzled. 'Farsight?'

'Being able to sense things beyond what can be picked up with eyes or ears.'

'Which is handy for tracking,' Coilla added.

'There's energy in the earth that governs the magic,' Stryke said. 'It's most powerful near water. I don't know why. But dwarfs with farsight can feel the energy's strength, and how it flows.'

'How does magic show itself with orcs?' Pepperdyne said.

'It doesn't. We've no command of magic, and neither do humans.'

'So if this world has only orcs and humans, nobody practises magic?'

'Right.' Stryke didn't mention the likes of Serapheim, who was an exception among humans anyway. Or the possibility that Jennesta was in this world. He saw no reason to tell Pepperdyne and his master any more than he had to.

Jup came back, slapping the dirt from his hands. 'I was right. There's energy here, and it's strong. Pure. I'd say there's a big concentration of it not far away, and the flow's southward.'

'Taress?' Stryke wondered.

'Suppose it must be.'

'We should be moving then.'

Wheam popped up. Somehow his beloved lute had survived intact, and he brandished it. 'Time for a song before we go? To put a spring in our step?' He saw their expressions. 'A tune then? A rousing air to send us on our—'

'If you do,' Haskeer told him, 'I'll kill you.'

'*On your feet, Wolverines!*' Stryke barked. '*We're marching!*'

The old shepherd was right about them arriving at sundown.

Standing on the crest of a steep hill, the band looked down at the settlement. They were surprised at how big it was. The fringes of the city consisted of acres of dwellings, shot through with alleys, lanes and crooked streets. Nearer the centre there were taller structures, with a dotting of towers and spires, and what could having been fortifications. Although it was dusk, few lights were visible.

Weapons concealed, they began their descent.

They arrived at the outskirts without seeing anyone, and came to a wide cobbled road leading into the city. Halfway along its length stood the first houses. They looked shabby, and there was no sign of the inhabitants.

'Orcs live here?' Coilla said.

'It looks as though nobody lives here,' Stryke replied.

They entered the maze of streets. Every door was closed, all windows were shuttered. There were no lights.

'Where is everybody?' Spurral wondered.

Jup pointed. 'Here's somebody.'

On the opposite side of the road, a lone figure was sprinting in their direction.

'Get out of sight, all of you,' Stryke ordered.

The band quickly retreated into the shadowy mouth of an adjacent alley.

As the running figure drew level, Stryke saw that it was a young orc, wrapped in a grey cloak.

'What's going on?' he shouted over to him.

The orc slowed and looked Stryke's way. He was obviously puzzled. 'What do you mean?'

'Where is everybody?'

'Don't you know what hour it is?'

'What's that got to do with—'

'It's almost *dark*! Get off the streets! They'll be here soon!'

'Who?'

The orc didn't answer. He ran on and disappeared round a corner.

Coilla emerged from the alley. 'What the hell was that all about?'

'Perhaps we found the only crazy orc in town,' Jup ventured.

'What now?' Haskeer wanted to know.

'We push on,' Stryke decided, 'and keep alert.'

They moved deeper into the silent, deserted metropolis. In street after street it was the same story; bolted doors, barred windows and unlit dwellings. They didn't encounter so much as a stray dog or prowling cat.

At length they came to a public square, bordered by houses on all sides and fed by a street at each corner. In its centre was a large patch of muddy grass, and in the middle of that was a tall wooden structure.

'Do you see what that is?' Coilla said.

Stryke blinked in the gloom. 'No, what?'

'It's a gallows.'

'So they go in for public executions here.'

'Yeah, but of who?'

'Stryke,' Haskeer said, looking restless, 'what's our aim? Where we heading?'

'I don't know. I didn't expect a ghost town.'

'Great. So we've gone into this half-arsed.'

'Think you could have done better?'

'I'd at least have a plan.'

'Gods protect us from any plan of yours.'

'I wouldn't have us wandering like tits in a trance.'

'Hold your tongue, Sergeant. Unless you want me to take that helmet and shove it up—'

Coilla put a finger to her lips. '*Sssshh!*'

'Stay out of this, Corporal.'

'No! I mean *listen*.'

Everyone froze.

Although a way off, the sound was unmistakable, and it was swiftly growing louder.

'Marching,' Jup whispered.

'Where's it coming from?' Stryke said.

'Can't tell.'

The sound was swelling, and close to hand.

'Take cover!' Stryke ordered.

The band began to move

None of them got more than ten paces before a group of humans entered the square at the next turning. They were about forty in number, and wore uniforms that in the half light could have been black or dark blue. All were heavily armed, and perhaps a third of them held shaded lanterns

At their head was the unit's commander, and it was he who bellowed, '*Halt!*'

His troop spread out to either side of him as they advanced, so that they approached almost in a line.

The Wolverines stopped in their tracks and looked to Stryke.

He knew they might have made a run for it, but he didn't want to risk scattering the band. In any event, running wasn't their way. He signalled for them to stay put.

He caught a glance from Coilla and mouthed, 'Maybe we can bluff our way out of this.'

She raised a sceptical eyebrow.

The human commander was short and thickset. He had a bushy black moustache that perched beneath his nostrils and didn't reach either end of his sneer. His raven hair was longish and slicked back.

When the line of humans were close enough to spit at, he barked an order and they halted. The commander himself continued walking, and two subordinates dogged him, one on each side, a pace or two to his rear. There was a practised air to the manoeuvre, an exhibition of military precision that was almost comical.

The trio stopped when they came to Stryke, Haskeer and Coilla, who were foremost.

'What the hell do you think you're doing?' the commander thundered.

'Just taking the air,' Stryke replied, feigning innocence.

'*Just . . . taking . . . the . . . air,*' the human repeated, his tone pure mockery. 'And the curfew be damned, is that it?'

'Didn't know there was one.'

The commander's face reddened. 'Are you trying to—' He checked himself and stared past Stryke at Jup and Spurral. 'What are *they*?'

'Not again,' Jup sighed under his breath.

Shoving forward for a better look, the commander caught sight of Pepperdyne and Standeven at the back of the crowd. His confusion doubled. 'Are you these creatures' prisoners?'

'No,' Pepperdyne told him, 'we're together.'

'*Together?* You're fraternising with the natives?'

'What'd you mean, natives?' Haskeer objected.

'We've got a troupe of jesters here,' the commander declared, loud enough for his men to hear. 'A company of fools. But we'll see who has the last laugh.'

'Doubt it'll be you,' Coilla said.

He turned to her. 'What did you say?'

'Won't be you laughing.'

'Is that so?'

'Sure. You need a heartbeat for that.'

'Which I have.'

'Not for long.'

'Are you *threatening* me?' He seemed to find the notion amusing.

'Call it . . . a prediction.'

'Well, here's a prediction of mine. You freaks are about to pay the price for disrespecting your betters.'

Coilla smiled. 'Bring it on.'

He clutched a pair of studded leather gloves. Seething with fury, he cracked her savagely across the face with them.

The band tensed.

Coilla lifted a hand to her cheek. Blood was trickling from the corner of her mouth. She spat it out, narrowly missing the commander's shiny boots. Staring into his eyes, she announced evenly, 'He's mine.'

The commander laughed. 'Oh, really. And since when did your kind have the guts to stand up to a superior?'

'How about since now?' she informed him pleasantly.

Quick as thought she delivered a mighty kick to his crotch. He let out an agonised yelp and doubled. She sprang forward and grabbed him by the ears. Pulling his head down, she pounded his face against her upraised knee a couple of times. There was a satisfying crunch of cartilage.

As she let him drop, Stryke and Haskeer whipped out their blades. Haskeer rammed his sword deep into the chest of one lieutenant. Stryke buried twin daggers into the flanks of the other.

It all happened so fast that the rest of the humans were too stupefied to act. Many wore expressions of shocked disbelief.

Then someone yelled, '*Terrorists!*' and mayhem broke out.

Weapons drawn, the mob of Wolverines and the line of humans rushed at each other. In the middle of the square they melded, then spiralled into a score of fights.

Though outnumbered, the more so as Standeven and Wheam effectively counted as non-combatants, the orcs made up the deficiency by battling with their habitual ferocity. And at first, they had another edge: the humans seemed stunned that orcs would fight at all.

There was a terrible harmony in the way the warband worked together. They hacked, cleaved, slashed and battered their way through obstructing flesh. If there was finesse, Pepperdyne was its only practitioner.

In this, his fighting style was nearer the humans. Where orcs pummelled, he engaged. Though whether employing savagery or swordsmanship the upshot was the same. Soon the cobblestones ran red and slippery. Of the human company's original number, only a third were still on their feet. The Wolverines had taken minor wounds, but no fatalities.

'We've got 'em licked!' Haskeer bragged.

'Don't crow too soon,' Stryke told him. 'Look.'

More uniformed men were running into the square from the streets on its far side. There were at least twice as many as in the unit the orcs were fighting.

Haskeer was contemptuous. 'Since when did we worry about odds?'

'They could be the van of a lot more.'

'So what do we do?'

'Kill 'em,' Stryke hissed.

'Why didn't you just say that in the first place?' He turned and swiped at an encroaching human, cleaving his ribs.

Fighting alongside Jup and Spurral, Coilla spotted the new-comers too. 'They've got back-up!' she yelled.

Jup shattered a skull with his staff. 'I see 'em. Never a dull moment with this band.' He spun to break a foe's arm, before toppling him into Spurral's path, who deftly finished the job with twin knife thrusts.

Coilla admired their teamwork.

'Maybe we shouldn't have taken on this lot,' Spurral said.

'And missed a scrap?' Coilla replied. 'We don't think like that.'

But she could see that the humans were taking heart from the reinforcements and fighting harder.

And then a fresh element was added.

As though obeying an unheard signal, the humans fighting the orcs began to disengage and pull back. They left their dead and dying where they fell.

Jup punched air. 'They're retreating!'

'I wouldn't count on it,' Coilla said.

As the humans hastily withdrew they moved aside, giving a clear view of the new contingent. At their head stood three figures dressed differently to all the others. They wore what appeared to be robes, and they were hooded.

Where there had been the cacophony of battle, there was now a deathly silence. The Wolverines held their ground, looking on.

'Are they priests or what?' Haskeer wondered.

Stryke shrugged.

'Whatever the fuck they are, what are we waiting for?'

'Steady. Something's going on.'

The three hooded figures pulled objects from their robes. It was difficult to tell what they were from a distance, but they resembled small metal tridents the size of long daggers.

'What the hell are they doing?' Haskeer said.

'Don't know. But I don't like it.'

The trio raised the tridents and pointed them in the orcs' direction.

Stryke bellowed, '*Everybody down!*'

There was a blinding flash of light. The tridents spewed intense shafts of red, green and yellow iridescence.

The band hit the ground a split second before the crackling beams of energy streaked above their heads. Two struck buildings behind the prone warband, demolishing a heavy door and punching a hole in a wall. Bricks and mortar rained down. The third bolt impacted the corner of the gallows, instantly igniting it.

A second volley had Wolverines rolling in the dirt to avoid the searing beams. The shafts raked the ground like small lightning strikes, dislodging cobblestones and throwing up sparks.

Stryke lifted his head and looked around. He saw Hystykk and Jad stretched out nearby. Both had bows. Hugging the ground, he slithered over to them.

'Bring those bastards down!' he ordered.

Awkwardly, the grunts wriggled the bows from their backs. They quickly nocked arrows and took aim at the robed figures.

An arrow zinged into the chest of one of the trident bearers. He staggered and fell.

'Eh?' Hystykk muttered.

He hadn't loosed his arrow. Neither had Jad.

Arrows peppered the other two robed figures. One unleashed a glaring energy bolt as he fell. It lanced straight up, illuminating the sky. Then died.

There was a roar.

Another mob swept into the square. They outnumbered the humans, and rushed to attack them.

Stryke clambered to his feet.

Coilla ran to him. 'They're orcs!'

'What the *fuck's* going on?' Haskeer exclaimed.

Stryke shook his head. 'Pull back the band. Get 'em into a defensive pattern.'

Obeying yelled orders, the Wolverines quickly came together.

Ahead, a bloody melee raged. A group of five or six orcs peeled off from it and raced their way.

The one leading them shouted, 'Who's in charge?'

'Me,' Stryke told him.

'Come with us.' He saw the humans and dwarfs. 'Prisoners?'

'No, we're together.'

The orc was taken aback. 'You're kidding.'

'They're with us,' Stryke repeated.

'We can't take humans,' one of the other orcs protested. He glared in turn at Standeven and Pepperdyne, and at the dwarfs.

'We'll sort this out later,' the leader decided. 'Let's move!'

'Where?' Stryke asked.

'More of them are on the way. Stay and you'll die.'

'Who *are* you?'

'*Come on!*' He began to move off.

Stryke hesitated for a second, then signalled the band to follow.

As they ran into the darkened streets, Coilla said, 'Stryke, those humans used magic!'

15

If the structures rulers occupy reflect their regard for the ruled, then the fortress that stood at Taress' heart spoke volumes.

Its entryways were heavily guarded and its gates were locked. Archers walked its ramparts. Lookouts were positioned on its towers, and a garrison was permanently stationed within its grim, impenetrable walls.

It was a measure of the castle's reputation, or more accurately the nature of its inhabitants, that few entered willingly.

An entire level at one of its highest points was the exclusive province of a single individual. Given his status, it would be reasonable to assume that the chambers were well appointed, if not actually luxurious. But they were sparse. Furnishings were minimal, there was little in the way of embellishment and nothing of comfort. In this, the apartment reflected the disposition of someone who had given his life to military service. To the subjugated, Kapple Hacher was commonly known as Iron Hand.

Yet his appearance and manner were at odds with the epithet. He was of advancing years; not yet old, but in the later stages of maturity. His close-cropped hair was silver, and those who didn't know him assumed that was the reason he was beardless. But he displayed no trace of vanity. He had the physique of a much younger man, for all that his face was lined and the backs of his hands were liver-spotted. His bearing was javelin straight, and he wore his immaculate uniform as though born in it. Overall, the impression was of a somewhat meticulous, kindly uncle. At least, that was the impression he gave to other humans.

For someone in such a position of authority he seemed to wear his responsibilities lightly. And the power he exercised was great. Hacher was both governor of what its conquerors regarded as a province, and commander of an occupying army. In the latter capacity he held the rank of general.

He was dining. As was his custom, he ate alone. He fed sparingly, and the fare was plain; fowl, bread and fruit. Wine was something he rarely drank, and when he did, it was watered. Which made him doubly unpopular with his poison tasters.

He was served by a pair of ageing orc females. They placed the food, such as it was, on a well-scrubbed table that constituted the main item of furniture, and performed their duties in silence. For all the attention Hacher paid to them, they could have been invisible.

There was a knock at the door.

'Come!' Hacher responded crisply.

Two humans entered, one in a dark blue military uniform, the other in a brown robe with the cowl down. Both men were half the general's age.

'Begging your pardon, sir,' the uniformed aide said, 'but we have news of—'

Hacher raised a hand to pause him, then dismissed the servants with a nod. They went out with heads bowed, the visitors looking on disdainfully.

'You were saying, Frynt?' Hacher laid down the knife he was eating with.

'There's been another disturbance. And during curfew.'

'Casualties?'

'We're still counting, but significant.'

'Including three members of the Order,' the robed one added, shooting Frynt a hard look.

'That's unfortunate, Grentor,' Hacher commiserated. 'The state recognises their noble sacrifice, and they'll be honoured for it.'

'Tributes are all very well. We would prefer adequate protection from the military. We have a right to expect that much.'

'Given your brothers' magical expertise, I would have thought they were quite capable of defending themselves.'

'I do hope you're not implying any criticism of my order's competence, General.'

'Far from it. I'm the first to acknowledge that their contribution is invaluable.'

Frynt glared at Grentor. 'They *were* afforded protection. The number of casualties we took confirms that.'

'Yet my brothers accompanying the patrol were slain.'

'You lost three. Our fatalities were much higher.'

'What of the losses we inflicted on them, Frynt?' Hacher intervened to ask.

'We killed a few, sir, and took half a dozen prisoners.'

'You see, Grentor? The balance wasn't entirely in their favour.'

'And that's supposed to be some kind of consolation, is it? What are the lives of those beasts compared to men's?'

'Every rebel we eliminate is one less. A step nearer purging Acurial of this . . . difficulty.'

'But it's a situation that shouldn't have arisen at all!'

'Let's keep things in perspective. The vast majority of orcs are placid, you know that. How much resistance did they put up when we conquered this land? The present trouble is being caused by a small minority. A bunch of throwbacks, no more.'

'And if these *throwbacks* should gain a hold on the rest of the populace? Fevers have a way of growing into a pestilence, General.'

'This is one contagion they won't fall prey to. It's not in their nature.'

'They have a rallying point; this Sylandya, their so-called Primary. She should never have been allowed to slip through our fingers.'

'No one's rallying to her. She could be dead for all we know. You're aggrieved at the loss of your brothers, Grentor. I understand that. But it's vital that our military and magical forces work in harmony.'

'So what do you propose doing?'

'More of a presence on the streets, a further drive to recruit informers, stricter punishments for those fraternising with the dissidents. And increased surveillance. The Order can be of great assistance in that respect, Grentor. If this nut requires a sledgehammer to crack, so be it. As for Sylandya, we'll step up efforts to find her or confirm her fate.'

'Your words are reassuring, General.'

'I'm glad you approve.'

'Approval depends on outcomes, not intentions. The Order will judge your measures on their results.'

'Naturally.' Hacher rose. 'Now if you'll excuse me, Brother Grentor, you'll appreciate that I have a great deal to discuss with my aide.'

Grentor glanced at Frynt. There was no warmth in either's gaze. 'Of course.' He gave an almost imperceptible nod, turned and left.

Frynt closed the door behind him and let out a weary sigh.

'I know,' Hacher sympathised, a faint smile playing on his lips. 'Our sorcerer confederates can be a trial at times.'

'Anyone would think they bore the brunt of these disturbances rather than us.'

'Quite. But I meant what I said about better cooperation between the services. We need everybody working together to be rid of incidents like tonight's.'

'Yes, sir. Talking of which, do you have any special instructions concerning this new batch of prisoners?'

'You know my philosophy, Frynt. We must leave the world a better place than we found it. Execute them. After extracting whatever intelligence they possess under torture, of course.'

'Sir. And you'll be issuing fresh orders pertinent to the tightening up of security?'

'I will.' He massaged the bridge of his nose with thumb and forefinger. 'In the morning.'

'I think you might have impressed Grentor with these new measures,' the aide ventured. 'You don't normally concede so willingly to his demands, if I may say so, sir.'

'It wasn't entirely to placate Grentor and the Order.'

'Sir?'

'It's a bad time for all of this to flare up again.' His tone had grown sober. 'Keep it to yourself, but I've been informed to expect a visit from a higher authority.'

'Is that a problem, sir?'

'When it comes to this particular superior, that would be putting it lightly.' He suddenly appeared weary. 'Leave me now, Frynt. I need to rest.'

'Certainly, sir.'

The aide quietly removed himself.

On the far side of the room there was a pair of doors. The evening being warm, they were wide open. Hacher walked out onto the balcony.

He was renowned for his unruffled nature. But even he felt a pang of dread as he looked down at the darkened city.

The gloomy streets the Wolverines were taken through looped and twisted so much that they soon lost their bearings.

Eventually they were led along a narrow alley to a darkened house that appeared no different to hundreds of others they'd passed. The orc guiding them rapped a signal on the door with the hilt of his sword. Everyone was quickly ushered in. The door guard's eyes widened when he saw the humans and dwarfs, but he said nothing.

The house looked abandoned. There was no furniture and the bare floors were carpeted with dust. The large group was kept moving until its head reached a small back room. A pile of rotting wooden planks lay on the floor. Swept aside, a trapdoor was revealed. Stryke hesitated for a moment, then stepped on to the ladder. The band filed down after him.

They found themselves in an extensive cellar. A large number of orcs were present, and their expressions were uniformly wary.

The orc who brought the Wolverines there was the last one down. In the light thrown by brands and lanterns they got their first clear look at him. He was around four and twenty summers old, and fairly tall, almost rangy, by the standards of his race. His features were strong and his bearing upright. Self-evidently he was robust, and a female might well have seen him as fetching. From the way those present regarded him, it was also plain that he had authority.

'We should take your weapons,' he said.

'You'd have to prise them from our corpses,' Stryke told him.

'I hoped you'd say that.'

'Why?'

'It's further proof you're like us. Special.'

'Special?'

'You *fight*. That's why you're here.'

'What's so unusual about—'

'But there's a way you're not like us.' He pointed at Standeven, Pepperdyne and the dwarfs, who had been herded together in a corner. 'Why are you mixing with *humans*?' He all but spat the word. 'And whatever they are,' he added, indicating Jup and Spurral.

Stryke had no choice but to elaborate on the story he told when they first arrived, and hoped these orcs were as parochial as the shepherd. 'We're not from these parts.'

'What?'

'We're travellers.'

'Where have you travelled from?'

Stryke took his gamble. 'The world's a big place. You know there's a lot more to it than Taress.'

'In what part of the world do orcs consort with humans and . . .'

'They're called dwarfs,' Stryke supplied.

'Where do orcs, humans and these dwarfs live together?'

Stryke had hoped to keep things vague. He was forced to take another stab in the dark. 'The north. Far north.'

A murmur went up from the onlookers.

'The wilderness?' the leader said. He seemed impressed, possibly awed. Or perhaps disbelieving. It was hard to say.

Stryke nodded.

'We know little of those climes. Things must be very different there.'

Stryke barely believed his luck. It took an effort not to let out a sigh of relief. 'Very.'

'But you fight like a disciplined unit, the way we do. We saw it. If humans and these others are in league with orcs, *who* do you fight?'

Yet again, Stryke had to think on his feet. 'Humans.'

'Then how—'

'Some humans, like our comrades here, condemn what their kind have done to our race, and make common cause with us. And the dwarf folk have always sided with us.'

'I've never heard of such a thing. Here, humans treat us like cattle.'

'As you said, you know little of northern climes. Our ways are unlike Taress'.'

'If what you say is true,' the leader replied thoughtfully, 'I can see benefits in having human allies. Assuming they can be trusted.'

'Some can.' Stryke knew that could be the biggest lie of all.

'What I don't understand is how you came to be fighters at all.'

'Where we come from, all orcs fight.'

There was another, even louder murmur from the onlookers.

'*All?*'

'Why be surprised?' Stryke said. '*You* fight.'

'I said we were special. Different. The norm in Acurial is that most orcs aren't warlike.'

'It's the other way round with us.' He made an effort not to look Wheam's way. 'But how did you come to this?'

'Who knows? Too soft a life for too long, maybe, before the invaders arrived. Some of us, a few, have a taste for blood. The citizens think of us as freaks because of it. We see ourselves as patriots.' He gave Stryke a hard look. 'So why did your group come south?'

That almost wrong-footed Stryke. He said the first thing that came into his head. 'To recruit fighters.'

'You thought it'd be the same here as in your land? That all orcs fought?'

'We hoped.'

'You must have felt let down.'

'We just arrived. We're still finding out how things are.'

'There's no cheer in what you're saying. If you come from a land where all orcs fight, yet you still can't overcome the oppressors . . . You haven't beaten them, have you?'

'No.'

'Then what chance have we, with hardly any willing to take up arms?'

'There are far fewer orcs in the north lands.'

The leader sighed. 'That's our problem, too. Not enough of us.'

'Who *are* you?' Stryke asked.

'I'm Brelan.' He beckoned to someone standing in a shadowy part of the cellar. 'And this is Chillder.'

A female orc strode into the light. Her resemblance to Brelan was remarkable. Except for obvious gender differences, they were identical.

'Never seen twins before?' she asked of Stryke, who was staring intently.

'Rarely.'

'And how are they thought of in your land?'

'As lucky,' he answered truthfully.

'Then that's another difference. Here we're seen as bringers of ill fortune.'

'Let's hope it's to your enemies.'

Chillder allowed herself a fleeting smile. 'We know you're Stryke. But who . . . ?' She waved a hand at the rest of the Wolverines.

'This is Haskeer, Coilla and Dallog,' he replied, 'my seconds-in-command.' He didn't think they were ready to accept the idea of Jup being an officer. Jabbing a thumb at the grunts, he added pointedly, 'The rest you'll get to know later, given a chance.'

'Perhaps,' she returned, her expression inscrutable.

Stryke scanned the watchful faces surrounding them. 'So this is the resistance?'

'Some of it.'

'And you lead them?'

'Along with my brother.'

'We're outsiders,' Coilla said. 'Tell us what happened here.'

'It must have been the same as happened to you,' Chillder replied. 'We had a good life for a long time. Maybe too good, like Brelan said. Then Peczan invaded.'

'Peczan?'

She eyed Coilla suspiciously. 'The human's empire.'

'Oh, *right*. We tend to think of them as just . . . filthy, brutal humans.' It sounded lame, even to her.

Chillder let it pass. 'When the invaders came, opposition was weak. They overran us between new moon and full.'

'Didn't anybody organise a proper defence?'

'Sylandya tried. Our Primary.' She saw Coilla's quizzical look. 'Acurial's leader. She was the only one in power who really strived to mount a defence.'

'What happened to her?'

Chillder paused before answering, 'No one really knows. But the upshot is that Taress is under the heel of foreign occupiers. We're a province of Peczan now. They *reckon*.' There was real venom in her voice. 'And life gets harsher by the day under Iron Hand.'

'Who?'

'His name's Kapple Hacher. Calls himself our governor.'

'And the humans use magic?'

'Too right! Don't say *that's* different in the north too?'

'Er . . . no, course not. Just wondered.'

'It works the same as in your parts, I guess. Magic's in the hands of an elite among the humans, the Order of the Helix. Most just call them the Order.'

Coilla nodded knowingly.

'Don't know how it was with you,' Chillder went on, 'but magic was the ploy they used to invade here in the south. Peczan said we had weapons of magical destruction and posed a threat to them. What a joke.'

'Did you?'

'I wish. If we did, *and* had the ability to use 'em, things might have been different.'

'We want to help fight the humans,' Stryke said.

'We always need recruits,' Brelan told him. 'But . . . We need to confer.' As he was turning away he noticed the tattoos on Jup's cheeks. 'What's that on his face?'

'I can speak for myself,' Jup informed him.

'So what are those markings?'

'A sign of enslavement.'

Chillder scrutinised the faces of several Wolverines and saw their fading scars. 'You all had them,' she said.

Stryke nodded. He assumed the twins took it for granted that humans were responsible.

Chillder and Brelan exchanged glances, then walked away. When they reached the farthest end of the cellar they were joined by several others. A hushed conversation ensued.

The Wolverines waited, several score pairs of distrustful eyes on them.

'That was some fine bullshit you fed them, Stryke,' Coilla whispered.

'I don't know. I'm not sure I'd have believed it.'

'The bit about coming from the north seemed to go down well.'

'Pure luck.'

'What do you think they'll do?' Haskeer asked.

Stryke shrugged. 'Could go either way.'

Wheam sidled up. 'Are we gonna fight 'em?'

'That's rich coming from you,' Haskeer sneered. 'I'd have thought you'd be right at home here with so many cowards around.'

Wheam was about to mouth a retort when Dallog motioned him to silence.

The twins were coming back, at the head of a small delegation.

'Well?' Stryke demanded.

'We said we could use recruits,' Brelan told him. 'But if you really want to be part of this, you'll have to prove yourselves.'

'You want to set a task, that's all right by us.'

'Let's call it a test. We lost some good orcs tonight helping you out. Nothing can be done about them. But seven of our group were captured, and they face certain death because of you.'

'I could argue with that.'

'Don't bother.' He looked to the humans, and pointed at Pepperdyne. 'The younger one looks the fittest.'

'For what?' Stryke said.

'He could be useful on your mission, being one of *them*. Like a key, you know?'

'What is this mission?'

'You're to free our captured comrades. You and your three officers, this human and ten of your band. You can pick which ones.'

'I'd need the full strength to pull off something like that.'

'No. The other human, the dwarfs and the rest of your unit stay here. And if you fail, they die.'

16

Dawn had yet to break, and the air was chill.

The compound was a bleak collection of slab-like buildings on the outskirts of Taress. It was surrounded by a high timber wall, and there were several lookout towers. Guards patrolled inside the perimeter, and a small contingent defended the only set of gates.

In a copse on the side of a nearby hill a number of figures were stretched out on the ground, surveying the scene. Stryke, Coilla, Haskeer and Dallog were there, along with Pepperdyne, ten Wolverine privates and two resistance members. Pepperdyne was wearing a dark blue military uniform.

'They use this place solely for interrogation and executions,' one of the resistance orcs explained. 'Prisoners are kept in the biggest block, over there.' He pointed. 'The smaller ones are the torture and death chambers.'

'Where will your comrades be?' Stryke asked.

'Could be anywhere.'

'Great,' Coilla said.

The orc pointed again. 'See those two buildings? With the thatched roofs? That's the officers' mess and the barracks.'

'They're your remit, Dallog,' Stryke said.

The corporal nodded, and in turn looked to Nep, Zoda, Gant and Reafdaw, who all had bows strapped to their backs. 'Think you can manage 'em?' The quartet gave the thumbs up. 'Those *and* the towers are asking a lot, Stryke,' Dallog reckoned.

'This whole mission's asking a lot.' He directed that at the resistance members.

'Curfew's going to end soon,' one of them said, 'so your timing's gotta be spot on.'

'We kind of knew that,' Coilla replied dryly.

'Least you'll have the element of surprise. They won't be expecting something so bold.'

'You mean you've never tried anything like this before?'

He shook his head. 'Nobody has.'

'This just gets better.'

'Can we count on you two for help?' Stryke wanted to know.

'We're only here to observe and report back. But we'll be waiting with transport if you get out again.'

Stryke bit off a response and turned to Pepperdyne. 'You all right with this?'

'Do we have a choice?' He wriggled a couple of fingers into the buttoned-up collar of his uniform and tried stretching it. 'Damn thing's too tight,' he complained.

'Fidgeting won't make it any bigger,' Coilla said.

'This concerns me more.' He pointed at a small, dark red stain on the breast.

'Guess that was from the last owner. You'll have to hope nobody notices.'

Pepperdyne stared at the compound. 'What if they want a password or something?'

'It's a risk we'll have to take,' Stryke told him.

'That's an officer's uniform,' one of the resistance members explained. 'High ranking. It should be enough to get you in.'

'What worries me,' Haskeer said, 'is there'll only be three of us.' He glanced at Pepperdyne. 'And one a human at that.'

'Any more would be too suspicious,' the resistance member pointed out.

Stryke sighed. 'All right, let's do this.' To Coilla he added, 'Be ready to shift, and fast.'

Keeping low, he moved away. Haskeer and Pepperdyne followed.

At the foot of the hill, and out of sight of the compound, they came to an open wagon. They clambered on to it.

'Time to bind you,' Pepperdyne said, taking up a coil of rope.

'I'm not happy about this,' Haskeer grumbled ominously.

'Bit late for that,' Stryke commented. 'Here, do me first.' He turned his back.

The human bound his wrists. Then Haskeer reluctantly allowed himself to be tied.

'I've made the knots loose,' Pepperdyne assured them. 'One good tug and you'll be free. Now sit down.'

He climbed into the driver's seat and flicked the reins over the pair of horses.

They bumped around the base of the hill and joined the road. A moment later the compound came into view.

As Pepperdyne steered the wagon on to the slip road, the trio of guards lounging by the gates straightened up. Recognising his rank, but not him, they hesitated for a second before offering salutes. Then the most senior of them came forward.

'Can I help you, sir?'

'Two prisoners,' Pepperdyne replied crisply.

The guard glanced at Stryke and Haskeer. 'We've had no orders to expect prisoners.'

'What did you say?'

'I said we've had no—'

'I was referring to the way you addressed me, Sergeant! Is that how you talk to all superior officers?'

'No, I . . . *Sir*! No, sir!'

'Better. There's far too much sloppiness in the ranks. Some might accept it, *I* don't. Now, you were saying?'

'Begging your pardon, sir. But we've had no notice that prisoners are due, sir.'

'Well, I had orders to bring them here.'

The sergeant looked uncomfortable. 'Sir, our instructions are plain. I'd need to check this with the camp commander, sir.'

'So you're questioning my authority.'

'*No* sir. I only—'

'You're saying you don't trust the word of a superior officer. You're adding insolence to insubordination. Perhaps you'd like to see my orders, is that it? *Is* it? Here.' He reached into his tunic pocket. 'I'm sure General Hacher would be more than happy to have a *sergeant* inspect the directive he issued to me personally.'

The sergeant blanched. 'General . . . Hacher, sir?'

'Don't let that stop you. I'm sure you can explain your actions to him when he has you flogged, *Private*.'

'I didn't mean . . . that is, I . . . Go right in, sir!' He turned to his two companions. 'Open up and let the officer through! *Move yourselves!*'

The gates were hastily parted and the wagon rolled in.

Inside, there were two more guards. Much further away, in the compound proper, other soldiers could be seen going about their duties.

To Stryke and Haskeer, Pepperdyne whispered, '*Be ready.*'

He brought the wagon to a halt, then glanced at the nearest watchtower. The lookout was paying them no attention. One of the guards approached, and Pepperdyne jumped down to meet him.

'What can I do for you, sir?' the guard asked.

'Take a nap.'

'Eh?'

Pepperdyne gave him a hefty crack to the jaw. The man went down like a felled tree.

Stryke and Haskeer shed their bonds and leapt from the wagon. They pulled out concealed blades, and Haskeer grabbed the sword of the unconscious guard.

The other guard stopped gaping and dashed for a wall-mounted alarm bell. Stryke lobbed his knife and hit him squarely between the shoulder-blades. The man fell headlong.

They hauled up the first guard and brought him round with a couple of slaps.

A blade was put to his throat.

'The ones outside,' Stryke said. 'Get them in here.'

'Go to hell.'

'You first. Now *do it.*'

Pepperdyne looked to the watchtower. Still the lookout hadn't noticed what was happening. He felt sure their luck wouldn't hold much longer. '*Stryke*, get a move on!'

Stryke raised the blade and held the tip a hair's-breadth from the guard's eye. 'Let's try this another way.'

'All right, all right! I'll do it!'

They shoved him towards the gates.

'Any tricks and you're dead,' Stryke promised.

He and Haskeer moved aside, leaving Pepperdyne with a dagger to the guard's back.

'What do I say?' the man asked.

'Just get their attention. I'll do the talking.'

Trembling, the guard rapped on the gate a couple of times. A few seconds later it was opened a crack.

'What is it?' They recognised the sergeant's voice.

'We need a hand in here.'

'Why?'

Pepperdyne put a little more pressure on the blade and took over. 'Sergeant, the axle's broken on the wagon. We need help shifting it.'

'*Sir!*'

The sergeant and one of the other guards sidled in.

Stryke and Haskeer leapt on them. A flurry of blows and kicks put them down.

They used the rope to tie them, and the guard Pepperdyne held. Securely trussed, they were dragged into a small gatehouse, along with the dead sentry.

'This is taking too long,' Haskeer complained.

As if on cue an arrow zinged towards the nearest watchtower. It struck the lookout and he dropped from sight.

'It's started,' Stryke said.

Haskeer scowled. 'We're not ready. There's still one of 'em outside.'

Another arrow soared overhead, winging its way to the second tower.

'I'll take care of it,' Pepperdyne told them.

He slipped out of the gates. Seeing him, the remaining guard snapped to attention.

'We need you too,' Pepperdyne said.

The guard hesitated. 'Sir, I—'

'What?'

'Standing order, sir. This post is never to be left unmanned.'

'But . . . Oh, to hell with it.' He booted the guard's solar-plexus. The man doubled and Pepperdyne dragged him through the gates.

While they were dealing with him, flaming arrows cut across the sky towards the thatched buildings.

'Get those gates opened wide!' Stryke ordered.

When they had, they saw Coilla and the other Wolverines tearing down the hill.

'Here they come,' Haskeer said.

'And here comes somebody else,' Stryke added.

A group of soldiers were running their way across the compound. Others were moving in another direction, towards rising black smoke.

'Onto the wagon!' Stryke yelled.

They jumped aboard, and this time Stryke took the reins. He urged the horses and drove straight at the approaching soldiers. Pepperdyne and Haskeer stood in the back, hanging on with one hand, outstretched swords in the other.

The wagon picked up speed. Stryke kept on course, and the advancing troops went from distant figures to clearly defined individuals. Several were shouting, but their words were impossible to hear.

Then the wagon was on them. Soldiers scattered, and there were yells and curses. Most leapt clear. Several avoided the wagon but fell prey to Haskeer and Pepperdyne's blades. One managed to loose an arrow. It flew hopelessly wide.

Stryke got his bearings and swerved. The wagon turned so sharply that on one side its wheels briefly left the ground. The jolt when they came down again all but dislodged everyone on board.

They glimpsed the thatched buildings in flames. Men were dashing in all directions. Buckets of water were being chained.

The wagon turned again and headed for the prisoners' block.

Coilla's team got to the main gates. There were just six Wolverines with her. Dallog and his archers were bringing up the rear and had yet to arrive.

There was no chance for Coilla's group to properly collect themselves. Eight or nine of the troops Stryke ploughed through had kept on to the gates. They reached them at almost the same time as the Wolverines.

Coilla took on the first of the troopers. He was an officer, and spitting mad. She liked angry opponents; it clouded their judgement.

He attacked in a frenzy, slashing wildly with his sword and bellowing incoherently. It took no great skill on her part to dodge his blows. Getting past his blade's lacerating passes was a bit harder. And she was all too aware that there was no time for delay.

She grew furious in her response. Flaying the man's blade, she laid siege to his defences, such as they were. Having bludgeoned her way past his guard, she bored steel into his chest.

Coilla looked about, ready to engage another foe. There was no need. The group was putting down the last of the humans without her help.

Seafe joined her. 'Not much of a scrap, was it?' He looked disappointed.

'I think they're not used to orcs standing up to them. But it won't take long to soak in.'

'*Corporal!*' one of the privates shouted.

It heralded the arrival of Dallog and his four archers.

He surveyed the corpses. 'You've made a good start then.'

'There's going to be more than just these. Now let's get organised. You and you.' She nodded at two grunts. 'Stay here and guard our exit. The rest, follow me.'

They hastened into the compound.

The wagon Stryke was driving arrived at the prison block. An imposing building, it was tall and windowless, save for a series of niches, like arrow slits, way up near the roof. They saw only one entrance; a pair of solid double doors, set smack in the middle of the facade.

As Stryke slowed down, one of the doors opened a fraction. Just enough to show a pale human face gazing out from the ill-lit interior. Ponderously, the door began to close again.

Pepperdyne vaulted from the still moving wagon and ran towards it.

'*Hold!*' he shouted.

The muscular doorkeeper froze. Pepperdyne saw that he held a length of thick chain suspended from a point somewhere overhead. It obviously worked a mechanism of pulleys and weights that operated the heavy door.

'Let me in!' Pepperdyne demanded.

The doorkeeper stared at Pepperdyne. Then his gaze flicked over his shoulder to Stryke and Haskeer pulling up in the wagon. 'I can't do that, sir.'

'This is an order!' Pepperdyne thundered.

Ignoring him, the man resumed hauling the chain. The door started to move again.

Pepperdyne tried to stop him. He put his shoulder to it, pushing with all his strength. The door inched closer to the frame.

Haskeer ran over and added his muscle. Straining, they halted the door's progress, but couldn't reverse it. The doorkeeper continued tugging mightily on the chain, face contorted with effort. For a few seconds, there was stalemate.

Then Stryke joined them. Drawing his sword, he stooped and thrust it through the gap in the door. The tip penetrated the doorkeeper's thigh. He cried out, but stubbornly hung on. Stryke jabbed at him repeatedly, staining the man's breeches crimson. Trying to squirm away from the blade and maintain his hold on the chain at the same time proved too much. He let go and fell. The tautness went out of the chain and it shot up, jangling. Released, the door suddenly gave under Haskeer and Pepperdyne's weight. They practically fell in.

On his knees, the gatekeeper was scrabbling for his own sword. Stryke cut him down.

Stepping over his body, they took in their surroundings.

They were in a chamber just about large enough to accommodate their wagon. Its ceiling was as high as the building itself, and near the top was one of the slit windows they saw from outside, presumably for ventilation. Apart from a couple of wall-mounted brands providing the only real light, the walls were plain and unadorned.

On the other side of the chamber was another, much smaller door. Hanging beside it was a bunch of keys on a metal ring the size of a female orc's anklet. The door was locked, unsurprisingly, and they went through the keys until they found a fit.

Entering cautiously, they found themselves in the core of the building. It was long, quite narrow, and simply laid out. There was a central aisle, with cages on either side. Not cells, as they might have expected, but what were essentially pens, fashioned from metal bars. They were too low for the occupants to stand, and their floors were covered in grubby straw. Each cage contained a despondent-looking orc, and the place stank.

'Kept like animals,' Haskeer growled.

'Why're you looking at me?' Pepperdyne said.

'Why do you think?'

'I didn't do this.'

'Your kind did.'

'*Shut up*,' Stryke hissed, 'the pair of you. We're not out of this yet.'

The prisoners had begun to notice what was happening and were growing noisily restive. At the far end of the aisle a door opened and a man in uniform entered. He didn't notice the intruders. His attention was on quietening the prisoners, and he went about it with something that looked like a javelin. Shoving the pole between the bars, he jabbed at them with its barbed point.

'I've had enough of this shit,' Haskeer declared. He headed down the walkway at a run.

'Leave him to it,' Stryke said, clutching Pepperdyne's sleeve.

Haskeer was halfway along the aisle and gathering speed before the human noticed him. For a second he just stared, bemused. Then he started withdrawing the pole from a cage, working frantically, hand over hand. He almost had it clear when Haskeer smashed into him.

The human was knocked backwards, losing his hold on the pole. He should have fallen, but Haskeer seized him by the shoulders in a steely grip. The man cried out. Haskeer propelled him to one side, savagely driving his head into the bars of a cage, the impact raising an almost melodic chime. He earned on pounding him against the cage until his skull was a bloody pulp. At length he let go, and the human dropped lifeless to the floor.

The caged orcs, who had been clamouring throughout, fell silent.

Stryke and Pepperdyne caught up. Stryke moved past Haskeer and made for the door the dead human had come out of. He booted it open. It was an empty guardroom.

He still had the bunch of keys. Walking back to the centre of the aisle, he held them up for the prisoners to see. 'We're here for the Resistance members captured last night!' he told them. 'We'll sort out who's who later! But remember: it's not over when we unlock these cages! If you want to leave this camp alive, be ready to fight! You'll have to scavenge weapons or improvise!' Glancing Pepperdyne's way, he added, 'And this human's with us!' He tossed the keys to Haskeer and said, 'Let 'em out.'

Outside, there was chaos. The barracks and officers' quarters were burning fiercely. Oily black smoke all but obscured the rising sun and the smell of charred timber perfumed the air. Most of the soldiers were fighting the fires; others milled in confusion. The Wolverine archers added to the turmoil by picking off random targets. For good measure they unleashed a few more flaming arrows at anything that might burn. A guards' hut was ablaze, and the wooden supports of a bulbous water tower.

Coilla and Dallog's group arrived at the two buildings given over to torture and execution. They had no idea which was which. Not wanting to split their forces, they went for the first they came to. Like the prison block, it was a featureless structure with no windows and a single entrance. But they didn't have Stryke's good fortune. The door was firmly closed.

'What now?' Dallog asked.

'When in doubt,' Coilla replied, 'blag your way through.'

A couple of the Wolverines toted two-handed axes. She ordered them to take down the door. As they hammered at it, the archers stood by with taut bows. The door proved as solid as it looked, and it needed repeated blows before the wood began to splinter and groan. Finally it gave.

They expected defenders to be waiting. There was no one to be seen. Kicking aside the jagged remains of the door, Coilla led the way into the building.

There was a wide flight of stone steps that went down to a short corridor, with a further door at its end. It was also locked, but nowhere near as robust as the one they just broke down. After a couple of strokes from an axe it sprang open.

Now they were in the heart of the building, and its function was immediately obvious. On one side stood a chest-high platform running the length of the room, with steps at each end. Above that was a sturdy beam of equal span, from which six ropes were suspended, each ending in a noose. Beneath each noose was a trapdoor. On the other side of the room there were tiers of benches for observers. The place seemed deserted.

'There's no doubt what they do here,' Dallog remarked grimly.

Coilla nodded. 'Let's get out. There's nothing—'

'*Corporal*,' Reafdaw whispered. He bobbed his head towards the dark hollow under the platform.

Everybody caught his meaning and listened. A second later

there was the faintest of noises. Coilla silently gestured to the two orcs nearest the platform.

Moving fast, they stooped and darted into the hollow. There was the sound of a scuffle and the smack of fists on flesh. Then they emerged dragging a human between them. His face was bloodied and his terror apparent.

'Just him under there,' one of the grunts reported.

'So what are you?' Coilla wondered.

'Bet he's an executioner,' Dallog offered.

Reafdaw slipped out a dagger. 'Shall we kill him?'

The man turned chalk white. He started to plead.

'*Shut up*,' Coilla said. 'Hold on for a minute, Reafdaw.' She moved her face closer to the quaking human's. 'You've one chance to save your neck. Can you get us into the torture block?'

His panicky gaze darted from her to Reafdaw to Dallog, then back again. He didn't speak.

'All right,' Coilla said, turning away, 'cut his throat.'

'*No!*' the human begged. 'I can do it! I'll get you in!'

'Then get going.' She shoved him towards the door.

The human resisted. 'Not that way.'

'Why not?'

'I couldn't get you through the main entrance. It'll be secured because of . . . whatever's going on outside.'

'No point keeping you alive then.'

'No, wait! There's another way. Under there.' He pointed to the space below the scaffolds. 'It's where I was going when you caught me.'

Coilla gave him a chilling look. 'If this is a trick . . .'

'It's *not*. I'll show you.'

They kept close to him as he moved underneath the platform. After hunching for about ten paces they came to an area where it was possible to stand. Overhead were the trapdoors.

The human carried on to the wall. 'Here,' he said.

At first, Coilla couldn't see what he meant. She reached out to touch the wall with her fingertips, and felt a ridge. Then she realised it was a doorframe, hidden in shadow. She pushed. There was light.

They were looking along a tunnel. It was softly lit by fat candles set in recesses.

'Straight from torture to death, eh?' Dallog said.

'And to tidily remove the . . . deceased,' the human told him.

'*Tidily*,' Coilla repeated, a note of menace in her voice. She gave him a hard shove. 'Keep moving!'

The tunnel ended at a series of metal rungs that climbed to a trapdoor.

'How many are up there?' Coilla whispered.

'I don't know,' the human replied. 'I really don't.'

Coilla looked back at the rest of her group, crowding the narrow tunnel. She didn't like the fact that they could only go up the rungs one at a time. It seemed perfect for an ambush. 'No lingering,' she told them. 'We get up there fast. And be ready for anything.' To the human she said, 'You first.'

He climbed the rungs and lifted the trap. Coilla went next, with Dallog right behind her.

They emerged in a building of roughly the same dimensions as the one they just left. But it was laid out differently. Ahead of them, hugging the left-hand side, was a paved walkway. The space to the right was divided into sections by floor to ceiling brick partitions, nine or ten paces apart, forming a succession of cubicles. It remind Coilla of a stable.

The rest of the orcs were beginning to surface from the tunnel, and Dallog was hauling up the slower ones by their scruffs. Coilla turned her head to check the bottleneck. That fleeting distraction was all their captive needed.

He bolted. Running along the gangway, he started shouting. Most of it was gabble, but the note of alarm was unmistakable.

'*Shit!*' Coilla cursed.

Before she could act, Dallog shot past her. He moved at a surprising clip given his age, and caught the human with apparent ease. There was a brief, futile struggle. Then Dallog seized the man's head and twisted it sharply. There was an audible crack as his neck broke. Man became corpse in the blink of an eye, and dropped.

But his shouted warning had a result. Up ahead, several figures came out of cubicles. They headed towards the orcs, weapons drawn.

'*Down!*' Coilla yelled.

It took Dallog a second to realise she meant him. He hit the deck. A small swarm of arrows soared over his head. They thudded into the first two humans, flattening them. The third and final man dashed for shelter as Wolverine archers loosed another volley. He almost made it.

'Nice move,' Coilla told Dallog as he got to his feet. 'Search the place,' she ordered the rest of the group.

Moments later she was called to one of the cubicles.

A manacled orc was suspended on the wall. He was unconscious and bloodied.

Nearby stood a brazier steeped with glowing coals. Cruel-looking irons were heating in it. Other tools of the torturer's trade were laid out on a gore-splattered bench.

'There's another one a few cubicles along,' a grunt told her. 'He's in a similar state.'

'Get them down. Have Dallog look at their wounds.'

A commotion arose along the walkway. She went out and saw several of her crew with a captive. They frogmarched him towards her.

'Look what we found,' one of them said.

The man was big and powerfully built. He wore the traditional black leather garb of an inquisitor, complete with integral skullcap and eye mask. His chest was bare and sheened with sweat from his labours.

'Your work?' Coilla nodded at the prisoner being taken down.

'And proud of it.' His manner was contemptuous, and he showed little of the fear their last captive displayed. 'Besides,' he added haughtily, 'your kind don't feel pain the way your superiors do.'

'If you say so.' She swiftly snatched an iron from the fire and drove it into his chest.

He howled. The smell of scorching flesh perfumed the air. Coilla contemplated doing it again, thought better of it and tossed aside the iron. Instead she raised her sword and cut off his shrieks with a clean thrust between the ribs.

'I reckon that's enough to hurt anybody,' she told his lifeless body. 'Improvise a couple of stretchers,' she ordered, 'we're getting out of here.'

They smashed the legs off two benches and used the tops to

transport the tortured orcs. Then they found the main entrance and left that way.

Out in the compound, confusion still reigned.

Somebody shouted, '*Look!*'

Stryke, Haskeer and Pepperdyne were running their way. They had a large number of freed prisoners in tow.

'All right?' Stryke asked.

Coilla nodded. 'Yeah. They've made suffering and death a fine art here.' She couldn't help eyeing Pepperdyne. He said nothing.

'At least we can get this bunch out,' Stryke replied.

There was a thunderous crash. The burning supports of the water tower had given way. Shattering as it hit the ground, the huge wooden container disgorged its contents. Several hundred gallons of water swept across the compound, knocking nearby soldiers off their feet.

'That should keep 'em busy,' Haskeer reckoned.

'Time to leave,' Stryke said.

They ran to the main gates and were joined by the pair of Wolverines they left as back-up. Almost as soon as they got out to the road, a couple of large covered wagons drew up. They were driven by the two resistance members who guided the Wolverines to the camp. The injured were put on board, then everyone else crammed in at the double.

It was still early, and there wasn't much in the way of people or traffic on the streets. In any event the journey wasn't too long. Instead of driving into the city proper, the wagons skirted it and made for a rural area. Soon, they came to a collection of seemingly abandoned farm buildings. The gateway was guarded by a contingent of orcs who waved the wagons through. They pulled up in a spacious yard.

Stryke got out. The place was full of resistance members. Brelan was foremost. Chillder hovered in the background.

'You asked for seven,' Stryke said, jabbing a thumb at the disembarking passengers, 'I've brought you thirty.'

'I'm impressed,' Brelan admitted.

'And here's something else for you,' Stryke added. He balled his fist and delivered a heavy punch to Brelan's jaw, flooring him. 'That's for putting my band in danger.'

On all sides, resistance members went for their weapons. A number moved forward.

Brelan raised a hand and stopped them. 'Right,' he said, spitting a mouthful of blood. 'I think we can work together.'

17

'What I still find hard to take in,' Brelan said, spearing a chunk of meat with his dagger, 'is the idea of humans taking the side of orcs.'

'The way I see it,' Pepperdyne replied, 'it's not about humans and orcs. It's about right and wrong.'

'And is that how your companion sees it too?' Chillder asked, staring at Standeven. 'He doesn't say much.'

'Er . . . I . . .' Standeven jabbed a finger at Pepperdyne. 'What he said.'

'He's a deep thinker,' Pepperdyne explained. 'Not much of a way with words.'

'Is he as good a fighter as I've heard you are?'

'You'd be . . . surprised at his talents, Chillder.'

Servers arrived to replenish their cups with wine, and conversation dwindled.

It was evening. Brelan and Chillder had invited Stryke and his officers to join them for a meal. The humans had been included, along with Jup and Spurral, though Stryke wasn't alone in thinking it was with some understandable reluctance on the twins' part. The rest of the Wolverines were taking their food elsewhere in the dilapidated farmhouse.

It was Stryke who broke the silence. 'So what's the plan?'

'Plan?' Brelan said.

'How are you going to stoke your rebellion?'

Brelan smiled. It was more cynical than amused. 'Rebellions need popular backing. Unlike your far northern lands, the orcs here have no taste for rising up. As I said, we of the resistance are different; we're prepared to fight the invaders. But we're no more than a thorn in their side. Though what you did today—'

'You could do every day,' Coilla assured him. 'Our numbers are small too, if you hadn't noticed. Resolve counts more than numbers.'

'Along with training and experience,' Stryke said.

'Not that you couldn't do with a much bigger force,' Dallog added.

'I'd give my sword arm for another thousand warriors,' Brelan agreed. 'But warfare's not in the nature of orcs. At least, not in this part of the world.'

Haskeer had been stuffing his mouth with fowl. He dragged a sleeve across his greasy chin. 'Yeah, why *are* they so gutless in these parts?'

Stryke shot him a look. 'Sorry. My sergeant's not used to civil company.'

Haskeer shrugged and tore a large chunk from a loaf of bread.

'Orcs tend to be blunt in their opinions,' Chillder replied. 'It seems we *are* like our northern brethren in that way, and long may it last. But he's right. Our race's weakness shames us.'

'And we find it puzzling,' Stryke remarked. 'That orcs should shy from a fight . . . well, that's something we don't understand.'

'I think we've become too civilised. It seems you of the northern wastes aren't as soft in your ways. Life here has been too easy for too long, and it's buried our natural passions.'

'But underneath the fire's still there. You're proof of that.'

'*You're* the proof,' Brelan said. 'We differ a little from Acurial's citizenry; you could almost be from another world.'

Stryke smiled stiffly. 'I wouldn't say that.'

'I would. You're unlike any orcs I've ever known. I mean, you even have ranks, like the humans. How did that come about?'

Stryke felt as though he was about to start walking on eggs again. He could hardly say it was imposed on them as members of a horde headed by an insane sorceress. 'We got organised, created a clear line of command so we could better fight the enemy. It's something you should think about doing yourselves.'

'It's so like the way humans do it, and what with those tattoos you all had, I thought you might have been press-ganged by them.'

'Is that something they do here?' Coilla asked.

'No. They've tried, mind you. But they find orcs poor material for fighting. We've been such an unwarlike race there isn't even a tradition of weapon-making. We have to forge our own, or steal them from the occupiers.'

'Things do seem in a bad way here,' Stryke reflected.

Chillder nodded. 'They are. But what your band managed in one day gives us hope. If you'd help us organise and train, we could do some real damage to the occupiers, not just harass them.'

'*Now* you're talking,' Haskeer said. He gulped his wine. Some of it dribbled down the front of his jerkin.

'We can help,' Stryke confirmed.

Chillder looked to the dwarfs. 'Jup, are your folk as warlike as these orcs of the north?'

'We hold our own.'

'As well as any in the band,' Stryke told her.

'And how do you see us faring against the humans here, Jup?' Brelan asked.

'I'd imagine their greater numbers would be a problem.'

'They aren't that great. Granted there's more than the resistance. A lot more. But not as many as you might think to cow a nation.'

'How so?'

'Isn't it obvious? With a population this meek, they don't *need* vast regiments to keep us down. That's why we were such a tempting prize. It's not force of arms that holds the balance, it's damn magic.'

'And with orcs lacking that ability, it's not likely to change.'

'Yet it was the lie that we could control magic that led to the invasion.'

'How is it with dwarfs?' Chillder said.

Spurral had been picking at her food. She looked up. 'What do you mean?'

'We know some humans can master sorcery. Is it the same with dwarfs?'

'We may look a little like them, but we don't share that particular gift. Our troubles would have been over long before now if we did.'

'Pity.' Chillder turned her gaze to Pepperdyne and Standeven.

'It's no good looking at us,' Pepperdyne said, raising his hands in denial. 'Magic's practised by an elite we've never been acquainted with.'

'You can't help us turn sorcery against them then,' Chillder sighed.

'Forget magic; it's not likely to be part of the orcs' armoury,' Stryke reckoned. 'But cold steel can match it.'

'How?' Brelan wanted to know.

'A dead wizard casts no spells. Humans are flesh, and they bleed. Concentrate on that.'

'It's easier said,' Chillder reminded him. 'What can we do to bring it about?'

'What you've *been* doing, only better. We've fought humans and we've fought magic. Both can be overcome. We'll share our skills with you, show you how to make the best of what you've got.'

'I had an idea about that,' Coilla ventured.

'Go on,' Brelan said.

'I noticed that you have a number of females in your ranks. But as far as I can see they're menials. Do any of them fight?'

It wasn't Brelan who replied, but his sister. 'Ah. You've touched on a sore point, Coilla. Of the resistance females, it's just me who takes on the enemy in battle. And that's only because my brother wouldn't dare deny me.'

'That's not really true,' Brelan protested. He saw how his twin was looking at him. 'Well, all right, it is. But as a general rule we don't let the females fight.'

'Why?' Coilla demanded.

'I'll say it again: we are few. We've a duty to protect the child-bearers.'

'Have you asked *them* what they think? Look, Brelan, you're an orc, but the way orcs are in Acurial isn't . . . natural. You need to understand that females of our race are as ferocious as the males. Or could be. They're an asset you're wasting.'

'That's never been our way.'

'Then change it. You're fighting for freedom for all. All should fight.'

Chillder backed that with, 'Hear, hear.'

Brelan was silent for a moment, and seemed to be mulling over Coilla's words. Then he said, 'They couldn't fight alongside the males. Their lack of skill would endanger them.'

Coilla nodded. 'That's what I thought. So why not let me put together an all-female band? Not to fetch and carry for you males, but to fight in their own right.'

Chillder smiled. 'It gets my vote.'

'I hope you'd be a part of it; and you, Spurral.'

'Why not?' Brelan conceded. 'If it helps the cause—'

'Good. There must be twenty or thirty females here who could form a warband.'

'You should ask Wheam to join,' Haskeer muttered.

'What did he say?' Brelan asked.

'Ignore him,' Coilla said, aiming a glare at Haskeer.

'All right then, we'll make a start in the morning,' Chillder promised.

Things wound down after that. One by one, the diners drifted from the table to find somewhere to sleep. Stryke and Coilla felt in need of air, and slipped out of the farmhouse. They propped themselves against a fence rail, well away from the patrolling guards.

'You look troubled,' she said.

'I don't like lying to these orcs. About who we are, where we're from, why we're here . . .'

'You think they'd find the truth more to their taste?'

'Hell, no. They'd probably burn us at the stake.'

'So you're doing the right thing. Just like Spurral did back there, denying dwarfs had any magical powers. They're not ready for the truth, however let down Chillder seemed.'

'Maybe.'

'Everything's on its head here. I mean, now we know why the humans haven't despoiled this place the way they did Maras-Dantia. They understand that the magic depends on the land staying hearty.'

'They'll find another way of fucking things up.'

'That's for sure.' She turned to look at him. 'I thought you might have been ticked off with me.'

'Why should I be?'

'This idea of a female warband. I should have asked you first. But just in the short time we've been here I've got crabby about the bullshit. You know, they call themselves civilised, but don't seem so damned civilised when it comes to females doing their bit.'

'Don't be too hard on them. They've lost touch with their roots, with what it means to be an orc. And no, I don't mind. Whatever gives the humans a kick in the arse is fine by me.'

'*Good.* I even thought of a name for the band. We're the Wolverines; I thought they could be the Vixens.'

He smiled. 'Sounds fitting.'

'But we're dodging the main issue.'

'Which is?'

'Jennesta. There's no sign of her. And she's why we're here, isn't she?'

'Part of it.'

'You saying we wouldn't be here if it wasn't for the chance to settle with her once and for all?'

'No. But we've barely seen Taress yet. Jennesta's not likely to be strolling around unprotected.'

'Getting even with her is why most of the band signed on for this mission. You shouldn't forget that.'

'I won't.'

'And it's all about a grudge for Pepperdyne and Standeven, too. They say.'

'That's another bucket of worms.'

'We're getting in deep here, Stryke. In more than one way.'

He raised a finger to his lips and nodded towards the farmhouse. Brelan was heading their way.

'There you are,' he said.

'I'm glad to have you without the others around,' Stryke told him. 'About that punch I threw at you—'

Brelan rubbed his chin, as though still stinging from the blow. 'I got the message. But that's done. I'm not here to go over it. We've had news.'

'What is it?'

'Seems an emissary of some kind's about to arrive from Peczan.'

'So?'

'The word is this isn't some lowly bureaucrat. They're high up. Important. And it's causing quite a stir among the governor's staff and the garrison.'

'How do you know this?'

'Not all orcs want to fight, but some of them are happy to pass on intelligence. This came down the line from servants in Hacher's headquarters.'

'So if we could get at whoever it is—'

'Perhaps. Or stage something that makes Hacher look inept in their eyes. Either way, with your help, we might be able to strike a blow.'

'And you've no idea who this envoy is, or how much power they wield?'

'None. Except that as far as Hacher's concerned, their coming doesn't bode well.'

'Yes,' Coilla said, 'but for who?'

18

The orcs of Acurial, and especially of Taress, were accustomed to having the military hammer on their doors at dawn. Usually it was a prelude to being locked up, tortured or summarily executed. Or perhaps to be forced to witness the execution of others. Sometimes it was part of a collective punishment for a real or imagined defiance of the occupiers' will; the citizenry made to watch as their homes burned, their cattle were slaughtered and their fields sown with salt.

It was much rarer for them to be turfed from their beds to line the streets. To be issued with pennants bearing the colours of their conquerors' nation and compelled to acclaim a visiting dignitary.

Most singular of all was to have the object of their ersatz approval gallop past at speed in a black carriage with its windows shuttered against curious eyes.

The carriage, accompanied by an entourage of similarly impenetrable vehicles and an honour guard of hard-faced elite troopers, made its way to the fortress at the centre of the city. As soon as it entered, the gates were hastily secured.

Near the castle's apex, in Kapple Hacher's eyrie, the governor awaited his guest.

As ever, he was outwardly calm. The sorcerer Grentor, who stood at his side, was less so.

'Tell me, Governor,' Grentor said, toying nervously with a string of worry beads, 'have you met our guest before?'

'I have. In Peczan.'

'And your impression?'

'I think . . . profound would be an appropriate word. And you, Brother? Have you been in the presence?'

'No. Although our visitor is technically the head of our Order, I've never had that pleasure.'

'Pleasure is a word you might wish to reconsider.'

'How so?'

There was a knock at the door.

'Come!' Hacher called.

His aide, Frynt, entered. 'They're here, sir.' He was breathless.

'You seem flustered,' Hacher said. 'I take it you've had sight of our guest.'

'Yes, sir. The party's on its way up.'

'All right. Leave us. No, use the other door.'

The aide went out, looking relieved to be going.

Grentor wore a perplexed expression.

'A word of advice, High Cleric,' Hacher told him. 'You'll find that the emissary is . . . let's say strong willed, and does not easily tolerate dissent. This is a person of enormous power and influence. It's as well to keep that in mind.'

Grentor would have replied, had not the double doors leading into Hacher's chambers not flown open with a crash.

Two figures walked in. They were human. At least, nominally so. Both were males, and impressively muscular. They were dressed for combat, in black leather trews, jerkins and steel-tipped boots, and they carried scimitars.

Beyond these superficialities, they were wrong. Their eyes were wrong. They had a fixed, glazed quality that seemed devoid of any spark of humanity. Their faces were wrong. The skin appeared overly taut and expressionless, and it had an unhealthy yellowish tinge. The way they moved was wrong. They progressed inflexibly, as though their spines were too rigid, and there was a slight tendency to shuffle.

The pair inspected the room, looking behind drapes and opening doors. They said nothing. Seemingly satisfied that no assassins lay in wait, they shambled to Hacher and the priest. One extended a beefy, parchment-coloured hand.

'I hope you've no intention of searching *me*?' Hacher complained indignantly.

'We'll let it pass this time.'

As they turned to the source of the voice, a female swept into the room. Even Hacher, who had seen her before, was taken aback by her appearance. For Grentor, it was a new and startling experience.

There was something perplexing, not to say downright disturbing, about the way she looked. The structure of her face was strangely off beam. It was just a little too flat and wide, especially across the temples, and her chin narrowed almost to a point. Her skin was curious. There was a light silvery green patina to it, as though stippled with tiny fish scales. Her nose was slightly convex, and her shapely mouth seemed overly broad. She had ink-black hair that fell to her waist.

What held Hacher and Grentor were her eyes. They were dark and undoubtedly mesmeric. But they had a deeper, more unsettling feature. Like portals, they allowed a glimpse into a realm of shadowy matter; infinite, merciless, chaotic.

Ignoring any rational definition of the word, she was beautiful. Beautiful in the way of a carnivorous plant, a wolf spider or ravening shark. Nightmarish yet alluring. Unwholesome.

She snapped her fingers. The sound was loud and brittle. In the silence that had settled on the room, it was almost shocking. The two dead-eyed bodyguards responded to it as surely as a spoken command. Turning as one, they strode out, Hacher and Grentor staring after them.

Hacher collected himself first, and greeted their guest. 'My Lady Jennesta.' He bobbed his head respectfully.

'Hacher.'

'May I introduce Brother Grentor, High Cleric of the Order of—'

'Yes, yes.' She waved away the rest of his sentence with a lazy motion of her hand. 'I'm aware of who he is.'

Grentor was halfway through a low bow. He straightened, looking uncomfortable.

'Please, ma'am,' Hacher said, gesturing to the best chair in the room, 'be seated.'

She regarded it with the disdain of someone expecting to be offered a throne. But she suffered the indignity, the silk of her emerald gown giving a gentle swish as she sat.

'Those bodyguards . . .' Hacher began, his gaze flashing to the door in anticipation of them returning any second.

'A fitting way to employ miscreants, don't you think, Governor?' Jennesta smiled.

Her teeth were small and white and quite sharp.

173

'Miscreants?'

'Enemies of the state. Dissenters. Those who would challenge our authority.'

Hacher felt sure she meant *her* authority, but kept that to himself. 'One of them . . . I thought I recognised—'

'You probably did. Disloyalty has no respect for position. The blight can even infect those quite high up in the administration.'

Hacher had no doubt that was a not very veiled warning directed at him.

'How better to punish traitors than having them serve the state they sought to undermine?' Jennesta went on. 'Dead yet undead; an exquisite fate.' Her relish was palpable. 'But I'm not here to discuss my pets. There are concerns, Hacher.'

'Ma'am?'

'You know my meaning well enough. The situation here is displeasing.'

'It's true we've had our problems. But there are stirrings in all the provinces from time to time. We have things under control.'

'Really? And what happened yesterday, was that an instance of how in control you are?'

'Ah, you heard about that.'

'I hear about everything, Governor. Have no doubts on that score.'

'We have a small seditious element. They got lucky.'

'They had a *human* with them.' She glared balefully. 'Is treachery rife here, too?'

'It was some kind of fluke. Such a thing has never been known.'

'Until now. How many more humans can we expect to side with the beasts?'

'The event was serious; I'm not denying that, ma'am. But it would be a mistake to take one incident and—'

'But it isn't just one. You have the makings of a rebellion here.'

'I wouldn't go that far.'

'Of course you wouldn't. You're complacent. What measures have you taken against the military who allowed the raid to succeed?'

'Reprimands have been issued and—'

'Have all those responsible executed.'

'Our own people?'

'To think they call you Iron Hand.' She laughed derisively. 'You're soft, Hacher. That's why the governance of this region is so dismal. Discipline will be imposed, and you'll start by signing death warrants as I dictate.'

'I protest at this blatant—'

'And if you don't want to see a warrant bearing *your* name nailed to the castle gate, they'll be some changes of attitude in this administration.'

In deference to her superior position, Hacher suffered the threat in silence.

Jennesta turned her attention to Grentor. 'There's no call for you to feel smug about this.'

'I can assure you, ma'am—'

'The Order has done as badly in Acurial as the military,' she ploughed on. 'The martial and magical wings are expected to cooperate and support each other. That obviously isn't happening.'

'I beg to differ. We've never faced this kind of situation before.'

'But it's just a handful of rebels, according to the Governor.' Her words dripped sarcasm. 'Oh, and a lone human who's made cause with them. But that's too much for you, even with the sorcery you have.'

'With respect, members of the Order have lost their lives fighting these rebels,' Grentor informed her gravely.

'Then they deserved to, and good riddance. Any who aren't up to the task have no place in any Order I lead.'

'That's a little harsh, if I may say so. As you know, ma'am, magic can be an imprecise art.'

'Fool. It's only as crude as those practising it.' Jennesta deftly unwound the silken scarf she wore, and bunched it. 'Here, catch.' She lobbed it at the priest as though it were a child's ball.

By reflex, he made to catch it. The ball sailed over his outstretched hand. It unravelled and became a streamer. Then it grew indistinct, and seemed to alter in form as it fluttered against his upper body.

Grentor gave an audible intake of breath. The scarf was wrapped around his neck. Only it was no longer a scarf. What had been embroidered silk was now a three-headed brimstone-coloured viper with a black zigzag stripe running the length of its scaly body. It constricted, choking off the priest's air. Forked tongues whipped from each of its hissing heads. Wickedly sharp fangs sought his flesh.

Despite knowing it had to be a glamour, Grentor began to panic. He tried to cry out, but only managed a croak. His face turned ashen. The snake squeezed tighter.

Hacher had looked on in horror. Now he moved in the priest's direction.

Jennesta made a casual hand gesture.

The viper disappeared. Grentor let out a sigh of relief. He staggered a few steps to the room's large oak table and leaned against it, palms pressed on its surface, head down. He was panting.

The scarf was in Jennesta's hand. She put it back on, heedless of the little drama playing out in front of her. 'There's no excuse,' she said. 'The magic flows strong through this land, pure and powerful. Unlike some places I've been.'

If Hacher and Grentor wondered what she meant, they were too awed or too discomfited to comment.

'Heed me, priest,' Jennesta continued. 'Things will improve. Because High Clerics can find themselves demoted to humble brothers. And worse.'

Grentor nodded, still dazed. He rubbed at his neck, and there was fear in his eyes.

A silence descended. It didn't seem to bother Jennesta, but Hacher found it awkward. For want of anything better to say, and incongruous as it sounded, he heard himself mouthing, 'You must think me a poor host, my Lady. Can I offer you refreshments?'

She fixed him with a stare he had difficulty holding. 'The refreshments I take are of a special order, and something I enjoy privately. But that does remind me . . .' She looked to the doors and, as if bending to her will, they opened.

Her pair of mindless bodyguards hobbled in. One had an ornately carved wooden box under his arm. This was presented to Jennesta. When she opened it, the minders' usual sluggish manner became something like excited. They licked their cracked lips with black, mottled tongues, and began to drool.

Jennesta fished something out of the box. It was russet in colour, and looked like a chunk of desiccated meat, or perhaps a greatly engorged worm. She dangled it at arm's length. In what appeared to be a well practised movement, the bodyguards sank to their knees, as though begging. She tossed the morsel.

There was a brief scuffle. Then one of the minders was stuffing the meat into his mouth and crunching it with pleasure. His companion was aggrieved, but brightened when she threw him a titbit of his own. They sprawled on the floor, chewing earnestly, brown juice running down their chins.

Jennesta noticed Hacher staring at the open box. 'They require sustenance,' she explained. 'I also find it convenient to neuter my subordinates. So in a spirit of waste not, want not . . .'

Hacher gaped at her. 'You mean . . .'

'Privy parts are very nutritious. I can attest to that myself.' She continued feeding them like dogs.

Grentor's complexion went grey. He put a hand over his mouth and turned his head.

Hacher steadied himself with a deep breath. 'What do you want us to do about the situation here, my lady?' he asked.

'I know orcs of old. However placid this Acurial variety may seem, I know what they're capable of. Particularly when exposed to a malignant influence from elsewhere, as I've reason to believe is happening.' Jennesta flung another piece of meat. 'What Taress needs,' she said, as her minions bit noisily into their treat, 'is a reign of terror.'

19

The sun rose blood red. A run of fine days looked threatened by drab clouds and chill breezes.

The weather was of no concern to a group concealed among the trees on the peak of a hill overlooking Taress. They were a motley collection of beings that would have dismayed both humans and orcs had they been seen. Which was why they employed means both practical and magical to make sure they weren't.

One of their number required solitude for the task she had to perform. At a distance from the others, she knelt by the edge of a pool. She had sprinkled certain herbs and compounds over its still waters while reciting the necessary incantation. The pool had bubbled and seethed, and took on the quality of a finely polished mirror.

Now Pelli Madayar of the elfin race looked down at the image of the human Karrell Revers. Through the power of sorcery she and the principal of the Gateway Corps conversed across dimensions.

'I think I made a mistake,' she confessed. 'I should have approached the Wolverines in Maras-Dantia.'

'Why didn't you?' Revers asked.

'There was little opportunity. The land was in such turmoil. I was afraid that if we revealed ourselves to them it would have been seen as hostile.'

'If that was your best judgement you acted wisely.'

'But *because* things in Maras-Dantia were so chaotic it might have been a better place to approach the warband, and do battle with them if necessary. Here, the potential for harming innocents is greater.'

'That you want to retrieve the instrumentalities by peaceful means does you credit, Pelli. But bear in mind that retrieve them you must, by whatever means.'

'Let me try it my way.'

'I'm content with that. But should you meet opposition you have what it takes to overcome it.'

'This is a much more regulated, oppressed world than Maras-Dantia. There are only two races, orcs and humans; and the orcs are cruelly subjugated. Our freedom of movement is greatly restricted. We wouldn't last a moment here without being spotted.'

'Then use the art to cloak yourselves.'

'We will if necessary. But you know how draining that can be.'

'I trust your discretion. And Pelli . . . I appreciate that you feel some sympathy for downtrodden orcs, and that's praiseworthy. But you must put that out of your mind. These creatures have a potential for savagery unmatched by virtually any other race. Be sure your compassion isn't misplaced.'

'I understand.'

'This is all the more important because of something that's just come to our attention.'

'Sir?'

'Our seers have picked up an anomaly in your sector.'

'Another set of instrumentalities?'

'We're not sure. But it's certainly a source of great magical power, and not far from your present location. It could be an individual, or a group. We can't tell at this stage.'

'Another player?'

'Perhaps. Whatever it is, you need to be doubly cautious.'

'We will.'

'What are your plans?'

'At the moment the group's recovering from the transference. We'll begin our surveillance shortly. As soon as an opportunity arises to confront the warband, we'll take it.'

'Good. Meantime, let's hope the Wolverines don't do anything that might lead to the instrumentalities falling into even more malign hands.'

'So we're agreed,' Stryke whispered. 'If either of us falls, the other takes the stars. If we both go down, it's Dallog's job.'

'And if he's not around?' Coilla wondered.

'One of the grunts.'

'Anybody but Haskeer, eh?'

'I'd trust Haskeer with my life. The stars are something else.'

'If he ever finds out we were plotting behind his back—'

'We're not *plotting*, just protecting something precious.'

'All right. But it's a pity we couldn't just hide the damn things somewhere.'

'Where?'

'Like I said, it's a pity we can't. Now can we concentrate on what we're supposed to be doing?'

They were in the centre of Taress. Although it was early, the streets bustled. Carts loaded with provisions vied with traders leading strings of mules. Costermongers hawked their trays of wares, and roadside stalls dispensed meat, flour and wine.

The vast majority of those abroad were orcs. But human patrols were much in evidence, and pairs of soldiers could be seen on many street corners, eyeing the crowds. Occasionally, troopers on horseback ploughed the throng.

Despite all the activity there was surprisingly little in the way of idle chatter or raised voices. The citizenry's mood seemed sombre. Up above, the sky was growing slate coloured, and the day was already uncomfortably muggy.

Stryke and Coilla kept their heads down and tried to look as though they were going about their business like everybody else. They dressed soberly in work clothes supplied by the resistance, and their weapons were well concealed.

Following directions they'd been given, they skirted the central, most populous part of the city. Across squares and through alleys, their pace even and expressions bland, they finally reached their destination. It was a quarter largely given over to storehouses and stockyards. But there was one, down-at-heel, tavern.

Brelan and Chillder were waiting for them, seated at one of the empty wooden tables scattered outside.

'We thought you weren't coming,' Chillder gently teased.

'Are we running to plan?' Stryke asked as he sidled between table and bench to sit.

'More or less,' Brelan replied. 'Though we'll be tight if there are foul-ups.'

'We'll have to be sure there aren't,' Coilla said. She had perched herself on the end of the table, one booted foot on the seat. 'Which there won't be if everybody follows orders.'

'Our side will.'

'No worries then.'

'Everything all right with Jup and Spurral, and the humans?' Stryke said.

'They're back at HQ helping with training, as we agreed,' Chillder told him. 'You do understand, don't you, Stryke, that we couldn't let them take part in this operation? If anybody saw them—'

'I understand.' He did, but also smelt an undercurrent of prejudice. Though it wasn't hard to see why, at least as far as the humans were concerned.

'Heads up.' Coilla nodded.

Haskeer and a quartet of non-ranking orcs were heading their way; and from another direction, Dallog with three more.

'Good place to meet,' Haskeer announced on arrival. 'How about a drink?'

'*No,*' Stryke said. 'We need clear heads for this.'

Brelan got up. 'The others will be in position by now. We should be moving.'

'Does everybody understand their part?' Coilla asked.

'Yeah, yeah,' Haskeer came back impatiently. 'Let's get on with it.'

They formed three groups. The first consisted of Stryke, Coilla, Chillder and two privates. Haskeer, Brelan and another pair of grunts made up the second. That left Dallog and the three remaining grunts as the third. The groups were mixed in such a way that each had at least one resistance member who knew the territory.

Without further word, the three groups moved off on their respective missions. Haskeer's and Dallog's went toward the city centre; Stryke's headed deeper into the warehouse district.

The streets were lined with substantial, faceless buildings here, and the roads were wider than in the residential quarters, to allow for heavier wagon traffic. There were few signs of life.

'Your plan's good, Coilla,' Stryke said.

'But?'

'There are risks.'

'We know that.'

'Not so much to us. There's going to be a lot of non-combatants in the path of—'

'We've been through this. Look at these streets. Tall buildings with hardly any breaks between. A perfect funnel.'

'It's not these streets I'm thinking about.'

'The other teams are going to channel the flow. Besides, the resistance will do their best to make sure the citizens are away from harm.'

'The humans will do that for us,' Chillder reminded them, 'because of what's happening today. That's the beauty of it.' She pointed. 'This is the place.'

Ahead, the road ended at chest-high wooden fencing. In its centre was a wide bar gate. Beyond the fence was rougher land, littered with outbuildings. Set well back was a large enclosure made of stout timber rails.

Even from a distance they could hear and smell what was housed there.

'Sure about guards, Chillder?' Stryke said.

'There'll be just a few. They don't think of this as a target.'

'And the guards are human?'

'Always. Orcs aren't trusted with arms. They get the menial jobs.'

Checking that no one was about, they approached the gate. It was simply secured with an iron bolt, and a length of chain looped over the gatepost. They undid it and slipped inside, leaving one of the grunts to stand watch.

There was churned, hardened mud underfoot, and not a blade of grass. Off to their right stood the largest building on site.

'Slaughterhouse,' Chillder mouthed.

As she said it, a door opened that they hadn't noticed before. A figure was outlined by a light burning inside. Then there was shouting, unmistakably human, and a group of men came out. There were four of them, matching Stryke's crew in number, and they carried weapons.

Striding forward, the thickset, shaven-headed individual leading them yelled, *'What're you doing here?'*

Stryke's team halted, but none of them replied.

'You better have a damn good reason for trespassing!' shaven-head growled.

The men fanned out in front of the orcs, weapons at the ready.

'Well?' the leader demanded, irate at the silence.

'They're too stupid to answer,' one of his sneering companions offered.

'If it's jobs you're after,' the leader said, 'you're out of luck. We've got all of your kind we need. Now *get out*.'

Stryke slowly folded his arms. No one spoke.

Shaven-head took a step nearer, and adopted a mock reasonable tone. 'Look, we don't want trouble.'

'We do,' Coilla said. 'We're orcs.'

Her hand darted into the loose-fitting sleeve of her shirt. Yanking a knife from her arm sheath, she flung it at him. The impact of blade against flesh knocked the human off his feet.

Stryke and the others weren't idling. Quickly drawing hidden weapons, they laid into the rest of the humans. The deed was short and brutal. Stryke and the grunt took down their opponents with two blows each. Chillder earned credit by needing only one.

'Now we *move*,' Stryke told them.

Leaving the bodies where they fell, they ran towards the enclosure, keeping an eye out for other humans.

The pen was a lot bigger than Stryke expected. Standing on one of the fence bars, he gazed out over an ocean of brown backs and jutting horns.

'Nearly a thousand head,' Chillder informed him. 'Somewhere the size of Taress gets through a lot of meat every day.'

'Well, it should do the trick.' He pointed at the grunt. 'Stay by this gate. When you see our signal, do your job and get clear. Coilla, Chillder; let's go.'

They jogged around the corral to its far end. From the folds of their peasant garb they produced flints, bottles of oil and three club-like torches with tarred heads. Stryke held one out. Chillder soaked it with oil, and Coilla brought the spark. It spluttered into yellow flame.

Stryke scrambled on to the enclosure's fence. The nearest cattle immediately grew alarmed. They mooed wretchedly and tried to back away from the flame. Holding the torch above his head, he waved it from side to side.

The two grunts he'd stationed saw the signal. They unlatched the gates, then ran for higher, safer ground.

Stryke shared the flame by touching his brand to Coilla and Chillder's. Mounting the fence, they goaded with fire and hollering.

At first, the spooked animals milled anxiously, and without accord. But herd instinct quickly took over. The cattle by the gate found it was open and began to spill out. With a vent for the mounting pressure, an exodus was triggered. The livestock poured from the corral and took the only available route. Charging across the mud-covered yard, driven by panic, they channelled into the path that led to the road. By the time they reached it, flight had turned into a stampede.

They thundered along the road, jamming its width, cows scrapping their hides against the walls on either side. The rumble of pounding hooves shook buildings as they passed.

Curving, the road took them towards the city's core. The cows met the bend at speed, striking sparks from the cobblestones as they swerved. A mature tree grew by the roadside. The living flood uprooted it. Carried along by the surge, it briefly stood erect, like the standard of some maddened bovine army.

The road narrowed, increasing the herd's terror. And as they approached more populous quarters, the streets were no longer empty. Orcs scattered, racing to sanctuary through open doors, or leaping to cling precariously from window frames. Some abandoned carts in the stampede's path. It made kindling of them.

But the streets had became a lot less crowded. Mostly due to what was about to happen in the city centre, partly because of discreet warnings from the resistance.

The rebels had been busy in other, more tangible ways. Aided by Haskeer and other Wolverines, they hijacked wagons and used them to block off certain streets. For good measure, and added chaos, they set fire to the roadblocks. The upshot was to direct the cattle along a particular path.

Most of the citizenry, and the occupying troops, were gathered in another part of the city. During the night, six Peczan ships had entered Acurial's waters. Hugging the coast, the flotilla nosed its way to an inlet and joined the land's principal river. They arrived at Taress' port with the dawn.

Close on fifteen hundred troops disembarked, reinforcements for Peczan's intended crackdown. Forming ranks on the quayside, they set off accompanied by the drums and pipes of a military band, and with pennants flying. The orc population, bar essential workers, were again dragooned into acting out a welcome. They crowded the sidewalks, but were kept behind wooden barriers in case affection for their glorious liberators got out of hand.

The conquering forces marched eastward, towards the centre of the capital.

The stampede moved in a westerly direction, heading for the capital's centre.

Increasingly frantic, the cattle downed more trees, destroyed kerbside food stalls and snatched away traders' awnings. The torrent wrecked discarded wagons and carried off riderless horses. Under the shock of countless pummelling hooves, cracks appeared on the road's surface.

The pipes and drums kept up a jaunty martial rhythm. Strutting proudly, the troopers passed browbeaten crowds cheering by rote. A cavalry division trotted alongside them, lances raised. Supply wagons and the buggies of officers' wives bobbed along in the multitude.

Even above the listless cries of the spectators, and their own marching, the soldiers became aware of a sound. More than a sound; a vibration. A tremor.

The buildings in this densely populated quarter were tall by Taress standards, and gave the impression of a shallow canyon. There was a sharp bend in the road ahead. The gorge of wood and stone turned, off to parts unseen.

On the corner directly in the marchers' path stood a house. It was three storeys high and extended nearer to the road than any of its neighbours. As they watched, it began to tremble. Dust and plaster fell, and as the building shook more violently, chunks of facing dislodged.

The marchers slowed. Behind their barriers, the orc spectators quietened. Now the mysterious, rhythmic sound could be heard more plainly, and felt through the soles of the troops' boots. Further scraps of stonework dropped from the quivering building. The marchers all but came to a halt.

A lone cow appeared. It loped along, but moved erratically, as though drunk. There was some ragged laughter from the crowd, and even from the column of soldiers.

Then a thousand head of enraged cattle rounded the corner.

It was a leathery deluge, with horses, ruined wagons and general detritus sucked in. The animals were steaming from their frenetic rush. Those in the vanguard foamed at the mouth and tossed their spiky-horned heads from side to side. If they were aware of the obstruction they approached, it made no difference. They kept on coming.

At first, the rear of the procession had no idea what was happening at the front, and continued marching. But the troops at its head had not only stopped; they were retreating into their advancing comrades.

As the stampede drew closer, what had been an orderly progression turned into milling anarchy. There was chaos, and a mounting sense of panic. Numbers of men tried scaling the barriers designed not to be scaled. A handful of cavalry officers, leaping from their saddles, actually managed it. But it proved no salvation for the majority.

The spectators, who had fallen silent, spontaneously resumed cheering, and what before had been half-hearted now took on a new vibrancy.

Some of the troops had the presence of mind to loose arrows at the cattle. It was a resourceful, if futile, gesture. A couple of the lead steers were hit and went down headlong. The animals behind piled into them, causing knots of squirming, kicking bedlam. But it didn't slow the stampede's pace. If anything, it increased the cattle's alarm. They either streamed around the stricken or simply ran over them. The column of troopers had compressed, and unable to back up further with any speed, made a stand, as though about to repel an enemy offensive.

The wave swept in. Men and beasts clashed in a shattering of bone and rending of flesh. Packed as the human ranks were, the cattle penetrated deep, and pressure at their backs kept them moving forward. The effect was similar to striking a block of butter sidelong with a mallet.

Scenes of mayhem were played out. A cow momentarily rose from the scrum, impaled on a trooper's spear. Another, running into a wagon at speed, was sent flying and smashed against the barrier. Soldiers attacked the cattle with swords, and only incensed the greater herd. Men were trampled.

The cavalry fared a little better, though many had their horses caught in an unstoppable tide that carried them off, the riders helpless. There were sorcerers amongst the shambles of the column. The flash and crackle of magical energy bolts erupted, and the smell of charred meat drifted across the crowd. Havoc spread.

The sullen sky birthed a clap of thunder. Fat raindrops started to fall.

The devastation played out in the shadow of the fortress. On a lofty balcony jutting from its bleak facade, Jennesta observed the scene. Her black cloak billowed in the wind, making her look like some oversized bird of prey, about to swoop. Her expression was unreadable. But she gripped the rail so tightly her knuckles were bloodless.

Not far away, on the rooftop of a lower and humbler building, other eyes took in the carnage.

'This is better than I hoped,' Brelan said.

'We aim to please,' Coilla told him.

Chillder turned to Stryke. 'Your band's proved itself today.'

'I thought we'd already done that.'

'More so, then. And now we think the time's come for you to meet somebody.'

'Who?'

'The most important orc in the country.'

20

The occupiers' retaliation was swift and brutal.

Homes were raided. Alleged sympathisers were dragged off for interrogation. Certain taverns, thought to be gathering places for dissidents, were closed down or put to the torch. There were arbitrary arrests and roadside executions. On the streets, there was an even greater military presence.

All of which made travel awkward and dangerous. But after more than an hour of dodging patrols and taking circuitous routes, the small group led by Brelan and Chillder reached their goal.

'Looks a shit place,' Haskeer reckoned.

'I knew we shouldn't have brought him,' Coilla sighed.

'Knock it off,' Stryke told them. He turned to Chillder, and said in an undertone, 'It does seem mean for somebody as important as you say.'

'Never judge a tome by its binding. Come on.'

The tiny house was situated in a narrow, filth-strewn alley. All the dwellings appeared shabby and tumbledown, but none were as unprepossessing as their goal. The windows were boarded and its timbers were rotting. It was hard to believe the place was occupied.

Brelan tapped a signal on the door. A cunningly concealed spyhole flipped aside. After a few seconds, bolts were drawn and the door opened.

'Inside,' Chillder prompted. 'Don't linger.'

A pair of stony-faced guards looked them over as they entered. The unlit interior was gloomy, and there was a pungent smell of decay.

The house was narrow but deep, and bigger than it seemed from outside. A long passageway stretched ahead of them, disappearing into shadow. On their left was a staircase. The twins motioned for them to climb it, and they ascended the creaking treads. On the first landing, they stopped at a door. Brelan rapped on it, and without waiting for an answer, pushed it open.

The cloyingly sweet aroma of incense wafted out, partly disguising the mouldy niff. Inside, the room was candlelit, and the first impression was of clutter. Most of which, on closer observation, proved due to books. They lined the walls and stood in uneven piles on the bare floor. Books of all sizes, bound in leather, vellum and plain boards. Most looked old, and not a few were greatly worn and crumbling. Some lay open. There was little in the way of furnishings beyond a crude table, covered in books, and a couple of chairs that had seen better days.

A female orc sat in one of them. She was mature, beyond breeding age but not yet old. Her dress was simple, consisting of a plain grey robe and slippers, and she wore no jewellery or other adornments. Yet there was something in her bearing that made the dilapidated chair seem like a throne.

'This is Primary Sylandya, true ruler of Acurial,' Chillder announced. To the female she said, 'These are the warriors we told you about. Stryke, Haskeer and Coilla. They've been of great help to the resistance.'

The female gave the trio a faint nod.

'I don't know how we're supposed to greet you,' Stryke told her. 'We're not keen on rulers. Most we've met didn't deserve bowing and scraping.'

'Yeah,' Haskeer agreed, 'we don't kiss arse.'

She smiled. 'Orcs who speak their mind. Refreshing.'

'We mean no disrespect,' Stryke assured her.

'Don't go spoiling it. I value honesty. It was so rare in politics.'

'You need more than talk to fix the problems you've got,' Coilla reckoned.

'Sylandya's aware of that,' Brelan said. 'She's head of our resistance group.'

'And our mother, as it happens,' Chillder added.

Stryke nodded. 'Should have guessed.'

'Family likeness?' Brelan asked.

'Same spunk.'

'I'll take that as praise.'

189

'You've come down in the world,' Haskeer judged, 'to end up in this shithouse.'

'I *knew* we shouldn't have brought him,' Coilla muttered.

Sylandya raised a mollifying hand. 'I said I favour plain speaking. Yes, I'm reduced. As are all orcs under the invaders' yoke. The least I can do is endure it with them.'

'More than endure,' Stryke said. 'Overcome.'

'You think we're not *trying*?'

'Too few of you are. You like straight talk, so I'll put it bluntly. Somehow, the orcs here have grown placid. Meek.'

'Cowards, more like,' Haskeer remarked.

'Like hell they are,' Brelan thundered. He took a step in Haskeer's direction.

Sylandya checked him with a wave. 'We can't deny it, son. They may not be craven, but their fighting spirit's been lost.' She looked to Stryke. 'Though that hasn't happened with every orc, it seems.'

'Your own offspring prove it,' Stryke replied, 'and those who volunteered for the resistance.'

'A pitiful few. There was a time, long ago, when our kind would never have allowed themselves to be subjugated. We were a fearsome warrior race, beholden to none. The way you still are, you orcs from the north. Or wherever you come from,' she added pointedly.

'Maybe our remoteness shielded us from the changes in regions where life's softer,' Stryke suggested, hoping to turn aside her suspicions.

'Perhaps. Though it seems strange that martial fortitude should be almost bred out everywhere but your homeland.'

'We can talk for ever about why,' Coilla intervened. 'What matters is how we get these orcs fighting.'

'I think the humans could help with that.'

'What do you mean?'

'They lied about us, and made war on us with words. The citizens of Acurial did nothing. They dreamed up excuses to invade us. We did nothing. They took our land and wealth. Still we did nothing. They treated us like cattle, humiliated us, and killed us at will. Except for the few, we suffered and did nothing. They impose ever harsher rule, and most of us do no more than shoulder the burden. But the time must come when the bough breaks under the weight of oppression. Then the spirit will reawaken.'

Haskeer snorted. 'I wouldn't hold your breath.'

'I believe that, deep down, our race still has its fire. Given a push, it could flare again.'

'What would it take?' Stryke asked.

'Two things,' Sylandya replied. 'First, we need to harass the humans, to hit them as often and as hard as we can. Your band can help greatly with this.'

'They won't take it lying down. There'll be reprisals.'

'We're counting on it.' She held his gaze. 'I know that sounds harsh. But it's no more than the harm humans will do us in the long run. If it lights the kindling of revolt, it's worth it.'

'You said two things.'

'At the critical point I'll call on the citizenry to rise up, and do my best to lead them.'

'And they'll heed you?'

'I'm hoping they'll heed Grilan-Zeat.'

'Who?'

'Not who, *what*,' Chillder said.

'Look about you.' Sylandya indicated the profusion of books littering the room.

'Books,' Haskeer muttered contemptuously. 'Never read one.' It was a proud declaration.

Coilla gave him a sceptical glance. 'You can *read*?'

'I've filled the many hours of my internal exile with these tomes,' Sylandya went on, 'looking for some clue from our past that might hold the key to our present. I may have found it in Grilan-Zeat.'

'You'll have to explain,' Stryke said.

'We have a history, for all the invaders have done to wipe it out. Had they not been rescued by patriots, these books would have been burned. We pored over their pages for anything that could aid us in our plight. It was ironic that we should find it in something as celebrated as the story of Grilan and Zeat.' She eyed him astutely. 'A story I would have expected you to know.'

'We're cut off from things in the north. Remind us.'

'A century and more ago, Acurial faced a crisis. Our leadership was still drawn from the clan chieftains in those days. It was hereditary, and two lines laid claim. Grilan was one contender, Zeat the other. The land was divided. Civil war threatened.'

'Between orcs who don't fight?'

'But they very nearly did. Passions were inflamed. It was the last time we came so close to warfare.'

'What stopped it?'

'A portent. A light appeared in the sky, and grew to fill it. As priests had been petitioning the gods to resolve the deadlock, many chose to see it as a sign. Not least Grilan and Zeat, who made peace and agreed to rule in harness. Well, as it turned out. They laid the foundation of our modern state. Before the comet faded from view it had already been named after them.'

'What's this got to do with now?' Coilla wanted to know.

'As we dug deeper into the chronicles we unearthed a curious fact. The comet had come before. It appeared more than a century prior to the days of Grilan and Zeat. And over a century before *that*. In all, we found records of four visitations, and mention of even earlier ones. We don't know if great events attended those past visits, as with Grilan and Zeat. But one thing we do know. The time between each arrival was exactly the same. It returns at precise intervals, and if it sticks to this pattern, it's due back. Soon.'

'Let's get this straight,' Stryke said. 'A comet stopped your ancestors taking up arms. Now you're hoping it'll come again and do the opposite.'

'And be seen as an augury,' Coilla added.

'There's a prophecy to do with the comet,' Brelan told them. 'It's said to arrive in times of most need, to light the way to salvation.'

'Oh, *please*. Prophecies are as common as horse shit, and less useful.'

'Maybe. But it's what the citizenry believes that's important.'

'The prophecy said something else,' Chillder explained. 'It spoke of the comet being escorted by a bodyguard of warriors. A band of hero liberators.'

Stryke stared at her. 'You can't mean—'

'If the helm fits.'

'*Bullshit*. That's laying too much on us.'

Haskeer gave a low whistle. 'Fuck me, we're heroes.'

'We shouldn't have brought him,' Coilla repeated.

'Old prophecies are one thing,' Stryke declared, 'but don't drag us into your fancies. We're fighters, yes, but we're just ordinary.'

'Hardly,' Sylandya replied. 'You came here at our time of crisis, didn't you? You're helping our cause, aren't you? And you have a taste for combat our own folk have lost. Whether you believe it or not, it gives us heart. The gods know we've little else to sustain us.'

Stryke was about to rebuff her. Then he looked at their faces and checked himself. Instead he said, 'When's this comet due?'

'We don't know exactly, not to the hour. But if it's true to form it should start to be seen around the time of the waning moon.'

'That's . . . when?'

'In thirteen days,' Brelan said.

'And you want to stir up a rebellion by then.'

'We have to,' Sylandya declared. 'Unless you have qualms about going against the humans.'

That puzzled Stryke. 'Why should we?'

'I've heard you consort with them.'

'Ah. You mean Pepperdyne and Standeven. I'll vouch for them.'

'You'd stand by humans?'

'These . . . yes.'

'I wonder if they'd stand by you.'

'They already have. One of them, anyway.'

'Run with humans and you invite trouble.'

'They're different,' Coilla interjected. 'They're not like the ones here. They've sympathy for the orcs' plight.'

'Sympathetic humans. I've seen many strange things in my life. I never thought to hear of that.'

'You'll have to take our word,' Stryke said, hoping Haskeer would keep his mouth shut.

'Part of me would like to meet these singular humans. But I have no taste for that just yet. I'd feel too much like a lamb seeking the company of a wolf. I would like to have met your other companions though, the . . .'

'The dwarfs, Mother,' Brelan supplied.

'But it wouldn't have been wise to bring them here. Some other time, perhaps.' Her eyes were on Stryke, and they were sharp. 'Compassionate humans and an unknown race of little creatures. So many riddles surround you.' She eased, and managed a slight smile. 'But I don't care, as long as you help us.'

'The two humans could be useful to us,' Brelan said. 'And the gods know we need all the allies we can get. Particularly with the arrival of this new Emissary.'

'Have you learnt any more about them?' Stryke asked.

'What we're hearing doesn't bode well. It seems we're up against a ruthlessness that makes even Hacher's governance seem kindly.'

'You can tell that already? The Emissary's only been here a couple of days.'

'But long enough for acts of cruelty and a vicious purge at the humans' headquarters. That's what our spies tell us, anyway. And what we did yesterday can't have gone well for Hacher. So score one for our side.'

'Can we get to this Emissary?' Coilla wondered. 'Their assassination would land a heavy blow.'

'Doubt it. They're bound to be well guarded, and by all accounts we'd be up against a fearsome target. They say there's something very strange about her.'

Stryke and Coilla exchanged glances.

'Her?' Stryke said.

'Didn't I say? They've sent us a sorceress.'

21

'No, no, *no!*' Dallog snatched the staff from Wheam and held it correctly. 'Like *this.*' He thrust it back. 'Try again.'

Wheam fumbled with it, and Dallog had to show him one more time. 'That's right. Now there's your opponent.' He pointed at a straw-filled dummy hanging from a beam. Its painted features depicted an orc's idea of a human face.

Wheam dithered.

'Don't just stand there,' Dallog told him. 'Attack!'

The youth gingerly approached the mannequin and swung at it feebly.

'You're going at it like a hatchling. This creature's going to kill you if you don't kill it first. Put some back into it!'

Wheam had another go. He summoned a bit more energy, but was no better coordinated. Taking a clumsy swipe with the staff, he missed the dummy and struck a wall-mounted oil lamp, shattering it.

'All right,' Dallog said, 'take a breather.'

Wheam dropped the staff and slumped to the floor. He propped himself against the wall, chin on raised knees. 'I'm useless,' he sighed.

'Not true.'

'So you say.'

'You're unskilled, that's all.'

'It's not just that. I'm . . .' He looked around to see if anybody was in earshot, and whispered, '*I'm afraid.*'

'Good.'

'What?'

'Nothing wrong with fear. Show me an orc who goes into battle without it and I'll show you a fool.'

'I don't understand.'

'Fear is a warrior's ally. It's a spur, a dagger to the back. Courage isn't being without fear. It's *overcoming* fear. If you're wise you'll make it your friend, and turn it on your enemy. Understanding that is what makes our race so skilled at warfare.'

'Then why don't the orcs here see it that way?'

'Somehow, I don't know why, they've gone wrong.'

'Have they? They live in peace. They're not bent on death and destruction the way we are. Maybe I should have been born in Acurial.'

'I'll pretend I didn't hear that. Look where their ways have landed them. You should be proud of your heritage.'

'You sound like my sire. He was always telling me what I should be, and saying I was a coward.'

'It's hard trying to follow in the footsteps of a great orc like your father. But he was wrong to call you a coward.'

'You must be the only one around here who believes that. Everybody hates me.'

'No they don't.'

'They hate me because of who I am. And those Wolverines who died . . . it was my fault.'

'It *wasn't*. Get that through your head. I know what it's like being an outsider too, and trying to fill somebody else's boots. But if you want the band's respect, don't throw away your birthright. Honour it.'

'That's easy said.'

'You can start by working on your training. *Really* working.'

Wheam stared at the discarded staff. 'I'm not very good at this.'

Dallog stooped, took hold of the staff and held it out to him. Wheam grasped it and allowed himself to be pulled to his feet.

'Look at your foe,' Dallog said, nodding at the swaying dummy. 'It's everything you feel bitter about. Everything you hate and fear. It's all the bile you've stored up about this warband, about yourself, about . . . *your father*.'

Wheam let out a piercing yell and rushed at the dummy. He set about beating it, swinging the staff wide and hard, delivering great clouts. After three or four blows straw started to spill from the dummy's split torso. Wheam carried on thrashing it.

'Good!' Dallog exclaimed. '*Good!*'

The farmhouse door opened. Stryke and Coilla came in.

As they passed, Coilla called out, 'Good job, Wheam!'

The youth beamed and continued the battering.

'He could be of some use yet,' she said.

'If we ever have to fight dummies,' Stryke replied.

They made their way to a large room at the back of the house that had been set aside as a refectory. Hardly any of the benches were occupied. They picked one farthest away from anybody else.

There was a water butt at the end of their table. Coilla ladled herself a cup, then took a swig. 'I still can't get over it.'

'Jennesta? It should be no surprise; Serapheim said she was here. It's why we came.'

'Knowing she's close makes it sort of more real. Back in Maras-Dantia we spent a lot of time trying to get as far away from her as we could. It seems strange doing the opposite.'

'I'd like to get near enough to slit her throat.'

'Who wouldn't? It'd certainly help bring on the rebellion Sylandya wants.'

'But an attack on Jennesta's going to be a suicide mission.'

'Is it? The resistance has spies in the fortress. Maybe they could get us in.'

'It's a thought. I'll talk to Brelan and Chillder. Though their minds are going to be on other things. Like trying to incite an uprising in thirteen . . . no, twelve days.'

'Surely they'd see how taking out Jennesta would aid that.'

'They might see the benefit; I don't think they'd be keen to allot their stretched forces to it.'

'They wouldn't have to. If we can get help from the inside it'd take just a couple of us to do the job. I'm thinking stealth rather than storming the place.'

'You're counting on Jennesta being that easy to overcome. Blades against sorcery; it'd be a close call.'

'I'm willing to try. See if the twins can get us a plan of the fortress. That'd be a start.'

'I'll ask.'

She raised the cup again and drained it. 'Talking of plans, what chance do you think they have with this comet thing?'

'It turns on a lot of maybes. But it's all they've got.'

She smiled. 'I nearly put my foot in it when they were talking about the waning moon. I didn't even know this world *had* a moon.'

'Me neither.'

'There's so much we don't know. I keep thinking I'm going to give us away. Though I wonder how bad that would be.'

'If they knew where we were really from? It's too big a risk. Orcs are different here. We don't know how they'd take it.'

'They're different all right, and not just in being so timid about fighting. I mean, a *state*? Cities? It's not what orcs do. If I thought we had no way of getting home again—'

'The star's still safe?'

'Don't look so anxious. Course it is.' She slapped the pouch at her waist. 'Stop worrying about it.'

The farmhouse door slammed loudly. They turned to see Haskeer swaggering in. Pausing only to throw a disparaging remark at Wheam and Dallog, he joined them at the table.

'How's my fellow heroes this morning?' he said.

'Oh, shut up about that,' Coilla chided.

'That's not showing much respect for the prophecy.'

'Only idiots believe in prophecies.'

He ignored the insult and looked about the room. 'Anything to drink?'

'Not the kind you want,' Stryke told him, nodding at the water barrel.

Haskeer pulled a face. 'No alcohol, no crystal, no action. Where's the fun? I thought we were getting a revolution started.'

'There'll be fighting enough, and soon.'

'Good. I'm keen for a bit of mayhem.'

'We all are. How are the new recruits shaping up?'

'All right.' He shot Wheam a scornful glance. 'Mostly.'

'I need to count on them. They have to work as part of the band and—'

'Don't sweat it, Stryke. They're knuckling down.'

'I'll hold you to account on that.'

Haskeer would have come back, had Jup and Spurral not arrived. He greeted them with, 'Ah, the pisspots.'

'How'd you like that water butt shoved up *your* butt?' Spurral asked.

'Ooohhh!' Haskeer lifted his hands in feigned dread. 'Call her off, Jup!'

'I'd prefer to help her. Only I'd use your head. It'd improve your looks.'

'I'd like to see you try, you little tick.'

'Whenever you're ready.'

They both stood up, glaring at each other.

'*Shut it!*' Stryke snapped. 'Sit down, the pair of you! We don't need this shit. Save it for the enemy.'

'I'll be lucky to see 'em,' Jup complained, sinking back into his seat. 'Spurral and me are going stir crazy stuck in this place.'

'I know it's tough,' Stryke said, 'but we can't afford letting you be seen.'

'So why the hell are we here? What's the point if we can't come out of hiding?'

'You'll have your part. Things are due to hot up over the next twelve days. You two on the streets is going to be the least Taress has to deal with.'

'I don't know whether to be flattered by that,' Spurral remarked. She looked to Coilla. 'We should be moving.'

'You're right. Come on.'

'Late for your sewing circle?' Haskeer teased.

'Yeah. Want to join us?'

Coilla and Spurral made for a door at the far end of the make-shift mess room.

They stepped out to a plot of land surrounded by a low dry-stone wall. A group of around twenty females were waiting for them. They were dressed for combat, and armed. Chillder stood at their head.

'Good turnout,' Coilla said.

'And champing at the bit,' Chillder told her.

Coilla faced them, and raised her voice so all could hear. 'You've been told the plan. Things are going to turn pretty lively in the days ahead, and we have to get combat ready fast. That means working together as a unit. The best way is to have the sort of set-up my warband has. A military structure, like the humans. I'm the most experienced, so I'm leading this group. If anybody objects to that, spit it out now.' Nobody spoke. 'All right. Chillder here is second-in-command. We'll be picking other officers if we need them.' She indicated the dwarf with a jab of her thumb. 'For those who haven't met her, this is Spurral. She's of a race you don't know, and you might see her as . . . different. But she's a good fighter and loyal to the orc cause. You can trust her.' Coilla couldn't tell what they thought about that. She carried on. 'We're hoping our first mission's soon. Very soon. So we'll be pushing you hard to get in shape. The resistance needs all the swords it can get, but the males in these parts don't seem to value what we have to offer. Let's show 'em what we can do, Vixens!'

They cheered, and there were catcalls. They waved blades in the air.

'That went down well,' Spurral whispered to Coilla.

'I don't think I've had that much to say since . . . well, I don't know when. But we have to—' Something caught her eye.

Just beyond the stone wall stood a row of stables. One had an open door. A figure was outlined there for a second, then disappeared.

'What is it?' Chillder asked, following her gaze.

Coilla shook her head. 'Nothing.'

Standeven drew back from the door and retreated into the gloomy stable. 'Look at them,' he said, his fury barely in check. 'They've even got the females involved now.'

'What's the problem?' Pepperdyne answered. 'They're just practising.'

'I should have known you'd take their part.'

'In what? They're only training.'

'They're getting ready for more trouble.'

'It's what they *do*. They're a warrior race.'

'These creatures are fighting against our side. Doesn't that worry you?'

'Our side?'

'Our race, then. Our *kind*.'

'They're fighting oppression. They want their freedom back.'

'They're provoking the wrath of the rulers of this place, and we're in the middle.'

'What you call the rulers are usurpers. This isn't their land. They took it.'

'Trust you to see it that way.'

'It's hard not to, given my people's history.'

'That's no excuse for going native now.'

'You've a short memory. It wasn't me who crossed Hammrik. We're in this situation because of you.'

Standeven's complexion turned a deeper scarlet. 'There was a time when you wouldn't *dare* speak to me that way!'

'That time's over. It's not about master and slave now. It's about survival.'

'And you think you'll ensure that by throwing in your lot with these creatures?'

'They've grounds for discontent. It's a just cause.'

'I wonder how interested they'd be in you as an ally if they knew what I know about you.'

'No idea. Maybe they look at these things differently. Why don't you try telling them?'

Standeven said nothing.

'Your threats don't wash here,' Pepperdyne told him. 'You need me to get through this and you know it. That's what sticks in your craw, isn't it, *master*?'

Outside, the Vixens had paired off to rehearse swordplay. The clatter of blades filled the air.

'I want to get out of this place,' Standeven said, more subdued. 'Preferably in one piece.'

'So do I. But it's not in our hands.'

'Well, it should be. It's only the instrumentalities that stand between us and going home.'

'Knowing how to use them might help. And taking them away from Stryke would need a damn sight more than luck.'

'Not that he has all of them.'

'What do you mean?'

'The female, Coilla; she's carrying one.'

'How do you know that?'

'There's a lot to be said for keeping low and using your ears.'

'It's called snooping.'

'I happened to overhear,' Standeven came back huffily. 'Seems Stryke wanted to split up the artefacts for some reason. Though we can only wonder why.'

Pepperdyne shrugged. 'Probably to stop somebody like you getting hold of them.'

'I got the impression it was something more than that.'

'None of this matters. We're not going to get the instrumentalities away from the orcs. Even if we could, we'd need that amulet Stryke has as well, *and* to make sense of it.'

'But we have to have them. If we do get back to our world we'd never be safe from Hammrik. They're the only thing we could barter with.'

'Sell to the highest bidder, more like. I know how you operate.'

'Buy off Hammrik with them, or sell them for enough to get us far away from him; either way they're our warranty.'

'*Our?*'

'I'd not be ungrateful to a loyal servant who stuck with me through this mess.'

'As I said, it'd take a miracle to get hold of them here. We'd have to try for it once we got home. If we ever do.'

'So we'll have to stay on the Wolverines' good side, if they have such a thing, in the hope they'll take us back. I'm not as sure of that as you seem to be.'

'What's the alternative?'

Standeven looked him in the eye, and there was a chill in his gaze. 'Perhaps there are such things as miracles.'

22

'Well, here we go,' Coilla said, adding a hatchet to her other concealed weapons. She wrapped a shawl about her shoulders.

'Think this is going to work?' Pepperdyne asked.

'A human and a bunch of orc females? We can't fail to get in.'

'Never did get the stain completely out of this.' He licked his fingers and rubbed at the front of his stolen uniform tunic.

'Stop fussing, it's all right.'

'We've pulled this trick once before. Are they going to fall for it again?'

'I'm counting on them thinking we wouldn't try it twice.'

'And if you're wrong?'

'Then they'll find they've got more than feeble menials to deal with.'

His expression turned sombre. 'You're trusting me with a lot, you know.'

'You've shown yourself as upright before. You going to change now?'

'I'm one of their kind, when all's said and done. The enemy.'

'Don't sweat it. If I think you're up to anything, I'll kill you.' She smiled pleasantly.

'Let's move,' he said.

The Vixens occupied two open wagons. Coilla and Pepperdyne climbed aboard the first, he taking the driver's seat. Spurral sat at the back, near the centre, wedged between a pair of females, a generous headscarf hiding her features. Like all the Vixens, she wore drab workers' clothing. Brelan drove the second wagon.

For a settlement founded by orcs, Taress was arranged along surprisingly organised lines, at least at its heart. Most of what a city needed to function – the storage and distribution of supplies, the provision of drinking water, the housing of livestock and so on –

had its own quarter. Since the invasion, the humans had added another, to direct the running of their colony. It was to this sector that the wagons headed.

Orc labourers were still repairing damage caused by the stampede. Under the cold watchfulness of human overseers, trees were being hauled away and walls rebuilt. Gangs of workers shovelled debris into fleets of drays.

The Vixens' journey was short, but not without risks. There were roadblocks to negotiate. The first, at the main thoroughfare leading into the administrative sector, was the most formidable. A guard-post stood on one side, and the road was sealed with a timber blockade. Sentries were out in strength.

The pair of wagons joined a queue of vehicles waiting to be let in. A couple were orc merchants' carts. There were several carriages bearing humans with an officious look; and a gig occupied by a woman who could have been an officer's wife, riding next to a beefy driver. The line was made up with a handful of men on horseback, mostly uniformed.

'They seem to be waving the humans through quicker,' Pepperdyne whispered.

'*Course* they are,' Coilla replied. 'What'd you expect? But don't count on it being the same for us.'

They finally reached the head of the queue. A sergeant stepped forward, saw Pepperdyne's rank insignia and saluted. If he noticed the ominous stain on the phoney officer's jacket, he gave no sign.

He held out a calloused hand. 'Your papers, sir?'

Pepperdyne gave him a folded sheet of parchment.

The sergeant studied it, paying particular attention to the seal. He nodded at the wagons' passengers. 'Who are they?'

'Clean-up detail,' Pepperdyne said.

'For where, sir?'

'Bureau of Tallies.'

The sergeant moved along the side of the wagon and looked in. All the females kept their heads bowed submissively. Several held wooden pails on their laps. Brooms, scrubbing brushes and other tools were laid on the deck. He walked to the second wagon and gave that a cursory once-over too. Then he sauntered back to Pepperdyne.

Coilla eyed the sergeant's jugular and fingered a concealed knife, just in case. He caught her look, read it as simple impertinence and glared at her. She dropped her gaze and tried for passive.

'Need any help keeping 'em in order, sir?' the sergeant asked Pepperdyne. 'I could spare a couple of troopers to go with you.'

'To mind these bitches? Waste of manpower. This lot are meek as cows.'

The sergeant glanced at the orcs and grinned. 'Take your point.' He handed back the parchment, then waved them on.

A safe distance later, Coilla turned to Pepperdyne and hissed, 'Bitches? *Cows?*'

'It's what they expected to hear.'

'You could have put a bit less bile into it.'

'Just playing my part.' He stuffed the parchment into his pocket. 'You humans have a high regard for your pieces of paper.'

'Too much, if that sergeant's anything to go by. It's not a very good forgery.'

'Good enough. It got us through.'

'Don't relax yet. We'll have to show it again soon.'

The second roadblock was less imposing. It consisted of a farm cart barring the way and a small company of troopers. Perhaps because the wagons had already passed the first checkpoint, scrutiny was casual. The counterfeit papers were given a token examination, and once a lone guard had made a lacklustre inspection of the passengers, the Vixens were let through.

They didn't have to do more than slow down at the third and final roadblock. An apathetic soldier barely looked up from his dice game to signal for them to keep moving.

'That went sweetly,' Coilla said.

'Let's hope it's as easy getting out. Assuming we live long enough.'

Coilla glanced over her shoulder to see how Brelan was doing on the second wagon. He gave her a cautious nod, working to keep a neutral expression on his face.

Being a restricted quarter, the streets were less crowded than the rest of Taress, and there were more uniforms about. Knots of troopers stood at crossroads and patrols walked the footpaths. Guardposts decorated the roadside.

As they passed, the occupants of the wagons drew stares. Most were dutiful, or idly curious, but it was attention they could have done without.

'This is uncomfortable,' Pepperdyne complained.

'Just look as though you've a right to be here. It's not far now.'

There were new buildings in the neighbourhood, erected by the invaders at the expense of older structures they requisitioned and tore down. It was to one of these that the wagons were bound.

They saw their goal as they turned into the district's core. In common with many of the buildings put up by the conquerors, hurriedly assembled in the early days of the occupation, it was functional rather than attractive. Standing back from the road, behind a tall iron fence, it was fashioned from plain stone slabs with few windows, set high. It looked robust enough to withstand an all-out assault.

The wagons halted at the gate. While they waited for a pair of guards to amble over to them, Pepperdyne beckoned Brelan. He climbed down.

'You're *sure* you've stopped the cleaning squad they're expecting?' Pepperdyne asked.

Brelan nodded. 'They're being delayed by a fake accident a dozen blocks from here.'

'Won't these humans be able to tell the difference when a new lot of faces turn up?' Coilla wondered.

'They can't tell us apart. Any more than we can them.'

'What about him?' Coilla jabbed her thumb at Pepperdyne. 'They'll know *he's* different.'

'These details don't always have the same escort.' He sounded a little exasperated. 'We've been over this a thousand—'

'*Quiet*,' Pepperdyne warned. 'They're here,'

The guards opened the gates sufficient to squeeze through, and approached.

They were brisk and moderately wary. The false papers came out again. There was the obligatory going over of the wagons, carried out indolently. The guards recited routine questions. Finally they nodded, parted the gates and guided the wagons through.

At the substantial doors of the building itself, the Vixens disembarked, pails in hand. There were worries that Spurral's height would attract attention, but no eyebrows were raised. As the resistance had explained, children were not unusual in work details.

Coilla had the uncomfortable thought that the group might be subjected to a body search. But again the fear proved groundless. The humans seemed to have no conception that females could present a threat.

One of the guards rapped on the door with the hilt of his sword. A panel slid aside and he spoke with someone. Then the door opened and everybody filed in.

The interior was a little grander than the outside. Cool grey marble faced the walls, and there were mosaics. The lofty ceiling had ornate carvings. But the embellishments were unfinished, a work in progress.

'They live a damn sight better than the rest of us,' Chillder whispered.

'Surprise,' Coilla said.

One of the guards leading the group turned his head and gave them a sour look. They fell silent.

The building was large. Brooms over their shoulders, and clutching their buckets, the Vixens tramped a seemingly endless passageway. They passed a number of doors. Some were open, affording glimpses of humans poring over benches strewn with paper and ledgers; or orcs hauling boxes. One room, bigger than most, held scores of artefacts. Under human supervision, orc servants packed straw-filled crates with gold statuettes, carved wooden relics and ornamental weapons.

'*Damn!*' Brelan muttered under his breath.

'What?' Coilla mouthed.

'Our birthright,' he hissed. 'Looted to decorate the parlours of empire quill-pushers.'

'*Hey!*' the guard yelled. 'This ain't a pleasure trip! Cut the mumbling!'

'Too right,' Pepperdyne said, stepping in. 'Button your lips! And don't dawdle!'

He underlined the point with a hard shove to Brelan and Coilla's backs. When Coilla turned, glowering, he gave her a wink. She didn't return it.

At length they came to a tall pair of double doors. Beyond lay a spacious, hall-like chamber. It contained rows of writing tables with high stalls. The walls were shelved from floor to elevated ceiling, and there were ladders for the upper reaches. Scroll cylinders, bound volumes and document boxes filled the shelves. Little light entered through the slit windows. Despite being broad day outside the room was lit by a series of wooden chandeliers, each bearing scores of stout candles, and by a plentiful scattering of lamps.

There were perhaps a dozen humans present, mostly clerks, seated at the tables. Two or three orc lackeys fetched and carried for them.

A stick-thin, gangly human approached. From his dress and bearing he could only be an overseer. The harassed look he wore strengthened the impression.

He clapped his hands like a prissy schoolmarm, his bony palms producing a strangely brittle sound. 'Listen to me!' he announced, his tone almost shrill. 'You orcs couldn't possibly understand what goes on here in the Bureau of Tallies. All you need to know is that it's much more important than the sum of your miserable lives. Sloppy work will not be tolerated. If you damage so much as a sheet of parchment, you'll be whipped. Is that understood?' He didn't wait for an answer. Which was just as well, given that the Vixens were in no mood for compliance.

Coilla and Spurral caught each other's eye. Coilla nodded, very faintly.

The overseer began issuing orders. Jabbing a lean finger at the ersatz cleaners, he dispensed chores. 'And you, you and *you*,' he decided, pointing at Coilla, 'can take care of the latrines.'

'I don't think so,' Coilla told him.

The overseer stopped short. He looked to Pepperdyne. 'Did that creature address me?'

'Why don't you ask her yourself?'

'*What* did you say?'

'Tell him, Coilla.'

'Clean your own fucking shithouse,' Coilla said.

The overseer turned scarlet. 'How *dare* you talk to your betters like that!'

'I just open my mouth and it comes out.'

A vein began pulsing in the overseer's forehead. 'This is gross disobedience!' He turned to Pepperdyne again. 'Have you no control over this creature?'

Pepperdyne shrugged. 'Looks like she doesn't want to clean your latrines.'

'I don't believe you're taking the brute's part. Are you drunk?'

'Chance would be a fine thing.'

'If this is some kind of joke—'

'Then the laugh's on you,' Coilla said. 'We might not understand what goes on here, but we sure as hell can stop it.'

Alarmed, the overseer backed away and started yelling, 'Guards! *Guards!*'

The pair of sentries who accompanied the group on the way in had been watching bemused as the scene unfolded. Now they stirred. The nearest made a grab for Coilla. She deftly swung the bucket she was clutching and struck him square to the forehead. He tottered. She swung again, landing another hard blow, then a third. The guard collapsed. His companion went down under a flurry of punches and kicks from a bevy of Vixens.

The overseer's crimson complexion gave way to pallid. Coilla turned to him. 'Now keep your mouth shut and do as you're told.'

She bawled an order. The Vixens produced their concealed weapons, and Pepperdyne drew his sword.

'Traitor!' the overseer spat.

Pepperdyne showed him the tip of his blade. 'She told you to shut up!'

The Vixens were levering out the false bottoms of their pails and retrieving sealed pots of oil.

'Splash that stuff around as widely as possible,' Coilla ordered.

The overseer's eyes widened. '*Louts!*' he shouted. '*Animals! How dare*—'

Pepperdyne drove his fist into the man's jaw. He went out like a snuffed candle.

Coilla nodded approvingly. To the Vixens, she said, 'Let's have the tithe detail.' Ten females stepped forward. 'You know your job. Sniff out the taxes these bloodsuckers have wrung from the citizens. Remember, every coin you find puts another sword in the hands of the resistance. Now get moving.'

The group went off.

Coilla looked around the room and saw that the human clerks and their orc menials stood frozen and gaping. She beckoned a trio of Vixens. 'Get the civilians clear, and don't let them out of your sight until we're done here.'

The onlookers were rounded up and led away, a couple of them dragging the overseer by his heels. As the orcs passed, heads bowed, Coilla needled them with, 'We wouldn't have to do this if you had guts!'

'Don't be too hard on them,' Chillder said. 'They've known no other way.'

Coilla shrugged.

'What about the treasures?' Brelan asked.

'What?' Coilla replied.

'Our birthright. The artworks they were—'

'Yeah. What about 'em?'

'We can't leave them here.'

'The plan was to grab the loot and torch this place. Nobody said anything about—'

'We *can't* leave them here,' Chillder echoed her brother. 'It'd be profane.'

'We barely have enough hands as it is.'

'We don't need your permission when it comes to our heritage,' Brelan stated flatly.

Coilla sighed. 'All right. You two take care of it.' She looked to her depleting forces. 'But we can't spare more than four to go with you. We'll meet up on the way out. And if anybody tries to stop you—'

'We know what to do.'

The twins quickly picked their helpers and made for the door.

'This we could do without,' Coilla grumbled.

Spurral nodded. 'It does spread us a bit thin.'

'So let's get on with it,' Pepperdyne urged.

The Vixens set to trashing the room. Files were torn from the shelves and papers scattered. Furniture was smashed and strewn around. They splattered oil over the debris.

'Right,' Coilla said. 'As soon as the others get back—'

There was movement farther along the room. A door they hadn't seen, set flush to the wall, sprang open. Three robed men came through it. Coilla recognised the trident-shaped weapons they clutched.

She exclaimed, '*Shit.*'

One of the robed figures pointed his trident.

Pepperdyne yelled, '*Get down!*'

The Vixens hit the deck.

A violet beam cut the air. They felt its heat above their heads. Its glow was so intense it pained their eyes. The bolt struck the shelving behind them, splintering wood and liberating a cloud of fluttering paper. Another blast came instantly. It glanced off a pillar, showering marble chips. A pungent, sulphurous odour perfumed the room.

The Vixens scuttled for shelter. Coilla and Spurral crouched behind an overturned table. Pepperdyne used a nearby heap of wrecked furniture.

As one, the robed humans advanced, tridents raised. A further purple energy shaft crackled past. It punched a wall, exploding plaster and fragments of stone.

'We have to take them out, Coilla,' Spurral said. '*Fast.*'

'Tell me about it.'

'Why the hell didn't we bring a couple of bows?'

'I've got these.' Coilla pushed up the baggy sleeve of her shirt, revealing an arm sheath of throwing knives. She plucked one and handed it to her. 'Don't use this 'til I tell you.' Coilla turned and attracted Pepperdyne's attention. She tossed him a knife. He caught it deftly. Then she mimed an order, holding up one, two, then three fingers, and indicated the approaching sorcerers. '*Together*,' she mouthed. He understood and nodded.

The robed figures kept coming, unleashing beams of dazzling vigour, ravaging wood, stone and glass.

As the trio passed a tangle of wreckage, one of the Vixens popped up from her hiding place brandishing a sword.

Coilla shouted, 'No!'

The Vixen made to swipe at the nearest sorcerer. He swung, aiming his trident at her. There was a blinding flash. The Vixen's blade took the brunt and instantly turned as red as a heated poker. She squealed and dropped the searing weapon. The sorcerer made to finish her.

'*Now!*' Coilla bellowed.

She, Spurral and Pepperdyne leapt up and tossed their knives. Coilla's throw was true. The sorcerer who blasted the Vixen's sword took it directly in the chest. Spurral's pitch was good too, though it incapacitated rather than killed her target. The blade struck his face and put him out of the running. Pepperdyne's shot was an honourable miss, but a miss nonetheless. It flew past his mark's left ear and embedded itself in the spine of a tome.

The sorcerer left standing reacted with a wild spray of energy bolts. Grabbed by her comrades, the Vixen who tried attacking was pulled out of sight as the rays demolished desks and gouged walls. The orcs resumed hugging the floor.

'To hell with this,' Coilla muttered. She gathered up her rough peasant skirt, revealing the hatchet in a scabbard strapped to her thigh. Tugging it free, she rose from her hiding place, arm back, ready to throw.

The remaining sorcerer was a dozen paces away. He saw her, and levelled his trident. There was a kind of stasis. It lasted no more than a split second, but seemed to stretch to eternity. His eyes narrowed as he took aim. Her arm came up and over, muscles straining. The axe left her hand.

It tumbled as it flew, end over end, its blade glinting reflected light. The sorcerer followed its path, his head going back, puzzled at the hatchet's unexpected trajectory. Not towards him, but upwards.

Above the sorcerer, and a little ahead of him, hung one of the massive chandeliers.

The hatchet's razor sharp edge sliced through the rope supporting it.

With a tremendous crash the whole affair plunged to the floor, smashing to pieces on impact. Lit candles bounced in all directions. The scattered oil ignited instantly.

A sheet of yellow-white flame sprang up. It engulfed the sorcerer. His wounded companion, on hands and knees, the throwing knife protruding from his gory cheek, was caught too. Their robes blazing, the shrieking men blundered about, spreading the flames.

The fire swiftly followed the trails of oil, probing the length and breadth of the room. It streaked to the shelved walls and began to climb. Where strewn candles came to rest, fresh gouts of flame broke out. Red tendrils snaked to heaps of furniture, setting them ablaze. A pall of smoke rapidly filled the room.

'*Get out!*' Coilla yelled. '*All of you! Out now!*'

Coughing and wheezing, sleeves pressed to their mouths, the Vixens groped for the door.

'*Come on, come on!*' Coilla urged, and with Pepperdyne's help shepherded the group out.

In the smoky corridor she undertook a quick head count and judged all present.

'Shouldn't we shut these doors?' Spurral asked, indicating the inferno raging in the chamber behind them.

'No,' Coilla said, 'let it spread.'

There was movement at the other end of the corridor. The Vixens went for their weapons.

'Easy,' Pepperdyne cautioned. 'They're ours.'

The unit Coilla sent to search for the chancellery were returning, along with the three who took away the prisoners. They were carrying four or five wooden chests.

The Vixen in the lead, a pleasingly muscular example of orc femininity, nodded at the fire. 'Thought you weren't going to set that off yet.'

'Change of plan,' Coilla told her. 'Any trouble?'

'Nothing we couldn't handle.'

'What'd you get?'

They lifted the lid on one of the chests. Gold and silver coins shone in the fire's glow.

'Good.' Coilla turned to another of the females. 'What about the prisoners?'

'We found a courtyard back there. Shoved 'em into it, barred the door.'

'All right. Now let's find Brelan and Chillder and get out of here.'

She took the lead, with Pepperdyne close behind.

The corridors grew hazy with smoke as they retraced their steps to the room where the looted art was stored. There seemed to be nobody about. That changed when Coilla, jogging ahead, passed a half-open door.

It was thrown wide, and a sword-wielding human leapt out. Alerted by cries from the Vixens, Coilla spun round while fumbling for her sheathed blade. The man lunged at her, sword raised.

He stopped dead in his tracks. The centre of his chest burst in a shower of blood, the tip of a blade protruding. The stunned human looked down at the flowing wound. Then his eyes rolled to white and he toppled, landing at Coilla's feet.

Pepperdyne stooped and wiped his gory blade on the dead man's tunic.

'Owe you again,' Coilla said.

'Forget it.'

They carried on, their mood warier, but met no one else until they reached their destination.

Bodies of several humans littered the storeroom floor. Chillder, Brelan and their helpers were placing artefacts in crates.

'Come on,' Coilla insisted, 'we've got to move!'

'Nearly there,' Chillder replied. She was ramming a figurine into a box.

'We can't take it *all*.'

'We know,' Brelan said. 'More's the pity. We've picked the best pieces.'

'Well hurry it up.'

Three more chests added to their spoils, the group made for the exit. By the time they got to it, the smoke was a lot thicker.

Checking that the street was clear, they quickly loaded the crates on to the wagons, and covered them with sacking. They slammed shut the entrance doors, and once the outer gate had been negotiated, set off.

Pepperdyne, again at the reins of the lead wagon, looked grim. 'If that fire's spotted before we get clear—'

'We'll have to hope it's not,' Coilla told him. 'So let's play it calm and innocent.'

'And if it *is* spotted?'

'You know the odds. We'll fight our way out.'

It was all they could do to stop themselves from constantly looking back. In their mind's eye a towering column of black smoke formed an accusing finger, pointing their way.

They approached the first checkpoint with trepidation, but in good order. It proved as slipshod as when they entered, and they were scarcely acknowledged, let alone stopped. The second was no different. Jaded sentries allowed them through with hardly a second glance.

At the third and most substantial roadblock there was less laxity.

There was no queue to get out, as on the way in, but they were obliged to stop.

The same sergeant they dealt with earlier was still on duty. On sight of them his expression turned chary.

'I wasn't expecting to see you back here so soon, sir.'

'No?' Pepperdyne answered.

'The clean-up crews usually take twice as long.'

'Do they?'

'Yes, sir.'

'Well, this is a particularly hard-working bunch.'

'That makes a change for these lazy devils, sir.' He fixed Pepperdyne with a hard stare. 'What's your secret?'

'Secret?'

'How do you make 'em move their arses?'

'No secret, Sergeant. Just a generous application of the whip.'

The sergeant grinned approvingly. 'Yes, sir.' He glanced at Coilla. She avoided his gaze.

He looked into the back of the wagon. His interest was held long enough to have Coilla suspecting he'd spotted the booty. She began slipping a hand into her folds of clothing in search of a blade.

The sergeant returned his attention to Pepperdyne. 'Thank you, sir. You can move out.'

Pepperdyne nodded and cracked the reins.

He and Brelan resisted the impulse to speed up. They kept to a steady pace even when the distant sounds of tumult rose behind them in the restricted zone.

Coilla and Pepperdyne exchanged brief smiles.

The wagons trundled past a patch of wasteland on one side of the road, an area where a house had stood before it was destroyed by the incomers. Now the lot was scrubby and overgrown.

An especially eagle-eyed passer-by, or someone particularly receptive to the ambience of magic, might have sensed an anomaly there. A pocket of nothingness slightly out of sympathy with the air around it. Like a transparent bubble which light was not quite capable of passing through. But so muted, so elusive, that an onlooker would likely dismiss it as a mote in their eye.

Wrapped in her cloak of sorcery, the elfin figure of Pelli Madayar observed the Vixens' exploits, and was troubled. There was no doubt that the renegade orc warband was seriously violating the Gateway Corps' precepts. They were playing with fire.

And she knew they had to be stopped.

23

There was a gathering in the grand hall at the fortress in Taress.

The room was crowded. Military top brass were present, along with representatives of the lower ranks. Robed members of the Order of the Helix were in attendance. Bureaucrats, administrators and legislators rubbed shoulders. They had stood waiting long enough to bring on a spate of shuffling feet and stifled sighs.

General Hacher was at the forefront. His aide, Frynt, and Helix luminary Brother Grentor flanked him.

'How much longer?' Grentor whispered. 'It's intolerable being treated like supplicants.'

'Perhaps you'd care to express that to the Envoy in person when she arrives,' Hacher suggested. 'She is, after all, the titular head of your order.'

Grentor shot him a poisonous look and returned to morose silence.

The sound of approaching footsteps brought on an involuntary stiffening of spines.

With a crash the doors to the hall were thrown open. Two elite guardsmen came in and positioned themselves on either side of the entrance.

Jennesta followed. The hem of her cloak, fashioned from the jet-black, glossy pelt of a beast that could only be guessed at, brushed the timber floor. The clack of her precariously high stiletto-heeled boots echoed throughout the hall.

She swept to the head of the room and climbed the steps to a dais. Then she discarded the cloak, letting it fall from her shoulders in a careless motion. Hacher wasn't alone in thinking of a snake shedding its skin.

Facing her audience, Jennesta spoke without preamble.

'I've been here only a short time,' she began, 'but long enough to see how this province is run. More importantly, I've seen *who* runs it. Is it the might of Peczan's armed forces? The empire's commissioners, or its lawmakers? The brotherhood of the Helix?' She scanned them coldly. 'No. Acurial's true rulers are the very creatures you are supposed to suppress. Rebels. Terrorists. Orc *scum*. How else can it be when the so called resistance strikes at will? When cattle stampede through the streets of the capital, patrols are ambushed and buildings torched. And when *humans* are reported to be aiding the insurgents.' She let that soak in for a second. 'Discipline is woefully lacking in this colony. Examples need to be set, and not only among the native population.' She nodded to the guards at the entrance.

They opened the doors. A pair of Jennesta's undead bodyguards shuffled in. Between them was a terrified looking soldier, his hands chained and his feet in shackles. The bodyguards' appearance, and unsavoury odour, had the crowd willingly parting to allow them through. They looked on in silence as the zombies shoved their prisoner to the front of the room and up to the dais, where he stood trembling before the sorceress.

'The outrage yesterday was the responsibility of many in this administration,' Jennesta announced, 'but let this man represent all who fail in their duty.' She turned her baleful gaze on the accused. He did his best to hold himself erect. 'You are a sergeant in charge of a roadblock barring access to the quarter housing the Tithes Bureau?'

'Yes, ma'am.'

'And you allowed a gang of orc terrorists to pass your check-point and stage an attack?'

'They were accompanied by a human officer, my Lady. I—'

'*Answer the question!* Did you let them through?'

'Yes, Ma'am.'

'Then you admit your dereliction and stand condemned. Negligence on such a scale demands punishment equal to the offence. Prepare to pay the penalty.'

The sergeant tensed, expecting perhaps to be hauled away and thrown in a dungeon, or even to be struck down by one of his undead captors. Neither happened.

Instead, Jennesta closed her eyes. The keen sighted might have noticed that her lips moved silently, and that her hands made several small gestures.

The accused looked on in troubled bafflement; the audience exchanged mystified glances.

'There,' Jennesta said, her singular eyes popping open. She sounded almost amiable.

For a moment, nothing occurred. Then the sergeant let out a groan. He lifted his hands and pressed the palms to his forehead. One of the bodyguards jerked the chain binding his wrists, pulling the man's hands back down. The prisoner moaned, gutturally, and his eyes rolled. He swayed as though about to fall. The groaning became constant and higher pitched.

The area of his temples and up into his hairline rapidly took on a purplish discoloration, as though bruised. His skull visibly swelled, and in the deathly silence a crackling could be heard as the expansion began to split his scalp. Writhing in agony, the sergeant screamed. Just once.

Like an overripe melon dropped from a castle battlement, his head exploded. The discharge scattered blood-matted chunks of hairy flesh, skull fragments and portions of brain. Headless, the stump gushing torrid crimson, his corpse took a faltering step before crashing to the floor. It lay twitching, its life essence pumping out into a spreading, sticky pool.

Many in the front row had their ashen faces and smart dress uniforms splattered by the eruption. An objectionable reek hung in the air.

One of the zombie bodyguards, noticing dully that blood and brain matter covered his bare forearm, started to lick it off with noisy relish.

'Note this well!' Jennesta intoned sternly. 'As this man confessed his guilt I chose to deal with him mercifully. Any others who transgress will not be treated with such lenience.' She touched a hand lightly to her brow. 'The effort has tired me. Go. All of you. Except you, Hacher. You stay.'

The spectators began to file out, several dabbing themselves with handkerchiefs. Some hurried, looking as though they sought the nearest privy.

Hacher was wiping the gore from his own face when Jennesta approached, her brace of undead hobbling a few steps behind.

'I trust the import of what you've just seen was not lost on you, General,' she said.

He glanced at the sergeant's corpse. Blood was dripping from the edge of the dais. 'Hardly.'

'Good. Then I expect to see change, *profound* change, in the governance of this colony. Otherwise your administration is going to become acquainted with my less compassionate side. Is that clear?'

'Yes, Envoy. Perfectly.'

'I know orcs. And I know the only thing they respect is force. If they raise a seditious hand, cut it off. If they slaughter a single trooper, send ten orcs to the charnel house. If they dare to rise up, grind their bones to dust. Leave them in no doubt who's master. Any less and you imperil our plans for this dependency.'

'Which are?'

'Exploiting the land's riches. And in particular, the most valuable resource of all.'

'I fear you may be disappointed in that regard. The few deposits of gold and silver we've found are hardly—'

'What I have in mind is worth more than mere gold.'

'I don't follow.'

'The greatest asset Acurial has to offer isn't to be found under the ground but walking upon it.'

'You mean . . . the natives themselves?'

'Precisely. The orcs have the potential to be the greatest fighting force this world has ever seen.'

'But these creatures are meek. Or at least most of them are. The ones who've taken up arms against us are the exception.'

'As I said, I know their true natures. I know what they're capable of. *All* of them.'

'Even if they do have an inborn aggression, and it could be brought out, why would they fight for us?'

Jennesta indicated her zombie retinue. 'They'd have no choice. Subject to my will, their obedience would be beyond question. Imagine it. A slave army, incomparably ferocious and totally subservient.'

'And this has the backing of Peczan?'

'As far as you're concerned, Hacher, I *am* Peczan. So why don't you leave the thinking to me and concentrate on instilling some terror in the population?'

Another meeting was taking place in the capital, not far from the fortress, in one of the resistance's many boltholes.

Making a rare excursion from her current hiding place, and having been brought under heavy guard by an elaborate route, Primary Sylandya was present. She sat at the centre of the small gathering, a goblet of brandy and water to hand.

'You pulled off a great feat yesterday,' she said, toasting her off-spring and Coilla. 'The Vixens acquitted themselves well on their first outing.'

'It's time the females got their chance,' Coilla replied.

'As I say, the raid was a triumph. The tithes you brought back have swelled our coffers, and I was especially pleased that you recovered those looted treasures.'

'Saving trinkets ain't going to win this fight,' Haskeer stated.

'Don't undervalue that act as a symbol,' Sylandya told him. 'It shows the citizenry that their heritage means something.'

'And that there are orcs who stand against our oppressors,' Brelan added.

Sylandya nodded. 'We need to deliver more blows like yester-day's. Who knows? Perhaps if the occupation here is seen to be failing, Peczan's enemies in the east and south will be embol-dened.'

'The eastern and southern lands are a long way off, Mother,' Brelan reminded her, 'and they're human realms too. Barbarous tribes, most of them. There's little hope of our enemy's enemy doing anything that might aid our cause.'

'I think that's right,' Stryke agreed. 'You can't rely on help from outside.'

'Shouldn't that be *we*?' Sylandya said. 'Or do you northern orcs see yourselves as apart from this struggle?'

'We see it as a fight for all orcs,' Stryke returned sternly. 'It's why we're here.'

'Can we get back to the issue at hand?' Chillder asked. 'Grilan-Zeat's due in not much more than a week and—'

'*If* it comes,' Haskeer said.

'We have to believe it will,' Chillder said. 'It's a thin hope, but it's all we've got. The question is, what more can we do to hasten an uprising?'

'Take out Jennesta,' Coilla replied. 'That'd strike one hell of a blow.'

'It'd also bring down some heavy reprisals.'

'Isn't that what we want? A kick that wakes up the populace and rallies them?'

'We've talked over the assassination idea,' Brelan explained, 'and we're agreed it should go ahead.'

Coilla smiled. 'Good.'

'But not right away.'

'Why wait?' Haskeer grumbled. 'Kill her now, I say.'

'Our contacts inside the fortress need time to prepare and make us a map of the place. Meantime we carry on harrying the humans. We've got a particular mission in mind that should rock them.'

'What is it?' Stryke asked.

'Don't worry, we'll keep you posted. But right now we need to get Mother out of here. She's too rich a prize for the authorities; we have to keep her out of their reach.'

'A new hiding place?' Coilla said.

'Yes. But I'm not saying where. What you don't know they can't get out of you.'

Brelan and Chillder left, accompanying Sylandya. The couple of other resistance members present went with them.

No sooner had they gone than Spurral and Dallog turned up. Shortly after, Pepperdyne arrived, still sweating from a training session. He had Standeven in tow.

'News,' Stryke announced. 'They've agreed to us targeting Jennesta.'

Pepperdyne was scooping a ladle of water from a barrel. 'Really?' He gulped the drink.

'You don't seem too excited about it.'

'Just cautious. It's bound to be a dangerous mission, isn't it?'

'That doesn't seem to have worried you up to now.'

'We still want revenge on Jennesta,' Standeven hastily interjected. 'But she's dangerous.'

'You're telling us,' Coilla said.

Stryke fixed the humans with a steady gaze. 'There's something I've been meaning to ask you two. When we ran into you, you said you were seeking Jennesta because she stole your consignment of . . . gems, was it?'

'That's right,' Standeven confirmed.

'But we know she hadn't been in Maras-Dantia for years. Why'd it take you so long to go after her?'

'It's a big world,' Pepperdyne replied. 'Well, the one we came from was.' He shook his head, as though clearing it. 'You know what I mean. It takes time to mount an expedition, and money. My master here had to recruit a small private army, then we travelled across continents and—'

'Seems to me you do a lot of talking for an aide, or servant or whatever you are. Why can't your master speak for himself?'

'He always had a silver tongue,' Standeven explained awkwardly. 'I often said he was capable of striking a better deal than I could myself. The words come more naturally to him.'

Haskeer eyed Pepperdyne suspiciously. 'You weren't a bloody wordsmith, were you? I hate the bastards. Making up stupid stories about us, branding us villains. According to them we're built like brick privies and hate the light. They say we eat babies, and everybody knows we only take human flesh when there's nothing else.'

'No, I'm not a storyteller.'

'Don't go spreading that talk outside the band, Haskeer,' Stryke warned. 'The orcs in these parts wouldn't understand it. Let's not give them more reasons to see us as different.' He turned back to the humans. 'I don't know about you pair. But just don't make the mistake of thinking we're fools.'

'Wouldn't dream of it,' Pepperdyne replied coolly.

'You're being too hard, Stryke,' Coilla protested. 'I owe Pepperdyne my life. He's proved himself.' It wasn't lost on any of them that she left Standeven out of her reckoning.

'Maybe,' Stryke said. 'We'll see.'

'Now do you mind if we eat?' Pepperdyne asked. Without waiting for an answer he headed for the door, Standeven at his heels.

Once it slammed, Coilla tackled Stryke with, 'Why are you so hostile to them all of a sudden?'

'I got to thinking about their story, and it doesn't stack up. Pepperdyne might be straight, but the other one . . .'

'Yeah, well, no argument there. But I wouldn't be here if it wasn't for Jode.'

'*Jode?*'

'You tend to feel pally to somebody who saves your neck.'

'Never thought I'd see the day when you'd count a human as a friend.'

'Just go easy on him, all right? He's been useful to us.'

Stryke looked to the others present, and Jup caught his eye. 'You've not said much, Sergeant.'

'About the humans? I've no opinion, beyond not trusting the race much.'

'More than that's ailing you,' Spurral said, slipping an arm round his waist. 'You've been morose for days. Spit it out.'

'Well . . . I'm not likely to play a part in the assassination, am I? Or anything else going on for that matter. It's not as though *I* can go out dressed as a female.'

'Why not?' Haskeer ribbed. 'It'd suit you.'

'Shut it, Haskeer,' Jup retorted. 'I'm not in the mood.'

'I know it's hard on you,' Stryke told him, 'but your time will come.'

'And when's that going to be?'

'There's something you could do tonight.'

Jup perked up. 'There is?'

'How about a little after hours mission? Part of the harrying.'

'What did you have in mind?'

'I thought we might pick a fight. Are you game?'

24

Taress' night-time streets should have been deserted save for patrols enforcing the curfew. But others were abroad.

A group of figures moved stealthily through the capital, slipping from one pool of shadow to the next.

They were ten in number, and Stryke had kept it a strictly Wolverine affair. He led the pack, with Coilla, Jup and Haskeer close behind, Orbon, Zoda, Prooq, Reafdaw, Finje and Noskaa brought up the rear.

Across cobbled lanes and along twisting alleys, the band made its way to a district that would have swarmed with citizens during daylight. Only once did they come close to a watch patrol, a squad of some two dozen uniformed and robed men illuminating their path with lanterns that gave off a violet glow so intense it could only be magical. The Wolverines hid until they passed, pressed into door spaces and the black mouths of narrow passageways.

At length they came to a broad avenue made desolate by the absence of life or movement. Only a gentle breeze disturbed the balmy summer air.

Using the corner of one of the larger buildings as cover, they peered round at their target. Situated on the opposite side of the road, it was a simple one-storey, brick-built structure, typical of many such scattered throughout the city. Serving as both a guard station and barracks, it had a single, robust door and slit windows. To one side stood a hitching rail where four of five horses were tied-up. A pair of guards were stationed outside the building's entrance.

'What do you think?' Stryke whispered.

'We've taken better places drunk,' Jup reckoned. 'Know how many are inside?'

Stryke shook his head. 'No idea.' He looked to Coilla. 'You all right with this?'

'Sure.'

He checked that the others were ready. 'Then *go*.'

Coilla stepped out from their hiding place and sprinted towards the guard post.

The sentries didn't see her at first. As soon as they did, they instantly bucked up and drew their weapons.

Coilla began to yell. '*Help! Help me! Please help!*'

That threw the guards. They exchanged perplexed looks, and though they kept a defensive stance, it was half-hearted.

Coilla carried on running, still shouting, and waved her arms about in what she hoped was a helpless female kind of way. The sentries stared at her.

Stryke barked an order. Two grunts rushed forward, their bows nocked. Coilla dropped and hugged the ground.

Arrows smacked into the guards. They went down.

As Coilla scrambled to her feet the guardhouse door flew open. Alerted by the commotion, men poured out. Many were minus their tunics or otherwise had their dress in disarray, having been off duty. But they had swords. Coilla drew her own and, bellowing, ran in their direction.

Her war cry was taken up by the Wolverines. Spilling from their hiding place, they charged.

Coilla reached the foremost of the troopers. He made the mistake of trying to bring her down with a tackle. She relied on her sword. As he dived at her, she lashed out, raking his torso. When he doubled, she drove her blade into his back.

A second man immediately moved in. Mindful of the fate of the first, he advanced warily. Coilla powered into him and their blades clashed. An exchange of blows ensued, the pealing of steel on steel echoing through the silent night. His swordplay had a certain finesse. Coilla had the edge in savagery. Knocking aside his incoming sword, she exploited the breach and punctured his lung.

With a roar, the rest of the orcs swept in. The two sides met and a bloody melee erupted. Then it quickly fragmented into a string of discrete fights.

Haskeer laid about him with a two-handed axe. The first human he engaged soon felt its sting. Screaming, he reeled away with a grievous wound that had his left arm hanging by a thread. A charging soldier was the axe's next patron. Swinging fast and hard, Haskeer struck him in the neck, cleanly decapitating the man.

The head bounced several feet and landed in Jup's path. He kicked it aside and faced up to a duo of spear-wielding guardsmen. They were dismayed by their first sight of a dwarf, and startled to see a basically humanoid creature battling alongside orcs. Exploiting their hesitancy, Jup piled into them.

He had the edge as a fighter. The troopers employed their spears by jabbing energetically but with little accuracy. Jup was master of his staff, and used it with greater skill. Some adroit footwork got him past the first spearman's defences to deliver a weighty blow that shattered his skull.

The second man drew back, brandishing his spear to keep Jup at bay. Feigning an advance, then quickly changing tack, the dwarf evaded the weapon and took a swipe at his opponent's head. The human shifted smartly, narrowly avoiding the strike. But Jup rallied instantly. Sweeping his staff low, he cracked it across the man's legs, flooring him, Reafdaw, fighting alongside, spun and plunged his sword into the prone trooper's guts. Dwarf and grunt exchanged a thumbs up and carried on brawling.

Someone started ringing an alarm bell mounted next to the guardhouse door. Its shrill din cut through the night like a hatchet. Zoda lifted his bow and launched an arrow at the bell ringer. It missed, its sharpened tip chipping the guardhouse wall. Zoda groped for another shaft.

Haskeer had fought his way nearer to the building. He brought his axe back over his shoulder, far enough that the head nearly touched the base of his spine. Then he swung it up and over, grunting with the effort of lobbing it. Spinning end over end, the axe flew above the struggling combatants, gathering impetus. It struck the chest of the man at the bell with enough force to pin him to the guardhouse door.

The door opened outwards, with the body still attached, and a couple of stragglers exited. It slammed behind them, the hanging corpse jiggling with the impact.

Stryke was embroiled in grinding combat with a heftily built sergeant. The man's weapon, through choice or hasty necessity, was a long-handled iron mallet, which he managed as nimbly as Stryke plied his sword. Seemingly tireless, the human kept the hammer in constant flight. Several times his swingeing passes came dangerously close to Stryke's head, and his greater reach barred retaliation.

Tiring of the cat and mouse, Stryke switched from targeting the man to concentrating on the weapon. As he dodged another swing, he twisted and brought his blade down on the mallet's haft. The steel bit into the wood near the head, but didn't entirely sever it. A brief tussle disengaged the weapons.

Retreating a step, the sergeant grinned and brought up the mallet for another blow. He did it with such force that the weakened head snapped off and flew over his shoulder. It landed on one of his comrades, braining him. Oblivious, the sergeant swept the weapon downward towards Stryke. It has halfway through its arc before he realised the head was missing. While he gaped at the splintered pole he was holding, Stryke ran him through.

The Wolverines had got the better of the guardsmen. Most lay dead or wounded, and the orcs were making short work of the few still standing. Stryke barked an order and the band rushed for the guards' station.

Coilla got there first. Wrenching open the door, with its dead trooper affixed, she stormed inside.

The interior was little more than a long dormitory. Cots lined one wall, lockers and stacked chests were heaped against the other. At the far end was a door ajar, leading to a privy. Coilla judged the place empty of troopers.

She was wrong.

As she walked past the row of cots, a figure leapt up. He had been hiding between two of the beds, pressed to the floor in sly ambush or trembling cowardice, and he hefted a sword.

He came at her fast, yelling something, the sword in motion. Coilla swerved, rapped the blade aside and booted his stomach. He landed on a cot, struggled to right himself, half rose. Then he fell back with a groan, her blade in his innards. She finished him with a thrust to the heart.

He was young, as far as Coilla could tell with humans. She

wondered why he didn't try surrendering, though she wasn't sure what she would have done if he had.

The door opened. Jup, Haskeer and Stryke came in, along with several of the others.

'All clear?' Stryke asked.

'Is now,' Coilla replied.

They checked the place, to be sure.

'Look at this,' Jup said, kneeling by an open chest.

The others gathered round. Somebody snatched a lantern and held it above the chest. It was neatly packed with military sabres, oiled and wrapped in muslin.

'New issue,' Stryke said, 'and nice pieces by the look of them. We'll take what we can carry.'

They lifted four boxes and hauled them outside. The door and attendant corpse slammed shut behind them.

'Do we torch the place?' Coilla asked.

Stryke looked to the sky. It was lightening. 'No. The sun will be up soon. We should be moving.' He turned to Jup. 'Feeling better?'

The dwarf smiled. 'A bit of bloodletting always blows away the cobwebs. It makes for a good—'

There was a commotion from the tethered horses. They shied and pawed the ground. A figure scrambled into the saddle of one and pulled away. As he galloped off, Coilla pitched a throwing knife at him. It fell short, clattering on the cobbled street. A couple of the grunts began chasing the rider.

'*Let him be!*' Stryke ordered, waving them back.

'He looked wounded to me,' Jup said.

Haskeer nodded. 'Reckon he was playing dead 'til he got his chance.'

'Doesn't matter now,' Stryke told them. 'We did what we set out to do. Let's get out of here.'

The rider wore no tunic, and his white combat blouse was stained with blood. Leaning forward in the saddle, in obvious discomfort, he rode hard to get away from the guardhouse.

The streets were still deserted. But dawn was breaking, and soon the curfew would lift.

Without knowing it, the wounded trooper careered past something incongruous. At the side of the road there was a small portion of space at odds with reality. A sachet of non-actuality that denied light.

Pelli Madayar was concealed in the anomaly's embrace. She had something like a crystal in her hand. It was the size of an egg, with markings that made it look like the abstract representation of an open eye, flecked with a mingling of colours resembling oil on water. She held it at arm's length and slowly panned across the scene several blocks distant, where the Wolverines were stealing into the dying night with their crates of plunder.

'You see?' she said, seemingly addressing no one but herself.

'I see,' came the reply. It emanated from the not quite crystal, oddly distorted by its passage across innumerable worlds. Warped, but recognisably the voice of Karrell Revers. 'And it further confirms that the orcs are interfering dangerously in the affairs of that plain,' he went on. 'But we knew this, Pelli. You must act.'

'I'm aware of what should be done. My fear is that, in trying to prevent any damage the warband may do, we further aggravate the situation. Things are complex here. We have to choose our time with care.'

'You're facing the inherent paradox the Corps has to deal with: to prevent interference, we must interfere.'

'So how *do* I deal with it?'

'You use your judgement. If I didn't believe you were capable of coping with the present irregularity you wouldn't be in charge of this mission. But be warned, Pelli. The longer you leave intervening, the more events will fester; and when you strike, it has to be decisively.'

'I understand.'

'Keep one thing in mind. The Wolverines have to be stopped, by whatever means you need to employ.'

'I can't help feeling that fate is about to deal them too harsh a punishment. They're starting to seem like no more than pawns in this drama.'

'That may well be so. But they are a martial race, and walk with death as a matter of routine. I say again that you must put aside any feelings of consideration you may have for these creatures. Don't go soft on me, Pelli. Because forces of great destruction have been set in motion, and they're on course for a collision.'

As the sun rose, there was a bustle of activity around Taress' fortress.

Orc labourers were toiling in the empty moat, clearing out debris that had taken years to accumulate, preparatory to it being flooded again. Crews were beefing up the other defences. New bars of thick metal were being affixed across lower windows. The main gate was reinforced with sheets of iron.

Kapple Hacher stood on the access road, watching the work progress. His aide, Frynt, was beside him, ticking items on a parchment list.

'It's a crying shame,' Hacher stated, 'that this place was allowed to fall into such a sorry state by the former regime. The defences are a joke.'

'They're not a warlike race, sir. I expect they didn't see the need.'

'But they saw fit to build the fortress in the first place, however long ago that was.' He grew thoughtful. 'Which makes me think . . .'

'Sir?'

'Nothing. Will the work be completed on schedule, do you think?'

'It should be if we have them working day and night.'

'Bring in more labour if you have to. I want it finished as soon as possible.'

'Do you really think the fortress could come under attack, sir?'

'The way things are going, anything's possible. And I don't want to leave us open to the Envoy's displeasure.'

'Ah, yes, sir. But is this enough to satisfy the lady Jennesta?'

'In itself, no. I wouldn't expect it to. It's just one measure. The crackdown I'm planning should mollify her to some extent. At least for a while.'

'Yes, sir. Let's hope so.'

'In that respect. . .' Hacher looked about, as though spying for eavesdroppers, and his voice dropped. 'In that respect there's been something of a breakthrough.'

'General?'

'Breathe a word of this and I'll have your tongue. Understood?'

Frynt looked offended at the idea of him being loose with the organ in question. 'Of course, sir.'

'We've got an informer. Not one of your usual low level turncoats either. This is somebody within the resistance itself. Close to the leadership, in fact.'

'Really, sir? May I ask who?'

If Hacher was going to answer the question, it wasn't to be at that moment.

There was a chorus of shouts from the guard detail supervising the workers.

A soldier had arrived on horseback. His shirt was bloodstained and he was yelling. The sentries rushed to him, and he fell into their arms.

25

'Will you stop that bloody row!' Haskeer barked.

Wheam cringed and quit plucking his lute. 'I was only—'

'You were only driving me crazy. Now stow the damn thing and follow me.'

'Where?'

'Stryke wants you in on something. Fuck knows why. Now move your arse.'

Haskeer led him to the rear of the safe house and a closed door. Typically, he ignored niceties and barged in.

The room was the largest in the building, and crowded. It looked as though all the Wolverines were present, along with a number of resistance members and a smattering of Vixens.

Stryke was standing near the door.

'Here he is,' Haskeer said 'Though why the hell you'd want him involved—'

'All right, Sergeant. Plant yourself somewhere.'

Grumbling, Haskeer went and lounged against a wall, arms folded.

Wheam looked up at Stryke and swallowed. 'What do you want me for, Captain?'

'A mission's being planned. We need everybody we can get. That includes you.'

'*Me?* But—'

'My band carries no dead weight. It's time you proved yourself.'

'I . . . I wouldn't want to let you down.'

'Then see you don't. Now shut up and find a place to perch.' He jabbed a thumb.

Wheam spotted Dallog. He weaved meekly through the throng and settled on a patch of floor next to him.

233

There was a lot of low level muttering. Whatever was going to happen hadn't started yet.

Brelan went to the head of the room and they quietened down. 'Everybody here? Good. As you all know, Grilan-Zeat's due to show itself soon. In not too many days' time it'll be at its most visible. When that happens, my mother's going to address the citizenry and the uprising begins. At least, that's what we're hoping. Before that, we need to soften up the enemy, and rattle 'em enough that they'll hit back and rile the populace. We want the pot boiling when the Primary makes her appearance. This is one of the ways we'll do it.' There was a crudely drawn map affixed to the wall behind him. He pointed to an area circled in red.

'What is it?' Coilla asked.

'Army camp. A small fort.'

'Where?'

'A bit beyond the city limits, to the west. Most of the likely targets here in Taress are better protected since our campaign started, so we're looking further afield.'

'What's that wavy line next to it?'

'A river. Fast flowing. And here,' he tapped a point near the river's end, 'there's a waterfall.'

'It might not be as secure as places here in the city,' Jup said, 'but it's still a fort. Won't it be a tough nut?'

'Which is why we need to muster as big a force as we can.'

'So the Vixens will play their part,' Chillder explained, 'and you too, Jup and Spurral, if you're willing.'

The dwarfs nodded. 'But what about us being seen?' Jup asked.

'The way we intend going about this, it won't matter. Besides, we'll keep you hidden until we're out of the city.'

From the back of the room, Pepperdyne raised a hand. 'What can we . . .' He glanced at Standeven, slumped beside him. 'What can I do?'

'Lend your sword arm,' Stryke told him. 'But we can't pull the uniform stunt again.'

'No,' Brelan confirmed, 'they'll be wise to that by now. Though what we have in mind doesn't call for it. But there's something else you all need to know about the raid. It'll be tomorrow.'

'That's one hell of a short notice,' Coilla remarked. 'Why so soon?'

'Two reasons. First, security. The longer between hatching a plan and carrying it out, the more chance it'll leak.'

'You've got turncoats in your ranks?'

'*No*,' Brelan came back huffily. 'But it's a rare orc who won't break in one of Peczan's torture chambers.'

'What's the second reason?' Stryke said.

'We've learnt there's going to be a changing of the guard at the fort. The new contingent's drawn from the reinforcements we welcomed with the stampede, and they're due to relieve the outgoing company today. Tomorrow's their first full day in a new camp. We'll know the layout better than they do. It's a good time to hit them.'

'Makes sense. But you still haven't said how we're going to get in there.'

Chillder smiled. 'We have a way.'

'Think it'll work?' Coilla said.

Stryke shrugged. 'What do *you* think? You're our mistress of strategy.'

'It's a smart plan, but it's complex. The more parts to a scheme, the more to go wrong.'

'What would you change?'

'I'd like us to have a good fallback. You know, a better escape route. Maybe more than one.'

'Any ideas on that?'

She nodded. 'But it'd take a few fighters out of the front line, and mean some hard work for us overnight.'

'Sort out the details soon as you can. I'll talk to Brelan about it.'

They were sitting on a weathered, low stone wall in a small inner courtyard of the house the resistance had commandeered. It was one of the few places they were able to find a little privacy.

'Are you sure about Wheam?' Coilla said. 'Him coming on the raid, I mean.'

'No, I'm not. But we need to make a good show of numbers. Brelan reckons they'll be a couple of hundred humans in that fort. We'll be lucky to scrape together as many on our side. Besides, he's never going to shape up if we don't put him in the field.'

'Unsupervised?'

'I'll get somebody to keep an eye on him.'

'And tie up a fighter.'

'Then I'll put him in some support role.'

'Is it worth the risk?'

'Look, if Wheam gets himself killed . . . well, too bad.'

'You mean that? Despite what his father said?'

'Fuck it, Coilla, I won't be cowed by threats from Quoll or anybody else. I thought we got away from all that shit when we left Maras-Dantia. If Quoll ends up with a beef we can settle it with blades. Nobody stops me getting back to Thirzarr and the hatchlings.'

'I'd go along with that. But you're being too hard on Wheam. It's not his fault he's in this fix.'

'Maybe.' He sighed. 'Guess I'm feeling a bit snappy.'

'Reason?'

'I didn't think things would be this knotty. I want to cut through it all and get to Jennesta.'

'You're not alone in that, Stryke. We all want it. But meantime we can help some fellow orcs. That's not bad, is it?'

'Suppose not.'

'Tell me something. You've been uneasy about Pepperdyne, but now he's in on this raid. Why?'

'I could say I prefer to have him where I can see him. Truth is, I'm not sure about him. But we need his skills, so . . .'

'I think you can trust him.'

'So you keep saying. I reckon you're a bit partial there.'

' 'Cos he's saved my life a couple of times? You bet I am.'

'Don't forget he's a human, Coilla. Blood will out.'

'Maybe we shouldn't judge others the way we've been judged.'

'And maybe some *should* be. Or would you prefer trying to reason with Peczan's army?'

She smiled. 'Looking out for tyros and humans you don't trust. You're going to have your hands full tomorrow.'

Several hours later, with most resistance members away preparing for the morrow and the shadows lengthening, a human furtively approached the safe house. Despite the clement weather he was bundled in a cloak, and wore an expansive hat with its brim pulled well down to hide his features. Looking to the right and left, he pushed open the door and slipped inside.

There was a room close by the entrance, its door half open. As the intruder crept past, Pepperdyne leapt out of it. They crashed into the opposite wall and a struggle ensued. The man's hat was ripped from his head.

'You!' Pepperdyne exclaimed.

'Take your hands *off* me!' Standeven demanded.

'In here!' Pepperdyne growled, dragging his master into the empty room. Ignoring his protests, he flung him into a chair. 'You're lucky I happened to be the one on guard duty. Where the *hell* have you been?'

'I have to account to you for my movements now, do I?'

'You do when you disappear for hours on end without a word. What's going on?'

Standeven dusted himself off with an exaggerated gesture. 'I had to get out.'

'What, for a stroll?'

'You've seen something of this place. I've only been shunted from one stinking hideout to another.'

'My outings haven't exactly been pleasure trips.'

'That's your choice. I needed air, and the sight of other faces. I wanted to get away from these creatures you're so fond of.'

'So you took a walk in a city full of them.'

'*Yes.* And how might that imperil this sordid little enterprise?'

'You fool. What if you'd been picked up by the authorities?'

'They're only interested in orc insurgents. Humans have privileges in this place, I saw that much.'

'They know a human's *working* with them!'

'So you can have free run of the outside but I can't. You're not my jailer.'

'It seems you need one.'

'If we ever get back home, I'll . . .'

'You still haven't got it through your head, have you? Things are different here. They're different between you and me.'

'Which might not last for ever.'

'You wish.'

'And in the event of things going back to the way they were, your fortunes are going to depend on how you behave now. You'd do well to keep that in mind.'

'I'm doing my best to keep us alive. Isn't that enough?'

Standeven adopted a conciliatory tone. 'And I appreciate it, Jode. I really do.'

'You've a strange way of showing it. How do I know what you were up to out there?'

'Wouldn't I be stupid to do anything that might jeopardise my own safety? My wellbeing's tied to this ragtag bunch of rebels, same as you.' He spread his hands and added reasonably, 'I've nowhere else to go.'

'You know the thing about you, Standeven? I can never be quite sure if you're a knave or an idiot.'

'On this occasion, probably the latter. I was foolhardy. I'm sorry.'

Pepperdyne considered his master's words, and said, 'If you ever do anything like this again . . .'

'I won't. I give you my word. Now forget my stupidity and save your anger for tomorrow.'

Pepperdyne expelled a breath and relaxed a little. 'Yeah, tomorrow. It's going to be an interesting day.'

'I'm sure of it,' Standeven agreed.

26

The fort was old. It was built in times long forgotten as part of Acurial's border defences. The pacifistic orcs of the present epoch had allowed it to fall into neglect, and its restoration was undertaken by the human invaders.

It stood on the edge of a rock-face, some thirty to forty feet high, and looked out over an expanse of open land that ran to the distant sea. Below the fort, nestling at the foot of the cliff, was a line of wooden buildings. They were of much more recent vintage, having been erected by orcs of the current era to store grain from nearby farms and to over-winter their cattle. With the coming of the humans these buildings were abandoned and left to rot.

The opposite side of the fort, where its entrance was situated, faced a grassy plain that stretched to the city of Taress. Not that the city could be seen. Even if it hadn't been too far away, a semicircle of squat hills obscured the view, and set the fort in a depression. As a result, the road that ran to its gates was on a slight incline. To the south-west, also hidden, a major river flowed.

A force of orcs, some ninety strong, had approached covertly, and now concealed themselves behind the hill crests. They brought three wagons, the horses' hooves muffled with sacking. The orcs took care to mask their advance. Patrols had been ambushed and lookouts purged.

Brelan commanded the force. Haskeer, Dallog and Pepperdyne were part of it, along with Wheam. Roughly half the Wolverines were present, and resistance members made up the rest.

Peeking over the ridge, Brelan surveyed the fort. It was constructed of stone. There were two towers, and sentries toured the battlements. But there was no moat or portcullis. The road swept straight down to its wooden gates, which were not unlike barn doors, albeit taller and sturdier.

Brelan pulled back and ordered the wagons to be brought up almost to the peak of the hill, where they were still out of sight. The horses were unhitched and quietly led away, and the wagons' shafts were removed. Each wagon carried a stout tree trunk with its fore-end iron-capped. These were hauled forward and securely lashed in place, so that the points jutted from the front.

The wagons had a central lever installed at the driver's end which connected to chains attached to the front axle.

Pepperdyne studied the arrangement. 'Clever. But how much control does the lever give?'

'Not a lot,' Brelan admitted. 'Just enough to steer it a little to the left or right, though it takes some strength to do even that. Which is why we'll have two pairs of hands on each.'

'How about braking?'

'There's only the wagon's brake. But we're not sure that'd work, given the weight we'll be shifting. We're relying on the things stopping of their own accord, once the gates and level ground slow them.'

'Bit iffy, isn't it?'

'It's the best we could do.'

Pepperdyne turned and saw Wheam standing nearby. His lips were silently moving and he wore a look of intense concentration. 'All right, Wheam?'

The youngster nodded, and said out loud, 'One hundred and four, one hundred and five, one hundred and six . . .'

'You're doing fine,' Pepperdyne told him. 'Keep it up.'

'One hundred and seven, one hundred and eight, one hundred and nine . . .'

'Good,' Stryke said. 'Try to keep to that pace.'

Spurral gave him a thumbs up and continued counting under her breath.

They were part of a group, numbering about fifty, cautiously edging their way along the base of the cliff below the fort.

Stryke lead them. Spurral, Jup, Coilla and Chillder were acting as his lieutenants. The remainder of the group comprised the balance of the Wolverines, all of the Vixens, and a contingent from the resistance.

They pressed as close to the cliff face as possible, sheltering beneath a narrow overhang to avoid being seen. Their path took them to the first of the derelict buildings.

'We need the third one,' Chillder reminded him in a whisper.

Stryke nodded.

He didn't want to take the risk of breaking cover and approaching the building they wanted head on. So he beckoned a couple of grunts and they set to carefully prising off rotting planks on the side of the first building. When a big enough gap was opened, Stryke began shepherding the group through.

The interior stank of mould, and the floor was strewn with rubble. Just enough light lanced through cracks in the building's fabric for them to see. Stumbling across to the opposite wall, they repeated the process, levering planks off with dagger blades.

Fortunately the buildings abutted each other, which meant no open space between them where the orcs might have been spotted. They had to get through two sets of planks, but they were so decayed it didn't present a problem.

The second building was very much like the first. Except that a mass of fallen timbers blocked the far wall and had to be cleared.

'How we doing, Spurral?' Stryke asked.

'Four hundred and seventy-nine, four hundred and eighty . . .'

'Right. *Move it*,' he urged the others. 'Time's running out.'

They got the timbers shifted and attacked the final wall. It was in the same state as the others and they were soon through.

The third building was the biggest so far, with barn-like dimensions and a high roof.

'This way,' Chillder said, heading for the rear.

Stryke ordered hooded lamps to be lit and they saw heaps of debris and wood stacked against the back wall.

'Here,' Chillder instructed.

They all piled into moving the obstructions and made short work of it. What was revealed was the bare cliff face. But when the lanterns were held close the light showed a large semi-circular area that wasn't the same colour as the rock.

'It's just mortar,' Chillder explained. 'We've already done the work. You've only to break through.'

Three or four orcs came forward with sledgehammers that had cloth wrapped around their heads to deaden the sound. They pounded at the mortar and it fell away in great chunks. Dust swirled in the already fusty air, and there was a chorus of coughing and spitting. In minutes an opening like a cave mouth had been excavated.

Stryke had more lanterns lit and torches fired.

'It's a labyrinth in there,' Chillder warned. 'I'd better go first.' She took one of the torches.

They found themselves in a long tunnel low enough that all but the dwarfs had to stoop. It sloped upwards on a steep gradient, and the floor was worn so smooth their boots had trouble gaining purchase.

At last they came to a level. Facing them were the mouths of two more tunnels. Chillder took the one on the right. It was taller than the one they entered by, but much narrower, making its transit oppressive. This led to a circular chamber. On its far side was a stairway carved out of the rock. They started to climb.

The stairs, perhaps a hundred in total, delivered them to a passageway. Along its length were the entrances to a dozen or more tunnels. Without hesitating, Chillder strode to one and entered. It was short.

They came out in a high but constricted gallery. On both sides were ledges of stone reaching to the ceiling. The ledges were packed with skulls. There were bones too. Thigh bones, arm bones, ribs, all neatly stacked and forming solid yellowy-white walls. Every few yards there were complete skeletons, standing to attention as though guarding the house of death.

If an archer had loosed an arrow from where they stood, it would have scarcely reached the far end of the gallery. The skulls and various bones, unmistakably from orcs, numbered in their thousands. Quite possibly hundreds of thousands.

'Welcome to one of the catacombs of Acurial,' Chillder announced, a certain awe in her voice.

'How long has this been here?' Coilla asked, taking in the display.

'It's ancient,' Chillder explained. 'Older than we can guess. At one time, long ago, all orcs were placed in galleries like this when their end came. Our ancestors have slept here for untold centuries.'

'The humans don't know about this?' Jup said.

'Most of our own don't know about it. It's just another part of our lost heritage. The resistance discovered it by accident when we were looking for a way into the fortress.'

'We should keep moving,' Stryke said.

They walked the length of the gallery, their footsteps echoing eerily. The empty eye sockets of the long dead seemed to follow their progress.

At the end of the gallery was another passage and yet more tunnels. Chillder entered the first they came to, and counted as she paced along it. It was so low they could touch the ceiling with ease. Suddenly she stopped and looked up.

'This is the place,' she stated.

Their torches showed a white cross marked on the ceiling.

'How we doing, Spurral?' Stryke wanted to know.

'Seven hundred and eleven, seven hundred and twelve, seven hundred and . . .'

'Let's get on with it.'

He called over grunts with picks and shovels.

'*Wait!*' Jup exclaimed.

They turned to see that he was standing with his arms held high and palms pressed to the wall.

'What is it?' Chillder demanded.

'Not here,' Jup said. 'It's not right.'

'What are you talking about?'

Stryke went to him. 'What do you sense, Jup?'

'Sense?' Chillder said, obviously bewildered.

'This isn't a good place,' Jup replied. 'There's a concentration of . . . I'm not sure. But above this point isn't where we want to come out. There's activity up there. Malevolent.'

'Will somebody tell me what's going on?' Chillder demanded.

'Jup has a . . .' Stryke faltered. 'He's sensitive to certain things. You're sure, Jup?'

'The farsight works well here. Clearer than I ever knew it in,' he glanced at Chillder, 'in the north. Believe me, this isn't where we should be. Can we move on a bit? Find another spot?'

'Have you gone insane?' Chillder fumed.

Stryke fixed her with a resolute gaze. 'If Jup says it's dangerous for us to break through here, then we'd better listen. He's never wrong about these things. Believe me.'

'If you think we're going to change the plan at the last minute on the say so of a—'

'Eight hundred and seventy-one, eight hundred and seventy-two . . .' Spurral chimed in, glaring at them.

'Trust us, Chillder,' Stryke said. 'That or stand aside. Only make up your mind now. There's no time for this.'

'Gods, you're all crazy,' Chillder decided. 'This was worked out with care.' She jabbed a thumb at the ceiling. 'Coming up here puts us behind an outbuilding, somewhere there's less chance of being seen.'

'We can't do it. Where else?'

She hesitated for a split second, took in the resolution on his face, and sighed. 'I must be damn crazy myself.' She turned and looked further along the tunnel. 'Let's see . . .'

'Hurry,' Coilla urged.

'Let me think!'

Chillder walked the tunnel, staring upwards as though trying to remember or imagine what lay above. The others shuffled along behind her. She stopped, looked as though she was about to say something, then moved on.

The tunnel was a dead-end, and they almost reached it before she halted again. 'Here. I think.'

'Jup?' Stryke said.

The dwarf put his hand to the ceiling and closed his eyes. Time slowed to a glacial pace before he opened them again and nodded.

'Move yourselves!' Stryke ordered.

Grunts rushed forward and attacked the ceiling with their picks.

'Nine hundred and thirty-four,' Spurral recited, 'nine hundred and thirty-five . . .'

'. . . nine hundred and thirty-six,' Wheam chanted, 'nine hundred and thirty-seven . . .'

'Right.' Brelan turned to Haskeer and Dallog. 'Get the wagons ready.' They went off to relay the order. To Pepperdyne he said, 'Clear about the timing?'

Pepperdyne nodded.

'And the archers?'

'Waiting on your word.'

'Good. Take your position.'

Pepperdyne left him.

'Wheam?' Brelan said.

'Nine hundred and forty-nine, nine hundred and fifty . . .'

Several dozen orcs were pushing the first wagon to the summit of the hill. The second and third were being readied for their turn. On either side of the road, teams of the resistance's archers were keeping low and looking Brelan's way.

He signalled to the first wagon. It stopped just short of the crest. Fourteen or fifteen heavily armed orcs scrambled aboard.

Brelan looked to Wheam again.

'Nine hundred and seventy-two, nine hundred and . . .'

Further down the hill, behind the waiting wagons, Haskeer was gathering together the forty or fifty warriors whose job was to provide the motive force, and later be part of the assault on foot. His method seemed to consist largely of swiping at their backsides with the flat of his sword and lots of muttered swearing.

'Wheam,' Brelan repeated.

'Nine hundred and eighty-nine, nine hundred and ninety . . .'

'Keep it aloud.'

'Nine hundred and ninety-one, nine hundred and ninety-two . . .'

Brelan unsheathed his sword and raised it. He could feel every eye on him.

'. . . nine hundred and ninety-four, nine hundred and ninety-five . . .'

The pushing crew flowed to the first wagon. Archers nocked their arrows.

'Nine hundred and ninety-seven, nine hundred and ninety-eight. . .' Wheam's voice strained with tension. 'Nine hundred and ninety-nine . . . *one thousand*!'

Brelan's sword came down in a decisive slash.

The archers leapt up, aimed and fired. Arrows winged towards the fort's battlements. Sentries fell.

The pushing crew shoved the first wagon to the crest of the hill, then over it. Once it reached the downward incline it began to move of its own accord and the crew let go. As it rumbled past Brelan he grabbed hold and scrambled aboard. The wagon picked up speed, bumping and bouncing on the potholed road, with Brelan and a fellow resistance member clutching the steering lever.

Orc archers kept up a steady stream of arrows, pinning down most of the fort's own bowmen. But the garrison had started to return fire. Arrows zinged over and around the careering wagon.

Wheam ran to Pepperdyne, by the second wagon. 'Do you think they'll make it?'

'If they don't, we've got two more tries. Now get to your place.'

Wheam joined Dallog at the last wagon.

Brelan's party was travelling as fast as a galloping horse and still picking up speed. They hung on grimly as the wagon bucked at every rut it hit. But it was halfway to its destination and still on course. Brelan hoped it would stay that way. He was doubtful they could steer with any accuracy if it deviated.

At the top of the hill the second wagon was trundled into place. Its crew climbed aboard, and Pepperdyne took the steering lever, along with Bhose. The pushers moved in, ready for the off.

'*Steady!*' Pepperdyne cautioned. '*Wait for it!*'

When Brelan's team started their descent the fortress looked like a child's plaything. Now it filled their world. They could make out the coarse texture of its stonework, the faces of the defenders on its battlements. And as the distance closed, the danger grew. The wagon became the prime target of the fort's archers, and bolts rained down on the orcs' raised shields.

There was a jolt as the road levelled, but no loss of momentum. Nor did the wagon vary its course. It hurtled into the fort's shadow, wheels blurred with speed. The defenders lobbed spears and rocks. Slingshot bounced off the orcs' shields.

Dead ahead, the towering gates loomed.

'*Hold on!*' Brelan bellowed.

Stryke saw nothing but blue sky.

He hauled himself up and cautiously poked his head through the opening. After a quick look he ducked back down. 'We need to move fast,' he told the others. 'Follow me.' He climbed out.

He was near one of the fort's outer walls, on the edge of its parade ground. The gates could be seen on the far side of the square. There were several stone buildings a short sprint from where Stryke stood. He could see men on the battlements above, but as far as he could tell, no one had spotted him.

The others began scrambling out of the hole. He hurried things on, directing them to shelter by one of the outbuildings.

When Chillder emerged he pulled her to one side. 'Where would we have come out if we stuck to the plan?'

She got her bearings. Then she pointed to a large building about a hundred paces away. It was plain, with few windows, set high, and could have been a barracks. 'On the other side of that.'

Stryke sent her to join the others. He kept an eye on the place she indicated until the last of his party came up. Then he hurried after them, keeping low.

'So what did we avoid?' Chillder wanted to know, still doubtful.

'Whatever it is,' Stryke told her, 'it's behind that barracks.'

A commotion interrupted them. They looked to the square. Dozens of soldiers were running towards the gates.

'They've spotted Brelan,' Stryke said.

Coilla drew her sword. 'Then let's stop 'em.'

'I don't like having that at our backs.' He nodded at the barracks.

'So what do we do?'

'Split our forces,' he quickly decided. 'You and the Vixens as one unit; Jup and me take the rest.'

Coilla fished out a coin. 'Call.' She flipped it.

'Heads.'

She caught the coin and slapped it on the back of her hand. 'Heads it is. What do you want?'

'You get the gate.'

She gestured to Chillder, Spurral and the other females. They peeled off from the group and followed her.

Stryke, Jup and the remainder of the party sprinted for the barracks.

They reached its nearest wall and flowed round to the side, lessening the chance of being seen from the square. It was a wonder to Stryke that no one up on the parapet had noticed them yet. But they seemed to be concentrating on whatever was happening outside the fort. He had a couple of his archers keep watch.

Signalling the others to hold their position, he and Jup crept to the corner and peered round it. Some twenty or thirty paces along, in the broad space between the barracks and the fortress wall, there was a large group of soldiers. They stood silently in a wide circle, weapons drawn, staring at the ground.

'That was our welcome,' Stryke whispered.

'How did they *know*?' Jup asked.

'Good question.'

They stealthily withdrew and rejoined the rest of the group.

With gestures and soft words, Stryke filled them in. Then he divided his force. Half, led by Jup, were sent to one end of the barracks. He took the other half to the opposite end. A lone orc lingered midway, ready to signal when they were in position.

Once he did, the two groups poured around the corners of the building. They charged the startled would-be ambushers from both sides, bellowing war cries, and fell upon them.

The Vixens were halfway to the gates before they were spotted.

Soldiers rushed to engage them. Arrows winged from the battlements.

Coilla, Spurral and Chillder were in the vanguard, and they tore into the humans with savagery. Thirty screaming females, wildly slashing steel, set about the troops like a flock of blood-lusting harpies. A dozen lethal brawls boiled in the middle of the square. More soldiers dashed towards the maelstrom.

There was a tremendous crash. The gates exploded inwards, crushing defenders on either side as Brelan's horseless wagon hurtled through. It ploughed into fleeing troopers, shattering their bones and bouncing over their broken bodies.

The wagon rumbled on across the square, humans scattering in its path. It demolished the corner of a storehouse, but kept going, though its speed reduced. Finally it smacked dead centre into the side of another, sturdier building, where its ram buried itself in the brickwork.

Its payload of bellowing orcs leapt free and charged into the fray.

Then the mayhem started in earnest.

27

'*Now!*' Pepperdyne yelled.

He and Bhose gripped the steering lever. Behind them, the orc attack team braced themselves. The pushing crew shoved the wagon over the lip of the hill and sent it on its downward path.

Pepperdyne could clearly see the damage to the fortress gates, and, on the battlements, more defenders than before. The orc archers sent out another volley, and human bowmen responded.

'We've used up the element of surprise,' Pepperdyne said, the wind whipping his hair. 'This could be rougher than Brelan's ride.'

Bhose nodded grimly.

As they gathered speed, the human gazed at the fortress and added, 'I wonder what the hell's going on inside there.'

Stryke and his team had made the space behind the barracks block a rat trap. Now it was a bloodbath.

The humans outnumbered the orcs two to one. Stryke's group had the advantage of ambushing the ambushers, and they had orchish ferocity. But with nowhere to run the humans fought with equal aggression.

It seemed to Jup that there was an endless supply of heads to crack and ribs to cave in. Deftly wielding his staff, he obliged. Though his style was somewhat cramped by fighting in such a confined space. He overcame the restriction, and his short stature, by employing a technique that had served him well in the past.

Attacking his opponents' lower limbs, he worked on toppling them. Brought down to his level they were ripe for lethal blows, or quick lunges from the thin-bladed dagger strapped to his palm.

Stryke preferred a sword and knife combination in close quarters combat. When a hulking trooper loomed up ahead of him, he lashed out with the knife, catching him in the chest. Then he used it the way a butcher uses a hook, hoisting the human forward, on to the sword's blade. The man had hardly dropped before another took his place. Stryke felled him too, hacking deep into his neck and letting loose a jet of scarlet.

Venting their hatred for the oppressors, the rest of the orcs toiled as hard, reaping a harvest of rent flesh and severed limbs. In short order the number of dead and wounded mounted. The surviving soldiers retreated, making a last stand with their backs to the wall. Stryke's team pressed in on them.

The fighting was much more widely dispersed on the parade ground. Brelan's group had got clear of their wagon and united with the Vixens. Half of them were archers, and they fell into exchanging fire with the bowmen on the parapets. The rest pitched into the general melee.

Coilla was embroiled with a young officer whose fencing skills were superior to any human she'd so far encountered in Acurial. It was the last thing she needed, and she battled hard to finish it quickly. But she was stymied by his flair for warding off every blow she threw at him.

She spent precious seconds thrusting, feigning, spinning and dodging before her impatience turned to fury. Ignoring caution she turned to brute might. Thrashing wildly, she powered through his defence. Before he got his guard back up she delivered a heavy whack to his sword arm with the flat of her blade. Her reward was a loud crack as the bone shattered. The officer cried out, the weapon slipping from his insensate hand. Coilla instantly followed through, landing a solid hit to his chest.

Internal organs ruptured, he went down spitting blood.

She found herself shoulder to shoulder with Brelan.

'Where's Stryke?' he yelled.

'They had an ambush planned. He's dealing with it.'

He looked shocked. 'But how—'

'Later, Brelan, later!'

They spiralled off into fresh opponents.

Moments later she noticed he'd gravitated to Chillder, and the twins were fighting in harmony.

Spurral eschewed her usual staff and chose to arm herself with a pair of long knives. Her other weapon was less tangible: the bewilderment of the humans when confronted by a dwarf. Moreover, a female dwarf. If incredulity meant a split second's hesitation she gladly exploited it, and more than one dumbfounded foe paid with his life.

Faced by a couple of troopers less impressed with her otherness, she nimbly plunged her knives into both their torsos simultaneously. Then she spun to avoid a rushing spearman, tripped him as he passed and planted the double blades in his back. The warrior who took his place reeled off clutching an open throat.

Coilla appeared at her side. 'We're forgetting the gates!'

Humans were massing there again, intent on closing the breach. 'What do we do?'

'Follow me!'

They weaved through the fracas, gathering as many Vixens as they could. With six or seven in tow they ran towards the gates. That caught the attention of several archers on the battlements. They targeted the sprinting females.

Barely ten paces had been covered when one of the Vixens was struck in the eye by an arrow. She was dead before she hit the dirt.

'*Shit!*' Coilla cursed.

'*Heads up!*' Spurral exclaimed, pointing with a knife.

A mob of troops had spilled out of one of the barrack blocks and was dashing to intercept them.

The small contingent of Vixens stood their ground. With a battle raging behind them, a crowd of troops milling at the gates ahead and knots of soldiers all around, there was little choice.

The fresh troopers swept in. Almost immediately one of the Vixens let out a piercing scream. A spear buried in her chest, she staggered a few steps before collapsing to her knees. Then she toppled, lifeless.

In short order one of her comrades was knocked senseless by a vicious head blow. Another sustained a wound that near severed her arm.

'This is getting hairy!' Spurral yelled. 'We need reinforcements!'

There was uproar at the gates. Soldiers went down like scythed corn as Pepperdyne's wagon ploughed through them. Nimbler humans leapt aside when it shot over the square. About halfway across, Pepperdyne applied the handbrake. The wagon skidded, turned almost end on end and came to a juddering halt. But its crew wasn't entirely unscathed. One was dead, and the defenders' arrows had injured a couple more. The rest jumped clear and joined the set-to.

'Looks like we got 'em,' Coilla said.

At the top of the hill, the third wagon was launched.

Dallog shared the steering lever with a dour resistance member. Wheam was in the rear with the rest of the attack team.

Turning, Dallog said, 'Expect this to be bumpy. Hang on back there.' He addressed it more to Wheam than the hardened fighters sitting with him.

The youth gave a weak nod, his complexion chalky.

Having seen off the wagon, Haskeer and the remainder of the force charged down the hill in its wake.

Stryke's group, dealing with the ambushers behind the barracks, had been oblivious to the greater picture. But with the last of the humans quickly and brutally dispatched, their task was done.

'We've wasted enough time here,' Stryke announced, jerking his blade from a trooper's lifeless breast.

'Then let's get back to the main event!' Jup replied in a tone that sounded almost gleeful.

They rushed out to the parade ground.

The scene that greeted them wasn't far short of anarchy. There were no defined lines of battle, just a mass of fighting orcs and humans.

'Where to, Stryke?' Jup asked, scanning the confusion.

'Looks like Coilla could use some help.' He pointed towards the ruined gates.

'Seems as good a place as any.'

Stryke swiftly formed his troop into a wedge formation and led them into the fray.

They traversed the square by the simple expedient of cutting down any humans who came near. Once they reached Coilla's group the wedge broke up and splintered into a dozen separate scraps.

'About time!' Coilla said.

'Been busy,' Stryke told her, batting away a soldier's blade.

'Hey, look!' Jup yelled.

Through the gap where the gates used to be they saw the third wagon heading towards the fort.

It was having a rough time. Arrows came down continuously.

With the orc archers part of the ground force running behind the wagon, their shields above their heads as though deflecting rain, no one was returning fire.

Apart from their helmets and chainmail, Dallog and his co-driver had no such protection. It proved telling. An arrow struck the co-driver in the neck. He fell heavily against the steering lever, then went over the side. The wagon veered sharply to the right and came off the road. Dallog struggled to control it.

One or two orcs in the back of the wagon managed to jump clear. The rest hung on grimly as it picked up speed. Dallog tried applying the brake. It snapped off in his hand.

Bumping over grassland, the wagon swerved further to the right. It passed the side of the fort, a spear lob to its left, travelling ever faster. Arrows were still raining down on them.

Dallog shouted something, but his words couldn't be heard. Wheam squealed.

Then the wagon ran out of land and plunged over the cliff.

A company of soldiers arrived furtively at the row of ramshackle buildings by the foot of the cliff. They forced the doors, and armed with lanterns poured in to begin their search.

The wagon of bellowing orcs shot over the precipice above. Like a great bird downed by a giant's slingshot, it crashed through the roof of one of the buildings. With a thunderous roar the entire structure collapsed.

The impact sent shockwaves through the unstable buildings on either side. Imitating a line of playing cards swiped by a spoilt child, the ripple effect had them falling into each other. Walls buckled and went down. Roofs caved in. Smoke and flame erupted from the debris, ignited by the lanterns and brands carried by the ill-fated troopers.

They heard the reverberation up in the fort, even above the noise of battle.

'Those *fucking* archers!' Coilla howled.

Stryke nodded. 'That's our next objective.'

The ground force, with Haskeer in the vanguard, jogged through the gates. Its archers immediately took issue with the bowmen on the ramparts and started swapping bolts with them. The others piled into the battle on the square, with Haskeer taking the lead.

Stryke spotted Pepperdyne finishing an opponent nearby. He left Coilla marshalling her Vixens and went to him.

'Feel like a task, human?'

'What do you have in mind?'

'Clearing those battlements.'

Pepperdyne glanced up at the archers. They looked to be at least thirty strong. 'I'm game.'

'We can't spare many for the job.'

'I said I'm game.'

'Right.' He cupped his hands. 'Haskeer! *Haskeer!*' Catching his sergeant's attention, Stryke waved him over.

Haskeer cut down a trooper on the way to keep his hand in. 'What?'

'We're going for the archers.'

'Good. The bastards.'

'We can't take more than six away from this. Grab three. Make 'em Wolverines.'

Haskeer's brow creased as he did the sum. 'That's five of us.'

'He's coming.' Stryke nodded at Pepperdyne.

Haskeer scowled but said nothing.

'And get our archers to lay down covering fire. *Go!*'

The sergeant dived back into the melee.

'How do we do it?' Pepperdyne asked.

Stryke pointed to a stone staircase set against the fortress' outer wall. It led directly to the battlements. 'Up that.'

'Bit exposed, isn't it?'

'Can you see another way?'

Pepperdyne shook his head.

Haskeer soon returned. He had Prooq, Zoda and Finje with him. All were blood-splattered.

'We ready?' Stryke said.

'The archers let rip when we get to the stairs,' Haskeer told him.

'All right. Let's move.'

They made for the staircase, allowing no opposition to slow them. That meant two or three skirmishes on the way, but nothing they couldn't handle.

A pair of archers were stationed at the base of the steps. When they saw a human with five orcs dashing at them they hesitated.

But only for a moment. They loosed arrows. Stryke's crew hit the dirt and the bolts flew overhead.

Haskeer was the first to his feet. As the bowmen nocked afresh he began running at them. He drew back his arm and hurled a hatchet. It struck one of the archers and took him out. The other had his bow taut and aimed directly at Haskeer. A fire-tipped arrow streaked past them and buried itself in the archer's chest. He went down with a cry, his jerkin in flames.

'Nice touch,' Pepperdyne said.

Then they were moving again. As they neared the steps the orc archers let go their covering shots, and again the arrows were tarred and burning. A dead human tumbled down the stairs, two flaming bolts embedded in his back.

Stryke at their head, the six tore up the staircase. They were almost at the top before anybody tried to stop them. A sentry came at Stryke with a broadsword, slashing it in a downward stroke. Stryke dodged the blow and kept going. He hunched himself and went for the man's legs. With a heave, he tossed him over the side of the stairway. The human dropped screaming to the ground.

They got to the parapet. Most of the archers were concentrating on the battle below and ignorant of their presence. But several of the nearest turned to defend themselves. There was no time for them to raise their bows so they went for swords. Stryke's crew were on to them instantly, and a short, vicious tussle cut short their resistance.

Stryke knew that the bowmen further along the parapet were the most dangerous, even with orc archers keeping them busy. Unlike the ones just killed, they were far enough away to use their bows and pick off his team.

'We need to get close to them,' he said. 'Finje, Zoda, Prooq; take these bows and keep 'em occupied.'

The grunts stripped the weapons and quivers from the dead humans as Stryke, Haskeer and Pepperdyne set off.

Their first encounter was with two sentries who, seeing the trio coming, charged at them. Stryke and Pepperdyne engaged the pair in swordplay. Haskeer raced on and barrelled into a lone archer in the process of drawing his bow. He battered the man, then proceeded to pound his head against the battlement wall, dashing his brains out.

Stryke and Pepperdyne, having finished the sentries, caught up. The three ran on.

They headed for a knot of four or five archers. Two of them loosed arrows in their direction. One was hopelessly wide of the mark. The other came so close to hitting Stryke he felt the displacement of air as it whistled past his ear.

Before they could take another shot, Pepperdyne, Stryke, then Haskeer hurtled into them. A bloody reckoning with blades, fists and boots left four sprawled on the walkway and one plummeting to the parade ground.

From the rear, Prooq yelled a warning. Stryke and the others dropped. A flight of arrows swept overhead and punched into three fast-approaching sentries. Back on their feet, Stryke, Haskeer and Pepperdyne darted onwards.

They didn't have to work for the next brace of kills. A couple of bowmen in their path succumbed to blazing arrows from orc compatriots below.

Ten paces later half a dozen sentries ganged up on them. Haskeer exposed the windpipe of the first one to venture near his blade. Pepperdyne punctured the second's chest. Stryke ran through the third with a savage thrust, then went on to eviscerate the fourth. Pepperdyne sliced into the fifth's belly, while Haskeer snapped the neck of the sixth.

There was no hiatus. The trio had left just a short trail of bloody footprints before they ran into the next clutch of defenders. And so it went, with a seemingly never-ending cavalcade of human flesh to be carved, stabbed and slashed.

Until at last they stood breathless at the parapet's end, surrounded by a litter of corpses.

Haskeer had hold of the remaining defender. He lifted the dazed, beaten human, with the intention of throwing him from the battlements and down the cliff face. Suddenly he stopped, seemed to lose interest in the man and casually dropped him on to the parapet's flagstones.

'What's going on down there?' he said.

Stryke joined him.

He saw the wreckage of the demolished hovels at the bottom of the cliff, with flames playing over them and billowing smoke. But what really caught his attention was the dozens of soldiers milling about the ruins, and what they must have been doing.

'They were going for the tunnel,' he murmered.

'Look at this!' Pepperdyne said. He was standing on the other side of the parapet, staring down at the fighting.

Stryke and Haskeer went to him.

A large number of troops were emerging from a maze of out-buildings and rushing towards the square.

'Must have been holding them back,' Stryke realised.

'Set us up,' Haskeer growled.

'There's got to be a hundred of them, or more,' Pepperdyne reckoned. 'Stryke, we can't—'

'I know. *Come on!*'

They sprinted along the parapet to the three grunts, and all of them pelted down the stairs.

The battle was still raging. Stryke spotted Coilla and made for her. He began yelling, 'There's a—'

'We see them!'

The first of the reinforcements were spilling into the square, forcing the orcs back.

Brelan arrived, panting. 'Look who's with them!' He pointed to a figure striding along in the midst of the troops.

'Who?' Stryke said.

'That's Kapple Hacher. The commander-in-chief himself.'

'This ain't by chance,' Haskeer stated. 'We've been stitched.'

'We can't beat these odds,' Coilla said.

'No,' Stryke agreed bitterly. 'Haskeer, sound the retreat.'

The sergeant took a curved horn from his belt and pressed it to his lips.

As its strident note rang out, Stryke bellowed, '*Pull back! Pull back!*'

28

The shrill, insistent note Haskeer sent out sparked an exodus.

All over the fort's parade ground, orcs disengaged and headed for the gates. Or at least most did. A few couldn't extricate themselves from overwhelming odds and imminent death. Others lay wounded, or were on the point of capture, and chose to turn their blades on themselves rather than fall into enemy hands. Those who did withdraw were hotly pursued, and rearguard actions were fought across the square.

The retreating Wolverines, resistance members and Vixens clustered at the gates, urging on stragglers and loosing arrows at the humans chasing them.

'Isn't that one of the Ceragans?' Coilla exclaimed, pointing into the heaving scrimmage.

Stryke nodded. 'It's Ignar.'

'He's in trouble, Stryke.'

The raw recruit had almost reached the edge of the scrum when a group of troopers caught up with him. He was trying to beat them off.

'I'm going in,' Stryke decided.

'I'm with you,' she said.

'Me too,' Pepperdyne announced.

With Stryke in the lead they ran towards the mob.

On their way they met the van of the pursuers. Four bawling soldiers blocked their path. Stryke hacked down the leader with a single potent blow. Coilla and Pepperdyne tackled the others as he sprinted on.

Ignar was battling two opponents. He was outclassed, and he was injured. Blood flowed freely from several wounds, not least a broad gash to the chest. It was all he could do to fend off his attackers, and as Stryke approached he slumped to his knees. One of the soldiers lifted his sword to deliver a killing stroke.

Stryke intervened. A powerful swipe of his blade all but severed the human's sword arm. The man screamed and stumbled away, gushing blood. Stryke spun to face his charging companion. Their swords clashed and they furiously hacked at each other. The flurry ended with the soldier taking steel to his belly.

Ignar had fallen. Stryke went to him and found him barely conscious. Coilla and Pepperdyne arrived.

'He's in a bad way,' Coilla pronounced as she examined the recruit. 'Lot of blood lost.'

'We'll get him clear,' Stryke said.

He and Pepperdyne half carried, half dragged Ignar while Coilla kept any other would-be attackers at bay. As they neared the gates, orc archers sent out covering fire for them.

They laid Ignar on the ground, and somebody propped his head with a folded jerkin. He seemed unconscious.

Stryke lightly slapped his pallid cheeks. 'Ignar. *Ignar.*'

The young orc's eyes flickered open.

'Here,' Coilla said, handing Stryke a canteen.

'With a wound like that,' Pepperdyne remarked, 'he shouldn't drink.'

'It doesn't matter now,' Stryke told him. He dampened Ignar's lips with a little water.

Ignar tried to speak. Stryke allowed him a drink from the canteen. He coughed, and murmured something. Stryke leaned closer.

'*I'm . . . sorry,*' Ignar whispered.

'No need,' Stryke replied. 'You fought well, and you die a Wolverine.'

Ignar managed a faint smile. Then his eyes closed for the last time.

Coilla hissed, 'Shit'.

'We can't hold here much longer,' Pepperdyne said.

'Get 'em moving,' Stryke ordered, rising.

'We've got comrades in there,' Brelan protested. 'We can't leave them.'

'We take losses,' Stryke said, glancing at Ignar's corpse. 'It's part of the price. Linger here and we'll lose more.'

'Or all,' Coilla amended. She pointed at the mass of humans across the square. They vastly outnumbered the orcs, and they were grouping for an all-out assault. 'We have to go. *Now.*'

Reluctantly, Brelan nodded assent.

Stryke turned to Coilla and Jup. 'They all know where the rendezvous point is. Any wounded or foot-draggers on the way get left behind. It's every orc for themselves. Pass it on.'

They moved off to spread the word.

He looked at Pepperdyne. 'Ready for a fast retreat, human?'

'Just say the word.'

Stryke signalled Haskeer. The sergeant gave another blast on the horn. Orc archers stepped up their flow of arrows.

The retreat began.

They poured out of the gates and on to the approach road. Shedding excess kit and even some weapons, they headed inland, their pace increasing to a sprint. The tail of the column had barely cleared the fort's precincts when the first of the humans came after them. Orc arrows helped slow the pursuit.

'We're fucked if they've got cavalry,' Coilla said, jogging alongside Jup.

'That's right,' the dwarf panted, 'look on the bright side.'

No riders appeared. But more soldiers exited and joined the chase.

The orcs topped a rise and swept down on to the plain beyond. They made for a stand of trees an arrow's flight ahead.

Pepperdyne, next to Stryke at the column's head, glanced back. He saw the pursuing humans on the crest, outlined against the cloudless sky. 'Doesn't look like all the garrison. Not by a long shot.'

'Good,' Stryke replied.

'But why aren't more of them following us?'

Stryke shrugged and upped the pace.

They got to the line of trees and through them. That put them in the first of a series of meadows. They crossed those too, trampling down hedgerows when there was no easier path. Another stretch of open pasture followed, with several copses at its far end.

The humans were still on their trail, but had fallen back some distance.

'Think we might outpace 'em?' Jup asked.

'Wouldn't hold your breath,' Coilla said.

'Not a lot left to hold. How much further is it?'

'I reckon we're near. Should see a wood soon. It's past that.'

They had a couple more fields to go across before they spotted the wood's edge. Putting on a spurt, they quickly reached it and moved into the trees.

'Be alert!' Stryke warned. 'This is a good place to get waylaid. And we've had enough ambushes for one day.'

Pepperdyne sidled up to him. 'Now I can't see them at all,' he said, scanning the open ground they'd just left. 'Maybe they've given up the chase.'

'Or they're sneaking round to lie in wait for us, like I said. C'mon, and stay awake.'

The legion of orcs crept through the woods, keeping vigilant and as quiet as over a hundred hastily retreating warriors could. As they penetrated deeper, dappled sunlight gave way to cool gloom under the leafy canopy. Silence wrapped them, overlaid only by their muffled footfalls on the loam.

After ten minutes of steady tramping they heard something else. A halt was signalled and they listened. It was the unmistakable sound of rushing water, close to hand. They pushed on. The trees began to thin and the light increased. Soon the riverbank was in sight. While the others held back, Stryke and Brelan carried on alone to the water's edge.

The river was wide and fast-flowing. It was thunderous, throwing off spray and spawning white foam where it churned around half-submerged rocks. On the river's far side the wood continued, and beyond it the tops of green hills were just visible.

Brelan cupped his hands over his mouth and gave a passable imitation of shrill birdsong. Further along the bank, five or six of his compatriots came out of hiding.

'Don't ask,' Brelan told them as they approached, anticipating their questions about how the raid had gone. Though his expression held all they needed to know.

'We've no time to waste,' Stryke said.

Brelan nodded. 'Get the others out here.'

Stryke gestured to their waiting companions. They started spilling on to the riverbank.

Directed to a spot not far from the rendezvous point, the troop set to clearing away a camouflage of undergrowth. It concealed ten rafts. They were simple but robust, consisting of thick tree trunks lashed together and sealed with tar. Each raft had a crude rudder, and the minimal protection of a waist-high rope on three sides, looped around several timber uprights.

As they were hauled to the water's edge, Coilla joined Stryke.

'Shame Dallog and Wheam aren't here to see this,' she said.

'Or Ignar, or any of the others we lost to deceit today.'

'You reckon it *was* treachery?'

'They weren't waiting for us by chance.'

'That means somebody in the resistance . . .' She let the implication hang.

'A mission this big, maybe too many knew the plan.'

'Not that many knew all of it. Like using the catacombs.'

'There were humans down there.'

'What?'

'When we were on the battlements I saw soldiers at the bottom of the cliff. They must have been going for the entrance. Looks like it was Wheam and Dallog's wagon that stopped 'em finding it.'

Coilla smiled. 'So they did some good.' She sobered. 'But if the humans knew about the catacombs—'

'There's a spy high up in the resistance? Maybe.'

'We're in trouble if there is, Stryke.'

'There's nothing we can do about it right now. We have to—'

A chorus of shouting broke out. Orcs were heading up the riverbank, towards a group of figures.

Jup ran past, Spurral in tow. Then Haskeer thundered by, with a bunch of grunts in his wake.

Stryke stared at the commotion. 'What the—?'

'This I don't *believe*,' Coilla exclaimed. 'Come on!' She joined the rush.

He followed, and seeing what all the fuss was about, increased his pace.

The advancing figures were orcs. Upwards of a dozen in number, they were bruised and bloodied, with several needing help to walk. And at the forefront were Dallog and Wheam.

Pepperdyne stared at them. 'How the hell . . . ?'

Dallog grinned. 'Just sheer good fortune.'

Coilla gave Wheam's arm a squeeze. 'We thought you were lost.'

'So did we,' the youth replied shakily.

Stryke elbowed his way through. 'Didn't think we'd see you again, Corporal. We'd written you off.'

'We were lucky,' Dallog told him. 'The shanties took the brunt when the wagon went over. Most of us came out with petty wounds. Didn't lose a hand.'

'There were soldiers,' Wheam piped up. 'Did you know there were soldiers down—'

'Yeah,' Stryke said, 'we did.'

'Bit of a shock for 'em,' Dallog reported, not without relish.

'And fortunate for us. They'd have ambushed us if we'd left through the catacombs. That or come up at our backs inside the fort.'

'But if they knew about the tunnel what's to say they know about this escape route too?'

'All the more reason to get out of here, and fast.'

Dallog scanned the orcs crowded round. 'I don't see Ignar.'

'He didn't make it.'

The corporal's face dropped. 'No?'

'No,' Stryke confirmed.

Wheam looked shocked.

'He died well,' Stryke added.

'That's a comfort,' Dallog replied. 'But I promised I'd keep an eye on those young ones.'

'So did I.'

Dallog nodded. He said nothing for a second, then added, 'But the raid was a success, right?'

No one spoke until Pepperdyne offered, 'That's debatable.'

'Your crew all right to carry on, Dallog?' Stryke asked.

'We'll be fine.'

'Then let's move.'

Stryke and Brelan snapped orders and the rafts were readied for launch. Each held twelve or more passengers. Wolverines, Vixens and resistance members boarded randomly. The way it fell out, Stryke, Jup and Spurral found themselves on the same raft. Haskeer and Coilla were together on another; Chillder and Brelan on a third; Pepperdyne, Dallog and Wheam on a fourth.

At Brelan's signal the vessels cast off, pushed clear of the bank with rudimentary paddles. The strong current took hold at once, tossing them about like corks and drawing them into midstream. Before things settled down there was some jockeying, the orcs paddling furiously to avoid collisions as the craft rapidly picked up speed.

The terrain slipped past at a clip. Copious trees and lush pastures. A glimpse of a small lake ringed with jade hills. Fields with flocks of sheep and startled shepherds. The sight of distant cerulean cliffs, shimmering in sunlight.

They rounded a bend. The river became wider and faster. They were drenched with the spume, rafts bouncing on the surge, bow and stern see-sawing.

'Hey!' Spurral yelled.

'What?' Stryke bellowed.

'Back there!' She pointed to the rear.

He squinted through the vapour and made out oblong patches of white. The mist cleared a little and he realised they were sails. They belonged to an armada of boats coming round the bend after them.

As they drew nearer they were noticed by the occupants of other rafts.

On Coilla's, she turned to Haskeer and said, 'Now we know where they disappeared to.'

'The bastards are on to our every move.'

'There's gotta be a spy.'

Haskeer snarled, 'If I get my hands on him—'

'We've more pressing problems. Hold tight!'

On the raft carrying Dallog, Wheam and Pepperdyne they were counting the pursuing craft.

'Twenty-one,' Dallog said.

'Twenty-*two*,' Wheam corrected. 'You missed one.'

'The number's not important,' Pepperdyne interrupted testily. 'Outrunning them is.'

'They're gaining!' Wheam cried.

Brelan and Chillder's raft was at the back of the orc flotilla. Close enough to the boats chasing them to see who stood at the prow of the leading vessel.

'It's him all right,' Brelan confirmed, shading his eyes with his palm, 'Kapple Hacher.'

'It was no fluke him being here,' Chillder reckoned. 'This whole thing stinks, brother.'

The river meandered for a mile or two, the turns and curves taming its pace. That slowed the rafts, dependent on current, and forced the orcs to work their paddles. The boats trailing them, under sail, began to close the gap. And even when the river straightened and flowed quickly again they continued to catch up, until the foremost were within an arrow's flight.

The humans proved the point by loosing a salvo. Arrows zinged over the orcs' heads, or fell short, cutting into open water. Orc archers returned fire. Their footing was unsure on the heaving rafts and the results were ragged. But the exchange carried on, and there were hits. Through skill or luck, two orcs were struck by bolts. One plunged overboard and was lost. The other fell wounded into the arms of comrades.

A human paid with his life, taking an arrow to the chest. Another was injured and dragged clear of the rail.

By this time the boats had closed in. But the rafts had a small advantage over the larger craft. They didn't have sails to tack, giving them a bit more leeway to manoeuvre. That kept most of the boats clear, though some got in close enough to engage. Spears were lobbed. Arrows, throwing knives and slingshot clattered against raised shields on both sides.

The speed of the river's flow hampered ramming attempts by the boats. Instead they tried to get alongside the rafts and board them. Others did their best to outpace the rafts, hoping to block their way. The orcs fought to stop them.

In this way the two small fleets played cat and mouse along the river. Harrying and assailing, bumping and swerving, hurling weaponry back and forth.

At length, a change came over the river. It flowed even faster, and up ahead it seemed to disappear into a boiling cloud. A deep rumbling could be heard.

'What the hell's that?' Jup said.

'Must be the falls,' Stryke explained.

'So what do we do?' Spurral asked, a little uneasily.

'Brelan's got it worked out. I hope. Just be ready to hold on tight.'

Every rudder operator on the orc rafts was a resistance member, briefed on what to do and when. As the chase progressed they steered nearer to the left bank and stayed alert for a signal.

The roar of water grew louder, the misty cloud loomed higher. Several boats were neck and neck with orc rafts.

On the bank, perilously close to the deafening lip of the falls, stood a cluster of mature trees. They were taller than any others on that stretch. From high up on the tallest there was a spiky flash of light. It repeated a number of times, proving it to be a confederate holding something reflective.

As one, the rafts veered sharply towards the bank. The orcs braced themselves. At the same time bands of archers ashore, some hidden in trees, peppered the human's boats.

The well chosen spot was shallow near the bank, and the majority of the rafts simply ground to a halt. Their occupants leapt off and splashed to shore. Some rafts were barred from quite reaching the shallows by the clutter of vessels. They tossed anchors of iron and rock overboard, then their passengers waded waist high to the riverbank.

The suddenness of the move confused the humans, though they must have known the orcs had no plan to go over the falls. A number of them tried copying the move and beaching in the shallows. But the deeper hauls of their bigger craft ran aground far short of the bank, leaving the troopers loath to brave the fast-flowing water.

Other boats dropped anchor in full flow, but had no benefit. There was such force in the tide that rather than holding, the anchors were dragged along the riverbed by the swiftly drifting boats. Some struggled to turn away from the attraction of the falls and head back the way they'd come. All the while, arrows rained down on them.

One boat, losing all control, slowly spun like a child's paper toy in a gushing stream as the river pushed it past the chaos of vessels and towards the falls. Men jumped from its decks, only to find that the river had as powerful a hold on them as their abandoned craft. Boat and men, black dots in a torrent of foam, rolled into the vast cloud of water vapour. The boat, dark outline showing through the mist, tipped, and for a second seemed to stand on its nose before plunging out of sight.

The last of the orcs swarmed ashore and into the trees. Humans who made it to the bank met a hail of arrows that kept them pinned down at the water's edge.

The resistance had horses waiting, along with a couple of wagons for kit and the wounded. Everyone quickly mounted. In minutes they were on a trail and heading out of the woods.

Their path took them to a rise that ran parallel with the river, so that they could look down to the tangle of vessels, and the humans milling on the bank. One figure was unmistakable. Kapple Hacher stood apart from his men, his fists balled. He looked up and saw the escaping orcs. Even from that distance they could sense his impotent rage. The orcs spurred their mounts and pushed on.

A while later, well clear of the river, they allowed themselves to slow down.

Riding next to Stryke and Brelan at the column's head, Pepperdyne had a question. 'Does that count as a rout or a success?' he wondered.

'Bit of both,' Stryke replied.

'I'd say that's a generous way of seeing it.'

'We did damage. And the way the humans tried to spring their trap could have been handled better, lucky for us.'

'I'm wondering if it was worth upward of forty of our lives,' Brelan said.

'And now we've got a traitor to contend with,' Pepperdyne added.

'We don't know that,' Brelan came back irately. 'It could have been chance.'

'Oh, come *on*.'

'Maybe Hacher was doing a snap inspection or something, and—'

'And at the same time they just happened to find the entrance to the catacombs minutes after we went in? Listen to yourself.'

'Face it, Brelan,' Stryke said. 'The odds are somebody informed on us.'

'The resistance are loyal,' Brelan stated indignantly. 'You'll find no betrayal in our ranks.'

'Didn't say there was.'

'What *are* you saying then? Because if there is a spy, and it wasn't an Acurial orc, that doesn't leave much scope, does it?'

'I'm as sure of the Wolverines as you are of your comrades.'

'Can you speak for all of them?' He glanced at Pepperdyne. 'Even those not of our kind?'

'I vouch for them all,' Stryke replied, unswerving.

'I hope you don't need to eat those word. I've things to do.' Brelan turned his horse and rode back down the column.

Pepperdyne looked to Stryke. 'Thanks.'

'I'm trusting you to deserve it. If I'm wrong . . . well, you'll know about it.'

Before the human could reply, Coilla galloped alongside.

'What's wrong with Brelan?' she asked. 'He shot past me with a face like a corpse.'

'He's pissed off about the way it went,' Stryke said. 'Only natural.'

'And he's tetchy about the idea of a traitor in his group,' Pepperdyne added. 'But I guess that's natural too.'

'What is it, Coilla?' Stryke wanted to know.

'I finished checking the wounded, like you asked. We've got two likely to lose limbs. The rest's all minor stuff. Not bad, considering.'

'No. I need to talk to you, Coilla. Alone.' He gave Pepperdyne a pointed look.

'Don't mind me,' the human responded. He dropped back along the column.

'Have you got it?' Stryke said.

Coilla's expression was blank. 'What?'

'The *star*.' He looked pained at her not immediately knowing what he meant.

'Oh. Course I have.' She slipped a hand into her jerkin and brought out the instrumentality just enough that only he could see it.

'Good. Guard it well. Above all else.'

'You know I will.' She stuffed it back. 'Really, Stryke, you're obsessed with this thing. Relax, and trust me.'

29

The resistance let a week pass to lie low and regroup before renewing their harassment of the occupiers. In turn, the authorities bore down ever harder on the occupied.

With the possibility of a spy in their midst, the rebels trod warily, conscious that they could be exposed at any time. Stryke wasn't alone in thinking that the humans and dwarfs in his group were looked on with suspicion. A feeling strengthened perhaps when Jup's power of farsight had been revealed to Chillder, for all that the Wolverines tried to brush it off as mere 'intuition'.

The band found itself fully employed helping to put pressure on the humans. The Vixens, too, played their part in stirring things up. As reward, the first signs of disobedience by the general populace showed themselves. The hoped-for revolution started to look like more than a possibility.

Adding to the tension, and assuming the prediction was true, the comet Grilan-Zeat was expected almost hourly.

But for Stryke and his band one mission was paramount.

The plot to assassinate Jennesta was known to very few, even within the Wolverines. Stryke kept his team small, picking only Coilla and Haskeer, with Eldo and Noskaa as back-ups. A sufficient number as the plan depended on stealth, not force of arms. Equipped with a rough map of the interior, supplied by sympathisers working as menials in the fortress, Stryke and the others set out on the first cloudy night.

Like all old castles, Taress' fortress was large and rambling, having been added to and refashioned over centuries. Such an acreage meant many walls to protect and doors to be kept barred. One particular annexe, projecting from the fort's eastern side and unprotected by the older moat, was where the daily needs of a garrison were most obvious. The kitchens and food stores were there, alongside the heaps of vegetable waste, stripped carcasses and other flyblown detritus waiting to be hauled away. It was the province of servants, and welcome to it.

There were guards, as everywhere on the perimeter, but they were few and Stryke had been told their routine. Furtive blades easily dealt with them, and their bodies were hidden in piles of refuse.

Finding a recessed door, Stryke softly knocked. The response was so long coming he was about to rap again when the sound of drawing bolts was heard. The door creaked open a crack and anxious eyes surveyed the group. Then it was pulled wide to usher them in.

The orc who admitted them was aged and crook-backed. He wore a once-white apron, grubby from toil and bloodstained.

'You know what you have to do?' Stryke said.

'It's little enough,' the servant replied. 'I get you in. After that you're on your own.'

'What about you?'

'I'll go missing as soon as you're in, and I won't be the only one tonight.' He stared at the group with rheumy eyes. 'I don't know who you are, but if you're here to put paid to that . . . hell cat, I pray the gods are with you.'

'You mean Jennesta.'

'Who else?'

'It'd be better if you didn't know why we're here. For your own safety.'

The old one nodded. 'I hope it's her. The bitch. You wouldn't believe the depravity since she got here.'

'I think we would,' Coilla told him.

'Time's pressing,' Stryke reminded them. 'It won't be long before those sentries are found and—'

'Follow me,' the servant instructed, reaching for a glowing lantern on a shelf by the door.

He led them through corridors and twisting passageways, up small flights of steps and down deep staircases. Until at last they reached a heavy door, which he unlocked with a brass key. There were more steps inside, going down to a dim passage.

'This is one of the tunnels we use to service our betters,' he all but spat the word, 'without them having to suffer the indignity of looking at us.'

'We seem to spend a lot of time in tunnels these days,' Haskeer observed.

The tunnel proved as ill-lit as they expected, and damp ran freely on the walls; a reminder that they were passing under the moat.

They came to another door.

'Beyond that, you're in the castle proper,' the old menial explained. 'That's when your map comes into play. Take this.' He thrust the lamp into Haskeer's hands. 'My eyes are used to the gloom down here. Now go! The door's unlocked, we've seen to that. And good luck.' He turned and shuffled off into the shadows.

They approached the door cautiously. On the other side was a corridor. It was unlit, but there were hangings and items of heavy wooden furniture against the walls, indicating that they'd moved from the world of servers to the served.

With Haskeer holding up the lamp, Stryke got out the map and laid it on an ornately carved half moon table. He'd already done his best to remember most of it, and what he saw confirmed his recollection.

'We should be here,' he said, tapping a finger on the parchment. 'Our quarry's high up. Five flights. So we need to go . . . that way.' He pointed to the right.

The corridor was long and branched off in various places. But they kept straight on to the end and a twisting stone staircase.

'This is only for servants too,' Stryke said, 'and if we've been told right, they'll not be using it tonight.'

'What about guards?' Coilla asked. 'There have to be some.'

'The map shows where the permanent ones are stationed. They're where you'd expect; the governor's private quarters and the like. We don't know about patrols.'

'Which are likely to be random, right.'

'So stay sharp.'

They began to climb.

A few hundred steps took them to the first landing. Two doors were there, both firmly shut. They crept past them. The next floor was the same; closed doors, no sign of anyone. Things were different on the third. Here the landing opened directly on to a corridor.

It was richly carpeted, and they caught glimpses of fine paintings as they stole by. The fourth level was again open, like the one below. On the fifth they found a door unlike any other. It was lavishly ornamented, too much so, though its decoration was old and beginning to fade.

'Remember,' Stryke reminded them, 'it's a sharp turn to the right then two passages down.' He looked to Noskaa. 'You're guarding this door. If we're not back soon, get out. Fast.'

The grunt nodded.

'Now let's see if this door's unlocked,' Stryke said, reaching for the handle.

'And if there's magic?' Coilla wanted to know.

'We trust our blades to better it.' He turned the handle.

The door opened on to a corridor that spoke of the status of those who walked it. Brightly lit, it was sumptuously carpeted and exquisitely embellished.

'You won't need that,' Stryke whispered, indicating Haskeer's lantern.

The sergeant gratefully dumped it on a nearby cushioned chair.

They took the right turn and padded along to the second corridor on their left.

'You're stationed here, Eldo,' Stryke ordered, strengthening his line of escape. 'Same as I said to Noskaa; if we're not back, or you think we're lost, get yourself out. Otherwise, if anybody comes near, drop 'em.'

'Got it, Captain.'

Stryke, Coilla and Haskeer entered the corridor. It was as handsome as the other, but there were no doors. Ahead of them, about as far as Haskeer could throw an enemy's leg, it turned sharply to the right.

When they got to the corner, Stryke whispered, 'We think they'll be a couple of them. It'll have to be quick, and true.'

Coilla nodded and plucked a throwing knife from her arm scabbard. She gave it to him and drew another for herself.

'Ready?' Stryke said.

She nodded.

'Now.'

They swiftly rounded the corner. They were in a short corridor that stretched to a set of imposing double doors. Two sentries stood by them.

Coilla, the better thrower, was first to get a bead. She tossed her blade and brought down one of the guards cleanly. Stryke's throw hit home, but it wasn't fatal, his target catching the blade near his shoulder. Coilla quickly grabbed a second knife, lobbed it and finished the job.

'Thanks,' Stryke mouthed.

Joined by Haskeer, they moved towards the doors. About halfway there, they noticed an opening on their right, which turned out to be a passageway. Its entrance was askew, the right side protruding further than the left, so that it was hard to make out until almost on it.

'Shit,' Coilla hissed, 'that wasn't on the map.'

As she spoke, the sound of muffled boots came to them. Before they could react, a guards patrol came out of the hidden passage. They looked as surprised to see the orcs as the orcs were to see them. But the spell was not long breaking.

The guards charged. The trio met them, steel on steel.

'We'll handle this!' Coilla yelled. 'Go! *Go!*'

Stryke dodged a swinging blade and sprinted for the double doors. He struck them at speed and they flew inward, nearly putting him on the floor of the room he tumbled into. Then by some agency the doors slammed shut behind him. He spun, gripped the handles and pulled, but they wouldn't be moved.

Jennesta's suite was extensive and opulently appointed. It also seemed empty. There was a grand bed, draped in sheerest silks and dotted with gold-tasselled cushions. But there was no sign of anyone having used it.

Stryke was about to try one of the two doors in the room when the nearest opened.

Kapple Hacher strode in.

'I don't think we've met,' he stated evenly.

'I know who you are,' Stryke said.

'Then perhaps you also know that no one enters this citadel uninvited. Not if they want to live.'

'My business isn't with you, and you won't stop me.'

'We'll see.'

'Just you, is it? No platoon of troopers to back you up?'

'You're not worthy of it. Besides, I need no help dealing with your kind.'

'Bigot.'

'*Liberator*, if you don't mind. We invaded this land to stop them using weapons of magical destruction against us.'

'That's bull. Orcs don't have a way with magic. Where were they, these weapons?'

'We haven't actually found any yet, but—'

'Lies. A ploy to invade. And who the hell were you liberating?'

'Those many orcs who wanted to avoid the consequences of their masters using their hidden magic against us. You could say we were invited, in an unspoken kind of way.'

'You can't believe that. You've seen the orcs here. They're placid. They'd never have threatened you.'

'Not all your kind are placid, it seems. Are you not from here?'

'You're right. Not all orcs are placid, not at heart. They're aggressive, tough. Warriors far greater than humans.'

Hacher laughed scornfully. 'Not on the evidence I've seen. And a few freaks of nature like you won't change it.'

'So why waste words?'

'Why indeed?' Hacher drew his sword.

Stryke pulled free his own and they set to.

For Hacher, old enough and high ranking enough to have been taught in a classical style, fighting was *fencing*. To him, a scrap was a duel. As far as Stryke was concerned, a scrap was a scrap.

It came down to undoubted skill and stylishness versus seasoned brute determination.

Hacher fenced, Stryke hacked. Hacher blocked passes with dexterity and put together complex attacks. Stryke battered away and thought only of skewering his opponent's lungs.

In the end an orc's fury and stamina proved the better. Bludgeoning the general's defences, he found a breach and sent his blade through it. The sword pierced Hacher between breastbone and shoulder. It wasn't a deep wound, but enough to offset him and he fell, losing his sword.

Stryke moved in to finish the task. Then stopped.

A presence had entered the room. Somebody who didn't have to speak to command attention. He turned from Hacher and stared.

Jennesta was dressed in black, with leather playing a major part in her ensemble. She wore a choker bristling with glinting spikes, and smaller versions on her wrists. There was something unnameable and almost palpable about her. It was a kind of allure, mixed with equal parts of revulsion. She exuded a power, and there was very little light in it.

Stryke couldn't quite stem a feeling of awe. He had a hint, deep down, of an emotion orcs found alien. Fear.

'It's been a long time,' she said, her tone surprisingly mild.

'Yes,' he said, tritely and feeling like a hatchling.

'You know, you should really bow to me. After all, technically you're still in my service. I never released you from it.'

'We don't bow and scrape since we took our freedom.'

'That wasn't all you took, was it?'

Stryke stopped himself from sending a hand to the pouch he carried the stars in. He said nothing.

'But we're going to put that right at last,' she told him. 'We're going to—'

Hacher groaned.

She swung her head to him, furious. 'Oh get out, you useless wretch. Go and have that seen to. Though why I don't let you bleed to death . . .'

'Will you be safe with him?' Hacher asked.

'You certainly weren't! There's nothing here that's beyond me. Now *get out!*'

The general climbed to his feet and limped to the door, a hand pressed against his bleeding wound.

When he left she refocused on Stryke. 'Where were we? Oh, yes, the instrumentalities.' Her face screwed with wrath. 'They were rightly *mine*. I searched years for them and you've added years more. That's not something I tolerate.'

'They're not for the taking,' Stryke informed her.

'Oh yes they are. The taking, and a lingering death as reward for your insolence.'

'Then you won't mind a condemned orc's last request. How did you escape? After you—'

'After my dear father consigned me to the vortex, you mean, in the hope that I'd be torn to pieces? No, I won't. I don't grant wishes. You can die wondering.'

'And you've climbed high in the world of humans. I'd like to know how.'

'Humans are scum. I've nothing but contempt for them. They're just a means. How I rose among them is something else I won't trouble you with. But it was absurdly easy, I'll say that.'

'Ever the conniver.'

'Realist.' Unexpectedly, her tone became even, almost conversational. 'You know, it's a pity things worked out as they did. You were a good slave once. I might have given you a high position in my service. And when I think about it, we do have something in common, don't we?'

'What in hell could that be?'

'No home. No realm in my case,' she added bitterly. 'Neither of us has roots, somewhere we can have allegiance to. But at least you have your own kind. There aren't many like me.'

'I believe it. What are you saying, Jennesta?' He felt a little flip in his stomach for using a term other than 'Your Majesty'. 'That you want me back in your service?'

'Gracious, no. I was just dangling something you couldn't have in front of you. No reprieves.'

Stryke lunged at her, bringing up his sword. She quickly moved her hands in some unfathomable way.

He froze. Try as he might, not all his strength could make him move. He stood like a statue, sword outstretched, body tensed for the thrust.

She laughed at him. Then she called out in some guttural, arcane tongue. Half a minute later two of her lumbering zombies shambled in.

'You know what to do,' she told them without bothering to look their way.

They shuffled to Stryke and began pawing at his clothes. Their soft, bony fingers probed his pockets. Yellow skeletal hands searched for his belt pouches. This close, the foul smell of the creatures was overpowering. But Stryke was powerless to shift, no matter how hard he struggled.

Inevitably one of the goons found the pouch of stars. When he upended it and they tumbled to the carpet, Jennesta's face lit up with an awful fire. She rushed to the spot, clouting aside the zombie who tipped the bag, as though in penalty for his disrespect.

Kneeling, she took up the stars with reverence. If she was disappointed at finding only four, she didn't show it. Which some small part of Stryke's writhing mind found strange.

'These will give me a power you can't imagine,' she boasted, flaunting the stars at Stryke. 'I won't have a mere realm. I'll have *realms*. The dominance of not one but many worlds. And it starts with an orc army as obedient as these two.' Jennesta nodded at the undead. 'Pity you won't see it.' She lifted a hand.

The double doors crashed open. Haskeer charged in, carrying a wooden bench, which he casually tossed to the floor. Coilla was right behind him, sword and dagger in hand.

The intrusion threw Jennesta, and for an instant her attention wandered, breaking whatever hold she had on Stryke. Freed, he carried through with the suspended thrust, no matter that Jennesta was no longer in front of him, and almost fell. Shaking himself, he made ready to strike again.

Coilla got there first. As Stryke thawed she sent a knife Jennesta's way. It struck her, hilt first, on the temple. The sorceress cried out, part in pain, mostly in fury. There was something like blood on her forehead, had it been blood's colour. Drawing back from what may well have been the only physical blow she had ever received, Jennesta called out in the secret tongue.

The pair of zombies immediately became animated. Moving surprisingly fast, they obeyed their mistress and attacked. Haskeer ran to meet them, straight off plunging his blade into the nearest one's chest. The tip erupted from the zombie's back, but in a plume of dust, not a surge of blood. Haskeer wrenched the sword free. The zombie, still standing, swayed for a second. Then he carried on as though nothing had happened. Haskeer tried again, and this time his sword went well into the belly. The zombie hardly broke step.

'We can't kill 'em!' Haskeer roared.

'Depends how you do it!' Coilla shouted back. Rushing at the next goon she gave a swipe that completely severed his arm. The limb fell uselessly to the floor, the zombie kept coming.

'Chop 'em into bits?' Haskeer queried.

He didn't get an answer. There was a commotion outside the wrecked double doors. Men shouting and running feet, heading their way.

More of a threat as far as Coilla was concerned, Jennesta seemed to have gathered herself, if the twisted expression she wore and the gestures she was making with her hands meant anything.

Coilla saw a route out. It was risky, and could have killed them as easily as staying here. But it was a chance. She grabbed Stryke and Haskeer's arms and drew them to her.

'Window!' she yelled.

'Huh?' Haskeer grunted.

'*Window!*' she repeated, pointing to the floor-to-ceiling framed glass doors at one end of the room.

Haskeer got it. 'Right!'

They began to run as shouting guards spilled into the room. Stryke, between Coilla and Haskeer, and as much propelled by them as his own efforts, was still woozy. His head cleared instantly when he saw the windows rushing towards them.

He managed to yell, 'She's got the sta—'

A cacophony of breaking glass and snapping wood drowned him out.

Then they were in silence. Falling. Seeing flashes of stars through cloud in the night sky. Followed by the tops of other buildings and the dark ground.

They landed in the moat quite close together, all things considered. The fall hurt them, but didn't irreparably harm them, though the water was cold and foul enough to instantly sober them. They swam to the edge and scrambled out. Eldo and Noskaa were waiting tensely nearby. All five melted into the night.

They left Jennesta playing with her toys.

'I can't believe you left it here!' Stryke grumbled as they were let into the current safe house, their clothes still wringing.

'*I* can't believe you took yours *with* you!' Coilla snapped back. 'Talk about a lion's den.'

'I thought carrying the stars was the best way of protecting them. I was wrong. But that doesn't excuse you putting yours at risk.'

'Stryke, if I'd had it on me back there she could have got them all. I thought hiding it was the safest.'

'And didn't tell me.'

'You only would have got . . . the way you are about it now. You need never have known.'

Moving into the house, they heard a commotion. Resistance orcs were hurrying to and fro, and there was a crowd in a side room.

'Oh, no,' Coilla groaned.

'What?' Stryke said, alarm rising.

'Better find out.' She headed for the crowded room, Stryke right behind her.

Elbowing in, they found Brelan, Chillder and Jup at the heart of it. They were staring at a small strongbox lying on the floor, its lid wrenched open.

'How did you fare?' Jup asked expectantly.

'We didn't,' Coilla admitted.

There were groans and words of sympathy from the crowd, which was increasing.

'What's going on here?' Stryke said.

'Oh,' Jup replied, 'yes, it's strange, and disturbing.'

'What happened?'

'It seems somebody broke in and cracked open this strongbox.'

'Got in? In this place? With so many around and all the security?'

'There's signs. Stove-in window at the back. Lock broke on this door.' He nodded to the entrance. 'What we're trying to figure out is who the box belongs to.'

'It's mine,' Coilla said.

'Don't tell me,' Stryke pleaded in an undertone.

Grim faced, she gave him a tiny nod.

'Yours?' Chillder said.

'I had it hidden behind that loose brick over there.' Coilla indicated the spot where the brick had been discarded, next to its empty hollow.

'Whoever it was, found it,' Brelan said. 'But they don't seem to have taken anything else. Was there something valuable in it?'

She paused for a moment, then answered, 'No, just some keepsakes. Junk mostly, but I was fond of it.'

'Why should anybody steal junk?' Chillder asked, her gaze fixed on Coilla.

'More important,' Brelan said, 'is *how*? If somebody can get in here this easily our security needs beefing up. A lot.'

'If it *was* somebody from outside,' Stryke offered.

'What?'

'There's another possibility.'

Brelan frowned as realisation dawned. 'Not that again, Stryke. I've told you the loyalty of our group is—'

'I'm just saying it's possible. So would it hurt to check everybody here?'

'*Search* them? Even if that wasn't repugnant it can't be done. There's been a steady stream in and out today, and I would have thought a thief wouldn't linger. But *search* them, for what Coilla's says is junk? Get a grip, Stryke. Making this place secure comes first. So if you don't mind, I'd like to hear about tonight's failure, but—'

'It could have been treachery again,' Stryke told him.

Brelan gave him a hard look and said, 'You might dry yourselves,' as he walked out.

The onlookers were largely silent now, and craned curiously. Stryke felt like he was in a zoo. He gathered Jup and, along with Coilla and Haskeer, went to find a quiet place. When they found it, round a table at the back of a noisy room, with a fire to steam their wet clothes, Stryke broke the news to Jup.

'Damn it, Stryke,' the dwarf came back, 'that's a blow.'

'You must hate my guts, Stryke,' Coilla said.

He shook his head. 'No. I gave you the responsibility, and you acted as best you could. I'm the greater fool for handing her the stars on a plate.'

'Do you think she's got the other one, my one?'

'Amazed if she hasn't.'

'Jennesta with all five instrumentalities,' Jup muttered. 'Doesn't bear thinking on.'

'And us stuck here,' Haskeer put in.

'It's going to be fun telling the rest of the band,' Coilla remarked.

'Oh, *no*,' Haskeer moaned. 'Does it mean we're stuck with those two humans?'

Standeven could be seen on the other side of room, sitting alone and sipping something from a tumbler as more productive work went on around him.

'I'm getting the stars back,' Stryke vowed darkly. 'They're going to be back in our hands if it kills me.'

'A good prospect with Jennesta,' Jup reckoned.

'So we're fucked,' Haskeer said.

'Oh, I don't know,' Jup replied. 'Look at it objectively. This is a fair land, nothing like Maras-Dantia. I don't know about Ceragan, but is that any better?'

'It isn't occupied by humans,' Coilla informed him.

'That won't last. There's a revolution brewing, and we helped fire it. So there's prospect for fighting, seeing the orcs in these parts right, which is what we set out to do, and a comely home at the end of it. Could be worse.'

Coilla smiled, not broadly. 'Nice try. Though I wonder how you and Spurral would feel in a world of orcs.'

'I'd be honoured.'

She raised her cup of wine to toast him for the compliment. 'Perhaps you're right and we'll have to make the best of it.'

'We'll have the stars,' Stryke promised. 'I meant it when I said—'

'Sssshhh!' Coilla had her finger to her lips. She nodded towards the door. Chillder was hurrying their way.

'It's here!' she beamed. 'Grilan-Zeat. The *comet*. It's arrived! Come and look!'

They got up and followed her. Everybody else in the room was heading for the doors.

Outside the farmhouse there was a silent, growing crowd of resistance members. All had their heads back, staring at the sky. Stryke and the others followed their gaze. They saw a light in the heavens. It was small, about the size of the smallest coin held out at arm's length, and had a misty, watery aspect. But it gave out light of a kind unlike anything else in the night sky, and it seemed somehow to have a purpose.

'Wonderful, isn't it?' Chillder said, sidling up to them. 'Now my mother can issue her call to arms. Then we'll see what the orcs of Acurial are made of.'

Stryke feared that might be the case.

'If they got this right,' Haskeer announced, 'maybe the heroes bit's true, too.' He sounded hopeful.

Stryke spotted Wheam in the crowd, looking up enraptured. Dallog was nearby, and most of the recruits from Ceragan. Staring. Transfixed by the wonder and mystery of it. He knew orcs all over Taress, all over the land, would be seeing the same, and he wondered what they'd make of it.

'It'll grow!' Chillder promised. 'The nearer it gets, the bigger.'

Coilla had drifted apart from the others. She found a stretch of low wall and sat to watch the sky. She felt contrition for her carelessness, but strangely that wasn't the major thing on her mind. As she gazed at the comet and heard the droned conversations from the crowd, she realised how different this land was. Not in big ways, but in small differences that were enough to throw you off. She felt drained, and very tired.

Jup had spotted her sitting alone and, guessing she might need cheer, left Spurral and made for her.

He hauled himself up next to her, his feet not quite scraping the ground, and said, 'It's not the end of the world, you know.'

'No,' Coilla said, 'but you can almost see it from here.'

ORCS

BAD BLOOD II

Army of Shadows

This Wolverines adventure is dedicated to
Elaine and Sam Clarke and Anna and Rod Fry,
with love and best wishes for the even greater
escapade they've embarked upon.

Of Omens, Revolts
and Legendary Heroes

After escaping Maras-Dantia, their chaotic birthplace, the survivors of orcs warband the Wolverines settled in Ceragan, a world populated solely by their own kind. Stryke, the band's leader, took native female Thirzarr as his mate, siring two male hatchlings. But by the time the oldest of Stryke's offspring was four, the band had grown restless with their bucolic life.

While hunting, Stryke and Wolverine sergeant Haskeer found themselves near the cave where the warband arrived in Ceragan, and were shocked when an unknown human emerged. But the man was mortally wounded, a dagger jutting from his back. A search of the corpse turned up an amulet bearing strange markings, and a gemstone.

The magical stone issued a message from Tentarr Arngrim, known to the Wolverines as Serapheim, the wizard who made possible their escape from Maras-Dantia. It included images of orcs in another world being cruelly subjugated by humans, and to Stryke and Haskeer's dismay they appeared not to be fighting back. Even more shocking, the architect of their oppression was shown as Serapheim's malevolent daughter, sorceress queen Jennesta, the warband's old enemy and once their ruler.

Arngrim's likeness asserted that it was in the Wolverines' power to help these fellow orcs and exact revenge on Jennesta. To do so they would have to use the five mysterious artefacts called instrumentalities – known to the orcs as stars – which Serapheim created and the warband still possessed. The instrumentalities allowed dimension-hopping, and perhaps more, and were the means by which the Wolverines were transported to Ceragan. Had someone not murdered him, Serapheim's messenger would have acted as the band's guide.

Wanting to accept the challenge, despite his suspicions of Arngrim's motives, Stryke guessed that the symbols on the amulet showed how the stars should be fitted together in order to travel to other worlds. Gathering the scattered members of the Wolverines, he found they were as keen on the mission as he was.

Stryke stood at the warband's head, as captain. Below him were two sergeants, one of whom was Haskeer. The other would have been the band's only dwarf, Jup, had he not elected to stay in Maras-Dantia. Under them came two corporals. Again, one was missing; but it was death, not the gulf between worlds, that separated Alfray from the Wolverines. The other corporal was Coilla, the sole female member, and their Mistress of Strategy. Beneath the officers were thirty privates. Or would have been if six hadn't fallen along the way.

To make up the strength, Stryke enlisted half a dozen native warriors, all tyros; and to replace Alfray as second corporal he chose an ageing orc called Dallog. None of which pleased Haskeer, who was even less happy when local chieftain Quoll forced Stryke to include his foppish offspring, Wheam, on the mission. Stryke decided that the band would go back to Maras-Dantia to try to find Jup, in hope of him resuming his role as sergeant. If he was still alive.

After an alarming transference, they found Maras-Dantia in an even worse state than when they left. The magical energy that coursed through the land had grown much weaker, and what remained was corrupted and malign.

Almost as soon as the Wolverines arrived they were attacked by human marauders. One new recruit, and Liffin, a seasoned member, were killed. As Liffin died defending Wheam, Haskeer's contempt for the youth increased. Stryke pushed the band onward to Quatt, the dwarfs' homeland, a journey fraught with peril.

An unknown number of instrumentalities exist, spread across the infinity of dimensions. Activation of the warband's set was detected by a covert group called the Gateway Corps. A multi-race assemblage of great antiquity, dedicated to the task of keeping the portals between worlds sealed off, the Corps hunted down instrumentalities. Corps leader Karrell Rivers, a human, ordered his second-in-command, elf female Pelli Madayar, to recover the instrumentalities held by the Wolverines. Her unit armed with potent magical weaponry, Pelli's brief was to stop at nothing to achieve her mission.

The Wolverines battled their way to Quatt and found Jup, and were surprised to discover he had acquired a mate, Spurral. Wearied by Maras-Dantia's increasing deterioration, Jup agreed to rejoin the band, but insisted that Spurral went along too.

Before they could leave, the Wolverines encountered humans Micalor Standeven and Jode Pepperdyne, who warned them of an imminent raid by religious fanatics. Despite their loathing and distrust of humans, the orcs heeded them, and with the dwarfs beat off the attack. During the fight, Pepperdyne, a superb warrior, saved Coilla's life. Standeven proved less heroic.

The Wolverines weren't aware that Pepperdyne was little more than Standeven's slave. Nor did they know that the pair were on the run from a despot called Kantor Hammrik, to whom Standeven was in debt. Standeven and Pepperdyne only avoided being executed by Hammrik because Pepperdyne played on the tyrant's desire to possess the fabled instrumentalities. Convincing him that they could locate a set in the so-called barbarous lands of Maras-Dantia, Standeven and Pepperdyne were dispatched there by Hammrik under armed escort, but overcame their guards. The tale they told the Wolverines was that they were merchants wronged by Jennesta, and were seeking revenge on her. In reality, Standeven coveted the instrumentalities the Wolverines held, intending to use them as a bargaining chip with Hammrik.

Irate that the Wolverines had brought trouble to their settlement, the dwarfs turned on them. The band, along with Jup, Spurral and the two humans, found themselves cornered in a blazing longhouse. Realising the only way to escape was by using the stars, Stryke aligned them for what he hoped was the world of their mission.

The warband materialised in the verdant terrain of Acurial, whose indigenous population of orcs had lost their martial instincts. Exploiting this weakness, the human Peczan empire had invaded under the pretext that Acurial possessed destructive magical weapons, and their occupation was brutal.

The Wolverines soon tangled with the invaders in Taress, the capital, and were startled to discover that the humans, a race with no talent for sorcery in Maras-Dantia, commanded powerful magic in Acurial. They had another jolt on learning that not all the orcs of Acurial were docile. Facing overwhelming odds, they were rescued by a group of orc resistance fighters, and spirited away by them.

Outbreaks of native opposition were a thorn in the side of Kapple Hacher, General of the occupying army and Governor of what the Peczan empire considered a province. He shouldered the burden alongside Brother Grentor, the High Cleric of the Order of the Helix, custodians and practitioners of the magic.

The resistance group was headed by twins Brelan and his sister Chillder. The movement's leader in hiding was their mother, Sylandya, who before the invasion was Acurial's ruler, bearing the title Primary. Stryke persuaded them that he and his band had come from the wilderness of the far north, where some humans allied themselves with orcs, to explain Pepperdyne and Standeven, and where dwarfs, unknown in Acurial proper, were commonplace. The mythical northern orcs, he told them, had never lost their taste for combat. Sceptical of Stryke's story, the resistance decided that the Wolverines could join them if they proved their mettle. Their task was to free resistance prisoners awaiting execution. With half the band held as hostages, under penalty of death for failure, Stryke liberated the prisoners.

The Wolverines set about helping to train and organise the rebels; and Coilla persuaded Brelan and Chillder to agree to her forming an all-female fighting unit dubbed the Vixens.

When the occupiers of Acurial sent a feared envoy to Taress to oversee the suppression of resistance, it turned out to be Jennesta. Having somehow survived her fate in Maras-Dantia, she had risen to a position of power and influence in the Peczan empire, and was also titular head of the Order of the Helix. The Gateway Corps secretly arrived in Taress too, and prepared to retrieve the instrumentalities, whatever the cost.

More than a century before, two chieftains had vied for leadership of Acurial. At the height of the crisis a comet appeared. It was taken as a portent, and the two agreed to rule in harness; a reign that proved beneficial. From old records the resistance discovered that the comet, named Grilan-Zeat in the chieftains' honour, returned at precise intervals, and that it was due back imminently. The resistance's hope was that the comet would be seen as an augury, and that, along with a rallying call from Sylandya, would inspire the populace to rise up. A prophecy connected to the comet stated that its arrival would be accompanied by a heroic band of liberators. To the Wolverines' astonishment, the resistance thought the warband might be these long-awaited saviours, or at least could be presented as such to inspire the masses.

The resistance stepped up their activity with the aim of provoking greater repression, in the hope that this would goad the placid majority of orcs into reacting. Sylandya's belief was that if pushed hard enough the orcs of Acurial would have their martial spirit rekindled.

A series of assaults on Peczan interests proved successful, until an ambitious raid on one of the occupiers' garrisons went disastrously wrong. Upping the stakes, the Wolverines launched a bid to assassinate Jennesta. This, too, was foiled, and ended with the sorceress gaining possession of four of the five instrumentalities. Stryke began to speculate that there could a traitor in the resistance ranks, or perhaps nearer to home. Among those suspected were the humans Standeven and Pepperdyne, despite their apparent support for the rebellion.

Then the fifth star, which Stryke entrusted to Coilla, was stolen from a resistance safe house. The presumption was that it, too, had fallen into Jennesta's hands.

As the comet made its appearance, dim but unmistakable, the Wolverines faced the prospect of being stranded in an alien world.

1

Only five of them were left alive.

They were four privates and an officer, the latter a female. Several bore wounds. All were close to panic.

The defence had been tough and bloody. But the company's ranks had finally broken under the onslaught, forcing the handful of survivors to retreat. They fell back from the breached gates and dashed for refuge. Behind them, the savage creatures poured in on a wave of fear and destruction.

Sprinting across the parade ground the five headed for a barracks block, a building of wood and stone, windowless and with a single door. They piled in and frantically barricaded the entrance with cots and lockers. Outside, the commotion carried on.

'This is one hell of a bolthole,' an infantryman complained. 'There's no way out of here.' He was near the edge, and like the others, sweat-sheened and breathing hard.

'I don't get it,' a comrade said. 'These animals are supposed to be docile.'

'Docile?' another retorted. 'Like hell!'

'What are we going to do?' the fourth wanted to know.

'Get a grip,' their captain told them, doing her best to sound calm. 'There'll be support. We just need to sit tight.'

'Reinforcements, ma'am?' the first queried. 'It'll be a while before we see any out here on the fringes.'

'The more reason to stand firm. Now let's get those wounds seen to. And stay alert!'

They ripped up bedding for dressings and set to binding their injuries. Their captain got them checking their weapons, and scouring the barracks for more. She had them further reinforce the door. Anything to keep them occupied.

'Hey,' one of the troopers said, halting the activity. 'It's gone really quiet out there.'

They listened to the silence.

'Could be they've gone,' a comrade offered, instinctively whispering.

'Maybe the back-up's arrived,' somebody added hopefully.

'So why can't we hear them?'

'Just the sight of reinforcements coming might've scared the creatures off.'

'Care for a wager on that?'

'Stow it!' the Captain snapped. 'Chances are the raiders have pulled out. All we have to do—'

A series of heavy thumps shook the door. They scrambled to it and threw their weight against the barricade. The pounding grew stronger, making the pile of furniture blocking it shudder. Fine clouds of dust began falling from the beamed ceiling.

Something hit the door with a tremendous crash, the shockwave jolting the defenders and sending part of the barricade tumbling. They hardly had time to brace themselves again when there was a second hefty impact. A cabinet toppled. Something made of pottery shattered.

The blows took on a regular, almost rhythmic pattern, each more jarring than the last. The door started to warp and splinter. The remains of their makeshift fortifications were weakening under the assault.

'We . . . can't hold . . . this!' a straining trooper warned.

A battering ram smashed through the door, demolishing what was left of the barricade. Swinging again, the ram destroyed the vestiges of the door and sent debris flying.

The troopers quickly moved away. Save one, caught in the confined space and entangled by wreckage. There was a high-pitched whistle. An arrow flashed through the gaping entranceway and struck him. Two more instantly followed. He went down.

His companions retreated, weapons drawn, and backed along the aisle between the lines of camp beds on either side. Shadowy figures were swarming through the ruined entrance. Ugly, grotesque beasts. Monsters.

The soldiers upended cots and tossed them in their pursuers' path, hoping to slow their progress. A couple of the troopers had shields and deployed them in fear of more arrows. No arrows came, but the repellent creatures kept up their remorseless advance, leaping the obstacles or simply kicking them aside.

Soon the fleeing group came to the barracks' end, an area uncluttered with furnishings, and had no option but to make a stand. They gathered in a knot, backs to the wall, bracing themselves to brave the coming assault as best they could.

There was no let in the creatures' progress. They rushed onward, heedless of the bristling swords intended to keep them at bay.

A frenzy of colliding blades and clashing shields ensued. Soon, screams were added to the cacophony. A trooper collapsed, his skull split by an axe. Another lost an arm to the sweep of a broadsword, then succumbed to multiple stabbing.

The fight grew yet more feverish. Fuelled by desperation, the two remaining defenders battled with ever greater ferocity. In the blizzard of stinging steel one misjudged the tempo of the battering and left open his guard. A sword found his belly; another stroke sliced cleanly through his neck, sending his head bouncing to one side. The headless corpse stood for a second, gushing crimson, before it fell.

Only the captain remained. Bloodstained, panting, her blade near slipping from moist fingers, she readied herself for the final act.

The monsters could have attacked en masse and finished her in an instant. But they held back. Then just one came forward.

It took the captain a moment to realise that the creature was waiting to engage her. She raised her sword. The being mirrored her and they set to.

Silence had fallen again, save for the pealing clatter of their blades. She fenced well, for all she had suffered and witnessed. The beast matched her in skill, though its method relied more on power and a boldness that was almost reckless. Their duel ranged back and forth across the cramped barracks, but none of the other creatures impeded her or tried to join in. They merely watched.

The finale came when the captain suffered a deep gash to her sword arm. A swift follow-through saw her take a further wound to the flank. Staggering, she lost her footing and went down.

The creature stood over her. She looked up into its eyes. What she saw was something more than brutishness. The bestial was there, but tempered with what she could only think of as a kind of empathy. And, perhaps, even a hint of nobility.

It was a fantastical notion, and it was the last one she would ever have.

The monster plunged its blade into the captain's chest.

Wrenching her blade from the female's corpse, Coilla said, 'She fought well.'

'They all did,' Stryke agreed.

'For *humans*,' Haskeer sneered.

More than a dozen other orcs were crowded into the barracks with them. All were Wolverines, with the exception of Brelan, a leader of the Acurial resistance. He elbowed through the throng, barely glancing at the human's body. 'Time we were out of here,' he told them.

They streamed from the barracks. There were over a hundred orcs in the compound, the majority resistance members, along with the rest of the Wolverines and the Vixens, the female warband Coilla led. They were busy scavenging weapons and torching the place. The few humans left alive were mortally injured, and they let them be.

As Brelan's order to evacuate spread, the force began to leave, moving out in small groups or singly. They took their own wounded, but by necessity left their dead.

Stryke, Haskeer and Coilla watched them go. Dallog, the Wolverines' eldest member, and one of the newest, joined them.

'We bloodied their nose good'n' proper,' he remarked.

Stryke nodded. 'We did, Corporal.'

Haskeer shot Dallog a hard look and said nothing.

'The tyros are shaping up well,' Coilla offered by way of compensation.

'Seem to be,' Dallog replied. 'I'm heading off with some of them now.'

'Don't let us keep you,' Haskeer muttered.

Dallog stared at him for a second, then turned and left.

'See you back at HQ!' Coilla called after him.

'Go easy on him, Haskeer,' Stryke said. 'I know he's not Alfray but—'

'Yeah, he's not Alfray. More's the pity.'

Stryke would have had something further to say to his sergeant, and in harsher terms, had Brelan not returned.

'Most have gone. You get going too. Hide your weapons, and remember the curfew starts soon, so don't linger.' He jogged away.

Their target had been well chosen. Being comparatively small, the garrison was a mite easier to overcome than some of its better manned counterparts. And its location, just beyond the outskirts of Taress city, meant it was conveniently isolated. Not that they could afford to ignore caution. There were likely to be patrols in the area, and reinforcements could be quickly summoned.

Outside the fort's broken gates, the last of the raiders were scattering. Donning various disguises, they left in wagons, on horses and, mostly, by foot. The majority would head for Taress, taking different routes, and melt into the capital's labyrinthine back streets.

Haskeer grumpily declared that he wanted to make his way back alone. Stryke was happy to let him. 'But mind what Brelan said about the curfew. And stay out of trouble!'

Haskeer grunted and stomped off.

'So, which way for us, Stryke?' Coilla asked.

'Haskeer's going that way, so . . .'

She pointed in the opposite direction.

'Right.'

The course they chose took them through a couple of open meadows and into a wooded area. They moved at a clip, anxious to put some distance behind them. At their backs the fort burned, belching pillars of black, pungent smoke. Ahead, they could just make out Taress' loftier towers, wine-red in the flaxen light of a summer's evening.

Not for the first time it struck Coilla how much Acurial's rustic landscape differed from Maras-Dantia, the ravaged land of their birth; and how it so resembled their adoptive world of Ceragan.

'I'm sorry,' she said.

Stryke was puzzled. 'About what?'

'Losing the star you trusted me with, probably to Jennesta. I feel such a *fool*.'

'Don't beat yourself up about it. I lost the other four to her too, remember. Who's the bigger fool?'

'Maybe we all are. We were betrayed, Stryke. It must have been somebody in the resistance who took the star I had.'

'Could have been. Then again . . .'

'You can't mean somebody in our band.'

'I don't know. Perhaps an outsider took it.'

'You really believe that?'

'Like I said, I don't know. But from now on we keep things close to our chests.'

She sighed. 'Whatever. Fact is we're still stuck here.'

'Not if I can help it.'

'What d'you mean?'

'I aim to get the stars back.'

'From Jennesta? From the whole damn Peczan empire?'

'There'll be a way. Meantime we've got our work cut out riling the humans.'

'Well, we struck a blow today.'

'Yeah, and the orcs of this world are waking up. Some of 'em anyway.'

'Wish I had as much faith in them as you do. The resistance's gaining a few new recruits, true. But enough for an uprising?'

'The more the screw tightens, the more we'll see joining the rebels. We just have to keep goading the humans.'

It was nearly dusk and shadows were lengthening. With the curfew looming they upped their pace some more. The edge of the city was in sight now and lights were coming on. Patrols were a real possibility the nearer they got, and they had to move with stealth. They crossed a stream and began skirting a field of chest-high corn that waved in a clement breeze.

Neither had spoken for some time, until Coilla said, 'Suppose . . . suppose we don't get the stars back. If we're stuck in this world, and whether it has its revolution or not . . . well, what's here for us? What place would we have?'

It was a thought that plagued Stryke too, although he was careful not to voice it to those under his command. His mind turned to what he would lose if they really were trapped in Acurial. He pictured his mate, Thirzarr, and their hatchlings, kept from him by the unbridgeable gulf that separated worlds.

'We'll endure,' he replied. 'Somehow.'

They turned their eyes skyward.

There was a light in the firmament, bigger than any star. It had an ethereal quality, as though it were a burning orb seen through many fathoms of water.

Stryke and Coilla knew it to be an omen. They wondered who it bode ill for.

2

On the other side of the city, beyond its periphery, the terrain was less fitted to growing crops. There were moorlands here, and large stretches of bog, where not much more than scrub and heather grew.

It was a place with a reputation. This was partly due to its poor fertility compared to the verdant land thereabouts. Although *poor* was not quite the right way of describing it. *Perverse* would have been a better word. There was something less than wholesome about the flora that bred here, and the animals that roamed were chiefly carrion eaters. The magical energy that coursed through the world had become corrupted in this spot.

The area also had a bad name because of certain artefacts it housed. These were scattered about the moor in an apparently senseless jumble, though there were those who thought they saw a pattern. The ruins were called monuments, temples, shrines and moot-places, but nobody really knew their true function. Certainly none could guess at the purpose of some of the more perplexing and bizarre structures.

The artefacts were fashioned in stone brought somehow from a distant quarry, and they were immensely ancient. No one knew who built them.

One particular stone formation, by no means the most extra-ordinary, stood at the bleak heart of the moor. It was an arrange-ment of columns and lintels, standing stones and ramparts, that made a whole yet seemed strangely at odds with geometry. Not so much in a way that could be seen, as felt. Through design or decay, sections of the edifice were open to the elements; notably a ring of stone pillars the colour of decaying teeth.

Inside the circle, a light burned.

A block of polished stone, chest high and weighing several tons, was set in the centre. It was worn smooth by age, but the smothering of arcane symbols it bore were carved deep enough that they were still visible. And now a copious quantity of blood, seeping from a pair of eviscerated corpses, made the markings even more distinct. The sacrifices, one male, one female, were human, opportunely provided by a summary judgement of felony.

A lone figure stood by the altar. Those who favour the night and the creatures that walk it would have called her beautiful. She had waist-length, jet-black hair framing a face dominated by dark, unpitying eyes. The face was a mite too wide, particularly at the temples, and the chin tapered almost to a point. Her well-formed mouth was marred only by being more than usually broad. But her skin was perhaps the most startling feature. It had a faint silver-green sheen, resembling tiny fish scales. In short, her beauty was confounding, yet undeniable.

As dusk slipped into full night she undertook a profane ritual.

On the altar before her, alongside the gutted bodies, lay the five instrumentalities stolen from the Wolverines, and which the warband coined stars. They were small spheres, each of a different colour: sandy, green, dark blue, grey and red. All sprouted radiating spikes of varying numbers and lengths. For the sandy sphere they numbered seven; the dark blue had four, the green five, the grey two, and the red nine. The instrumentalities were made from an unknown material – unknown to all but a sorcerer élite, that is – and the Wolverines had found them indestructible.

Next to the instrumentalities stood a small, unembellished silver casket, with its lid open. It contained a quantity of material that was, impossibly, both organic and inert. The substance's texture was part waxy, part old leather, part lichen. It was unpleasant to the touch, but had a sweet aroma. In the parlance of wizards it was known as Receptive Matter. Sorcerers using it for benign purposes sometimes called it Friendly. But never Safe.

The sorceress recited invocations of tongue-tying complexity, and performed certain other rites both intricate and dreadful. Beads of sweat stood out on her brow. She briefly wondered if such a spell might be too taxing even for her.

Then, at the ritual's climax, she thought she heard the instrumentalities sing.

She had a moment of fusion with them. There was a kind of

symbiotic connection, a melding, and brushed by their energy she glimpsed a fragment of their power. What she felt, and saw, was terrifying. Or would have been to any except those who lived by terror. She found it heady.

The Receptive Matter accepted the transfer. It divided and began transmuting into the required shapes. Not long after, exhausted, she gazed at the fruits of her toil and reckoned herself satisfied.

It was not entirely true to say that she was alone in the stone circle. Several others were present, standing at a respectful distance. But as they were technically dead the question of their presence in the normal sense was debatable. They were her personal guardians and fetch-its, the select few nearest to her, whose loyalty was unflinching because they had no other option.

Outside the circle, far enough away for privacy, stood a ring of more conventional protectors in the form of a detachment of imperial guards. Farther back still there was a road, or more accurately a rough track, on which a fleet of carriages was parked. In one of them, two men conferred in whispered tones.

To the conquered orcs of Acurial, Kapple Hacher was known as Iron Hand. He was Peczan's highest representative in the province. Or had been until the empire sent the female they were waiting for. But for all her hints and threats he remained, at least in name, governor; and commander of the occupying army, with the rank of general.

He was entering his years of later maturity. There were lines on his face and hands, but he was as fit as many a younger man, and had seen action before climbing to his present position. His hair, close-cropped, was silver; and he went against tradition somewhat in being clean-shaven. He was a meticulous individual, ramrod-backed and always clad in a pristine uniform. His rivals – and every official had critics in the mire of imperial politics – saw him as being too much in thrall to bureaucracy.

Where Hacher represented the civil and military authority in the province, his companion embodied the spiritual. Brother Grentor was something like half the general's age. It was a measure of his ability that he had risen to become prominent in the Order of the Helix in so short a time. Unlike the general he sported a beard, albeit close-trimmed, and an ample shock of blond hair. The expression he wore was invariably solemn; and as dictated by his title of Elder, he always dressed in the simple brown robes of his order. Grentor had his own detractors, and they held that he too jealously guarded the Order's secrets and privileges.

The soldier and the holy man personified the twin pillars on which rested the Peczan empire. Inevitably, there were tensions between these factions, and a continuous tussle over power and influence, making Grentor and Hacher's relationship occasionally fraught.

Grentor had a lace kerchief pressed to his nose and mouth. He said something, but the words were muffled.

'For the gods' sake speak clearly, man,' Hacher told him.

The Elder gingerly removed the cloth and made a face. 'I said, how you can stand this vile smell of rotting vegetation?'

'I've known worse.'

'It wouldn't be so bad if we hadn't been forced to endure it for so long.' He glanced towards the stone circle. 'Where *is* she?'

'More to the point; what's she doing?'

Grentor shrugged.

'I would have thought you of all people might have known. She is the head of your Order, after all.'

Grentor gave a short, mirthless laugh. 'M'lady doesn't take me into her confidence. I'm only the Elder, after all.'

'I've never heard you sounding so disrespectful of such an important personage,' Hacher needled gently.

'I give respect where it's due. But in this case . . .'

'I did try to warn you about her.'

'No amount of warnings can prepare you for the reality of Jennesta.'

'I'll concede that. But seriously, what do you think she's up to out here? Between ourselves, of course,' he assured him.

'I don't know. Except that it's something important to her, and obviously involves the Craft.'

'It must be vitally important for her to be spending so much time here when there's rising trouble on the streets.'

'Ah, so you're no longer insisting it's all down to a few hot-heads?'

'I still think the number of rebels is comparatively small. But a few can make a lot of trouble.'

'I know. My Order's bearing the brunt of it.'

'Along with the military, Brother,' Hacher replied with a trace of irritability. 'We're all having to deal with it.'

Grentor looked to the stone circle again. 'It could be that whatever she's doing has a bearing on the situation.'

'Some magical solution, you mean? A weapon, perhaps?'

'Who knows?'

'I think it more likely that our lady Jennesta's pursuing some goal of her own. She often seems to put herself before the interests of the empire.'

Grentor didn't take the bait. There was a limit to how far anyone in his position would dare go in criticising Jennesta. 'You've heard what the creatures here think about what's happening in the sky, no doubt,' he said, steering the subject into somewhat safer waters.

'I know they have a name for it. Grilan-Zeat.'

'Yes, and my Order has undertaken some research on the matter.'

Hacher nodded. He knew that in the sect's vernacular so called research often involved torture. 'And what did you find?'

'It's appeared before, apparently. More than once. And there seems to be a regularity about it.'

'I daresay that's of interest to scholars, but what do the comings and goings of heavenly bodies have to do with us?'

'The populace see it as a portent. Or at least some do.'

'Comets are just one of Nature's oddities,' Hacher responded dismissively.

'Signs in the sky should never be ignored, General.'

'Such matters are in your province. They're of no concern to the military.'

'The important thing is how the populace reacts. If they *believe* it to be an omen—'.

'No doubt the rabble-rousers will exploit the masses' superstition. That doesn't mean we can't handle the disturbances.'

'Which will get worse, given the way Jennesta's clamping down on any hint of dissent. She's stirring things up.'

Hacher stiffened. He didn't want to be drawn into the stormy waters of politics any more than Grentor. 'Please don't involve me in the internal machinations of the Order.'

'I'm not trying to. I'm just saying that her actions affect us all. Don't pretend you think she's not making things worse. I don't believe in leniency any more than you do, but we're holding down an entire nation here, and we're few in number. What sense is there in provoking them?'

'You might as well provoke a flock of sheep.'

'Did you know there was a prophecy attached to the appearance of Grilan-Zeat?'

'No, I hadn't heard that particular piece of flummery.'

'It says that the comet is accompanied by a band of heroes. Liberators.'

Hacher snorted derisively. 'Heroes? The orcs are too spineless.'

'Not all of them, evidently.'

'We're talking about a small group of . . . freaks. Generally these creatures are meek. Why else do you think we occupied this land at so little cost?'

'Our research suggests that might not always have been so. The records are far from complete, but they hint that the orcs had a martial history.'

'And you think their fighting spirit could be revived somehow.'

'It's possible. Again, it turns on what they believe.'

'Omens, prophecies, a lost warlike temperament; you're seeing too much in this, Grentor.'

'Perhaps. But isn't it better to be prepared?'

'Planning for contingencies is good military practice, agreed. But you're petitioning the wrong person. Our lady Jennesta holds all the cards now.'

Grentor tugged at the general's sleeve and nodded to the carriage's window. 'Talking of which . . .'

'At last,' Hacher sighed.

Jennesta was returning. She wasn't alone. Three of her personal bodyguards were with her. They were human. Or had been. Considered challengers to her power, Jennesta's sorcery had consigned them to an undead state and made utterly obedient slaves of them. Their eyes were set and glassy, and lacked any vestige of benevolence. Such skin as could be seen was stretched tight, and was of an unwholesome, parchment-like colour. The zombies were combat dressed, in black leather and steel-toed boots, and they were armed with scimitars. One of them carried a steel-banded chest.

Hacher and Grentor were out of the carriage when the little procession arrived. Close to, the zombies stank, and the Elder had his kerchief out again.

'Were your endeavours successful, ma'am?' the general asked.

Jennesta shot him a look laced with suspicion before replying, 'Yes. The energy is particularly strong here, and of a . . . *flavour* I find gratifying.'

She turned away from them to supervise the loading of the trunk into her carriage. From the way she scolded her minions it obviously contained something significant. Not that Hacher or Grentor would have dared ask what.

For his part, Hacher was glad that whatever she had undertaken seemed to have gone well. He thought it might improve her temperament. It was a hope swiftly crushed.

Satisfied that her precious cargo was safely stowed, Jennesta's attention came back to the pair. 'I'm displeased,' she announced.

'Oh?' Hacher responded. 'I thought—'

'Don't. It doesn't become you. There's been more trouble on the streets. Why?'

'A minority inciting the rabble, ma'am. Nothing more.'

'Then why can't you stamp it out?'

'With respect, we can't be everywhere. The territory the imperial forces have to cover—'

'It's nothing to do with numbers, General, as you said yourself. It's what you do with those you have. These upstarts should be hit hard. I know orcs and their inherent savagery, and I've always found that brutality is the best course in a situation like this.'

'If I may be so bold, my lady,' Grentor ventured hesitantly. 'Isn't it possible that harsher action might further aggravate the insurgents?'

'Not if they're dead,' she replied coldly. 'You seem particularly dense on this subject, Elder. You both do. The equation's simple: rebellious heads rear up; we cut them off. What's so hard to understand about that?'

Grentor was anxiously fingering his string of beads and summoning the nerve to say something more.

'*Wait*,' Jennesta said, stilling them with a raised hand. She looked up, an expression of concentration on her face, as though she heard something they couldn't.

They stood in silence for what seemed an eternity. Grentor and Hacher began to wonder if this was another of Jennesta's eccentricities. Or, knowing her, the prelude to unpleasantness.

Something swooped out of the darkness. They thought it was a bird. A hawk, perhaps, or a raven. But when it came to rest on Jennesta's outstretched arm they saw it had only the superficial appearance of a bird. In subtle but noticeable ways it was like no bird that ever flew. It had the look of magic about it.

The creature moved along her arm and chirruped gutturally into Jennesta's ear. She listened intently. When it finished she made a gesture, as though brushing a speck of dust from her sleeve. The enchantment was annulled in a soundless explosion, instantly transforming the ersatz bird into a myriad of shimmering, golden sparks. The glowing pinpoints gently faded as they were carried away by the evening breeze. All that lingered was the pungent smell of sulphur.

'I have tidings,' Jennesta told them, her face like flint. 'It seems your minority of troublemakers have wiped out one of our garrisons. If you want a more graphic example of my point, just say so.'

Neither man spoke.

'You two need a little adjustment to your attitudes,' she went on icily. 'Things are going to be different in this land, even if I have to have every orc in it put to the sword. Be assured, change is coming.' She turned and strode towards her carriage.

Hacher and Grentor watched her go. Then, as on every other night during the past several weeks, their eyes were drawn skyward.

There was a new star in the firmament, larger and brighter than all the rest.

3

'*Keep your eyes on the road!*' Stryke bellowed.

'*All right, all right!*' Haskeer yelled, knuckles white on the reins.

In the back of the open wagon Coilla, Dallog, Brelan and new recruit Wheam hung on grimly.

They took a corner at speed. The wagon's wheels lifted on one side, then crashed down at the turn, jarring all of them. Seconds later, half a dozen mounted troopers rounded the bend in hot pursuit. They were quickly followed by a much larger contingent of riders. Some of them had open tunics flapping in the wind, or were minus jackets and headgear altogether, due to the sudden, unexpected start of the chase. Behind them were several wagons filled with militia, and even a buggy carrying a couple of officers. Farther back still, a mob of troops dashed to keep up on foot.

The Wolverines' wagon was in one of Taress' main thorough-fares now, a wide avenue lined with some of the city's more substantial buildings. It thronged with mid-morning crowds, and startled orcs dived clear of the speeding wagon and the humans chasing it.

Stryke's crew weaved through a sea of merchants' carts, lone riders, occupiers' carriages and strings of mules. There were scrapes and collisions, and much cursing and waving of fists. The wagon clipped a trader's handcart, flipping it. Turnips and apples bounced across the road, getting underfoot of horses and passers-by. Riders and pedestrians went down.

Those at the roadside weren't immune. Some of the pursuing humans took to the walkways, scattering bystanders and ploughing through peddlers' stalls. In the process, several riders struck low-hanging awnings and projecting beams, and were unhorsed.

Despite the chaos a substantial number of humans stayed in the chase. And they were beginning to close in on the fleeing wagon. To press their point, they loosed a stream of arrows at it.

A bolt narrowly missed Coilla's head and zinged on over Haskeer's shoulder. He swore loudly and whipped the foaming horses. Another arrow landed at Wheam's feet, embedding itself in a plank. He froze, staring at it. Dallog pulled him to the floor and held him there. The arrows kept coming, zipping overhead and peppering the tailboard.

'Fuck this,' Coilla growled. She took up her own bow and started returning fire.

Brelan, the only other one on board with a bow, followed her lead. The wagon juddered and shook so much that their first shots were wild. Then Coilla got a bead and sent a shaft into the chest of one of the leading humans. The force of the hit catapulted him from his mount. His falling body collided with the riders behind him, downing several more. But it didn't slow the rest.

It didn't do more than briefly interrupt the flow of arrows either. The only solace was that firing from the saddle spoilt the humans' aim. Bolts flew high, wide and low; a couple veered towards the wayside, narrowly missing onlookers. In the rear of the wagon Coilla and Brelan were bobbing up, firing, then bobbing back down. Their shots weren't much more accurate than the humans', but at least kept them busy. At the wagon's front, Stryke and Haskeer were hunched, trying to offer the volatile bolts as small a target as possible.

'Damn!' Brelan cursed. 'I'm out!'

Coilla loosed her final arrow. It missed. 'Me too,' she said.

They quickly ducked as a small swarm of shafts came back at them.

'Try this,' Dallog said. He passed them a thick coil of rope.

Muscles rippling, Coilla flung it at the pursuers, like someone casting a heavy fishing net. Resembling an ungainly discus, the coil spun in a descending arc. It landed in the path of a rider. His horse came to grief on the obstacle, throwing him down to be trampled by the mounts behind. Pounded by hooves, the coil unravelled, tangling several more horses in lashing rope and adding to the confusion.

Brelan hefted an empty crate and launched it over the tailgate. It smashed when it hit the road, strewing wreckage and claiming more casualties. Meanwhile, Dallog and Wheam were zealously ripping up the planks that served as benches. Passed to Brelan and Coilla, they were hurled at the enemy. One human tried to catch the plank hurtling his way. The force of the impact carried him out of his saddle, slamming him to the ground still clutching his dubious prize.

'How much further, Brelan?' Stryke called out.

'Couple of blocks!' He realised where they were. 'Take the next left! Here! *Here!*'

Haskeer tugged viciously on the reins. The wagon swerved sharply and took the corner half on the sidewalk. It also took out a kerbside stall, striking it square on and ploughing through its display of pottery. There was an explosion of broken bowls, flying platters and terracotta shards.

The road they entered was no less crowded. More so, as this was one of Taress' major junctions. The pedestrians who saw them coming ran for their lives. Once it passed, the crowd closed again in the wagon's wake, only to have the horde of humans tear round the corner at their backs. The cavalry fell to hacking at them with sabres as they battled their way through.

The mêlée put a little distance between the orcs and the humans, but Haskeer didn't slow. At their rear, the humans were already emerging from the scrum and picking up speed again. By this time the street ahead was clearer, those further along having seen what was happening and made for cover.

Wheam was shouting. They all turned to look, and saw another wagon gaining on them. It was harnessed to a team of four horses, as opposed to their two, and carried five or six troopers. Haskeer urged on his team, but the greater horsepower of the humans' wagon had it rapidly closing the gap. In seconds, it drew level. The occupants brandished swords, and a couple had spears. As the two wagons neared each other the orcs took up their own weapons and braced themselves.

The humans side-swiped the orcs with a bone-rattling crash. Swords met and the chatter of whetted steel commenced. There was little finesse. Hacking and slashing outbid grace, and the spur was frenzy.

Brelan spilt blood first. More by luck than judgement, one of his swings bit deep into a human's arm, nearly severing it. The man screamed and fell back, showering his comrades with blood. Coilla was next in, driving forward and piercing somebody's lung. She withdrew quickly, narrowly avoiding the thrusts of blades and spears.

Emboldened, Wheam got to his feet and began hacking at the humans too. His efforts were spirited but feeble, his swipes erratic and wide of the mark. Then he overreached himself. Leaning half out of the wagon, stretching to get to a target, his jerkin was grabbed by one of the humans. The man tugged mightily, doing his best to pull the tyro out. Struggling, Wheam let go of his sword. It clattered on the road and was lost. Another human joined in. Wheam started yelling. Coilla and Brelan got hold of him and tried hauling him back. A tug of war developed, with Wheam as the squealing rope.

Dallog joined in, slashing at the pullers. He caught a blade for his trouble. It raked his forearm, forcing him back.

'You all right?' Coilla said.

'Yes!' he shouted, winding a cloth around the wound to staunch the blood flow. 'Look to Wheam!'

'Right,' she replied grittily, and commenced yanking with more determination. Wheam carried on howling.

Up front, Stryke was crossing swords with his human counterpart opposite. The wagons were parting, then bumping and scraping together again, making their duel a strangely disjointed affair. When the gap widened, stretching Wheam and raising his yelping, Stryke and his foe could do no more than exchange scowls. When it closed, they resumed their hacking with renewed zeal.

In the back, they finally freed Wheam. Dragging him into the wagon, Coilla shoved him to the floor and barked, 'Now stay down!'

'Watch out!' Brelan yelled.

Ahead, a driver had abandoned his hay wagon and made off in panic. It was side-on, blocking two-thirds of the highway, its pair of dray horses still hitched.

Haskeer had already seen it. He gave the reins an almighty heave, causing his frothing team to swerve sharply. They avoided the deserted wagon with a hair's breadth to spare. Passing so close spooked the already nervous drays. They lumbered forward a few paces into the gap the orcs had just shot through, blocking more of the road.

The driver of the wagonload of humans, a heartbeat behind, saw the obstruction too late. He tried the same manoeuvre Haskeer had pulled off, tugging desperately on his reins in a bid to steer clear. But the turn was too sharp. The wagon tilted at a crazy angle. Then it jack-knifed and went over, flinging its occupants out and crushing several. As it flipped, the shaft snapped, freeing its team. The quartet of horses bolted, dragging the shaft and striking sparks off the cobblestones.

'That's them fucked,' Haskeer remarked.

'It's not over yet,' Stryke told him, looking over his shoulder.

Their pursuers had reached the wreckage and were bodily shifting it. Those on horseback weaved around.

The orcs' wagon picked up speed again.

'One more turn!' Brelan shouted, indicating a road coming up on their left.

They took the bend at a clip, and found themselves in a narrower, much less crowded street. The humans were still at their backs.

As they progressed, Stryke and the others gave no sign of noticing the shadowy figures positioned in alleyways, in upper windows and on rooftops. They did drop speed, allowing the depleted pack of humans to catch up, but adopted a meandering course to hamper them overtaking.

Once the humans were bunched and slowed, the trap was sprung.

From their hideaways and high places, the resistance loosed a torrent of arrows on their cluster of targets. The cascade of bolts instantly struck down over a score of men. As many were wounded. Some took shelter behind their halted wagons, or used shields to deflect the shafts. Those who tried retreating found their escape route blocked; resistance confederates had rolled hijacked carts across the entrance to the street. Archers were stationed there too, adding to the storm.

Pounded from all sides, the militia lost interest in their quarry.

'Get us out of here,' Stryke said.

Haskeer lashed the horses and they made off at a trot.

Under Brelan's direction, they weaved through Taress' backstreets, keeping to a pace and demeanour they hoped wouldn't attract attention. After a number of twists and turns, taken partly to throw off anyone who might be following them, they arrived in a particularly ill-lit and dilapidated blind alley. It terminated at an apparently solid wooden wall, which to even a close observer passed for the rear of a building whose frontage presumably stood in an adjoining street. It was an illusion. The wall held cunningly concealed doors large enough to admit the wagon. It rolled in, and the doors were hastily secured behind it.

They got out of the wagon in an area the size of a barn. A couple of dozen resistance members were milling around, and several moved in to tend to the sweating horses. Somebody brought Dallog a flask of brandy and dressing for his wound.

Brelan went off to report to his comrades.

Stryke jabbed a thumb doorward. 'That gave 'em something to ponder.'

Coilla stretched her back, fists balled. 'Yeah. Went well.'

''cept for him,' Haskeer complained, glaring at Wheam.

The tyro quaked and started babbling excuses.

'Ah, shut it,' Haskeer growled.

'I was only trying to explain.'

'Dribbling bullshit's what you're doing. As usual.'

'Give the kid a break,' Dallog said. 'He's a tyro.'

'And you're not?'

'I'm saying he's young. We should—'

'We? Not with us long enough to wipe your arse and you're telling me what's what.' He was beginning to seethe.

'No,' Dallog replied evenly, 'I'm just telling you he needs to find his feet.'

'He needs a backbone! He could've fucked the mission!'

'But he didn't.'

'No, I didn't,' Wheam echoed.

'I've had it with you two,' Haskeer said menacingly. He took a step in Dallog's and Wheam's direction.

Stryke put himself in his path. 'You running this band now?'

Haskeer took in his captain's expression. He said nothing and looked away.

'I've had enough of this shit,' Stryke went on. 'So cut the sniping.' With a tilt of his head he indicated the resistance members busy at the far end of the room. 'If any of these local orcs get wind of where we're really from—'.

'Yeah, yeah,' Haskeer muttered.

'I *mean* it, Haskeer. I won't let this thing get screwed by you or anybody else in the band. Got it?'

'Why we doing this?'

'*What?*'

'Why're we fooling around with these rebels when we should be trying to get the stars back?'

It was quite a speech for Haskeer, and for a second, Stryke was stymied. In part, his hesitancy was due to the fact that he held himself responsible for the instrumentalities' loss. 'We help the resistance 'cos it's right,' he said at last. 'As for the stars . . . I'm gonna find 'em.'

'Well, I wish you'd get on with it.'

Haskeer held Stryke's gaze this time, and neither looked likely to back off.

'Lighten up,' Coilla told them. 'We've been in spots tight as this before.'

'Have we?' Haskeer said.

Then he turned and walked away.

4

There was turbulence throughout Acurial, and particularly in its most densely inhabited sector, the capital city of Taress. Responding to civil unrest with a heavy hand, the human occupiers had further increased their repression. Known or suspected dissident haunts were torched. Public gatherings of any size were brutally dispersed. Wayward opinions were silenced. Arrests were arbitrary, torture routine, executions commonplace.

It was what the resistance wanted. Their attacks on the invaders were designed to bring about retribution, in hopes this would goad the citizens out of their passivity and reawaken their slumbering martial spirit. Fed by whispering campaigns, clandestine meetings and daubed slogans, sedition spread. And now the comet Grilan-Zeat hung in the sky for all to see, promising hope for those who believed.

Events balanced on a knife edge, with revolution possible but by no means inevitable. To speed it on, the rebels determined to continue throwing oil on the smouldering embers. To this end the Wolverines had pledged their support.

Early morning saw the warband gathered in one of the resistance's growing number of safe houses. Though under the circumstances 'safe' was a word they used loosely.

The humans Standeven and Pepperdyne were there, as were Brelan and his twin sister, Chillder. Because of the latter – and in some minds the former – the warband were cagey while they were present. But once the twins left, tongues were loosened.

'I'm worried about what she's thinking,' Jup said.

'Who?' Stryke wanted to know.

'Chillder. Her attitude's been different to me ever since she saw me using the farsight. Haven't you noticed?'

'No.'

'Well, you haven't been stuck in these hideouts with the rebels as much as Spurral and me.' There was more than a hint of resentment in the dwarf's tone.

'We told her you just had a hunch.'

'But did she buy it?'

'Your warning stopped us walking into a trap. I reckon that made Chillder grateful enough not to question how you came up with it.'

'I'm not so sure. Like I say, she's been cooler towards me ever since.'

'She's a lot on her mind.'

'Shit, Stryke,' Jup flared, 'it's bad enough that me and Spurral stand out so much as it is without them thinking I'm . . . odd.'

'You are fucking odd,' Haskeer muttered.

'There's no call for you to chip in on this,' Spurral said, fixing him with a look of flint.

'Gods forbid I should take the piss out of somebody called Pinchpot,' Haskeer mocked.

'Lay off,' Jup warned, 'I'm not in the mood.'

'Fuck you.'

'In your dreams.'

Seeing the heat building, Stryke stepped in. '*You*,' he said, pointing at Haskeer, 'rest that jaw or I'll break it.' He turned to Jup. 'And *you* stop taking the bait. Any more bullshit and I'll be cracking skulls. *Got it?*'

They nodded, sullenly.

'All of us are wound up,' Stryke continued, his tone mollified. 'But there's a rebellion coming and we've gotta be united.' The band's grunts, lounging at a distance, were listening attentively. He looked at Jup. 'Way things are going, you'll be out in the thick of it soon enough.'

'You keep telling me that.'

'It'll happen. That thing in the sky, the prophecy, the rallying call Sylandya's going to make; it'll all rouse the orcs in these parts. We've got to get behind 'em. That's the main thing for us.'

'Is it?' Coilla ventured.

'What do you mean?'

'I have to say it, Stryke. Doesn't getting the stars back come first?'

He sighed. 'I admit I fouled up over that, but—'

She raised a hand to still him. 'I'm not knocking you. I was as much to blame over the one you trusted me with. 'Course we're pledged to helping the rebels. But knowing we can get home's more important, isn't it?'

'On my oath, we'll have the stars back.'

Silence descended. It was the younger of the two humans, Jode Pepperdyne, who broke it. 'What can we—' He glanced at his companion, Micalor Standeven. 'What can I do to help?'

Stryke's reply was a cautious, drawn out, 'Well . . .'

'We're stuck here too, you know,' Standeven protested.

'We have to keep plans close to our chests,' Stryke explained. 'For security.'

'You mean you don't trust us,' Pepperdyne said.

'Nobody's saying that,' Coilla assured him.

He scanned the room, taking in their wary eyes. 'What folk say and what they think aren't always the same.'

'Not with me,' Haskeer told him. 'I don't mind saying I reckon too many outsiders know about this band's business.'

Coilla glared at him. '*Haskeer*,' she hissed through clenched teeth.

'And when too many know,' he ploughed on regardless, 'we get treachery.'

'I don't have to take these . . . *insinuations*,' Standeven announced, puffing up his fleshy chest.

'Whatever *they* are,' Haskeer said.

'You're questioning my honour.'

'Well ain't that a shame. If you don't like it, you can fuck off.'

'That's enough,' Stryke warned.

'I know when I'm not wanted!' Standeven responded, summoning up what passed for his dignity. He gestured at Pepperdyne, as though signalling to an obedient cur. 'We're leaving!'

Pepperdyne hesitated, catching Coilla's eye for a moment, then followed his departing master.

'Jode!' she called out.

They slammed the door behind them.

Coilla turned on Haskeer. 'You fucking . . . *moron*! You oaf! We're beholden to Jode. *I* owe him my life.'

'Yeah, *him*,' Haskeer replied. 'What about the other one?'

'I . . . I don't know about Standeven.'

'We can't trust either of 'em; they're humans. And you're getting too chummy with the younger one.'

Before Coilla could hit back, Stryke took a hand. 'Seems we're forgetting something.' His expression grew dark. 'This is supposed to be a disciplined band,' he told them all. 'Only some of you are acting like it's not. But there's just one way we're gonna get through this, and that's in good order. That means respecting the chain of command, and obeying orders without bellyaching. *And it means an end to this bickering!*'

Wheam, along with a couple of the other tyros, visibly winced.

'We're gonna see more discipline in this band,' Stryke went on, 'and less backbiting. I'm not asking, I'm *telling*. And if anybody here thinks they can do a better job than me, now's the time to say it.' No one broke the hush that had fallen, and few met his eyes. 'Right. So no more bullshit. *Clear?*'

There was a general murmur of agreement.

'What *can* we do about the stars, Captain?' Dallog asked.

'Hold your horses. *Noskaa!*' The grunt sprang to his feet. 'Check that we're not overheard.'

Noskaa went to the door, looked outside and gave a thumbs up. Then he stood watch there.

'Whether any of you like it or not,' Stryke continued, taking a brief look at Coilla, 'there could be a traitor, in the resistance or nearer home. So any plan about Jennesta's best kept to us for now.'

Dallog said, 'This might seem stupid—'

Haskeer cleared his throat, making a noise that implied ridicule but stayed just short of insubordination.

Dallog shot him a glare and tried again. 'It could be a dumb question, Chief, but how do we know Jennesta has all the stars? Including the one Coilla had, I mean.'

'We don't. But it's a good bet she has.'

'You mentioned a plan,' Jup chipped in. 'If it involves getting into the fortress . . . well, that didn't turn out too brilliant last time, did it?'

'There could be another way.'

'Such as?' Coilla wanted to know, her irritability about Pepperdyne still apparent in her tone.

Stryke chose not to pull her up about it. 'Something I heard

317

from the resistance might be useful. Seems Jennesta's been making regular trips to some kind of sacred place on the edge of the city. A stone circle.'

'What for?'

He shrugged. 'Who knows? Something rank, I expect.'

'Anyway, what about it?'

'She goes in a carriage, in convoy. It's one time when she might be exposed.'

'Why not go for her at the circle?'

'Too well guarded there, and the ground's too open.'

'What makes you think she'd have the stars on her?' Haskeer asked.

'Wouldn't you?' Stryke replied. 'After all she's been through to get 'em?'

'Even on the road she'd have a heavy guard,' Coilla reckoned. ''*Specially* on the road.'

''Course. But the escort peels off for their barracks just before the fortress. That could be our chance.'

'Sounds tight.'

'I didn't say it'd be easy.'

'Brelan and Chillder aren't going to wear another assassination attempt,' Jup decided.

'I'm not saying we should try killing her. Though if we got the chance . . .'

'Whether we try to kill her or not, Stryke, the resistance won't want to be involved,' Coilla said.

'That's another reason we're keeping this to ourselves. We do it without them knowing.'

'How?'

'We'd need a cover story. And if we do this right it'd only take about half the band.'

'We had a small team last time, and look how that turned out.'

'This is different. It's an ambush. We've done plenty of those in the past.'

'Never against somebody like Jennesta.'

'If you've got a better idea, Coilla . . .'

'No, I haven't. But I still think we should let Pepperdyne in on this.' Haskeer let out a loud groan. Coilla ignored him. 'He's an asset. He could help us.'

'And he'd keep it a secret from Standeven?' Stryke said.

'I don't think that'd be hard for him.'

'I don't trust 'em,' Haskeer stated.

'*So you said*,' Coilla responded ominously.

Stryke shook his head. 'No. We won't need Pepperdyne. Not the way I'm thinking of doing it.'

'What if he and Standeven get wind of it?' Spurral wondered. 'Could happen, with all of us cooped up together.'

'If they do, we'll kill 'em.'

Coilla frowned at that, but said nothing.

'So it's settled,' Stryke said. 'We'll work on a plan. Meantime, we fight with the resistance. Pepperdyne can help with *that*. They'll need all the blades they can get with a rebellion coming.'

'*If* it comes,' Haskeer muttered.

'Have faith.'

'I leave that to the temple priests.' He drew his sword and held it up to catch the light, turning its glistening length fiery. 'I put my faith in this.' He gazed at it almost reverently.

Stryke smiled. ' 'Course you do. You're an orc.'

'We can't be sure a rebellion's going to work,' Coilla reminded them. 'This is such a different world. Most of the orcs here are like sheep, and the humans have *magic*. Not to mention the odds we'd be—'

'It's simple,' Stryke interrupted. 'We fight, they die.'

The grunts gave a ragged cheer at that.

'Hope you're right,' she said. 'But trouble has a habit of popping up in this place.'

He shrugged. 'I reckon we'll be fine as long as humans are all we have to cope with.'

Not too far away, outside the city limits in one of the sparsely populated, less fruitful areas, stood an abandoned, semi-derelict water mill. The wheel itself was broken, and the watercourse that fed it had dwindled to a weed-choked trickle. Even an astute observer would see the place as desolate and forsaken.

Except perhaps for those possessing the skills of sorcery, or the gods-given power of farsight. These rare individuals might have detected the coppery taste and faintly sulphurous odour of magic cloaking the place. If they were particularly gifted they may have sensed a certain prickling in the atmosphere, a galvanic quality that made the hairs on the back of their necks stand up, signifying an enchantment intended to deceive.

The mill *was* nearly a ruin, but it wasn't uninhabited. Behind the magically generated façade a special operations unit of the multi-species Gateway Corps had commandeered it.

The group's leader was another deception, in a way. Pelli Madayar, a youthful female of the elven folk, had a petite frame and looks of such delicacy that she could be mistaken for frail. It was a false impression. Her energy and strength were prodigious, her determination inexhaustible.

She was in consultation with a lieutenant, a short, stocky individual with the sour expression habitual to the race of gnomes. All about them, the rest of the unit busied themselves with various chores. Gremlins, centaurs, goblins and a satyr were present, along with pairs of brownies and harpies. A small band of pixies and several trolls laboured beside entities that might have been considered exotic even in such diverse company, including a chimera and a wendigo; creatures normally preferring solitude. It was testament to the Corps' mission that so various a collection of races had chosen to put aside their natural inclinations, and their differences, to join in a common purpose.

Mid-sentence, Pelli Madayar broke off, closed her eyes and lifted a hand to her brow. Then she excused herself and hurried away. Her subordinate understood, having seen her do the same thing many times before.

She climbed the slats of a rickety staircase to the mill's upper level. In one corner stood a barrel, larger than she could have got her arms around, its metal bands red with rust. It was full of rainwater from a breach in the roof, and there was a rainbow film on its oily surface. The water was filthy and foul smelling, but that didn't concern her; it was still a suitable medium. In any event she had no option if this was the way her leader chose to get through to her.

Hands on the barrel's edge, she gazed down at it. The water immediately became agitated and began to gently bubble as though coming to the boil. Then it changed its nature. It became something other than simply water; a kaleidoscopic eddy of churning matter suffused with radiance. Shortly it settled and an image came into focus.

She was looking at Karrell Revers, supreme commander of the Gateway Corps, his likeness projected across an infinity of worlds. He was in late middle age, his close-trimmed beard and hair turning silver. But he was still enormously energetic, and acuity lit his eyes. Revers was exceptional among humans in being a possessor of magical abilities.

'Pelli,' he said, 'there's been a development.' His voice had an echoing, ethereal quality.

Even though they were separated by an unimaginable void, she could see he was troubled. 'What is it?' she urged.

'I told you we thought there could be another player in the little drama you have unfolding there, and that there are indications someone other than the orcs has the instrumentalities. Now we've detected a further anomaly, making for a new possibility.'

'Yes?'

'There could be another set.'

'*Another? Here?* How likely is that?'

'The odds are . . . incalculable. But I should sound a note of caution. Because this is unprecedented we could be misinterpreting the signs. Though I have to say it's hard to reach any other conclusion.'

'So now we've got two sets to track down.'

'Yes. Well. . . perhaps.'

'Please, Karrell, help me on this. I can't operate properly if I don't know what—'

'I'm sorry. The thing is, it isn't clear. We're getting different magical signatures from what *might* be two sources. Their characteristics vary in a way we've never seen before.'

'All right. So what do we do?'

'We're working hard on resolving this. But you can see this makes your mission even more vital.'

'Yes, but what's my brief now?'

'Essentially, it remains the same. If you can recover the instrumentalities we know exist, those held by the orcs, or that were held by them, we can eliminate them from our search. The important thing is that you act quickly.'

'I can see that.'

'And I have to say, Pelli, I'm concerned that you haven't acted already.'

'Time spent on reconnaissance is never wasted, you know that. Also we've had to be sure that no innocents get caught up in this. Trouble's brewing here. Relations between the native population and their oppressors look as though they're coming to a head, and—'

'We don't concern ourselves with local affairs. It's one of the Corps' primary rules, as you're fully aware. I just hope it isn't some element of sympathy you feel for the orcs that's staying your hand.'

'It's true I think they've blundered into something they don't understand, and in that sense perhaps they're not to be blamed. That's why I hope to use persuasion to get the instrumentalities back before taking the ultimate step.'

'I've told you before that your compassion is understandable, and it reflects well on you.' His tone came across as a mite petulant. 'But these are *orcs* we're talking about. Some races are beyond the pale, even for the Corps. Your sympathy could well be misplaced. The outcome of your mission is more important than mere individuals You must use *all* means to achieve our objective. Is that understood?'

'Yes, it is.' She mulled things over for a second and added, 'There's something I've been meaning to ask you. You gave me no orders about what would become of the warband once we've taken the instrumentalities from them.'

'Assuming they survive their encounter with you and your superior weaponry.'

'Yes, assuming that. Am I to return them to their home world?'

If she didn't know him better, Pelli would have thought the look Revers gave her was unduly hard. 'You have no such orders,' he told her.

Without further word he broke their connection.

5

Like a chunk of ordure floating in the middle of a cesspit, the great fortress at Taress never failed to draw the eye.

Its baleful walls and haughty towers subjugated the city as surely as the human invaders who had annexed it. Built long ago, by orcs when they were warlike, recent events had turned the pile from defensive to offensive. From a place of sanctuary to a place of dread. It stood as a perpetual reminder of the native population's loss of independence and dignity.

There was a great deal of bustle in its spacious central courtyard. A detachment of uniformed men, and some women, were square-bashing. Others were paired off in mock combat. Weapons were being issued, horses groomed, wagons loaded.

From the balcony of his quarters high above, the stern figure of Kapple Hacher surveyed the activity. His aide, and probably closest professional confidant, the young officer called Frynt, stood beside him.

'Now we're training clerks and medics to patrol the streets,' Hacher said.

'I understand more reinforcements are due for dispatch from Peczan soon, sir,' Frynt informed him.

'I'm not sure there'll ever be enough for Jennesta.'

'Sir?'

'Taress is to be entirely purged of subversive elements, to quote our mistresses' own words. How many troops do you think that would take?'

'With respect, General, you've often said that the troublemakers are a minority.'

'I still think that's so. But it's a question of definitions. Who *are* the dissidents?'

'Isn't it our job to weed them out, sir?'

'Good question. But not one that unduly troubles m'lady Jennesta. Her view is that any orcs who arouse suspicion should be rounded up. And eliminated if they resist. In effect, they're *all* revolutionaries to her. So we have this ever-increasing clamp-down.'

'You can't deny that incidents have increased of late, sir.'

'Yes, they have. What do you expect when you prod a hornets' nest? I believe the resistance, the actual core, is quite small, but I've never said they weren't dangerous, and I'm all for coming down on them hard. But I can't help but feel that Jennesta's policy is only making matters worse.'

'Perhaps this comet the orcs are so excited about is what's really stirring them up, sir.'

'And who's putting the idea into their heads of linking it with omens and prophecies? No, we should be using a rapier here, not an axe.'

'Regrettably, sir, your counsel is unlikely to sway the lady Jennesta.'

'You're telling me.' Hacher grew thoughtful. 'Though there is one weapon in our armoury that could be useful in winkling out the real insurrectionists.'

'Your . . . source,' Frynt said knowingly.

The general nodded. 'Although it isn't entirely certain that I can keep that channel open, it might prove invaluable.'

'But surely, sir, all this talk of rebellion is somewhat academic in light of the nature of the orcs we're governing. The majority are passive.'

'Jennesta doesn't think so. She maintains the entire race is capable of something like savagery. Though what experience she might have had with them to reach such a conclusion is open to question.'

'And you, sir? Do you think they have some buried appetite for combat?'

Hacher turned and surveyed the city. 'Perhaps we're about to find out.'

At one of the resistance's safe houses, hidden in the tangle of the troubled capital's back streets, Jode Pepperdyne and Micah Stand-even had found a secluded room.

'How often do I have to tell you?' Standeven angrily protested.

'Try me one more time,' Pepperdyne said.

'I had nothing to do with Coilla's star going missing!'

'Why do I find that hard to believe?'

'So why do you bother asking me? You know, back where we come from, your badgering would have been seen as gross disobedience.'

Pepperdyne laughed in his face. 'But we're not there, are we?'

'More's the pity.'

'I don't like being stuck in this world any more than you do. Assuming you *do* mind.'

'What's *that* supposed to mean?'

'If the stars hadn't gone missing we wouldn't be here.'

'*And that had nothing to do with me,*' Standeven repeated.

'So you say. But given we are stranded here, why do you keep needling the band? They're the only allies we've got, and they don't trust us.'

'They never did.'

'Speak for yourself.'

'They're *orcs*. Humans aren't exactly their favourite race, in case you hadn't noticed what they're doing to them here.'

'I think they know when somebody's treating them straight. Most of them, anyway.'

'You're a fool, Pepperdyne. The only reason we're still with them, why we're still *alive*, is because it suits them. Don't go misplacing your trust.'

'What, I should put it in *you*?'

'You could do worse.'

'Only if I'd gone insane.'

Standeven's bile was rising again. 'You might do well,' he uttered vindictively, 'to think about your position if we ever get back home.'

'Your threats don't wash here. Or hasn't that dawned on you yet?'

'I'm just reminding you what our relative positions were, and how they could be that way again. How you behave here's going to have a bearing on how I choose to treat you in future.'

'You don't get it, do you? The way things are going, we might not *have* a future. And if we're into reminding each other about events, remember that you wouldn't be here . . . hell, you wouldn't *be* at all, if it hadn't been for me.'

'One of your obligations is to look after your master's safety. It's your duty!'

Pepperdyne lunged and grabbed him by the scruff. 'If you think you don't owe me your life, maybe I'll take it back.'

'Take your filthy hands off me, you—'

The door opened.

Pepperdyne let go of Standeven.

Coilla came in. 'Jode? Are you— Oh.'

Standeven transferred his red-faced glare from Pepperdyne to her. '*Don't mind me*,' he snarled. Shoving past her, he left.

'Let him go,' Pepperdyne said.

'I wasn't thinking of stopping him,' Coilla replied. She closed the door. 'You were arguing.'

'Very perceptive.'

'If you want to be let alone I can—'

'Sorry.' His tone was conciliatory. 'It's just that he gets under my skin.'

'You're not alone.'

He nodded. 'What was it you wanted, Coilla?'

'Well, first off, I thought you could use some of this.' She handed him a brandy flask.

He accepted it, took a swig and gave it back. 'And second?'

'You two left in such a hurry, I just wanted you to know that not everybody in the band thinks badly of you.'

'What, both of us? Me and . . . him?' He nodded at the door.

'I was thinking of you.'

'Thanks.' He smiled. 'But I reckon you're in a minority of one.'

'Oh, I don't know. I reckon Stryke has some regard for you. Maybe a couple of the others.'

'They've a funny way of showing it.'

'You've got to understand how it is between orcs and humans. And not just in this world. We've got . . . history.'

'Maybe that's something I can understand.'

'Can you?'

'You think orcs were the only downtrodden race on our world?'

'You're a human. Your kind does the treading.'

'There are humans and humans.'

'Isn't it time you came clean about yourself?'

'What's to tell?' he came back stiffly.

'Don't close up on me.'

'Would knowing my past change anything? I mean, haven't I proven myself yet?'

'You have to me. But most of the others . . .'

'I give you my word that I had nothing to do with the theft of the star.'

'And what would your partner say if I asked him about it?'

'Standeven's not my partner,' he returned sharply. 'And he'd give you his word too.'

'What value could I put on that?'

'As much as I do.'

'How much is that?'

'If Standeven says he didn't—'

'Why are you so loyal to him, Jode?'

He sighed. 'Habit, I suppose. And not wanting to believe certain things even of him.'

'What *is* the bond between you two?'

'Complicated.'

'Not enough. Tell me more.'

He had to grin. 'You're persistent, Coilla, I'll give you that.'

'So reward me. Open up a bit. I'd like to know something about the man I owe my life to.'

'How about that flask again?'

She dug it out. He took another draught. Coilla had one too.

'Well?' she said.

'I'm a Trougathian.'

'You're a *what*?'

'A Trougathian. After Trougath, the place we come from.'

'Never heard of it.' There was a chair by her, and she sat.

He followed her lead and perched on a barrel of nails. 'The world you and I come from is much bigger than the part you call Maras-Dantia.'

'And your race renamed Centrasia,' she replied with a trace of bitterness.

'*Some* humans did. My sort didn't get to name places.'

'So what sort are they?'

'A little like you orcs.'

'Yeah?' She couldn't keep the scepticism out of her voice.

'Well, I said a *little* like. But there's a couple of similarities. One is that my race has a martial tradition, too.'

'That explains your skill with a blade. So your race fights as a living, like we do?'

'No. It's not inborn with us; it's learnt. Though over so long a time it practically *is* inborn now. But we're not fighters by inclination, or even choice. It was just practical. Most of my race would prefer untroubled lives.'

'If you didn't choose to fight, you must have something to defend.'

'Ourselves. And our land.'

'The first I understand. But dying for land, that seems odd to me. Maybe because orcs never had any.'

'They did here.'

'And your race took it from them.' She raised her hands. 'Sorry. Tell me about your land.'

'Trougath's an island off . . . well, it doesn't really matter where it is. It's large enough for us and the soil's good. So's the fish harvest. We're islanders, we have an understanding with the sea. Most of all, it's our homeland. But it's got one flaw.'

'Its location.'

'You're smart.'

'For an orc, you mean?'

'No, just smart.'

'Stands to reason you'd only have enemies if there's something you've got they want, or if you're in the wrong place.'

'I can see why you're the band's Mistress of Strategy. But you're right; a very wrong place. At least, that's what it became. Trougath stands at a point where it could threaten free passage for its several neighbours, had we wanted to do that, which we didn't. So we sat in the middle of a wheel, each spoke sharpened and pointing at us. All the neighbouring states had a lustful eye on such a favourably placed island. Whoever took it could cow the others. That's why my people embraced warfare, and kept them out.'

'How come, if those nearby states were so strong?'

'My people had been there since long before the rise of the powers that came to surround us. We were numerous and well established. We knew the terrain. And we fought well, as people will when they're protecting all they've got. We were always on alert, and often under actual siege. We did without enough arms, we did without salt. Even water, at times.'

'How long did that last?'

'Generations. Eventually it dawned on them that they couldn't conquer us, so they took to flattering us. So in addition to the skills of combat, we learnt the black art of politics. The game became playing one off against the other. That, and occasional wars, kept us sovereign for a long time.'

'But I'm guessing your luck ran out. Otherwise you'd be there now.'

He nodded. 'Our leaders sided with the wrong tyrant. Not through any liking of him, but by necessity. That caused a schism among my people. Not a civil war exactly, though that came close, but enough of a distraction for us to drop our guard. The very warlord our leaders befriended was the one who took advantage.'

'There's a surprise.'

'It seemed like treachery to us. Hell, that's what it *was*. Those were dark days, and we all did things we weren't especially proud of, in the name of patriotism. None less than me. I won't bore you with the ins and outs. The upshot was that our nation was smashed and what survived of the population scattered. We became drifters, peasants in foreign lands, impoverished merchants, even mercenaries. Some were enslaved.' The latter came out with particular vitriol.

Coilla kept her peace for a moment, then, 'You said there was more than one way your race was like mine.'

'We're both maligned. And once your enemies stigmatise you, they can justify any crime, any indignity they heap on you. Our name was blackened and it sticks. Even false ignominy carries on, like a rock cast down a hill.'

She could relate to that. 'The storytellers, the scholars with their books; they're from the winning side, more often than not. You wouldn't believe the shit they spew about orcs. They say we favour human flesh, or even that we eat each other. They put it about that we sprang from *elves*, for the gods' sake. All lies!'

'They said we conjured demons and sodomised goats.'

Coilla burst out laughing. Pepperdyne looked stern for a moment, then joined her.

'So,' she said when that was subsiding, 'how does Standeven come into all this?'

Amusement died in his face instantly, like a snuffed candle.

'Is he a . . . Trougathian too?' she asked.

'No, he's a bastard.'

'But one with some kind of charge on you.'

'Let's say I'm working a debt off with him.'

'Even while you're in this world? Doesn't that change anything?'

'Only here. Back home . . .'

'We might never see our homes again, Jode!' She checked herself. 'Shit. That's not good for morale, is it? Stryke'd hate hearing me say that.'

'It's no secret, Coilla. I reckon we all think that staying here's the most likely thing.'

'Well, it'd be no different to what's happened in the past.'

'What do you mean?'

'Something we were told before we left Maras-Dantia the first time. Do you know why the elder races came to be there?'

'*Why?* They . . . you . . . were just . . . always there. Weren't you?'

'No. I don't say I understand it, but out there—' she waved a limp hand in the general direction of away '—out there, there are whole worlds of elves and centaurs, and pixies and gnomes, and all the rest. And orcs,' she added hastily. 'Crowds of the races . . . I don't know . . . *fell through* to Maras-Dantia. Scooped up like fish in a net by a powerful sorceress.'

'Humans too?'

'We were told you were our world's true race.'

'Ironic.'

'We didn't think so.' There was a flash of steel in her eyes.

'So all orcs would have originally come from Ceragan.'

She frowned. 'I don't know. The world we've been living in has only orcs too. But a damned sight more spirited than the ones here.'

'So humans might not have started off on Maras-Dantia. Who's to say where orcs, humans or any other race could have originated? Or how far they've spread. Doesn't that intrigue you?'

'No, it makes my head hurt. I see things simpler. Like, maybe we should look at this as being just like moving from one camp to another. Your people are drifters; you must understand that.'

'It's a hell of a trek, Coilla. Sure you're not just making the best of it?'

'' 'Course that's what I'm doing. It's the orc way. We never say die.'

'That could have been Trougath's motto.' He grew sombre. 'But lately I feel almost like—'

He broke off at the sound of approaching footsteps. They were loud and hurried, and could mean trouble. Pepperdyne and Coilla got up, hands on sword hilts.

Chillder burst into the room. She was breathing heavily.

'We've got a situation,' she announced, 'and we need all the swords we can muster.'

6

A crowd had gathered in one of Taress' largest squares. The mob was several hundred strong, and tempers were fraying. What began as a series of protests – against taxes, restricted access to holy places, the razing of certain venerated buildings, food rationing, curfews, heavy-handed policing and any number of other grievances – had distilled into a general outpouring of bitterness at the occupation. The situation was near flashpoint. But it wasn't an incipient riot that drew the resistance. Their aim was to use it as cover.

A number of the rebels were present, along with most of the Wolverines, and the Vixens, the all-female unit Coilla had formed. Scattered around the square, they were dressed soberly, with weapons well concealed.

'Not that long ago these orcs wouldn't have been this restive,' Stryke whispered in Brelan's ear.

'They wouldn't even have come onto the streets.'

The pair were standing together at the edge of the milling crowd. There was a knot of human militia nearby, disquiet on their hard faces.

Stryke could see Haskeer not far off, and a little way on, Dallog with a team of grunts. Further afield, Chillder stood alongside several Vixens. But there was no sign yet of the comrades they were waiting for.

'Sure everybody knows what they have to do?' Brelan asked softly.

Stryke replied pointedly, 'My band does. I hope *your* facts are right.'

'There's no doubt. What we want is there.' He flicked a glance at a building on one side of the square. It stood apart from its neighbours on either side, and looked recently constructed. A squat, one-storey structure, its facing was white, with barred windows. Weapons drawn and watchful, a group of nervous militiamen stood guard outside its heavy door.

Stryke was careful not to be seen staring at the place. 'So what happened?'

'Seven of our comrades were in the area checking out a target. They got unlucky. The troopers took them without blood being spilt.'

Stryke raised an eyebrow at that.

'We don't know how they came to be caught, except they were outnumbered.'

'How come they're in this guards' station?'

'They couldn't be taken to a proper prison for fear of the crowd. We reckon they'll be kept in there until this blows over. Or until an escort arrives.'

'Plenty of soldiers around as it is,' Stryke said, scanning the scene.

'They'll have other things to think about soon.' He chanced another quick peek at the guardhouse. 'If we don't get them out they'll be at the mercy of Iron Hand's torturers. They're good patriots, and loyal, but they'll talk. And that could be a real blow for us.'

Stryke nodded, then gave Brelan a nudge. Robed members of the Order of the Helix were weaving through the crowd. 'Looks like we'll have more than military to deal with.'

'Where's that human of yours?' Brelan wondered irritably.

'He's not *mine*. And he's— Hang on. There he is.'

Pepperdyne came into sight. He was wearing the stolen officer's uniform that had served them well on previous missions. Coilla and two members of the Vixens were with him, walking a couple of paces behind, as though being led.

'The females should be shackled,' Brelan said. 'It'd look more convincing.'

'Even Acurial's tame orcs might find that hard to swallow. Unless you want this crowd tearing him to pieces.'

'Granted. Though I never thought I wouldn't want that to happen to a human. It's time to set things in motion, Stryke.'

Stryke nodded, then raised a cupped hand to his mouth, as though stifling a cough. The other nearby Wolverines, watching for it, began passing the signal on. Brelan did the same with his resistance members. The unspoken order passed through the crowd.

Pepperdyne and his little entourage were making for the guard-house. They met no open opposition on the way, but there were plenty of hostile stares and the odd shouted comment. That the females were following him with no sign of compulsion seemed to confuse the onlookers, and mollified many of them. In fact, their reflexive passivity, and the sense of obedience to authority that had been drummed into them, meant most of the crowd cleared a path.

Pepperdyne kept his eyes firmly on the target and maintained an unhurried pace. The females in his wake ignored shouts directed at them.

The rebels stationed around the square knew to hold back until Pepperdyne's group had reached the guards' station. Shortly after that, they would act.

Pepperdyne and the others were coming to the crowd's outer edge, which like the rest of the perimeter ended at a thin line of soldiers. Behind them was an empty space in front of the guard-house, perhaps thirty paces in depth.

Coilla moved closer to him and whispered, 'Remember, you're an officer. Act like it.'

'I never would have thought of that,' he hissed sarcastically. 'Now leave the talking to me.'

She glared at his back.

The soldiers containing the crowd took Pepperdyne at face value. They saluted, and let him and the females through. The party of sentries at the guardhouse door seemed less sure. They were obviously surprised to see this unknown officer and his charges. They looked quizzical. All were noticeably tense.

As Pepperdyne and his retinue approached, one of the guards shouted, '*Halt!*'

The man who spoke stepped forward, and after a second's hesitation offered a perfunctory salute. He was short and wiry, with a pencil-line moustache and features that reminded Pepper-dyne of a rodent. The stripes he wore showed his rank as sergeant.

Pepperdyne returned the salute in a languid fashion he hoped was fitting to his supposed status. He was about to speak.

'Can I help you . . . sir?' the sergeant got in first. There was a tinge of scepticism in his manner.

Pepperdyne adopted an authoritative tone. 'I've got three more detainees to join the ones you're holding.'

'I've had no orders to that effect.'

'I'm ordering you now.'

'On what authority?'

'By the authority of my rank. And you'd do well to address a superior officer in the proper fashion.'

'Yes, sir,' the sergeant replied, but it was cursory, almost insolent. 'However, my brief's strict. I'm to take no prisoners here without official say-so. That means a direct order from an immediate superior or written authorisation from—'

Pepperdyne pointed at the crowd. 'We have a situation here, Sergeant,' he blustered, 'in case you hadn't noticed. Sticking to the rules does you credit, but things are moving fast on these streets. These captives are linked to the rebels and they need locking up.'

'So why aren't they restrained, sir?'

'Are you implying that I can't control a few females, Sergeant?'

'I wouldn't know about that, sir.'

'I'm getting tired of this. Are you going to obey my order and take these prisoners?'

'If I have the proper authority.'

'*Which I'm giving you.*'

'Your name and division. Sir.'

Pepperdyne stared at the unsmiling pedant. 'What?'

'To check your credentials. I'll have to send a runner to HQ and—'

'You should know that I act under the direct mandate of General Hacher himself. I don't envy your position when he hears about this.'

'That may be so, sir. But we've had reports of bogus officials. It's my duty to verify the credentials of any . . . *officer* presenting themselves at this station.' He was maddeningly cool.

'Are you questioning my patriotism?'

'That's not my place, sir.'

'Don't you care that apart from your insubordination, your worship of the rulebook's stopping me from carrying out my duties? That's a serious step for somebody in your position, Sergeant.'

'My commanding officers would be the best judge of that, sir.'

'Of which I'm one!'

'Perhaps it would help if I went through it again, sir. Once you give me your name and—'

Pepperdyne capped his rising tension by maintaining a stern face. He saw that the other soldiers were eyeing him with something close to hostility. He was aware of Coilla shifting uncomfortably behind him.

From their vantage point, Stryke and Brelan were growing restive too.

'What the hell's going on?' Brelan muttered. 'He should have got them to open that door by now.'

'Maybe we've pulled this trick once too often.'

'What do we do?'

'Stick to plan. Be ready to give the signal.'

Pepperdyne made a show of listening as the sergeant spouted regulations, but his mind was on contingencies. And his hand was drifting towards his scabbard.

'So if you'd care to give me those details, sir,' the sergeant concluded, 'we can clear this up.'

'Eh?'

'Your *details*, sir. As I explained.'

'Look, if you're going to persist in—'

'*Oh for fuck's sake.*' Coilla came out from behind Pepperdyne and thrust a dagger into the sergeant's midriff.

He looked down at it dumbly, swayed, then fell.

'*Shit!*' Pepperdyne said. 'What the *hell*, Coilla?'

'Just moving things along.' She swiftly drew her hidden sword. The pair of Vixens did the same, and so did Pepperdyne.

The other guards, stunned into immobility for a second, now raised their own weapons and closed in.

'That did it!' Brelan exclaimed from his place at the crowd's edge.

'Signal!' Stryke bellowed.

Any thought of concealment gone, they began frantically gesticulating at their confederates. As the order rapidly spread,

Stryke and Brelan started forcibly elbowing their way towards the guardhouse.

Pepperdyne and the females fell into a defensive semi-circle, their blades jutting like a predator's fangs. They gambled that their backs were safe. The nearest in the crowd, who had seen what happened, were reacting. So had some of the guards keeping them in check, but they were torn between joining in and holding the line.

The dead sergeant's comrades advanced, spitting rage. Pepperdyne, Coilla and the Vixens braced themselves.

A great roar went up from the crowd.

There were whirlpools of violence in that churning mass. Attacked by well placed rebels and Wolverines, the scattered groups of militia were already beleaguered. And here and there, ordinary orcs, civilians, were taking part. Hastily improvised weapons appeared. Some used their bare hands. The points where the fighting started were like raindrop impacts on the surface of a lake. They sent out ripples of agitation that built to waves.

The soldiers defending the guardhouse froze at the uproar. Pepperdyne didn't. He tore into the nearest trooper. They battered away at each other, blades pealing, and Pepperdyne instantly proved himself the better swordsman. The man's defence crumbled under the onslaught. He took a hit to the groin, and while he was busy with that, Pepperdyne followed through with a chest thrust. Another guard slid into the fallen one's place and the fight carried on seamlessly.

Coilla had already downed her first opponent and was hacking at two more simultaneously. Her speed and agility vexed them, and they struggled to land a blow. She inflicted a wound on one man, putting him on the back foot with a streaming shoulder, then improved the odds by dropping his companion. The next to step in was more seasoned, or at least cannier, and she found herself fencing rather than hacking.

Battling shoulder to shoulder, the duo of Vixens gave a good account of themselves, despite their relative inexperience. They fought with a zeal not far short of savagery, and a sense of ruthlessness that had their foes wary of engaging them at too close quarters. Glancing from his own labours, Pepperdyne was in awe of the females' aggressiveness. But with at least ten guardsmen still on their feet, and who knew how many more zeroing in, fervour might not be enough.

The crowd was boiling now, with brawls all across the square. Wolverines and rebels were at the centre of nigh on every storm, and the Vixens were fighting with particular resolve. Dead and wounded soldiers were underfoot. To a lesser degree, so were orcs, resistance and civilians alike. But far from sobering the horde, the casualties fuelled its anger.

Haskeer was in the thick of things, cutting a swathe for the bunch of privates in his wake. He favoured an axe, which he swung with abandon, cleaving heads and severing limbs. In another part of the crowd Chillder and a gaggle of Vixens were beating in the brains of several hapless troopers. Not far off, Dallog led a contingent of the Ceragan inductees. Wheam wasn't among them. It was thought better to confine him to lookout duties beyond the fighting.

Joined by hand-picked rebels and Wolverines, as planned, Stryke and Brelan were a spit away from the guardhouse. By the time they arrived the crowd had become a mob. But the sentries holding the line against it weren't a problem. There was no line. The whole area was one seething mass of fighting orcs and humans, and they gave off a deafening roar.

The arrival of Stryke's crew was timely. Pepperdyne and the three females were holding their own, although several sentries from the broken line had attached themselves to the guardhouse defence, upping their numbers. Pepperdyne was dragging his blade from a guard's guts. The toll was starting to show. His movements were growing leaden and his sword arm was cramping. One of the Vixens nursed a wound, but kept fighting. Coilla was covered in foes' blood. She was smiling.

Stryke, Brelan and their back-up came in like steel surf. The balance was tipped, and after a brief flurry of bloody confrontation the remaining guardsmen were overcome.

'Took your time,' Coilla said.

'We were picking wild flowers,' Stryke told her, deadpan.

'Come *on*,' Brelan urged. 'Time's running low.'

They searched the dead sergeant's pockets and found a bunch of keys. While most of the group kept watch, Brelan made for the door and began trying them. On the third attempt the locked turned.

Brelan gave the door a shove. 'It's not the way we thought it'd go,' Brelan said, shooting a glance at Pepperdyne, 'but—'

'*Look out!*' Coilla yelled, pushing him aside.

An arrow flew out of the open door, barely missing him. It zinged into the crowd and struck a gesticulating protestor, piercing his raised arm.

Stryke rushed through the door, with Coilla, Brelan and Pepperdyne close behind. Inside, a sentry was groping in his scabbard for another arrow. Stryke got to the man first and thrust a blade into his chest.

'*To your left!*' Pepperdyne shouted.

Stryke spun just fast enough to block a sword swipe. Its wielder had come from the only blind corner, and he attacked with an ardour born of desperation. His frantic state suited Stryke. A panic-stricken opponent rarely had sound judgement; and so it quickly proved. After a couple more of his blows were deflected, the human looked spent, and his defence was sloppy. Stryke reaped the benefit by puncturing his heart.

There were no other humans in the building. At its far end were two cells, essentially cages, and the seven resistance members were crammed in one of them. None of the sergeant's keys undid the cell's robust lock, and it didn't succumb to a battering. But a hasty search turned up another ring and they got the door open. The prisoners had obviously been maltreated. They had black eyes, cuts and bruises, but no worse injuries. Their rescuers gave them weapons, some brought, some taken from the dead guards.

If anything, the riot outside had stepped up.

'That was sweet,' Brelan said, leading his freed comrades.

'We're not out of here yet,' Stryke reminded him. He turned to Pepperdyne. 'Ready?'

'This bit I don't like,' the human told him.

'You can't just walk away with us,' Coilla said. 'This mob would go wild. Wilder.'

'They'd kill you,' Stryke summarised. 'But if they think you're our prisoner—'

'Right, right. I get it.' He looked unhappy.

They surrounded Pepperdyne as though escorting him, and

started off. Their route would keep them close to the frontage of the square's buildings, skirting the edge of the crowd, until they came to a side street and waiting transport. The rioters who noticed the human officer in the group's midst assumed he was being taken hostage. Some cheered.

Stryke and the others had hardly set out when there was a series of brilliant flashes. They erupted in the heart of the crowd; scintillating bursts of red, green and violet that scarred the eye.

'The Helix!' Brelan exclaimed.

'The more reason not to linger,' Stryke said. 'Keep moving.'

There was another vivid flash in the crowd. A rioter collapsed with a smouldering hole in his chest. The odour of charred flesh permeated the air as those around backed off in dread. Robed men were discharging the magical beams almost wantonly, targeting anyone in their way.

Close by, Haskeer was tangling with a trooper. The man was armed with sword and shield, and had proved stubborn in preventing the orc from killing him. Haskeer relished the challenge. He rained the trooper with boneshaker blows, forcing him into a purely defensive mode. The man was flagging when a particularly intense bolt of magical energy went off near to hand. Dazzled by the light, Haskeer and the trooper stilled, blinking.

Haskeer snapped out of it first and resumed his assault. The militiaman, still in a daze, managed only a confused resistance. Several hefty jolts from Haskeer's axe was enough to throw him completely. A meaty strike to his head had him first on his knees, then keeling over.

There was another flash, as brilliant as the last, and a further victim succumbed to a fiery bolt. As Haskeer's vision seeped back he could just make out the figure of a Helix member no more than twenty paces away. He had seen Haskeer and was raising his power wand. Haskeer dived. A searing beam swept over him, close enough for its heat to be felt. Scrabbling on hands and knees, he made for the fallen trooper as the Helix initiate took aim again. Reaching the corpse, he wrestled the shield from the human's death grip. Then, still kneeling, he flung it with might at the Helix. It skimmed like a discus and struck him squarely in the neck, nearly decapitating him.

Onlookers got the message. Fearsome as their trident weapons might be, the Helix weren't invulnerable. In seconds they were under siege. Haskeer and his troop melted into the throng.

Stryke and the rebel party stayed out of such clashes. They moved as swiftly as they could towards the turning that led out of the square. But when they were almost at the corner, they halted.

'Oh, great,' Coilla grumbled. 'More shit.'

Two wagonloads of troops came along the street they were heading for. When the wagons reached the square they stopped, blocking the road. The troops began getting out.

'Time for these,' Brelan said, digging into the canvas bag hanging from his shoulder. He produced a number of earthen cylinders, similar to water bottles, and handed them out.

Coilla grabbed one gleefully. 'I *love* these things.'

'What is it?' Pepperdyne asked.

'Acurialian fire,' Brelan told him. The human looked blank. Brelan mimed throwing one, then mouthed '*Boom.*'

'I've seen similar,' Pepperdyne realised.

'*Use 'em,*' Stryke grated.

They struck sparks against the oil-soaked wads of fabric stuffed into the containers' necks. When the cloth fuses were well alight they started lobbing. The cylinders soared in the direction of the wagons and disembarking soldiers. They shattered on impact, exploding in plumes of orange fire. The burning oil had been mixed with certain compounds that made it viscous. It stuck fast to whatever it touched, igniting the wagons, the walkway and any troopers unlucky enough to be in range. Converted to fireballs, they stumbled aimlessly, yelling and beating at their clothes. The wagons were blazing.

The few soldiers untouched by fire were either making futile efforts to put out the flames or loosing sporadic arrows in the direction of Stryke's group. But panic made their aim wild. And now they had another problem: the crowd was turning on them. Chunks of paving stone rained down on a scene already engulfed by fiery chaos.

'Should keep 'em busy,' Coilla remarked with satisfaction.

'Let's go,' Stryke said.

With Pepperdyne back in the middle of the scrum, they bypassed the mayhem and charred bodies without challenge. All over the square the other Wolverines, rebels and Vixens were slipping away too. Singly or in small groups they would make for hideouts or the cover of false identities.

Off from the square, in near empty streets bled clean by the riot, Stryke, Coilla and the rest met up with their transport.

Bumping along in a covered wagon, moving slowly to avoid attention, they allowed themselves to relax a little.

'Looks like the uniform trick's stopped working,' Coilla said.

Pepperdyne nodded. 'They were bound to catch on eventually. Your Vixens fought like she-devils, by the way. I've not seen them that ferocious before.'

'Then you haven't been moon-gazing lately,' Coilla told him.

'Moon-gazing?'

'Not well up on the ways of females, are you, Jode.'

Comprehension dawned. 'Oh. You mean—'

'The time of the moon's cycle when my sex can get a little . . . cranky.'

'From what I just saw I'd have used a slightly stronger word. Like murderous. But how come you *all*—'

'You *really* don't know much about females, do you? When any number of us spend time together in the same place it's not unusual for our cycles to tally. That's what happened today.'

Pepperdyne grinned. 'A whole squad of moon-crazed she-orcs. Gods help the enemy.'

'Gods *damn* 'em,' Brelan said. 'But the citizens acted well too. I'm proud of them.'

'They do seem to be finding their orcish natures a bit more,' Stryke agreed. 'But are they ready for a full-scale uprising?'

'The tipping point's near. Very soon my mother, as Principal, will come out of hiding and make her rallying call. After that, what happened today's going to look like a picnic.'

'Let's hope,' Coilla remarked cautiously.

The wagon was arriving at its destination. It pulled through high gates and into the courtyard of an abandoned villa the resistance had occupied. It looked as though none of the other rebels had got back yet.

As they were climbing out, Wheam said, 'Today was a great success, wasn't it, Brelan?'

'It was a success. Not sure about great.'

'But the sort of thing orcs will be telling tales about for generations. A tipping point, you said.'

'If it helps bring about the revolution,' Brelan conceded, 'it could be remembered as a key day.'

'And the wordsmiths will tell tales about it, and the balladeers will sing songs.'

Coilla groaned. 'I can see where this is going.'

'As it happens,' Wheam sailed on, 'I've already begun composing an epic ballad about this great day.' He pointed at his brow. 'Here. In my head.'

'I'm surprised there's room for it,' Coilla observed.

'I don't have my lute with me, of course . . .'

'Oh, good,' Pepperdyne said.

'. . . but I'm sure I could give you a recital without it.'

'Yes, well—' Stryke began.

'But bear in mind that it's a work in progress.'

'Aren't they all,' Coilla muttered.

They were walking towards the safe house's doors. As Wheam spoke, everyone increased their pace.

'I call it The Battle of the Square,' he intoned grandly, and cleared his throat.

> *''Twas upon that fateful day we beat the foe to their dismay*
> *With blade and axe we thrashed them sound*
> *All round the square and into the ground*
> *And all who were there, you could hear them say*
> *That was the day we made the humans go away*

'That bit needs some work. It goes on . . .

> *'Oh let the humans wail, oh let them grieve*
> *Oh let their hearts bleed, oh let—'*

'Oh, let *up!*' Coilla snapped.

'Wouldn't you like to hear the bit about how—'

'Moon!' she barked threateningly, jabbing a finger at her chest. Wheam flinched and fell silent, crestfallen.

As they approached the doors they were thrown open. A couple of resistance members came out, and Jup and Spurral were close behind them. Their expressions were grim.

'What's happened?' Stryke said as he pushed his way in.

'We've had an . . . incident,' Jup replied.

'What?' Brelan demanded.

The dwarfs exchanged glances. 'Best to show you,' Spurral said.

The place was in turmoil as they led them through the house and down steps to the extensive cellars.

Passing through an arch and into one of the smaller rooms, Jup pointed. 'There.'

The others crowded in. On the rough flagstones the corpse of an unknown orc lay in a pool of blood. On the other side of the chamber Standeven was held fast by a pair of rebels.

'What the hell have you done?' Pepperdyne said.

7

'Somebody better tell me what happened here,' Brelan demanded.

'This is how we found it,' one of the rebels holding Standeven said. 'With him standing over the corpse. And he had this.' He held up a bloody knife.

'Who is he?' Stryke asked, nodding at the dead body.

They all shook their heads.

'He's a stranger to me,' Brelan confirmed. He turned to Standeven. 'Did you do this?'

'Yes.' He was pale, and he was shaking. There were beads of sweat on his pallid brow.

'Have you gone *insane*?' Pepperdyne exclaimed.

'Let him speak,' Stryke said.

'It was self-defence,' Standeven claimed. 'I'd no choice.' He was growing agitated. 'I'm not the villain here! You should thank me for—'

'*Calm down,*' Stryke told him firmly. 'Get a grip and tell us what happened. From the start.'

The human swallowed. 'I was told this was going to be a storage area, and I was moving boxes of rations in.'

'Seeing as you're no good for anything else,' Coilla muttered.

'Button it,' Stryke grated. 'You were moving stuff.'

Standeven nodded. 'When I came in, he was here.' He indicated the body, but avoided looking directly at it.

'Seen him before?'

'No.'

'What happened?'

'He attacked me.'

'Just like that? He didn't speak?'

'Not a word.'

'But you had a knife.'

345

'Er . . . no. That was his.'

'You took it off him?' There was scepticism in Stryke's voice.

'I. . . Yes.'

'You're no fighter,' Pepperdyne sneered.

'I expect you to back me!' Standeven flared. 'You know I'm not the sort to—'

'I know you'd rather run than fight.'

'I couldn't! I was *attacked*!'

'And you, no fighter, disarmed a knife carrier and killed him. You expect us to believe that?'

'You find . . . reserves when your life's at stake. He pulled the knife and we struggled. It was more luck than anything else that he ended up with the blade in him.'

'Then what?' Stryke asked.

'What do you mean?'

'What did you do after you'd stabbed him?'

'I called for help.'

'Not until then? Not when you were actually fighting him?'

'It all happened so quickly, I—'

'Right. What was he doing when you came in?'

'Doing? Nothing that I could see.'

'What do you *think* he might have been doing?'

'How the hell should I know? He was an intruder; maybe a spy for all I know. I would have thought I'd be congratulated for stopping him.'

'Is there anything to identify him?' Brelan wanted to know.

'No, we looked,' one of the rebels confirmed.

'How did he get in?' Coilla wondered.

'That wouldn't have been too hard,' Brelan admitted.

'*What?*'

'We're fighting *humans*, not fellow orcs. You must have noticed we have all sorts through here; citizens who might not be actual resistance members but secretly support us. Offering information, donating supplies, bringing messages . . .'

'Could that be what he was? A messenger?'

'We tend to know them by sight.'

'So by and large,' Stryke summed up, 'you let anybody in except humans. Which is fine if you think all orcs support your cause, and can keep their mouths shut.'

346

'We're not that sloppy,' Brelan protested. 'We take measures. And yes, I do believe the orcs of Acurial support us, at heart.'

'Hope you're right. But you need to beef up security.'

'We're off the point,' Brelan came back defensively. 'All I know is that a human's killed an orc, right here in a safe house. And if there wasn't doubt about why—' he jabbed a finger at Standeven '—*he'd* be dead now.'

'Why don't you make sure the intruder wasn't known to anybody here?' Stryke suggested.

'You bet I will. What do we do with him?' He glared at Standeven again.

'I want to talk to him. Privately.'

There was a hint of suspicion in Brelan's eyes. 'Why?'

'He's attached to my band. It's my charge. Just like you discipline your group. You've my word that if there's more to come out about this, you'll know.'

'And if it turns out to be murder, plain and simple?'

'Why should I?' Standeven protested heatedly. 'What could I possibly gain by—'

'*Shut it*,' Stryke ordered. 'If that's what happened, Brelan, he'll pay for it. Dearly.'

'He'd better.' He gestured at the rebels holding Standeven to let him go. 'We'll take the body out when you've finished here.' Then, grim faced, he led his comrades from the room. The door slammed behind them.

Stryke turned to Dallog and Wheam. 'You, too. Out.'

'Aaaahh,' Wheam complained, disappointed.

A look from Stryke silenced him. 'But stay close, Dallog. I might be needing you.'

They went out, leaving Stryke, Coilla and Pepperdyne with Standeven.

'Right,' Stryke said, confronting him, 'what really happened here?'

'I told you. But—'

Stryke grabbed him by the scruff and wrenched him close. 'You're saying that was the whole story?'

'I'm trying to explain! There was . . . something I didn't mention.'

'I knew it!' Pepperdyne snarled.

'No, wait, wait!' Standeven pleaded. 'I couldn't say it in front of the others.'

'What?'

'Let go, Stryke, and I'll show you.'

Stryke hung on to him for a moment, eyes locked on his. Then he let go and pushed him away. 'This better be good.'

'It is,' Standeven said. 'Least I reckon you'll think so.'

'*Get on with it.*'

'After *that* happened—' he waved a hand at the dead orc '—I didn't call for help right away. I searched the body.'

'Why?'

'I like to know who's trying to kill me. I was just curious.'

'Looking for valuables, more like,' Pepperdyne remarked.

'Oh, I found something valuable all right.' Standeven thrust a hand into his pocket. What he brought out filled the palm of his hand. It was a green sphere with five projecting spikes of varying length, made of a material no one had been able to identify.

'*The star,*' Coilla gasped.

Stryke snatched it and began scrutinising it. 'It's the one stolen from you, Coilla,' he decided at last. He looked to Standeven. 'And this was on the body?'

The human nodded. He was still flushed and had a lustre of perspiration.

'You *say* you found it on the corpse,' Pepperdyne speculated, 'but how do we know that's true?'

'Where else would I have got it? And if I had anything to hide, why would I give it to you?'

'To save your skin?' Coilla put in. 'It's a good bet we might go easier on you after getting a prize like this.'

'For all we know you could have been walking around with it ever since it disappeared,' Pepperdyne added.

'Why would I do *that*?' Standeven asked. 'I know you all think I stole it. But if I had, how come I've still got it? Wouldn't I have sold it or—'

'Or given it to Jennesta,' Coilla said.

Standeven made no comment.

Stryke sighed. It was part exasperation, part bafflement. 'Let's get this straight. You're set upon by an orc you've not seen before.

You kill him.' He hefted the instrumentality, 'And you find this on his body.'

'Yes.'

Coilla spoke for all of them. 'It makes no sense.'

Stryke put the star into his belt pouch. 'Sense or not, least we've got it back.'

'But it doesn't add up, Stryke. Who was he?' She pointed at the body. 'What was he doing here? Why did he have—'

'Yeah, I know. But unless you two have any bright ideas, I can't figure it.'

'Assuming what we've been told is true,' Pepperdyne said, staring pointedly at Standeven.

'I meant what I said to Brelan. If something deeper's going on here, there'll be a price to pay. Otherwise . . .'

'We accept his story,' Coilla finished, eyeing Standeven.

'Could be out of our hands.'

'Meaning?'

'We're strangers here. If it turns out this dead one *was* connected to the resistance, or they decide they don't believe what happened, it'll be their call.'

'So where does that leave me?' Standeven asked.

'You're not a member of my band.'

'Thank the gods,' Coilla mumbled.

'You're not in the band,' Stryke repeated, 'but we brought you here, and we stand together. So whatever I feel about you, which ain't good, I'm still responsible for you. Call it Wolverine pride.'

'I understand,' Standeven said, 'and I really—'

'I'm not finished. But if it turns out you've been lying about all this, you're alone. And I'll kill you myself. Understand *that*?'

He nodded.

'Keep yourself to yourself. Avoid the rebels' company, if you can, and stick near band members. Maybe this'll blow over.'

'Think it will?' Pepperdyne wondered.

Stryke shrugged, then went to the door and called Dallog in. 'Escort Standeven to our billet. Make sure the band keeps an eye on him for at least a couple of days.'

'How much do I tell 'em about all this?'

'They've a right to know. But I'll take care of it. Now get him out of my sight.'

Dallog took Standeven by the arm and hustled him out.

Stryke looked to Pepperdyne and Coilla. 'What do you think?'

'It stinks,' Coilla offered. 'Only I can't see where the smell's coming from.'

'Pepperdyne? You know him best.'

'He's a lying, two-faced bastard. But I never saw him as a killer. Not because he isn't ruthless, mind you, but because he's a coward.'

'Lots of murderers are cowards.'

'I suppose I'm saying . . . I don't know what to think, Stryke. He's twisted enough to kill if it furthers his ends, or at least not to fret if somebody loses their life over him. But he's got no guts. Fuck him. He *always* screws things up.'

'He's not doing that to us.'

'We're going to have to baby-sit him now,' Coilla said, 'That's not what I signed up for.'

'Me neither,' Stryke agreed. 'But I'm more worried about our bond with the resistance. We've worked hard for their trust. This could break it.'

'Ever get the feeling we aren't in control? Not just over this, but what's going on here in Acurial?'

'It's what troubles me most; not having control over our own fate.'

'Well, we fought hard enough for it in Maras-Dantia, and once a race gets a taste for freedom they cling to it.'

'I'll second that,' Pepperdyne contributed.

Stryke gave him a quizzical look, then glanced at Coilla.

'Jode's a Trougathian,' she told him.

'A *what*?'

'Long story. Maybe he'll tell you sometime.'

Pepperdyne didn't offer to explain.

'But you're right about control,' she went on. 'We've got no easy way out. Not as long as we've only got the one star.'

'We're going to go for the others.'

'When?'

'We need to make a plan, scout Jennesta's route, think of a cover story for Brelan and Chillder—'

'*When*, Stryke?'

'Tomorrow.'

8

Stryke kept the team small. He decided on Coilla, Haskeer and Dallog, the latter the only new recruit; along with eight privates, none of them tyros.

It was late the following day, and the shades of night were falling. Stryke's group had established that Jennesta was at the stone circle on the outskirts of Taress, and the route she usually took back to the fortress was confirmed. Now they waited in hiding by a road leading to the redoubt.

'I'm surprised the resistance let us out of their sight,' Coilla said. 'What did you tell them?'

'Brelan and Chillder think we're freelancing,' Stryke told her, 'helping to keep the pot boiling. Reckon they were glad to have us out of their way after what happened with Standeven.'

'How's that going? I've been here all day, remember.'

'The rest of the band's looking out for him. Pepperdyne's closer than his shadow. The rebels are as cold as a dead witch's arse to him. But it turned out the orc he killed isn't known to them, which might make it easier.'

'I still don't see how we're going to keep this mission from them. They're bound to hear about it.'

'The humans won't boast about a defeat.'

'And if they do?'

'They're not going to say anything about the stars.'

'That's not what I meant. My worry's about what Brelan and Chillder are going to do when they know we went after Jennesta again behind their backs.'

'What *can* they do about it?'

'Shut us out?'

'We can still help bring about an uprising. That's what we came here for.'

'It'll be harder if we make enemies of the resistance.'

'We thrive on enemies, Coilla. But you're right; we don't need the rebels on our necks.'

'So how do we avoid it?'

'Like I said, Jennesta wouldn't boast of a defeat, so the resistance won't hear about it. But she would crow if it goes wrong.'

'You mean we can't screw this up.'

'Right.'

'What I wanna know,' Haskeer said, 'is do we kill her if we get the chance?'

'Not if it gets in the way of snatching the stars,' Stryke decreed. 'Otherwise . . .'

'The rebels would hear about *that*,' Coilla remarked.

'And wouldn't bellyache if we pulled it off. Killing the Peczan envoy'd be a big boost for them.'

They fell silent and returned to watching.

Their hiding place was just beyond a fork in the road. The turnoff led to the main barracks, which were out of sight, where the majority of the fortress's garrison was billeted. The road Stryke, Coilla and Haskeer overlooked went to the fortress itself.

Despite being near the city's heart, the area was almost semibucolic due to the acres of land belonging to the fortress. Land once used for leisure and hunting by long-dead rulers, and now employed for drill by the citadel's battalion. Graced with more trees than anywhere else in Taress, it was quiet compared to the rest of the metropolis, with little traffic and few passers-by. The reputation of the place was such that citizens preferred to avoid it. But there were patrols of troops to be wary of.

'How much longer we got to wait?' Haskeer grumbled.

'Most times she's back around now,' Stryke said.

'Waiting's the bit I hate.'

'It's part of the job. Take it easy.'

'Count your toes,' Coilla suggested.

Haskeer scowled at her.

They waited until it was nearly dark, and were passed only by the odd rider or wagon, usually travelling at speed to get through the district as quickly as possible. Haskeer grew more restless, and Stryke was beginning to think the mission would have to be scrubbed.

It was Coilla who snapped them out of it. 'There,' she said, pointing up the highway.

A convoy was coming along the main road and approaching the fork. It was headed by a group of mounted cavalry, followed by two coaches, each with a trooper sitting alongside the driver. Another contingent of cavalry brought up the rear. The procession moved at a clip, but short of breakneck speed.

'Hope the others are watching this,' Coilla added.

'If they're awake,' Haskeer muttered.

Stryke shot him a frown.

'Well, Dallog's with 'em.'

'He's a pro,' Stryke told him, 'and so are the grunts with him. So quit sniping.'

Haskeer grunted in a noncommittal kind of way.

The convoy had reached the fork. The cavalry in the lead peeled off and headed for their barracks, as did the contingent bringing up the rear. The unescorted pair of carriages picked up speed for the home run.

Coilla gazed into the trees on the other side of the road. She couldn't see anything. Not that she expected to. 'They're cutting it fine.'

'The timing has to be spot on,' Stryke reminded her. 'Relax.'

She smiled at the thought of relaxation as she reached for her bow.

The convoy was almost on them. Coilla and Haskeer nocked their arrows.

'Make those shots count,' Stryke told them. 'You might not get a second chance.'

'I know, I know,' Haskeer came back irritably.

The convoy was almost level with their position when a loud crack rang out. Ahead of the first carriage a mature tree crashed down in a flurry of leaves, blocking the road. The carriages skidded to a halt. Another substantial tree fell behind the second carriage, boxing them both in.

'*Now!*' Stryke yelled.

Coilla and Haskeer loosed their arrows. Coilla's struck the trooper next to the driver on the lead carriage. It was a righteous hit, pitching the man from his seat. Haskeer's arrow missed. Stryke and Coilla glared at him.

Cursing, he fumbled for another bolt. Coilla reloaded first, took aim and brought down the trooper on the second carriage. Haskeer's next shot was true. It killed the first carriage's driver. By that time the driver of the second had scrambled down on the far side and disappeared into the tree-line.

'Remember,' Stryke warned, 'Jennesta's magic can be lethal. She should be in the first carriage, so leave that to me. Now *move*!'

They came out of hiding and charged toward the road. Before they were halfway the rest of the raiding party, with Dallog to the fore, emerged from the foliage. Several of them still clutched the axes they used to fell the trees. Two grunts ran to stand lookout at each end of the halted convoy. The rest made for the carriages.

An arrow shot out of the open window of the second coach. It was aimed at Coilla, and came near to claiming her. She dropped and hugged the ground. Stryke and Haskeer did the same. Coilla got off an arrow of her own. It smacked into the carriage door. Whoever was inside returned fire, but the bolt flew over their heads. Haskeer unleashed an arrow, sending it through the window. Somebody in the dark interior shrieked.

The sound of battering came from the far side of the carriage. Dallog's crew were laying siege to it. Stryke, Coilla and Haskeer got up and raced for their goal. As they approached, the door of the second carriage burst open and four troopers spilled out.

'You go ahead!' Coilla shouted to Stryke.

He sprinted off.

Swords drawn, the troops came at Haskeer and Coilla, who rushed forward to meet them. The chime of steel on steel echoed through the twilight. Almost immediately, Dallog and the others poured around the carriages and joined in. Jennesta's guards fought with spirit, but had no hope of not being overwhelmed.

Stryke reached the first coach. He hesitated for a fraction of a second at its door, then wrenched it open.

A bulky, shadow-swathed figure filled the doorway. It half fell, half leapt on Stryke, pinning him to the ground and knocking the wind out of him. His sword was dashed from his hand.

Stryke immediately knew his foe as one of Jennesta's zombie bodyguards, if only from the foul odour it gave off. Struggling under the creature's oppressive weight, he was aware of its skin, dried out and wrinkled like ancient parchment. He saw the black chasm of its dead eyes.

The zombie encircled him with its fetid arms. Fists balled, Stryke pummelled the once-human, landing hefty blows to its head. But he couldn't break its iron grip. The zombie's abnormal strength began to crush the life out of him. Stryke writhed and kicked, but the bear-hug held.

Then his flailing hand touched metal and he grasped the hilt of his dropped sword. He brought it up and round in an arc, striking the zombie's side. The blade cut deep, but brought only a puff of grey dust from what should have been a wound. It hardly troubled the zombie. Gasping for breath now, Stryke tried another tack. He hacked frenziedly at the creature's arm. After three blows it severed, exuding more rank dust. The arm fell away. Half free, Stryke exerted pressure and rolled the thrashing zombie far enough for him to scramble clear. Quickly, he found his feet.

The creature rose too. It looked about itself, lifeless eyes unblinking, and saw its amputated arm. Reaching down, he grabbed it, hefted it as though it were a club, and lumbered in Stryke's direction. Stryke charged and plunged his blade into the thing's chest. It met little obstruction. Its tip exploded from the zombie's back, liberating yet more dust. Stryke yanked the sword out and withdrew a couple of paces. The zombie kept coming, apparently unharmed. Stryke made to attack again.

Haskeer appeared and darted between them. 'It's mine,' he growled, facing the creature. 'You *go!*' Ducking to avoid its fleshy club, he commenced chopping and slashing at the zombie.

Stryke ran for the open carriage door, leapt up and jumped in.

Jennesta sat alone. She wore an expression that could have been called serene.

He seized his chance and thrust his sword at her heart.

It felt like the blade had struck an anvil. The impact sent a shockwave up his arm that instantly suffused his entire body. It was a pain unlike any he had ever known. He imagined that being stung by a dozen venomous serpents would be like this. An energy ran through him, a malevolent force, bringing agony to every fibre.

He was flung backwards, landing on the floor, his back to the opposite seat. The pain immediately began to fade.

Jennesta was swathed in a semi-transparent aura that looked like air rippling on a hot day. It was shot through with a brilliant violet patina that shifted, melted and reformed itself. Stryke knew a mere sword was no match for such sorcery.

'Did you think to find me unprotected?' she said.

'It was worth a try,' Stryke grated. He was fighting against his inbred deference for her, and his wariness of her powers.

She laughed. It was a disturbing sound. 'Your race may be unparalleled fighters, but you hardly excel when it comes to thinking.'

'If brainwork means something like you,' he replied defiantly, 'I'll stay dumb.'

'Insolent cur!' She made a movement with her hand, as though lobbing an invisible ball.

Stryke was hit by a jolt as powerful as the shock he'd just recovered from. He bit his lip to stop himself crying out.

'So you came here to kill me?' she added. Her tone made it sound conversational.

He said nothing.

'Or perhaps you hoped for a different prize,' Jennesta went on. For a fraction of a second, and apparently involuntarily, her eyes flicked to a bulky silk pouch on the seat beside her.

Stryke hadn't noticed it before, and now he willed himself not to look at it. 'Your death's the best prize I can think of.'

'Then you really do lack imagination, dullard.' She made the hand gesture again.

He took another punch of psychic force. The hurt inundated every cell in his body. He felt it in his bones, his teeth. And he knew he couldn't take much more; assuming she didn't simply kill him outright.

'Your view of the universe is so depressingly limited,' she said. 'You grasp no more than a sliver of the truth. If only you had the intellect to see how much *more* there is to reality.'

Stryke thought that was an odd thing for her to say. But then, most of what she said had always struck him as bizarre. He held his silence.

'Why am I bothering?' Jennesta asked. 'You and your kind have the acumen of worms. And to think I once believed that you, Captain Stryke, had the wit to rise above your animal state.'

'You never showed it.'

'You never earned my trust.'

It was Stryke's turn to laugh, even if it risked a further jolt. 'You talk as though your trust's a gem, and not a sham of paste and glass.'

'What a poetic turn of phrase. For an animal. You could have been great, Stryke.'

'I'm flattered.'

'Low sarcasm. I shouldn't expect more. But what you're too dim to understand is that by your treachery you've traded my patronage for a life of struggle and hardship.'

'We call it freedom.'

'It's overrated,' she sneered.

The carriage door was still open. Outside, the sound of fighting continued, but it was strangely faint, as if heard from a distance.

Stryke said the first thing that came into his head, purely to keep her engaged. 'You might have the upper hand now, but—'

'Oh *really*. Foolishly, I expected more of you than empty threats and petty chatter. Let's not beat about the bush. Neither of us are mentioning the enormous basilisk in the room. The *instrumentalities*, dolt.' She fleetingly glanced at the pouch again. He took that as confirming his hunch and tensed himself.

'What about them?'

She rolled her eyes. '"*What about them*," he asks. So you're happy that you no longer possess them, is that it? No answer? Perhaps a little encouragement's in order.' She raised her hand.

Stryke sprang forward, snatched the pouch and dived out of the carriage. Thinking he'd be struck down at any instant, he ran towards Haskeer.

His sergeant had decapitated the zombie and was staring down at it. Even headless, the creature still showed signs of life, writhing and twitching in the dirt.

'*Move it!*' Stryke yelled. '*Run!*'

Haskeer fell in behind him.

Stryke looked back. He expected to see Jennesta coming out of the coach, but there was no sign of her. Up ahead, Coilla, Dallog and the others were surveying the corpses of the troopers littering the road.

Loosening the drawstrings on the pouch, Stryke checked its

contents. The instrumentalities were inside. Triumphant, he stuffed the pouch into his jerkin.

'Got them?' Coilla asked as he approached.

He gave her a thumbs up.

'*Company!*' Dallog shouted, pointing with his sword.

A detachment of cavalry was heading their way from the direction of the barracks, and they were moving fast.

Stryke ordered a retreat. They ran into the trees and mounted hidden horses. In her carriage, Jennesta smiled.

They split into four groups to avoid attention, with Stryke, Coilla and Haskeer staying together. As a precaution, the safe house had been changed following the incident with Standeven, and they rode hard for it to beat the curfew. But they slowed their pace when they got into the inner city's narrow, winding streets, where many others were hastening home before full dark. Finally, finding the lanes too crowded to ride, they had to dismount and lead their horses.

'Now we've got the stars back,' Haskeer said, 'we can leave anytime we want.'

'Not until things are settled here,' Stryke replied sternly.

'Didn't say we should. It's just good to have the option.'

'I'll drink to that.'

'Now you're talking.' Haskeer spat plentifully, narrowly missing the feet of an irate passing citizen. 'My throat's as dusty as a troll's crotch.'

'Is it just me,' Coilla wondered, 'or did this mission seem just a little too easy?'

'You wouldn't say that if you'd been in there with Jennesta,' Stryke replied.

'You're still alive, aren't you? And, all right, we met some opposition; but nothing we couldn't handle.'

'We got lucky.'

'Don't you think Jennesta would've taken more precautions? Not just for herself, but the stars?'

'You know what it's like with rulers. They get full of themselves. Too brash. They never think anybody'd dare go against 'em. The important thing is we got these back.' He patted his jerkin.

'Guess so.' She didn't sound entirely convinced.

'We're nearly there,' Stryke said, changing the subject. 'Expect the rebels to be nosey about what we've been up to today, and stick to our story. Remember, we've just been harrying the militia.'

Coilla and Haskeer nodded.

But when they got to the disused grain store the resistance were using they found the place abuzz. No one seemed interested in where they'd been. Eventually, Chillder located them, and she was animated.

'What's happening?' Stryke asked.

'The resistance council's decided the Principal should come out into the open. Isn't it great? Our mother's going to issue her rallying call!'

'When?'

'In the morning.'

'That soon?'

'The time's right, Stryke. Make sure your band's ready; we're heading for the revolution!'

9

Hacher had grown used to Jennesta's nocturnal habits. Or at least accepted them. In the weeks she had been in Taress as the empire's special envoy, he had reason to wonder if she ever slept at all. And if she didn't sleep, those who served her were expected to be awake and on hand, whatever the hour.

So it was that Hacher found himself in her chambers near dawn, having been at her beck and call for most of the night. Jennesta herself was outside on the balcony, watching Grilan-Zeat. The comet was big in the sky, a boiling light to rival the sun that was soon to rise.

Hacher was alone in her apartment. His aide, Frynt, had been dispatched on some errand Jennesta demanded, and Brother Grentor had likewise been dragged from his bed to attend to her whims. Her undead personal guards were nowhere to be seen. Hacher suspected that they were slumbering in some state of coma necessary to revitalise their strength, but preferred not to dwell on the thought.

He was bored as well as exhausted. Though the anxiety Jennesta always managed to generate in everyone gave his fatigue an edge. It was rather like the way he remembered feeling as he prepared to enter a battle when he was a younger man. But this night trepidation had reached new heights, given Jennesta's ambush during the evening. Not that she had done more than mention it, almost in passing, let alone discussed it with him. He wasn't so naïve as to think it would end there, and his concern was when and how she might show her displeasure.

As he pondered, she entered the room. Hacher intuitively stiffened, almost to attention, as he always did when she was around, and doubly so when there was a chance she was going to be wrathful.

Worn out by anticipation, he decided on the risky strategy of pre-empting her by broaching the subject first, greeting her with, 'I owe you an apology, my lady. The assault you were subjected to earlier was inexcusable.'

'Yet you are about to make excuses for it, no doubt.'

'No, ma'am. I merely wish to express the military's regret that you should have been put in harm's way.' He consulted a parchment he'd been reading. 'And I see from the report that you lost a personal possession to the outlaws.'

'The item in question is not your concern, General, and in any event it was unimportant, trifling.'

'I'm pleased to hear it, ma'am.'

'The matter of my personal security, however, is not insignificant. In allowing my convoy to be attacked, those under your command were both incompetent and cowardly.'

'A number of men gave their lives for you, ma'am.'

'But not all, I think.'

'Ma'am?'

'Who survived the raid?'

Hacher scanned the report. 'A coach driver, and one of the troopers accompanying you, though he's severely injured.'

'Execute them.'

'With all due respect, ma'am, I think—'

'Only you don't, do you? Think, that is. The only way you're going to put down this growing rebellion is by being utterly ruthless with your underlings. They need to be toughened to pass that mercilessness on to the scum on the streets.'

'I have complete confidence in our armed forces,' Hacher protested indignantly. 'Their expertise and bravery are next to none.'

'The rulers of every nation tell their subjects lies. Do you know one of the biggest? That they have the best army in the world. While in actuality armies are a rabble, a dumping pit for felons and cutthroats. Only absolute obedience, born of the rope and the lash, enables them to function.'

'Our forces *are* properly disciplined, ma'am. And as a result, as fighters they're peerless.'

'You don't know the meaning of the word. Nor will you until I fashion a force that's *truly* peerless. Merciless and totally compliant. The executions will go ahead. As to your own behaviour, as the one ultimately answerable, I've issued you with enough warnings about your behaviour. Be sure that this is the last one.'

'Ma'am.' For all his iron reputation, and his position of command, he lowered his eyes from hers.

'Cheer up, General,' Jennesta told him. 'Your forces will have the chance to prove you right very soon.' She looked out at the rising sun, bloody red on the horizon. 'Something tells me it's going to be an interesting day.'

On a periphery of the city, in a location passed on by word of mouth in marketplaces, taverns and cornfields, a crowd was gathering. The area was shabby, with little to tempt visitors, and dawn had barely broken, yet a large number had collected. More were arriving by the minute, on foot, by horseback, in packed wagons.

Up above, the comet was plain, even when rivalled by the climbing sun.

The quarter was one of mean dwellings, stables and depositories, largely derelict. The focus of the crowd was a particular warehouse, some three-storeys tall, that once served as a grain store. There was a gallery, or veranda, projecting from its second floor, onto which sacks were hoisted. It was a perfect point to address the crowd from.

Inside the building the atmosphere was tense. Many rebels were assembled, along with all the Wolverines. The humans, Pepperdyne and Standeven, were not present, and nor were Jup and Spurral. It was thought best to keep them out of sight of the crowd.

Principal Sylandya, Acurial's aged matriarch, was the centre of attention. She sat as though enthroned, on a hastily found, down-at-heel chair, and she wore the scarlet robe that signified the office she had never renounced. A small army of rebels buzzed about her. But her offspring, the twins Brelan and Chillder, stayed closest. A privilege that had been temporarily extended to Stryke and Coilla, though Stryke at least suspected this was because Sylandya found the Wolverines intriguing, and perhaps a bit exotic.

'Do you have your speech prepared, Mother?' Chillder asked.

'No. This is not a time for lectures. I'll speak from the heart, and the words I need will come.'

Brelan smiled. 'A typically wise decision.'

'You always knew how to flatter your old mother,' Sylandya told him. 'But no soft-soap today, I beg you. I need an honest steer from both of you on what we're doing here.'

'You have doubts?' Chillder said, frowning.

'*Of course* I have doubts. I hope I've raised you well enough to know I would. What I'm about to say to that crowd is going to have a price. A price paid in blood. Citizens are going to suffer.'

'They're suffering already, and the way things are it'll never stop. Surely it's better to pay that price to rid ourselves of the occupiers?'

'That's what my head says. My feelings aren't so clear-cut.' She turned to Stryke. 'What do our friends from . . . the north think?'

Stryke didn't miss her slight hesitation, and not for the first time suspected she was more sceptical about his band's story than her children were. 'The orcs here have a choice. They can be cattle fit for slaughter or snow leopards lusting for prey. If they're going to throw off the yoke they need to remember what they are. Your call to arms and that thing in the sky could do it.'

'Snow leopards? That's a class of beast I'm not familiar with in what I know of Acurial. They must be confined to your northern wastes.' She eyed the necklace of leopards' fangs he wore as a trophy about his neck, and gave him a look half quizzical, half amused.

Stryke cursed himself for mentioning something unknown in this world. He said nothing.

'But of course you're right,' she went on. 'Most of this land's orcs have lived too long in a dream. My hope is that we can wake them. Whether Grilan-Zeat and my poor words can bring that about is moot.' She smiled. 'Oh, and the prophecy concerning a band of heroes. Let's not forget that.'

'How much stock do you put in it?' Coilla asked.

'Prophecies and comets? It could all be so much moonfluff. Though I wouldn't tell your Sergeant Haskeer that; he seems rather taken with the romance of it.'

'A big old softie, that's our Haskeer,' Coilla told her with a straight face.

'I've no idea if the legends and omens have any real meaning,' Sylandya repeated, 'and frankly I don't care. I'll use whatever it takes to gain our freedom. Needs must.'

'You've no qualms about telling the citizens a lie?'

'I didn't say it *was* a lie. But even if it is, sometimes a lie in the service of truth is tolerable.'

'Makes sense to me,' Stryke remarked.

Brelan came forward. 'It's time, Mother. Are you ready?'

'Ready as I'll ever be.' She clutched his hand, and reached for his sister's. 'We're about to enter an abyss, in hope of finding the light beyond. You two have to promise me that whatever happens you'll keep faith with our cause.'

'You'll be here to make sure we do,' Chillder replied.

'The fate of the nation doesn't depend on one individual. Things change. *Promise.*'

'I promise.'

'Me, too,' Brelan echoed. 'But I think you're being—'

Sylandya placed her fingers on his lips, stilling him. 'You said it was time.'

The twins nodded. She rose and they moved to either side of her, taking her arms.

A little procession formed, led by the Primary and the siblings. Several members of the resistance council followed, with Stryke and Coilla falling in at the rear. They made their way up a staircase to the floor above, and from there out onto the balcony-like veranda. A number of rebels were already there, as were a handful of Wolverines, including Haskeer.

From their vantage point they could make out the size of the crowd, which had further swollen. More orcs were arriving. When they recognised Sylandya, their roar was like thunder.

'How's she going to make herself heard over this din?' Coilla bellowed into Stryke's ear.

He shrugged.

When Brelan raised his arms, the crowd immediately fell silent. They boomed again when he announced the Principal, then resumed an expectant hush.

Gently refusing her children's support, Sylandya stepped forward. Straight-backed, her face a picture of resolve, she seemed the exact opposite of the frail oldster of a moment before. And when she spoke it was in an impressively strong, loud voice. 'Citizens of Acurial!' They roared once more at that, and even louder when she amended it to, 'Citizens of *free* Acurial!'

When the clamour died down she continued, 'We have suffered greatly in recent times! Our liberty has been stolen and our land defiled! Too long have we stood back and endured the indignities heaped upon us and the assaults on our pride!'

Archers were on the veranda, scanning the crowd. In the horde itself, rebels, Wolverines and Vixens were watchful for any sign of opposition.

'The time is long overdue for us to throw off the shackles the outsiders have forged for us! And now we have a sign!'

Stryke couldn't say what drew his eye to a figure way over beyond the farthest edge of the crowd. It was true that whoever it was wore a cloak and hood that obscured their features, but many in the crowd were dressed that way, for fear of being identified. And the figure was far enough away to present no threat to the Principal; too far even for an arrow to be unleashed with sufficient strength or accuracy. Yet Stryke still stared.

'We have the blessings of our revered forebears! We have the assurance of a prophecy! There! There in the sky!' She pointed to the heavens. The crowd went wild.

Stryke saw the figure take something from the folds of their cloak. He couldn't make out what it was.

'Peczan has held us in bondage long enough! Now Grilan-Zeat has come, a hammer to break the chains that bind us!'

The figure cast the object into the air. Or rather, released it. Whatever it was soared upward, seemingly of its own volition. Then it levelled out and started moving over the crowd.

'We have a heritage! A heritage of ferocity and battle, of victory over our foes! A heritage we have allowed ourselves to forget! Well, now the time has come to reawaken that slumbering spirit! To set free the hounds of war!'

As it got nearer, Stryke could see that the object had wings. At which point he stopped thinking of it as an object and started thinking of it as a bird. A white bird, not particularly large, flapping unerringly in their direction. He wondered what harm a bird could do.

'Coilla,' he whispered, nudging her. 'See that?' He pointed, but not obviously so.

She squinted. 'A bird? Looks like a dove.'

'Yes, I think it is a dove.' He noticed that the figure who released it had gone.

'What about it?' she asked slightly peevishly, irritated at him talking over Sylandya's speech.

'It's . . . not right.'

'When we raise arms against our oppressors it is in pursuit of a righteous cause! The cause of freedom!'

'What do you mean, not right?' Coilla hissed. 'It's a fucking *bird*.'

'No,' Stryke replied. 'I don't know what it is, but . . .'

The dove was a stone's throw away and heading straight at them.

'No longer will we dwell miserably in the dark! We shall take up our blades and carve our way to the light! No matter how much human flesh stands in our path!'

'Brelan! Chillder!' Stryke yelled. '*Danger!*'

The principal faltered, and looked at him. Everyone else on the veranda did likewise, some open-mouthed, others with angry expressions.

'Something's coming!' Stryke shouted. 'There!' He thrust out an arm to indicate the approaching threat.

As he did so, a change rapidly came over the dove. It became somehow indistinct, and began to alter its shape. But it kept coming. Some in the crowd noticed it and reacted noisily.

Stryke snatched a bow from one of the rebels, drew it and took aim.

The dove transformed into a swirling black cloud, with streaks of gold and silver pulsing at its core.

Everyone on the balcony was in disarray. Stryke loosed his arrow.

A bolt of pure white light, blindingly vivid, erupted from the cloud. It covered the distance to the balcony in an instant, striking Sylandya. She collapsed, a smouldering wound in her chest.

The cloud that had been a bird that wasn't a bird, dissolved.

There was uproar. Brelan and Chillder, ashen with shock, half carried, half dragged their stricken mother inside. Stryke, Coilla and a number of the rebels went with them.

The crowd was in turmoil.

They laid Sylandya on some sacking. Brelan slipped out of his jerkin and folded it as a pillow for her head. He and Chillder seemed distraught to the point of panic. A rebel medic elbowed his way through. One look at the gaping, charred wound told him all he needed to know. He turned to the twins and slowly shook his head.

Sylandya was still conscious. Her lips moved feebly. Brelan and Chillder moved closer.

'Remember,' she whispered, 'remember . . . your . . . promise.'

'We will,' Brelan pledged, squeezing her hand.

Then Sylandya's eyes closed and the last breath went out of her.

The twins surrendered to despair.

Chillder rose. She wore a look of hurt and bewilderment.

Coilla went to her and put her hands on her shoulders. 'Courage,' she said.

'She knew,' Chillder replied, as though separated from the world by a great distance. 'Somehow, she knew.'

The crowd was making a tremendous racket. Stryke went back outside.

Haskeer was still there, surveying the scene below. '*Shit*,' he said. 'And on our watch.'

'We couldn't have foreseen it,' Stryke assured him, though he wasn't entirely sure that was true. 'I'll tell you one thing. I doubt that was Helix magic.'

'Jennesta?'

'Who else? Getting some minion to assassinate the one orc who could rally the populace would be right up her alley.'

'To cow them?' He gazed at the frantic crowd. 'They don't look too put off to me. Just the opposite.'

'No,' Stryke agreed. 'This could be Jennesta's biggest mistake.'

10

Stryke was proved right, and in short order.

Far from intimidating Acurial's population, the murder of Sylandya enraged it. Attacks on the occupiers immediately increased ten-fold. Not just in the city but throughout the country. Many of the assaults were opportunistic, and carried out by individuals or small *ad hoc* groups. One of the resistance's tasks was to coordinate these actions, and to organise the growing number of dissidents into a coherent fighting force. Within days they had the makings of a rebel army.

Brelan and Chillder channelled their grief into these activities, working with demonic energy in their mother's name; and the Wolverines were heavily involved in training the new intake. But the warband drew most satisfaction from doing what they did best: confronting occupiers on the streets of Taress.

In this, Jup and Spurral, and the human, Pepperdyne, were given roles to play. The dwarfs in particular, after being confined for so long, found it a pleasing outlet. Though none of the trio ever ventured out unaccompanied by fellow band members or rebel fighters, lest they be taken for enemies or freaks. For Standeven, little changed. Useless in any kind of combat function, his contribution was centred on manual work at various safe houses, which he undertook grudgingly. But he mostly confined his complaints to the Wolverines. The incident of the dead intruder had been eclipsed by the burgeoning uprising, but not forgotten.

For his part, Stryke kept the instrumentalities with him at all times, even in combat. He was not about to repeat the mistake of entrusting any of them to anyone else, even the most loyal of his comrades. There were mixed feelings about this in the band.

One discovery of the Wolverines, which dismayed them, was that some orcs allied themselves with the occupying humans. They were small in number and didn't dare do it openly, preferring to act as fifth columnists and informers, but the effect on morale was something else to be countered. Chillder and Brelan were especially shocked by this development, having regarded their fellow citizens as patriots, and they dealt with traitors harshly when they were caught. It was an element that added another variable to an already chaotic situation.

The resistance's growing numbers meant the way the occupiers were engaged was changing. There were still plenty of guerrilla raids, but large-scale, more conventional face-offs were starting to replace them. For these, the Wolverines' expertise was invaluable.

So it was that a week after Sylandya's death, which many were already calling her martyrdom, the entire band stood together on one of Taress' main thoroughfares. At their backs was a force of several hundred insurgents, ragtag and ill-armed, but eager for blood. Ahead, a good lance throw away, an equal number of human militia was gathered. They were better ordered and better equipped, but unused to being challenged by creatures with a newfound passion for warfare.

Events were at the sham stage, as the Wolverines knew it, with both sides exchanging catcalls, insults and threatening gestures. A standard practice before a battle.

'How'd you think they'll hold up?' Coilla said, jerking a thumb at the ranks behind them.

'What they lack in know-how they make up for in rage,' Stryke reckoned.

'Still gonna get most of 'em killed,' Haskeer muttered. 'Fucking amateurs.'

'Even a legendary band of heroes can't have a revolution without an army,' Stryke replied.

Jup guffawed.

'What's *your* problem, pisspot?' Haskeer snapped.

'I'm standing next to you.'

'Hang on while I die laughing.'

'Don't mind him, Jup,' Coilla said. 'He's still swollen-headed about a human he killed yesterday.'

'Why? What's so special about that?'

'It wasn't a soldier.'

'What was he?' Pepperdyne asked.

'A tax gatherer.'

Pepperdyne considered that for a moment. 'Well, fair enough.'

They all murmured agreement.

'When's this going to kick off?' Dallog wanted to know as he surveyed the enemy line.

'Yeah,' Wheam piped up. 'When we gonna *fight*?' He swished around the sword he was clutching.

'Careful with that thing!' Haskeer protested. 'You'll have somebody's eye out!'

'It'll start soon enough,' Stryke said. 'Remember the tyros are your charge, Dallog.' He glanced at the new band members, those recruited on Ceragan. They looked tense and ashen. 'Especially him,' he added, nodding at Wheam.

Wheam looked discomfited.

'They'll be fine,' Dallog assured him, though his expression was grim.

'Come on, *come on*,' Spurral muttered, impatiently drumming the cobblestones with her staff.

'Your female's keen for the off, shortarse,' Haskeer observed. It was said not without a trace of admiration.

'Yes, and she'll take it out on you if this thing doesn't hot up soon,' Jup came back.

'Here we go,' Coilla said. 'They're moving.'

The human troops began to advance. Subject to rigid military discipline, they progressed in an orderly fashion.

'*Advance!*' Stryke yelled, raising his blade.

The crowd of orcs was more shambolic as it went forward, but its passion was high. They started to beat their shields and bellow war cries.

As the humans picked up speed and added their own battle cries to the din, they found the orcs had hidden allies. From rooftops and high windows, citizens proceeded to rain objects down on their heads. A volley of tiles, bricks, pots and the occasional arrow fell like lethal hail.

When the opposing forces were near enough to see the expressions of fear, bloodlust, fury and foreboding on each others' faces, both sides broke into a charge.

The two living tides swept together and melded in a brutal frenzy.

The battle, the latest in a series that occurred almost daily, took place in the hub of the city. Central enough, in fact, that although it couldn't quite be seen from the fortress of Taress, it could certainly be heard.

For Jennesta and Hacher, ensconced in her quarters at one of the redoubt's loftiest points, it was a near permanent background noise. Not that they were consciously listening. The events in Jennesta's chambers took precedence over death's raucous clamour.

'Well, I'm waiting,' she repeated, arms folded resolutely.

'I'm at a loss to know what you expect of me, ma'am,' the general replied.

'Yes, and that's the problem, isn't it? Perhaps you could start by telling me what you intend doing about the anarchy out there.' She waved an arm at the window.

'The present situation, with respect, ma'am, has been brought about by the assassination of the female the orcs called their Principal. I could almost believe it was an act designed to stir things up even further, and—'

'Are you questioning my methods?'

'I think I am, my lady. Even before the Principal's death we made certain moves that only worsened the situation in this province. Actions, I have to say, that you drove.'

'*Now* you find the guts! It's a pity you didn't have the resolve you're now showing towards me when you were supposed to be defending Peczan's interests.'

'I've always worked as diligently as I could in service to the empire,' he responded irately.

'No. You might think that, but you haven't. Your actions have undermined everything that should have been done here. And *would* have been done by a competent commander.'

Hacher was allowing himself to grow heated. 'Before your arrival, *my lady*, we had a situation here that was manageable. Your . . . *initiatives* have turned simple law enforcement into a much graver problem.'

'Let me tell you the *real* problem, Hacher.' She counted items off on her bejewelled fingers. 'You failed to anticipate the potential for rebellion these animals harboured, or to recognise their capacity for savagery, despite me telling you so. You led your forces in a shambolic way. You weakened the effectiveness of the imperial presence here because of political infighting with the Helix. Above all, you stubbornly refused to accept that the only thing the natives of this godsforsaken land understand is strength. In short, General, *you* are the problem.'

'Look where an excessive show of strength has got us, ma'am. Look at the streets. See what we've bought with our display of strength and brutality.'

'Too *little* brutality, too *late*! You know, you really do baffle me. Your reputation was of a governor who didn't allow mercy to cloud his judgement. They call you *Iron Hand*, for the gods' sake! Yet you shy from taking that hand from its silken glove.'

'Don't mistake my objections for a taste for leniency, my lady. Mine is not a moral stance. I'd execute the whole population of Acurial if it furthered our purposes. And I would have ordered the death of the Principal myself if I thought it would do some good. It's the strategic line we've taken that I argue with. Your measures, not least the elimination of Sylandya, have soured the air and stretched our forces to breaking point.'

'I'm never going to get through to you, am I?'

'I prefer to say that we have an honest disagreement over policy, ma'am.'

'I don't tolerate disagreement. I tell subordinates where they've gone wrong and they conform to my will. That's how it works.' She threw back her head in a gesture of exasperation. 'Oh, why am I wasting my breath on you? And not just you. The whole system in this place is riddled with far too much free-thinking, and you're not the only culprit. But that's going to change. Radically.'

'Ma'am?'

There was a sound at her chamber door. It wasn't so much a knock as a series of thumps and a coarse scratching. A couple of seconds later the door opened, and a pair of Jennesta's undead bodyguards shuffled in carrying something wrapped by a black winding cloth, not unlike a shroud. They dumped their bundle at Jennesta's feet and looked up to her as though they were faithful curs bringing their mistress an outsized bone.

'Ah,' she said, 'the first fruit of my reforms.'

Rather than assign the task to her clumsy servers, she knelt and began to undo the sheet herself. What she revealed when she threw it open shocked Hacher to the core.

'Brother . . . Grentor?' he murmured, not entirely sure his identification was correct.

His uncertainty arose from the state of the cleric's corpse. It had been horribly mutilated, and to Hacher's disgust some parts of the body bore signs of having been gnawed upon. A perk allowed Jennesta's zombies, he suspected.

'You appear taken aback, General.'

'Of . . . of course I'm shaken. How did he come to this? Was he a victim of the rebels?' He added the latter in desperate hope that it was the explanation, as opposed to the only other alternative.

'No, he fell victim to me,' she informed him evenly and confirming his fear. 'The leadership of the Order has fallen into as parlous a state as the military. It was time for a change.'

'But this is surely too harsh a way to bring it about?'

'It's the *only* way.' She was talking through gritted teeth. 'I keep *telling* you: a demonstration of ruthlessness is the best remedy for keeping underlings in check. Why should I stand by and watch the Helix squabble and deliberate endlessly before they throw up another Grentor to take this weakling's place? Better that I decide the matter swiftly, with a lesson for them as part of the bargain.'

There was another rap at the door. But this was a proper knock, brisk and crisp.

'Come!' she called.

Hacher's aide, Frynt, entered, giving Jennesta a slight bow of his head as he came in.

The general was confounded to see him. 'Frynt? I thought you were occupied on the west side today.' There was no reply. Hacher's gaze flicked to Grentor's remains. 'I'm afraid the good brother has met a rather unfortunate—'

'Don't bother,' Jennesta said. 'He knows.'

'I . . . I don't understand, my lady.'

'Meet the new Governor of the province of Acurial, and Commander-in-Chief of its army.'

'Am I to understand—'

'You are hereby relieved of all your duties and titles, Hacher. Frynt steps into your clumping boots.'

He turned to his erstwhile aide. 'Frynt? Is this so?'

'Sorry, sir.' He didn't look it. 'But a servant of the empire has a patriotic duty to stand up when called.'

'Or to further their own selfish interests. I thought you were loyal.'

'I am, sir. To the emp—' Jennesta caught his eye. 'To our lady Jennesta and the empire. There is no personal dimension involved.'

'How could you condone this?' Hacher indicated Grentor's body. 'In what warped view can it be considered a positive act?'

'The lady Jennesta has convinced me of the need for change, and for that change to be instigated with a certain . . . vigour.'

'I thought better of you, Frynt. You disappoint me.'

'Then you know how I feel about you,' Jennesta told him. 'There's no point in arguing. Let's save your breath, shall we?'

'Argue I most certainly will, my lady. I'll take this high-handed deed to the ears of the highest in Peczan. If I'm to be sent home in disgrace—'

'Oh no, General; you're not going home. I have a much more useful role for you.'

Her zombie slaves had positioned themselves as the living spoke. Now at her signal they moved in with surprising speed and seized the deposed general. He cried out, protested and cursed, but they held him fast.

Jennesta approached the struggling figure, her hands raised preparatory to casting a glamour. 'As I said,' she intoned, 'let's save your breath.'

Frynt watched, stunned. He didn't know this was going to happen, let alone that he would be obliged to witness the general's fate.

The horror of it gave him an inkling of what it would be like serving his new mistress.

When Hacher started screaming, Frynt closed his eyes.

11

By the end of the third week of the uprising proper, with the ranks of the resistance growing still further, the balance of power started to radically shift. As the Peczan military suffered daily trouncings by armed insurgents, and civil disobedience became widespread, a tipping point was reached. The invaders, until so recently masters of a conquered land, were on the back foot.

Although it was a change the rebels had worked, hoped and died for, even the most optimistic of them were stunned by the speed with which it came about. Ever larger sections of the population shed their former meekness to reveal the inherent fighting spirit that had lain buried for so long. Their pent-up grievance drove a thirst for freedom, and inspired by the radiant presence of Grilan-Zeat, they unleashed a savagery unlike any the humans had faced before.

It was around this time, when fighting was at its most intense, that Wheam took the first small step to redeeming himself.

He had performed competently in the clashes he was allowed to take part in. Or at least he hadn't brought a major disaster down on the warband's heads or got himself killed. Though nor had he managed to slay, wound or greatly inconvenience any of the enemy. Nevertheless it became almost a matter of routine to include him in missions, under the watchful eye of Dallog and other more experienced band members.

The Wolverines had been allotted a role in a raid on a house where army officers were billeted. It didn't go to plan. Due to foresight on the part of the authorities, or possibly because of an informant, a company of soldiers had been concealed nearby. What should have been a clean hit and run attack turned into a pitched battle in one of the few street markets still functioning in the capital. In the process the band was scattered, and Coilla, Haskeer and Wheam found themselves sheltering in a narrow, foul-smelling alley off the main highway.

Haskeer was less than pleased to be stuck with the novice. 'Get in here!' he growled, pulling Wheam back from the alley's mouth. 'You wanna lose your fucking head to an arrow? Not that I should care.'

'Sorry,' the young one replied tremulously.

'Go easy on him,' Coilla said. 'He's still cutting his teeth, remember.'

'Wish he was cutting his damn throat. And what's with *this?*' He slapped at the lute Wheam had strapped to his back. 'What the hell you doing bringing a thing like that to a fight?'

'It's the only way I can be sure not to lose it,' Wheam explained, 'what with us always moving safe houses and—'

'Yeah, yeah. Should have known you'd have some bullshit reason. Just keep it out of my face.'

'Is it clearing out there?' Coilla asked.

Haskeer poked his head round the corner. 'Looks like it.'

'Shall we make a break?'

'Yeah. Our lot are somewhere down on the right.' He turned to Wheam. 'That's *that* way.' He jabbed his thumb rightward. 'Case it's too hard for you to work out.'

'Soon as we're out of here, Wheam, just run,' Coilla told him. 'Fast.'

He nodded.

'Ready?' Haskeer said. 'Right. Three . . . two . . . *go!*'

They came out of the alley at a dash, swerved right and started racing through the debris of the ruined market. There were overturned stalls, and fallen orcs and humans among the trampled fruit and vegetables, broken pottery and strewn clothing.

Coilla looked back. '*We've company!*'

A large gang of soldiers had appeared and were chasing them.

Wheam, at the rear, was struggling to keep up with Coilla and Haskeer.

'Come on!' Coilla urged. 'Move it!'

One trooper, a strong runner, was well ahead of the pack and gaining on Wheam. The tyro himself was flagging, and the soldier got near enough to brush his back with his fingertips. Then he caught hold of the strap holding the lute and wrenched it free.

Wheam ran on. The instrument fell clattering to the ground. Two of the strings snapped melodiously. The human, still running hard, kicked the lute out of his path. It sailed across the street and landed with a crash, breaking into pieces.

Wheam stopped, turned and gasped.

Coilla and Haskeer shouted at him. 'Come *on!* Leave it! *Move your arse!*'

The rest of the soldiers were sprinting forward and closing the gap.

'My . . . lute,' Wheam whispered. His eyes moved to the approaching soldier. '*Bastard.*'

An uncharacteristically crazed expression came to Wheam's face. He drew his sword. Seeing this, the running soldier slowed and went for his own.

Wheam charged him, waving his blade and screaming incomprehensibly. He launched himself at the man like a wild thing, thrashing and slashing a storm. Such was the force of his attack that the trooper fell back a pace or two. He had his sword up, but purely defensively.

Coilla and Haskeer had stopped by this time. They watched Wheam laying about the soldier; and beyond, the human's thundering group of comrades, getting nearer.

'We have to go and fetch the little fucker,' Coilla said.

Haskeer made a disturbing noise somewhere deep in his throat and balled his fists. He nodded, curtly.

They unsheathed their weapons and headed back.

Wheam's deranged battering had the trooper retreating at a steady pace. He had no hope of overcoming the pint-sized whirlwind, but could only try to fend him off until his companions arrived.

In the event, it was in vain. Wheam landed a blow on the human's forearm, opening a deep, copious wound. Next he thrust his blade into the man's midriff, setting him staggering. Yelling what sounded like gibberish, though the word *lute* seemed to feature quite a lot, he pummelled his foe mercilessly, shredding flesh and cracking bones.

He was still hacking at the corpse when Coilla and Haskeer got there. Wheam swung round and growled at them, eyes blazing, sword raised.

'*Whoa!*' Coilla shouted. 'It's us!'

Wheam blinked and focused. A little of the bloodlust drained away. He looked at the sword in his hand, then down at his victim.

'Nice one,' Haskeer complimented.

'Don't believe it,' Coilla said. 'A good word for Wheam.'

'Don't sweat it,' Haskeer grated. 'I'm not giving him a fucking medal.'

'Er . . . the soldiers,' Wheam interrupted, pointing along the street with his blade.

They were almost upon them.

'No time to run now,' Coilla decided.

'We stand,' Haskeer agreed.

The three of them stretched out in a line across the road and braced themselves. Near enough that their features could be plainly seen, the soldiers began whooping and waving their swords.

An open wagon careered round the corner from a side street and came to an abrupt halt between the two sides. A couple more followed, loaded with rebels who hastily leapt out to take on the mob of soldiers.

Stryke was in the back of the first wagon, alongside Brelan. He gestured for Haskeer, Coilla and Wheam to jump on. They quickly clambered aboard and the wagon moved off at speed.

Coilla expelled the breath she'd been holding. 'Good timing.'

'Glad you could make it,' Stryke replied. 'How'd you get on?'

'Killed our share,' Haskeer informed him bluntly.

'Wheam gets the gold feather,' Coilla said. 'Claimed his first kill.'

Stryke looked impressed. 'Well done. You'll find it'll come naturally now.'

Wheam mumbled something that included the words *lute* and *bastard*.

'What?'

'Broke my lute,' Wheam grumbled. 'Swine.'

Stryke gave Coilla a quizzical look.

'Human broke his thingamabob,' she explained. 'Lit Wheam's fire.'

'We'll find you another one,' Stryke promised.

'No we fucking won't,' Haskeer exclaimed, alarmed. He saw Stryke's face and shut up.

'Where we going?' Coilla asked.

Brelan spoke for the first time. 'Not far. A place we commandeered near the centre. There's something you Wolverines need to know.'

He wouldn't be drawn on what, and the rest of the journey was spent in silence through streets much emptier than they had been before the uprising took hold.

Soon they came to a large civic hall, complete with columns and surrounded by ornate iron fences. It was an old building, originating in the orcs' distant, more glorious past. Latterly it had been taken over by the occupiers. It was testament to the progress the rebels had made that they had taken it back.

Brelan suggested that Coilla, Wheam and Haskeer clean up and feed themselves while he talked with Stryke. Reluctantly, they obeyed.

Stryke was taken along crowded corridors and past faded embellishments to a room empty but for Chillder.

'We have news,' Brelan stated without preamble.

'So spit it out,' Stryke suggested.

'We thought we'd made things bad for the humans. Now we know it. We've heard that Jennesta's getting ready to flee the city.'

'How do you know this?'

'Oh, the word's reliable. We've an army of informers, some in high places. They say she's got together a bunch of military loyal to her and they're about to make for the south coast, probably to a waiting ship. She might have left already.'

'You can't let her get away.'

'Unfortunately, we can.'

'But—'

Brelan stilled him with a raised hand. 'We can't spare the forces. And when it comes down to it, she's just one individual. It's all the same to us if she's gone or dead. She'll still be out of our way.'

'Brelan, you can't—'

'*But* you and your band are free agents. And we know you have some kind of personal grudge against Jennesta, so—'

'A grudge?'

'We're not stupid. You know, our mother never quite believed your story, and we've always had doubts about where you were from and what you were doing here.'

'There's no need to say anything, Stryke,' Chillder assured him. 'We're grateful enough to you and your band that anything that's gone before isn't important.'

'Will you do it?' Brelan wanted to know. 'We've fresh horses for you, and supplies. What we can't let you have is any of our fighters.'

'Wouldn't want 'em. Though a guide would help.'

'We've maps.'

'Good enough. But I need to talk this over with my band.'

'They're gathered downstairs. Don't be long. Jennesta might already have a head start.'

Stryke was taken to a large chamber that looked as though it had served as a grand feasting room in olden days. All the Wolverines were there, as were Pepperdyne and Standeven. Jugs of water and of wine had been put out for them. Haskeer was sampling the wine. Wheam was being made a fuss over by his fellow tyros, and not a few Wolverines.

'We've got to make this quick,' Stryke informed them briskly. 'You been told what's going on?' Just about everybody shook their heads. 'Story is Jennesta's about to run for the coast. Might have started by now.'

'What are the rebels doing about it?' Coilla wanted to know.

'It's down to us. If we want the mission.'

'Do we fuck,' Haskeer thundered. 'Let's go after the bitch.'

There was a general murmur of agreement.

'Anybody see why we shouldn't?' Stryke said.

No one did.

'So what's the plan?' Pepperdyne asked.

'Wait a minute,' Haskeer objected. 'Who said you were coming along?'

'I'm not wasting time arguing about these two,' Stryke declared, waving a hand at Pepperdyne and Standeven. 'Choice is between leaving them here or taking them with us. I reckon it's better to take 'em.'

'Why?'

'They have a grievance against Jennesta too,' Coilla reminded him. 'Don't you, Jode?'

'Er . . . yes.' He knew this was no time to deviate from the cover story he and Standeven had concocted.

'And we know Jode's more than handy in a scrap,' Coilla added.

'Maybe,' Haskeer granted. 'But why do we need this other one? He's no use in a fight.'

'Talk about me like I'm not here, why don't you,' Standeven protested.

'Yeah, we will,' Stryke assured him. 'I reckon I'd rather have you where I can see you, 'specially given how the rebels feel about that thing with the intruder. Or whatever he was.'

'How many more times,' Standeven responded, 'do I have to explain—'

'We're not going through it again. You two are coming. And like I said, we're not debating this. All of you; get yourselves ready, on the double. We leave as soon as I've seen Brelan and Chillder.'

'I'll come with you,' Coilla decided.

They left the band collecting their gear.

The first thing Chillder said when they found her was, 'You're going?'

Stryke nodded.

'I have a feeling we won't be seeing you again.'

'Who knows?' Strangely, he had a similar feeling.

'I hope we will,' Brelan offered.

'Way things are going,' Coilla reckoned, 'you two are probably going to be too busy running the country.'

'Thanks in part to you. And we're grateful.'

'Yeah, well,' Stryke told them, 'let's not get sloppy. We could lose Jennesta and be back tomorrow.'

'Perhaps.'

'I'd like to have a minute with the Vixens,' Coilla requested.

'Most of them are outside,' Brelan said.

'That all right, Stryke? I'll be quick.'

'Go.'

She wished the twins good luck and went out.

Chillder smiled. 'Whatever your true goal is, Stryke, we hope you reach it.' As he was leaving she added, 'That bit in the prophecy about a legendary band.'

'What of it?'

'Maybe it was true.'

12

There was only one main road leading to the southern coast. Or more accurately only one that was likely to be suitable for the small army accompanying Jennesta. The Wolverines took it.

Before they left, they learned a little more from the rebels' spies. General Hacher, it seemed, had mysteriously disappeared. Having promoted some aide or other to fill the gap, Jennesta had promptly abandoned the successor to his fate. Of more interest to the band was that she had insisted on being transported from the city by carriage, and that supply wagons had been taken along. The Wolverines, on the other hand, travelled light.

After a quarter day's hard riding they got a first glimpse of the sea. Their approach was on high ground, and they could look down on the bay and its tiny harbour.

'No ship,' Coilla said.

'And no Jennesta,' Stryke replied.

'Could she have got away?'

'Doubt it. There's not been time. You'd at least expect to see a sail on the horizon. I reckon the ship she's summoned hasn't got here yet.'

'So where is she?'

'Dunno. Send out scouts.' He had an idea. 'No, wait. *Jup! Over here!*'

The dwarf galloped to him. 'Chief?'

'There's no sign of her.'

'So I see.'

'Think your farsight could help? Might be quicker than searching.'

'I'll give it a try.'

He climbed down from his horse, not without difficulty given his size, watched by an amused Haskeer. Jup flashed him an offensive gesture. Then he walked a little way from the others, knelt down and began worming his fingers into the sandy earth. The tyros and the two humans, unused to Jup's gift, watched with interest.

'What if she *has* gone, Stryke?' Coilla said. 'Maybe she did catch a ship. What then?'

He sighed and gave it some thought. 'Maybe the rebels could help us find out where she's gone, and maybe we could—'

'Follow her to this Peczan empire? A fucking *empire*, Stryke. Want to fight one of those?'

'Or we could go back and carry on with the resistance.'

'We've done about as much for them as we can, and you know it. And what do we do when the revolution's over? Go home, knowing we only coped with half the mission?'

'If she's really got away, we might have to.'

'Shit on that,' Coilla hissed.

Jup shouted and beckoned them over. Stryke gave the order to dismount, and the band went to him.

'Any luck?' Coilla wondered.

Jup nodded. He still had his hand half buried in the ground.

'Where?' Stryke said.

'A little inland and to the west.'

'Sure it's them?'

'Well, farsight isn't like seeing a picture somebody's painted or a page from a book. It. . . it's hard to explain. Just say that what I'm getting is like a spread of gems on a black cloth. There's lots of 'em. That means a sizeable number of living things. Not animals either; they flare differently. And right in the middle of all that there's a big, blood-red diamond, pulsing like . . . well, I don't want to think like what.'

'That's Jennesta?'

'I'd bet a year's pay on it. If we got paid. It has to be them, Stryke. But . . .' He looked troubled.

'What?'

'There's something else. Back the way we came, and further off, but even stronger despite the distance.'

Heads turned in the direction he'd indicated.

'What you saying? Another force?'

'Maybe. I've never seen anything like it before.'

'Could *that* be Jennesta,' Coilla asked, 'and the bunch westward somebody else?'

'No. They have a totally different . . . *flavour*. Jennesta's a murky diamond. Whatever this is, it's . . . a whole string of them, only shining white. If I was using my eyes for this I'd be blinded.'

'Could it be natural?' Stryke said.

'Possibly. Sometimes you get a particularly strong impression from something like a large, fast-flowing river, or certain rich mineral seams. And of course we don't really know Acurial very well; there could be any number of things that affect farsight. Still damn strange though.' He pulled his hand from the earth. 'Like a second opinion from Spurral? Her gift's at least as strong as mine.'

Stryke pondered the offer. 'That won't tell us any more than we know, will it?'

'Unlikely.'

'Then we'll hope it's natural, and harmless. Forget it. It's Jennesta we're concerned about. Let's head west.'

As Jup said the distance wasn't too great, Stryke ordered the band to lead their horses, the better to approach with stealth.

In the event their march took them into the lengthening shadows of evening. Until at last a pathfinder returned noiselessly to tell them the encampment was ahead.

It lay in a grassy hollow at the foot of a chalk cliff. There were guards, but they would be easily dealt with. On their bellies, the band peered down at the camp from the cliff-top. There were perhaps a couple of hundred humans present, mostly uniformed. Three covered wagons stood to one side of the clearing, and a carriage, presumably Jennesta's, was parked near its centre.

'How we going to deal with that many, Stryke?' Coilla said.

'We've faced bigger odds.'

'Hmm. Something wily might be better.'

'You're our Mistress of Strategy. So strat.'

She smiled. 'I'll think of something.'

Stretched out full-length nearby, Spurral idly worked her fingers into the grassy sward. She closed her eyes.

'*Shit!*' The ground could have been boiling hot going by the speed she pulled out her fingers.

'*Ssshhh!* Keep it down,' Jup whispered. He saw how she looked. 'What is it?'

'I just used the sight. Think I picked up what you did, only this seems a hell of a lot stronger and closer. It's really intense, Jup.'

'Where?' Stryke demanded.

She turned and pointed to the darkening plane behind them.

Stryke looked up and down the Wolverine line. 'Anybody see anything out there?'

Nobody could.

'If that's another bunch of Jennesta's supporters,' Coilla speculated, 'it could be a flanking action.'

'That makes us sitting ducks. All of you: back from the edge and down to the plain.'

They withdrew, moving furtively. They knew Jennesta would have more guards stationed around the camp, and probably patrols. The last thing they needed was to alert them.

Back on the plain, they peered into the gathering gloom.

Haskeer glared at Jup. 'You sure your female's right about this? I can't see a fucking thing.'

'*His female*,' Spurral told him, 'is quite capable of speaking for herself; and yes, I'm sure.'

Haskeer grunted but otherwise kept quiet.

They all stood motionless for several silent minutes, surveying the plain. Stryke wasn't alone in starting to think it was some kind of mistake.

It was Pepperdyne who pointed and said, 'What's that?'

Stryke strained his eyes. 'Can't see anything.'

Coilla chimed in with, 'I can! Look, just to the right of that stand of trees.'

Something was coming out of the murk. As it got nearer they realised it was someone mounted on a white horse. A slight figure, lean and straight-backed.

It came near enough for them to make out what kind of being it was.

'What the *fuck?*' Haskeer exclaimed, voicing the amazement they all felt.

The rider was unmistakably of a race that didn't exist on Acurial.

Halting just short of the band, the rider lifted her hand in a gesture of greeting. 'I'm here in peace. I intend you no harm.'

Stryke found his tongue. 'Who are you?'

'My name is Pelli Madayar.'

'You're an elf.'

'Very observant of you.'

'What the *hell* is—'

'There are some things you'll have to take on trust.'

'Like a member of the elven race turning up here?' Coilla said. 'We need more than trust to take that in our stride. Where are you from?'

'That's not important.'

'Is there a tribe of elves living in Acurial we didn't know about?' Stryke persisted.

'As I said, that's not important.'

'If you're not from this land you must have come from . . . elsewhere.'

'As you did.'

Stryke was taken aback by that, as they all were. 'You seem to know a hell of a lot about us.'

'Perhaps. But I repeat: it's not my intention to do you harm.'

Jup said, 'You wouldn't have come from Maras-Dantia, would you?'

'No. My kind are not confined to any one world. No more than orcs are, as you have found.'

'You with Jennesta?' Stryke wanted to know.

'No. My allegiance lies elsewhere and shouldn't concern you.'

'Helpful, ain't she?' Haskeer muttered.

'There are some things it's better you should not know.'

'Is that so? So how about we beat it out of you?'

The elf was unruffled. 'I wouldn't advise you trying that. We don't want to hurt you.'

Haskeer laughed derisively. 'Hurt us? You and whose army?'

No sooner had he spoken than some of the grunts started shouting and pointing along the plain. A group of riders, about equal in number to the Wolverines, was emerging from the shadows. Many in the band went for their swords.

As they slowly advanced, the nature of the newcomers could be seen. There were goblins, trolls and harpies in their ranks, along with centaurs, gremlins, gnomes, satyrs, kobolds, were-beasts, changelings and individuals from many other races, including some the orcs hadn't seen before.

'This just gets creepier,' Jup remarked, clutching his staff with rapidly whitening knuckles.

'Who the hell are you, Madayar, and what do you want?' Stryke demanded.

'We've come to parley.'

'About what?'

'You have certain things that don't rightfully belong to you. Our duty is to retrieve them.'

'What things?'

'She means the stars, Stryke,' Coilla reckoned.

'Yes,' the elf confirmed. 'The artefacts more properly known as instrumentalities. They cannot stay in your possession.'

'They're ours by right!' Stryke thundered. 'We fought and bled for them. Some of us died on the way.'

'Yeah,' Haskeer added, 'you want 'em, you rip 'em from our corpses.'

'You have no understanding of their power.'

'We've got a pretty good idea,' Stryke said.

'No, you haven't. Not their *real* power, and what they represent. What you've seen so far is just a fraction of their true potential.'

'All the more reason not to hand them over to the first bunch of strangers who come begging.'

'We're not begging, we're asking.'

'The answer's no,' Haskeer told her. 'Now fuck off.'

She ignored that. 'The instrumentalities pose a terrible threat. Our task is to make sure they don't fall into the wrong hands.'

'And yours are the right hands, are they?' Stryke came back. 'I don't buy that.'

'In the name of reason, consider what I'm telling you. If you knew what you were meddling in—'

'So tell us.'

Pelli faltered. 'As I said, some things must rest on trust.'

'Not good enough. You want something from orcs, you've got to take it. If you can.'

Her tone took on a more conciliatory note. 'The ferocity of the orcs, and their bravery, are well known, for all that so many malign you. I know your tenacity and of your valour. But you can't hope to prevail against us.'

Stryke looked to the rest of her group, now at a standstill a short arrow's flight away. 'In our time we've killed many from just about all the races in your ranks. Nothing I see makes me think you'd be any different.'

'Don't judge us by your past experience, Stryke. Your instinct is to fight, I understand that. It's your birthright. But you don't have to surrender to that impulse this time. Rather than lift your blades against us, try thinking instead.'

'You saying we can't think?' Haskeer rumbled.

'I'm saying that in the end you have no choice but to surrender the instrumentalities.'

'Surrender's a word we don't grant,' Stryke replied icily.

'Don't see it as surrender, but rather as a triumph of good sense.'

'And if we don't?'

'Then I have to demand that you turn over the artefacts. Now.'

'We don't take demands either.'

'This is pissing me off,' Haskeer fumed. 'You're *pissing me off*, elf!'

'That's your final word?' Pelli asked.

Stryke nodded. 'Any other parleying gets done with blades.'

'I'm sorry we couldn't reach an agreement.'

'What you going to do about it?'

'Reflect, and consult with my companions.' She turned her mount and began to leave.

'You reflect away!' Haskeer shouted after her. '*And all the fucking good it'll do you!*'

In common with others in the band, several of the new intake had nocked arrows when the strange group appeared. Now one of them, raw and jumpy, accidentally let loose his string. The arrow shot past the retreating elf's head so close she felt the air it displaced.

Pelli Madayar swung about to look their way.

Stryke started to shout. He wanted to say that it was an accident. That the band would fight to the last drop of blood and without mercy, but had no need to put an arrow in the back of anybody under a truce. He didn't get the chance.

The elf pointed her hand their way, then swept it left to right, rapidly. A wave of energy, red-tinged, flew at the band as fast as thought. It hit them with the force of a tempest. All of them. The entire company went down, knocked off their feet as surely as if they'd been struck with mallets. With it, the wave brought pain that coursed through their bodies for a good couple of seconds.

'Gods,' Coilla groaned as she struggled to get up.

'*Stay low!*' Stryke hissed. 'All of you: head for the tree-line. But keep down!'

They scurried for the trees, bent double, trying to zigzag and make themselves harder targets. Halfway there, the air above them lit up with intense, multicoloured beams of light. Rays crackling all around them, they put on a burst of speed and made it into the tiny wood.

'Anybody hit?' Stryke panted.

Miraculously, it seemed no one had been.

'Who the fuck *are* this bunch?' Haskeer said.

'Doesn't matter. Main thing is getting out of the way of their magic.'

'A frontal assault's not on then?' Coilla ventured.

'What do you think? Magic that strong, we'd be lucky to get ten paces.'

'They're coming!' Dallog warned.

The bizarre multi-species company was approaching, riding in a line, steadily.

'We'll get to safer ground and figure out how to fight this,' Stryke decided.

Jup, who with a couple of scouts had penetrated the wood further than the others, came dashing back. He was breathing heavily. 'Not that way. Jennesta's troops.'

'Shit,' Coilla cursed. 'They must have picked up on the racket.'

'Great,' Haskeer grumbled. 'Jennesta and a couple of hundred humans that way, the freak circus over here, and us in the middle.'

'What do we do, Stryke?' Pepperdyne badgered.

'Depends how you want to die.'

Coilla shook her head. 'No, Stryke. There's one other course.'

He didn't have to be told what that was. But he hesitated.

They could hear Jennesta's army now, tramping through the wood and making no effort at furtiveness. The riders were much nearer, too.

'Hurry up, Stryke!' Coilla pleaded.

He reached for the pouch where he kept the stars.

Standeven stared, open mouthed. 'Surely you're not going to—'

'*Shut it,*' Stryke told him as he began pulling out the artefacts. His other hand went to the amulet at his throat.

'There's no time!' Coilla yelled.

The Gateway Corps had reached the tree-line. In the other direction the foremost of Jennesta's troops could be seen moving through the wood, a spit away.

Stryke let go of the amulet and concentrated on the stars, quickly slotting them together in a random pattern.

The whole band instinctively gathered about him.

Standeven started to shout. The words were unintelligible and slick with panic. It almost drowned out the noise Wheam was making.

Stryke took one last look at the comet through the branches overhead. It shone like a night-time sun.

Then he clicked the final instrumentality into place.

13

The bottom had dropped out of the universe.

They were living sparks, sucked through an endless, serpentine tunnel of light. On its supple walls flashed endless images of other realities, moving so fast they were almost a blur. And beyond, outside that terrible shaft, an even more breath-taking actuality; a limitless canopy smothered in countless billions of stars.

The band's only sensation was of helplessly falling. A ceaseless and unremitting plunge into the black maw of the unknown.

Then, after an eternity, they dropped towards a particular chasm, a whirlpool of sallow, churning light.

It swallowed them.

They landed hard. The collision with what seemed to be solid ground was bone-shaking. But they had no leisure to recover from the impact. Wherever they had fetched up was hostile. Murderously so.

The place was in the grip of a violent sandstorm. Trillions of grains of sand lashed them like shards of glass or tiny diamonds, bathing them in pain. The sand not only pummelled them, it all but blinded them; they could see practically nothing. It was hard to stand, let alone walk. The heat was terrific, and in no way mitigated by the never-ending, roaring wind. Even for a group of warriors as toughened as the Wolverines, it was intolerable.

Coilla was vaguely aware of other figures clustered about her. She happened to be standing next to Stryke when he slotted the instrumentalities together. If she hadn't, she probably wouldn't have been able to find him now. But by luck, when she stretched out her hand she brushed his arm. She took it in an iron grip.

Thrusting her mouth to his ear, she bellowed, '*Get us out of here!*'

Coilla had no way of knowing that was exactly what he was trying to do. The cluster of stars was still in his hands, and hampered by being unable to see what he was doing, he was battling to rearrange them.

After what seemed an agonisingly long time, choking with the sand filling his mouth and nose, he managed to slot them into another random assembly.

The void snatched them again. They were back in the swirling, never-ending spillway, taking a stomach-churning tumble to another unknown goal.

The band was pitched into a blizzard, exchanging insufferable heat for unspeakable cold. All they could see was white. Stinging snow pricked them like innumerable needles. The temperature was so low they found it difficult to breathe. Stryke's fingers froze instantly, and it was all he could do to manipulate the stars. Teeth chattering, hands shaking uncontrollably, he finally altered them.

Once more, the cosmic trapdoor flipped open.

They were standing in torrential rain in a landscape that seemed to consist solely of mud that was nearly liquid itself. The air was uncomfortably humid. In seconds they realised that the rain was corrosive. It nipped at their flesh and singed their clothing as though it was vitriol. Stryke manipulated the stars.

A jungle embraced them. At first it seemed endurable. Then gigantic swarms of flying insects appeared, tenacious and hungry. They covered the band, fibrous wings beating, stingers seeking unprotected skin. Stryke manoeuvred the stars into another configuration.

They were deposited on a vast, featureless plain, the only variation being a distant range of blue-black mountains. Three suns beat down, one of them bloody red. Of more immediate import were the two armies the Wolverines found themselves between. One consisted of creatures resembling giant lizards, with purple hides and flicking, barbed tongues. The other was made up of beasts that seemed to be a cross between bears and apes, only with four arms. Each horde numbered in the hundreds of thousands, and they were moving rapidly forward, with the warband squarely in their path, like a nut in a vice. Stryke fiddled with the instrumentalities.

Icy salt spray splashed their faces. They were on a tiny rock in the middle of a turbulent ocean, battered by winds and towering waves, beneath an angry sky. The rock was jagged and slippery, and the band clung on to each other for fear of falling and being swept away. Stryke acted.

He kept on readjusting the stars as they were transported from world to world in search of somewhere bearable.

In dizzying succession they flashed in and out of lands of startling diversity, including some they found incomprehensible as well as hostile. In one, they were attacked by carnivorous birds; another was an environment that had a noxious gas for its atmosphere that they were lucky to escape in time. They witnessed abundant orc-sized fish emerging from a huge lake, revealing legs, and jaws bristling with fangs; sentient snakes as big as elephants, devouring each other; a land of perpetual earthquakes where enormous fissures opened and closed with frightening rapidity; a world stifled by sulphur and riddled with blue lava flows; a mighty river inhabited by multi-tentacled beasts with the faces of rodents; gigantic flies that supped on struggling spiders in sticky webs that spanned valleys; a place where great prides of felines waged war amongst themselves; rampaging worms as large as mature oaks; dominions ruled by plagues of rats, and on and on.

Eventually they materialised somewhere that didn't seem immediately threatening. It was a dead world. They couldn't tell if the desolation was the result of war or natural disaster, but it seemed complete. Not far away stood acres of debris and twisted uprights, just recognisable as the ruins of a city. There was no sign of life anywhere, not even vegetation, which the soil looked incapable of supporting in any event. Everything was grey and spent.

The Wolverines stood wordlessly for several minutes, in anticipation of something unfriendly happening. When it didn't, they did more than relax. They collapsed exhaustedly. They were in a sorry state; drenched, tattered, bruised and bleeding. The tyros were near unhinged, and Standeven was a wreck. Some of the band were vomiting. Others nursed wounds or crouched with their heads in their hands.

'*That was . . . one . . . hell of a . . . ride,*' Coilla said when she stopped fighting for breath.

'*Couldn't . . . set the . . . stars . . . properly,*' Stryke gasped back. '*No . . . chance to.*'

She started to pull herself together, as most of the others were. 'I . . . know. Who would . . . have thought. . . so many . . . of the worlds were . . . . so shitty?'

'Least it looks safe here.'

'Maybe.' She surveyed the barren landscape suspiciously.

'We'll rest for a bit, tend wounds. Then I'll fit the stars for Ceragan.'

She nodded and perched herself on a half-melted rock, head down, arms dangling.

As soon as he could, Stryke got some of the recovering grunts to mount guard. He had Dallog look at injuries, none of which fortunately called for major treatment, and ordered iron rations to be broken out.

They spent the next hour or more recuperating and getting their heads straight. During which, Jup came to Stryke with a question.

'What do we do about the humans?'

'Do?'

'Yeah. You planning on taking them back to Ceragan with you? Come to that, what about me and Spurral?'

'I've not been thinking straight,' Stryke confessed. 'That's a problem I hadn't weighed.'

'Can't be blamed for that. But what *are* you going to do with us non-orcs?'

'You and Spurral are welcome to join us in Ceragan. You'd be the only dwarfs, but you wouldn't be without comrades.'

'That's a generous offer, Stryke, and I thank you for it. But I'm guessing it's not one you'd be happy making to Pepperdyne and Standeven.'

'No, there'd be no place there for *them*. But suppose we took them back to Maras-Dantia?'

'*That* I hadn't thought of. Seems right, seeing as it's where you picked them up in the first place.'

'We could do the same for you. Get you back to your own kind.'

Jup sighed. 'I dunno, Stryke. We had good reasons for leaving. I'm not sure either of us would relish going back, for all that we were born there. Maras-Dantia's fit only to break hearts these days.'

'Then my offer of Ceragan stands. Who knows? Maybe we can figure out how to use the stars to find a dwarf world for you.'

Jup grinned. 'Trying to get rid of us already and we're not there yet. But I reckon we've got no real option. Though I've doubts about us ever finding a dwarf needle in that haystack of worlds we've just seen.'

'Maybe. Anyway, that's settled. Maras-Dantia for the humans and you two with us.'

'I'll have to talk it over with Spurral, mind. But I reckon she'll agree with me.'

Stryke nodded. 'Don't be too long about it. I want to get out of this place.'

The dwarf glanced at the bleakness surrounding them. 'You're not alone.'

He left.

Coilla took his place. 'Had any ideas on who they might have been?'

'Who?'

'You're not working with a sharpened sword yet, are you, Stryke? Who do you think I mean? That mixed bunch of races that tried frying us, of course.'

'No. We've seen a lot we can't explain these last few hours; they got kind of pushed out of my head.'

'But what do you reckon? Bandits? Mercenaries?'

'With the way their ranks were made up? And with magic? Really *powerful* magic? I've never seen any marauders like them before.'

'And all they wanted was the stars. Why?'

He shrugged. 'Damned if I can figure it.'

'Know what I can't understand? Why didn't that elf . . . what was her name?'

He thought about it. 'Madayar. Pelli Madayar.'

'Right. Why didn't she kill us when she had the chance? I reckon she could have, with magic that strong. Don't you?'

Stryke nodded.

'Yet she just gave us a bit of a knock. And those magic beams or whatever they were; funny how none of them took any of us out, isn't it?'

'It does seem . . . odd,' he conceded. 'Maybe she lied about being with Jennesta, or maybe they *were* mercenaries who saw the value of the stars.'

'How did they know we had them? Or even that they existed?'

'I . . . don't know. But does it really matter? How likely is it we'll run into them again?'

'There's something you're forgetting. That Madayar more or less told us they'd come from somewhere else, *like we did*. That can mean only one thing, Stryke. They can world-hop, too.'

'But they'd have to have stars to do that.'

'Unless there's another way we don't know about. Mind you, who says we've got the only set there is?'

'If they've stars of their own, why did they want ours?'

'Search me. Maybe they collect the bloody things. What I'm trying to say is that if they have stars, could be we haven't seen the last of them.'

She left him to ponder that.

Shortly after, he gathered the band.

'We've had an interesting day,' he told them, raising a few wry laughs. 'But now we've had a chance to steady ourselves I can use the stars to take us where we want to go.'

'Where's that?' Standeven asked.

'Us and the dwarfs to our world, Ceragan. You two back where we found you.'

'Centra— Maras-Dantia?'

'Unless you want to stay here.'

'But . . .'

'But what? Enjoy our company so much you can't leave us, is that it? Or maybe you'd prefer being taken back to Acurial. I'm sure the orcs there'd be glad to see you again.'

'Don't we get a say in this?'

'What say do you want? Stay here or go back to Maras-Dantia. That's your choice.'

'I think you're being very high-handed,' Standeven protested, 'and you should at least—'

'Let it go,' Pepperdyne told him. He knew his one-time master still harboured thoughts of gaining the instrumentalities, and thought even less of the idea now than he had originally.

'When I want *your* opinion—'

'*Let it go*,' Pepperdyne repeated coldly, laying an emphasis on the words that he hoped would convey to Standeven exactly what it really was he should let go of. 'We're lucky Stryke doesn't leave us here. Or somewhere worse.'

'Too fucking right you are,' Haskeer interjected. 'Though I reckon it's what we ought to do.'

'We do things my way,' Stryke reminded him. 'Maras-Dantia it is.' He took out the instrumentalities and laid them on a rock beside him. Then he reached into his shirt for the pendant. 'Get ready to brace yourselves.'

He was becoming more adept at fitting the stars together, and now he did it with great care, careful to follow exactly the order that would get them to their old home world.

Just before he clacked the fifth one into place he took a look at the faces staring at him. Many were apprehensive. Several, notably Standeven and Wheam, wore expressions that were positively sickly. Stryke couldn't altogether blame them. He wasn't looking forward to what came next himself.

He slammed the star into position.

Reality instantly dissolved and the now familiar, dread sensation of falling was on them again. They were drawn through the hellish kaleidoscope with no more means of controlling their passage than if they had been leaves in a gale. The only scrap of comfort they had was knowing where they'd end up.

Several lifetimes later, as it seemed, they came to themselves in another actuality.

They were standing on a large circular rock that had been raised like a dais and smoothed flat. The rock was inside a colossal cavern. Surrounding it were a hundred or more startled dwarfs, apparently in the throes of some kind of ritual. Stryke began fumbling with the stars. The dwarfs moved faster. Scores of them swarmed up onto the rock podium, and in a second the tips of multiple spears were pressing against the Wolverines' throats.

'I don't think this is Maras-Dantia,' Coilla said.

14

Two things saved the Wolverines' lives: their seemingly miraculous arrival and the presence of Jup and Spurral.

All the dwarfs surrounding the warband were male. They wore kilts woven from coarse material, and sandals, but were bare-chested. Many had necklaces of animal teeth, and a few sported brightly coloured feather headdresses. They were armed with daggers and the stout, bone-tipped spears that currently menaced the warband.

It was obvious that the dwarfs had never seen anything like orcs before, and regarded them with open amazement. The humans they looked upon with disdain, if not actual hatred. But they were confounded most by Jup and Spurral, and it was apparently because of them that they stayed their hand. They either gaped at the couple with something like awe or avoided their gaze almost shyly, keeping their eyes downcast.

'They seem 'specially taken with you and Spurral, Jup,' Stryke said, a spear pressing against his throat. 'Talk to them.'

Jup looked doubtful but gave it a go. 'Er . . . We come in peace.'

'That was original,' Coilla muttered.

'Doesn't look like it worked,' Stryke said.

The dwarfs had blank expressions.

Jup tried again, carefully mouthing, 'We are friends. There's no need to fight us.'

'Kill us, you mean,' Coilla remarked under her breath.

Still the dwarfs were baffled.

'Try Mutual,' Stryke suggested.

Jup raised a sceptical eyebrow. 'Really?'

'Got a better idea?'

'We mean you no harm and we're here as friends,' Jup said in

Mutual, the common tongue used by most of the races of Maras-Dantia.

Comprehension dawned on the dwarfs.

One of them, an older individual with a particularly impressive headdress, and presumably some kind of elder, replied in Mutual, 'You come from the sky?'

'Well, what do you know,' Haskeer whispered hoarsely.

Jup glanced Stryke's way for a lead. Stryke managed to give him the tiniest of nods.

'Yes,' Jup announced, feeling faintly ridiculous. 'Yes, we are here from the sky.' He raised his eyes heavenward, theatrically.

A chorus of gasps and exclamations of wonderment came from the dwarfs.

'These are your servants?' the elderly one asked, indicating the band.

'Oh, yeah,' Jup confirmed. 'They serve my every need.'

'And these?' He pointed his spear at Pepperdyne and Standeven. 'They are your prisoners?'

'Uhm. Well . . .'

'Do you want them executed now?'

'Exe— No. *No.* They're . . . I've decided they should be my slaves.'

'It's never wise to allow these creatures to live.'

'With you there,' Haskeer agreed in an undertone.

The humans, unfamiliar with Mutual, hadn't a clue about what was being said.

'What's going on?' Pepperdyne asked Stryke softly.

'Don't worry about it,' he mouthed back.

Jup having faltered somewhat, Spurral decided to push their luck, and took a hand.

'We choose to allow them their lives,' she told the elder imperiously, 'for the time being. Now release us. *Immediately!*'

The elder flinched, then looked alarmed. He snapped something to his fellows in their own, slightly guttural tongue.

The spears were lowered and the dwarfs stepped back from the Wolverines. The dwarfs moved away from the two humans more reluctantly, and carried on eyeing them with suspicion. Stryke quickly stuffed the instrumentalities into his pouch, hoping no one had noticed.

'You must crave sustenance after your journey,' the elder stated ingratiatingly. 'Please allow us to lay humble offerings before you.'

'Let us at it,' Jup replied, trying for an air of command.

The elder ushered them down from the dais and led them away from it. To the band's bemusement, dwarfs bowed as they passed. Not a few prostrated themselves. Pepperdyne and Standeven were viewed less respectfully. They got glares.

'They think we're gods,' Coilla whispered.

'Band of heroes,' Haskeer boasted, 'that's us.'

'Don't get above yourself,' Jup said. He gave Spurral's arm a pat. '*We're* the gods. You're just a servant.'

Powerless to start anything, Haskeer clenched both his teeth and his fists.

It was obvious that the cavern was a natural formation. Enormous and cone shaped, it had a round opening in its roof, far above. They could see blue sky through it.

They were taken to one of a number of tunnel openings. The passage was wide and sloped upwards. Their way was lit by flaming brands fixed to the walls. Soon they came to where two tunnels crossed, and they turned right, still climbing. Several more twists and turns brought them to daylight.

They emerged at a high point, giving them a perfect view of where they were. It was a tropical island; sizeable, but not so big that they couldn't see its limits. Around two-thirds of it was swathed in lush jungle. There were white beaches against which an azure sea gently lapped.

The dominant features were a pair of volcanoes towering out of the jungle. One was considerably taller than the other, and strands of grey smoke rose from both. Looking back, the band realised that they had just come out of a third volcano, bigger than either of the other two. The only difference being that it was extinct.

The day was warm, getting on for hot, and no cloud marred the sky. As the Wolverines followed their elderly guide they started to attract a retinue of dwarfs. There were gangs of children, and for the first time, females. Like their men-folk, they went bare-chested. Jup found that of particular interest until Spurral elbowed him sharply and cooled his ardour.

Coilla gave Stryke a nudge too, but more gently and in order to draw his attention to something. He followed her eyes. High up on the volcano they'd just exited there was a broad ledge on the seaward side. Standing on it was a line of five or six trebuchets. The catapults were large, similar to ones the orcs had seen, and used, in sieges.

A little further on they passed a low wooden structure not unlike a squat barn. Its doors were closed and half a dozen stern-faced dwarfs stood guard outside.

The crowd stared, grinned, laughed and shouted as the procession made its way to a clearing. Dozens of huts of various dimensions stood there. They were taken to the biggest, a one-storey affair on piles, with a porch on its front. The elder threw open its door and welcomed them in.

The longhouse was generous enough in size that even the Wolverines and their hangers-on didn't overfill it.

'My own dwelling,' the elder explained. 'I trust it isn't too humble for you.'

'It'll do,' Jup said.

There was a gaggle of females present. Members of the elder's family perhaps, or his wives or servants. They were gaping open-mouthed at the strange visitors. The elder snapped something at them and they fled, giggling, out of the open door.

'I will send you refreshments,' the elder told them. 'Is there anything else you need?'

'No,' Spurral replied in her queenly tone. 'You may leave us now.'

The old dwarf bowed awkwardly and backed out.

When he'd gone, Haskeer said, 'Fuck me.'

'You've a skill, Spurral,' Stryke told her. 'You should have been a troubadour.'

'They seemed to think we were somebody important. I just played on it.'

Haskeer took in their surroundings. 'Not bad, this place. Better than some of the shit-holes we've seen lately.'

'Yes, it's all very fine,' Coilla said, 'but what the *fuck* are we doing here? Stryke, how come we're not in Maras-Dantia?'

'I don't know.'

'Did you make a mistake setting the stars?'

'I'd swear I didn't.'

'One way to be sure,' Dallog offered. 'Try them again now.'

'No,' Stryke decided. 'If they got it wrong this time they could again.'

'And we might not end up somewhere as sweet,' Jup finished for him. 'There are worse places for a billet.'

'Maybe it's not as sweet as you think,' Coilla argued. 'Did you notice those catapults? They have to be here for a reason.'

'And they've got something in that hut back there they don't want us to see,' Pepperdyne added.

'I agree with Jup,' Stryke declared. 'We'll hold up here.'

'How long for?' Coilla wanted to know.

'For as long as I need to think about why the stars got it wrong. We're all bushed. It won't hurt us to take a furlough here.'

The door opened and a multitude of female dwarfs came in bearing platters of food. They laid out a feast for them and withdrew bowing. The timber dining table that dominated one end of the room was laden with breads, fish and fruit, much of a kind none of them recognised. There were also flasks of something that resembled rice wine. Pepperdyne, born an islander, told them he was pretty sure it was distilled from seaweed. That made some of them doubtful, but it tasted good.

Sitting at the table eating their fill, which was considerable, they allowed themselves to relax a little. Though Stryke did take the precaution of stationing privates by the door and the several windows. The guards took heaped dishes of food with them and stuffed themselves as they stood watch.

'What do you think of this as a dwarf world?' Dallog asked of Jup and Spurral.

'Well, they don't seem as advanced as our tribes in Maras-Dantia,' Jup replied, 'but it's pleasant enough.'

'If you happen to be a fucking god,' Haskeer murmured.

'Any more of your insolence and I'll have you whipped, underling,' the dwarf teased.

'We're not gonna be here for ever,' Haskeer promised darkly. 'Just you wait.'

Jup laughed in his face.

'That language you were speaking,' Pepperdyne said. 'What was that all about?'

'In Maras-Dantia, or at least what used to be our part of it,'

Stryke informed him, 'just about everybody spoke Mutual. How else would so many different races figure out each other?'

'And now we've found it here,' Coilla remarked. 'How can that be?'

'Looks like there's more moving between worlds than we thought.'

'How long was it used in Maras-Dantia?' Pepperdyne asked.

'For ever,' Coilla told him. 'Nobody knows who first thought of it.'

'So maybe it didn't start there. If the worlds have bled into each other more than we know, it could have originated anywhere.'

'Possible, I suppose.' Coilla knew that the elder races weren't native to Maras-Dantia; it was the humans' world by birthright. It seemed logical to her that when the various races were inadvertently deposited there, long ago, they might well have brought something like Mutual with them. But she didn't mention any of that. Instead, she said, 'From what we heard, it seems humans aren't too well liked in these parts, Jode.'

'We gathered that much.'

'Yeah, well, I think it goes a bit deeper than a tiff. Take care.'

'Ahhh, ain't it cute?' Haskeer mocked. 'She's worried about her little pet.'

'You'll be worried about the one between your legs if you don't pipe down,' she promised him.

Nobody spoke for a moment until Wheam wondered, 'How do you think they're getting on in Acurial?'

'Just fine, I should think,' Stryke reckoned.

'You can't help thinking what they made of us, can you?' Dallog speculated.

'Maybe we'll go down in their history books,' Coilla said, only half seriously.

'Yeah!' Haskeer enthused. 'As a band of legendary heroes who—'

He was drowned out by the catcalls of the rest of the band.

'I think you're right about the resistance winning out there,' Pepperdyne said when it quietened. 'I'm more puzzled by who that bunch were who wanted your stars, Stryke.'

That put a damper on the band.

'Damned if we can figure it out,' Stryke confessed. 'But if they really did come from somewhere other than Acurial, like that elf said, they could turn up here. We're going to have to be alert for that.'

'Not much of a furlough then,' Coilla came back dryly.

'If these dwarfs don't try to stop us we'll find ourselves a good defensible hold-out first thing. We'll be better prepared if they come again.'

'Against the magic they have?' She paused a moment before braving the next thing she wanted to say. 'Stryke, about the stars . . .'

'What about them?'

'Given they're precious, and now we might have this new bunch trying to get their hands on them, why don't you divide them up between five of us and—'

'No.'

'Don't just dismiss it, Stryke. It could be a good way of protecting the things.'

'If we lost just one, that's enough to make the others useless.'

'This isn't just about you, you know. The stars are our only way home too.'

'No Coilla. Not after what happened last time.'

'You're blaming me for that, are you?'

'You know I'm not. How could I when I lost four of them to Jennesta myself?'

'So you won't consider it?'

'It's better my way.'

'You can be such a stubborn pig sometimes!' she flared. 'When are you going to get it through your head that—'

There was a commotion outside. They heard shouts and screams.

Rushing to the door, they saw dozens of dwarfs running in all directions in panic.

The band flooded out of the longhouse. At sea, a flotilla of small boats was heading for the shore. In the distance, a ship was at anchor.

The Wolverines headed for the beach. There were more dwarfs there, desperate to get away from the advancing boats. They stopped a few to ask what was going on, but got no sense out of them.

'Look!' Coilla yelled, pointing at the nearest boats.

They were manned by humans.

'I'm guessing it's not a social visit either,' Stryke observed.

'Now we know why the dwarfs aren't keen on Jode and Standeven.'

A number of male dwarfs were now running onto the beach as opposed to away from it. They were armed with their spears.

'What do we do?' Dallog asked.

'We make a stand with them,' Stryke replied, 'what else?'

'Pity they've got nobody operating those trebuchets.' The corporal pointed to the ledge on the volcano.

'No time. They've been caught unawares.'

'Yeah,' Coilla agreed, 'probably because they were too concerned with us.'

'Here they come!' Haskeer bellowed.

The first of the humans were wading ashore.

'So let's get to it,' Stryke ordered, drawing his sword. '*Come on!*' He led them into the surf. Only Standeven held back, skulking far up the beach.

They met the invaders in knee-deep water and laid into them. The humans were shocked to be facing an unknown race, and one so ferocious, and were equally dismayed to find Pepperdyne among their attackers. That gave the band an initial edge. Soon, the surf was stained red.

But it didn't take long for Stryke to realise he'd made an error. This wasn't the incomers' main or only force. Further along the shoreline more boats had come round the island's curve. Humans had already got well inland in that direction. They were fighting dwarfs on the beach, and the dwarfs weren't coming off best.

Stryke ordered some of the band to stay where they were and finish off the dwindling number of humans still exchanging blows. He took the rest up the beach to confront the bigger influx happening there. Spurral, who proved a good runner, had seen what was happening and streaked off even before he issued the order. She was well to the fore and not far short of a group of humans wading ashore.

Running abreast with Haskeer, Jup and Coilla, and the other band members on their heels, Stryke yelled a warning. A party of humans who must already have penetrated the island's interior were returning to the beach, and their path crossed the Wolverines'. The humans, perhaps twenty strong, were dragging and carrying screaming dwarfs towards the waves.

Stryke's band and the kidnappers all but collided. Startled by the sudden appearance of a group of creatures they were unlikely to have encountered before, the humans let go of their captives to defend themselves. The freed dwarfs, most of them young, began fleeing back into the jungle.

The warband tore into the boatmen, savagely hacking them down. Pepperdyne, taking a great swipe with his blade, parted one of them from his head. Haskeer, employing both hatchet and knife, hurtled into a duo simultaneously, stabbing one and braining the other. Dallog plunged his spear into a foe with such force it lifted the man off his feet. Even Wheam gave a good account of himself, in Wheam terms. He managed no fatalities, but attacked with gusto and inflicted mean wounds on a couple of opponents.

They worked as fast as they could to get through the obstruction and reach the greater number of humans beyond, where more struggling dwarfs were being hurled into the humans' bobbing craft.

As the last man in their path was downed and dispatched, several of the grunts started raising a clamour. Stryke and the others looked to where they were frantically pointing.

Out in deep water, Spurral was grappling with three men. As the band watched, they pummelled her senseless and flung her into a boat, then hauled themselves aboard.

'*Shit!*' Jup cried. He began running.

The band took off in his wake, arms pumping, heads down.

A burly human tried blocking Jup's way. He cracked the man's skull open with his staff while barely breaking step. He ran on, splashing into the water.

'Spurral!' he shouted. '*Spurral!*'

The boat she was in had begun moving away, four men pulling mightily on the oars.

Jup was wading now, finding the going increasingly harder the further he got. Breakers battered him and he almost lost his footing.

The others were close behind. By the time they caught up with him he was more than chest high and battling impotently against the water's sluggish impediment.

They saw Spurral's boat, along with dozens of others bearing snatched dwarfs, rapidly departing.

All they could do was watch helplessly as it headed for the ship waiting on the horizon.

15

Jup was frantic, and seethed with a cold fury, but knew that keeping his head was the best hope of finding Spurral.

Stryke did the logical thing and ordered the band to find a boat. They scoured the shore and came up with nothing except small canoes, totally unsuited for venturing out to sea. He considered building a boat, or possibly a raft. But with time at a premium, and his doubts about whether they could construct something truly seaworthy for who knew how long a voyage, that looked impractical.

Boat or no, their biggest problem was finding out where Spurral might have been taken. Jup's farsight was useless because a vast body of water like the ocean, he explained, gave off an energy of its own that swamped the pinpricks generated by living beings riding it. So they needed the dwarfs' help. Which proved harder than they first thought, simply because the natives seemed to have disappeared. Some had obviously been taken by the raiders. They could only guess that the rest had gone into hiding, probably in the depths of the jungle, or perhaps in the labyrinth of tunnels that riddled the dead volcano.

Stryke decided to concentrate their efforts on finding them. Surveying the terrain from the highest point they could easily get to, which turned out to be the outcropping where the catapults stood, he hastily scrawled a crude map of the island. This he divided into more or less equal segments. Then he split the band into eight groups of four or five members each and allotted them a segment to search.

His own group included Jup, Coilla and Reafdaw, who was one of the Wolverines' more experienced scouts. Stryke made a point of having Haskeer lead one of the groups assigned to the farthest tip of the island. He wanted to keep him and Jup apart for now, given their tendency to aggravate each other. That was a complication they could do without.

Stryke's team had an area of jungle to search. It wasn't one of the densest parts, and they were able to pace out most of it, looking for any sign that might betray the dwarfs.

'Those humans had to be slavers,' Coilla said as they trudged. 'No other reason I can see for taking prisoners alive.'

'Oh, great,' Jup groaned. 'And that's supposed to cheer me, is it?'

'Yes. Slaves have a value. It doesn't serve the slavers to be careless with their wares.'

'Assuming they *are* slavers. Who knows what goes on in this world?'

'I think Coilla's right,' Stryke said. 'They sought out the young and fit, so it figures. Spurral might not be having too good a time of it, but they don't gain by harming her too much.'

'Not *too* much,' the dwarf repeated bitterly. 'This isn't lifting me, Stryke.'

'I know. But don't we like to try working out the odds before any mission?'

'Yes,' he sighed, 'I suppose we do.'

'Well,' Coilla remarked by way of steering the subject elsewhere, 'one thing we've found is that this world isn't made up of just dwarfs.'

'Worse luck.'

'And if there's humans here too,' she went on, 'there could be other races.'

'Like Maras-Dantia?' Stryke said. 'The way they got here, I mean.'

'Could be. From what we know, Maras-Dantia was like a big sink hole once, sucking in all those races, including ours. Could have been the same here.'

'Why does it have to have been once?' Jup wondered, taking an interest despite his worry. 'You mean some time in the past, right?'

She nodded. 'Has to have been. All the races were too well rooted. That must take time. Other thing is, no new races were turning up out of nowhere. We never heard of anything like that, did we?'

409

'Doesn't mean to say it only happened way back in the past and can't happen now. Why did it stop?'

'It'd take better heads than ours to know that.'

'Maybe it's happening all the time,' Jup persisted. 'If not in Maras-Dantia, in other places. Like here.'

'Could that have been how that crew who wanted the stars got to Acurial?' Coilla wondered. 'By chance? You know, perhaps they fell into—'

'Don't think so,' Stryke interrupted, 'not from what Pelli Madayar said. I got the sense they weren't the sort to be tossed around like corks.'

Reafdaw had been walking ahead, scanning the greenery. Now he stopped and held up a hand. They cut the talk and froze. He used gestures to indicate a point on the jungle floor that to them looked no different to any other. They quietly caught up with him.

He pointed downward. Two things became clear with scrutiny. There was trampled vegetation in a particular spot. And when they grew accustomed to the scene they could make out a patch of ground that had a phoney look to it. It was just about possible to see the lines that hinted at something like a trapdoor. They silently positioned themselves around it, weapons drawn. Stryke began issuing orders via signing.

Jup and Reafdaw crouched and inserted their blades into the almost invisible slits. On a signal they levered the trap out of true, and with Stryke and Coilla's help, lifted and tossed it aside.

A piercing scream came from the pit they exposed.

They looked down. A young female dwarf was cowering below in a hollow not much bigger than herself. She wasn't alone. Three dwarf children, all males, clung to her. Their dirty, upturned faces were terrified.

Jup spoke softly to them in Mutual, assuring them they were safe. The orcs stepped back out of sight while he did it, to save spooking them. At last Jup won their confidence, and got them to accept that the orcs were friendly. They were helped out of their dank pit and given water, which they bolted.

Stryke judged it best to take them to the elder's longhouse. On the way they were silent, and noticeably still fearful. But the orcs, and even Jup, despite his anxiety, held back on questioning them.

Being in the more familiar surroundings of the village, and then the longhouse, seemed to reassure the quartet. If not exactly relax-ing, they at least became easier in themselves. They were given food, and more to drink.

The girl's name was Axiaa, or something very much like it, and she was related in some obscure way to the three children. Obscure because, as she haltingly explained, in the closed community of an island, everyone was related.

The boys were called Grunnsa, Heeg and Retlarg, as far as Stryke and the others could nail it. Their names didn't translate to Mutual, and the dwarfs' throaty first language made understanding no easier. Grunnsa was the oldest, at ten or eleven seasons. Heeg and Retlarg were perhaps seven or eight, and brothers. Grunnsa was their cousin, and possibly their uncle too, such were the island's tangled relationships.

It seemed that the brothers' parents had been taken by the humans. Grunnsa's might have been too, or could be in hiding somewhere. It was unclear.

'Who were those raiders, Axiaa?' Stryke asked.

Being addressed by an orc, and the servant of a god to boot, made her a little shy, but she answered, 'Gatherers.'

'Seen them before?'

'Oh, yes. They come from time to time and take away some of our kin. Never all. They like for there to be more when they return.'

'Why do they take you?'

'To trade. Sell. For work on other islands.'

'Are there many other islands?'

'Yes. Many.'

'The dwarfs have visited them?'

'A few have. The brave ones. But most of us never leave here.'

'Why?'

'Outside—' she waved a hand in the direction of the sea '—is death.'

'Oh good,' Jup said.

'Axiaa,' Coilla asked, 'do you know where our friend was taken? The she-dwarf we came with?'

'The goddess.'

'Er, yes, that's her. Where did she go?'

'Bad place.'

'But do you know *where*? How could we find it?'

The girl didn't seem to grasp that.

'We know!' Retlarg piped up.

Coilla turned to them. 'You do?'

'Yes,' Heeg confirmed.

'The grown-ups don't know we know,' Grunnsa confided. 'But we found out.'

'How?'

'Show you?' Retlarg asked.

She nodded, puzzled.

The three youngsters leapt to their feet and tore to one side of the spacious room. They fell upon a piece of furniture not unlike an ottoman; a couch that doubled as a storage chest. Throwing aside its coverings, they raised the top. There was a jumble of household possessions inside, which they cheerfully tossed onto the rush-matted floor as they burrowed. At last they retrieved a rolled, yellowing parchment, about the length of an orc's arm, secured with a round of smooth twine. They ran back to Coilla and gave it to her.

Along with Stryke, Jup and Reafdaw, she took it to the feasting table. Sweeping aside the remains of their earlier meal, she unfastened the scroll and rolled it out. They weighed down its corners with coconut drinking vessels and fat candles.

It was a chart. Whoever drew it, quite a while ago from its state, had a fine hand. It had been executed in different coloured pigments, now much faded.

The map showed a world dominated by ocean. But sprinkled with islands of all shapes and sizes, some in close clusters, others alone, a few isolated. There were hundreds of them.

'I'm guessing the one we're on,' Stryke said, 'is here.'

He pointed to a shape quite far south, but reasonably close to a number of others. A red cross had been drawn inside its outline, and there were some crude symbols underneath. None of the others had that, save one. This bore a stylised skull in its centre and it had been circled in black. It was north-west of the first, and without knowing the chart's scale, they thought it looked not too far away.

'Gotta be that one,' Jup reckoned.

The three kids clamoured to see, the table being too high for them. They were hoisted up onto chairs.

'Is this where we are?' Coilla wanted to know, pointing at the island with the cross.

They confirmed it.

'And the place these Gatherers come from?'

'*There!*' they chorused, plonking grubby fingers on the island with the skull.

'That clinches it,' Stryke said.

'Now how do we get there?' Jup inquired gloomily.

'In a boat,' Grunnsa suggested.

'They're all too small,' Coilla reminded him.

'*No,*' Heeg insisted. 'The *big* boats.'

'There are big boats? Where?'

'In the boathouse, of course,' the boy replied in a way that sounded like he was the adult and she the child.

'Where is this boathouse?'

'Outside the village.' Grunnsa pointed vaguely in the direction of the extinct volcano.

'Must be that place we saw them guarding,' Stryke reasoned.

'So what are we waiting for?' Jup said.

At that point the longhouse's door opened. Haskeer and a pair of grunts came in. They had the elder with them.

'Found him and a couple of others hiding in the tunnels,' Haskeer explained. 'He's pissed off with us.'

The elder's angry expression verified that.

'Why?' Jup wanted to know.

'Ask him yourself. He doesn't talk to mere *servants.*'

Jup addressed the elder. 'We're sorry about your trouble with the Gatherers. What can we do to help?'

'Your offer comes too late. You should have stopped them.'

'We tried.'

'Those who fall from the sky must be more powerful than the Gatherers. Yet it seems you are not.'

'We want to avenge you, and to get your islanders back. But we need your help.'

'*Our* help? What can we do that those who come from the sky cannot?'

'We need boats that can put to sea, so we can pursue the Gatherers and punish them.'

The elder became tight-lipped.

'We know you have such boats,' Stryke told him. 'And where the Gatherers are to be found.'

The elder shot the children a sharp, disapproving look. 'It is forbidden.'

'What's forbidden?'

'Our customs forbid any from leaving here and voyaging to other islands. It brings wrath upon our heads. We believe the Gatherers would not have known of us if some of our kin had not ventured out and been captured.'

'We understand,' Jup sympathised, 'but we aren't bound by your customs. And one of our number was taken by the Gatherers. We want her back.'

'It isn't just the Gatherers. There are other dangers on the outside. Great dangers.'

'We can deal with them,' Stryke came back harshly. 'But what about the *boats*? Do you hand them over or do we take them?'

He said it with sufficient force to give the elder pause. 'There are two,' he admitted. 'We took them from certain of our kin who were building them secretly, in defiance of custom. They would have used them to leave here and try to make a new home free of the Gatherers.'

'Might not have been a bad idea.'

'Did you not survey this world from your vantage point in the sky? You seem to know little about it. For all that we suffer from the Gatherers, this island is safe compared to what dwells beyond it.'

'We'll take our chances.'

'When we seized the boats they were incomplete. They are not yet seaworthy.'

'Would it take much to finish them?'

'I think not.'

It occurred to Coilla to ask, 'If you don't allow sea-going craft, why did you keep them?'

'We had no intention of keeping them. They were to be publicly burnt, as a warning to any who would try the same foolishness. But then you arrived.'

'Lucky we came when we did.'

'Can we get any of your islanders to help us make the boats ready?' Stryke said.

The elder shook his head. 'It would go against our customs and stir up unrest.'

'And the same goes for any of you helping us sail them?'

'It does.'

'To hell with your stinking customs then. We'll manage alone.'

'Not quite,' Coilla said. 'Jode was island-born, he told me so. He'll have sailing skills.'

'You seem to know more about those humans than we do,' Haskeer jibed.

'Good thing I do, isn't it?'

'That's settled,' Stryke decided. 'We'll start work on the boats right away. As to you.' He fixed the elder with a hard look. 'Forget any idea you might have about taking it out on these kids for aiding us. Or we'll bring wrath down upon *your* head.'

'Have we done chin-wagging?' Jup pleaded. ''Cos while we're standing here flapping our tongues there's no saying what Spurral's going through.'

16

Spurral had been knocked cold by the blows she took on the beach. When she came to, in the rowing boat, the island was just a speck in the distance, recognisable only by the columns of smoke curling from its pair of active volcanoes.

There were five humans in the boat; four rowing, one at the helm. Three dwarfs, apart from herself, were aboard, lying on the boat's deck. Two male, one female, all young. Like her, their hands were tied. The humans said nothing, contenting themselves with scowling at their captives from time to time and raising a sweat at the oars. When Spurral tried to speak to them they told her to shut up in coarse terms.

They were hardy, weather-beaten men, with skin the colour of old hide from a life under the merciless sun. Most were bearded, and several bore scars. Their clothing suited the needs of fighting and sea-going.

Cautiously lifting her head, Spurral looked over the rail. She saw that their boat was one of dozens of identical craft heading in the same direction, and she guessed they held dwarf captives too. The boats were making for a large triple-masted ship whose sails were being run up as they approached.

When they reached the ship it towered over them like a cliff-face, making the row-boats toys by comparison. Rope ladders dangled from its side. Spurral and the others had their bonds cut, amid threats against misbehaviour, so they could climb them. The ascent was precarious, and as she made her way up she could hear the ship's timbers creaking and the waves lapping against its hull.

On deck, they were herded together facing the bridge. Spurral estimated there were forty or fifty dwarfs present. The humans numbered about the same, and most of them set to hauling aboard the boats for stowing, or making them fast to be towed. Nine or ten men kept an eye on the dwarfs. Not that they were trouble-some. They were browbeaten, and some of the females were weeping. And apart from the occasional whispered exchange, they were silent.

A man appeared on the bridge. He was younger than the majority of the crew, surprisingly so for someone Spurral took to be their skipper. His face was hairless, his head was a mane of black curls. There was something about the way he looked and moved that was almost sensuous, calling to mind a predatory feline eyeing its next meal. Of his robustness there was no doubt, and even from a distance he radiated a vitality that spoke of harsh command.

He rapped loudly on the bridge's balustrade with the hilt of his richly embellished sword. There was no real need. He already had their attention.

'I am Captain Salloss Vant,' he announced in a strong, carrying voice. 'It's normal for the master of a vessel to welcome guests aboard. But I've a feeling you'd find it hard to take my words to your hearts.' The crew laughed. He smiled at his quip, then turned stern. 'But take *this* as holy writ. If you have any other gods, forget them. *I* am your deity now.'

Spurral was aware of dwarfs giving her furtive glances. She began to regret the band letting them believe something so fanciful.

'As far as you're concerned,' Vant went on, 'I am the god of this vessel for as long as you're on it, and my word is your only law. And have no doubts that law-breakers will feel a wrath that only a god can bring about.' His expression slid to ersatz amiable. He spread his hands in a gesture of reasonableness. 'We are Gatherers. You are the gathered. Accept your fate and allow us to fashion ours. And don't look so glum! Your new lives as servants, oarsmen, menials and the like will no doubt bring you great satisfaction.' The crew laughed again. 'A pleasure you can begin practising for straightaway,' he continued, the mask going back to severe. 'There are no passengers on this ship. You will work.'

With no further word he turned his back on them and strode away.

'That's one god I can't wait to see fall,' Spurral said, just loud enough for those nearest to hear.

Twilight on the island brought cool breezes, along with a reminder that time was getting on.

The pair of boats the elder surrendered were quite large. Big enough between them to take the whole warband and their provisions, with a little room to spare. They were essentially oversized rowing boats or undersized galleys, depending on how it was looked at. Both were fitted out for between eight and ten rowers. In addition they had a short mast to add the power of a sail. The rudders were a mighty affair, and would need two pairs of hands in rough weather. There were no covered areas on the boats, but lockers had been built in.

They needed most work on their hulls, which were unfinished, and both craft lay keel up, with the band swarming about them. Wood was shaped, twine woven, tar boiled. Hammering, sawing and chiselling filled the air. Supplies were being gathered for the voyage; water, and such food as they thought might keep.

True to their elder's word, the dwarfs didn't assist. But many looked on, some in open curiosity, a few disapproving. The three children, Grunnsa, Heeg and Retlarg, were the band's shadows, though even they were wary of being seen to actually help.

Under the pressure, from time and Jup's growing unease, tempers were wearing thin. As Pepperdyne, the only one with any real experience of seamanship, was effectively in charge of getting the ships ready, he was the lightning rod.

'Can't you get them to work any faster?' Jup demanded.

'They're performing miracles as it is,' Pepperdyne assured him. 'Be patient.'

'That's easy for you to say. Your woman's not out there somewhere, suffering the gods know what.'

'Trust us, Jup. We want Spurral back as badly as you do.'

'I doubt that!' He checked himself, and relented. 'Sorry. I know you're doing your best.'

'And we'll keep on doing it.'

'It's funny. I never thought I'd be making common cause with a human, let alone over something as important as this. No disrespect.'

'None taken. Life has its little ironies, doesn't it?'

'Never thought I'd be bossed again by a human either,' Haskeer muttered darkly as he worked nearby.

'Jode's not bossing us,' Jup told him. 'He's helping.'

'Oh, so it's *Jode* now, is it? That's what Coilla calls him. Seems to me some in this band are getting a bit too pally with his kind.'

'Jode happens to be his name. And I reckon he's earned his part in this.'

'You know where putting your trust in humans gets us. Or is your memory as short as your legs?'

'I've not forgotten. But when somebody proves their worth—'

'Know what humans are worth? *This* much.' He spat.

'Nobody's saying you have to like me, or my kind,' Pepperdyne said. 'Or that I should have any great regard for you. None of that matters. Fact is, we need to work together.'

'It might not matter to you—'

'For fuck's *sake*,' Haskeer,' Jup butted in, growing incensed. 'Won't you rest it? This isn't about you. It's about finding Spurral.'

'Yeah. Right.'

'What's *that* supposed to mean?'

'All this fuss for a mate.'

'*What?*'

'They come along regular as whores. You can always get another one.'

'*You bastard!*' the dwarf exploded, leaping forward.

He delivered a couple of low punches in quick succession, and while Haskeer was still reeling, seized him by the throat. He hit back with a vicious kicking at the dwarf's legs.

Then Stryke and Dallog were there, grabbing Haskeer from behind. Pepperdyne did the same to Jup, and the pair were pulled apart.

'*Are you two insane?*' Stryke bellowed. 'There's no time for this shit!'

Jup glowered. 'He said—'

'Do I look like I care? You're sergeants in this band. *Sergeants*. But you're going the right way to getting yourselves broken to the ranks. Understand?'

'Yeah,' Jup muttered, and Pepperdyne let him go.

Haskeer didn't respond.

'Haskeer?' Stryke said. He and Dallog still had hold of him. Stryke applied a little less than gentle pressure.

'*Yes!*' Haskeer replied. 'Yes, damn it!'

They released him. He was enraged, and gave Dallog a particularly poisonous look, but curbed himself.

'Spurral's one of our band.' Stryke directed the statement at Haskeer, suggesting he *had* heard what was said. 'And this band sticks together. If any of us is in a fix, all of us get them out of it. *Whoever* they are,' he added pointedly. 'Now get this job finished.'

They went back to work. Some with better grace than others.

When he'd moved away from the rest, Coilla went to Pepperdyne. 'Don't take it too personal. Haskeer can be a swine, but he comes through when it counts.'

'What's his beef?'

'It's a thing between him and Jup. It goes way back.'

'He wants to watch his mouth. I thought Jup was going to kill him.'

'Nah. Cripple him maybe.'

Pepperdyne had to grin.

'Seriously,' Coilla asked, 'when do you think we're going to get these things launched?'

'They might be finished tonight. But no way should we put to sea in the dark. So first light, I guess.' He glanced Haskeer's way. 'Let's hope we all hold together that long.'

'Yeah, and we need to. These islanders don't say much, but from what I've picked up we could run into anything out there.'

They gazed at the vast expanse of water and the disappearing rim of the sinking sun.

Pelli Madayar stood on the peak of a hummock and watched as day began slowly turning to night.

Her second-in-command, Weevan-Jirst, was by her side. A member of the goblin race, his kind were known to be nimble and tough. He had a gaunt build, almost sinewy, and the texture of his knotty, jade-coloured flesh resembled taut leather. His elliptical head had no hair. His ears were tiny and half enclosed by flaps of rough tissue. His mouth was little more than a slit, and his compressed nose had nostrils like slashes. His eyes were disproportionately large, with inky black orbs and sallow surrounds.

The foreboding appearance of goblins often led other species to assume they were hostile; an impression not always without foundation, though unjust in Weevan-Jirst's case. He had devoted his life to the Gateway Corps, and met the high standards of probity the Corps demanded. Which was not to say that he was incapable of performing acts of violence in pursuit of their cause.

'I communicated with Karrell Revers again,' Pelli revealed, 'shortly after we got here.'

'And what did the leader have to say?' The goblin's inflection was sibilant, containing traces of a throaty hiss that formed the greater part of his native tongue.

'More or less what I expected. He was unhappy with the outcome of our first encounter with the orcs.'

'It would be difficult to count that as a triumph.'

'I know. But Karrell gave me a free hand on this mission, and he knew I wanted to try dialogue before force.'

'No one could argue against that being the ideal. But I've yet to see a world where ideal is the norm.' He grew reflective. 'It occurred to me that it could have been the goblin presence in our party that enraged them.'

'How so?'

'Traditionally, goblins and orcs haven't seen eye to eye, shall we say. And not always without good reason.'

'I don't think it was that. The fact is I handled it badly.'

'You're too hard on yourself.'

'No harder than our cause demands. This is my first real mission; I'd hoped to have made a better start.'

'There are few precedents to guide us, Pelli. Instrumentalities being so rare, these assignments are very uncommon. Some go their whole lives without having to do what the Corps has asked of you.'

'That's hardly an excuse.'

'Perhaps not. But it serves as a reason. What conclusion did Karrell reach?'

'He's still content to leave it to my discretion. Just. But he warns that, given the nature of the race holding the artefacts, force is probably the only option.'

'He could well be right. Can anybody negotiate with orcs?'

'I'm starting to think not.'

'Then what choice do we have?'

'There's something else. Karrell warned me earlier that another force had entered this game. Some individual or group with command of the portals. Their presence was detected in Acurial. And if they were there—'

'I take your point. Do we know more than that about them?'

'No. Which is worrying. To have one set of instrumentalities in irresponsible hands is bad enough. To have two—'

'Must surely be unprecedented.'

She nodded. 'This is a dangerous enough world as it is without another variable being thrown in.'

'All the more reason for us to bow to the leader's wisdom in the matter of the orcs.

'Yes, I suppose it is.'

'Do we have any idea where they might be?'

'We do now. Or at least we do roughly. Karrell gave me coordinates.'

'So your orders are . . . ?'

'We go after them at dawn. And when we find them, we hit them hard this time.'

They watched the last fragment of the sun vanishing below the horizon.

The patchwork of islands spread out before them fell into night.

17

It wasn't long before Spurral witnessed the nature of Salloss Vant's justice.

The captives had immediately been given various onboard chores, most of them mindless and all of them hard work. Spurral was put with five other dwarfs in an ill-lit, dank area below decks containing enormous lengths of unyielding rope, thick as her arm. They had to roll it into coils on great wooden cylinders that took two to turn. Spurral's job was to guide the rope onto the drum so that it wound neatly. In no time they all had bleeding, blistered hands.

There was a single crewman overseeing their labours. After an initial bout of shouting and threats he deposited himself on a heap of filthy sacking and promptly dozed off. Spurral took the opportunity to try to engage the others in whispered conversation. Most were too frightened to respond, but two answered, and they got a conversation going, of sorts.

One was male and a bit older than the majority of prisoners. He seemed to be called Kalgeck, and Spurral thought he had spirit. The female was in some ways his opposite. Her name was something like Dweega. She was among the youngest on board, and timorous, yet found the guts to reply, which Spurral had to give her credit for. It was only later that Spurral discovered Dweega had spoken not out of courage, but desperation.

Several hours of hard labour passed before a bell sounded somewhere. The guard woke up, ran a quick eye over what they'd done and ordered them out. As they shuffled forward, Spurral saw that the girl was having trouble walking. But before the crewman noticed, several others, principally Kalgeck, crowded round and hid her limp from view.

By now, night had fallen. The captives were herded into the

ship's hold, and when it was Dweega's turn to descend the ladder, Kalgeck kept close enough to disguise her faltering progress.

For the first time since being seized, they were given sustenance. It was hard, stale bread and suspect water. The hold was badly crowded, but Spurral made sure she got floor space next to Dweega. She noted that Kalgeck had bagged the space on the girl's other side.

The prisoners were forced to keep silence throughout. But once the few meagre candles had been snuffed, and the hold was locked down, whispers were exchanged. Though quiet weeping was more prevalent.

Spurral wriggled nearer to the girl and spoke low. 'You all right?'

'Are any of us?'

'You in particular. What's wrong with your leg?'

Dweega didn't answer. But Kalgeck leaned in close and said, 'She's lame.'

Spurral sensed the girl stiffening at the words.

'It happened when they caught us?' Spurral asked.

'No,' Dweega said. 'I've always . . . been like this.'

'And you don't want the Gatherers knowing.'

'They can't get a good price for damaged goods,' she mouthed bitterly.

'You've been lucky so far. How much longer do you think you can hide it from them?'

'I was hoping that when we get to wherever we're going I might slip ashore and—'

'Can't see that happening. Not the way they've got things set up.'

'I thought you might be able to help.' There was anger in Dweega's voice, and obvious despair. 'You're supposed to be some kind of god.'

'She can't be,' Kalgeck whispered, 'or she wouldn't be here.'

'It was your elder who assumed we were gods,' Spurral told them. 'I'm flesh and blood, just like you.'

Dweega sighed. 'Then that's our last hope gone.'

'You don't have to be a god to do something about our situation.'

'Like what?' Kalgeck wanted to know.

'There are as many of us as there are of them. If we could overpower a few of them and get hold of their weapons—'

'*Mutiny?* We wouldn't stand a chance.'

'What's our choice? We can go meekly to our fate or make a stand. I know which I'd prefer.'

'Then you go ahead,' Dweega said.

'I can't do it alone. We need to organise ourselves.'

'You don't know the Gatherers like we do,' Kalgeck rasped. 'They'd show us no mercy.'

'They'll certainly show none to Dweega when they find out she's lame. Isn't that reason enough to strike at them first?'

'And assure our deaths. Maybe she can get off this ship; and at least the rest of us will be alive as slaves.'

'You might call it a life. I don't.'

'I don't relish it either. And if I thought we had a hope of overcoming the Gatherers I'd be with you. But I can't see the others having much of an appetite for taking them on.'

'What about you, Dweega?' Spurral asked her. 'How do you see it?'

'I'll take my chances.' She turned over and showed Spurral her back.

Nothing more was said, and exhausted, they gave in to fitful sleep.

It seemed no time at all before the morning came.

At first light they were roughly roused with kicks and curses, and allowed a little of the brackish water to gulp. Then they were steered to their labours.

But this time they were given different tasks. Instead of working with the rope, Spurral's group was set to scrubbing the decks. Again, Kalgeck and some of the others did their best to shield Dweega, but it wasn't as easy as when they were working in the dimly lit winding room.

Inevitably, something happened that made it impossible for Dweega to hide her disability.

One of the crewmen ordered her to move away from the small cluster of companions trying to shelter her, and swab a different part of the deck. Dweega wavered, which only attracted more attention to her. Under an impatient tirade from several of the crew, she finally rose, and clutching her pail made her way to the indicated place. She did her best to walk normally, but was obviously struggling, and the effort could plainly be read on her face.

It was only a short distance, but it was an ordeal for her. Doubly so as everyone watched her progress in silence. As she knelt, painfully, one of the crew slipped away. A moment later he returned with the captain.

Salloss Vant went to Dweega and towered over her, sour faced.

'Stand up,' he ordered coldly.

She did it, although awkwardly.

'Now walk,' he said. 'That way.' He pointed to the spot she had just come from, where Spurral and the others were standing.

The deficiency in her leg was apparent, and when she got there she all but collapsed into Spurral's arms.

'We've no room on this ship for any who can't pull their weight,' Vant boomed, 'or who have no value to us! They're a waste of precious food!'

'I can work!' Dweega pleaded.

'But not very well, it seems. We Gatherers aren't a charitable trust, and we carry no passengers.' He nodded to several crewmen, and started to walk away.

The men advanced on Dweega. A tussle developed as they tried to prise her away from Spurral. None of the other dwarfs did anything except look horrified.

'*Captain!*' Spurral shouted.

Salloss Vant stopped in his tracks and turned, a look of surprise on his face that one of his chattels should dare address him.

'You don't have to do this,' Spurral told him. 'We can do her work for her. She doesn't have to be a burden on you.'

Vant gave the crewmen another curt nod. One of them landed a heavy blow to the side of Spurral's head with a linchpin, breaking her grip on Dweega and knocking her down. Then they began dragging the girl away.

At that point Kalgeck came alive and tried to intervene. He rushed forward, shouting, '*No! No!*'

He, too, was viciously downed.

'*I'll have no defiance on this ship!*' Vant roared, glaring at the captives.

None of them moved as Dweega, screaming now, was forced to the ship's rail.

'Heed this well!' Vant said. 'And be certain that the same fate awaits any who challenge my authority!'

The crewmen lifted the struggling Dweega by her arms and legs. They swung her back and forth a couple of times, building momentum, then tossed her over the rail. There was a shriek as she fell, followed by a distant splash.

Gasps and screams came from the horrified dwarfs.

'*Bastards!*' Spurral yelled. '*Stinking, cowardly bastards!*'

Vant turned his attention to her, and to Kalgeck, quaking beside her on the deck.

'Spirit's a good thing,' he stated, looming over them. 'Slaves with grit usually make good workers, and that increases the price we'll get for you. Once you've been broken, that is.'

'Go to hell,' Spurral spat.

'We're already there. And should you doubt that, I'm happy to underline the point.' He gestured to the crewmen who threw Dweega overboard.

They hoisted Spurral and Kalgeck to their feet, and shoved them to the central mast. Chests to the column, arms hugging it, their wrists were tied. The backs of their shirts were ripped open.

All the other captives were gathered and made to watch what happened next.

Vant barked an order. A muscular crewman stepped forward, unfurling a leather whip.

'Six for a start, I think,' the Captain decided.

The whip cracked across Spurral's back. She felt indescribable pain, but was damned if she was going to cry out. The next lash was for Kalgeck. Agony racked his body, but he followed her lead and kept silent.

They were beaten alternately, with lingering pauses between the blows, until each had received their six strokes. Neither made a sound throughout. Trickles of blood ran from their lips due to them clenching their teeth so hard.

Somebody doused their gore-clotted backs with buckets of sea water. The salt stung like fire. Then they were left there, still tied, as examples to the rest as they filed past on the way to their labours.

At length, Kalgeck whispered, 'That . . . mutiny.'

'What . . . about it?' Spurral managed.

'How do we . . . start?'

The Wolverines finished work on the boats during the night. They were up again as soon as the sun rose, lugging the vessels down to the water's edge and loading provisions. The day was already warm.

The band was fatigued, and tempers were still taut, particularly in the case of Haskeer and Jup. Given the tensions, Stryke had the additional problem of carefully choosing who went on which boat. He decided that Jup, Dallog and himself would represent the officers on one of them, along with Pepperdyne as a sort of unofficial master. He thought it best to have Standeven along too, so he could keep an eye on him. The second boat had Haskeer and Coilla aboard, with the latter put in charge. Haskeer didn't like a corporal being given primacy over a sergeant, but Stryke couldn't risk him being in command when he was in such a volatile mood. He did take a chance by including Wheam on the second boat, however, in the hope that Haskeer wouldn't find that too provoking. The tyros were just about evenly distributed between the two craft, as were the Wolverine privates. Turns would be taken at the rowing, and with operating the rudders.

The trio of dwarf children, Grunnsa, Heeg and Retlarg, were also up with the dawn, if they had slept at all. When the final preparations were being made, they shyly approached Stryke and Coilla.

It was Grunnsa, the oldest, who came right out with, 'Can we go with you?'

'No,' Stryke told him. 'Sorry.'

The children chorused their disappointment.

'It'd be too risky,' Coilla explained patiently. 'Besides, you're needed here to lend a hand getting things back in shape after the raid.'

'Will you see our parents?' Retlarg said.

'I don't know,' Stryke admitted. 'But if we do, I promise we'll help them if we can.'

Heeg put a question they'd rather wasn't asked. 'When will you be back?'

Stryke and Coilla knew that for good reasons or ill, they might never return.

Coilla softened the blow. 'It could be soon. So look out for us, won't you?' She felt bad giving them what could well be a fruitless task, but didn't want to dash their hopes completely.

'Thanks for your help,' Stryke told them. 'We couldn't have done this without you.'

Grunnsa beamed. 'Truly?'

''Course.' He brandished the chart. 'How else would we know where to go?'

'Time for us to get on,' Coilla announced. 'And you three should be getting back to your duties.'

The kids puffed their chests at the implication of their importance and ran back up the beach shouting.

'Talking about the chart,' Coilla said as she watched them go, 'how do we know these Gatherers are heading for their base? Maybe they've gone straight to whoever they want to sell the islanders to.'

'It's all we've got to go on. If they're not there, we'll be waiting when they get back.'

'That won't be much use to Spurral.'

'I know. But like I said, we've no other option.'

Before they left, Dallog performed a short ceremony invoking the Tetrad, commonly referred to as the Square, the four principal orc deities. He called upon Aik, Zeenoth, Neaphetar and Wystendel to favour their voyage and keep their blades keen. It wasn't something the band normally did, except before major engagements. But Stryke had given permission for morale's sake, and because he thought they could use all the help going.

As Dallog recited the simple ritual, the band veterans remembered Alfray, his fallen predecessor, who always undertook the same duty. A very few, Haskeer among them, wore expressions that showed they considered the comparison unfavourably.

When it was done, Stryke ordered everybody to board the boats. It looked as though all the islanders had gathered, the elder at their forefront, to watch the warband depart. They took in the scene in complete silence.

Stryke stood at the bow of his vessel. Almost without thinking, he patted his pouch containing the instrumentalities.

Then the oars cut into the foaming water and they set off.

18

The young officer who brought Jennesta the news had been part of the retinue that accompanied her from Peczan. So he knew her temper, and dreaded her reaction.

When he presented himself at her tent in the makeshift camp near the coast in Acurial she was alone. At least as far as other living beings were concerned. As usual, several of her undead bodyguards were present, shuffling vacantly in the background.

'What do you want?' she asked languidly as he entered. She didn't bother looking up.

He bowed. 'M'lady, I've word of the hunt for the Wolverines you ordered.' She said nothing so he ploughed on. 'I regret having to tell you that they . . . got away.' He braced himself for the storm.

But she was calm. 'How?'

'That's what's extraordinary, my lady. We had them in sight, in the woods. Then they . . . somehow they . . . *vanished*. Or not quite vanished. They . . . I have no words to describe it, m'lady.'

She didn't seem surprised. 'Then don't try. It's obviously beyond you.'

'There's more, ma'am, if it pleases you.'

'We'll have to see, won't we? What is it?'

'Ours wasn't the only force out there. There was some other group. Small, but possessing powerful magic. They seemed to be after the orc band, too. ma'am. And once the orcs . . . went, we were anxious this group might have turned their magic on us.'

'How was this group made up?'

'That's another strange thing, ma'am.'

'It has been an unsettling night for you, hasn't it, Major?'

'We didn't get too close a look at them, my lady, but many of the men swear they weren't human. Not like orcs or—' He was about to say *you*, and thanked the gods he checked himself. 'Not like orcs. These were many different kinds of creatures, unlike anything we've ever seen before.'

'If you're to thrive in my service you'll learn to take *strange things* in your stride. Is that all?'

He was surprised, if not shocked, that she took what seemed to him bad news so evenly. 'We've also had reports that bands of liberated . . . that's to say *rebellious* orcs are roaming this area. We're not in the most secure of positions, ma'am.'

'We won't be here long.'

'What are your orders, my lady?'

'My intention is to follow them.'

'My lady?'

'The band of orcs. The *Wolverines*.'

He was baffled. 'Begging your pardon, my lady, but . . . how? By ship?'

'No, you fool. There never was a ship expected. And no vessel could follow where they went.'

'Then, my lady, how . . . ?'

'I have the means. Though I warn you that you might find the journey a little . . . exhilarating. What's the matter, Major? You look uneasy.' She was poking fun, not inquiring after his well-being.

'Nothing's wrong, thank you, ma'am.'

'Good. Because if I thought that you or any other of my followers might baulk at the manner of our going from this place . . . Well, perhaps an illustration will serve.' She reached for a small silver bell standing on the arm of her couch. It tinkled lightly.

In response, the tent flaps rustled and were clumsily pulled aside. A figure lumbered in. It was another of her zombie slaves. Superficially, it looked like all the others the major had encountered. Its eyes were glassy, and lacked any hint of compassion. The skin that could be seen, on the face and hands, had the sickly pallor of a long mummified corpse.

The being lurched forward a few steps, then halted, adopting a grotesque parody of standing to attention. And the major couldn't help but notice that it gave off the vile odour of decomposing flesh.

'The latest of my attendants,' Jennesta explained. 'Study him closely. I think you may have been acquainted, albeit loosely.'

He stared at the swaying abomination.

'Come on, Major!' she urged. 'There's enough of the original features left for you to make out who this is, surely? He was a man of some distinction, for a while.'

Realisation began to dawn. The major's face took on an appalled expression.

'Ah, I see you *do* recognise our visitor. But let me formally introduce you. Say hello to General Kapple Hacher, late governor of this province.'

The creature that had been Hacher was drooling.

'Consider him closely,' Jennesta said, icy now. 'Because in him you see the destiny of any who would seek to thwart me or disregard my wishes. Make no mistake, Major; I could as easily command an army of his kind as a rabble of free-thinkers. Make sure you and your comrades give me no reason to do so.'

He nodded, words being hard for him to summon.

'Prepare for our departure,' she ordered. 'Oh, and do spread the word about the general's new status, won't you? Now leave me.'

He bowed and turned to go.

'And, Major.'

'Ma'am?'

'See to it that I'm not disturbed.'

The officer gave another quick bow and departed, ashen-faced.

Ignoring the undead Hacher and her other flesh puppets, she stooped and pulled a small chest from under the couch. It was steel-banded and had an elaborate lock, but its real protection lay in the enchantment Jennesta had cast upon it; a spell only she could negate without fatal consequences. Inside the chest was another, slightly smaller, fashioned from pure silver. This, too, was bound with a charm. Once opened, she gazed at her greatest treasure.

The instrumentalities were identical to the ones she had purloined from the Wolverines: sandy coloured, green, dark blue, grey, red; each with varying numbers of projecting spikes. Knowing that even her magic wasn't powerful or subtle enough to create a set from scratch, she had studied and laboured for years to perfect a way of duplicating them. The faultless copies she now ran loving fingers over vindicated her efforts. She knew they would do everything the set the doltish orcs possessed. They could do *more*, given she was so better versed in their potential.

She looked forward with relish to pursuing the warband. But first she had somewhere else to go.

Beyond the veil of the worlds, the Wolverines' two sturdy boats sailed on.

They were lucky with the weather; the sea was calm and the sky clear, which meant the pair of craft could travel within a short hailing distance of each other. That was useful for Pepperdyne, who was able to bawl instructions to the second vessel when it was doubtfully handled. Coilla, in charge of the second boat, was grateful for the guidance. Haskeer was less enamoured of a human bellowing orders at them.

Stryke, Jup and Dallog were the high-rankers on the boat Pepperdyne skippered. Standeven was aboard too, typically seated as far from the others as possible, and looking bilious despite the millpond sea.

Pepperdyne had been navigating by the sun, and earlier, by the fast fading stars as dawn broke, using a basic star chart he got from the elder. It was a crude method, and he was anxious for some kind of landmark to confirm their position. At around noon, he got it.

Jup pointed. 'There!'

Far off, they could just make out three or four dark bumps rising from the sea's otherwise featureless surface.

'You've good eyesight,' Pepperdyne complimented.

'But they are islands, right?'

'Have to be,' Stryke replied. He had the chart spread on a bench, and tapped a particular spot. 'These, I reckon.'

Pepperdyne leaned in for a look. 'I think you're right.'

'So we're on course?'

The human nodded. 'More or less.'

'But how much can we trust the map?' Jup wondered.

'It seems true so far. Though my hunch is that it covers just the immediate area.'

'Is that a problem?'

'Only if we have to go outside what the map shows, for any reason. Into what would be, for us, uncharted seas. If this world's all ocean there are probably a damn sight more islands than on here.'

'I heard one of those dwarf children come out with an old saying,' Dallog informed them. 'It was about there being as many islands as there are stars in the sky.'

'Poetic, but not very helpful if we have to travel further than this chart.'

'I don't see the need to,' Stryke said. 'The map tells us where we started and where we need to get to. Anything else happens, we'll deal with it.'

'Hope you're right,' Jup remarked, 'For Spurral's sake.'

They had seen the chain of islands on the second boat, too.

Wheam was particularly excited at their first sight of landfall. 'This is an important moment. It should be celebrated. It will be, in the epic ballad I'm going to make out of this voyage.'

'Oh joy,' Haskeer intoned flatly.

'If only I had my lute. I always found it so much easier to word-weave with that in my hands. It was such a blow losing it.'

'Yeah, a real tragedy.'

'You'll just have to compose it in your head,' Coilla suggested.

'If there's enough room in there,' Haskeer muttered.

Wheam was oblivious to barbs. 'This ballad could be the making of me as a song-smith. Once I perform it—'

'You know,' Coilla told him, 'you really showed some promise back there in Acurial. When you lost your temper with that human over your lute.'

'He made me angry. But—'

'Exactly. It brought out your orcishness. Don't you think it's better to try being what you were born for than—'

'Poncing about like a limp-wristed fop with water for blood,' Haskeer finished for her.

'Not *quite* the way I'd have put it,' Coilla admitted, 'but not far off.'

'Why can't I be a warrior and a bard? A *warrior-bard*.'

'Don't think there have been too many of those among our race.'

'Then I'll be the first!'

'Just focus on the warrior bit. It's more likely to keep you alive.'

'I don't see why I—'

'Just a minute.' She was staring out to sea.

'But—'

'*Quiet*. Look.' Coilla stretched an arm to indicate something she'd seen.

'What?' Haskeer said. 'Another island?'

'No. Something small, and not far off. See it?'

He squinted, a hand shading his eyes. 'Yeah. What is that?'

'Dunno. Could be just a bit of flotsam. *Hang on*. Something moved.'

'I think it's somebody waving,' Wheam reckoned.

'You could be right,' Coilla agreed. She stood up and hailed the other boat, then gestured towards the object.

Stryke judged it something worth investigating, and ordered the boats to alter course.

As they got nearer, they saw that it was indeed a figure, clinging to a chunk of driftwood.

'It's a dwarf!' Jup exclaimed.

'And female,' Pepperdyne added.

When they reached the castaway, oars were upped on one side of Stryke's boat and she was hauled aboard. They laid her on the deck. She was obviously exhausted, and parched from exposure to the sun, but didn't seem to be seriously hurt. Though she was very frightened.

'It's all right,' Jup soothed. 'Here, drink this.' He pressed a canteen of water to her lips. 'Steady, steady. Not too fast.'

'I recognise her,' Dallog decided.

'I think I do, too,' Pepperdyne said. 'From the island.'

Jup grew animated. 'Then she must have been taken with the others.' He began lightly slapping the girl's cheeks. 'Come on. Wake *up*.'

'Go easy on her,' Stryke warned. 'She'll come out of it in her own time.'

'Here.' Pepperdyne handed Jup a brandy flask, 'Try her with a little of this.'

A trickle of the fiery liquid had the girl coughing, but it put some colour into her cheeks. Her eyes fluttered and opened, and she looked up at them fearfully.

'Everything's all right,' Jup assured her gently. 'How're you feeling?'

She groaned and tried to say something.

'What's your name?'

She managed, 'Dweega.' Then she focused and recognised him. 'The . . . god.'

'Well, not really.'

'I . . . know. She told . . . me.'

'She? Who told you? Was it Spurral, Dweega? Remember? She was with us on your island.'

Dweega nodded.

'She's alive?' Jup asked, not daring to hope.

'Yes.'

Jup punched the air. 'I knew it!'

'But. . .'

He sobered. 'What?'

'The . . . Gatherers . . . Salloss Vant . . .'

'Who?'

'She's done in,' Stryke declared. 'Let her rest for a while. At least we know Spurral's alive.'

'Or was when this one last saw her.'

'Which probably wasn't that long ago,' Pepperdyne offered. 'You don't get much time when you're adrift, what with the sun and lack of water. She might only have been out here for a matter of hours.'

'Which means the Gatherers' ship can't be far off.'

'Yes. Assuming that's where this girl came from, which seems a good bet.'

'But which direction?' Jup scanned the ocean.

'Our best plan's to keep going for the Gatherers' base,' Stryke decided. 'Chances are that's where they're heading.'

Jup nodded at Dweega. 'So how come this one ended up in the drink?'

'Noticed her leg?' Dallog asked.

They looked, and saw that one of the girl's legs was twisted and distended.

'That's not a recent injury,' Dallog continued. 'I'd say it's been like that for quite a while. Maybe she was born that way.'

Jup's face clouded. 'You're saying those bastards dumped her overboard because of it?'

'They're slavers. They've no use for faulty produce.'

437

'Shit. What's Spurral gotten herself into?'

'They've no reason to do the same with her,' Stryke reminded him.

'Far as we know. And she's not one to take bullshit from anybody. She could provoke them and—'

She's smart, Jup. Seems to me she'll know how to play it.'

The dwarf nodded, but looked doubtful.

'We push on,' Stryke said. 'Give this girl dry clothes and see if you can get some food down her. Once she rallies she might tell us more.'

It was about time to relieve the first set of rowers, so Stryke ordered the changeover. He got Coilla to do the same on her boat. With fresh bodies at the oars, they set off again at a clip.

A couple of hours passed before Dweega started to come to herself. Hesitantly, she told them what she knew about Spurral, and Salloss Vant.

'You know where they were going?' Stryke asked her.

She shook her head.

'Or where they are now?'

'Roughly. The course they were on, anyway.'

'Will you help us track 'em?'

'I'm . . . frightened. I don't want to go back to . . . *that man.*'

'It'll be different this time,' Jup promised. 'Nobody's going to hurt you.'

She looked around at the warband, taking in their weather-beaten, scarred faces, and the flint in their eyes. 'All right.'

'So how far are we from their ship?' Stryke asked.

'Maybe closer than we think,' Dallog interrupted. 'Look.'

Well to their stern was a ship. It was distant enough for the details to be hazy, but the white of its sails was plain to see.

'Could that be them?' Jup wondered, a real edge in his voice.

'No,' Pepperdyne said. 'It's a different class of ship from the one they had.'

'What do you think, Dweega?' Jup said. 'Recognise it?'

'He's right. It's not the Gatherers' ship I was on.'

'Who says they've only got one ship?' Dallog speculated. 'Might be more of 'em.'

'Could be,' Stryke conceded. 'Then again, there must be lots of ships, this being a world of islands.'

'I don't think so,' Pepperdyne said. 'I've been watching it for quite a time, while you were tending the girl. It never varies its speed, never falls back or forges on. It's always at the same bearing. I'd say whoever that is, they're shadowing us.'

19

The casting overboard of Dweega galvanised many of the captive dwarfs. But they knew the Gatherers of old, and their terrible reputation. Angry as they were, and grief-stricken over Dweega, the dwarfs wanted to act but remained fearful. Spurral did her best to change that.

The whipping she and Kalgeck had taken left them pained and badly sore. There was no ministration from the Gatherers, not that they expected any, but their fellow captives rallied round. They had been stripped of their few miserable valuables, with the exception of a small number of items even the slavers thought worthless. These included certain herbs and salves the dwarfs habitually carried. They gave some relief, and speeded healing.

Although she didn't welcome the thrashing, Spurral was perversely grateful for it. It sharpened her appetite for revenge, and her fortitude earned her kudos among the other prisoners, making them more open to her whispered seditions. Kalgeck, too, seemed to find resolve in his punishment.

Spurral immediately set them to work making weapons. Nothing resembling blades could be pilfered. So they improvised bludgeons from pieces of timber and sacking. They made slingshots with strips of cloth, and sneaked peach-stones out of the crew's swill buckets, for shot. Part of the reason they got away with it was because the slavers had no regard for them. They were too used to plundering the dwarfs' island without opposition, and saw them as timid, unresourceful creatures. The Gatherers had grown complacent, which suited Spurral.

The only time they could really work on the weapons was at night, below decks in their makeshift dormitory. In almost complete darkness, by touch.

Satisfied that lookouts were posted, Spurral and Kalgeck,

sprawled on their mean sacking, were busy fashioning wooden hatchets.

'How can we fight with these?' Kalgeck whispered, holding up his crude effort.

'They only need to work once or twice. To get us some real weapons.'

'Oh. Right. You know a lot about fighting, Spurral.'

'I've done a lot *of* it. You?' She knew he hadn't.

'Not really.'

'Then trust me.'

'I overheard something Vant said today.'

'What?'

'He said we'll be at our destination soon.'

'How soon?'

'Didn't say. But it sounded like very soon.'

'So the quicker we strike—'

'Wouldn't it be better to wait until we get wherever we're going? You know, and maybe make a break for it?'

'No. We don't know what we'll be up against when we dock. Here, we've got just the crew to deal with.'

'*Just?*'

'They're flesh and blood. They bleed and die like anybody else.'

'Including us.'

'Listen, Kalgeck; characters like Salloss Vant dominate others in two ways. First, by force. Second, *fear*. They trade on their victims being afraid of what they *might* do. To overcome the Gatherers you have to overcome the fear.'

'That's easy said.'

'What's the worst they can do?'

'Kill us?'

'That depends on whether you think death's worse than enslavement and misery.'

'And you don't.'

'I don't want to die any more than you do. But I like the idea of this scum staying alive even less.' She tried to make out his expression in the poor light. 'You are still with me on this?'

He was a moment answering. 'Yes.'

'And the others?'

'Most of them, I think. But all of us are . . .'

441

'Afraid? There's no shame in it, Kalgeck. It's something we have to get over.'

'Even you?' He sounded incredulous.

'Of course.'

'You credit us with more courage than we deserve. We're not known for bravado.'

'So-called courage isn't about doing something without fear. It's doing something *despite* fear. Show me somebody who doesn't feel dread in a fix like this and I'll show you a fool.'

'Can we hope for help? From those who dropped from the sky with you?'

She had to smile, though he couldn't see it. 'I know Jup and the others will be doing their best to find us. But we can't count on that. We have to suppose we're alone.'

'What do you want us to do?'

'We need to seize an opportunity, and soon. Pass the word for everybody to be ready to act, and watch for my lead.'

The sky was a breathtaking canvas of crystal clear stars.

Night had not deterred or slowed the ship stalking the Wolverines' boats. It maintained the same distance and rate of knots, and had no trouble staying on course despite the orcs' vessels being completely unlit. The ship itself did bear lights, or at least gave off a soft illumination that couldn't be accounted for by lanterns. It progressed in an eerie glow, like a ghost ship.

On the first boat, Pepperdyne had managed to avoid contact with Standeven since they started out. Now he felt obliged to check with the man who, in spite of himself, he still thought of as his master.

Standeven remained in the seat he'd occupied since they began the journey. He hadn't exchanged more than a few words with anyone. It was a measure of how the others thought about him that, full as the boat was, he sat alone. He was staring at the ship trailing them when Pepperdyne perched beside him.

'Who do you think they are?' he asked in an undertone.

Standeven shrugged. 'Who knows? But it's obvious what they're after.'

'Is it?'

'Of course. What are the most valuable things on this boat?' He looked around furtively before answering his own question in an animated whisper. 'The instrumentalities!'

'How would they know we've got them?'

'How did that group that attacked us in Acurial know?'

'You reckon it's them?'

'Perhaps. Or some other. It doesn't matter. What's important is that they understand the worth of the artefacts.'

'What's your point?'

'We've let ourselves lose sight of what prizes they are.'

'I thought we'd seen the sense in abandoning that idea.'

'You might call it sense. I say anybody who turns their back on a fortune must be a fool.'

'You can't still be thinking they could be taken. From an orc's warband? That's *insane*.'

'Given the power at stake, and the riches, it'd be worth the risk.'

'Say we did get them. What then?'

'We'd use them to get out of this wretched world and—'

'How? We'd need Stryke's amulet too, and there's no way he'd let either that or the stars out of his sight.'

'There's always a means, Pepperdyne.'

'Like stealing them? The way the one Coilla had was taken back in Acurial?'

Standeven's face twisted. He raised his voice. 'How often do I have to tell you—'

'*Ssshhh!* Keep it *down*. If the others get a hint of what you're thinking . . .'

Heads had turned. Pepperdyne gave them a bland smile. When they lost interest he added, in an even lower tone, 'You're forgetting something. The damn stars aren't working properly anyway. So what are you going to do? Keep trying in the hope of them taking us home? And if by some miracle we got there, what do you do about the debt you owe Kantor Hammrik?'

'There'd be no need to pay debts with the instrumentalities in our possession. Or to go home. We could find ourselves a pleasant world somewhere. Maybe one where the natives are so backward we could rule them. We'd be *kings*, Pepperdyne.'

'Have you been drinking sea water? All this is crazy.'

'Only to someone with the imagination of a worm.'

'You're quite something, aren't you? It never entered your head that these orcs have become friends. Well, comrades at least. And you'd abandon them here.'

'Maybe they're . . . *friends* to you, but we've been in nothing but trouble since you got us tied up with them. And what are they dragging us into now?'

'We're trying to help one of our own. It's called loyalty, if the word means anything to you.'

'It means getting us killed.'

'Stryke said he'd take us home. I believe him.'

'Even if he kept his word, he'd still have the instrumentalities. I . . . we *must* have them.'

'Let it go. It's wild talk.'

Standeven didn't seem to be paying attention. He had a distracted look, and his head was half tilted, as though he was concentrating on something.

'What is it?' Pepperdyne asked.

'Can you hear anything?'

'Hear? Hear what?'

'I've been hearing a . . . melody. No, not that. It's faint but . . . it sounds like . . . voices, singing. *There*. Hear it?'

Pepperdyne listened. There was only the swish of oars cutting through water and the occasional murmur of other conversations. 'No, I can't hear anything.'

'You *must* be able to hear it.'

'There's nothing. It's just the sea. It can play tricks.'

He looked bewildered. 'Is it? Perhaps you're right. I can't seem to . . . I don't hear it now.'

'You've not been getting enough rest. None of us have. That probably accounts for it, and what you've been saying.'

'My judgement's sound,' he replied indignantly. 'I can see the logic of it even if you can't. I have to have the stars. They *want* me to.'

'What? Get a grip, Standeven.'

'You wouldn't have dared talk to me like that not long ago.'

'That was then. Now's a different game. I don't know what's going on in that devious head of yours, but understand this: if you do anything stupid you're on your own.'

'Obviously,' he sneered.

'Look, there's no way I'm going to—'

He stopped when he saw Stryke rise and make his way to them. 'Everything all right?' the orc said.

It could have been Pepperdyne's imagination, but he thought there was a hint of suspicion in Stryke's voice. He considered telling him what Standeven had just said, but decided against it. 'We're fine,' he told him. 'Just fine.'

On the Gatherers' ship, dawn brought another round of drudgery. The dwarfs were hurried through their usual meal of stale bread and water. Then they were steered, blinking, to the deck, for chores to be handed out.

The slavers had divided the prisoners into arbitrary work gangs when they were first brought aboard, and seemed content to let them carry on. So Spurral and Kalgeck were again in the same group, making intrigues easier. They were assigned to the galley.

It was sizeable, longer than it was wide, and oppressively hot, even so early. A row of wood-burning kilns occupied one side of the room. All were in full flame, with a variety of pans, pots and kettles on their tops, seething and steaming. The two biggest stoves were being used to heat cauldrons of water, vessels large enough to accommodate a crouching dwarf.

The not too clean work surfaces were littered with cooking utensils and victuals; principally fish, along with some doubtful-looking meat, wheels of rock-hard cheese and loaves of the musty bread. There were a few bunches of limp, shrunken vegetables.

It was among these that Spurral noticed the protruding hilt of a knife. There were no other blades to be seen. Presumably they had been hidden from the captives, and this one was overlooked. She nudged Kalgeck and indicated it with a subtle glance.

As the crewman watching them turned his attention to some bawling, Spurral whispered, 'Can you sidetrack him?'

Kalgeck was taken aback, then looked resolved and nodded.

While the dwarfs were being gruffly assigned their tasks, he edged his way towards a shelf of stoneware. At its end stood a tall jug. Kalgeck shot an anxious look at the crewman's back. Then he reached up and swotted the jug off its shelf. It went down with a crash, and shattered.

Silence fell, and the crewman spun round, looking furious. He strode to Kalgeck, red-faced.

'What the hell you playing at?'

'It was an accident. I—'

'Accident? You clumsy little swine!' He took a swipe at Kalgeck, landing a meaty smack. 'I'll give you accident!' The blows continued to rain down on the dwarf's head and shoulders.

While everyone was distracted, Spurral quickly palmed the knife and slipped it up her sleeve. It had a short blade, but it was razor sharp, and the coolness of the steel against her skin had a reassuring feel to it.

Kalgeck was still being clouted by the swearing crewman, and his arms were raised as he tried to protect himself. Spurral had a flash of regret at having involved him, and wondered how far the punishment would go. It crossed her mind to intervene and use the knife now. But no sooner had the thought occurred than the human, fury spent, ceased his pounding. He replaced it with even more colourful invective as he ordered Kalgeck to clear up the mess.

Down on hands and knees, gathering the pieces, Kalgeck caught Spurral's eye and gave her a wink.

Their group was set to washing dishes, carrying and fetching, bringing firewood from the hold to feed the kilns, and a variety of other duties. But nothing that involved anything sharp, such as preparing food. The galley crew took care of those tasks themselves, and Spurral feared they might notice a blade was missing. When there was no outcry she concluded they weren't methodical enough to realise.

The morning progressed in a grinding routine. One menial, back-breaking job after another was assigned, with the dwarfs spurred on with curses if they were lucky, kicks and punches if they weren't. At around noon all the captives were allowed out on deck to be fed. As usual, the fare dished up for them was even worse than the crew's own lacklustre chow. But the dwarfs, their appetites sharpened by the ceaseless labour, bolted it anyway.

Slumped on the sweltering deck, waiting for their short break to be rudely ended, some of them catnapped. Others exchanged whispers under disapproving gazes, or simply lounged, exhausted. For Spurral and Kalgeck, sitting with their backs to the rail, it was the first time they had a chance to confer since Kalgeck's earlier hiding.

'You all right?' she asked from the corner of her mouth.

He nodded. Though his developing bruises seemed to tell a different story.

'Sorry I got you into trouble,' she added.

'Don't be. It was worth it.'

'Yeah. We got our first real weapon.'

'And I pilfered these.' He discreetly opened his hand. In his cupped palm were four or five objects that looked like pegs, made of wood with metal tips.

'What are they?'

He smiled. 'Don't know much about seafaring, do you? They're kevels. You use them to secure ship's ropes. They'll make good shot for the slings.'

She was impressed. 'Smart thinking.'

'When do we act, Spurral? Everybody's ready. Well, ready as they'll ever be. They're just waiting on your word.'

'We have to pick the right—'

Kalgeck kicked the side of her leg and nodded up deck.

Salloss Vant had appeared. It was the first time they'd seen him since the day before. He was accompanied by a couple of particularly rough-looking henchmen, and he didn't look happy. Moving in the peculiarly slinking, almost feline manner that struck Spurral when she first saw him, the Gatherer captain positioned himself before them. As he did, other crewmen placed themselves around the captives.

'*On your feet!*' he barked.

The dwarfs reluctantly rose.

'Someone here has betrayed my trust,' Vant said.

'What trust?' Spurral remarked under her breath.

'When I took you aboard I asked you to surrender to your fate,' he went on. 'It seems not all of you saw the wisdom in my advice.' He regarded them with a baleful glare. 'A knife has gone missing.'

Spurral could have kicked herself for assuming she'd got away with it. 'Looks like you'll get the word sooner than you thought,' she whispered to Kalgeck.

His eyes widened. He began stealthily slipping a hand into his partly open shirt, seeking a weapon.

Spurral was aware that some of the dwarfs nearby were surreptitiously glancing her way.

447

'Is anyone going to own up to it now and take their punishment?' Vant demanded. Nobody spoke or moved. 'So you're cowards as well as fools. Just what I expected from inbred scum. You'll *all* be flogged for your insolence. Those assigned to the galley this morning, stay on your feet! The rest of you, back on your arses!'

'Here we go,' Spurral muttered.

She, Kalgeck and the five or six others in their group were left standing. They were more or less bunched, like a cluster of corn in a field otherwise flattened by a storm.

Vant scanned them. His malevolent eye fell upon Spurral and Kalgeck. 'You two,' he rumbled ominously. To his crew, he snapped, 'Bring them here!'

The nearest pair of sailors headed for those still standing. They didn't bother to draw their weapons, taking it for granted there would be no resistance.

One of them made straight for Spurral, approaching with a merciless smirk on his grizzled face. She had her arms behind her back, out of his sight, and let the stolen knife slide down her sleeve and into her hand.

'Move, bitch,' he grated.

Spurral swung round the blade, fast and hard, and buried it in his midriff. For good measure she thrust it into him twice more. The man looked as much bewildered as pained, staring down at the widening crimson patch with a bemused expression. Even as his legs buckled and he started to fold, she grabbed the hilt of his cutlass and dragged it from its scabbard. He was hitting the deck when she turned on the second man. This one appeared dumbfounded, too. She took the benefit of his slow reaction and drove the blade into him, putting all her force behind it. He went down.

A pall of silent, disbelieving shock descended. Everyone, captives and crew, seemed spellbound. For one stomach-churning moment Spurral thought she was alone, that none of the others would move to support her.

Then Kalgeck shouted, 'Now! *Now!*'

There was an explosion of movement and sound.

Dwarfs and men were shouting. Some screamed. Spurral saw three dwarfs piling into a crewman, pummelling him with their improvised hatchets. Somebody tugged free the man's sword and turned it on him. Another crewman staggered past with a female dwarf clinging to his back, repeatedly stabbing him with a seized dagger. Yet another was borne aloft by half a dozen captives and hurled, yelling, over the side. One of the henchmen beside Salloss Vant took a faceful of slingshot. He sank, writhing, to his knees. Everywhere there was chaos.

Kalgeck had got hold of the cutlass from the second man Spurral downed. He was no master with a sword, but the energy of his rage made up for the lack. Bellowing inarticulately, he laid into a knot of crewmen already besieged by his fellow islanders. Forced back to the rail, they were desperately trying to fend off their attackers.

Taken unawares, the Gatherers were faring badly. But Spurral knew the element of surprise wouldn't last long, and if the dwarfs didn't capitalise on it straightaway, they never would. Vant was wading into the dwarfs, swinging his sword like a madman. Spurral determined to settle with him.

She hadn't gone six paces when one of the crew blocked her way. He was armed with a cutlass and bent on stopping her. Spurral would have been happier meeting him with a staff, but she was as comfortable with a sword as just about any other weapon. And now the bloodlust was on her. She charged.

He was strong. When their pealing blades collided it sent a jolt through her. The blows they exchanged were harsh, like rock on rock and just as unyielding. Despite her strapping dwarfish build, Spurral was nimbler, which kept her from reach. But her opponent was the single-minded sort and came on relentlessly. He was good at blocking her thrusts, too, frustrating every attempt at breaking his guard.

They were close to stalemate when chance intervened. Spotting a crewman in the rigging, several dwarfs targeted him with their slingshots. The stinging bombardment made him lose his grip. Screaming, he plummeted to the deck, landing with a bone-shattering crash just behind Spurral's foe. It was enough of a distraction to make him turn, simultaneously dipping his guard.

Spurral didn't hesitate. She ran at him, cutlass at arm's length. The momentum took the blade deep into his chest. He went down heavily, falling backwards, the force of his collapse whipping the sword out of her hand. Thudding her boot on the corpse, she wrenched it free.

She straightened, panting, with sweat trickling from her brow. When she looked up, Salloss Vant was standing in front of her, bloody cutlass in hand.

He wore a demonic expression. His eyes burned like searing coals. When he spoke, he struggled to get the words out through his choking wrath. 'You . . . are going . . . to . . . *die.*'

'You can try,' she replied, trying to keep the foreboding out of her voice.

Done with words, he bellowed and came at her.

20

Vant's rage swamped any finesse at swordplay he might have possessed. He hurled himself at Spurral like a maddened bull. And now she saw that in addition to his cutlass he brandished a long-bladed knife. He swung the weapons like some kind of demented juggler, smearing the air with a metal haze.

Spurral hastily withdrew, trying to stay supple and anticipate where and how he might strike. An impossible task when facing someone as crazed as Vant, she soon realised. All she could do was keep moving. It was a strategy with limited value; inevitably he closed in on her and she was forced to engage.

The impact of the first blow she blocked had her staggering. The second came close to putting her down. She retreated once more, just a few steps this time, then feigned going in again. It was intended to wrong-foot him. Instead, she had to quickly duck as his blade whistled over her head.

A cacophony of yells, screams and clashing blades served as background. All around them, dwarfs and Gatherers battled. The surprise element had more momentum than Spurral guessed, and the islanders were driving home their advantage. Taken unprepared, dead and wounded crewmen littered the deck, or fought desperate rearguard actions. Some of the crew, those from the night watch, were sleeping when the rebellion broke out. Their awakening was rude.

Not that the dwarfs had it all their own way. They were facing hardened brigands and, as proof, the bodies of their dead and wounded were nearly as plentiful.

Avoiding two blades wielded by someone demented with fury was taxing Spurral. Already she was less light on her feet, and her arms were starting to feel leaden. Taking the offensive, she opted to rush Vant, sweeping her sword like a scythe. It was his turn to swerve. He moved just fast enough to elude her low swipe. His anger further heightened, he was back on the offensive without pause. Another round of battering followed, rattling Spurral's bones.

It was shaping up as less than an even match, and Spurral knew she had to find a different strategy or lose. The thought occurred that if she couldn't change the *way* he fought, perhaps she could change *where*. She turned and ran. Bellowing, he dashed after her.

She headed for one of the few parts of the ship she was familiar with. That meant leaping over corpses and skirting fights. At one point a Gatherer tried to bar her path. She deflected his cutlass on the run, and left him to cope with a trio of dwarfs closing in at his rear.

Spurral arrived panting at the galley door. It was half open. She kicked it in, Vant close behind. Inside, she was relieved to find the place empty, and raced to the interior. A second later he crashed in behind her.

'You little freak!' he screamed, lips foaming. 'Stand and take what's coming!'

'You want me,' she hissed, 'you come and get me.' It was a bold challenge; he was between her and the only way out.

Her hope was that the restricted space would cramp his movements and perhaps give her, with the smaller frame, a slight edge. A bonus was that there were plenty of potential weapons in the galley. Or rather, missiles. She grabbed an iron cooking pot and lobbed it at him. It fell short, clattering at his feet, and Vant furiously kicked it aside. He began to advance. Spurral took to bombarding him with anything that came to hand. She threw kettles, pans, a wooden mallet, skillets, flagons, trenchers and a heavy ladle. Several of the objects struck him, but he seemed oblivious to any hurt they might have caused. The only obvious effect was that his vehemence rose to even greater heights. She started to wonder if anything would stop him.

There being nothing else within easy reach to throw, she braced herself for his onslaught. Oblivious to the broken crockery and utensils underfoot, Vant stormed her way. She stood her ground. There was little choice; the narrow, windowless galley's farthest wall was no more than ten paces behind her.

Spurral had to hold her sword two-handed to hang on to it, such was the energy of the pounding he delivered. She managed, just, to stop any of his passes getting through, but her every attempt at turning her defence into an attack was thwarted. He staved her off with almost contemptuous ease. Despite her resolve to stand firm, the sheer power of his pummelling was forcing her to retreat. And she knew that if her back touched the wall her chances of survival would be vanishingly slim.

Desperation breeds ingenuity. Or insane recklessness. Something she noticed out of the corner of her eye, and the idea it gave her, could have fallen into either category. They had drawn level with the two largest kilns. Their fires had recently been banked, and the water in the massive cauldrons they supported was boiling vigorously. The clouds of steam they gave off misted the room. Condensation ran down the walls and dripped from the ceiling.

What Spurral had in mind was potentially as harmful to her as Vant, and she wasn't sure if she'd be nimble enough to steer clear of injury. But she did it anyway.

She swung her sword as hard as she could, not at the captain, but at one of the cauldrons. As it struck, she flung herself backwards. She hit the floor at the same time as the cauldron toppled from the oven, drenching Vant in scalding water.

He screamed in agony. Letting go of both his blades, he sank to his knees, a cloud of steam rising from his sodden clothes. His skin was already raw and blistering. A few drops of the boiling water had splashed on Spurral, and stung like hell. She could hardly imagine how it felt for him.

His screams cut through her like a knife, and she was sure they could be heard throughout the ship. Then he collapsed completely to writhe on the floor moaning.

She got to her feet and looked down at him. A quantity of the water had hit his face, inflaming it to the point where it was almost unrecognisable. There was an odour of seared flesh.

Spurral didn't know if the burns were severe enough to kill him, but if they were, it would evidently be a lingering, painful death. As much as she had grown to hate Salloss Vant and all he stood for, as much as she resented the humiliation he had heaped upon her, it wasn't in her to be sadistic.

Somehow she had been parted from her cutlass. It was by the kiln, whose fire had been extinguished by the cascade of water. The

453

sword's blade was broken in two, presumably from when it struck the iron cauldron. She picked up Vant's long-bladed knife.

He was squirming, and perhaps trying to speak, or curse, but the sounds were strangled and unintelligible. His eyes, though glazing, still had a spark of malice. If he recognised Spurral as she leaned over him, he gave no sign.

She lifted the knife high, two-handed, and plunged it into his heart.

Once the deed was done, the wider world seemed to re-establish itself. For the first time she noticed the fusty smell from the quenched fire. Again she was aware of noises from the rest of the ship; distant cries, running feet, chiming blades.

The door flew open. Several figures barged in. She snatched up Vant's cutlass, then realised it was Kalgeck and two or three of the other dwarfs.

They stared at Vant's gently steaming corpse, and at Spurral. Their saucer-eyed expressions mixed disbelief with admiration.

'My gods,' Kalgeck whispered. 'You all right, Spurral?'

She nodded. 'How's it going out there?'

He tore his eyes away from Vant. 'We've managed to deal with most of them. Some are holding out.'

'They'll lose heart quick enough when they know their chief's dead. Let's get him to where he can be seen.'

They dragged the body out to the deck. It left a wet trail, and they dumped it in plain view, the knife still jutting from its chest.

There was a stand-off. The majority of the Gatherers who hadn't given up were occupying the bridge. But possession of the wheel meant nothing when the dwarfs had mastery of just about everything else, and most importantly, the rigging. Without control of the sails, the ship was going nowhere.

When the hold-outs saw Vant's corpse their resolution crumbled. The dwarfs gave them assurances that they wouldn't be harmed. Whether they believed it or not, the crewmen had little option but to surrender.

The islanders found themselves with getting on for twenty able-bodied prisoners and about a dozen wounded. They herded them below decks to the prison hold they'd had to endure.

As they watched them descend, Spurral remarked, 'Looks like you have your own slaves now.'

'That's not our way,' Kalgeck told her.

'It's to your credit that it isn't. Hostages, then. To deter the Gatherers from raiding your home again.'

'I was thinking we might be able to trade them for some of our kin who got taken.'

'Good idea.'

'If we can find out where they are, of course. Which might not be easy.'

'I know. But you could see this as an opportunity.'

'To do what?'

'To venture out from your homeland. You've got a whole world to explore. Fear has kept you prisoners on your island as surely as the Gatherers held you captive on this ship.'

He hadn't looked at it that way. 'Yes,' he replied thoughtfully, 'maybe we could.' The sound of a splash turned their heads. Dwarfs were pitching the bodies of dead humans overboard.

'I can't believe we beat them,' Kalgeck said. 'It seems . . . unreal.'

'We did it because they didn't expect it of us. It's a good lesson. Remember it.'

'We did it because of you. If you hadn't—'

'You did it yourselves. You just needed to know you had it in you. That you could overcome the fear.'

'At a price.' He nodded towards a line of dwarf bodies, covered in blankets, laid out on the deck.

'Freedom always has its price, Kalgeck. I hope you'll come to believe it was one worth paying.'

'What do we do now?'

'We sail this ship back to your island.'

'How? I mean, we know a bit about seafaring, but we've only ever really done close-to-shore stuff, like canoeing.'

'We'll manage. If we have to, we'll get some of those humans to help us.'

'Would they?'

'What's their alternative? Drifting out here with us for ever? We'll make 'em think their lives depend on it, if need be.'

He smiled. 'Right.'

'You're learning. Only let's get underway soon, shall we? There's somebody whose company I've been missing.'

Jup had sunk into melancholy. He spent most of his time standing alone at the prow, searching for a sail or any other sign that might give him hope.

Stryke laid a calloused hand on his shoulder. 'There's no sense brooding.'

'There's little else to do.'

'Take a turn on the oars when we change over. Work off some of those worries.'

Jup smiled wryly. 'That's what I like about you orcs. You see everything so . . . *direct*. But some feelings can't be got rid of that easily.'

'You'll snap out of it when we catch the Gatherers.'

'You think we will?'

'Whatever it takes.'

'Thanks.' The dwarf eyed his captain. 'Expect you think I've gone soft.'

'No.'

'We dwarfs tend to mate for life. So to win Spurral and then lose her . . .'

'I know how I'd feel if anything happened to Thirzarr, Jup, or the hatchlings.'

'She sounds a good sort, your Thirzarr. Wish I could have met her.'

'You'd get on. You've something in common.'

'What's that?'

'You're both stubborn as mules.'

Calthmon, one of the veteran Wolverine privates, called out from the oars, 'They're gaining on us!' He pointed at the mysterious ship stalking them.

'He's right,' Pepperdyne confirmed. 'They're putting on some knots.'

Stryke hailed the second boat. 'See that?' He indicated the ship.

'We noticed!' Coilla yelled back. 'What do we do?'

'Row double-time and put some distance between us.'

'Run?' Haskeer exclaimed. 'Since when did we dodge a fight?'

'If it's the same lot who ambushed us in Acurial,' Stryke told him, 'I don't want to face their magic in open boats. Now up the pace!'

All hands to the oars, the boats increased speed, and at first, they widened the gap.

'They're catching up!' Dallog warned.

Pepperdyne looked back. 'At this rate they'll be on us in no time.'

'There's no way of outrunning them?' Stryke asked.

'Not with the wind-power they've got. Only thing I can suggest is we take our boats on different courses. Spread the targets.'

Stryke considered it. 'No. If we have to make a stand we'll do it together.'

Sails billowing, the ship came relentlessly closer. Finally it slowed and was looming over them. Seeing no point in wasting the rowers' muscle power, Stryke ordered the oars to be drawn. But he passed the word that they should be ready to resume at short notice.

'Now what?' Jup wondered, staring up at the massive wooden wall overshadowing them.

Figures appeared at the ship's rail and looked down at the boats. They were of diverse species, and familiar to the orcs.

'It's them all right,' Dallog said. 'The bunch from Acurial. And there's that elf who leads them.'

'*Attention, Wolverines!*'

'What the hell?' Jup exclaimed.

'*This is Pelli Madayar.*'

'How is her voice that . . . *loud*?' Dallog said.

'It's being amplified in some unnatural way,' Pepperdyne reckoned.

'Must be magic,' Stryke agreed.

'*Hear me, Wolverines! We have to talk.*'

'About what?' Stryke yelled.

'*The topic I broached with you in Acurial.*'

'She's on about the stars again,' Jup said.

Stryke nodded. 'You've had your answer on that!' he shouted back. 'Nothing's changed!'

'*I have to insist that we negotiate. Heave to and board our ship.*'

'No way!'

'*Would you prefer that I came down to you? To show good faith.*'

'You don't get it, do you? There's nothing to talk about!'

'*Refusal isn't an option, Captain Stryke. If you won't negotiate, I must demand that you hand over the artefacts.*'

'Demand be fucked!' Haskeer thundered loud enough for all to hear.

'Who the *hell* do they think they are?' Coilla added, enraged.

'Steady!' Stryke cautioned. To Pelli Madayar he bellowed, 'You were told before: we don't take kindly to demands!'

'*Then we cannot be held responsible for the consequences of your obstinacy.*'

'Why can't she talk plain like everybody else?' Haskeer grumbled.

'Pass on the word to be ready to move,' Stryke told Dallog under his breath.

'*This is your last chance, Wolverines,*' Pelli warned. '*I strongly advise you to lay down your arms and parley with us.*'

'Go!' Stryke roared. '*Move!* Get those oars moving!'

The boats glided away, the rowers straining. Stryke was no seafarer, but he knew a sailing ship couldn't set off from a standing start the way his boats could. He just hoped they'd get enough of a head start to stand a chance.

But the Gateway Corps had no need of pursuit.

The orcs had barely escaped the shadow of the ship when the air crackled. A blinding luminous beam struck the short stretch of water between the two boats. More shafts of incandescent light, red, purple and green, immediately followed. All came close to the vessels, but like the first, punched the ocean. Where they landed, the water boiled and gave off clouds of steam.

'Are they warning shots?' Pepperdyne wondered.

'Either that or they're lousy at aiming,' Stryke came back.

No sooner had he spoken than a fiery bolt struck the craft Coilla commanded. It wasn't a direct strike; the beam sliced into the rail and clean through one of the oars, neatly severing it. The impact was enough to rock the boat.

'To hell with this,' Stryke cursed. 'If one of those hits dead-on we're done for.'

'So what do we do?' Jup said.

'Give 'em something back.' He yelled an order stridently enough that it could be heard on both boats.

Stryke had had the foresight to place a more or less equal

number of the band's best archers in each vessel. The order he issued, using phrases that meant nothing to outsiders, told them which strategy to use.

They plucked prepared arrows, with tips wrapped in tar-smeared windings. Sparks were struck, igniting the bolts. Then, at Stryke's signal, they were loosed in the direction of the ship; not at any of the beings on board, but at the sails. Most of the viscous, flaming missiles found their target, igniting the sheets. In seconds, several patches were ablaze. Figures could be seen running about the deck.

'Now let's move!' Stryke shouted.

The boats pulled off again. To their rear, the sails were well alight. Several more energy beams flared from the ship, but they were wide of the mark.

'That'll give the bastards something to think about,' Jup commented.

'For now,' Stryke said. 'But I don't think they're the sort to give up too easily. *Come on, rowers! Put your backs into it!*'

It didn't take them too long to put a respectable distance between themselves and the burning ship. Nevertheless, Stryke didn't let the boats slacken their pace. He wanted to get as far away as possible.

'What do you reckon to the damage on the other boat?' he asked Pepperdyne.

'Hard to say without actually being over there. But it doesn't look too bad from here. It's not been holed, that's the main thing. We should be able to patch it up soon as we get the chance.'

'Good enough.'

Throughout the whole episode Standeven had done exactly what they expected of him; he kept low and cowered. Now he rose and gingerly made his way to Stryke and Pepperdyne.

Seeing him approach, Stryke said sarcastically, 'Come to help, have you?'

'No,' the human replied soberly, as though it was a genuine question. 'I wondered . . .'

'Spit it out.'

'I wanted to be sure the instrumentalities were safe.'

Stryke glared at him. '*What?*'

'They're secure, right?'

'What the hell's that got to do with you?'

'It concerns all of us. They're our only way to—'

'They're just fine.' Despite himself, Stryke's hand instinctively went to the pouch.

'You're sure that they—'

'Why the interest? What business is it of yours?'

'Like I said—'

'Ignore him, Stryke,' Pepperdyne intervened. 'It's just his weak-minded fear talking.'

Standeven shot him a venomous look.

'Well, he can keep his fears to himself in future and let me look after the stars.'

'Of course, Captain,' Standeven said, oozing with sycophancy. 'I wouldn't have it any other way.' He turned and picked his way back to his seat.

Stryke glanced at Pepperdyne. The human didn't meet his gaze.

21

Jennesta enjoyed few things more than a spot of mayhem and arson.

Having relished the former, she brought about the latter.

The surprise attack, using overwhelming forces and aided by her magic, had succeeded. Now the settlement burned. Some of the creatures fought on, as she fully expected their kind to do, but the pockets of resistance were isolated. And as the camp was on the small side there were few of them to defend it; even she might have hesitated before venturing into one of their more densely populated regions.

She had given strict orders about which of the creatures her followers were to search for, and that they were on all accounts to be taken alive. The rest she had no concern for.

But now she was growing impatient. The ones she sought had not yet been found. Her underlings would rue the day if she had to take a hand herself. It was true that many of them were unnerved by the crossing, but that just made them weaklings in her eyes, not needy. She filled her time with some creative thinking about the form punishments would take.

Her reverie was broken by the arrival of a nervous officer. In the best tradition of those who wish to keep their heads, he broke the good news first. Their principal quarry had been caught, albeit at the cost of several of Jennesta's followers' lives and only by using an awe-inspiring number of troops. The less than good news was that the two other targets, the younger ones, had got away.

She expressed her anger at the less than perfect outcome, but it was really just a matter of giving the officer what he expected of her. In truth she was content. She had the important one.

The prisoner was brought to her. It was chained and well attended, yet still needed several of her undead guardians, including Hacher, to keep it in check. The creature was haughty, and when Jennesta approached, it spat at her face. She had it beaten for that.

Once the beast was further secured, and as fire and bloodshed held sway outside, Jennesta set to work.

Spurral was right. The Gatherer prisoners had seen the futility of not cooperating and helped the dwarfs with the ship, though they weren't allowed any leeway that might permit them to cause trouble. No one doubted the prisoners agreed in the hope of lenient treatment. But the boost to the dwarfs' confidence in having their tormentors in their power was considerable. Relations between the surviving Gatherers and their one-time captives were hardly cordial, but so far there had been no serious discord.

As the ship headed back to the dwarfs' island, something like normality was imposed.

Spurral and Kalgeck stood on the bridge, watching dwarfs and Gatherers trim the sails.

'But *why* do we have to slow down?' Spurral asked, irritated at the prospect of delay.

'Because of what the Gatherers told us,' Kalgeck explained, 'backed up by these.' He slapped his hand on Vant's charts spread out before them. 'Right now we're in deep water. Very deep. But soon it gets shallow. There's a reef or something down there, and we have to steer a careful path through it.'

'Why can't we just go round?'

'That really would add to the journey, and we'd have to pass through waters with treacherous currents.'

'Great,' she sighed. 'So what do we do, exactly?'

'Slow to a crawl and measure the depth. Look.' He pointed down at the deck.

A group of dwarfs were at the rail. They had a large coil of rope with a lead weight at its end. Knots in the rope marked out the fathoms.

When the ship was little more than drifting, the measuring line was lowered over the side. They played out almost its entire length before the bottom was reached.

'How deep's that?' Spurral said.

'Getting on for fifty fathoms,' Kalgeck replied. 'No danger to us there.'

The ship crept on as the sun made its lazy way across the azure sky. Measurements were taken at regular intervals, but showed practically no variation.

Spurral grew more impatient at the sluggish progress. 'Are we ever going to get to this shallow patch, Kalgeck?'

'According to the chart, we're already in it.'

'Somebody should tell the sea.'

'These maps aren't always exact. Least, that's what the Gatherers say.'

'Well, I hope we're going to see some—'

There were shouts from the measuring team.

'Now what?' Kalgeck wondered.

'Let's see,' Spurral said, heading for the ladder that led to the deck.

When they reached the measurers, one of the dwarfs held up the end of the rope. It was severed and the weight was gone.

'What did it?' Spurral asked.

'Don't know,' the young dwarf with the rope told her. 'But whatever it was happened at about twelve fathoms.'

Kalgeck examined the rope. 'Looks like it was cut, or . . .'

'Or what?' Spurral said.

'It probably just got caught on something down there.'

'So let's try again.'

They brought another coil of knotted rope and fitted a new weight. It was fed overboard, and a dwarf was set the task of calling its progress.

'One fathom . . . two . . .'

'This should sort it out,' Kalgeck offered.

'Yeah, most likely,' Spurral replied, though there was a jot of uncertainty in her voice.

'. . . four fathoms . . . five . . . six . . .'

'I expect it's just a fluke.'

'Hmm.'

'. . . eleven . . . twelve . . . thirteen . . .'

'Seems it's all right this time,' Kalgeck announced.

'. . . fourteen . . . fifteen . . .'

'Good. Now maybe we can get on and—'

The line suddenly went taut. Then it began playing out at a rapid rate. The end of it would have disappeared over the side if several dwarfs hadn't grabbed hold of it. But they struggled, and the rope was sliding painfully through their hands. Kalgeck, Spurral and the others joined in, and still they fought to keep a grip.

'We're going to lose it!' Spurral warned.

'It must be snagged,' Kalgeck reckoned.

'Then why's it moving about so much?'

The rope was going from left to right then back again, and it was twisting in their hands. Kalgeck called for help. Three dwarfs ran to them and seized the rope. Now there were no less than nine of them clutching the line, but the bizarre tug of war went on.

It ended abruptly. Without warning, the line went slack. The release was so sudden it put them all on their backs. Scrambling to their feet, they quickly hauled the rope in. This time there was no resistance. Again, it had been severed.

'What the hell's going on?' Spurral said.

Kalgeck was blowing on his reddened palms. 'Maybe it got caught on a sunken wreck.'

'That's *moving about?*'

'The currents that deep can be strong. Maybe if—'

A weighty thump echoed through the ship. It originated somewhere far below. A second later there was another impact, louder and more powerful. The ship bobbed, tilting the deck and making the dwarfs' footing unsure.

Someone yelled and pointed. No more than an arrow's flight away a large segment of sea bubbled and boiled. The churning water was white with foam.

'What the hell is *that?*' Spurral exclaimed.

One of the Gatherer prisoners, working on some tedious chore nearby, had abandoned it and come to the rail. He stared at the seething mass of water with a fearful expression.

'Do you know what it is?' Spurral asked him.

He nodded, but seemed unable to speak.

'Well?' she insisted.

He whispered, *'The Krake.'*

'What's that?'

The human gave no answer. She looked at the others. Kalgeck

had gone pale, and the other dwarfs in earshot looked just as drained of colour.

'Kalgeck?' she appealed. '*Kalgeck!*'

He tore his eyes from the restless water. 'We've heard the stories. The Krake are lords of the deep. Some say they're gods. They can crush any size of ship, or pull it down into the abyss.'

'To do that they'd have to be . . . gigantic.'

'Bigger than islands, they say.'

'But you've never actually seen these things yourself?'

'Not . . . until now.' He was staring over her shoulder.

She turned.

Something was rising from the angry water. At first, with spray and mist obscuring the view, it was hard to make out what it was. As it continued to rise it became clearer.

It was an appendage, a tentacle with the girth of a temple pillar. Like a blind cave worm it was greyish-white, and its gristly skin was dappled with thick blue veins. Soon it had risen to the height of the ship, and was still growing.

Another tentacle erupted from the water, much closer to the vessel; near enough to rock it and send a wave over the rail. Soaked and dazed, the dwarfs retreated.

Shouts and screams had them turning to the opposite rail. On that side, too, tentacles were rising. The dwarfs stood transfixed as more and more emerged. In minutes the tentacles, swaying grotesquely, stood taller than the mainmast. All around the ship the water frothed wildly.

One of the tentacles came down, striking the deck a tremendous, sodden blow. Another swept in horizontally, demolishing the rail and causing dozens to duck. When a third crashed into the bridge, the dwarfs snapped out of their stupor.

They set about attacking the odious limbs with cutlasses and axes. The rubbery flesh proved resilient. Blows glanced off, and only continuous hacking made any impression. When blades did break through to tissue they released copious amounts of a glutinous ochre-coloured liquid. Its disgusting stink had them reeling.

The tentacles weren't just causing damage to the ship. Somehow sensing the dwarfs and humans, they slithered at remarkable speed to entwine any they could catch. Screaming victims were hoisted into the air and over the side.

Encircled by a muscular tentacle, the mainmast snapped like matchwood and toppled, pinning dwarfs and humans alike. So dire was the situation that even the Gatherers joined the effort to repel the Krake. They were using improvised weapons, or snatching up swords and axes dropped by dwarfs that had been taken. In the face of disaster the slavers and their one-time captives made common cause. Not that it made much difference.

'This is hopeless!' Spurral yelled as she battered at a writhing tentacle.

'We'll have to abandon ship!' Kalgeck returned. He was smothered in the foul-smelling yellowish-brown life fluid.

'I wouldn't give much for our chances on the open sea!'

'What, then?'

'Just keep fighting!'

A bellowing human was dragged past, a tentacle wrapped around his legs. Spurral and Kalgeck tried to hack him free, but their blades made practically no headway. The unfortunate Gatherer was whipped over the rail and disappeared.

Ominous creaking and rending sounds came from the ship's bowels. Above deck, tentacles ripped through timber as though it were parchment. Planks buckled, the remaining masts shuddered, canvas fell.

The ship lurched violently. Then it began to descend.

'We're going down!' Kalgeck shouted.

Water began pouring over the rails and swamping the deck. It was ankle deep in seconds, then knee and quickly waist-high. Panic broke out.

Spurral felt as much as heard the hull crushing. Dwarfs and humans were swept overboard. She looked around for Kalgeck and saw him being carried over the rail by a torrent of water.

There was a dizzying drop as what remained of the ship was pulled beneath the waves.

Spurral was immersed. Underwater, all was chaos. The sinking craft, with fragments shedding. A jumble of barrels, chests, ropes, scraps of sail, struggling bodies, twisting tentacles.

Just briefly she glimpsed animate forms, deathly white and grotesque in appearance. They were of enormous bulk, and their repugnant flesh pulsated horribly. She saw gaping, cavernous mouths lined with fangs the size of broadswords. And she caught sight of a single massive eye, unblinking and afire with greedy malevolence.

Then mercifully, total darkness closed in on her.

22

Once the ship they set on fire was out of sight, the Wolverines inspected their second craft. According to Pepperdyne, the only one with any real knowledge of boats, the damage was worse than he first thought.

'That magic beam punched through the hull in a couple of places,' he explained. 'Kind of sprinkled it. Look, you can just see the burn marks around the holes.'

Stryke leaned and nodded. 'And?'

'It left us with a number of leaks. Small and slow, but a nuisance. We can patch them up, and get somebody bailing.'

'So what's the problem?'

'I don't know how much the timbers might have been weakened by the hit. It could get worse, and we don't have what we need for a major repair.'

'What can we do?'

'Stop at the next island we come to and hope it's got trees.'

'We'd have to change course. That'd slow us.'

'We'll slow a damn sight more if we sink. Where is the nearest island?'

Stryke took out the chart and unfolded it. 'There,' he said, jabbing at a spot.

'I'm not sure if this boat would make that.'

'Great,' Stryke sighed. 'Any ideas?'

'When this sort of thing happened back in Trougath we'd lash the boats together.'

'If this one sinks won't it take both boats down?'

'You have to look at it the other way round. The buoyancy of the good one keeps them both afloat. It's not ideal, Stryke, but it should get us there. Though joining the boats will slow down our speed, of course, and it'll steer like a cow.'

'With that Pelli Madayar after us, this isn't a good time to fetter ourselves.'

Pepperdyne shrugged. 'Only other thing I can come up with is abandoning this boat and squeezing everybody into the good one. Mind you, *that* would slow us down a lot too. Not to mention things would be kind of crowded.'

Stryke considered it. 'No, we won't do that. It'd cramp our style too much if we have to fight. Take as much help as you need and see to the lashing. But do it fast; I feel like a sitting target.'

'Right. Jup'll have to be told about the delay.'

'I know, and he's not going to like it. You get on here. I'll tell him.'

The boats were already linked by a couple of lengths of rope. And they were near enough to each other that he could easily step over.

Jup was at the prow of boat one as usual. He was leaning over the side and stretching his arm to get his hand in the water.

'What you doing?' Stryke asked.

Jup straightened and wiped his wet hand against his breeches. If anything, the sombre expression he'd worn since they set out was more intense. 'I was trying farsight.'

'I thought this much water stopped it working.'

'It does, mostly. I'm . . . I wanted to do *something*, you know?'

Stryke nodded.

'And I picked something up,' the dwarf added.

'You did?'

'A life force. Or maybe a whole lot of them clustered together. Really massive. Big enough to counter a lot of the water's masking effect.'

'Any idea what it is?'

'No. But it's got an . . . atmosphere that I don't like. Definitely didn't feel friendly.'

'How far away?'

'Hard to say. The amount of energy it threw out, it could be a long way off. But my guess is that it isn't too far.'

'Is it a threat?'

'Who knows? But like I said, it didn't come over as pleasant.'

'We'll be on our guard.' He considered his sergeant. 'There's nothing to say it's anything to do with Spurral.'

'No. Not directly. But knowing she's out there with . . . whatever isn't a good feeling.'

'We've got to detour, Jup.'

'*What?* Why?'

'Pepperdyne says the other boat might sink if we don't find an island and fix it.'

'Shit' He looked over at boat two. Pepperdyne and several Wolverines were starting work. 'What're they doing?'

'Lashing the boats together.'

'Doesn't that mean if one sinks—'

'I thought that. Pepperdyne says no.'

'Damn it, Stryke; first that elf tries to fry us and now this. Am I ever going to get to Spurral?'

'I'll make it as quick as I can. We'll be working all out.'

'I'm counting on it.'

'Meantime, you keep doing whatever it is you do with the farsight. We could use a warning if what you picked up comes our way.'

'Sure. But if what I sensed comes our way a warning's not going to help much.'

It didn't take long to get the boats secured and plot a new course. The two-boat behemoth they created was ungainly and difficult to manoeuvre, but Pepperdyne maintained it would get them to land.

After a faltering start, due to how cumbersome the vessel had become, they got the hang of handling it. They rowed hard, and there was enough of a prevailing wind to make it worth raising the small sails.

Those who weren't on rowing duty speculated on the mystery of Pelli Madayar's group. Some looked forward to tangling with the Gatherers by recounting previous battles, as orcs were wont to do, and garnished their tales with some light boasting. A few concentrated on sharpening their weapons. Jup stayed at the prow, looking grim and occasionally dipping his hand in the water. Standeven continued to occupy his lonely place at the stern. He seemed restless, and Pepperdyne, too busy to spend time with him, nevertheless noticed that his one-time master's eyes were rarely off Stryke.

They quickly fell back into toiling at the oars combined with breaks for rest and bluster. A couple of hours into this routine, with the sun well past its highest point, a lull developed. Wheam tried filling it.

He stood and cleared his throat. No one paid any attention. He cleared his throat again, louder and theatrically. Two or three heads turned but most ignored him.

'Comrades!' he declared. '*Shipmates!*'

Haskeer groaned.

'It occurred to me,' Wheam said, 'that this could be the perfect time to give you all the first taste of the epic ballad I've been composing.' He pointed a proud finger at his temple. 'In my head.'

'You haven't got your lute,' Coilla reminded him desperately.

'It doesn't matter. All good verse should be as powerful whether spoken or sung.'

'How powerful is it if you keep it to yourself?' Haskeer said.

Wheam ploughed on. 'This particular extract is about what we're doing right now. It goes:

'They were cast upon the briny deep
for their solemn oath they would keep
to rescue a lost comrade true
from the sea so very blue!

'Ooohh *they battled magic mean and nasty*
and their victory was proud and tar-sty . . .

'That should be tasty. I need to work on something else that rhythms with nasty.'

'End my life,' Coilla pleaded, 'Now.'

'Tasty?' Haskeer murmured, baffled.

'We could throw him overboard,' Stryke said with no trace of humour.

'Anyway,' Wheam continued, 'the next bit is a kind of chorus. Feel free to join in.

'They fought the elf
they fought the witch
one was a pest
the other a bitch!

'Raise your flagons
raise your trumpets
the Wolverines
are no dunces!

'Things get really gripping now, In the next thirty verses—'
'*Land ahoy!*'

It could have been a lie. A frantic attempt by a tormented grunt to ease the pain. No one cared.

In reality, land was in sight. The dark, bumpy outline of an island could be seen on the horizon.

Haskeer raised his eyes heavenward and muttered, 'Thank you, gods.'

'How we going to handle this, Stryke?' Coilla wanted to know. 'If it's inhabited, that is.'

'Choices?'

'The usual. Sneak, full frontal or parley.'

'Nothing special in mind?'

'Not knowing what the hell we'll face, no.'

'We'll try parley. After scouting the lay, of course.'

''Course.'

'If it's inhabited and they're hostile,' Dallog said, 'what then?'

'Friend or foe, we'll get what we need,' Stryke vowed. 'We've no time to waste.'

When they got nearer and the island's features became clear, they saw that several ships were anchored in its largest bay.

'So it is inhabited,' Coilla said. 'Or at least somebody's visiting.'

'I'd say there's a settlement,' Stryke reckoned. 'Look. Just by the tree-line there. Those are some sort of buildings, aren't they?'

She squinted. 'Yes, I think they are.'

'Then we'll circle from a distance and see if there's somewhere quiet we can land.' He turned and shouted, '*Get those sails down, now! We don't need spotting!*'

When they got round to the island's far side they could see no signs of habitation. They headed for a small, deserted cove, and managed to land on its sandy beach. Stryke ordered the twin boats to be hauled ashore and into the trees, then had them camouflaged. Four privates, including Wheam, were assigned to guard the boats.

Standeven was told to stay, too, though he uncharacteristically tried to object. Stryke led the rest of the band into the interior.

'Why are we going inland anyway?' Jup asked. 'Don't we have what we need where we landed?'

'Not really,' Pepperdyne answered. 'We could use good seasoned timber for the repairs, and there's nothing suitable. Some serious tools would be handy too.'

'And our food and water are running down quicker than I thought they would,' Stryke admitted. 'That settlement we saw seems the best place to restock. Maybe we can pick up news of the Gatherers there, too.'

The island's heart was dense with jungle, and hacking their way through was inevitably a slow job. Anxious to speed things, Jup had suggested taking the much less obstructed coastal route. Stryke thought that would leave them too exposed and vetoed the idea.

But the island was small, certainly compared to the dwarfs' homeland, and the sun had still to set when they arrived at the beachside settlement. They surveyed it from hiding places at the jungle's edge.

There were around half a dozen dwellings of various sizes. An odd feature was a largish pool that had been dug in the clearing in front of the buildings. It was fed with salt water by channels connecting it to the sea, and there was a stout wooden barrier all around it. There were creatures of some kind splashing about in the water. They were of a fair size and dark skinned, but it was hard to make out what they were.

Other beings were present, and obviously in charge. These were instantly recognisable to the orcs.

'Fucking goblins!' Haskeer growled.

'I gather they're not one of your favourite races,' Pepperdyne said.

'We've had run-ins,' Stryke told him.

'Maybe they're different here,' Coilla ventured.

'Yeah, right,' Haskeer came back acerbically.

Pepperdyne was curious. 'So what is it about them?'

'They're ugly, back-stabbing, two-faced, mean, greedy, underhand, stuck up, cowardly, stinking bastards.'

'Those are their good points,' Coilla added.

'Given what we've known of them in the past,' Stryke said, 'we'll forget the parleying. Now let's get some scouts out.'

When the pathfinders had left, stealthily blending into the jungle, the others settled to watch what was happening in the encampment.

After a while, Coilla said, 'Those creatures in the pool; I reckon they're horses. Or maybe ponies.'

'Why would goblins keep horses in a salt-water pool?' Jup reasoned.

'I think Coilla could be on to something,' Stryke said thoughtfully.

'You reckon they're horses? What are the goblins trying to do, teach them to swim?'

'No, not horses. Not exactly. And if I'm right, they wouldn't need teaching.'

'So what do you think they are?'

'I want a closer look to be sure. Let's think how we can do that.'

Zoda, one of the scouts he sent out, returned at that point. 'Chief, you better come and see what we've found.'

Stryke beckoned Coilla, Jup and Pepperdyne to accompany him. He left Haskeer in charge.

They followed Zoda into the jungle. It took just a few minutes to reach a clearing, an area where the vegetation had been trampled flat and several trees bodily uprooted. Gleadeg, one of the other scouts, was waiting for them. He wasn't alone.

Stryke took one look and said, 'I was right.'

The creature before them did look like a horse, but not entirely so. It was about the same size as a pony, but much more muscular and powerful looking. With the exception of its mane, which was dark grey, it was completely black with no markings of any kind save a little patch, again grey, about its eyes. Its skin wasn't like a horse's at all; it was smooth and oily in appearance, resembling a seal's coat. There was a very unusual aspect to its mane, too; it exuded a steady trickle of water, as though it were a gently squeezed sponge. The water ran down the creature's shiny flanks and fell in drops.

'You're a kelpie?' Stryke asked.

'I am,' the water horse replied, its voice low and throaty. 'And you are orcs.'

474

'You know us?'

'I know of your race.' He looked to Jup, 'And I have communed with dwarfs.' The kelpie bobbed its great head in Pepperdyne's direction. 'And I am more than familiar with his kind. Unhappily so.'

'I can vouch for this human. He means you and your kin no harm.'

'That's hard to believe of his race. But he hasn't yet struck me down or tried to enslave me so I must take your word for it.'

Pepperdyne looked embarrassed.

'Your kind are rare where we come from,' Coilla said. 'They say it's wise to keep away from you, that you lure hatchlings to watery graves so you can eat their hearts. It's even said that you're really the spirits of evil creatures who have died badly.'

'Many untrue things are said about orcs too,' the kelpie replied. 'Do you eat your young? Are you the twisted offspring of elves? Do you murder the innocent for the sheer pleasure of it? Like you, we kelpies are subject to hatred and fear simply because we are different and prefer a solitary path.'

'Well said.'

'There is one true story told about us, however. Above all else we value our freedom.' The subject was painful enough to mist the kelpie's startlingly blue eyes. 'To us, enslavement is worse than death.'

'Yet it looks like that's been your fate,' Stryke commented. 'Why are you here?'

The kelpie looked to Pepperdyne again. 'Because his folk brought us here by force, as they have since time out of mind.'

'Why is no one ever pleased to see me?' Pepperdyne asked.

'Now you know how we feel,' Coilla told him.

'The ones who brought you here,' Jup said, 'are they called Gatherers?'

'Yes,' the kelpie confirmed.

'So how do the goblins fit into this?'

'The Gatherers are the catchers of slaves. The goblins buy. A few for themselves, but mostly to be sold on in turn. They stand between the slavers and their prey's ultimate masters. Their role is to match suitable slaves to the tasks they will undertake. So it's trolls or gnomes for islands where mining takes place, elves and brownies for houses of pleasure, gremlins for the drudgery of scholarly work. Even orcs, to provide bodyguards for petty tyrants. Though they are notoriously hard to break, you'll be proud to hear.'

Coilla frowned. 'There are islands here where orcs live?'

'Oh, yes. None near to this one, however, and even the Gatherers hesitate to try plundering them.'

'And what about kelpies? What sort of so-called owners are found for you?'

'We are in demand on many islands.'

'You have special skills?'

'No. It seems we make good meat.'

The silence that followed was broken by Jup. 'How did you escape the goblins?'

'Purely by chance. A rare lapse of attention on their part let me seize the opportunity to get away. I believe the only reason they haven't mounted a search for me is because, as my kind counts time, I am old. Very old. My flesh would be too tough!' He gave a watery, snorting laugh. 'There's no profit to them in wasting energy on me. Particularly as they are presently small in number.'

'How small?' Stryke wanted to know.

'Barely two score. Normally there are many more present, but the rest are away delivering the latest batch of . . . *goods*. That's why there are only kelpie prisoners here at the moment.'

'Why haven't you tried to overcome them yourselves, while their numbers are low?'

'We are hampered in two ways. First, we have no leadership. It's not our way. We are a fiercely independent breed.' He sighed. 'And look where it's got us.'

'And second?'

'Can you who dwell solely on the land imagine what it is to be dependent on water? We have to wallow in its life-giving essence several times a day. Our lives depend on it. A kelpie deprived of water dies a horrible and lingering death. We can hardly mount an uprising when weighed down with that necessity. I myself have to visit the shore daily to bathe. I don't doubt they will catch me there one day and kill me.'

'No they won't. We're gonna help you.'

'You are?'

'You bet,' Coilla said.

'Definitely,' Pepperdyne and Jup chorused.

The kelpie was taken aback. 'The human too? What have we done to deserve this?'

'Let's just say we're like you; we value freedom,' Stryke said. 'Do you have a name?'

'Of course.'

'What is it?'

'It would do you no good knowing, unless you're able to talk under water.'

'Er, no. That's not one of our skills.'

'Just call me the kelpie.'

'You have our protection. Come with us. You could probably use something to eat. What *do* you eat?'

'Not the hearts of hatchlings. Our appetites are wide-reaching, but given the choice we favour fish.'

'We'll see what we can do.'

On their way back to the others, Stryke asked Jup how he felt.

'I'm fearful of Spurral falling into the hands of scum like these goblins.'

'So take it out on them until we find the Gatherers.'

'I intend to.'

'Good. I knew that'd cheer you up.'

They waited for dark.

Under cover of night they positioned themselves around the goblin compound. Stryke had sent for the five guarding the boats, to up the numbers. But he kept Standeven well out of things, and relegated Wheam to a back-up.

There were perhaps a dozen goblins visible. Most of them bore the metal-topped trident spears they favoured, but also carried blades. The rest of the goblins were either in the various buildings or on the beach near the anchored ships.

'We keep this simple,' Stryke whispered to Coilla. 'Get in fast, kill 'em.'

'So how's that any different to what we usually do?'

'Ready?'

She nodded.

He signalled, and it was passed on.

The first move was down to the archers. They shot bolts into the compound that dropped five or six of the goblins before the others caught on. The next volley was of flaming arrows aimed at the buildings' rush roofs, for chaos' sake.

The blazing arrows were the signal to charge. Out of hiding, the Wolverines swept in from all sides. The goblins who survived the arrow bombardment were recovering their balance, and the ones in the now-burning buildings had spilled out. Those on the beach, alerted by the fires, were hurrying back.

So the orcs faced the full complement, and relished it.

Stryke lashed out at the first goblin he met. His blade severed the sinewy neck, sending its head bouncing across the sand. The next took steel to its guts. He disarmed a third by simply doing just that; he lopped off the creature's sword arm, then ran it through.

For Coilla, the lure of her throwing knives had proved too strong. Plucking them from the holsters strapped to her arms, she lobbed in rapid succession. A goblin fell with a blade in its eye; another stopped one with its back. Spotting a goblin rushing at her, its trident levelled, she struck it square to the chest. Yet another caught a knife in what would have been its privy parts, if it had had any.

Pepperdyne had the by now familiar experience of confronting foes surprised to be facing a human. For the goblins, he guessed, humans meant Gatherers and grubby mutual interest. They were stunned to be attacked by one. Their initial hesitation was a bonus he seized. His sword hewed wiry flesh.

Haskeer, battling nearby and trying not to admire the human's style, spat on subtlety, as usual. He brought down the first goblin he came across with bare fists, then snapped its curved spine over his knee. The one after that he eviscerated.

All acquitted themselves well, even the seasoning tyros. But Jup outshone. He fought with a ferocity to equal the matchless orcs. Spurred by frustration and fury, drunk on bloodlust, he gave no quarter. Armed traditionally with his staff, and having a long-bladed knife to hand, he thundered into the goblins like a pint-sized tsunami. He shattered skulls and ripped through throats. Landing a particularly vicious blow, he propelled a goblin over the fence and into the kelpie's pool. They put paid to it with thrashing hooves and snapping teeth.

The moment arrived, as it does in every battle, when it dawned on the victors that there was no one left standing to fight. A quick search of the buildings that escaped the fire, and the surrounding area, confirmed it.

The kelpie prisoners were liberated. They scrambled from the pool and shook themselves. Some pawed the ground, as though that was a pleasure they had long been deprived of.

Stryke got his officers together, and the ageing kelpie joined them.

'We've got to make a choice,' Stryke told them. 'Either we push on to the Gatherers' island or we stay here in the hope that Spurral and the slavers turn up. You should have first say on this, Jup.'

'I . . . I honestly don't know, Chief. My instinct is to go on. Then again, knowing this is where the slaves are brought . . .'

'It's one place they are brought,' the kelpie corrected. 'This isn't the only island where goblins, and other races, collect slaves.'

'Shit. So Spurral might not be brought here?'

'Don't despair. This is the most likely place. But your mate has not arrived yet, which given when she was taken, makes me think the Gatherers are sticking to their pattern.'

'What do you mean?'

'The time when they come has never been predictable, but the *order* of their coming is always the same. The Gatherers next port of call after raiding the dwarfs' island is invariably our own. Take us to our island, Wolverines, and there's a chance this Spurral of yours can be found. There's nothing here for us. We want to go home.'

'What do you think, Jup?' Stryke asked.

'Gods, this is getting so complicated. But it seems to make sense.'

'You're forgetting that we've only got two small boats,' Coilla reminded them, 'and one of those damaged.'

'And you're forgetting those,' the kelpie said. 'He tilted his head to indicate the beach and the anchored craft. 'Why use a boat when you can have a ship?'

'I'd feel a damn sight better in one of those,' Haskeer announced.

Stryke turned to Pepperdyne. 'Could we handle one of those goblin ships?'

He took a look. 'I reckon so.'

'All right then. We leave at first light.'

The kelpie nodded contentedly. 'Good. I can assure you of a warm welcome. Few are as hospitable as the kelpies.'

23

The darkness dissolved, to be replaced by a blinding light.

Spurral was on her back, staring up at the sun. She turned her head to avoid its punishing glare. There were fiery floats in her eyes and she blinked to rid herself of them. She had no idea where she was. As the floats faded and her faculties returned, so did the memory, of the ship, the Krake and what had happened.

She became aware of the sound of pounding waves, and when she reached out a hand it came into contact with wet sand. Water was lapping at her feet and thighs. Her sodden clothes were steaming gently in the heat.

Slowly, painfully, she got up and tried to make sense of her surroundings.

She was on a long, golden beach. Wreckage and general debris was deposited along the shoreline, including a couple of large sections of ship's decking. She guessed that she had probably clung to one of them, although she had no recollection of it.

Behind her, the beach stretched back a long way until it met a jumble of palm trees and other vegetation. Above the trees she could see the peaks of several small mountains of greyish rock, gleaming in the sunlight. There was no sign of habitation.

She stilled. Mixed in with the crash of waves and shrieking gulls there seemed to be something else. It took her a moment to realise it was someone shouting. As she attuned herself to it she grasped that there was more than one voice.

Looking along the beach to her left, she saw nothing. It was a different story to her right. In the far distance she could see figures. There appeared to be seven or eight of them. They were humanoid in shape and looked as though they were waving. As she watched, trying to make out who or what they might be, it became obvious they were heading her way. Spurral hesitated for a moment. Then, spurred by hope, she began to run towards them.

It felt as though it took for ever to cover the expanse of beach between her and the approaching figures. As she moved, her legs growing leaden with the effort of running through the obstructive sand, she became conscious of how much she ached. The battering she had taken when the ship went down, and presumably afterwards when she was at the mercy of the tides and drifting flotsam, was starting to make itself felt. Her elbows were grazed, there was a dull pain in her back and she noticed large blue-black bruises coming up on her pumping arms. But the prospect of someone else being on an island she thought deserted kept her going.

When she finally got close enough, she saw that the figures were dwarfs. Closer still, she recognised Kalgeck among them. Then they met and she was hugging him, relieved and frankly amazed that her friend had also survived the catastrophe. His companions, five males and two females, all young, clustered round joyfully.

'Are you injured?' Kalgeck asked, surveying her.

'I was lucky. Just a few knocks. How about all of you?'

'Fortune smiled on us, too. Our injuries are slight. It was a miracle.'

'It's hard to argue with that. But . . . are you all there is?'

His expression turned solemn. 'As far as we can tell. We've not been looking for too long, but apart from each other, and now you, we've seen no one else.'

'You couldn't have looked everywhere. It could be survivors have washed up elsewhere on this island, or even other islands.'

'Yes, we'll have to hope for that. But it does seem a mockery by fate if my kin should beat the Gatherers only to perish because of the Krake.'

'It would,' she agreed glumly. 'How about the Gatherers? You've not come across any of them?'

Kalgeck shook his head. 'But most of them were imprisoned below decks, remember.'

'Yes, of course. I could almost feel sorry for them.'

'It's hard for us to think that way about them. They caused us so much misery.'

'I know, and I can't blame you for it. Still, it's possible some of them might have made it here. We should take care.'

'What do we do now?'

'Do you know where we are? Or anything about this island?'

'No.'

'All right. So let's find out if it's inhabited; and if it is, whether the natives are friendly or not. But first we ought to look through the wreckage for anything useful, like provisions.'

'I already found this.' He held out a water flask.

'Oh, great. Can I? I'm parched.'

As she drank, Kalgeck said, 'It doesn't look like there's a lot else, though.' He was staring at the wreckage she washed in with.

That proved almost right. In fact they were lucky enough to find another flask, containing coarse brandy this time, though it was only half full. A nip each raised their spirits a little. They also scavenged some chunks of timber that would serve as clubs. Nothing else was of much use. But a couple of the dwarfs had managed to hang on to weapons from the ship; a Gatherer knife and one of the wooden hatchets the captives had made clandestinely.

They set off inland. Just inside the tree-line they came across bushes with a crop of yellow, spiky fruit about the size of apples. They were unfamiliar to Spurral but the dwarfs knew them and were delighted. Once the tough skin had been peeled off the sweet, juicy white flesh proved delicious. They ate their fill and then some.

'Right,' Spurral said, licking her fingers, 'let's see what else this place has to offer.'

Fortified, they continued their journey.

The jungle was thick and difficult to get through. After they'd trekked for some time, with Spurral in the lead, hacking at foliage with the knife and stumbling on vines, they were beginning to wonder if it was worth going on. Then she stopped, raising a hand for the others to be quiet. There was an extensive clearing just ahead. There seemed to be nobody about, so they gingerly stepped into it.

Trees had been felled, or more accurately uprooted, and dragged to form several heaps at the glade's edge. The undergrowth was trampled flat. In the centre of the clearing was a sizeable pool.

Spurral cupped her hand and tried the water. She spat it out. 'Salt. Must be fed by the sea.' Looking round, she added, 'Nothing here is natural except the pool. Somebody cleared this area.'

Kalgeck held a finger to his lips and pointed. There was a rustling in the undergrowth. They raised their meagre weapons. More rustlings came, but from several directions. The dwarfs drew themselves into a protective circle, eyes peeled.

Some kind of creature crashed through the vegetation, then several more. They were big and black.

'Horses?' Spurral exclaimed. As soon as she said it she saw her error.

The creatures entering the clearing looked superficially like horses but with important differences. Their skin was wrong, resembling a seal's, and their luxuriant manes oozed water. They were much more muscular and robust looking than commonplace horses. Above all, they had eyes that betrayed far greater acumen than any steed.

Kalgeck confirmed it. 'They're not ordinary horses. They're—'

'Kelpies,' one of the creatures grated, trotting forward. 'And we would like to welcome you to our island if we were sure you meant no harm.'

'We don't,' Spurral replied, recovering her poise. 'Do we look like raiders?'

'No, you look like bedraggled dwarfs. And as there is no ship off our coast I assume the sea cast you here.'

'Yes. We survived a wreck.'

'Then you are most fortunate, given some of the perils in these waters.'

'We met one of them.'

'Doubly fortunate then.' He surveyed the dishevelled group. 'You must forgive our suspicion. We have few visitors, and those who do come are usually unbidden and mean us no good.'

'You wouldn't be talking about humans, would you?'

'They can be among the worst of races, as you dwarfs must surely know.'

'You mean the Gatherers.'

'That's a name reviled by my kind. Even more so now, as we believe a visitation from them is due. And that always means pain and grief.'

'I can set your mind at rest about that. They went down with the ship we were on.'

'*Truly?*'

484

'Yes.'

'And their vile captain?'

'Salloss Vant? Dead.'

'You're sure?'

'I saw it.'

'Spurral's being modest,' Kalgeck interjected. 'She's the one who killed him.'

Insofar as they could read the kelpie's expression, he looked impressed. 'We have been in hiding, hoping against hope that the slavers might pass us by this time. Now you bring us this glad news. Come, your injuries will be tended and you can rest. Then there will be celebrations and feasting in your honour.'

'Now you're talking,' Spurral told him. 'We've had nothing but gruel for days. But tell me, what do we call you?'

'Before I can answer that question,' the kelpie said, 'I have one for you. How good are dwarfs at talking underwater?'

By the time Pelli Madayar's group put out the flaming sails, the Wolverines had made their getaway. She ordered a clean-up and went to her cabin.

The nature of the magic she used to communicate with the Gateway Corps' homeworld was such that it utilised any suitable medium. Sea water was the simplest, most plentiful and by far the most effective channel. She stared into a large bowl of it. The application of certain compounds to make it more receptive, followed by a gestured conjuration, sparked the enchantment.

The water simmered and ran a gamut of colours before settling down. At which point Pelli found herself looking at an image of Karrell Revers, human head of the Corps.

'I hope you have more cheering news for me this time,' he said without preamble.

'We've had our second engagement with the orcs.'

'And it wasn't a success. I can tell from your expression, Pelli.'

'They *are* a prime fighting unit.'

'So are you. Or you're supposed to be.' His tone had been much more prickly of late. The strain was telling on him. 'Could it be that your failure to overcome the warband is due to you exercising too much restraint?'

'It's true I began by trying negotiation, but—'

'This situation requires a remedy, quickly and decisively. You should have known better than to try parleying with orcs. Force is what they understand.'

'I thought we were supposed to stand for moral principles.'

'There'll be no principles, moral or otherwise, if instrumentalities fall into the hands of orcs, or worse.' Revers softened a little. 'I'm sorry, Pelli, but the gravity of what's going on makes it vital that we draw this to a close quickly. Forgive me for saying this, but the impression I have is that things are getting beyond your control there.'

'They're not,' she assured him, though she didn't entirely believe that herself. 'I intend to clear this matter up.'

'Then you'll follow my earlier advice.'

'Sir?'

'Use the special weapons.'

'That could involve the loss of innocent life.'

'Not if you proceed with caution when you use them. You've had no luck taming the Wolverines. This could be the only way you'll triumph over them.'

'I'll give your advice serious consideration.'

'Do it. Pelli.'

Without further word his likeness faded and disappeared.

She sighed and got up.

Out on the deck, her second-in-command, Weevan-Jirst, was gazing at his open hand. He held a palm-sized gem of fabulous rarity. Its iridescent surface flashed a series of images.

'Traced them yet?' she asked.

'I think so,' he rasped. 'They have altered their course, but their destination is predictable.'

'Then we'll continue the pursuit as soon as we can.'

He looked up from the gem. 'You look troubled. Can I ask the outcome of your communication with our leader?'

'We take the gloves off.'

24

Stryke didn't choose the biggest goblin ship. He thought that might stretch the ability of his band to crew it. Pepperdyne would effectively be commanding the vessel, and he agreed.

At first light they loaded whatever provisions they could forage from the ruins of the goblin encampment, got the freed kelpies aboard and set off. The journey, their new allies assured them, would not be lengthy. For Jup, wracked with anxiety and unusually distant, it couldn't be fast enough. He kept himself to himself, and the others mostly let him be.

The ship ploughed on uneventfully until well into the day. During all that time Pepperdyne was up at the wheel, with Coilla beside him.

'You really look in your element,' she said.

'It's the first thing I've got real pleasure out of since we set off on this crazy escapade.' He gave her a sideways glance. 'Apart from the few chances we've had to talk, that is.'

She smiled. 'Yeah, I've enjoyed that too.' She broke eye contact and said, 'This ship's certainly much faster than those dwarf boats.'

'That's the power of sail.' He nodded at the billowing sheets. 'And we've been lucky with the wind so far.'

'This must be like old times for you.'

'Sort of. Though on Trougath we lived more like the dwarfs do here. Coastal sailing mostly. But we had ships too, of course, for trade.'

'So you've captained one this big before?'

'Well . . . not quite. But don't tell the others.'

They laughed conspiratorially.

'The principles are more or less the same though,' he continued. 'Sailing's sailing.'

'We couldn't have done this without you, you know.'

'I think you could. If there's one thing I've learnt about the Wolverines it's that you're resourceful.'

'We've had to be. But whether it runs to commanding a ship . . .'

'It's easy. Here, try.'

'Really?'

'Sure. Come on, take the wheel.'

He stepped aside and she grabbed hold.

'Wait a minute,' he said, and moved behind her. Arms round her, he took her hands and guided them to a slightly different position. 'That's the best way. And don't grip so tightly. Relax. A light touch is best.'

'This is fun.'

'If you did it long enough you'd get a feel for the vessel. I mean, a *real* feel for it. Those who do this all the time can sense the mood of the ship.'

'Ships have moods?'

'Oh, yes. They're like people. Sorry. They're like people or orcs or . . .'

She smiled. 'You don't have to keep correcting yourself, Jode. I know what you mean.'

'Maybe it's because I find it easy to forget our differences.'

'We are different.'

'In how we appear, sure. But there are deeper things; ways in which all races share certain similarities. That's another thing I've learned during our time together, and I'm grateful for it.'

'But you're from Maras-Da— Oops. Now I'm doing it, aren't I? You're not from there, are you? Not in the way I mean.'

'No. Same world, different part. The area you come from was always shrouded in mystery for the rest of us. It was a forbidden place. Only when I got there did I realise how many different forms life takes. *Whoa!* You're letting her drift a bit.' He corrected the wheel. 'When I said a light touch I didn't mean *that* light. You have to keep in control or she'll start to rove.'

'That's something I've never understood.'

'What is?'

'Why ships are *her* or *she*. Is it because males build them?'

'I hadn't really thought about it. Maybe.'

'So it's to do with males seeing females as something they own and can control?'

'I like to think it's because a ship has grace and charm, like a female.'

She grinned. 'Quick thinking.'

'It was rather, wasn't it?' He had to smile too. 'I can never imagine anybody controlling you, Coilla.'

'Gods help the male who tried. What about you?'

'How do you mean?'

'Was there a *her* or *she* for you in Trougath?'

His smile went away, and it was a moment before he answered. 'Once.'

'And?'

'Like my nation and my previous life, she was . . . swept away.'

'Sorry. I didn't mean to dredge anything up for you.'

'That's all right.'

'I won't ask anything about—'

'No. What's done is done. I'm not one for dwelling in the past.'

'I understand. You know, your story, your people's story, isn't that different to ours in a way. We lost our birthright too.'

'I know. But not the details. You've never told me how your band came to leave Maras-Dantia.'

'It's a long story.'

'I'd like to hear it some time.'

'Sure. Though you might find it a bit boring.'

'I doubt that.'

They heard footfalls on the ladder leading to the wheel deck. Stryke appeared. Pepperdyne quickly stepped away from her.

'What's going on here?' Stryke said, seeing Coilla at the wheel.

'Nothing!' the two of them replied simultaneously.

'That is,' Coilla elaborated, 'Jode's giving me a lesson in seamanship.'

'Maybe that should be seaorcship,' Pepperdyne suggested. He and Coilla sniggered.

'Yeah, right,' Stryke replied, failing to see the joke. 'You've been at that wheel quite a while now, Pepperdyne. Got anybody to relieve you?'

Pepperdyne took back control of the wheel. 'Hystykk and

Gleadeg had a turn earlier. They seem to have the knack. But I'm fine for now, Stryke.'

'Sure?'

'It's a long time since I did anything like this. I'd like to savour it a bit longer.'

'Suit yourself. Just shout when you want a break. I'm going back to the others.' He started to leave.

'I'll come with you,' Coilla told him. She flashed Pepperdyne a quick grin and followed.

Down on the main deck, out of earshot, Stryke said, 'You seem to be growing very friendly with him.'

'We get on.'

'That might not be for the best.'

'What do you mean?'

'Do I have to remind you about the way humans are? Getting close to any of them—'

'Jode's different.'

'Is he?'

'He's helped us. He's helping us *now*. Not to mention I owe him my life a couple of times over. I reckon that entitles him to a little of my time.'

They came to a row of barrels standing by the rail. Stryke stopped and sat. Coilla lingered for a moment, considering the unspoken invitation, then sat down herself.

'I'm only saying this for your good,' Stryke assured her. 'We know that as a race humans can't be trusted.'

'Hold it right there. We came on this mission because of a human. Serapheim, remember? How's he different?'

'He saved us in Maras-Dantia.'

'And Jode saved some of us in Acurial, like I said.'

'Serapheim gave us the means to help the orcs in Acurial, and to get our revenge on Jennesta.'

'And how's that worked out? All right, we aided the Acurial rebels, but there's been precious little in the way of a reckoning as far as Jennesta's concerned. And we wouldn't be in the fix we're in now if it hadn't been for Serapheim.'

'You could always outargue me,' Stryke admitted. 'But I stand by what I said about humans. You've only got to look at the other one, Standeven, to see how low they can get.'

'We're not talking about *him*. Jode's out of a different mould.'

'We aren't going to see eye to eye on this, are we?'

'Nope.'

He reached into his jerkin and brought out a flask. 'Drink?'

She smiled and nodded.

Several healthy swigs of brandy mellowed them both.

'Talking of Serapheim,' Coilla said, relaxing, 'do you ever question why he sent us on this assignment?'

'We know why. To help fellow orcs and for revenge on Jennesta.'

'Think about it. Why should he care about orcs? And Jennesta's his own daughter, don't forget.'

'Being his flesh and blood might be more reason for wanting to punish her. He feels disgraced by her evil, and wants to atone for it by taking away the life he sired.'

'And us orcs?'

'He said he was ashamed of what his race was doing to ours in Acurial.'

'Ah, so the nasty humans *can* act nobly.'

Stryke said nothing. He had another drink.

She went on, 'There's something about all this, Stryke . . . I don't know; it doesn't ring true somehow. I mean, his servant turning up in Ceragan with a knife in his back; what was that about? Who killed him? Why? Come to that, how did Serapheim himself survive the collapse of the ice palace in Ilex?'

'That's an awful lot of questions.'

'Here's another one. How come Jennesta's still alive after going through the . . . What did they call it? The vortex. Not only didn't die but ends up helping to run a human empire. How did that happen?'

'I don't know, Coilla. And I *do* dwell on these things. But sometimes I think there are some mysteries we'll never solve.'

'Perhaps.'

He stood. 'I need to check on Jup.'

'What's he doing?'

'Trying to use his farsight. Remember that big life force he detected? I thought it'd be a good idea to have some warning if we're going to run into it.'

'Has he seen anything?'

'Not so far. But Haskeer's been needling him again, and it throws him off. That's what I need to check on.'

'All right. I'll be with the kelpies if you want me.' She nodded to the far end of the deck where the sea horses were herded together. A bunch of grunts with buckets on ropes were hauling up water to douse them with.

He finished by telling her, 'You remember what I said about Pepperdyne.' Then he turned and walked away.

He passed a stack of chests stowed nearby. What he didn't notice was Standeven sitting on the deck behind them, chin resting on raised knees, listening.

The rest of that day and most of the next passed without incident.

They were into the afternoon when land was spotted. The kelpies grew excited in their rather stately way, and the band prepared to disembark.

When they were close enough to see the island in detail, the old kelpie who first befriended them was puzzled.

'My folk are on the beach,' he rumbled.

'What's strange about that?' Stryke asked.

'You don't understand. My kin shouldn't be cavorting openly in the sea, and certainly not in the daytime, for fear of the Gatherers.'

'Could they have come and gone?' Jup wanted to know, his heart sinking.

'If they had, you can be sure kelpies wouldn't be enjoying them-selves in broad daylight.'

As they nosed in and dropped anchor, things became clearer. The kelpies on the beach were joined by a group of two-legged beings, waving frantically.

'They're . . . dwarfs,' Jup whispered, not daring to get his hopes up.

He didn't wait for the gangplank. Tossing a length of rope over the side he agilely shinned down it. Splashing knee-high through water, then onto the flaxen sand, he saw someone running towards him.

Spurral flew into his arms.

The following hours were filled with explanations and renewed camaraderie, for orcs and kelpies alike. At one point, Haskeer marched up to the couple, slapped Spurral heartily on the back and bellowed, 'Well done! Always knew we'd find you.'

Jup watched open mouthed as he swaggered past.

'Maybe he's not so bad after all,' Spurral said.

Haskeer barged his way to Stryke and asked, '*Now* can we get out of this place?'

'Soon as we can.'

'Good. Ceragan's starting to look really good compared to some of the places we've been.'

'Yeah, well, hold on. The stars didn't get us there last time we tried. We have to work that problem out.'

'That must have been something you did wrong, Stryke.'

'If I did, I did it wrong a lot of times.'

'So how we going to sort *that* one?'

'I don't know. Maybe—'

'Excuse *me*,' Spurral interrupted, 'but what about these dwarf survivors?' She waved a hand in their direction. They were sitting morosely by themselves further along the beach.

'What about 'em?' Haskeer said.

'We've got to take them home. Back to their island.'

'Shit, can't somebody else do that?'

'Who? The kelpies aren't a seafaring race. And even if the dwarfs thought they could crew a ship, what would they do for one once we've gone?'

Coilla nodded. 'She's right.'

'Yes,' Stryke agreed. 'We take them back. Then we'll think about the stars.'

'But we won't think about them tonight,' Spurral announced. 'The kelpies are laying on a celebration for everybody, and they're keen on celebrations, I can tell you.'

'And to spice it up a bit,' Coilla added, 'I've got a little something here I found in a cabin on the goblins' ship. Didn't mention it before; thought it might be a surprise.' She took out a small black pouch, loosened its strings and poured some of the contents into her hand.

The others crowded round and instantly recognised the heap of tiny pinkish crystals.

'Pellucid,' Haskeer all but drooled.

Coilla clamped her hand shut. 'But only with the permission of our captain, of course.'

'What do you say, Stryke?' Spurral wanted to know. 'Do we deserve a little relaxation after all we've been through?'

'There were a couple of times when crystal led us to some bad outcomes,' he replied stern faced. A smile cracked it. 'But I don't think this is going to be one of them.'

25

The celebration was good. It must have been, because most of those present would never be able to remember it.

There was drinking, feasting, boasting and inane giggling. The latter was due to the pellucid, which bathed the proceedings in a dreamy, kaleidoscopic haze.

A high point, for Wheam if no one else, came when the tyro, sober and without the benefit of crystal at that juncture, came to them excitedly. He was holding something.

'Look what I found on the ship!' he exclaimed.

'What'd ya say?' Haskeer mumbled, his eyes red pinpoints.

'I thought that if Coilla found that crystal lightning on the ship there might be other things of value. And I found *this*!' Beaming, he held up the object.

'Whassit?'

'A *lute*! It's not like any I've seen before, it's a goblin one I suppose, not that you'd think those creatures would appreciate music, but you never know, do you, anyway it's more or less the same as the sort I'm used to, so I thought—'

'*Aaarrghh!* Talk plain. And slow.'

'Ah. Yes. I found this lute.' He held it aloft once more, and wobbled it. 'It'll replace the one I lost. I can sing my ballads again.'

'If I could get up, I'd kill you.'

'So you don't fancy hearing anything now then?'

They say that even when Wheam started to run, Haskeer was still crawling after him.

There were a lot of thick heads the next morning, and Dallog was kept busy tending minor wounds inflicted during the horse-play. But the band was accustomed to quick recoveries after revelry, and dunkings in the tepid brine, voluntary and otherwise, sobered the majority.

Anxious as everybody was to be off, the kelpies insisted on a prolonged farewell ceremony complete with rambling speeches and numerous toasts. Though Stryke ordered that the latter should be in coconut milk as opposed to alcohol.

They finally shipped out mid-morning.

The journey back to the dwarfs' island was without event, which at least gave the band a chance to fully recover. Jup's spirits had soared. Not that much was seen of him and Spurral during most of the voyage. The only damp blanket was Standeven, unsurprisingly, who continued to brood when he wasn't dogging Stryke's footsteps.

At first, their arrival caused something of a panic. The islanders assumed that the advent of a three-master meant another visitation by Gatherers. Once that was sorted, and it soaked in that the slavers had been defeated, there were joyful scenes. The Wolverines, partied-out, accepted the accolades with fixed, clenched-toothed smiles.

As soon as they could, Stryke and his principal officers slipped away. Pepperdyne accompanied them, and Standeven tagged on, like a dependent cur. They made their way up to one of the dead volcano's lower ledges.

Stryke surveyed the view. 'Seems fitting that we should leave this world from the place where we entered it.'

'And good riddance,' Haskeer offered.

'Oh, I don't know,' Coilla said. 'Just look at it. There are a lot worse places.'

'To hell with it; I want to get back to Ceragan.'

'We're assuming we *can* get back. I mean, we didn't intend being here.'

'Remember what the kelpies said?' Spurral reminded them. 'About there being islands occupied by orcs? If the stars let you down maybe you could make a life here. Perhaps we could even find an uninhabited island and—'

'You're forgetting something,' Stryke said. 'Some of us have mates and hatchlings in Ceragan.'

'Sorry. Of course you have. I was being thoughtless. But . . . and don't take this the wrong way; there should be a fall-back plan if the stars don't get you home.'

'But we won't know that until we try them,' Coilla reminded

her. 'And if they take us somewhere other than Ceragan, what's the odds they'd bring us back here?'

'It's a good point, Stryke,' Dallog reckoned. 'Surely the only real decision is whether we try using the stars or not.'

'I know. My head's full of it. But my instinct *is* to try. I want to do all I can to get back to my brood.'

'I can understand that,' Jup said.

'It gets my vote,' Haskeer chipped in.

'I think you might have been right about me making a mistake, Haskeer,' Stryke admitted. 'I must have set them wrong.'

Coilla nodded. 'And no wonder, given how rushed we were.'

'Think you can get it right this time, Stryke?' Standeven wanted to know.

'What's it to you?' Haskeer sneered.

'I just want to be sure we do it properly this time.'

'*We?* What makes you think *you're* included?'

'You can't just leave us here!'

'Why not? We're not your mother!'

'We've been through all this,' Stryke returned sternly. 'We've already said we'll take the humans back to Maras-Dantia. I gave my word.'

'What are we now,' Haskeer grumbled, 'wet nurses?'

'I'll have no more argument. It's decided.'

'Well, sorry to go on about it,' Jup put in, 'but did we ever really resolve what happens to Spurral and me?'

'We said you'd be welcome in Ceragan,' Coilla replied.

'Yeah, and we appreciate it,' Spurral responded. 'But with respect, I don't know if we want to spend the rest of our lives in an orcs' world.'

'And you haven't changed your minds about being in Maras-Dantia? You don't want to go back?'

Jup and Spurral exchanged a look. They shook their heads.

'Why can't they stay here?' Haskeer wanted to know, jabbing a thumb at them. 'This is a place for dwarfs.'

'It isn't a dwarfs' world,' Spurral explained, as though to a hatchling. 'It's a . . . dumping ground.'

'Let's stick to what we agreed,' Stryke decided. He indicated Pepperdyne and Standeven. 'We take these two back to where we found 'em, in Maras-Dantia. Jup and Spurral can come with us to Ceragan.'

'Then what?' Jup wanted to know. 'For me and Spurral, I mean.'

'We can try to figure out the stars, and the amulet. Maybe—'

'Maybe we can find a way to send them to a dwarf world?' Coilla finished for him. 'It's a long shot, Stryke. What if we never—'

'Can you think of anything better?'

'No.'

'Then that's what's on offer.'

'This is all moot if we've no way of knowing the stars work,' Pepperdyne said. 'There's no point going round in circles.'

Stryke nodded. 'You're right. We all need to cool off, and I need to think. We'll try the stars again, but a bit later today, after I've had a chance to study them and you've all cooled off. Anybody object to that?'

Nobody did.

When everyone had dispersed, and Stryke had gone off somewhere quiet to try figuring out the instrumentalities and the amulet, Coilla and Pepperdyne found themselves alone.

'This is a rare thing,' he remarked.

'It is unusual not to be part of a mob, isn't it?'

'While it lasts. What's the betting somebody's going to barge in on us any minute?'

'We could avoid that.'

'How?'

'These volcanoes are supposed to be riddled with caves. And the view from up there must be quite something. Fancy exploring?'

'I'm game.'

The climb was actually very gentle, so they went as far up as they could reach, reasoning that the higher they were the less likely they'd run into anybody else. Before long they found a cave and seated themselves just inside its mouth.

Pepperdyne expelled an appreciative breath. 'It's pleasantly cool in here.'

'Said it'd be good, didn't I?'

'What's really good about it is having the chance to spend some time with you. You know, without anybody wanting something carried or trying to kill us.'

She smiled. 'And I've got something that should brighten things.' She pulled the small black pouch from her pocket. 'I kept some of this back.'

'The crystal?'

'Yeah. I noticed you didn't have any last night.'

'I've never had any. I've heard about it, of course, but never really saw the need.'

'It's not something you need; it's just nice now and again. You're in for a treat.' She began filling a clay pipe, then stopped. 'If you want to, that is.'

'Why not? And I'd rather do it without a crowd watching my first time.'

She got the pipe going, took a lungful and passed it to him. They felt the effect almost instantly.

After a little while she asked, 'How is it?'

'Not how I imagined.'

'Is that good, bad . . . ?'

'Mellow. Relaxing.' He took another pull on the pipe, held it, let it out. 'So . . . ges, yood. Uhm. I mean, yes . . . good.'

'Your face!' She started to giggle.

'What about it?'

'Just looks funny, that's all.'

'You look pretty comical yourself.' Then he caught the giggles too.

They laughed until they shook, then fell back and sprawled helplessly on the ground.

When the laughter subsided a tranquil mood came over them. They lay staring at the cave's roof, admiring the patterns reflected sunlight made on the soft stone.

At length, Coilla said, 'After today . . .'

'Yes?'

'It looks like we might not see each other again.'

'I was trying to put that out of my thoughts.'

'Me, too. But it keeps creeping back.'

'Mind you, if Stryke can't make the stars behave maybe you will be stuck with me. Somewhere.'

'I know Stryke. Somehow he'll make them work. Even if it takes a hundred tries. He's stubborn.'

'A hundred different worlds like the ones we saw before? Doesn't bear thinking about.'

'But if he does make them work, that's it. You'll be in Maras-Dantia and I'll be back in Ceragan.' She turned her head and regarded him. 'I'll miss you. You've been a good comrade in arms.'

'Coming from an orc, I take that as a high compliment.'

'It's meant to be. We fight well together. That's important to my kind. Particularly for a—'

'For a what?'

'Nothing. Tongue running away with me there. Expect it's the crystal.'

'Is it?'

'Would you do something for me, Jode?'

'What?'

'Scratch my back. It's itching like hell in this heat.'

They laughed.

'Sure,' he said. 'Give it here.'

She sat up and he commenced scratching.

'Hmmm, that's good. This isn't something you can get just anyone to do, you know.'

'Then I'm honoured.'

'Bit higher. Yes, there. Aaaahh. Nice.'

The scratching turned to a gentle massaging. The massage became a series of caresses. She turned her face to his.

They kissed.

26

It was nearly evening when Stryke emerged from the longhouse the dwarf elder had put at his disposal. He had ordered the band to gather on the beach, ready for what they hoped would be an initial hop to Maras-Dantia. But when he got there not everyone was present.

'Where's Coilla?'he asked.

'No idea,' Jup reported. 'Pepperdyne and Standeven are missing, too.'

'Words I've been longing to hear,' Haskeer said.

'Don't start that again,' Stryke told him.

'Well, if the pair of 'em got left behind it'd be no great loss.'

'But it's not like Coilla to miss a roll call.'

'To be fair,' Jup said, 'I don't think she's been seen since we were all together earlier. Chances are she didn't know about your order to be here now.'

'Anybody seen Coilla lately?' Stryke wanted to know. None of them had. 'Give it a couple of minutes, Jup, then start the roll call. If she's not here by the time you're done I'll send out a search party.'

Jup nodded and set to getting the ranks into order.

Not far off, on the other side of the volcano, Coilla and Pepperdyne were climbing down from the cave. They turned a corner on the narrow path and saw the beach.

'Shit,' she said. 'Looks like Stryke's mustered the band. They must be getting ready to leave. He'll kill me for missing the roll. Come on!'

'Wait!'

'What is it?'

'Down there.' He pointed to a spot further along the beach and just round a bend. 'That's Standeven.'

501

'What the hell's he doing sitting out there?'

'Who knows? He's been behaving very oddly lately.'

'Doesn't he always?'

'Not usually this much.'

'You know, Jode, this could be a golden opportunity for you to dump him.'

'What, leave him here?'

'Doesn't he deserve it?'

'Well, yes. But . . . No, I can't do it.'

'Really?'

'No. I mean, how could I inflict him on those innocent dwarfs?'

She laughed. 'That's what I like about you, Jode; you've got values. Even if they are wasted on a rat like Standeven.'

'You get to the band. I'll go and fetch him.'

'Don't be long. There are some who'd like to see you two left behind.'

'Would Stryke allow that?'

'Don't look so alarmed. Of course he wouldn't. Just don't keep him waiting.'

'I'll drag him there if I have to.'

'Right. Hey, before you go.' She leaned over and kissed him, then they dashed off in opposite directions.

Standeven was sitting by the shore, throwing pebbles into the waves.

Pepperdyne arrived, panting. 'What are you doing?'

'Nothing.'

'The band are gathered up the beach there. I reckon they're getting ready to leave.'

'So what?'

'*So what?* You want to be left behind?'

'Hardly seems to matter.'

'Are you insane? Stryke's going to take us back home.'

'Maybe he's going to *try*.'

'You're scared of the transition, is that it?'

Standeven flared indignantly, 'How dare you imply—'

'Oh, stow it. You've hardly proved yourself a hero on this little jaunt, have you? Cowardice's a fair assumption.'

'It's not that.'

Pepperdyne doubted it. 'What, then?'

'Suppose he does get us back. We'd be no better off, Hammrik's going to be on our trail again, and Stryke will still have the instrumentalities.'

'That again, is it?'

'What do you mean?'

'The stars. You've become obsessed with them. We can sort out the situation with Hammrik, if only by getting as far away from him as possible, but you have to have the stars. Is there a limit to your greed?'

'It's not that.'

'What, then?'

'I just think . . . I think they'd be better with me.'

'The instrumentalities would be better with you,' Pepperdyne repeated incredulously.

Standeven nodded.

'You have gone crazy.'

'It's hard to explain. I—'

'Don't even try. We've no time for your ravings. On your feet.'

He stayed where he was.

'If we don't get to the band right now,' Pepperdyne warned him, 'we're going to spend the rest of our lives in this place.'

'Suits me. But then, you wouldn't be with your little friend, would you?'

'What?'

'Coilla. Grown close, haven't you? But you should have a care. The others don't like it. Stryke's certainly not keen. Do you think he might have ambitions in that direction himself? After all—'

'Right, that does it.' He grabbed hold of his one-time master and bodily hauled him up.

'Take your filthy hands off me you—'

Pepperdyne punched him in the solar plexus, hard. Standeven doubled, gasping. Pepperdyne took hold of his arms and began frogmarching him along the beach.

Jup was just finishing the roll call when Coilla turned up. She was breathless.

'Where've you been?' Stryke demanded.

'Sorry,' she gasped. 'Didn't . . . know we . . . were supposed . . . to be here.'

'You would if you'd stuck around. Where were you?'

'Just . . . taking a walk.'

She got some odd looks for that.

'Picking wild flowers?' Haskeer mocked.

Coilla glared at him. 'I was taking a last look at the island. That all right with you?'

Haskeer shrugged.

'You seen the humans?' Stryke asked her.

'Jode and Standeven?'

'Know of any others tagging along with us?'

'Oh, right. No. Er, yes.'

'Which is it?'

'I saw them back there. Just briefly. They're coming.'

'They'd better be quick.'

'Here they are!' one of the grunts shouted.

The pair of humans were hurrying their way. Pepperdyne was no longer propelling Standeven, though the latter was limping and looked rough.

'Sorry, Stryke,' Pepperdyne said.

'Let's do this, shall we?' He took in their expectant, and in some cases apprehensive, faces as he dug out the instrumentalities and the amulet.

'Try to get it right this time,' Haskeer muttered.

Stryke shot him a murderous glance. 'I've been studying the markings for most of the day. It'll be done right.' He started to assemble the stars.

Everybody gathered round and watched him carefully slot together all but one of the artefacts.

'Right,' he said, 'brace yourselves.'

Coilla and Pepperdyne exchanged a furtive look. Jup and Spurral linked hands. Dallog gave Wheam's trembling shoulder a supportive squeeze. Standeven wore an expression similar to a cornered rodent's. Everybody tensed.

Stryke began easing the fifth and final star into place.

There were shouts and screams. Along the beach, dwarfs were scattering in panic. The source of their terror was a ship that seemed to have appeared without any of the band noticing.

'Ah, fuck,' Haskeer cursed, 'not again!'

Stryke stayed his hand.

'Do it!' Haskeer urged.

Stryke removed the fifth star.

'What you doing?'

'We've got company.' He nodded at the ship.

'You mean *they* have.'

Stryke glanced at the running dwarfs. 'We don't abandon comrades.'

'For the gods' sake, Stryke!'

'We're *not* leaving. Not till we know what this is.'

'Recognise that ship?' Pepperdyne said. 'It's the same bunch that attacked us earlier.'

'Remember what they did to us last time, Stryke,' Coilla warned. 'They've got strong magic.'

'Still,' he replied calmly, 'don't you want to know who they are?'

'No!' Haskeer protested.

'Just because you want to dodge a fight—' Coilla began.

Haskeer bridled. 'Who you accusing of—'

'*Button it*,' Stryke growled. 'This isn't the time.' He put away the stars and stuffed the amulet back down his shirt.

Kalgeck arrived at a sprint. He made straight for Spurral. 'Is it them? Have they come back?'

'The Gatherers?' she said. 'No, it's not them. You know it can't be. But they're as deadly in a different way. Get your kin clear of the beach.'

'They're already doing that. I want to fight.'

'Not this time, Kalgeck. We're facing something too powerful.'

'Then why not use the trebuchets?' He pointed to the volcano.

'Of course!' Coilla exclaimed. 'The catapults. Stryke?'

'It's a good idea. Let's get up there.'

'Catapults ain't going to dent those bastards,' Haskeer grumbled.

'*Come on!*' Coilla yelled.

'You get to cover!' Spurral sternly instructed Kalgeck.

The band dashed for the path leading to the ledge on the mountainside. All but Standeven, who under cover of the uproar slunk away.

When they got to the line of catapults they immediately began to prime them, working with an efficiency born of much experience.

'We don't know how far their magic can reach,' Dallog said. 'We could be sitting targets up here.'

'All weapons have a limit,' Stryke reminded him.

'Even magical ones?'

Stryke ignored that and continued barking orders.

The ship was at the shoreline when the first volley of heavy rocks was unleashed. All fell short, but close, making great splashes that swamped the ship's deck. The next battery was better aimed.

A rock crashed into the side of the ship, demolishing a large section of the rail. Seconds later, another struck one of the masts, neatly severing it. Timber and sails fell in a jumble.

Something like a slow lightning bolt issued from the ship. Purple and crackling, it flashed to one of the catapults and blew it to bits. Orcs were thrown back by the impact.

'*Casualties?*' Stryke roared.

Dallog dashed around checking. '*Nothing bad!*' he yelled back.

The arms of several catapults went up and over, launching another cascade. They were all misses, some very near, others soaring over the ship and splattering down on its far side.

This time, there was a different response from the ship. What emanated from it was a sort of pattern, similar to ripples in a pond, only travelling through the air. Like the lightning bolt it travelled fast, but not so rapidly that the band didn't have the chance to flatten themselves. The ripples, alternately black and glowing gold, wiped out all of the catapults, shredding them to splinters in a deafening cacophony.

'So much for being out of range,' Haskeer complained.

Coilla pointed. 'Look! They're coming ashore!'

A small flotilla of boats was heading for the beach.

'It's fight or run time,' Stryke announced.

'We don't do run,' Coilla reminded him.

'So let's meet 'em, shall we?'

He gave out a battle cry and they followed him down.

27

If the Wolverines thought they would engage the strangers conventionally they were soon disabused of the notion.

Even before the group of boats hit the beach their multi-race occupants were on the offensive. Variously coloured beams of intense energy flared. Bolts struck the sand, throwing up clouds and gouging deep pits. They seemed to be shots designed to get the firers' eye in. The next round came a lot closer to the band.

On Stryke's order they ran to shelter behind a scattering of large rocks occupying the space between beach and island proper.

The Wolverines replied with arrows, some flaming. They were sticks against a hurricane. Some of the bolts were obliterated by piercing energy shafts. Others simply evaporated before they got near their targets. The orcs saw that this was because an almost invisible energy shield of some sort shimmered around the beings wading ashore.

'We're not touching 'em,' Coilla said.

'At this rate we'll be overrun,' Dallog warned. 'What'll we do, Stryke?'

'Maybe we'll have better luck hand to hand with them.'

'Dream on,' Haskeer growled. 'Those wizards are too powerful for steel to make any headway. Use the stars and get us out of here.'

'No. Even if I wanted to, the band's scattered all over the place. We'd leave half our strength behind.'

'Here they come!' Coilla shouted.

A good dozen of the attackers were drawing close. Pelli Madayar was at their head. Behind her tramped a colourful assortment of elder races.

'There's a couple of fucking goblins with 'em!' Haskeer exclaimed.

'Should have known those bastards would have something to do with this,' Jup snapped.

The advancing party was still spraying the area with their magic beams.

'Ready to engage!' Stryke ordered.

Orcs drew second weapons, nocked bows and primed slingshots.

When they were no more than ten paces distant, Pelli Madayar held up her hand. The group stopped, as did the bombardment.

'We don't have to do this, Stryke!' she called out.

'She knows your name,' Coilla said. For some reason she found that especially disquieting.

A chill had gone up Stryke's spine on hearing it too, though he would never have admitted it. Ignoring the others' gestures to stay put, he stepped out from behind the rock.

'Who are you? What do you want?'

'We're not your enemies, whatever you think. You know what we want. The instrumentalities, that's all.'

'*All?*'

'You can save yourselves further grief very simply. Just hand them over.'

'Like hell we will.'

'You have no right to them.'

'And you do?'

'Morally . . . yes.'

'Fancy word from somebody who just tried to kill us.'

'We weren't trying. Look, if you're worried that giving up the artefacts means we'll leave you stranded here, don't be. Maybe I can arrange to have you sent to your home world.'

'Maybe? That doesn't sound too promising to me.'

'I have to consult a higher authority.'

'This is my higher authority,' Stryke told her, holding up his sword. 'And it says *no.*'

'Be sensible. What you've just seen is only a taste of the power we command. If we turned it on you full force you wouldn't stand a chance.'

'We'll play those odds.'

Pelli sighed. 'This is so pointless. Why are you so intent on wasting your lives for the sake of—' She stopped, as though hearing a voice no one else heard. Then she turned to look out to sea.

A small armada of ships was making for shore.

All of the strangers turned to look, contemptuous of offering their backs to the Wolverines. The band, too, came out from their shelter and stared.

'This place is as busy as a whorehouse on pay day,' Haskeer muttered.

It was obvious that the arrival was as much of a surprise to the strangers as it was to the orcs.

Feeling as though he'd been virtually dismissed, Stryke backed off and rejoined his crew.

'Who the hell's knocking at the door now?' Coilla said.

'I don't know. More Gatherers?'

'No,' Pepperdyne told them. 'Definitely not Gatherers. Look!'

One of the fleet of five ships was engaging with the strangers' vessel. And it was doing it magically. Vividly hued beams shot from craft to craft.

Seemingly having forgotten the Wolverines, Pelli and her ill-assorted group began jogging towards the shoreline. Before they reached the waves they were sending out shafts of their own.

'What the *fuck* is going on?' Haskeer demanded.

'Looks like our enemy has an enemy,' Stryke replied.

'Which would be fine,' Jup pointed out, 'if our enemy's enemy wasn't our enemy too.'

'What the hell are you talking about?'

'Take a look at that ship coming into shore, the leading one. It's prow-on. See? Now do you notice somebody standing there, right at the front, bold as shit?'

'Yeah,' Haskeer said, blinking and with a hand shading his brow.

'Recognise who it is?'

It was Coilla who answered. 'Jennesta,' she whispered.

28

'I thought the stars were supposed to be incredibly rare,' Coilla said, 'but it looks as though everybody's got them.'

'Maybe we've just run into everybody who *has* got them,' Pepperdyne suggested.

Down on the beach, the magical battle raged. The new arrivals had sent in boats of their own. They were running a shuttle, dropping troops off in shallow water and going back for more. The soldiers were Jennesta's human followers, along with a much smaller number of her zombie personal guard. But they seemed no more able to overcome the strangers' magic than the orcs were. That was for Jennesta. Ashore now, and sweeping majestically up the beach, she was essentially waging the war single-handed and, considering her opponents' might, making a good job of it.

Stryke figured that if they couldn't fight the strangers' magic, they could fight Jennesta's army. As there was no way to escape, he argued, they could at least kill something.

At first, it went well. They charged into the fray and gave a good account of themselves, downing troops and hacking zombies to pieces. But it didn't take long for both Jennesta and the strangers to notice them. A bombardment of enchantments forced the band to retreat. Though Stryke wasn't alone in thinking that, vicious as their magic was, neither side was actually trying too hard to kill them.

The band pulled back to the edge of the beach and the shelter of rocks.

'The stars!' Haskeer pleaded. 'Use 'em now!'

'Lay off!' Stryke snapped. 'Coilla! Are we all here?'

'No. We're missing Dallog, Wheam and a couple of the other tyros.'

'Bloody typical,' Haskeer moaned.

'I'll go and look for them,' Stryke decided.

'I'll come with you,' Coilla told him. 'No, no argument. You'll need somebody to watch your back.'

'All right.'

'Me too.' Pepperdyne said.

'No.'

'Going to stop me?'

'If I have to. But better that you stay here and help hold our position.'

'But—'

'Do it, Jode,' Coilla said. 'I'll . . . We'll be fine.'

'If you're going,' Haskeer grated, 'you better get a fucking move on.'

Stryke tossed his head. 'Come on.'

They ran towards the scrum.

The bodies barring their way were all human or zombie. The wizardry was taking place further down the beach, at the water's edge. But soldiers and the undead were still a formidable obstacle.

Stryke and Coilla hacked, slashed, stabbed and battered their way through them. They had a few errant energy bolts to dodge on the way. Some of Jennesta's horde weren't so lucky.

'I see 'em!' Coilla yelled. She pointed.

Dallog and a couple of tyros were slugging it out with twice their number of soldiers.

Coilla and Stryke fought their way to them.

Their blades quickly turned the tide. A bloody exchange saw the attackers overcome.

'Where's Wheam, Dallog?' Stryke asked.

'Down there!'

Further along the beach, Wheam was trying to hold off a pair of zombies. He had his new musical instrument strapped to his back, and looked more worried about protecting it than himself.

'I'll get him,' Stryke said.

'We'll come!' Coilla and Dallog chorused.

'*No*. I'll not have the band scattered again. Get yourselves back to the others. *Now*.'

They left reluctantly. He plunged back into the fray.

Coilla, Dallog and the tyros had as tough a path to travel on the way back as she and Stryke had on the way out. The troops seemed to be everywhere, and none left them unchallenged. By the time their goal was in sight, their blades ran with gore.

'Can you make it alone from here, Dallog?' Coilla said.

''Course.'

'Get on then.'

'What about you?'

'I'm going after Stryke.'

'But he said—'

'Just get these two back, all right?' She ran off.

Stryke came at one of the zombies from the back and ran it through. True to experience it hardly registered the blow. So he took to chopping at it, as though he were felling a dead tree. When enough major damage had been inflicted the armless creature hopped on its one leg for an instant then collapsed. The second zombie Stryke simply decapitated, sending its head bouncing in the blood-soaked sand.

'Am I glad to see you, Captain,' Wheam panted.

'I'm going to get you out of here. Stay close.'

Before they could move, Coilla arrived.

'I thought I told you—'

'You need me,' she said. 'Look around. Somebody's got to cover your back.'

'All right. Let's go.'

It was getting harder to steer a way that didn't have troops in it. So they were compelled to carve a path. But still the increasing opposition made them take a different route back. It took them past a large outcropping of rock.

It was only very shortly after what happened next that Stryke started to think they'd been deliberately herded that way.

Jennesta stepped out from behind the rock.

The trio stopped in their tracks.

'Run, Wheam!' Coilla pleaded. 'Get out of here!'

The youth fled.

Jennesta laughed, disturbingly. 'It seems not *all* orcs are courageous.'

Stryke and Coilla rushed her as one, their blades levelled.

She made a swift hand gesture. The pair instantly froze in their tracks, rigid as statues.

Strangely, the fighting seemed to have frozen too. Or at least the sound and sight of it had. It was either more of Jennesta's magic, or her followers had fallen back, reinforcing the suspicion that it had been a set-up.

'Now that I've got you nicely calmed,' Jennesta said, 'we can have a civilised conversation.'

Stryke and Coilla were helpless. They struggled to move or make a sound but couldn't.

'When I say conversation, of course, that doesn't imply that you'll be taking part in it. Actually, Stryke, I've got someone here who knows you. Or did.' She snapped her fingers loudly.

Two zombies lumbered into sight. They walked on either side of somebody.

It was Thirzarr.

Stryke's mate showed no sign of recognising him. She looked healthy enough, apart from a few bruises, but seemed to be in a light trance or coma.

'Surprised?' Jennesta mocked. 'I thought you might be. She isn't fully undead, like my servants here. She's . . . let us say she's in the stage before that, and could go either way. A zombie or back to how she was. You can decide which.'

For all his torment, Stryke couldn't break through her enchantment.

'My proposition is straightforward,' she informed him. 'I'll free your mate if you and your band surrender yourselves to me. Just the orcs; I've no need for the other types you have hanging on. Do that, Stryke, and you'll not only free Thirzarr, you'll also be part of a wonderful enterprise. The Wolverines will form the nucleus of my zombie-orc army. Quite a combination, yes? Unquestioning obedience coupled with your peerless fighting skills and robust fitness. A great improvement on the present sort.' She indicated her zombie slaves with a casual flick of the hand. 'Think of it, Stryke. You'll be able to fight and conquer to your black heart's content. Not just in one world, but many. *All* of them. With the instrumentalities turned out on a mass scale . . . Oh, yes. That's how I come to be here. I copied yours. And now I know I have the means perfected, I can start to build an army of totally compliant orcs to conquer . . . well, everywhere really. Anyway, that's the proposition. I'm going to sever the bonds holding you now so you can give your answer. One move and you'll go back to helplessness.' She gestured with her hands again.

Stryke thawed. Despite his rage and anguish he fought back the urge to leap for her throat. He knew it would be futile, and he needed to bide his time. If he had any. He kept his bile for words. 'You stinking bitch! What have you done to Thirzarr? And what about our hatchlings? Where are they?'

'You don't expect me to tell you, do you? Your brats are not the issue. Your mate or your band. What's your answer?'

'I can't agree, not on behalf of the others. They fought hard for their freedom. I can't be the one to make them forfeit it.'

'Then your mate becomes a mindless slave. Perhaps you'd *like* a mindless slave for a mate. I could see it might have some advantages. Is that it, Stryke?'

'If you'd only face me one to one, in a fair—'

She burst out laughing. 'Oh, *please*. As if I'm going to do that. But perhaps there's another way of resolving this.'

'How?'

'If you won't capitulate, then settle it in a way more to your liking. In combat. If my champion wins, you succumb. Well, you'll be dead actually, but you would have conceded defeat. You win, you have your mate back, good as new.'

Coilla struggled against her invisible bonds futilely.

'Who's your champion?' Stryke said.

'She's standing right next to me.'

'*Thirzarr?* I won't do it. She wouldn't either.'

'Really?' Jennesta waved a hand at Thirzarr.

She seemed to come alive, yet not quite.

'Fight him,' Jennesta ordered, 'to the death.' She handed Thirzarr a sword.

She snatched it and immediately made for Stryke. He stood stupefied for a second, not believing his eyes. Then he had to move fast to evade her singing blade.

Stryke twisted and turned to avoid the rain of blows she sent his way. He only reluctantly raised his own sword when he had no other way of fending her off. Every move he made was defensive. Her every stroke was calculated to kill.

It was getting desperate. Stryke was being driven to up the ante in the face of her inexhaustible attack. He dreaded his instincts taking over and, Thirzarr or not, striking back in like kind.

Suddenly Wheam reappeared. He popped from behind the outcropping. Of all the things he might have done next, Stryke would never have guessed the one he chose.

He threw a rock at Jennesta. It struck her on the shoulder and she cried out, more in injured pride than hurt.

The unexpectedness of the attack broke her concentration and whatever mental power she exercised to maintain her enchantments.

Coilla unfroze. Thirzarr stopped, lowered her arms and dropped the sword. She seemed to have re-entered the state she arrived in.

As Jennesta raged, and presumably struggled to re-establish her hold, Coilla grabbed Stryke and began pulling him away. He struggled at first, wanting to go to Thirzarr, but even in his frenzy he saw that was hopeless. He let Coilla and Wheam guide him.

They ran. Something like a thunderbolt followed them, but boomed harmlessly overhead.

The fighting had died down considerably, and although they faced opposition, which fell to Coilla to deal with, they got back to the others unscathed.

What had happened was quickly relayed to the band. Most took the news in dumb silence.

Coilla said, 'Take us to Ceragan, Stryke. We'll raise an army and come back here to kick Jennesta's arse so hard—'

'We don't know if the stars would get us there. But there's worse.'

'How could it be worse?' She had an icy churning in the pit of her stomach.

'Don't you see? Jennesta must have been there, to get Thirzarr. And Thirzarr wouldn't have come willingly. No orc would. They would have fought. It wouldn't be beyond Jennesta to wipe out every orc there if she could manage it. Coilla, we don't even know if Ceragan still exists.'

ORCS

BAD BLOOD III

Inferno

For Jacob Harry Fifer,
who will hopefully read this one day,
and probably wonder what the old boy
was up to.

Into the Fire

Discontented with life in pastoral Ceragan, orcs warband the Wolverines were intrigued to receive a message from Tentarr Arngrim, the wizard known as Serapheim, who had previously aided them. Arngrim described a world where orcs were brutally dominated by human invaders. Worse, their oppressors included Serapheim's depraved daughter, the sorceress Jennesta, once the warband's ruler, whom they believed dead. Although suspicious of Arngrim's motives, Stryke, the Wolverines' captain, persuaded his band to embark on a mission to help their fellow orcs, and possibly exact revenge on Jennesta.

The Wolverines held five peculiar artefacts called instrumentalities, created by Serapheim, which they referred to as stars. The means by which the band was deposited on Ceragan, the stars could carry their possessors between worlds, though Stryke was untutored in operating them. But he also had an amulet, taken from the body of Arngrim's murdered messenger, and its markings provided a key.

At full strength the warband consisted of five officers and thirty privates. Stryke commanded. Beneath him were two sergeants. Haskeer was one; the other, Jup, the band's solitary dwarf, had stayed behind in Maras-Dantia, the Wolverines' anarchic birthplace. There should have been a pair of corporals too. Coilla, the only female member and its Mistress of Strategy, was present. But her counterpart, Alfray, had fallen in battle. Death had also taken six of the privates.

To get the numbers back up, Stryke recruited a clutch of Ceragan novices, and replaced Alfray with an ageing orc called Dallog. This was less than popular with some of the Wolverines. They were even more disgruntled when local clan chief Quoll forced his popinjay of a son, Wheam, onto the band.

Bidding farewell to his mate Thirzarr, and their hatchlings Corb and Janch, Stryke first took the band to Maras-Dantia to search for Jup, in hope of him resuming his role of sergeant. They succeeded, and Jup, along with his partner Spurral, rejoined. But one of the new recruits, and Liffin, a veteran member, were killed by marauders. Haskeer in particular blamed Wheam and the other tyros for this, and openly expressed contempt for them.

Before they left Maras-Dantia the band encountered two humans, Micalor Standeven and Jode Pepperdyne, who posed as merchants. In reality, Pepperdyne was Standeven's slave, and they were running from tyrannical ruler Kantor Hammrik, to whom Standeven was indebted. Standeven's plan was to steal the orcs' instrumentalities to pay off Hammrik. Stryke would have abandoned the duo, or worse, had they not warned him of an impending raid; and in the fight that followed, Pepperdyne saved Coilla's life. So when the Wolverines had to quickly exit a life-threatening situation, using the stars, Pepperdyne and Standeven went with them. Their destination was the world of the warband's mission.

The Wolverines were unaware that an indefinite number of instrumentalities existed, scattered across endless worlds. Nor did they know that a clandestine group, the Gateway Corps, was dedicated to tracking them down. The activation of Stryke's stars was detected by the Corps, and its human leader, Karrell Revers, ordered his deputy, female elf Pelli Madayar, to recover them at any cost. Accompanied by a multi-species snatch team, and armed with potent magical weaponry, Pelli set off in pursuit of the Wolverines.

Arriving in Acurial, a world as luxuriant as Maras-Dantia was corrupted, the Wolverines were horrified to discover the orc populace had had their martial spirit bred out of them. Playing on this docility, and the ploy that Acurial possessed non-existent weapons of magical destruction, Peczan, a human empire, had invaded.

Tangling with the occupiers, who had a command of magic – rare among humans – the Wolverines found that not all orcs in Acurial were placid when they were rescued by a resistance group whose members' fighting instincts had reawakened. It was headed by Brelan and his twin sister Chillder. Its leader in hiding was their mother, Sylandya, Acurial's deposed ruler. The Wolverines joined the insurgency. They trained the rebels, and Coilla formed an all-female warband dubbed the Vixens.

Opposing the resistance were General Kapple Hacher, Governor of what Peczan regarded as a province; and Brother Grentor, High Cleric of the Order of the Helix, wardens of the magic. As heads of two of the empire's main pillars in the prefecture, the military and the spiritual, Hacher and Grentor were often at odds. But the arrival of Jennesta, Peczan's pitiless emissary and both men's superior, overshadowed their differences.

Pelli Madayar's Gateway Corps unit also arrived, covertly observed events and plotted to seize the Wolverines' stars.

The resistance discovered that a comet named Grilan-Zeat, which had appeared at crucial points in Acurial's history, was soon to return. Their hope was that it would be seen as an omen, and along with a call to arms from Sylandya would inspire the submissive populace to revolt. A prophecy was attached to Grilan-Zeat. It said that a party of liberators would accompany the comet. Some in the resistance believed the Wolverines might be these longed-for champions, and portrayed them that way to further encourage the citizenry.

With comet and prophecy as carrots, the rebels applied a stick. They increased harassment of the occupiers with the intention of bringing down their wrath, which in turn would spur the masses to react. The Wolverines were involved in a succession of attacks on the invaders. Until one particularly ambitious raid went badly wrong; an attempt to assassinate Jennesta was foiled, ending with her snatching four of the five stars. Stryke wondered if there could be a spy in the resistance, or even among the Wolverines themselves. Then the fifth instrumentality, in Coilla's care, was stolen from a rebel hideout. There was little doubt that this was also Jennesta's doing. As the comet became visible it looked as though the Wolverines would never see Ceragan again. They had no choice but to fight on alongside the resistance. And in the weeks that followed, the bellicose nature of the orcs of Acurial began to resurface, to their human oppressors' cost.

The Wolverines didn't know that Jennesta had used esoteric sorcery to duplicate their instrumentalities. But the Gateway Corps was aware through their own magical means that another set of instrumentalities had been brought into play, making their mission of containment all the more urgent.

Despite the animosity between their races, Coilla and Pepperdyne grew close as the insurrection built, and the normally reticent human related some of his history. He was a Trougathian, a member of an island race on Maras-Dantia whose misfortune was to occupy a strategic location between rival nations. Trougath was afflicted by war for generations, until finally betrayed by a supposed ally, and broken. Its population scattered, and some were enslaved, with the upshot that Pepperdyne became little more than Standeven's chattel. The largely nomadic Trougathians were maligned and reviled, not unlike orcs.

Events in Acurial took a dramatic turn when, in a resistance safe house, Standeven was found with the dead body of an orc intruder, though he denied any wrongdoing. The mystery deepened when the dead orc turned out to have Coilla's stolen instrumentality. Wolverines and resistance alike were suspicious of what Standeven might have been up to, but nothing could be proved.

Their spirits lifted by regaining the star, the band set out to get the others back from Jennesta. Staging an ambush, they achieved this; although some in the band thought it went a bit too easily.

Sick of Hacher's running of the province, Jennesta transformed him into one of her zombie bodyguards. She had Brother Grentor murdered. And when Sylandya came out of hiding to rally the populace, Jennesta assassinated her. That proved a miscalculation. Far from stifling revolution, it stoked the flames.

With the resistance close to victory, Jennesta and a group of loyal human followers fled for the coast, the Wolverines in pursuit. But as the band prepared to attack her, the Gateway Corps appeared and Pelli Madayar demanded the Wolverines' instrumentalities. Stryke's refusal unleashed an onslaught of powerful magic from the Corps. Sandwiched between them and Jennesta's advancing force, Stryke activated the instrumentalities, though he had no time to set their coordinates.

The band travelled through a succession of hostile realities, staying in each only long enough to randomly reset the stars and escape. Finally arriving in a barren but unthreatening world, Stryke calibrated the instrumentalities properly. His plan was to return

Pepperdyne and Standeven to Maras-Dantia, then take the band back to Ceragan.

But the stars inexplicably deposited them in a world of islands, on an isle inhabited by dwarfs. The orcs' seemingly miraculous arrival saved them from massacre by the dwarfs, who took them for gods. Shortly after, the island was raided by human slavers, the Gatherers, who carried off a number of dwarfs, including Spurral. Securing two boats and a crude map, the Wolverines set out to rescue her. The Gateway Corps, who had followed the warband to this world, were on their trail.

Spurral found herself at the mercy of the Gatherers' ruthless leader, Captain Salloss Vant. She immediately began fermenting mutiny among her fellow captives, one of whom, a lame female called Dweega, was thrown overboard by the slavers. Picked up by the Wolverines, Dweega was able to tell them the Gatherers' course. But the band had to fend off a seaborne attack by the Gateway Corps before continuing their hunt. And Standeven was growing morbidly obsessed with the warband's stars.

On board the Gatherers' ship the dwarfs rebelled, and Spurral faced up to Vant and killed him. Taking control of the vessel, the dwarfs began sailing it back to their home. En route they were attacked by a fearsome creature called the Krake – one of 'the Lords of the Deep' – and the ship was sunk.

One of their boats having been damaged by the Corps, the Wolverines landed on a nearby island for repairs. It turned out to be occupied by a group of goblins who held captive a number of kelpies who, despite being sentient, were traded as meat. The orcs made common cause with them and killed the goblins. Learning that the Gatherers sailed a predetermined route, and the kelpies' island was their next port of call, to gather slaves, the Wolverines took a goblin ship and headed there. They didn't know that Spurral and a handful of other dwarf captives, having survived the shipwreck, had washed up on the kelpies' island, and been nur- tured by them.

Jup and Spurral were finally reunited. Feeling honour-bound, Stryke agreed to return the liberated dwarfs to their island home. On the way, Coilla and Pepperdyne's friendship, frowned on by many in the band, escalated and they secretly became lovers.

Shortly after the orcs reached the dwarfs' island, the Gateway

Corps appeared, and Pelli Madayar again demanded Stryke's instrumentalities. His refusal sparked a battle, with the Wolverines facing the Corps' sorcery. The band narrowly avoided being overwhelmed when Jennesta arrived with her force, and magical combat broke out between her and the Corps.

At the height of the chaos, Jennesta confronted Stryke. And to his astonishment she was with his mate, Thirzarr, who was in an hypnotic trance, one step from the full zombie state, and under Jennesta's control. With horror, Stryke realised that Jennesta must have travelled to Ceragan to capture Thirzarr, and could have inflicted untold destruction on his adoptive world.

Jennesta offered Stryke a deal: surrender the Wolverines to her, for conversion to undead servitude, and Thirzarr would be freed from her bondage. Refuse and Thirzarr would become a zombie, never to recover. Stryke struggled with the proposition, and turned it down. At which point Jennesta declared that the outcome would depend on one-to-one combat between Stryke and Thirzarr. At Jennesta's command, Thirzarr launched a murderous attack on Stryke. He desperately fought to suppress the killing instinct that could have had him slaying his mate. Only chance, and the intervention of Coilla and Wheam, prevented it.

Rescued from Jennesta's malign presence, Stryke yielded to despair. The Wolverines, retreating in disarray, saw no prospect but failure.

Five years earlier

Events were finally coming to a head in Maras-Dantia.

Jennesta had led an army to the snowbound north, into the shadow of the advancing glacier. Once there, they laid siege to Ilex's great ice palace.

She didn't care about the fate of her Manifold Path army. An alliance of humans, orcs and mercenary dwarfs united in common cause against the God-fearing forces of Unity, the Manis were no more than a convenience to her. The only thing that interested Jennesta was inside the palace.

The situation had been compounded by treachery. Mani dragon mistress Glozellan had sided with Jennesta's enemies and brought her charges into play. A squad of leathery behemoths, saw-like wings beating furiously, spewed gouts of flame over the army. And Jennesta's father, Serapheim, used his sorcery to paint the grim sky with images that grossly lied, to sway her militia and break its spirit. Though she expected no better from that quarter.

As more snow began to fall, stinging the troops' flesh and blinding their vision, she grew impatient. Accompanied by her orc commander, General Mersadion, and half a dozen of her ablest Royal Guardsmen, she gained entry to the palace.

Its murky corridors held the stench of age-old corruption, and aberrant, inhuman sounds echoed through the crumbling pile.

Jennesta and her group were not the first to get in. Several advance parties of Manis had entered before them. Their corpses littered the place. Without exception they were terribly mutilated, and in many cases it looked as though they had been partially consumed. Despite his orcish spirit the general's disquiet was palpable, and the guardsmen, holding aloft oil-fed lanterns, were plainly anxious. Jennesta paid no attention.

They had hardly penetrated the labyrinth of twisting passageways and cavernous chambers when misshapen figures began moving from the shadows.

The Sluagh, a loathsome shape-changing race reckoned by many to be demons, infested the palace. Alien in form and in deed, they were entirely merciless. As they swiftly proved when the two hindmost guards in Jennesta's party were brought down and torn apart. Ignoring their screams she hurried on, the general and the other troopers, ashen-faced, close behind.

They hadn't gone far before the creatures struck again. Lurching from the gloom, fibrous hides glistening moistly in the dim light, one of them snared a guardsman with sinewy tentacles. At the ready this time, the soldier's comrades and the general turned to hack at the Sluagh.

'Leave him!' Jennesta snapped.

Their fear of her outweighed any feelings of solidarity. They abandoned the shrieking trooper. Glancing back, Mersadion caught a glimpse of the man's fate, and shuddered.

There was a respite as Jennesta strode on, looking for a way to reach the palace's lower levels. But it was short-lived. Turning into a narrow passage they found a pack of Sluagh ahead. Slavering and giving off a confounding babble, the beasts advanced. With her own safety at stake, Jennesta acted, fashioning a spell with an intricate movement of her hands, though with an air of blasé impatience rather than any kind of dread. A searing flash lit the darkness. The Sluagh burst open like ripe melons sliced with an invisible axe, liberating their steaming viscera as they fell.

Jennesta continued walking, lifting the hem of her gown above the mess. The others followed, gingerly stepping over the carcasses, hands pressed to their faces to keep out the stench.

They came to an arched doorway opening on to a flight of steps that went down into pitch blackness. A faint rhythmic throbbing could be heard from below. Jennesta ordered two of the three remaining troopers to stay at the entrance and stand guard. From the expressions the pair wore it was obvious they didn't know whether to be relieved or alarmed. There was no such ambiguity on the third soldier's face when she pointed to the stairs and told him to take the lead.

After descending for only a short time there was a commotion from the guards left above. It began with yells and ended in screams, quickly stifled. Unmoved, Jennesta told her two surviving underlings to keep *going. The light from the lamp carried by the leading trooper wavered in his unsteady hand, casting grotesque shadows on the moist walls.*

The periodic throbbing grew louder the deeper they went. But now it was mixed with other, discordant sounds; the grind of stone on stone and the creaking of timbers. There was a trembling underfoot. Tiny fragments of ice started to fall, shaken loose by the vibration. The sensation was like a minor earthquake.

The stairs came to an end, depositing them in a wide corridor that ran into darkness in both directions. Except not quite. To their right, there was a weak glimmer of light. Jennesta ordered the guardsman to extinguish his lamp. In the ensuing blackness the pulsating light could be seen clearly, outlining the shape of a sizeable door. They went towards it.

Small chunks of debris were falling now, and seeps of dust. The rumbling grew, pounding the soles of their feet. And there was something strange about the air. It felt charged, oppressive, and far too warm given the chill atmosphere.

There was a movement to their rear. Looking back, they could make out one of the Sluagh at the foot of the stairs, and several more behind. The guardsman lost his nerve. He dropped the snuffed lantern and ran, past the door bleeding light and along the passageway. His dash lasted less than twenty paces. A Sluagh's feelers whipped down from the ceiling, snared him and hoisted him up. Howling, legs kicking, he disappeared into shadow.

Taking advantage of the distraction, Jennesta hurried to the door, General Mersadion in tow. It was unlocked, but heavy and hard to move. She let him take the brunt of shifting it. On the other side was another, much shorter corridor, leading to an archway. The space beyond was bathed in beating light.

She got him to secure the door, then said, 'Looks like it's just you and me, General.'

Pointing at the source of the light he asked, 'What is it, my lady?'

'Think of it as a . . . gateway. It's very old, and it was what inspired my father to create the artefacts that rightly belong to me.'

He nodded, as though he understood.

'Activating the portal has released the energy that's destroying this palace,' she added offhandedly.

Mersadion looked no more comfortable for the explanation.

They approached the arch. It led to a set of wide steps that swept down to a capacious chamber that housed five massive, rudely worked standing stones, arranged in a semicircle. At its centre was a low granite dais, studded with what appeared to be gems. Issuing from the dais' surface was something wondrous.

It was as though a waterfall had been upended. But it wasn't a liquid cascade. It was light. Countless millions of tiny multicoloured pinpoints, spiralling, twisting, surging upwards in a never ending, constantly replenished flow. The dazzling vortex was the source of the throbbing beat, and a sulphurous odour hung in the air.

There were a number of beings present. Standing just beyond the arch, Jennesta scanned them. Her father, Tentarr Arngrim, known to the covert world of sorcery as Serapheim, was at the forefront. Jennesta's sister, Sanara, the most human in appearance of Arngrim's brood, was by his side. The rest were Wolverines, the wretched orc warband who had subjected Jennesta to the bitterest of betrayals. All were transfixed by the glittering spectacle.

Jennesta saw the female orc, Coilla, standing close to the dais and staring at the torrent. Coilla mouthed, 'It's beautiful.'

Standing next to her the dwarf, Jup, nodded and said, 'Awesome.'

'And mine!' Jennesta declared loudly as she lost patience and strode down the stairs, Mersadion in her wake.

All heads turned to them. For a split second Jennesta's steely poise faltered. But she was confident in the superiority of her magic over anything here, spell or weapon.

'You're too late,' Serapheim told her. His tone was cooler than Jennesta cared for.

'Nice to see you too, Father dear,' she returned acerbically. 'I've a contingent of Royal Guards at my heels,' she lied. 'Surrender or die, it's all the same to me.'

'I can't see you passing on the opportunity to slay those you think have wronged you,' Sanara said.

'You know me so well, sister.' She thought how prissy Sanara was. 'And how pleasant to see you in the flesh again. I look forward to despoiling it.'

The Wolverines' leader spoke. 'If you think we're giving up without a fight, you're wrong.' He indicated his troop with the sweep of a sturdy hand. 'We've nothing to lose.'

'Ah, Captain Stryke.' She cast a derisive eye over his warband. 'And the Wolverines. I've relished the thought of meeting you again in *particular.' Her voice hardened with the tenor of authority. 'Now throw down your weapons.'*

There was a flurry of movement. Someone came out of the host, sword drawn. Jennesta recognised him as the band's healer, an aged fool of an orc called Alfray.

Instantly, Mersadion was there, blocking the attacker's path. The general's blade flashed. Alfray took a blow. He swayed, his eyes rolled to white, and he fell.

There was a moment of stasis, an immobility of all present as they took a collective intake of breath.

Then Stryke, Coilla, Jup and the hulking brute Haskeer fell upon the general and hacked him to pieces. The rest of the band would have joined them if it hadn't been over so quickly.

Jennesta saw no reason to spend any of her magic intervening. But she quickly acted when the vengeful orcs turned to her. An apple-sized ball of fire manifested on the palm of her outstretched hand. Its intensity immediately grew, the brilliance hurtful to the eyes of everyone looking on.

Serapheim cried, 'No!' at the backs of the advancing Wolverines.

Jennesta hurled the fireball at them. They scattered and it missed, passing close enough to several that they felt its scorching heat. The fiery globe struck the far wall and exploded, the sound of its report filling the chamber. Chunks of masonry came down with a further resounding crash. She had already begun forming another fireball when Serapheim and Sanara stepped in.

Jennesta wrapped herself in a cloak of enchantment, a conjured field of protective vigour, near transparent save for the slightest tinge of shimmering green. Her father and sibling did the same, and a duel of sorcery commenced.

Blistering spheres and searing bolts were exchanged, needles of energy and sheets of power were flung. Some volleys the bubble-like defensive shields absorbed; others were deflected, causing the hellish munitions to ricochet. Multicoloured streaks sliced the air. There were intense detonations throughout the chamber, cleaving wood and stone.

All the orcs could do was take shelter. Except for a small group, oblivious to the mayhem, who clustered around their fallen comrade.

Under the onslaught, and the building power of the vortex, the palace was beginning to destruct. The rumblings grew louder. Fissures rippled across the flagstone floor, cracks appeared in the walls.

The combined might of Serapheim and Sanara was proving too strong for Jennesta. Her forehead was sheened with perspiration, her breath was laboured. She fought to maintain concentration. Her stamina, and her confidence, were waning.

Sensing that she was weakening, her father and her sister increased the ferocity of their assault. Her protective shield started to waver. When its emerald tint slowly changed to a pinkish crimson Serapheim and Sanara knew the sign. They upped their barrage.

Jennesta lost her hold. The shield silently burst into a golden nimbus that dissolved to nothing. She staggered slightly, then steadied herself with an effort of will. She let out an exhausted breath.

Serapheim darted forward and grabbed her wrist. She was in too much of a daze to stop him. He began dragging her across the chamber.

The Wolverines wanted to kill her. They came forward with blades in their hands.

'No!' Serapheim bellowed. 'She's my daughter! I've a responsibility for all she's done! I'll deal with this myself!'

Reluctantly, they obeyed.

Serapheim was pulling Jennesta towards the dais and the sparkling portal. When they were almost there she came to herself, and realised what he intended doing. She showed no fear.

'You wouldn't dare,' she sneered.

'Once, perhaps,' he told her, 'before the full horror of your wickedness was brought home to me. Not now.' Holding her in an iron grip, he thrust her hand towards the portal's cascading brilliance, the tips of her fingers almost in the flow. 'I brought you into this world. Now I'm taking you out of it. You should appreciate the symmetry of the act.'

'You're a fool,' she hissed, 'you always were. And a coward. I've an army here. If anything happens to me you'll die a death beyond your wildest imagination.' She flicked her gaze to her sister. 'You both will.'

'I don't care,' he told her.

Sanara backed him.

It seemed to Jennesta that they might have had tears in their eyes. She thought them weaklings for it.

Serapheim said something about evil and some prices being worth paying. He pushed her hand nearer to the sparkling flux.

She looked into his eyes and knew he meant it. She tried to conjure a defence, but nothing came. Her cocksure expression faded and she began to struggle.

'At least face your end with dignity,' he said. 'Or is that too much to ask?'

She spat her defiance.

He thrust her hand into the vortex, then retreated a pace.

She squirmed and fought to pull her hand free but the gushing fountain of energy held it as tightly as a vice. A change came over the trapped flesh. It began to liquefy, releasing itself as thousands of particles that flew into the swarm of stars and spiralled with them. The process increased apace, the vortex gobbling up her wrist. Rapidly she was drawn in to the depth of her arm, which likewise disintegrated and scattered.

The band was rooted, their expressions a mixture of horror and macabre fascination.

Her leg had been sucked in now, and it was melting before their eyes. Strands of her hair followed, as though inhaled by an invisible giant. Jennesta's disintegration speeded up, her matter eaten by the surging vortex at a faster and faster rate.

When it began to consume her face she finally screamed.

The sound was instantly cut off as the energy took the rest of her in several gulps.

She was plunging down an endless tunnel. A tunnel that sinuously twisted and turned. A tunnel without walls, like a vast, transparent tube; transparent but faintly iridescent. Outside, if the word had any meaning, there was both nothing and everything. Nothing in the sense of being utterly devoid of recognisable points of reference. Everything in that the dark blue velvet beyond the walls was peppered with countless stars.

She fell, helplessly. And caught a glimpse of a pinpoint of light, far, far below. It grew at a remarkable rate, rapidly swelling to the size of a coin, a fist, a shield, a wagon wheel. Then it was all-embracing and rushing at her, obliterating everything else.

She dropped, not into light, but complete darkness.

To her amazement, she woke up.

She was on her back, lying on what felt like soft grass. The air was balmy, and she could smell the sweet perfume of flowers in full bloom. Other than distant birdsong, all was quiet. Blinking at the sky, she saw *that it was a perfect blue, adorned with a smattering of pure white clouds. The sun was high.*

Two revelations occurred as her mind began to clear. First, she was alive. Second, this obviously wasn't Maras-Dantia. It also dawned on her that she was naked.

Her limbs were leaden, and she felt battered, though it seemed she had no major injuries. She tried to raise her head, but she was weak and nauseous, and found it too much of an effort. Her sorcery was also apparently depleted. She struggled to conjure the simplest of rejuvenation spells, and got nothing.

But she had enough of her senses intact to feel the power coursing through the ground beneath her. The raw magical energy in this place was of a strength and purity that far outdid the almost spent vitality of Maras-Dantia.

So she had no option but to lie where she was, in hope of regaining her vigour naturally.

She couldn't tell how long she was there; she was feverish, and such rational thoughts as she had were on matters other than the mere passing of time. They mostly concerned the retribution she would exact on her father, her sister and the hated Wolverines. If she ever got to see them again.

The day slid into evening. It began to get dark, and cooler. Overhead, stars were appearing.

She heard a sound. It took a moment for her to identify it as an approaching horse. The animal was plodding slowly, and coupled with the squeak of wheels and the jangling of chains it became obvious it was pulling a wagon. It came to a halt close by. Someone dismounted. There was the crunch of boots on gravel, then an absence of sound as whoever it was walked onto the grass.

Somebody gazed down at her. She could only make out that it was a human male, and he was robustly built. He stared for what seemed an age. Not just at her nakedness, but her general appearance. By any yardstick she was beautiful, but her beauty had aspects most observers found disquieting. Her singular eyes were part of it, as was the perplexing configuration of her features: a face a mite too wide, particularly at the temples; a chin that came almost to a point; a vaguely convex nose; a shapely but overly broad mouth, and a mass of coal black, waist-length hair. But it was her skin that was most arresting. It had a slight silver-green lustre, and a dappled character that gave the impression she was covered in minute fish scales.

She was fully aware of the depraved nature of the man's race, more than once having admired their inexhaustible cruelty. If his intentions had been dishonourable in any way there wouldn't have been much she could have done about it.

But instead of subjecting her to lust or brutality he performed an act of compassion he would later, albeit briefly, regret. Stirring himself, he spoke. His tone was kindly, concerned. When there was no reply he bent and wrapped her in his rough cloak. Then he gathered her up with the ease of a mother lifting her child, and as gently. He carried her towards his wagon.

Jennesta finally got a better idea of where she was. Even in the dying light she glimpsed a verdant landscape. She saw meadows, cultivated fields and the rim of a forest. Not far away stood a range of rolling green hills.

They came to a road, and the wagon. The man put her aboard tenderly, slipping a couple of folded sacks under her head as a pillow. When they set off he drove carefully.

Lulled by the swaying of the cart, she lay, fatigued, looking up at the rising stars. Despite her fever and her weakness she turned the same thought over and over in her mind.

She had had the luck to come across a good man.

The following week was a blur.

She had been taken to a farmhouse. It was modest, and needed thatching. There were chickens and pigs in the yard. In the house was the farmer's wife and her brood; four youngsters, all boys.

The farmer and his wife tended Jennesta. They fed her, bathed her and spoke soothingly to her until she got back her senses.

She feigned memory loss, and let them assume she had been attacked and robbed of everything. They just about accepted that the odd greenish patina of her skin was the result of a childhood malady, and soon seemed to ignore it. And it wasn't so outlandish, they told her, in a world that had orcs in it.

The reference to that particular race revitalised Jennesta. She interrogated the couple, demanding all sorts of information. Where were these orcs? Were they the only non-human race in this world? What was the humans' political set-up and where did its power lie?

They found her questions baffling, and couldn't understand why she didn't know the simplest of facts. Jennesta blamed her contrived amnesia, pretending to recall a blow to the head.

What she learned was that she was in Peczan, the cradle of a great empire. It was incomparably mighty, though it had its enemies. Most of these were barbarian kingdoms, often at each other's throats, and of little account. Peczan's only possible rival was the orcs, who occupied a far-off land called Acurial. But even they posed little threat, Jennesta was told, given their aversion to warlike ways. Naturally she couldn't accept her hosts' talk of the orcs of Acurial being docile, and felt sure they spoke from ignorance. But she held her tongue on the subject.

What she learned set her planning. Now there was a goal, and she turned her will to achieving it.

She had almost entirely recovered physically. Her magical abilities were another matter. They had started to return, but feebly, though she still felt the land's amazing fecundity. Her plan could hardly be realised from a decrepit farmhouse in the middle of nowhere. She needed to move on. That meant fully regaining her powers, and the use of people to serve her purpose.

Jennesta applied another kind of power to the oafish farmer. His conquest took just days. Once seduced, he was clay in her hands, and she remade him in her own image. Where there had been humanity, now there was only a dim-witted devotion to her whims. Where there had been tenderness towards his family, now there was callous indifference.

Such was her hold on the man that he willingly conspired in replenishing her powers. In the event, his wife's contribution was poor fare, mean and stringy. But the hearts of the four boys proved extremely nourishing. Her abilities restored, Jennesta had no further need of the farmer. She dispensed with him by simply removing the cloud from his mind and allowing him to see what had been done. His suicide provided her with a fleeting distraction.

The farmer was her first acolyte. There would be many more.

She had heard of a nearby town, and lost no time getting there, taking the farm's wagon and what little money she could find. The so-called town turned out to be not much more than a village. But it did have a tailor. Finally rid of the farmer's wife's drab hand-me-downs, she made sure her new clothes included a hood and a veil, should her appearance be an issue.

She also learned something she found intriguing, and which the *farmer hadn't bothered mentioning. Unlike the vast majority of humans in Maras-Dantia, in this world they had a command of magic. At least, some did. These adepts belonged to the Order of the Helix, a sect with as much sway in the empire as its political masters.*

The Order's nearest lodge was in the region's administrative centre, a provincial city a day's ride away. Compared to the sleepy hamlets and villages she passed on the road, its bustling streets gave her a measure of anonymity. More importantly, it connected her with a strand of the empire's web.

Jennesta had no trouble finding the Helix lodge; prominently located, it passed for a major temple. She was less lucky trying to penetrate it as anything other than a supplicant. The Order was male dominated. There were females in its ranks but they were few, and hardly any had real power. Rebuffed, she looked for a weak spot.

The Order's local overseer was an elderly, addle-headed bachelor who had never met anything like Jennesta before. She captivated him with ease. In half a year she had become his indispensable aide, and was grudgingly admitted to the Helix ranks under his patronage. By year's end she occupied his position, thanks to the judicious administering of poison.

She had a power base.

The ruthless efficiency with which Jennesta ran the lodge, and reports of her outstanding magical abilities, attracted the attention of the Order's upper echelons, as she intended. The upshot was a summons to the capital, and Helix's headquarters.

Competition for preferment was much stiffer once she entered the Grand Lodge, and advancement was frustratingly slow. Applying pressure on obstructive officials, swearing oaths she would later break, forming fragile alliances, corrupting the susceptible, bullying the weak and eliminating rivals needed all her guile. It also took time.

Another two years went by before the Order of the Helix was hers.

She immediately turned her attention to infiltrating government. As magic and politics intermingled in Peczan, she had already earned a certain notoriety that opened previously slammed doors. By virtue of her position at the pinnacle of Helix, she was automatically granted access to the citadels of the ruling class and the parlours of the influential, despite their thinly-veiled resentment of a female. Once again, she set about climbing.

A further year of machination and murder passed. She completed it as an upper-ranking official; a position of considerable power, though short of the highest. Any hopes she might have had about reaching the apex of empire were allowed to slip away. It wasn't that she didn't have an insatiable appetite for power. It was simply that she had all she needed, and saw no point in wasting more time laying siege to the summit, where she would be too noticeable in any event.

Jennesta never stopped thinking about orcs. She thought of the Wolverines in terms of revenge. And she thought of the orcs of Acurial as an opportunity.

It had long been her ambition to command an unparalleled army, and given their inexhaustible passion for warfare, no race was better suited to fill its ranks than the orcs. In this, Jennesta was perpetuating the dream of her mother, the sorceress Vermegram, who long ago mustered the orcs of Maras-Dantia. With such a force, and armed with the instrumentalities, Jennesta saw no limit to conquest. But like Vermegram, the magical means to totally control the race had eluded her. The orcs who served her in Maras-Dantia were kept in line with iron discipline and brutal punishments; the doctrine of fear Jennesta applied to all her underlings. That had proved insufficient, as the actions of the cursed Wolverines attested. The irony was that she had all but perfected a method of control when her father consigned her to this world. A world whose only orcs inhabited a distant land.

So she was intrigued, during her fourth year, when she started to hear rumours about military action against Acurial. This wasn't because Acurial posed any kind of threat to the empire or its interests. It was motivated by a desire for expansion, a hunger for natural resources and to bolster Peczan's influence in the region. But even a dictatorship must occasionally placate the opinion of its subjects, particularly when planning to send their young into combat. The orcs reputed passivity went some way to assure people that an invasion would be a walk-over, but a pretext was needed.

It was Jennesta's idea to put out that the orcs had magic at their disposal, destructive enough to menace the empire. Ignorance about far-off Acurial was so prevalent that this story was widely believed. Jennesta earned kudos for the ploy, but her request to accompany the invasion force was ignored. She set about fresh intrigues to get what she wanted.

The invasion was launched, and succeeded, with minimal Peczan casualties. Which seemed to confirm that Acurial's orcs were too passive to resist; something Jennesta still found hard to believe. The empire's bureaucracy ground into action and started to administer what was now a province. Draconian laws were enforced. Helix lodges were established. While all this was going on, Jennesta fought to curb her impatience, never an easy task, and continued her campaign to get to Acurial.

Half a year into the occupation she gained a concession. On the principle of knowing your enemy, she had argued for being allowed to study the orcs. Her hope was that this would take her to Acurial. It didn't. But Peczan shipped back a sizeable number of orc captives. They were paraded through the streets of the capital as living tokens of the empire's triumph, then handed over to Jennesta for what was officially referred to as 'appraisal'.

She was confounded by what she saw. These orcs did indeed seem passive, even submissive. Her instinct was to test their apparent meekness to its breaking point. On her orders they were humiliated, demeaned, beaten, tortured and subjected to arbitrary executions. The majority offered no more resistance than cattle sent for slaughter. But a few, a very few, snapped out of their apathy and tried to fight back with a ferocity she knew of old. This convinced her that the race's martial tendencies were not so much absent as dormant, and could be reawakened.

She told her superiors about it. She demonstrated it to them by having selected subjects goaded to fury. The fact that at least some orcs were capable of defiance was no surprise to them. The situation in Acurial was becoming troublesome. There had been organised attacks on the occupying forces, and they were escalating. Jennesta persuaded them of the need to send an emissary to shake things up in the province. Her Helix reputation, and not least her ruthlessness, landed her the role.

But shortly before she was due to leave, she saw her father.

From time to time, Jennesta would walk the streets incognito, usually at night. She did it partly to gain a sense of the city's mood, but mostly to hunt for victims when she felt in need of sustenance. She went out alone, certain that her powers could better anything the city might threaten, though there were those who would have assassinated her given the chance.

She found herself in one of the more sordid quarters, as she often did.

Such places tended to have an abundance of people who wouldn't be missed. There had been the usual minor inconvenience of men trying to approach or harass her. Most turned away when they saw her look. The persistent were given a taste of the Craft, leaving them stung or injured or worse. Jennesta remained unperturbed.

Weaving through a street that seemed to house nothing but taverns and bordellos, something caught her eye. A man was walking some distance ahead. Like her, he was hooded, and he had his back to her. But she thought she recognised his frame and gait, although there was sign of a slight limp. Certain she must be mistaken about who it might be, nevertheless her curiosity was stirred, and on impulse she followed him. He was doing his best to keep to the shadows. She did likewise.

After trailing him for some time through bustling streets they came to a quieter but no less run-down district. At one point the man slowed and looked back. Luckily for her, Jennesta was able to take refuge in the gloom of a cloister. Hidden by a crumbling column, she got a fleeting glimpse of his face. It was thinner than when she last saw him, and he looked drawn. But there was no mistake.

Very little shocked Jennesta. This was a rare and notable exception. But surprise was soon replaced by cold fury.

It seemed her father hadn't seen her, and continued his journey. She followed, doubly careful not to be spotted. He led her deeper into the low neighbourhood. Others lurked in the shadows here, but father and daughter both radiated something the night dwellers found unsettling, and they went unmolested. The streets became lanes and the lanes narrowed to twisting alleys. At last they arrived at a blacksmith's shop with adjoining stables, so ramshackle they were presumably abandoned. Her father paused at a side door and again looked back. Jennesta was well hidden. Satisfied, he pushed the door just far enough to slip in, then quietly closed it behind himself.

She lingered where she was for a moment. There was no question that she would act. Her dilemma was how. Remembering the last encounter with her father, she considered summoning Helix and military reinforcements. But there was a good chance he wouldn't still be here when they turned up. More importantly, he looked far less robust than he used to, and perhaps not so much of a challenge. Although she didn't know who else might be in there with him, of course. In the end her rage at his presence, and a hunger for vengeance, overrode any other considerations. She made for the door.

It wasn't locked, and opened at her touch. Inside was a short wooden passageway leading to another door that stood slightly ajar. She approached it stealthily. Peering through the crack, she saw a barn-sized interior lined on two sides with stalls for the horses, all derelict now. Ahead of her were stacks of powder-dry bales of hay. She crept to them and hid there.

There was a murmur of voices. The interior was ill-lit, but she could make out two figures. One was her father. The other was a much younger man, no more than a youth, with a striking mop of red hair and a freckled face. Like Serapheim, he carried no obvious weapon. The pair were conversing earnestly. Serapheim dug into a pocket, took out an amulet on a chain and handed it to the youth. The young man stared at it for a moment, then put the chain around his neck and tucked the amulet into his shirt. They carried on talking, and Jennesta, keeping low, moved forward in an effort to hear.

Serapheim held up a hand to halt whatever the youth was saying, then turned in her direction. 'You can come out,' he said, his voice clear and steady.

Jennesta cursed herself for thinking he wouldn't detect her presence. She stepped out of hiding. The youth looked shaken. Her father displayed no such reaction. He seemed calm as she walked towards them, though she judged his appearance as weaker than when they last met.

'You look a mess,' she told him.

'You haven't changed,' her father replied.

'Thank you,' she gave back wryly.

'It wasn't a compliment.'

'I thought you were dead.'

'Don't you mean hoped?' He didn't wait for a response. 'Luck and the Craft got me out of the palace. Just.'

'And not without cost, by the looks of you.' He said nothing and she added, 'So how do you come to be here? Or need I ask?'

'I thought the . . . task was done in Ilex. It was only later that I realised you hadn't perished, or had at least arrived somewhere you could do no harm. And when I saw what you were up to in this world . . .'

She wanted to say You can do that? *but bit it back. 'You can't be that far-looking if you weren't aware of me tracking you tonight.'*

'I let myself be preoccupied. Humans do that. We're not perfect.'

'That wins a prize for understatement. I assume your arrival at this particular time has some significance?'

'I've been here a while. I've watched you. I know you're intending to go to Acurial.'

'Ah. Your beloved orcs. So that's why you came here.'

'We owe them, Jennesta. For what we've done to them. What Vermegram tried to do.'

'My mother was a visionary!' she snapped. 'I'll never understand why she got entangled with a weakling like you.'

'Perhaps I was weak in turning a blind eye to her . . . misguided notions. But I believe she came to see the error of her ways.'

'There was no error in her ambition', Jennesta replied icily. 'It was right, and she almost achieved it.'

'I can't allow you to carry on what she started.'

'And how do you think you'll stop me? By repeating what you did to me in Maras-Dantia? You failed.' She rapped her chest with a fist. 'I'm here, in front of you. You'll fail again.'

'I'll have allies.'

'Not in this world. None in the empire and certainly none in—' She checked herself as a thought struck.

His thin smile seemed to confirm her suspicion. 'Not all orcs are like those in Acurial. As you well know.'

No, she thought, not in this world. She turned her attention to the youth, as much to give herself thinking time as anything. He looked awed. 'And is this one of your . . . allies?' she asked, contemptuously.

'Parnol's an apprentice; a very promising one.' He laid a hand on the boy's arm and fixed Jennesta with an even gaze. 'And he's under my protection.'

She didn't think her father would have made that point if this Parnol was capable of defending himself magically at any high level. So he had to have another function. She was beginning to guess what that was. 'Careful, Father,' she said. 'You don't have Sanara here to help you.' She flicked a glance at the youth. 'And he doesn't look comparable.' Parnol shifted uncomfortably.

'I'm warning you, Jennesta,' Serapheim bristled.

'Do it now.'

'What?'

'If you're so confident you can defeat me, why bother with plots and schemes? We can settle this now. Right here.'

'It doesn't have to be this way,' he reasoned. 'Reflect on the course you're taking.'

'Oh, save your breath, old man,' she retorted disgustedly.

'If you can see the light,' he persisted, 'as your mother did—'

'To hell with this.' She swiftly brought up her hand and lobbed a fistful of flame at him.

For all his age and brittleness, Serapheim was faster. A swathe of energy instantly appeared, embracing him and his apprentice. When Jennesta's searing volley struck, it dissipated harmlessly. She summoned a defensive shield of her own and continued her fiery assault. At first, her father didn't respond, until, under the increasing salvo, he retaliated. Blast and counter blast illuminated the cavernous barn.

It was all too reminiscent of their duel in Ilex, but Jennesta was determined on a different outcome. She invested all her concentration and considerable skills in overcoming her father's defences. Yet despite her resolve, and Serapheim's apparently diminished state, she couldn't break through.

Then she noticed her father produce an object from the folds of his cloak. Or rather, a cluster of objects, interlocked. In a heartbeat she realised it was a set of instrumentalities. Her eyes widened at the sight. She burned with frustration at having what she most desired so near yet beyond her reach.

Her aggravation heightened when she saw that her father was manipulating the artefacts. He had them directed at Parnol, who was doing little beyond looking terrified. Jennesta guessed what was about to happen, and nothing in her magical armoury seemed able to pierce Serapheim's barrier and prevent it.

In a rush she realised the flaw in her father's strategy. The barricade of energy he conjured was focused solely on repelling magic, which left another possibility. But Serapheim was slotting the last instrumentality into place, and she had just seconds to do something about it. More in desperation than in hope, she acted.

The sunburst spell she unleashed was simple. It was merely the generation of an eruption of light, but blindingly intense. When she opened her eyes she saw that it had left Serapheim and Parnol in disarray, and both had instinctively turned their backs on her. But her father was still fumbling with the instrumentalities. Gathering up her gown, Jennesta plucked out the dagger she kept strapped to her thigh.

She drew back her arm and flung the blade with all the strength she could muster.

In that speck of time, two things happened simultaneously. Serapheim activated the instrumentalities, and his apprentice, still dazzled, lurched into the dagger's path. Unimpeded by the shield, it struck the youth square between his shoulder-blades. Serapheim cried out. Parnol staggered from the blow, then whipped away by the power of the instrumentalities, he vanished.

Shocked by what had happened, his concentration broken, Serapheim lost his hold on the protective shield. As it dissolved, Jennesta began to conjure a further, lethal strike. Her father hastily adjusted the instrumentalities, and with a last look mixing sorrow and anger, he disappeared too.

She stood alone. There was disappointment at not having eliminated her father, and particularly at letting the instrumentalities elude her. But she judged it at least a partial victory.

The sulphurous tang of magic hung in the air. It mingled with the smell of burning timber, stray bolts from their battle having started several fires in the building.

She left it to burn.

Jennesta set out for Acurial not long after, and many were glad to see her go.

She had no way of foreseeing what would unfold there. No hint that she would triumph in her quest for the instrumentalities, yet see her other plans ruined, thanks to the intervention of the detestable Wolverines.

Nor could she imagine that she would eventually find herself on a corpse-littered beach on a world of islands, poised between the prospect of victory and having everything turn to ashes.

1

There was chaos.

All across the island, battles were raging between Jennesta's loyalists and the Gateway Corps. Most of the dwarfs who inhabited the isle, and who had survived the initial clash, had fled to their boltholes or the upper slopes of the sacred volcanoes. Seashore and jungle resonated with the flare of magic and the ringing of blades.

The Wolverines were gathered in the strip of pebbly land between beach and tree-line, sheltering behind an outcrop of rock. They were still reeling at what Stryke and Coilla had told them.

Two of the band's best scouts, Hystykk and Zoda, had been dispatched to discover Jennesta's whereabouts. They returned crestfallen.

'She's not where you last saw her, Captain,' Zoda confirmed. 'There were too many of her troopers about for us to look much further afield.'

'So where the fuck is she?' Haskeer said.

Coilla shrugged. 'Could be anywhere by now.'

'This island's not so big,' Stryke told them. 'We can find her.' As the effect Jennesta's spell had on him wore off, it was being replaced by pure anger.

'Where's she likely to have gone?' Pepperdyne asked.

Haskeer gave the human a venomous look. 'If we knew that, pink face, we wouldn't be flapping our gums here.'

'I mean, figure it out. It wasn't as though she was actually winning the battle, was it? It was a draw at best. And it looks to me like that elf's group holds the beach. So she'd maybe think twice before going for her fleet.'

'Makes sense,' Coilla said.

'Trust you to back him,' Haskeer muttered.

Coilla shot him a dagger look but kept quiet.

'So what does she do?' Pepperdyne went on.

'Goes inland,' Jup supplied.

'Not a lot of choice,' his mate Spurral added, lightly ribbing him.

Pepperdyne nodded. 'Right. But is she going to tramp about in the jungle? I don't think so. She'd make for something more practical.'

'The dwarfs' village!' Wheam exclaimed.

The others had worked that out already, and he didn't get the hurrah he expected.

'What do you think, Stryke?' Coilla asked.

'I think we're wasting time,' he snapped, 'when Thirzarr needs me.'

'Yeah. So, the village?'

He sighed. 'As good a place as any, I s'pose.' To the rest he announced, 'We're moving out! We run into anybody, we cut 'em down!'

'Don't we always?' Haskeer wondered.

'She won't be alone,' Dallog warned, drawing another contemptuous look from Haskeer.

'I know,' Stryke said. 'We can deal with it.'

'What about Jennesta herself?' Jup asked. 'What happens if—' He saw Stryke's expression. '—*when* we find her? How do we handle *that*?'

'I'll think of something,' his captain returned gruffly, and without further word turned and set off at a pace.

The band fell in behind him.

Coilla slipped an arm around Pepperdyne's waist as they walked. It drew looks.

'How bad was it back there?' he wanted to know.

'Pretty bad. I've never seen Stryke so . . . out of control.'

'He seems all right now.'

'Don't kid yourself. Take my advice: steer clear of him. He's just about bottling the fury.'

'Can't blame him after what happened to his mate. I know how I'd feel if something like that happened to . . . somebody I care for.' He smiled at her.

Coilla returned it, then sobered. 'It's not just Thirzarr. He's got

Corb and Janch to think about too. His hatchlings,' she added by way of explanation. 'And who knows what mayhem Jennesta might have wreaked in Ceragan. This is one pissed-off band, Jode.'

'How can I tell?'

'What'd you mean?'

'You're orcs. Pissed-off seems to be the natural state.'

She grinned again, despite herself. 'Not all the time.'

'Thankfully, no.'

'Mind you, it was good that Wheam got pissed-off back there just when we needed it.'

'Sounds like he did well.'

'Yeah. Not that Haskeer believes it.'

They glanced at Wheam. He was jogging along next to Dallog. But Dallog seemed more interested in Pirrak, one of the other tyros from Ceragan, with whom he was engrossed in conversation.

'Looks like Dallog's neglecting him,' Pepperdyne observed.

'He has to mentor all the newbies.'

'I've noticed he's spent a lot of time with that one recently.'

'Maybe Pirrak needs some kind of guidance. The fresh intake are new to this, remember.'

'Been quite a baptism of fire for them, hasn't it?'

'Yes. It's a wonder we haven't lost more of 'em, thank the Tetrad.'

'The what?'

'You've not heard any of us say that before? It's our congress of gods. There are four of them. I'll explain some time, if you're interested.'

'I'd like to hear about it. And you . . . believe in these gods? You appeal to them?'

'Usually when somebody's trying to part me from my head.'

Pepperdyne smiled. 'I know that feeling. It was the same with my people.' He cast an eye over the trudging band. 'I guess there's a certain amount of appealing going on right now.'

'You bet.'

'So how do your— *Damn*. Heads up.' He nodded.

Coilla followed his gaze and saw Standeven elbowing their way. She rolled her eyes.

Pepperdyne's one-time master arrived sweating. 'I need to talk to you,' he insisted to Coilla in an undertone.

'About what?'

He looked around, anxious not to be overheard. 'The instrumentalities,' he mouthed.

Pepperdyne groaned. 'Not this again.'

Standeven glared at him and turned indignant. 'I only want to ask the Corporal here if they're still safe.'

'What's it to you?' Coilla said.

'A lot. As it should be to everybody here. Our only chance of getting home depends on—'

'I know. They're safe. You'd have to kill Stryke to get 'em. Unlikely in your case.'

He ignored the jibe. 'And has he mastered them yet? Has he worked out what's wrong with them?'

She jabbed a thumb in Stryke's direction. 'Why don't you ask him?'

Standeven looked to Stryke, forging ahead at the column's prow. He saw the broadness of his back, the rippling muscles and, when he turned his head to scold those following, the murderous expression he wore. 'I'll . . . wait until he's free.'

'He does have a couple of other things on his mind,' Pepperdyne informed him dryly.

'But they're secure, right? The stars, they're—'

'*Enough*. You're getting obsessed with the things. Give it a rest.'

Standeven flushed redder. 'There was a time,' he grated angrily, 'when you wouldn't have dared speak to me like that.'

'So you keep telling me. And I keep saying that time's past. Live with it.'

Shaking with impotent fury, his old master fell back in the column, where he was given a wide berth.

'I think he's going crazy,' Pepperdyne said, at least half seriously.

Coilla shook her head. 'Don't know about that. I do know the effect the stars can have.'

'Effect?'

'Spending too long with 'em can make things a bit weird. We've seen it in the band.'

'Weird?'

'You turned into an echo, or what?'

'Just explain, Coilla.'

'Later. It's a long story. But the stars have the power to get a hold on some, make 'em act . . . well, a bit like Standeven.'

'What about Stryke? He's with the things all the time.'

'Yeah, and that's a worry. But like I said, it affects some, not all. He seems to handle it. Most of the time.'

'Oh, great.'

'What I'm saying is, keep an eye on Standeven.'

'I usually do.'

They marched in silence after that, turning things over in their minds.

Stryke was leading the band along the upper lip of the beach, keeping the jungle to their right. Soon they would reach a line of sand dunes marking the point where they needed to turn inland, onto the path that headed toward the dwarfs' settlement.

As dwarfs themselves, Jup and Spurral felt a natural sympathy with the natives, but their empathy was with Stryke. Marching four or five ranks to his rear, they found themselves eyeing him constantly.

'He looks in a state,' Spurral commented, 'near frenzied. Is he going to hold it together?'

'Course he will. He's tough. What beggars belief is how history's repeating itself.'

'Me and the Gatherers.'

Jup nodded. 'So I know how he feels.'

'He helped you get through that.'

'Yeah. I owe him.'

'Now you can repay. He needs your support. And maybe more down the road, depending on how this plays out.'

'There's no going near him at the moment, the mood he's in.'

'Well, you'll just have to—'

'*Wait!* Look.' He pointed at the sand dune they were approaching.

A number of humans were swarming over it, their Peczan uniforms marking them as Jennesta's followers. Several of her undead slaves were with them. Their movements were lumbering and jerky, and their deathly pallor was evident even at a distance. The looks of surprise on the troopers' faces testified to this being an unexpected encounter rather than an ambush.

'*Damn,*' Spurral said. 'Just what we needed.'

'Yes, it is,' Jup told her.

'More *trouble*'s what we need?' She drew her short-bladed sword.

'Better to be at the enemy's throats than each other's. It'll bleed off the tension. 'Specially Stryke's.'

As Jup spoke, Stryke rushed at the troopers, bellowing a war cry. The rest of the band took it up and thundered after him. All but Standeven, who hung back, looking fretful.

The two lines met in a bellowing roar and the clatter of steel.

Stryke tore into the human ranks like a hot cleaver through pig fat. A pair of troopers went down in a brace of heartbeats, and instantly he was engaging a third. He fought like a berserker, oblivious to whistling blades and lunging spears. His only aim was rending the flesh of anything in his way.

Coilla and Pepperdyne worked in unison, carving a path deep into the enemy's ranks, until they ran into one of the undead. The process by which Jennesta magically created her zombie adherents endowed them with a strength and stamina most lacked in life. This one was an exceptional example, and must have been hulking even before he met his fate. Armed with what looked like a tree trunk, he took a hefty swipe that caught Pepperdyne off guard. The blow was glancing, but enough to bring him to his knees. A follow-up would have brained him, had Coilla not rushed in, sword swinging. She struck the zombie at its waist, cutting deep. Back on his feet, Pepperdyne rejoined the fray, adding his weight to the fight. Together they hacked their foe to pieces.

Jup and Spurral also fought in harmony. Given their height, this was as much necessity as choice. Employing a well-practised technique, Jup used his staff to crack kneecaps, toppling opponents and bringing them in range of Spurral's blade.

Haskeer had no truck with anything like finesse. Having felled a trooper with a thrust to the man's chest, he had his sword dashed from his hand by a stray blow. Menaced by a trio of advancing soldiers he swiftly hoisted the corpse and hurled it at them. They went down like a row of skittles. Snatching up his sword, Haskeer followed through.

The new recruits instinctively fought as a group, with Dallog marshalling them, and gave a good account of themselves. Even Wheam, his confidence growing, managed to inflict some damage.

The whole band, steeped in frustration, vented their anger with orcish fury. They stabbed, slashed and pounded at the enemy mercilessly, intent on nothing short of a massacre.

At length, Stryke wrenched his blade from the innards of the last human and stood panting as he surveyed the slaughter.

'Feeling better?' Coilla said.

He wiped blood from his face with the back of a hand. 'Some.'

Jup arrived. 'Casualties light,' he reported. 'Dallog's patching up those who need it.'

Stryke nodded. 'Then let's keep moving.' He set off.

They took the jungle path leading to the dwarfs' village, alert to any further danger. The journey was uneventful until they were almost at the settlement, when they spotted columns of black smoke beginning to rise above the trees. Shortly after, they entered the clearing.

All but two or three of the huts were burning, and a dozen or so dead dwarfs were scattered about. Some of the band caught the briefest glimpse of movement in the jungle. It was judged to be natives fleeing to their hiding places. Coilla called out to them, but got no reply. The remaining huts were searched, along with the surrounding terrain, and proved deserted. Lookouts were posted, and the private with the best head for heights, Nep, was ordered to climb one of the taller trees to spy out the land. Stryke set half a dozen grunts on the more or less endless task of finding suitable wood to replenish their store of arrows. The rest of the band gathered around him.

'No Jennesta,' Haskeer said tightly, glaring at Pepperdyne. 'So much for your brilliant plan.'

'It was a reasonable assumption,' the human protested.

'And nobody had a better idea,' Coilla added.

Haskeer switched his baleful stare to her. 'That's right, take his side. As usual.'

'It was the best idea,' she repeated deliberately.

'Yeah, right.'

'If you've got some kind of beef, Haskeer, let's hear it.'

'I'm not keen on humans having a hand in how this band's run.'

'I haven't,' Pepperdyne told him. 'I was just trying to help.'

'And a fat lot of good that turned out. We don't need your *help*. So why don't you—'

'*Shut it,*' Stryke warned, his tone ominous. 'We're all in this together, and I'll have no bickering.'

'Now *you're* taking his part,' Haskeer grumbled.

'I said *shut . . . it*. There'll be no indiscipline in this band. And if anybody thinks otherwise they can step up now.'

Haskeer looked as though he just might, except they were interrupted by a shout from Nep at the tree top.

'*What?*' Stryke bellowed back.

'*The ships! They've gone!*'

'*Which?*'

'*All but ours!*'

Stryke signalled for him to come down.

'So Jennesta *has* left the island,' Jup said.

'And that other bunch too, by the sound of it,' Spurral put in.

'Shit,' Haskeer grated through clenched teeth.

'*Now* what do we do?' Coilla said.

2

The Gateway Corps ship had sailed beyond sight of the dwarfs' island. But the Corps elf commander, Pelli Madayar, who had taken the wheel herself, was uncertain which course to set. For that, she looked to her goblin second-in command, Weevan-Jirst. He was gazing at a plump, gleaming gem nestling in his palm.

'Anything?' Pelli asked.

'Nothing.'

'Take the wheel. I'll try.'

They swapped places. She warmed the gem in her hand, then stared hard at it. Its swirling surface was cloudy.

'Is something wrong with it?' Weevan-Jirst asked in the rasping timbre peculiar to his race.

'There shouldn't be, given the quality of its magic. I'll check.'

'How?'

Pelli was aware that although high in the Corps' magical hierarchy, her deputy still had a lot to learn. 'By comparing it with a set of instrumentalities we already know about,' she explained.

'Those held by the orc warband?'

She nodded. 'You're aware that each set of artefacts has its own unique signature; what some call its song. We know the tempo of the ones the Wolverines have. I'll see if I can attune to them. One moment.' Face creased in concentration, she softly recited the necessary spell. At length she said, 'There,' and showed him the gem.

Images had appeared on its façade. They were arcane, and continuously shifting, but to adepts their meaning was plain.

'The orcs' instrumentalities,' Weevan-Jirst interpreted, 'on the isle of dwarfs.'

'Yes. Which confirms that the fault doesn't lie in our method of detection.'

553

'I see that. So why can't we trace the artefacts Jennesta has?'

'Because I'm now certain that she's done something unpreced-ented, or at least extremely rare. The instrumentalities she's using are copies, presumably taken from the originals the orcs have. Their emanations are unlike those given off by the genuine articles, which is why we're finding it difficult to track them.'

'Copies? That would be a remarkable achievement.'

'Oh, yes. There's no doubting her extraordinary magical talent. Moreover, I believe she's also tampered with the originals in some way, giving her a measure of control over them.'

'Which would explain the erratic way the Wolverines were world-hopping before arriving in this one.'

'Indeed it would. She's toying with them.'

'But I'm puzzled.'

'How so?'

'Our mission is to retrieve the orcs' instrumentalities, and we know where they are. So why have we left them behind on the island?'

'We now have not one, but two sets of instrumentalities in irresponsible hands. And Jennesta's ability to duplicate them is potentially catastrophic. Imagine dozens, scores, *hundreds* of instrumentalities in circulation. The Corps could never control a situation like that.'

'It doesn't bear thinking about,' Weevan-Jirst agreed gravely.

'We've two options. We can go back to the island to tackle the orcs again, and run the risk of losing Jennesta for ever. Or we concentrate on her, knowing we can find the orcs as long as they have the artefacts, which they're unlikely to part with.'

'We don't know where she is.'

'I think we can find out by recalibrating our detection methods on the basis that her instrumentalities are copies.'

'Is that possible?'

'In theory. Only it might take a little while. But there's some-thing else that could work to our advantage. Jennesta has Stryke's mate, and we can almost certainly count on him pursuing her too. With luck, we'll be able to bag both sets at the same time.'

'How will *they* know where she's gone?'

'Don't underestimate how tenacious a race the orcs are. I'd put a large wager on them working it out.'

The goblin looked doubtful. 'Isn't this deviating from our orders?'

'I have autonomy in the field, to a degree.'

'Yes,' he hissed, '*to a degree*. Are you going to consult higher authority?'

'Karrell Revers? No. At least, not yet.'

'Can I ask why not?'

'I have total respect for his judgement, but he's not here.'

'You mean he'd likely order you to stick to our original mission.'

'Probably. And we'd lose precious time while the situation's debated on homeworld.' She gave him a concerned look. 'Of course, I appreciate that you might be unhappy with my plan. But I'll take full responsibility for—'

'I'll be glad to abide by any decision you make, Pelli. For the time being.'

She decided not to pursue that comment. 'Thank you. Meantime, we have something else to attend to.' She looked along the deck. The bodies of three of their comrades were laid out, wrapped in bloody sheets. 'Then we have a score to settle with Jennesta.'

There were dead on Jennesta's ship too. Some walked and breathed, after a fashion. Others would never do either again.

Several of the latter were being pitched overboard by a party of the former.

The corpses being disposed of were dwarfs, broken and bloodied following Jennesta's creative interrogation methods. Apart from mundane necessity, the fate of the discarded cadavers had the additional effect of chastening her followers. But although Jennesta embraced, indeed revelled in the appellation tyrant, she was coming to understand the value of tempering stick with carrot when it came to her subordinates' loyalty. This took several forms. The promise of power and riches under her dominion was one way. Another was the dispensing of pleasure, her sorcery being capable of conferring sensations of wellbeing, even ecstasy, as readily as terror.

But there was a kind of follower for whom neither punishment nor bliss was the spur. These rare individuals shared her taste for cruelty. And Jennesta had found one. His name was Freiston. He was a young low-ranking officer in the Peczan military, one of those who had thrown in their lot with her in the hope of extravagant rewards. He was a human, so naturally she distrusted him. Not that she didn't distrust all races, but she was especially suspicious of humans. After all, her father was one.

Freiston had caught her attention because of his skill as a torturer, and his passion for it, which had proved useful. On the strength of that she promoted him to her notional second-in-command.

Following the debacle on the island, they were in Jennesta's cabin. She was seated, regally; he was required to stand. Also present was Stryke's mate, Thirzarr, who lay insensible on a cot. She looked as though she was sleeping, but it was a state only Jennesta's sorcery could rouse her from.

'Did you get what you want, ma'am?' Freiston asked.

She smiled. 'My wants exceed anything you could imagine. But if you mean the information I needed to set our course, then yes.'

'If I may say so, my lady, it's ironic.'

'What is?'

'That those dwarfs should have given their lives for something as mundane as a location.'

She gave him a withering look. 'It's hardly mundane to me. But it was a case of making them understand, rather than them trying to withhold what I wanted. Not that you're complaining, surely? You obviously enjoyed it.'

'I'm ready to serve you in any way necessary, ma'am.'

'Perhaps you should have been a diplomat rather than a soldier.' He started to respond. She waved him silent. 'We'll be in a combat situation at landfall. I need my force in good order and well briefed on what they'll be up against. You'll see to it.'

'Ma'am. We're going to be a *little* under strength in a couple of key areas due to a few of our people being left behind on the dwarfs' island.'

'Do I look like someone who cares about that? If they were too slovenly to obey my evacuation order I don't need them.'

'Yes, m'lady. Can I ask when we'll reach our destination?'

'In about two days. What I seek turned out to be nearer than I suspected. So you're going to be a busy little man, Freiston.' She rose. 'Let's set the wheels turning.' Glancing at Thirzarr's recumbent form, she led him out of the cabin.

From the deck, the other four vessels in her flotilla could be seen, ploughing in her flagship's wake. On the deck itself, one of Jennesta's undead stood motionless over a dwarf's body. She swept that way, Freiston in tow.

Approaching, she saw that the zombie was General Kapple Hacher. Or had been. He was staring at the cadaver. Freiston showed no emotion at seeing his one-time commanding officer so hideously reduced.

Jennesta was furious. 'What are you doing, you *dolt*?' she raged. 'You had your orders. Take that—' She jabbed a finger at the corpse. '—and cast it overboard.'

The drooling hulk that had been a great army's general and governor of a Peczan province carried on staring.

'*Do it!*' Jennesta insisted, further incensed. 'Obey me!'

Hacher lifted his gaze to her, but otherwise stayed motionless. Her patience exhausted, she continued haranguing, and took to cuffing him with a rings-encrusted fist, raising puffs of dust from the tatters of his decaying uniform. After a moment his eyes, hitherto glassy, flickered and showed something like sentience, and perhaps a hint of defiance.

Freiston's hand went to his sword hilt.

'*Do . . . as . . . you're . . . told,*' Jennesta commanded, fixing Hacher with a look of smouldering intensity.

The light died in his eyes and they returned to insensible. With a kind of rasping sigh he bent to the corpse. He lifted it with no sign of effort and, straightening, tossed it over the rail. There was a distant splash.

'Now get back to your duties,' Jennesta told him.

Hacher slowly turned and trudged away, heading for the prow and a group of fellow zombies hefting supplies.

Jennesta saw Freiston's expression and answered his unspoken question. 'Sometimes, when their original force of will was strong, subjects can be less compliant.' She indicated the party Hacher was joining. 'They're imperfect beings; far from the ideal I have in mind.'

'Can they be improved, ma'am?'

'Oh, yes. In the same way that a peasant using poor clay makes poor pots, this first batch has flaws that carried over from the material I was forced to use. But with the right subjects, and

557

refinements I've made to the process, the *next* batch is going to be far superior. As you'll soon see. But you have something on your mind, Freiston. What is it?'

'We have the orc's female,' he replied hesitantly.

'Stryke's mate, yes. What of it?'

'If he's as pig-headed as you say, my lady, won't his band be after us?'

'I'm counting on it.'

'Ah.' He knew better than to query her reasoning, but ventured another thought. 'And the group that attacked us? Who *were* they?'

'They can only have been the Gateway Corps. I thought they were a myth, but it appears not.'

'Aren't they another threat?'

'They're meddlers. Self-appointed so-called guardians of the portals. There'll be a reckoning for what they did today.'

Freiston had doubts about that, given that Jennesta had just had to retreat from them. But naturally he kept his opinion to himself.

'Neither orcs nor a ragbag of interfering elder races are going to stand in my way,' she went on. 'There's going to be a very different outcome the next time our paths cross.'

3

Stryke's fury had subsided. Cold purpose took its place.

He set about getting things organised. As it was nearly dusk, the dwarfs' remaining undamaged longhouses were commandeered and the surrounding area secured. A group was sent to the goblin ship the band had arrived in, to replenish its rations and to guard it. Scouting parties were dispatched to comb the island.

Having done as much as he could for the time being, Stryke sat down on the steps of one of the longhouses and fell to brooding. Everybody in the band knew better than to approach him. With one exception.

Jup came to him with a steaming bowl and a canteen. 'Here.' He offered the food. Stryke barely looked at it, and said nothing. 'You've got to eat,' the dwarf told him. 'For Thirzarr. You'll be no good famished.'

Stryke took the bowl. He stared at its contents. 'What is it?'

Jup seated himself. 'Lizard. The jungle's full of 'em. That other stuff's leaves and roots,' he added helpfully. 'There's fruit too, but I figured you need meat.'

Stryke began eating, without enthusiasm.

After a moment, Jup ventured, 'About Thirzarr . . .' He ignored Stryke's baleful expression and pushed on. 'I'll tell you what you told me when Spurral got taken. Your mate has a value to Jennesta. And you don't damage something of value.'

'What value? Why should Jennesta give a damn about Thirzarr's life?'

'Don't know. It could be as simple as antagonising you. What's important is that Jennesta kept Thirzarr alive; she didn't leave her lying on the beach back there.'

'But the state she was in. Like one of the bitch's damned undead.'

'Not quite. Jennesta *threatened* to make Thirzarr that way. But she didn't do it. That's more reason for hope, Stryke.'

'We don't know she hasn't. And it's not just Thirzarr. There's Corb and Janch. What value are *they* to her?'

'There's no reason to think—'

'And Ceragan itself; what might she have done there?'

'Stryke.'

'Come to that, what if—'

'*Stryke*. Could she have made Ceragan more of a shit hole than Maras-Dantia?'

Jup was gratified when that drew a thin smile. 'Where do we go from here?' Stryke said.

'Not sure. We just have to believe that a way's going to open for us. But you know we're with you, Stryke. The whole band. Whatever it takes.'

Stryke nodded and went on eating mechanically.

They sat in silence.

Not far away, just inside the jungle's lip, Coilla and Pepperdyne were foraging.

He stooped and ripped up a handful of purplish leaves. 'Do you think these are all right?'

Coilla looked, then sniffed the bouquet. She made a face. 'I wouldn't risk it unless you want to poison everybody.'

He tossed the clump away. 'This is harder than I thought. Things seem more or less the same in this world as ours, but when you take a closer look . . .'

'Yes, there are differences in the small stuff. But think about how big some of the differences were in those other worlds we went to. We were lucky with this one.'

'Talking of which, you started to tell me how what we call our home world isn't really *your* home world, despite you being born there. What the hell was that all about?'

'It's not the real home of any of the elder races. As we were told it, it rightly belongs to your race.'

'And?'

'You want to hear it now?'

'What else is there to do? Unless you'd prefer to—' He reached for her.

She wriggled free, laughing. 'Whoa! Steady. All right. It's complicated, and I don't even know if it's true, but—'

'It's just a fairy story then.'

'The stories *they* tell would freeze your blood. No, we reckon what we heard's probably true, but . . . who knows?'

'So spill it.' He sat, then patted the sward next to him and she sat too.

'All right.' She gathered her thoughts. 'The story goes that the world we both come from was the humans' world. All we knew was our land; what we called Maras-Dantia and your race called Centrasia. We thought Maras-Dantia belonged to all the elder races living there, and that humans came from outside much later and fucked everything up.' She saw the look he gave her. 'No offence.'

He smiled. 'None taken. So what was the truth?'

'There were humans in Maras-Dantia before the great influx, or at least a few. One of them was Tentarr Arngrim, who calls himself Serapheim.'

'*Before* the influx? You said he set you off on this mission. How *old* is this man?'

'Very, I guess. But he's a sorcerer, so . . .' She shrugged. 'Anyway, Serapheim's mate was a sorceress called Vermegram. Whereas he's human, she was . . . I don't know. Something else. They had three offspring, all female. One was Jennesta. Then there was Adpar, who was part nyadd.'

'What's that?'

'A kind of water sprite. Jennesta killed her.'

'Charming.'

'The third sister's Sanara, who must take after her father 'cos she looks human. She helped us out of a fix in Maras-Dantia.'

'What's all this got to do with—'

'I'm getting to it. What we know about those early days—'

'What you *think* you know.'

'Yeah, right. Now shut up. Serapheim or Vermegram, or maybe both of 'em, found a way to move between worlds. It's what led to the stars Serapheim made. Or discovered.' She waved a dismissive hand. 'It's all a bit vague. But their messing around opened . . . sort of cracks between worlds. Holes, if you like. And elder races fell through from their worlds to Maras-Dantia.'

'Including orcs.'

'Yeah. Which set us on the road to servitude, and wound up making us the backbone of Jennesta's army. But that's another story. The one I'm telling you ended with Serapheim and Vermegram falling out . . . somehow. Some say they turned from lovers to enemies, and there was a conflict. I don't know anything about that. Vermegram's reckoned to be dead, though nobody's sure how or when.'

'Hang on. You said she wasn't human.'

Coilla nodded. 'You only had to look at Jennesta and Adpar to see that.'

'How could she be anything *but* human if she was in Maras-Dantia before the elder races arrived?'

'Fucked if I know, Jode. I'm not an oracle.'

'What you said about your people going into servitude; how did—'

'Enough questions. Some other time, all right?'

He was taken aback by the sharpness of her reply, but shrugged and said, 'Sure.'

She changed the subject and softened her tone. 'It's getting cooler.'

He slipped an arm round her. She moved closer and laid her head against his shoulder.

There were shouts from the clearing.

'Damn!' Pepperdyne complained. '*Every* time we get a quiet moment together . . .'

'Come on,' Coilla said, scrambling to her feet.

They headed back to the village.

One of the scouting parties had returned. They had four human prisoners with them, their hands tied behind their backs. Looking terrified, their uniforms dusty and tattered, they were forced to their knees. The band gathered around them, Stryke to the fore.

Orbon, who led the scouts, reported. 'Found these stragglers further along the beach, Captain. There was no fight left in 'em.'

Grim-faced, Stryke approached and walked slowly along the line of crouching captives. All of them avoided his gaze and kept their heads down.

'I've just one question,' he told them. 'Where has your mistress gone?'

A couple of the prisoners glanced nervously at each other, but none of them spoke.

'I'll make myself plain,' he said, walking back and forth in front of them, his unsheathed sword in his hand. 'I get an answer or you get dead.' He went to the first in line. 'You! Where's Jennesta?'

The man looked up. He was trembling. 'We . . . That isn't . . . the sort of thing she'd . . . tell the likes of us.'

'Wrong answer,' Stryke told him. He drove his sword into the prisoner's chest. The man toppled, and lay twitching before he was still.

Stryke moved on to the next human. 'Where's Jennesta?' he repeated, his gory blade pressed to the captive's throat.

This one was more resolute, or perhaps it was bravado. 'You can go and fuck yourself, *freak*,' he grated, and made to spit in Stryke's face.

He didn't have the chance. Stryke brought back his sword and swung it hard. The blow was savage enough to part the man from his head, which bounced a couple of times before rolling to a halt at Standeven's feet. His face drained of all colour and he hastily stepped back, looking queasy. The decapitated torso sat for a moment, gushing, before it fell.

The next man in line was older than the others and wore an officer's uniform. He was splattered with his dead comrade's blood.

Stryke turned to him. 'Has that loosened your tongue? Or do I do the same to you?'

The man said nothing, though it was as likely from fear as courage. Stryke drew back his blade again.

'*Wait!*' Pepperdyne yelled, pushing his way forward. 'What the *hell* are you doing, Stryke?'

'This is band business. Stay out of it.'

'Since when was it your business to slaughter unarmed prisoners?'

'You've a lot to learn about orcs, human.'

'I thought I'd already learned that you were honourable.'

That seemed to give Stryke pause for thought, but he didn't lower his sword. 'I need to know where the bitch's taken Thirzarr.'

'You'll not get anything out of dead men.'

'Force is all their kind understands.'

'My kind, you mean. And isn't that what humans say about orcs?'

'We *do* understand it,' Haskeer protested.

Pepperdyne jabbed a thumb at the dead prisoners. 'Not working too well here, is it?' He turned back to Stryke. 'Let me try. Come on. I'm one of *their kind*; maybe they'll open up to me.'

'Why don't you keep your snout out of this?' Haskeer said. 'You're not in this band.'

'He's proved himself,' Coilla told him. 'I say we give it a chance.'

'Here we go again.'

'And what's that mean?'

'You're backing him. Again. Seems to me you should be siding with your own, not outsiders.'

'*We're* outsiders, you idiot! Everybody shits on us, curses us, hates us. You might think of that when you're busy judging. Jode's suffered as much as we have, in his way.'

'You're talking about a human. They're more shitters than shat upon, I reckon.'

Jup burst out laughing. 'Sorry.' He tried to sober himself. 'But . . . *shitters*? *Shat upon*? You outdo yourself, Haskeer.' He started laughing again. Several of the privates joined in. He made a better fist of composing himself. 'Coilla's right. Maybe Jode could make 'em talk.'

Haskeer was seething now. 'You too, eh?'

'What have we got to lose? If it doesn't work we can move on to cutting off a few of their fingers or toes or . . .' He glanced at the pair of alarmed prisoners. 'Failing that, Stryke can finish 'em.'

'What is it you want, Stryke?' Pepperdyne asked. 'Information or revenge?'

'There's a lot to be said for revenge.'

'My people have a saying: "If you go out for revenge, build two pyres."'

'I'll build a hundred,' Stryke replied coldly, 'a thousand . . .'

'Make the biggest for Jennesta. But you won't learn where to find her from dead men.'

Stryke slowly lowered his sword. 'Try. But be quick.'

'Thanks. Might be better if you all left us. I think you're making the prisoners nervous.'

Stryke snapped an order and everyone retreated to the other end of the clearing, Haskeer mumbling unhappily as they went. Pepperdyne crouched by the two remaining humans and began some earnest talking.

The band settled down to wait.

Stretched out on the compacted earth of the clearing, Haskeer said to no one in particular, 'How do we know he ain't plotting with 'em?'

'*What?*' Coilla said. 'When did you swap your brains for horse shit? Jode's trying to *help.*'

'Yeah, we know how helpful humans can be.' He looked sharply at Standeven, sitting nearby, making him fidget uneasily.

'You're full of it, Haskeer. You should wise up about who our friends are.'

'Friends, Coilla? Are you trying to tell me that—'

'You're bruising my ears!' Stryke declared. 'Give it a rest, you two.'

Haskeer and Coilla fell into aggrieved silence.

The band quietened down too. Pepperdyne carried on talking with the prisoners.

The orcs were just starting to get restless again when one of the perimeter sentries, Gant, called out to them. The second scouting party had returned.

It was led by Dallog, who had the tyro Pirrak at his side. Wheam walked alone, further back. But what caught everyone's attention was who the scouts had with them; a party of dwarfs, three of them youngsters.

Spurral stood. 'Isn't that Kalgeck? And those kids who got us the map?' She ran towards them, Jup and some of the others close behind.

Kalgeck, with whom she had suffered captivity by the Gatherers, rushed forward to meet her and they embraced. The children, Heeg, Retlarg and Grunnsa, gathered round too.

'Am I glad to see you,' she told them, speaking in Mutual, the universal tongue. 'Are you all right?'

Kalgeck nodded. 'We managed to get to one of our hideaways. It was close though. We ran into some human soldiers, like those over there.' He pointed at the captives with Pepperdyne. 'They would have killed us, except some of that other bunch with all the different races came along. Who were they?'

'We don't know,' Spurral admitted. 'Not exactly.'

'Anyway,' Kalgeck went on, 'they protected us. They sort of sprayed fire at the soldiers and scared them off. Then they told us to run and hide.'

Coilla looked thoughtful. 'Interesting.'

'Heads up,' Jup said. 'Here comes Jode.'

Pepperdyne arrived, clutching a small piece of parchment.

'Luck?' Stryke asked.

'Some. It didn't take much for them to see the light. They know roughly where Jennesta's gone, but not why. One of them drew this.' He handed Stryke the paper.

It was a roughly drawn map, showing a cluster of islands, with one island, set apart from the rest, bearing a cross. The only other thing was a rudimentary set of arrows indicating the compass points.

'So it's east of here,' Stryke said. 'But how far?'

'They weren't sure, but thought it was a couple of days' voyage. So not too far.'

'Why not compare it with the map we've already got?' Spurral suggested. 'The one these kids found for us.'

'Just about to,' Stryke told her. He fished it out of a pocket.

They unfolded it, laid it on the ground and compared the two.

'There,' Pepperdyne said, pointing to one corner.

'Yeah,' Stryke agreed. 'They match, more or less.'

'We know about that island,' Retlarg announced.

'Do you?' Coilla asked. 'How come?' All three children started to clamour. She held up a hand to still them. 'Kalgeck? You know anything about this?'

'Yes. A couple of the elders were with us for a time when we were hiding. We heard them talking about it.'

'What did they say?'

'The humans, those soldiers, they were trying to find out where the island was. They took away some of our tribe to make them tell.'

'What's so special about it?'

'It's where your kind live.'

'What do you mean?'

566

'He means orcs,' Spurral said.

The youngsters all nodded vigorously and chorused agreement.

Pepperdyne, who had picked up enough Mutual to have a sense of what was being said, looked taken aback. 'There are orcs in this world?'

'Why not?' Coilla reckoned. 'There seem to be plenty of races here, just like in Maras-Dantia.'

'This is all about Jennesta's scheme to create a slave orc army, isn't it?' Jup put in.

'Orcs wouldn't let her,' Coilla declared.

'Unless they're a bunch of pussies like that lot in Acurial,' Haskeer contributed.

'How likely is that? They'd wipe the floor with her.'

'Yeah? With her magic—'

'We're wasting time,' Stryke said. 'We've got a destination. Let's get to it.'

Pepperdyne indicated the prisoners. 'What about them?'

'We'll leave 'em to fend for themselves.'

'How'd you feel about that, Kalgeck?' Spurral wanted to know.

'There are parts of the island that are deserted. They can go there. We won't interfere with them if they leave us alone.'

'Fair enough,' Stryke said. 'Now let's get to the ship.'

4

Rather than wait for dawn, Stryke insisted they set sail that evening. There was a crimson sunset as they upped anchor and moved away from the island, promising a torrid following day.

So it proved. Even at dawn it was hot, though a constant, moderate wind gave some relief and kept the sails full. The cabins and cargo holds were stifling, and most of the band preferred the relative comfort of the deck. In scattered pairs and groups, the main topic of whispered conversations was Stryke's treatment of the prisoners. Some backed him, others had doubts. Stryke himself spent most of his time alone at the prow, as though willing the ship onward.

Pepperdyne was amidships, at the wheel. As an islander born and bred, it would normally have been a pleasure, had not Standeven been plaguing him.

'You saw what he did to those soldiers. Didn't that alarm you?'

'Stryke did what he felt he had to do,' Pepperdyne replied, his response measured. 'I can't say I liked it, but—'

'It was the act of a savage.'

'I'd take what you're saying more seriously if you didn't have a cloud over you about that dead orc back in Acurial.'

'How many times do I have to tell you—'

'Yeah, sure.'

'Those two Stryke killed were *human beings*,' Standeven persisted. 'Our kind.'

'And not just a lowly orc, eh?'

'Forget that! My point is that Stryke's the one with the instrumentalities.'

'Here we go again.'

'They're our only way home.'

'And there's no way you're getting them.'

'That's not it. I'm saying is he the best one to be in charge of them?'

Pepperdyne laughed. 'It should be you, is that it?'

'No! But he's unstable. He showed that yesterday.'

'Maybe he is, maybe he isn't. But he's what we've got, whether you like it or not. No way is he going to give them up.'

'Of course he isn't. But I'm thinking that if we spoke to him, reasoned with him, maybe we could get him to take us back home before we get dragged deeper into this madness.'

'You say *he's* unstable then you come up with an idea like that. It's not going to happen, Standeven. Do you really expect him to break off searching for his mate to ferry us home? Not to mention how erratic the stars have been. How could he be sure of *getting* us home? Or of getting himself back here?'

'So you're admitting he can't control them.'

'I'm not sure anybody could. Anyway, I'm not inclined to run out on the band. Not now, when they're trying to find Thirzarr.'

Standeven was puzzled. 'Why?'

'It's called loyalty. A notion you're not familiar with.'

'What about loyalty to Humanity? To *me*.'

'It has to be earned. The band's done that. You haven't.'

'Your trust in these orcs is misplaced. This . . . relationship or whatever it is you're having with Coilla; they're laughing behind your back about it, you know. Those who don't hate you for it, that is. Why don't you stick with your own?'

'I think you just answered that question yourself. For all of what you call their savagery these beings aren't devious like you and most of our race. Whatever you might think, they don't hide their true opinions behind mealy-mouthed words. They speak plain and act out what they feel. I quite like that.'

'And that's your excuse for your disgusting union with one of them, is it?'

'I don't have to explain myself to you or anybody else. And I don't have to listen to this shit. Now clear off.'

'Since when did you get to give orders?'

'I'm the skipper as far as this vessel's concerned, and that makes my word law.' Pepperdyne gave his erstwhile master a flinty look. 'And if that isn't enough for you, I can back it with this.' He took a hand off the wheel and made a fist of it.

Standeven blanched, then, mumbling curses, turned and stamped off. Coilla was coming up the stairs to the wheel as he went down, and he pushed past her wordlessly.

'What was *that* about, Jode?' she asked.

'The usual.'

'Still keen on the stars, eh?'

'He says he isn't.'

'Yeah, right.'

'He said something else.'

'So stop creasing your brow and spit it out.'

'What do you reckon the rest of the band think about . . . us?'

'Do they know?'

'Standeven said they did, and that they're not happy about it.'

'Nobody's said anything to me. Well, apart from Haskeer. But he's always moaning about something, and humans aren't his favourite race.'

'Maybe we should be a little more discreet.'

'Why? What the fuck's it got to do with them?'

'Well, it's not as though our situation's that normal, is it?' He saw her expression and started rowing back. 'Not that there's anything *abnormal* about it, of course. I mean—'

'All right, you can stop digging now. It's rare, yes, but that's no reason for anybody to get sniffy about it. Anyway, Standeven's probably just trying to vex you. Don't let him get under your skin.'

'Expect you're right. But I'd be happier if—'

'Hold it. Here comes Wheam.'

'Damn it. It's busier than a town square on market day up here.'

She favoured him with a smile. 'Give the kid a break. He looks low.'

Wheam trudged up the steps dejectedly.

'Why so glum?' Coilla asked.

'Oh, this and that,' the youth replied.

'Anything in particular?'

'Dallog just chewed me out.'

'Why?'

'He says we haven't got enough drinking water on board, 'cos we left in a rush and didn't load enough, and everybody's drinking more in this heat.'

'How's that your fault?' Pepperdyne said.

'He's not blaming me for it. But he sent me to tell Stryke.' He glanced at their brooding captain at the bow.

'And you're not keen on the job?'

Wheam shook his head.

'Why can't Dallog tell Stryke himself?' Coilla wondered.

'Dunno. He seems to be more involved with the other tyros right now. Well, one; Pirrak.'

'That's his job, isn't it? Looking after you neophytes.'

'S'pose.'

'How low *is* the water?'

'Not enough to get us where we're going, he says.'

'All right. I'll talk to Stryke about it.'

'You will?'

'Sure.'

Wheam broke out in a grin. 'Thanks, Coilla. I was hoping you'd say that.'

'I figured. Now lose yourself while I sort it.'

He went off with a lighter step.

She looked to Pepperdyne. 'Where's the map?'

He hauled it out of a pocket and handed it to her. 'Think you can get Stryke to wear a stopover?'

'Sounds like we've no choice.'

'Rather you than me.'

'He'll see the sense of it.'

'In his present mood?'

'Leave it to me.' She unfolded the map. 'Where are we?'

He leaned over for a look, then pointed. 'Around there.'

'So the nearest place to stop would be . . . here?' She jabbed at a string of islands, two quite large.

Pepperdyne nodded. 'They seem as good as any. Assuming they have water, of course.'

'How far are they?'

'Half a day. Less with a favourable wind.'

'Right.' She waved the map under his nose as she left. 'I'll bring this back.'

'Good luck,' he muttered.

Coilla was aware of the band's eyes on her as she made her way to the prow.

Stryke must have heard her approaching, but he didn't turn or speak.

'Stryke?' she said, then more firmly, '*Stryke.*'

'Come to tongue-lash me about those prisoners?'

'No. That's done.'

'What, then?'

'Something you need to know, and act on.'

He turned to face her, and she saw that he looked haggard. 'What is it?'

Coilla drew a breath. 'There's been a screw-up on the rations.'

'*What?*'

'We left in such a rush—'

'We can do without food for a couple of days.'

'Sure. But it's the water.'

'*Shit.*' His features darkened further. 'Whoever's responsible should get a whipping for this.'

'Give it to yourself.'

'That's close to insolence, Corporal.'

'Maybe. But it's closer to truth. If we made a mess over the provisions it's because you were driving the band too hard.'

'I'd drive it to its bloodied knees when I'm trying to find Thirzarr.'

'When *we're* finding Thirzarr. You seem to have lost sight of what we are. We're the Wolverines. We look out for our own. But we won't get a chance to do that if we die of thirst.'

Stryke mulled over her words. At length he said, 'Where do we get water?'

She showed him the map. 'We're here. The nearest islands are these.'

'When would we get there?'

'Jode reckons not long after noon.'

'Suppose we rationed the water.'

'Dallog wouldn't have raised the alarm on this if he thought that'd work. I know you're frantic about Thirzarr, Stryke, and any delay's a pisser, but we've no option.'

Again he weighed things up. 'Do it. But I don't want to spend any more time there than we have to.'

'Got you.' She jogged back towards the wheelhouse.

They altered course immediately. The winds stayed friendly,

even increasing by a few knots, and they made good time. Not long after the sun passed its zenith they spotted one of the necklace of islands. It was tiny, little more than a rock jutting out of the ocean, and they passed it by. The next two or three were about the same. When they reached the first of the bigger islands it proved almost as barren, and in any event there was nowhere to land, unless they wanted to climb sheer cliffs. A couple more minor islands came into view, and true to form they were tediously small and desolate. Everyone on board started to worry. Stryke paced ominously.

The second large island was a different proposition. Even from a distance they could tell it was verdant, so Pepperdyne steered the ship towards it. Stryke ordered the ship to circle the island, and they found that it, too, was protected by tall cliffs. But not on every side. There was a long stretch of beach, its fine, almost white sand stroked by gentle, foam-topped breakers. The beach stretched to a dense, sun-dappled jungle. Stryke had Pepperdyne take them in.

They dropped anchor as near to the shore as they could. The three boats their stolen goblin ship carried were unlashed and lowered. Stryke decided on leaving just a skeleton watch and taking most of the band as the landing party. He wanted a quick excursion, and the more hands the better. Standeven was one of those left on board, to his and everyone else's relief, and the rest of the watch were told to keep an eye on him.

Before setting out, Stryke told Haskeer to hail the island.

'Why warn 'em?'

'Because we've come peaceably. If anything lives here I want them to know that.'

'Our ship's done a pretty good job of announcing us anyway,' Jup said.

'I still want to make ourselves known,' Stryke insisted. 'Do it, Haskeer.'

'Why me?'

'You've got the biggest mouth,' Jup told him.

Haskeer glared at him, then cupped his hands and bellowed.

Stryke got him to repeat several times. There was no response.

'We saw no signs of habitation, and there are no ships. It's got to be deserted,' Jup argued.

'Probably,' Stryke agreed. 'But we won't take any chances. There'll be three search parties. Haskeer, you lead one; and you,

Jup. I'll take the third. We'll decide the groups once we hit the beach. Now move.'

They swarmed over the side and filled the boats.

The trip was brief, and soon they were splashing ashore through the shallow, crystal-clear water, colourful fish darting from their path. On the beach, Stryke addressed them.

'Our only job is to fill those.' He pointed at the heap of canteens and cow-gut sacs they'd brought. 'You know what to do; look for natural springs or anywhere that might catch rainwater. And hurry. I don't want us lingering here or—'

Jup was signalling him with one hand and pressing a finger to his lips with the other. He pointed at the jungle. The whole band quietened and looked that way.

They stood in silence for some time, scanning the greenery. It got to the point where they began to think it was a false alarm. Then there was movement in the foliage. Restricted to just one or two places, making it unlikely to be the wind, it was accompanied by a rustling and the snap of dry twigs.

In the undergrowth there was the briefest flash of what appeared to be a pair of vividly red eyes.

'Looks like we're not alone after all,' Coilla said, reaching for her blade.

5

'Spread out!' Stryke bawled. 'And have your weapons ready!'

The band fanned out, swords, axes and spears in hand.

'Do we go in?' Haskeer asked, nodding at the area of jungle where they'd seen movement.

'No,' Stryke decided. 'If they're friendly they'll come to us. If they're not, it's a trap.'

'We can't stay here for ever,' Coilla said.

'I know that,' Stryke came back irritably.

Minutes passed. Nothing happened.

Pepperdyne broke the silence. 'Whatever's in there, how likely are they to come out when we're standing here fully armed?'

Spurral nodded. 'Good point.'

'Yeah,' Jup agreed, 'perhaps if we looked a little less confrontational . . .'

'Stryke?' Coilla said.

He sighed. 'All right, stand down. But *stay alert.*'

The band relaxed, or at least made a show of it. Some sat, or leaned on their axes, though their eyes stayed fixed on the jungle.

More time passed.

Stryke grew increasingly restless, and finally declared, 'I can't be doing with this.'

'And?' Coilla said.

'I'm thinking we should go in and deal with whatever we find, friendly or otherwise.'

'Just say the word, chief,' Jup replied.

Stryke took up his sword again. 'Right. Forget groups; we're going in mob-handed. Anything tries to stop us, we down 'em.'

The band brightened. They were keen to relieve their frustrations with a fight.

"bout time,' Haskeer mouthed, speaking for them all.

575

Stryke at their head, the band moved towards the tree-line.

'*Hold it!*' Dallog yelled. 'Look!'

A figure was emerging from the jungle. It walked upright and was taller than most of the orcs. As it came nearer its features were revealed. From the waist upwards it resembled a human, albeit with a thin covering of dark fur. Below the waist it had legs resembling a goat's, with a thicker, gingery pelt, that ended in hooves. It had a long tail, similar to some kind of monkey. The creature's beard, like the hair on its head, was black, curly and luxuriant. A small pair of horns, again like a goat's, protruded from just above the hairline. Its face was close to a human's, except for small, upswept ears and eyes with intensely red orbs.

'What the hell is *that*?' Pepperdyne whispered.

'A faun,' Coilla explained. 'Back in Maras-Dantia they're forest-dwellers.'

'Are they friendly?'

'We've not had a lot to do with them. Though we've killed a few in our time.'

'I suppose that's not having a lot to do with them.'

The faun approached boldly, seeming undaunted by the sight of a heavily armed orc warband accompanied by dwarfs and a human. His step was certain, and he wore an expression that could have been called imperious. He bore no obvious weapons.

Stryke went forward, raised an open hand and addressed the faun in Mutual. 'We're here in peace. We mean you no harm.'

'You come well armed for beings with peaceful intent,' the faun replied. There was a commanding edge to his voice, a tone that suggested he was used to being obeyed.

'It's a violent world. But you're right.' He made a gesture and the band put away their weapons. Though more than a few did it with reluctance.

'Who are you?' the faun asked.

'I'm Stryke, and this is my . . . these are my companions, the Wolverines.'

'I am Levanda. If you really are here in peace, welcome.' He looked them over, his gaze lingering on Jup, Spurral and Pepperdyne. 'If I may say so, you seem rather broad-minded in your choice of . . . companions.'

'We like to get on with everybody,' Stryke replied, straight-faced.

'Why are you here?'

'We need water. Nothing more.'

'Of course.'

'We'll trade for it if—'

Levanda waved the offer aside. 'Your presence is payment enough.'

From behind her hand, Spurral said to Jup, 'Bit of an old smoothie, isn't he?'

'You will honour me by accepting our hospitality,' Levanda told Stryke, 'for which the fauns are renowned.'

'Thanks, but we've pressing business elsewhere. So just the water. No offence.'

'My clan will be disappointed. We put great value on visitors. Come.' He turned and made for the jungle.

Exchanging glances, the warband followed.

It was much cooler, and a lot darker, when they entered the greenery. At first, trailing the faun, they had little sense of where they were heading, beyond it being deeper into the tangle. But at length they met a well-trod path and the going became a mite easier. The path meandered, veering round large clumps of bushes, dipping through gullies and over vegetation-smothered hillocks. Eventually it calmed and widened, and led them to an open space. This housed dozens of sturdy, mature trees, and the trees cradled dwellings. They looked a little like huts that had somehow been hurled and caught in the trees' embrace. A mixture of timber, wattle and wicker, many of their frontages had loggias. There were fauns clustered on these, looking down.

More were in the clearing below. They were going about their daily occasions; preparing food, tending several fires in pits, or just lounging and passing time. One sat on a stump playing softly on a bone flute. Every so often fauns scampered up and down stout ropes dangling from the trees. Despite their ungainly physiques, they did it with remarkable ease.

As the band arrived, the fauns stopped whatever they were doing and stared.

Looking around, Pepperdyne said, 'I can't see any women. Or do they all have beards too?'

577

Coilla stifled a giggle. 'There aren't any females.'

'What, they hide them?'

'No, there are no female fauns. That's how it was in Maras-Dantia anyway.'

'No females? How do they—'

'It's said they breed with nymphs. But they only come together when they need to. So I guess there's an island in these parts where nymphs live.'

'You saw those other islands. Nothing lived on them.'

'Well, further away then.'

'Yet these fauns don't seem to have ships, or even boats. We didn't see any.'

'Maybe the nymphs come to *them*. Does it matter?'

'I suppose not.'

The piping of the flute tailed off as the band halted. There were many fauns present, but they kept their distance, standing all around. They were silent.

'Where's the renowned hospitality?' Jup mumbled.

'Where's the *water*?' Spurral said.

Stryke echoed that. 'If you'll just show us to your spring, Levanda, we'll be on our way.'

'Are you sure I can't press you to food and drink?' the faun replied.

'Like I said, we're in a hurry.'

'Pity. It could be your last chance for a while.'

There was a smattering of laughter from the fauns surrounding them.

'What do you mean?'

'We like to fatten up the merchandise.'

More laughter, and louder.

'We've no time for jests.' Stryke's anger was rising.

'Oh, this is no joke. Not for you, anyway.'

'So what the hell is it?'

'Trade. With his kind.' He nodded at Pepperdyne. 'Gatherers.'

Given recent events that was particularly inflaming to Stryke, and to Jup and Spurral.

'*What?*' Stryke grated.

'The Gatherers bring us nymphs in exchange for whatever

beings fetch up on our shores. Your race is a valuable commodity; we'll get a good price. All you have to do is surrender.'

Again, Haskeer spoke for them all. 'You can kiss our arses, goat breath.'

'We know you to be a belligerent race, but you can see that you're outnumbered.' He pointed at Haskeer. 'Throw down your weapons, or we'll disarm you.'

'We do the disarming,' Stryke told him. In one smooth, rapid movement his sword was out and swinging.

The blade sliced through Levanda's outstretched arm. He screamed, staggered back and sank to his knees, blood gushing from the wound. His severed limb lay twitching wetly on the ground.

There was a split second of shocked immobility on the part of the fauns. Enough time for the Wolverines to draw their weapons.

Then all hell broke out.

Producing hidden blades, the fauns rushed in on all sides, and the band spun to meet them.

It wasn't the orc way to stand and wait for the tide to hit, and Stryke was the first to move. He charged at the oncoming wave, sword and long-bladed dagger in his hands, a roar in his throat. And there was no fancy swordplay or mannerly rules when he met the foe. His only aim was carnage and he dealt in it wholesale.

Under his onslaught a faun collapsed with a split skull, and the next took steel to his gut. Advancing in unison, a trio tried to bring Stryke down. He dispatched the first with ease, slashing his neck with a vicious blow. The second he came at low, hamstringing him; and the third succumbed to a thrust to his chest. Vaulting over their bodies, Stryke set about another opponent.

The rest of the band weren't idle. Coilla employed the store of snub-nosed blades she kept in her arm sheaths. Confirming her status as the best knife-thrower in the band, her first couple of lobs were true, striking a faun square between its eyes and another in the windpipe. Her third effort merely wounded, though grievously. Then the enemy were too close for throwing knives and she switched to her sword.

Pepperdyne fought beside her, their blades expertly carving flesh as the fauns kept coming. Wrenching his sword free from a foe's innards and spinning to face the next, he caught a glimpse of

Haskeer. He had a hatchet in one hand and Levanda's amputated arm in the other, which he was using to bludgeon a particularly muscular adversary. Sprawled in a crimson pool, Levanda himself looked on, his expression a mixture of agony and open-mouthed amazement.

As was their practice, Jup and Spurral worked as a team. Favouring his staff, Jup cracked heads adroitly, or used it to tumble opponents, bringing them within range of Spurral's wickedly keen pair of knives. In unison, the dwarfs penetrated deep into the fauns' ranks, leaving a trail of dead and injured in their wake.

The new recruits had also got into the habit of fighting together, like a small band within the band, less able but improving with every engagement. Wheam, Keick, Pirrak, Harlgo and Chuss, steered by Dallog, gave a good account of themselves, valour making up for their lack of experience.

No sooner had the Wolverines bettered something like half of their attackers than a further group emerged from the jungle. Armed with spears and battleaxes they swept towards the fray. The veteran band members needed no order to react. Those who could, peeled off from the battle and headed for the fresh incomers; Seafe, Gleadeg, Prooq, Gant, Reafdaw, Nep and Breggin among them.

Leaving Pepperdyne to deliver a death thrust to a wounded faun, Coilla caught up with Stryke. He stood over his latest kill, eyeing a bunch of circling foes.

'Need a hand?' she asked.

He gave her a sidelong glance and she saw that he was in a killing state, an almost dream-like reverie that came on when the bloodlust took hold. It was something she knew and respected.

No words were necessary. Together, they advanced. One of the fauns who had been holding back warily lost his nerve and fled. It was enough to trigger the others. They turned and ran, and it had a knock-on effect. Those fauns still standing began to withdraw.

'I think they've broken,' Coilla said.

Stryke was coming to himself. The crazed look was leaving his eyes. 'Maybe. But we have to—'

There was a high-pitched whistling sound. Something hit the ground close by.

'Archers!' Coilla yelled.

Several more arrows winged from the tree houses, peppering the sward.

'*Everybody down!*' Stryke bellowed.

Those of the band who weren't still actively engaged with the enemy dived for whatever cover they could find. Several, including Stryke and Coilla, used faun corpses for shelter, meagre protection as that was.

Band members armed with bows, principally Reafdaw, Eldo, Zoda and Finje, immediately began returning fire.

The advantage wasn't entirely with the faun archers. They had to avoid hitting their own kind remaining below. The orcs had no such restraint.

A faun was struck and fell, drawing a ragged cheer from the orcs. Seconds later another plunged to earth.

'We'll never get 'em all at this rate,' Coilla complained. 'They could keep us pinned here till doomsday.'

Arrows continued to rain down.

There were shouts behind them. Stryke and Coilla looked to their rear. An orc had taken an arrow.

'Can you make out who it is?' Stryke said.

'One of the tyros,' Coilla told him. 'I think it's Chuss. But it looks like it's just his arm.'

'And who the hell's *that?*'

A Wolverine was dashing towards Chuss. He was running a zigzag path, trying to avoid the arrows zinging all around him, and it was hard to make out who he was.

'It's another newbie,' Coilla realised. 'Harlgo.'

'*Take cover!*' Stryke shouted at him. '*Get down, Harlgo!*'

Too late. An arrow pierced Harglo between his shoulder-blades. The impact threw him off his stride but he kept going. Slowing, his stride uncertain like a drunk's, he managed a few more steps before a second arrow struck the back of his neck. He went down, a dead weight. It was the fauns turn to cheer.

'*Shit!*' Coilla hissed.

'*Burn 'em!*' Stryke hollered. '*Burn 'em out!*'

The Wolverine archers were prepared. Their kit included bolts wrapped with tarred cloth. Quickly striking sparks, they began igniting them. In seconds, flaming arrows zipped towards the tree houses.

It must have been some time since rain, because the dwellings were tinder dry, as was the foliage they nestled amongst. The burning arrows hit the houses' walls, and passed through open doors and windows. Fires instantly broke out.

Even as the houses blazed the fauns carried on showering arrows on their tormentors. The orcs likewise continued sending up their fire-tipped bolts. Soon almost all the lofty huts were alight and the fauns were forced to bail out. Some climbed down, braving orc shafts. Others fell, in many cases burning and shrieking.

It was the final blow for the surviving fauns in the clearing. Those who were capable fled into the jungle, chased off by vengeful band members.

But the Wolverines' triumph was tempered.

Stryke and Coilla stood and jogged to Harglo. He was surrounded by a group of kneeling comrades. Dallog was there, wearing a grim expression, and as they arrived he looked up and shook his head. As they suspected, Chuss' wound was nasty but in no way life-threatening. It made the loss of Harlgo bitterly ironic.

Stryke came away from the huddle and headed for Levanda, who still lay where he fell. A number of the band tagged along, Jup and Spurral among them.

They gathered around the faun chief. He was conscious, but had lost a lot of blood, and his eyes were growing dull.

Spurral pushed her way to the front and gazed down at him. 'You know the joke?' she said. 'There are no Gatherers anymore.' Then she took her blade and plunged it into his heart.

No one begrudged her. But Haskeer looked disappointed at being cheated out of the act himself. He made do with spitting on the corpse.

'Yeah,' he said, wiping the back of a hand across his mouth. 'Don't mess with orcs, shithead.'

6

'I say it's *your* fault,' Haskeer contended, aggressively jabbing Dallog's chest.

'And how do you work *that* out?'

'You're supposed to be looking after these rookies, ain't you?'

'That's the job Stryke gave me, yes, but—'

'Not doing it too well, are you?' He pointed to Harglo's body.

'Not fair,' Dallog countered, trying to contain his own fury. 'We were in a battle, and that means casualties.'

'*Battle?* That was no battle, it was a skirmish. Not that you'd know the difference. You're wet behind the ears for all your great age.'

Half of the band looked on, waiting for a fight.

'We Ceragan orcs might be new,' Dallog said, 'but we've paid our dues on this mission. Harglo isn't the first we've lost, remember. There was Yunst and Ignar too.'

'Proves they weren't up to it!' Haskeer came back triumphantly. 'And talking of remembering, *we* lost Liffin. All 'cos of you, and him.' He nodded Wheam's way. The youth looked at his feet, shamefaced. 'But I blame you more. You should have known better.'

'You're staining Harglo's name. He was brave.'

'Stupid, more like.'

'I resent that.'

'Resent it all you want.'

'Take it back!'

Haskeer balled his fists and leaned in menacingly. 'Make me.'

Dallog raised his own hands. 'Any time.'

At that point Stryke arrived and roughly separated them. 'What the fuck's the matter with you two?' he demanded. 'I turn my back and in no time—'

'Just a few home truths,' Haskeer told him.

'If there's any truth telling to be done, I do it, Sergeant!'

'I'm just saying—'

'You say too much. I don't care what your beef is, either of you. All I'm interested in is getting out of here and finding Thirzarr. If that's too much for you both, I'll leave you here to fend for yourselves.'

They knew he meant it, and that seemed to sober them.

Noskaa and Vobe trotted up.

'We found the spring, Captain,' Vobe reported, 'a couple, in fact. We got all the water we needed, and the fauns kept well away.'

Noskaa grinned. 'Yeah, they're shy of us now, and they've enough to do fighting the fires.'

'Good work,' Stryke said. He turned to Dallog. 'How's Chuss?'

'He'll be fine,' the corporal answered sullenly.

'Any other casualties?'

'Only minor.'

'Right, we're leaving.'

'What about Harglo?'

'We haven't got time for a proper send-off for him. Sorry.'

'We're not going to leave him here?'

'Sometimes, when an orc dies in the field, we've no choice.'

'It wouldn't take long to build a pyre. If we all—'

'No.'

'I've got to face his kin when we get back, Stryke, *if* we get back, and I don't relish having to tell them we couldn't dispatch him decently with a few words said.'

'I feel as bad about it as you do, but we've got to move,' Stryke insisted.

'Do you?' There was an edge to Dallog's voice.

'Can I suggest something?' Pepperdyne said. All heads turned his way, more than a few looking resentful at a human apparently interfering in something so orcish. 'Why don't we take Harglo with us and bury him at sea? That'd give you time to do it properly and have whatever sort of service you want. It's what my people used to do.'

'We're not your people,' Dallog muttered.

Stryke nodded. 'All right, we'll do it.'

'We can't,' Dallog protested. 'An orc should go out of the world in flame, or at least be buried deep. Not flung into the sea like some—'

'It's that or we leave him.'

For a moment it looked as though Dallog would keep arguing. Instead he replied, 'Whatever you say, Captain.'

They loaded the water and caught the tide. The winds were fair and they made good progress. Even from afar, tall columns of black smoke could be seen rising from the fauns' island.

When they were well under way they turned their attention to Harglo. Dallog insisted on taking care of everything. As keeper of the band's standard he carried spare pennants. A couple were stitched together and used as a shroud, tightly bound.

The band gathered on deck. As the mate of a Wolverine, there was no objection to Spurral being present. But Stryke worried that having humans there could antagonise the band. So Pepperdyne stayed up on the bridge, along with Standeven, although they could hear what was said.

Dallog carried on the tradition started by his dead predecessor, Alfray, and conducted the ceremony. Given the respect for Alfray, and the hostility some felt towards the new intake, that didn't please everybody; particularly Haskeer, who stayed sour faced throughout.

After saying something about Harglo's character, qualities and clan background, Dallog evoked the Tetrad, the orcs' quartet of principal deities, commonly known as the Square. The young recruit's spirit was commended to Wystendel, god of comradeship, Neaphetar, god of war, Aik, god of wine, and Zeenoth, goddess of fornication. Then the corpse, sliding from a tilted plank, was consigned to the depths.

Normally this would have been followed by the taking of excessive amounts of wine and pellucid, accompanied by overblown stories about the deceased's exploits and the singing of heroic songs. But given the circumstances this was deferred to a later date. Wheam announced that he was composing an epic ballad honouring Harglo, the performance of which was also deferred, to a date to be decided.

When it was over, and the band had scattered to their duties, Stryke took Dallog aside.

'That was done well,' he said.

'Not well enough for some in the band, I think,' Dallog replied frostily.

'It's true you're not Alfray, and a few begrudge that. But you're your own orc and you did as good a job as he would have, in your way.'

'The belief seems to be that I don't care for my charges as well as he did.'

'Don't listen to Haskeer. Harglo's death wasn't your fault. None of them were.'

'No. Yet I feel liable. It seems . . . unjust that they should pass so young when I've reached the years I have.'

'Call it fate, or the whim of the gods. We all live in the Reaper's shadow.'

'But think how good it would be if we didn't.' There was a spark of real passion in the corporal's eyes. 'If we could turn back the years and cheat death . . .'

'It comes to us all, Dallog, sooner or later.'

'It's unfair, this rapid piling on of time. One instant you're young and strong, the next near dotage. Least, that's the way it feels.'

'Most of us orcs don't have the luxury of ageing, living as we do. Born as fighters, despised, all hands against us. A short life's the likely outcome. You've survived. Count yourself lucky in that regard.'

'But if only—' He had been in a kind of reverie as he spoke, now he came out of it. 'Forgive an old one's rambling, Stryke. You've got enough on your platter worrying about Thirzarr without my musings.'

'Anybody would think you had one foot in the pyre. There's life in you yet.'

Dallog gave a thin smile and nodded, and without further word they parted.

At the other end of the ship another meeting was taking place. Coilla had made it her business to seek out the tyros, to offer them condolence on the loss of their comrade. Only Pirrak had eluded her, and now she found him. He was at the rail, staring out to sea.

'Pirrak?'

He started and spun to face her, and he seemed alarmed. 'Corporal?'

'Steady. You look as jumpy as a frog on a hot griddle. You all right?'

'I'm . . . yes, I'm fine. I was just . . . You startled me.'

'You're pale.'

'Am I?' He touched a hand to his cheek, self-consciously.

'Thinking about Harglo?'

'Harglo. Yes. Yes, he was on my mind.'

'Did you know him long, back in Ceragan?'

'Since we were hatchlings.'

'That makes it harder.'

Pirrak nodded.

'You're young,' Coilla went on, 'and you've not seen as much action as the rest of us. You'll . . . well, you won't get used to losing a comrade but you'll learn to accept it. It's one of the costs of what we do. Of who we are.'

'That's what Dallog says.'

'He's right. And you can take some comfort from the way Harglo died. He was trying to help Chuss. That showed good fellowship. He was brave.'

'Yes. Brave.'

'Look, if you ever need anybody to talk to—'

'Yes, thanks. I'm all right. Really.'

'Well, take it easy.'

Coilla turned and left him, but couldn't help noticing that he went straight to Dallog, further along the deck.

She climbed the stairs to the wheel, and Pepperdyne. Standeven had gone off to fill a corner somewhere.

'You look thoughtful,' Pepperdyne said.

'I was just talking to Pirrak. He was really tense.'

'Can you blame him? He's a rookie, and going through a lot.'

'Yeah, s'pose. But sometimes I wonder about the tyros. Like, whether they're going to hold it together.'

'They have so far. And they've got Dallog. He seems grounded.'

'Hmm. I guess things are a bit fraught.'

'Yeah, we're all on edge.'

'You too?'

'Not as long as you're here to protect me.'

She smiled. 'Fool.'

Mid-morning of the next day they passed a group of mountainous islands. They were on the chart Stryke had and came as no surprise. What was unexpected were the three ships with black sails that came round the headland of the last island and followed them.

Orbon was at the wheel of the orcs' ship. He was one of the privates who had proved to have some talent for steering, and Pepperdyne was training him as a relief. Pepperdyne himself was down on the deck with the rest of the band.

'They look just like this ship,' he reckoned, shading his eyes with a hand.

'Goblins?' Jup said.

'A lot of them got killed when the band freed those kelpies,' Spurral reminded them. 'Could be more, out for revenge.'

'Maybe they're not goblins,' Jup suggested.

'They're goblin ships, ain't they?' Haskeer retorted.

'*We're* on a goblin ship. That doesn't make us goblins, does it?'

'Could it be that Pelli Madayar's bunch again? Coilla wondered.

'Well, I say we stop and face the bastards,' Haskeer declared. 'Whoever they are.'

'No way,' Stryke told him.

'You reckon this could be innocent, Stryke?' Coilla asked.

'Plenty of ships in this world.'

'Yeah, but *goblins* . . .'

'We keep going.'

'So what we going to do; lead them to our destination?'

'We'll deal with it.'

'But—'

'Fuck the goblins. Or whoever it is. All I care about is getting where we're going.' He looked to Pepperdyne. 'Can we have more speed?'

'We're going just about as fast as we can now.'

'Try.'

'I'll get up to Orbon and see what we can do.' He made for the stairs.

'I can't believe we're running from a fight,' Haskeer mumbled disgustedly.

Pepperdyne applied his skills and they did manage to put on a few more knots. Steadily, they increased their lead over the trio of ships. By the middle of the afternoon they had fallen back and out of sight.

Some time later the Wolverines came across a pair of islands. Again, they were marked on their map, and they were the largest islands they'd seen so far in this world. One was lush, with golden beaches. The other was its complete opposite; rocky and stark, its shoreline nothing but shale. The islands were close together, separated by a narrow channel.

'You sure we have to go between them?' Stryke asked.

'According to the map this area's strewn with reefs,' Pepperdyne explained, 'except for this strait. Otherwise we'd have to make a big detour.'

They had to slow down to navigate the channel safely. No sooner had they entered when a grunt on lookout in the rigging began to shout. He pointed to the verdant island, on their starboard side. A large number of canoes were coming out to them.

That drew most of the band to the rail, straining to see. Given recent events, they assumed hostility.

'Can anybody make out who they are?' Stryke said.

'Think so,' Jup replied, squinting. 'They look like . . . elves.'

'Yeah,' Spurral confirmed, 'you're right.'

'They haven't given us trouble before,' Coilla said.

'Really?' Stryke replied. 'What about Pelli Madayar?'

'Back in Maras-Dantia, I meant.'

'Who knows how they are here? This place is full of surprises.'

'They don't *look* hostile.'

'I don't care. We're not taking any chances.'

'The speed we're travelling we can't stop them reaching us,' Pepperdyne told him.

'And we really can't go faster?'

'Too risky in a strait this tight.'

'Prepare to repel boarders, then.'

The band took up their weapons and watched as the armada of canoes approached.

When they arrived, the boats kept up with the slow-moving ship without too much trouble. They were numerous and carried many elves, along with heaps of trinkets, craftworks and general bric-a-brac.

'Do they want to trade?' Coilla wondered.

Jup shrugged. 'Dunno. But they've fallen unusually quiet for traders.'

He was right. The hubbub to be expected from hawkers who infested ports was absent. The elves had become muted as soon as they saw that the ship was crewed by orcs. Now most of them simply sat and stared. They seemed bewildered.

One of the boats was much bigger and more ornate than the others, resembling river barges the Wolverines had seen on their travels. Rowers were seated at the bow end. The stern held an elevated platform covered by a gold and blue fabric canopy. On the platform was a seat, and in it sat an elf of mature years, dressed a little more finely than the rest. Behind him stood a much younger elf controlling the rudder. With some difficulty this boat was manoeuvred until it lay alongside the orcs' ship.

'Stay sharp,' Stryke warned the band. 'This could be a ruse.'

'They don't look like ambushers,' Jup said, 'what with all that junk they're carrying, and no sign of weapons.'

'Anything's possible in this place.' He had ordered the archers to nock their bows; now he signalled them to stand ready. Then he hailed the boat. *'Who are you?'*

The regal-looking elf called back, *'I was about to ask the same question!'*

'Identify yourself!' Stryke repeated.

'Mallas Sahro! I'm the Elder of this clan!' He indicated the bobbing flotilla with a sweep of his slender hand. *'And you?'*

'Captain Stryke of the Wolverines!'

'You're orcs!'

'Obviously!'

'Then I confess to being confused!'

Stryke was puzzled by the exchange. *'Explain!'*

'We thought you were goblins!'

'You were expecting goblins?'

'Yes!' He pointed to the boats' cargoes. *'This is tribute for them!'*

'Do you think he means those three ships we saw?' Coilla asked.

'I don't know,' Stryke confessed. He yelled again. *'There are no goblins on this ship!'*

'I see that! It seems we are again mistaken!'

'Again?'

'You're not the first of your kind we've seen lately!'

'What do you mean? When?'

'Yesterday! Ships passed with humans on board, and an orc!'

Stryke's heart took a leap. He had to force himself to ask the question. *'Was it . . . a female?'*

'Yes! We glimpsed her standing on deck!'

'Could it be?' Coilla whispered.

'We need to talk!' Stryke called. *'Will you come aboard?'*

'I will not set foot on a goblin ship!'

'I said there are no goblins here!'

'It's taboo!'

'Shit,' Stryke hissed. *'This bellowing at each other is no good! How can we parley?'*

Mallas Sahro considered that. *'Come ashore! We'll meet on the beach!'*

'Careful,' Haskeer warned. 'Might be a trap.'

Stryke ignored him. *'All right, we'll trust you!'*

'As we will you! I return, you follow!' He signalled his rowers and the boat pulled away. All the canoes did likewise and headed back to the island.

'They seem harmless enough,' Coilla said as they watched them leave.

'So did the fauns,' Jup reminded her.

'We'll take no chances,' Stryke assured them. 'Bring us to a halt, Pepperdyne.'

'Are you sure? I thought we were in a hurry.'

'We are. But if these elves can tell us anything to speed our journey I want to hear it. Now do as you're told.'

The anchor was dropped and the sails taken up.

Stryke decided to leave Dallog and the tyros on board to guard the ship. The elderly corporal looked as though he thought this might be some kind of slight, but said nothing. Not knowing how the elves would react to humans, bearing in mind the Gatherers' reputation, Pepperdyne and Standeven were left behind too. Figuring dwarfs would probably be acceptable, Stryke included Jup and Spurral in the landing party. By the time all that was sorted out the elves had got back to their island. The band piled into their three boats and followed.

Mallas Sahro was waiting for them on the beach, seated in his throne-like chair. He had only a couple of functionaries or servants with him. The rest of his clan had pulled well back, to the tree-line, where they sat watching. None of them seemed to have weapons. Stryke took that as a promising sign of good faith.

The Elder greeted them with, 'You come well armed for talking.'

'Where have we heard that before?' Coilla whispered.

'We're always armed,' Stryke said, and tried to reassure him by adding, 'To us it's like the fine jewellery your clan wears.'

Mallas Sahro was indeed bedecked with rings, bracelets and necklaces, all fashioned from silver, though tastefully simple in design. From his expression he was less than convinced by the comparison, but replied, 'Very well.'

'I should tell you that we've dealt with the elven folk before, and they've had no cause to regret it.'

'And we know the orcs, for all your fearsome nature, to be honourable and fair.'

'Yeah, we'll kill anybody,' Haskeer muttered.

The elf raised his thin eyebrows.

'Don't mind him,' Stryke said, giving Haskeer a murderous sidelong glance, 'he's got an odd sense of humour. *How* do you come to know about our race?'

Mallas Sahro seemed puzzled by the question. 'The same way you know ours, I suspect. This is a world of many races, and many meetings.'

'Of course.' He saw no point in explaining that the Wolverines were not of this world. The Elder would probably think him insane. 'What concerns us is the orc you saw yesterday.'

'The female.'

'Yes. What did she look like?'

'We only had the briefest glimpse. She was tall, and straight, and her hair was like flame. I can't tell you more.'

'It could be Thirzarr, couldn't it, Stryke?' Coilla said.

'Perhaps. And you say she was with humans, Elder?'

'Yes.'

'Did you see another female with them? One of . . . unusual appearance?'

'No. But we did not linger too long near those ships. You see, we made the same error as we did with you today.' A troubled look came to his face. 'We thought it was *him*.'

'Who?'

'Gleaton-Rouk. A goblin with command of dark magic, and a nature utterly ruthless. More than once we've suffered his wrath.'

'That's who the tribute was for?'

'Yes. We're traders, not fighters. We make things, like this jewellery you admired. There are silver seams here and we mine them. The goblins have no such skills, or the patience to learn them. They only *take*. Their talents lie in cruelty and destruction, and we pay tribute to keep them from our door.'

'Yeah, we've encountered goblins before,' Coilla said.

'With respect,' the elf told her, 'I think even the formidable orcs would find Gleaton-Rouk a daunting foe.'

'So when you saw our ship you thought it was him,' Stryke reasoned.

'Yes. That and the fact that he's due.'

There was a commotion from the crowd of elves at the rear of the beach. They were pointing out to sea.

Three black sails had appeared on the horizon.

7

There was something close to panic on the elves' island. But the populace wasn't disappearing into the jungle; they were running down the beach towards their boats.

'What's happening?' Stryke said as they streamed past.

'We must meet them with the tribute!' Mallas Sahro replied.

'Or what?'

The Elder seemed not to understand. 'I thought I made that clear.'

'This Gleaton-Rouk's going to cut up rough.'

'To say the least!' The elf was agitated. 'He'll ruin our crops, burn our homes, put us to the sword!'

'Why?'

'*Why?*'

'Because he's threatened to, right?'

'Yes. And he's punished us in the past. Several of my clan have been killed by him.'

'That's tough, but it's a just few. He hasn't killed you all or burnt you out.'

'No, because we pay the tribute!'

'And if you didn't, or offered less, what would he do?'

Mallas Sahro was at a loss for an answer. 'As I said, he would kill us and . . .'

'Wrong,' Stryke said. 'If you were wiped out he'd have no tribute, no silver. Why should he do that? Can't you see what's going on here? He kills a few to keep you in line. The rest's bluster.'

The Elder threw up his hands. 'But what else can we do?'

'Ever thought of defying him?'

'We're not warriors!'

'We are.'

'This ain't our affair, Stryke,' Haskeer said.

'I reckon it could be. Remember what Spurral here said earlier, about them maybe being out for revenge on account of what we did to those goblin slavers. More I think about it, the more sense it makes.'

'I thought you wanted to waste no more time.'

'My hunch is we won't have the choice. And you were right, Coilla, about leading them to where we're going. We don't want that.'

Haskeer snorted, 'Oh *come on*, Stryke.'

'You're not up for a fight, Haskeer? *You?*'

'Well . . .'

'Please,' Mallas Sahro implored, 'I must go!'

Stryke grabbed his arm. 'You could put a stop to this now.'

'It's easy for you to say. We have to live here.'

'Living in fear isn't living.'

'And we're not keen on tyrants,' Coilla added, warming to the prospect.

'You're asking me to put my folk at risk,' the elf protested.

'I'm asking you to free them. With our help.'

'Those ships are moving at a hell of a lick,' Spurral observed.

They were much nearer than they should have been since the band last looked. Their black sails billowed fit to split.

'It's magic,' the Elder said. 'I told you he commanded powerful sorcery. Even the wind obeys him.'

'Don't you elves have magic too?' Coilla asked.

'Yes, but on a different scale. Ours is healing, benign, protective.'

'So use it to defend your clan and leave the fighting to us.'

'I don't know . . .' His eyes were darting to the shoreline. Most of the elves were with their boats now, obviously anxious, waiting for his order to set off.

'Does Gleaton-Rouk normally come in three ships?' Stryke wondered.

'What?' The Elder dragged his gaze back to him. 'Oh. Er, no. Usually just one. We thought yesterday was an exception, when we saw the female of your kind. Then today, when you—'

'Right. I've a hunch they've come in force because of us.'

'You?'

'They feel they owe us a debt. Of blood. Well, you going to make a stand?'

'You can't fight him. He has exceptional skills.'

Stryke slapped his sheathed sword. 'So do we.'

'I'm sorry. I appreciate what you're saying, but I can't take the risk. I have to think of my clan.' Head low, as though in shame, he hurried off accompanied by his keepers.

'You gave it your best shot,' Haskeer said. 'Let's get out of here'.

'I meant it when I said we've no choice. You think they're just going to let us sail away?'

'Not to mention that we can't leave these elves at the goblins' mercy,' Coilla added.

'What's more important to you, Stryke,' Haskeer rumbled, 'these elves or Thirzarr?'

'I'd knock you down for that if I didn't know you said it because you're an idiot. I figure it *was* Thirzarr the elves saw yesterday. If Jennesta's kept her alive this long there's a chance she'll survive longer. But before we can find out we have to get through this.'

Haskeer had nothing else to say.

They watched as the Elder's boat went out, surrounded by his clan's many canoes. The trio of goblin ships was near enough that figures could be seen on their decks.

'So what do we do?' Jup said.

'If I'm wrong,' Stryke told him, 'the tribute gets handed over and the goblins leave. If I'm right, then we do what we're best at.'

They looked on as the goblin ships drew nearer and the elves' boats headed for them. Then things took an unexpected turn. Manoeuvring nimbly, despite the narrowness of the channel, one of the ships changed course.

'Should they be doing that?' Spurral said.

'What the hell—' Jup exclaimed.

Without slowing, the two ships carried on towards the elves' motley fleet.

'This doesn't look good,' Coilla said.

The ships ploughed through the swarm of elves' boats. Many were swamped, overturned or shattered. Elves jumped from boats to avoid the oncoming prows. Soon the water was peppered with bobbing heads, wreckage and the debris of tribute. There were shouts and screams from the swimming elves.

Emerging from the chaos, the ships began coming round, to close in on the shore.

'Looks like they're not in the mood for trinkets today,' Jup said.

'It's us they want,' Stryke told him. *'Weapons!'*

The band filled their hands.

'Hey!' Coilla yelled, pointing. 'There!'

They hadn't been paying attention to the third goblin vessel. It was making straight for the orcs' anchored ship.

Those on board had been watching. They saw the pair of goblin ships sail into the elves' boats, sinking or upsetting scores of them, and leaving a trail of wreckage. Now the third ship was coming their way.

Pepperdyne glanced at his companions. Dallog, Wheam, Pirrak, Keick and Chuss; none of them veterans and one nursing a wound. And Standeven, who could be relied on to be useless or worse. So six defenders. He looked to the approaching ship. There were perhaps four times that number of goblins visible on its deck.

As Pepperdyne wasn't a member of the band, and the band operated on military principles, he had no authority. Dallog's rank put him in charge. Pepperdyne had his doubts about the wisdom of that, but rather than waste time arguing he opted for conciliatory.

'How do we handle this, Corporal?' he asked.

'The fewer who get aboard the better.'

'That's what I figured. How many archers we got?'

'Good ones? That'd be Keick and Chuss. But Chuss—'

'Yeah, right.' He glanced at the tyro. Chuss' wound meant his arm was bound and in a sling.

'I'm not too bad with a bow,' Dallog added. 'You?'

'I'm a blade man. But I can use a spear.'

'So me and Keick as archers, Wheam, Pirrak and you with spears. Chuss'll have to do what he can. Luckily it's not his sword arm.'

The goblin ship was coming alongside; no mean feat in so narrow a channel.

'Unless you're going to fight,' Pepperdyne told Standeven sarcastically, 'you'd better hide yourself.'

Standeven nodded, and avoiding the others' eyes, scampered for the hold.

'Here they come!' Dallog shouted.

The goblin ship glided in, its rail no more than a hand's span from the orcs'. A splash sounded as its anchor went down. Goblins were rushing forward with grappling hooks to secure their charge on the Wolverines' ship.

Dallog and Keick loosed arrows. One caught a goblin in the chest, the second found another's windpipe. They kept firing as Pepperdyne, Pirrak and Wheam used their spears to impede the boarding, while Chuss slashed at groping hands and jutting heads.

The first, modest wave of would-be boarders lying dead or wounded, a second dashed to the rail. Mindful of the first wave's fate, most of them carried shields. Now hits were rarer as orc arrows clattered against the shields and spears were deflected. The battle at the rail turned into a slog, and Pepperdyne discarded the spear in favour of his sword and knife. No goblin had set foot on the orcs' ship, but the battle to keep them off was steadily being lost.

The orc archers carried on firing and managed to drop a couple more of the enemy despite their shields. Then an arrow came at them. Not from the mob trying to get aboard but from above. The bolt penetrated the deck close enough to Dallog that its flights brushed his leg. They looked up. A goblin was high in the rigging of the attacking ship, armed with a bow and aiming again. They scattered as his second arrow pierced the deck.

Keick nocked a shaft and sent it up at the sniper. It missed. The arrow carried on and curved in a great arc to disappear over the other side of the goblins' craft. The goblin in the rigging returned fire, and would have struck Keick if Dallog hadn't barged him aside, narrowly avoiding being hit himself. Dallog swiftly took his turn at the goblin archer. His effort was a much wider miss than Keick's, who by then had his own bow drawn. Holding down the urge to let loose immediately, he took time getting his eye in. When he fired, his arrow sped true. It impacted in the goblin's midriff. He hung on grimly but briefly before plunging to his ship's deck with a shrill cry, landing on two of his comrades.

The distraction had taken Dallog and Keick's eyes away from the rail. Now they saw that it was a scrum, with several goblins aboard and more about to follow. They dropped the bows, drew their blades and ran to join the fight.

Because there were so few defenders to repel boarders they were well spaced out along the rail. Which meant Wheam was a good twenty paces from Pirrak, the next in line, and could expect no aid. He thought he needed it. Still clutching his spear, he was pointing it at an advancing goblin. The goblin was armed with an ornate double-headed iron axe and a boiling fury.

The tyro had the benefit of reach, but the goblin had the skill and confidence of a seasoned fighter. As he had been taught, Wheam used his spear to make it as hard as possible for his opponent to properly deploy his weapon. The goblin, his anger stoked by Wheam's determination to keep him at bay, tried to dislodge the spear with wild swings. When they connected, Wheam could feel the transmitted impact in his sweating hands, and struggled to hold on.

The goblin was dealing blows with the axe's flat, the better to knock the spear aside. Now he deftly flipped the axe, lurched to one side and swiped downwards. The spear was sliced in two, leaving Wheam clutching about a third of the broken shaft. Certain of a kill, the goblin advanced, still swinging. Wheam backed-off fast, lost his footing, stumbled and fell. Then the goblin was standing over him, a grimace of triumph on his face, the axe raised for a death blow.

Wheam still had the broken shaft in his hand. In desperation, bellowing with the effort, he thrust it upwards with all his strength. The shaft, unevenly severed so its head was like a stake, plunged deep into the goblin's belly. Crying out in shock and pain, he staggered rearward, the axe slipping from his horny fingers. Then he fell and lay writhing, his hands on the protruding shaft. Wheam scrambled to his feet, fumbled his sword from its sheath and buried it in the creature's chest.

He turned away. He was panting for breath and shaking. But he had never felt so good. More goblins were climbing over the rail. Wheam brought up his sword and prepared to meet them.

For Pirrak, the situation Wheam had faced was reversed. Many of the goblins now getting aboard carried their traditional weapon: a spear-length metal trident, its forks sharpened to a wicked keenness. Armed now with a sword, Pirrak was at a disadvantage, and he didn't dare try to retrieve his spear. So he took to dodging, stooping and sending in low blows. One such pass had him hacking into a goblin's sinewy leg, liberating a gush of dark, almost black blood. Wailing, his victim fell away, to be replaced by another trident-bearing goblin.

They circled, Pirrak turning away the trident's thrusts with his blade. The goblin lunged, driving the trident forward, and only Pirrak's nimble footwork saved him. He managed to hit the trident's metal shank a couple of times, but his blade merely raised a melodious din. Pirrak knew that at any instant he could be set upon by further opponents, but he couldn't overcome the goblin's defence or experience. He opted for a charge, dashing parallel to his foe, slashing as he went. The best he could do was catch the other's shoulder, opening a gratifying but superficial wound. That only outraged the goblin, who renewed his efforts to impale Pirrak.

The duel continued for what felt like an age to Pirrak. He was beginning to believe that he would be the first to weaken, or make a wrong move from inexperience. Feigning, thrusting, stabbing and swiping at each other, they moved through a bizarre lethal dance.

Suddenly it was over. In a brief hiatus at his front, Dallog looked for Pirrak. What he saw had him reaching for a hatchet. The goblin was closing in on Pirrak again when the hatchet struck the creature between the shoulder-blades. He spun and fell. Tyro and corporal exchanged a look, then both returned to fighting.

Dallog and Keick had entered the fray together and stayed that way. Their work was a grind of hacking and chopping, ducking and twisting. Keick slashed his blade across a goblin's face, forcing him back. Knocking a shield clear, Dallog plunged his sword into an opponent's trunk, crunching through its hard, almost insect-like carapace.

A sword and knife combination was Pepperdyne's choice. He could use them with a surgeon's skill or apply brute force as necessary. Facing a charging goblin, he employed both. Leaping aside at the last moment, he spun and brought his blade down on the goblin's outstretched arm. The amputated limb dropped still holding its trident. Howling, the wounded goblin fell away. Pepperdyne flicked his pair of blades into the deck and scooped up the trident. He hurled it at a goblin just climbing over the rail. The trident caught him square, propelling him backwards and out of sight. Pepperdyne plucked his quivering sword and knife from the deck, and looked for the next target.

For his part, Chuss made himself useful by finishing off the wounded left by the others. He had a hairy moment when one of the injured goblins seized his ankle in an iron grip. But the creature was dying, and a blow from Chuss' sword completed the job.

Shortly, the flow of boarders thinned and stopped. On the goblins' ship the remaining uninjured attackers withdrew and scrambled over the far rail. Presumably to wade ashore and join the fight there.

The defenders stood in silence, breathing hard, bloodstained, muscles aching.

'Is that it?' Wheam panted.

'Think so,' Pepperdyne replied.

'Could be more hiding over there,' Dallog said, pointing at the other ship with a gory blade.

'We'll check. But I think we got the better of them. I reckon they underestimated us and didn't want to spare many from the main assault on the beach.'

Dallog nodded. 'Likely.'

Pepperdyne looked at the tyros. 'I have to say your charges gave a good account of themselves.' He touched the hilt of his upright sword to his chest, saluting them.

They looked bashful. Youngsters again.

'They're orcs,' Dallog replied. 'They come alive in blood.'

'I should make sure Standeven's all right,' Pepperdyne said. 'Though why I bother . . .'

He went to one of his former master's favourite hideaways; a storage locker under the bridge. Wrenching the door open, he found him curled up inside.

'Have they gone?' Standeven asked tremulously.

'Yes, you're safe.'

'It's not me I'm worried about,' he came back with faux indignation.

'No? Then who?'

'Not who, *what*. Do you think Stryke's keeping the instrumentalities safe? I mean, with all this fighting going on—'

Pepperdyne slammed the door on him and rejoined the others.

'I wonder how things are going on the island,' Dallog said.

'Should we join them?' Keick wondered.

'I don't think Stryke would be very pleased if we abandoned our post,' Pepperdyne replied.

'He's right,' Dallog added. 'We should stay put. They're on their own.'

8

On the beach, Stryke and the rest of the band were watching.

They saw their ship attacked by the goblins, during which Coilla at least had concerns for those on board. Now the goblin ship, which almost completely blocked the view of the orcs' own, was being evacuated.

Jup pointed at the goblins jumping or lowering themselves over the side on ropes, then splashing towards the shore. 'Looks like Dallog and the others did well.'

Coilla nodded. 'Good for them.'

'Yeah,' Stryke said. 'But we've got our own problems.'

The other two goblin ships were anchored, and their crews were also wading to the beach, their tridents held above their heads. Elves were arriving too, staggering out of the waves, some supporting kin.

'It's too open here,' Coilla decided. 'We're better off facing them inland.'

'*Run away?*' Haskeer growled.

'A strategic retreat to a position that benefits us.' She nodded at the unfolding scene. 'Look at their numbers.'

'Coilla's right,' Stryke said. 'We're not at full strength. Makes sense for us to pick the terrain. We'll get ourselves into the jungle back there and waylay the bastards.'

Spurral was looking at the surviving islanders struggling ashore. 'Let's hope the elves stay clear.'

'No worries there,' Haskeer sneered. 'They've no guts for a fight.'

As the band jogged towards the greenery, the first of the goblins were emerging from the water.

Once into the coolness of the jungle, Stryke had the band gather round. 'This is how we're doing it. Four groups. There . . .' He pointed to a large downed tree. '. . . there . . .' A big, moss-covered rock. '. . . there . . .' A thick stand of trees just inside the lip of the jungle. '. . . and there.' The remains of an abandoned elf cabin, rotting in the tropical climate. 'They likely saw us come in so they'll be following. And they'll be expecting a trap, so we need to be well hidden and *quiet.*' He glanced at Haskeer. 'Archers fire at my order, not before. We don't want to give 'em a chance to retreat. Sergeants, get the groups sorted.'

Jup and Haskeer quickly divided the reduced band into four units and headed one each. Haskeer's group took the rock as its hideaway, Jup's the fallen tree. Coilla led the third unit, and made for the ruined hut. Stryke's group hid themselves in the stand of trees. He had chosen the hides because they formed the four sides of a corral or box. The task for Stryke's group was to secure the fourth side, the corral's gate, once the enemy were in.

They took their positions and waited.

What seemed like an age passed, and Stryke wasn't alone in thinking the goblins would simply wait them out. Then there was movement in the boundary between beach and jungle. Leaves rustled and dry bark cracked. Dark shapes could be made out.

The goblins came into the jungle. They used a measure of stealth, but seemed more reliant on their greater numbers. The orcs bided their time, well hidden and silent, waiting for the enemy to enter the snare. Soon, as many goblins as were likely to had moved into the area, and they were starting to fan out. The trap had to be sprung while they were still bunched.

'*Fire!*' Stryke bellowed.

The archers had been spread across the hiding places. Now they let loose from all sides. Arrows slammed into the outermost of the pack of goblins. A good half dozen fell, dead or wounded. No sooner had they gone down than a second wave of arrows came in. At which point practically all of the goblins went down, whether hit or not, to avoid the shower of bolts. Some had bows. Kneeling, they began to return fire. But the orcs were playing shoot and hide. Bobbing up or round their cover, they fired then instantly ducked back out of sight.

This went on for a while, and not to the goblins' advantage. Their only hope was to break the impasse. At an order gutturally barked, presumably by one of their commanders, they rose and charged. Like the blooms of some exotic black flower bursting open, goblins hurtled towards all four hides.

The orcs got off a few more shots, but things were about to get too intimate for bows. Blades and hatchets took their place.

The greatest number of goblins headed back to where they entered the jungle, hoping to regain the beach. They were confronted by Stryke's unit, the gatekeepers, slipping from the trees to block the exit. This group was slightly larger than the other three, given it would bear the brunt, but it was still desperately small compared to the pack of charging goblins. And it wasn't only the goblins' numbers that gave them an edge; many had tridents.

The orcs met them head-on, a resolute line of barbed steel, determined to deny a way out. It was a savage clash, and Stryke was to the fore. His first encounter was short and brutal. A goblin charged, trident levelled. Stryke nimbly side-stepped, batted away the trident and followed through with a second swipe, to the creature's throat. No sooner had the goblin been floored than it was instantly replaced. Stryke and his unit stood their ground, dodging and downing the press of opponents.

The slab of rock sheltering Haskeer's group was swarming with goblins, while others were trying to round it. Attrition was the name of the game. The goblins were bent on overrunning the orcs, and the orcs were as keen to stop them. With fighting up close and vicious, tridents proved too cumbersome, and most were discarded. The goblins switched to their serrated, snub-bladed swords and crimped daggers. But trying to scale the barrier was a challenge. The rock ran with blood, making traction difficult.

A cleaver in each hand, Haskeer swung at the encroaching goblins, cracking skulls and shattering bones. When one of the hatchets caught in the hilt-guard of a goblin's sword it was wrenched from Haskeer's grip. Enraged, he struck out with the remaining hatchet, scything the creature's belly and releasing its stinking contents. Swiftly bringing up the weapon he swiped at another goblin, striking him on the side of the head with the flat of its blade. As he fell, others took his place. Haskeer's detachment fought on.

Jup and Spurral were in the vanguard of the group stationed at the fallen tree. Compared to Haskeer's unit their cover was minimal. But they were just as resolute. They stood behind a barrier bristling with blades and spear-tips, and clad with shields, which the frantic goblins all but threw themselves against. Dispensing with staffs, the dwarfs employed their short swords and knives, thrusting and slashing at goblin flesh.

The pummelling on the Wolverines' shields was as relentless as a rainstorm on a field of wheat. And when one of the rangy goblins struck Spurral's shield particularly hard it was dashed from her hands. The creature followed through with a lunge to her breast. Fortunately, Jup's reactions were quicker. He blocked the blade; and Spurral, swooping low, buried her sword in the goblin's guts.

The shuffling of the combatants' feet caused her shield to be kicked away, beyond reach. A goblin tried exploiting that vulnerability, slashing his blade as he moved in on her. She could expect no further help from Jup, who had his own problems with an axe-wielding opponent. Not that she needed it. Her stocky, robust physique belied the speed and agility she was capable of, as her foe discovered. Ducking, weaving, she eluded the blade, then gave the goblin's shin a couple of hefty kicks. It was enough of an irritant to jolt the creature, and let Spurral deliver a lethal thrust. The vengeful goblins kept coming.

At the decaying lodge, Coilla perched on a heap of collapsed timber, looking down at the raging conflict. She was picking off goblins with her cache of throwing knives, plucked from her arm holsters. Choosing her mark, she lobbed a blade and struck a creature's head, downing him. On reflex born of experience she instantly yanked out another knife. There was no shortage of targets, and her next shot winged to a goblin's exposed neck.

She got a bead again, and threw. But the goblin it was aimed at managed to raise his shield. The knife bounced off it and landed a few paces away. Stooping, the goblin retrieved it, and swiftly hurled it at Coilla. It was an able throw, though not quite good enough. The blade embedded itself in the lodge wall, a hand's breadth from Coilla's head. That enraged her. As the goblin charged her way she tugged the quivering knife free, and with a grunt of effort pitched it at him. The blade caught him in the eye. Coilla reached for her sheath. There was one knife left. She flung it at the nearest attacker. It struck the creature's midriff, not killing but inflicting a grievous injury. Her arsenal spent, she drew her sword and jumped into the fray.

Fighting raged on, close quarters and bloody. The orcs took wounds, but could have suffered worse had they not had the protection of their hides. Even so, the unfavourable odds were starting to grind them down.

A cry went up from the goblins engaging Stryke's group at the trap's entrance; a rasping, keening outburst quite unlike the gruff roar a similar-sized mob of orcs would have made. It was a yell of triumph. Stryke and his unit had given a good account of themselves, but finally, perhaps inevitably, they buckled. The goblins had broken through. With no choice but to withdraw as they flooded out, Stryke's crew readied themselves to continue the battle as a brawl. But the corralled goblins stampeded past them and spilled onto the beach, leaving the killing floor littered with their dead and mortally wounded.

Stryke bellowed an order, calling the other three teams to him. They jogged his way, trampling over the corpses and cutting down the injured still game for a fight.

'Let's finish it!' Stryke yelled, pointing seaward with his sword.

They gave chase, emerging from the jungle's rim and dashing for the beach. What they saw there stopped them.

The fleeing goblins had joined the rest of their incoming contingent, a group of almost equal size, and they were forming up to face the orcs.

'*Shit*,' Coilla mouthed.

A hush fell as the two groups eyed each other.

Then a goblin pushed through the ranks and swaggered out into the separating gap. He was more finely dressed than the others, and had a long bow slung over one shoulder. It was black, elaborately embossed with tiny hieroglyphs in gold, and made from a material it was hard to identify, appearing to be neither wood nor metal. At his waist was a leather quiver holding arrows that were likewise black and marked with golden symbols.

'Who leads you?' he demanded, his voice coloured by the distinctive sibilance peculiar to his kind.

'I do,' Stryke said, stepping forward.

The goblin looked him over, a contemptuous expression on his face. 'I am Gleaton-Rouk.'

'I guessed that.'

'You owe me,' the goblin grated.

'How?'

'You killed some of my brood siblings.'

'The ones using kelpies for meat, you mean.'

'Whatever they were doing wasn't your concern.'

'We made it our concern.'

'And for that you owe a debt of blood.'

'You think you're going to collect it?'

'Have no doubts on that score, orc. Now throw down your arms.'

The Wolverines broke into derisive laughter.

Stryke's smile melted. 'That's something we don't do,' he informed the goblin evenly.

'Give yourselves up or die.'

'Like fuck we will,' Haskeer said.

The goblin glared at him. He indicated his force with a sweep of his bony arm and hissed, 'Consider the odds.'

Stryke coolly appraised them. 'Yeah, it does seem a bit unfair on your lot.'

Gleaton-Rouk began to seethe. 'So you refuse?'

'What do you think?'

'Then suffer the consequences.'

'Fine by us,' Stryke told him.

The goblin turned his back on them and headed for his line. His parting shot was 'So be it! Ready yourselves for hell!'

'See you there!' Coilla piped up cheerily.

The goblin ranks parted for him and he disappeared.

'Not taking the lead himself, I see,' Jup observed.

Haskeer nodded. 'All mouth and breeches.' He spat on the ground contemptuously.

The Wolverines watched as the goblins prepared for an attack. They could have fallen back to the jungle and faced them there, or stayed put and met them with a defensive formation. But their blood was up.

Stryke didn't need to give an order. By a kind of osmosis, intent spread through the band like a contagion.

As one, they charged.

Bellowing and whooping war cries, the Wolverines thundered towards the startled goblins.

They struck their lines at speed, wrong-footing the enemy and throwing them into confusion. The orcs laid into them with savage fury, severing limbs, piercing lungs and hacking off heads. Unprepared for wrath on such a scale, dozens of goblins fell like corn before the scythe.

Coilla worked a pair of swords as she ploughed through the chaos. She stove in a ribcage to her right, crushed a skull to her left. One blade slashed a goblin throat as the other slid deep into his comrade's belly. Weapons ranged against her were dashed aside, their wielders' impertinence paid for with cold steel. Like the rest of the band she was driven by bloodlust, the matchless trait of her race.

The ferocity was shared by Jup and Spurral, who battled with a berserk fierceness that near equalled the orcs'. They had become separated when they penetrated the enemy line, but proved as formidable fighting singly as they had as a team. For Spurral, the goblins were so much flesh to nourish her ravening blade. Jup, brandishing a pair of daggers, followed in his mate's wake, bringing down her leftovers. Blocked by a particularly obstinate foe, he came at the goblin low and with force, toppling the creature onto Haskeer's waiting sword.

Typically, Haskeer had attacked with as much, if not more frenzy, than any in the band. Heaving his blade from the goblin Jup tossed his way, he swiftly reemployed it, severing another's leg. The mass of targets kept it busy.

Stryke had made it his business to seek out Gleaton-Rouk and settle with him. But there was no sign of the goblin chieftain. And now Stryke's attention was on his band. The shock of their charge was wearing off and the goblins were rallying. A counter-attack was beginning, pushing the Wolverines back by sheer weight of numbers, and the band was taking wounds.

To Stryke's right, no more than a good spit away, one of the veterans, Bhose, was tussling with a trident-wielding goblin. Bhose lost. The goblin breached his defence and struck him with the trident, its razor-sharp tines passing clean through the orc's shoulder. Bhose went down under the impact, causing his assailant to lose his grip on the lodged trident. The goblin leapt forward, stamped his bony foot on Bhose's chest and attempted to pull the trident out. Hands clasping its shaft, face wreathed with pain, Bhose struggled to stop him.

Stryke quickly disposed of the opponent he was facing, then waded Bhose's way. By the time he got there the goblin had wrestled his trident free and was raising it for a killing blow, while Bhose stretched a hand for his sword, lying just beyond his reach. Stryke buried his blade in the goblin's back. Retching blood, the creature collapsed.

Bhose wasn't the only orc to sustain a wound. For all their bravado and martial skills, the Wolverines were being too severely challenged by the recovering goblins and were close to becoming overwhelmed. Stryke judged it prudent to disengage and regroup. On his signal a couple of nearby privates took hold of the recumbent Bhose and began dragging him clear. Then Stryke yelled an order. As one, the band pulled back. All got clear, as much by luck as dexterity. Wary of some kind of ruse, the goblins didn't pursue them.

The Wolverines arrived back at the spot they started from. They were paying the toll of combat. Some had injuries, and all of them ached from the exertion of battle. They were blood-splattered and out of breath, and Jup and Spurral ran with sweat.

Stryke quickly assessed the wounded. Supported by a pair of comrades, Bhose looked the worse. Coilla was checking his shoulder.

'How is he?' Stryke asked.

'It's a nasty wound,' she told him, 'and it's bleeding a lot.'

'I'm fine,' Bhose protested.

'Pity Dallog's not here to dress it,' Jup reckoned.

'Balls,' Haskeer said. 'Who needs him? Anybody could staunch a wound like that.'

'Anybody but you, maybe.'

'How'd you like me to cut a piece out of you and try?'

'*Shut it!*' Stryke barked, jabbing a thumb at the goblins. 'Save your bile for them.' He turned to the grunts holding up Bhose. 'Get him to the rear.'

'I'm fine,' Bhose repeated weakly.

'Do as you're told.'

They hauled him away.

The goblins were forming up for an attack.

'*Brace yourselves!*' Stryke warned.

The orc archers had a few arrows left, and nocked them. Everyone tensed.

There would be no charge from the Wolverines this time. That tactic was spent. It was the goblins' turn.

Somebody on their side shouted an order. They began to advance, slowly at first, then with gathering speed.

'*Steady!*' Stryke yelled.

The goblins broke into a trot, then started to run.

When they covered about half the distance to the Wolverines, something strange happened.

An abnormality occurred in the space between orcs and goblins. The air itself seemed to turn heavy, and took on a ruddy, dusty glow. A film appeared, shimmering like the surface of a giant soap bubble, rippling with pulsing scarlet. It stood as a semi-transparent veil across the charging goblins' path.

Most slowed or stopped. Some, the brave, foolhardy or crazed, kept running. Deceived by the veil's translucence, these few dashed headlong, thinking to break through. Three or four of them struck the barrier simultaneously. It repelled them. They flew back as though flung by a giant invisible hand. And from the instant they touched the glistening wall, they ignited. Wreathed head to foot in flame, they landed heavily, to writhe and scream as they burned.

The Wolverines felt a wave of heat, and involuntarily stepped back.

Haskeer gaped. 'What the—'

Coilla pointed. '*There!*'

Farther down the beach a large group of elves had gathered. Mallas Sahro, their elder, was to the fore.

'They're using their magic,' Stryke said.

'So they do have some backbone,' Haskeer muttered.

The burning goblins' comrades were vainly trying to beat out the flames when another, stronger heat wave throbbed from the veil.

The band drew back again. They saw that the veil had emitted a sheet of fire that swept towards the milling goblins. When it reached the first of them, those tending the fallen, they too burst into flames. It didn't stop. Continuously regenerating itself, the burning curtain kept moving at a walking pace. Ignoring the agonised screams of those on fire, the remaining goblins backed away, then quickly retreated as it herded them in the direction of the shoreline.

The band noticed that one goblin risked himself to retrieve a dropped trident. He went for that particular weapon rather than any number of others, even though it put him in danger of contact with the advancing wall of flame. Once he had it, he ran full pelt for the sea, holding the trident high above his head as he splashed in. The others entered the water close behind. To their rear, the fiery veil halted at the shore's edge.

Stryke and the band watched as the mantle of fire slowly faded, along with its heat. Beyond it, the goblins were waist-deep, making for their ships.

Jup was shielding his eyes with a hand. 'Is that their chief?' he wondered.

A figure was standing on the prow of the biggest ship.

'Yeah,' Coilla confirmed.

'Fucking coward,' Haskeer murmured.

'What's he doing?' Jup said.

Coilla squinted again. 'Looks like he's drawing his bow.'

Haskeer gave a derisive snort. 'Bloody fool. What's he hope to hit from that distance?'

'What's up with them?' Spurral asked, nodding at the crowd of elves along the beach. They were shouting and gesturing, but they were too far away for their words to be made out.

'Probably celebrating,' Stryke suggested.

From his ship, Gleaton-Rouk loosed an arrow.

'It's way off target,' Haskeer sneered. 'Even if it got this far it'd miss us by a mile.'

Most of the Wolverines agreed, showing disdain with mocking jeers. Their scorn appeared justified as the arrow soared well to their right and far too high to do any damage except to treetops.

But then there was a change. Defying nature, the arrow altered course. It turned sharply and began to descend, heading straight for the band.

'*Down!*' Stryke bellowed.

Everyone dropped and hugged the ground. Bhose was already sitting, nursing his wound. One of the attending grunts gave him a shove and with a moan of pain he slumped onto his back.

The arrow soared towards them, and for a moment it looked as though it would pass overhead. Instead its trajectory became more acute. Impossibly gathering speed, it descended so fast they couldn't see it.

The arrow struck Bhose in his chest.

'*Back!*' Stryke yelled. '*Pull back!*'

The band hastily retreated, making for the trees, keeping low and dragging Bhose with them.

As soon as they reached shelter, Jup examined their comrade.

He looked up at the circle of Wolverines. 'He took it square to the heart. He's dead.'

Coilla gazed out at the departing goblin ships and said, 'How the *hell* did they do that?'

9

Surrounded by his brothers-in-arms, an orc lies dead on the edge of a beach, his blood seeping into the sand.

The sand consists of an untold number of grains. The number of grains of sand on all the beaches of all the islands is trivial compared to the number of worlds that exist.

The void between them is unimaginably great, and terrible. But tenuous, spider-web bridges connect the worlds, woven by the power of the instrumentalities.

An endless expanse. A blue-black canvas speckled with infinite points of light.

One speck, no brighter and no dimmer than most, was verdant. Ceragan, a blue-green world, was home to orcs. It was largely unspoilt, but a small part of it had been defiled.

At the encampment, they were still clearing up the damage. Their own dead had gone to their pyres; the attackers' corpses, far greater in number, had been disposed of less ceremoniously. Now the orcs were repairing their dwellings.

Nearly half of the lodges had been wholly or partly destroyed by fire. The corrals were broken and the livestock had scattered. Wagons were upended, and a barn stood in ruins. The carcasses of horses and cows were being hauled away.

The settlement echoed to the sounds of hammering and sawing. Timber was unloaded from overburdened wagons. Smiths pounded anvils next to braziers of glowing coals. Lengths of rope were woven and roofs re-thatched. New fortifications were being erected.

Wandering through all the activity were two young male hatchlings. They were siblings, the eldest over four summers old, his brother three. Each clutched a skilfully crafted hatchet. They were much smaller versions of the weapons carried by the adults, but just as sharp, and woe to anyone who tried parting the pair from them. Not that it would occur to orcs to do so.

The hatchlings roamed with no particular purpose, driven by boredom, curiosity and a certain amount of anxiety. Their parents had been snatched from them, and although they were being cared for, they were adrift and fretful. They were more careless than they would have been if adults they respected were watching over them. It showed in their mud-caked boots and mucky britches.

The younger of the two moved with less certainty than his brother. In common with the very young of many races, he walked like a small drunk, stumbling occasionally. Only when he toppled and couldn't right himself did his brother stretch out a hand to him.

They watched as roofs were fixed, fences rebuilt and debris heaved from the well. Some greeted them with a nod or a few distracted words. Most ignored them. Their offers to help were dismissed with gruff laughter or sharp words. They were resigned to staring.

'There you are!'

They turned at the sound of the familiar and not altogether welcome voice, and saw the clan's chief, Quoll, sweeping their way. He was still big and powerfully built, despite his advancing years, and seemed incredibly ancient to them. Festooned with the arm-lets, bangles and leopard-tooth necklaces signifying his position, he was accompanied by his usual entourage of kin and dogsbodies.

He stood over the hatchlings, his followers looking on. 'Where have you been?' he demanded.

'Right here,' Corb told him.

'You're the oldest. It's your duty to look after your brother.'

'He does!' Janch protested.

Quoll fixed him with an icy gaze, which to the youngster's credit he held and tried, less successfully, to return. 'Judging by the state you're both in I'm not sure about that. What have you been doing?'

'Just playing,' Corb replied casually.

'Hmmm. Getting under everybody's feet more like.'

'No we haven't,' Janch muttered, his eyes now on his own feet.

'The time is coming to put aside childish things,' the chieftain declared portentously. 'What with your parents lost and—'

'They're not!' Corb protested.

'Not this again. Listen to me, both of you. Part of growing up is learning to accept what the gods have in store for us. You have to resign yourself to them being gone.'

'Don't say that!'

'It's the truth, Corb. You must come to terms with it.'

'*No*. They're not dead. I *know* they're not. Don't care what you say.'

'*How* do you know?'

'They're great warriors. Nobody could kill them. I just . . . feel it.'

Janch nodded vigorously in agreement.

Quoll sighed, and his forceful tone softened a little. 'Yes, Stryke showed his valour many times; and Thirzarr matched him in bravery and skill. Look at the price paid by the force that took her. But look too at the commander of that force, the witch.'

Corb and Janch shuddered inwardly, remembering the stories their mother told about the witch, and the raid that confirmed them.

Quoll himself recalled the ferocity of her attack, but stayed master of his emotions. And he resolved not to criticise Stryke in front of the hatchlings, though he half blamed their father for bringing near ruin on them all. 'Going against a power like hers is pissing into a gale,' he continued, 'even for an orc. I admire your loyalty to your parents, and your faith in them. But it's best not to rely too much on hope.'

'What about Wheam?' Janch piped up.

The chieftain held his steadfast expression, no matter what was going on inside. 'I have to suppose that my son is lost too. He was a disappointment to me. My wish is that he met his end with some dignity, and courage, as an orc should.' He had spoken in a kind of mild reverie, avoiding their eyes. Now his clarity returned and he looked to them. 'Face it. Stryke and Thirzarr are probably dead, thanks to the witch.'

She was no witch. She was a sorceress, and resented being thought of otherwise. And Jennesta's resentment was not to be stirred up lightly.

She stood on a beach on a world unimaginably distant from

Ceragan. Night was falling and the moons were beginning to appear. Not that she was in any way softened by the sight.

A figure approached. She recognised it as her latest aide, a major whose name she had already forgotten. He was another field promotion, his predecessor having been killed earlier in the day. This replacement was a younger man, and moderately bright for a human, but she saw little in the way of a future for him. He came to her with eyes averted and an uncertain step.

She didn't wait for him to begin his no doubt stumbling report. 'How are they?'

'They seem to have settled, my lady.'

'Not too much, I hope. I need their ferocity as well as their obedience.'

'Yes, ma'am.'

'You look uncertain, Major.'

'Well, my lady, they . . . they're a little . . . troublesome.'

'I'd expect them to be. Though more to my enemies than us. Come.' She turned and strode towards the island's heart, her aide following at a safe distance.

They came to a makeshift camp. Like youngsters caught in mischief her troops quickly turned solemn when they saw her, and presented themselves stiffly. She ignored them and swept past. Her goal was at the centre of the camp, adjacent to her own tent.

Several large wooden cages stood there. They were well built, and by necessity robust. Guards were posted all around them. Two or three of Jennesta's zombie servants were present. Trusted with simple tasks, they were pushing hunks of meat and water jugs through the slats. The captives stared at the offerings but showed scant interest in eating or drinking. Most of them were standing motionless. A few crouched in the dirt with vacant gazes, and one or two shuffled aimlessly. They came more to life, of a sort, when they noticed Jennesta approaching.

A kind of roar went up from them, part frustration, part fury, but strangely distorted, as though it should have been less muted. They became agitated, after a fashion, and moved to rattle the bars of their cages, still howling.

Jennesta raised her arms. *'Silence!'*

They instantly quietened. But they obeyed without exactly being cowed, and close scrutiny might have shown a tiny hint of something like defiance in their eyes.

'Good,' she said, studying them. 'They look promising.'

'Promising, ma'am?' the major ventured, shooting a nervous glance at the cage's occupants.

'I need their fire,' she explained. 'But there also has to be submission to my will. It's a balance.'

'May I ask what use these creatures will be put to, my lady?'

'Initially, revenge,' she replied, ignoring his impertinence in querying her. 'I've been exiled from the Peczan empire because of those terrorists in Acurial, and the Wolverines played their part in that. But it was an ill wind that's brought me nearer to attaining my goal. There'll be a reckoning the next time I encounter that wretched warband.'

'Begging your pardon, ma'am, but if we're to engage with them again we might have to consider the level of our forces. Not a few have fallen in your service. Today alone we lost—'

'I'm aware of that,' she informed him icily, and embedded in her tone was the inference that she didn't particularly care. 'But here, in front of you, is a beginning; the reinforcements to swell our ranks, more pliable and much more ferocious than those sorry efforts.' She indicated the trio of once human zombies milling near the cages.

One of them was Kapple Hacher, formerly a man of power and influence who had made the mistake of inviting Jennesta's anger. Her contempt seemed to faintly register with him. There was the merest flicker of recognition, an echo of the dissent in the captives' eyes. It went unnoticed.

'We're leaving here. Now,' she announced abruptly. 'Issue the orders.'

'Ma'am. And the Wolverines?' the major asked.

She glanced towards her grand tent. Its flaps were open. Inside, sitting in plain view, was Stryke's mate, Thirzarr. Her bearing was rigid and her expression was vacant.

'The Wolverines will come to me,' Jennesta said. 'And they won't be alone.'

Pelli Madayar was in a dilemma, and plagued with uncertainty. The dilemma was how best to act in what was an increasingly complex situation. The uncertainty came from questioning her own abilities.

She was at the rail of her ship, the many races of the Gateway Corps unit busy around her. Her second-in-command, Weevan-Jirst, stood by her side.

'You're making too much of it,' he hissed.

'Am I?'

'Your orders are simple enough: recover the instrumentalities.'

'You make it *sound* simple. The reality turns out to be a lot messier.' She gave him a sidelong glance. 'Or is that just my elven way of looking at things?'

'Perhaps. Then again, maybe we goblins have a tendency to see events as a little too black and white.'

Pelli smiled. 'That's quite an admission.'

'One thing about being in the Corps and mixing with other races is that it exposes you to different views. But I stand by what I said. Our mission has a plain objective.'

'It *did*. But now there are *two* sets of instrumentalities, and at least one other player in this drama. Those factors increase the variables. I'm in a quandary about how to tackle the problem.'

'We have the weaponry. Resolve to use it against the orcs and that sorceress alike. And not just a mild dose, like before.'

'Again, easily said. But it doesn't take into account the innocent casualties that could cause and—'

'It's not for me to remind you, but what the Corps believes in and what it expects is getting back instrumentalities, whatever the cost. If that can be done without harming the blameless, well and good. But it's not the primary consideration.'

'That's where my doubts set in. It's been generations since the Corps had to do anything like this, and those rules were formulated long ago.'

'That doesn't make them wrong.'

'I think they are. Which is why I'm wondering if I'm best suited to lead this unit.' She sighed. 'The way things are going, my first assignment looks like being my last.'

'Karrell Revers gave you this job because he knew you could do it. And you can, if you get over your scruples and see our work as being for the greater good.'

'So a few deaths of bystanders along the way is an acceptable price, yes, I know. I can't accept that.'

Weevan-Jirst studied her face, his own remaining typically expressionless. 'Who exactly are these bystanders?' He jabbed a lean hand at the ocean. 'How many true innocents are we likely to meet on the islands out there?'

'Enough.'

'Or is it that you have sympathy for one group in particular?' It was hardly a question.

'The orcs? You know I have . . . not sympathy, but some regard for the fix they're in.'

'You can't see *them* as innocent.'

'I see them as unwitting.'

'Don't forget they attacked us.'

'I don't think that was deliberate.'

'Not deliberate? You're talking about a savage, destructive race. One of a very few never granted membership or knowledge of the Corps.'

'Many races are maligned. There are those who would tar all goblins with the same brush because of the actions of a few.'

He nodded soberly. 'I'll grant you that.'

'So how can we be sure that what's said about orcs is true? And even if it is, it's the nature they were born with. Who are we to judge?'

'The Corps judges all the time. It decides who can't have instrumentalities, and the means necessary to enforce that. Having the instrumentalities fall into the hands of a race beyond the pale like the orcs, and that sorceress, is what the Corps was set up to prevent.'

Staring at the distant horizon, again she sighed, more in resignation this time. 'I suppose you're right. There is a bigger picture. I'll be mindful of it.'

'You will forgive me for what I am about to say. And I would not like you to think . . .'

She had never known him to be hesitant before. 'Yes?'

'I would not like you to think that my words are inspired by anything other than making our mission a success.'

'All right. Go on.'

'Gratified as I am to hear that you intend acting more decisively,

I understand this might prove . . . difficult for you. In that event, I would be prepared to assume leadership of this unit.'

Pelli needed a moment to take that in. 'You're challenging my command?'

'No. I'm merely stating that if you're unable to fulfil your function I will step in.'

'That would be your duty in any event, if I were killed or badly wounded or—'

'Those aren't the eventualities I have in mind.'

'What is?'

'Your possible reluctance to employ the force necessary when it comes to the crunch.'

'I see.'

'I have the right to take over,' Weevan-Jirst reminded her. 'It's laid out in the Corps' tenets. You would be bound to give me access to your means of contacting Revers, and I would report your incapacity to him.'

'Did he put you up to this? I mean, were you briefed that you might need to take such action?'

'Only . . . in so many words.'

'So Revers doesn't trust me?'

'He mistrusts your inexperience. As a responsible leader, he had to plan for any . . . shortcomings.'

'At what point am I considered incompetent? Am I to make every decision with your reaction in mind? I can't see that making my position easier.'

'Naturally I would apply common sense. But if the success of this mission were to be threatened by inaction on your part, I would move to relieve you of your command. Not that I would lightly adopt such a course.'

If there was a way of telling when a goblin looked embarrassed, she didn't know it. But it was obvious he was serious.

'You won't have to,' she told him.

10

The Wolverines built a funeral pyre on the beach of the elves'
island.

Stryke would have preferred to skip the ritual and push on. But
the discontent about Harglo's burial at sea felt by many in the band
was something he didn't want to rekindle.

Assuming the function that was once performed by his predecessor, the late Alfray, Dallog again conducted a ritual in which
he entrusted their fallen comrade to the care of the gods. Not
everyone in the band was happy with the corporal fulfilling this
role; Haskeer in particular wore an expression showing more than
simple grief. But he and the few other dissenters held their peace.

Bhose's corpse was laid on the pyre. His weapons, helm and
shield were distributed amongst the band, as was the custom, but
his sword was placed in his hand. Then Stryke said a few words,
paying tribute to Bhose's courage and loyalty, and they consigned
his body to the flames.

All the elves had gathered, watching from a distance in respectful silence. Mindful of not stoking tensions in the band, Pepperdyne saw to it that he and Standeven also stood apart. Coilla would
have preferred Pepperdyne at her side, but throughout the ceremony contented herself with sidelong glances that caught his eye.

It took some hours for the pyre to do its work. The Wolverines
stayed to the end, in a mood close to reverential, while the elves
slowly drifted back to their settlement. At length, Stryke broke the
spell with an order for the band to stand down.

As he passed, Haskeer said, 'Another good comrade gone.'

Stryke nodded. 'Yeah.'

'This mission's costing us dear in lives.'

'It's the price we have to pay sometimes.'

'Did Bhose have to pay it today?'

'What do you mean?'

'I don't know that the way we fought made much sense. Trying to box those goblins in, then taking it out to the beach.'

'What would *you* have done?'

'It ain't just that; it's this whole mission. It started simple. Now we're floating round these lousy islands with a bunch of hangers-on and the band bleeding members.'

'You're painting it too black. We fight and some of us die, you know that. It's the orcs' lot.'

'Yeah, but—'

'And we've no choice. At least, I haven't as long as Thirzarr's out there somewhere. Even if we were ready to leave we can't rely on the stars anymore. So like it or not, we're stuck with what we've got.'

'And if we don't make it home?'

'Then we'll settle for getting our own back on Jennesta.'

'Some chance.'

'Taking chances is something else we do, even slim ones. But you don't have to. If you don't like the way things are going you can stay here with the elves.'

'No, no. I only—'

'Or if you think you can do better at leading the band, be my guest and try.'

'Look, Stryke, I just—'

'*Otherwise*, stop bellyaching. Got it?'

Haskeer sighed and mumbled, 'Got it.'

'Right. Now let's see if we can find out what happened to Bhose.' He turned and walked away. Haskeer followed, and the rest of the band fell in behind them.

Stryke led them to the elves' village. It had become a sombre place. The elves had dead of their own, many of them, and the bodies were laid out in front of Mallas Sahro's lodge. He sat on an imposing, throne-like chair overlooking the scene, a couple of attendants at his side. When he saw the Wolverines approaching he rose to meet them.

'On behalf of my clan,' he said, 'allow me to express regret at the loss of your comrade.'

Stryke nodded. He glanced at the rows of elven dead. 'Your folk have suffered too. Our sympathies.'

'Thank you. We have an old saying: "There will be tears enough to rival the ocean". That never seemed more apt.'

'Why did you decide to use your magic after all?'

'The answer lies before you. In the past the goblins have taken a life here, a life there. Never before have they slaughtered us on such a scale. That, and because of what you said about us using our powers to throw off their yoke.'

'You aided us, and we're grateful. But it was our fault. They were here because of us. We brought you trouble, and for that we owe you an apology.'

'No, you don't. We already had that particular trouble. The goblins have plagued us for a long time, but it took today's events to force us to act. It was a lesson. A hard one, to be sure, but necessary.'

'I'm pleased you see it that way. Though you must be aware that they might return for vengeance.'

'In which case we have our defensive magic. Hopefully it will be enough to ward them off. In any event, given the beating you inflicted on them, I suspect it will be a while before they brave our shores again.'

'I trust you're right about that. But you probably aren't the only islanders in these parts to be tormented by them. You might think of making common cause with your neighbours. There's strength in numbers.'

'A wise thought. I'll set about it once our period of mourning ends.'

'Don't leave it too long,' Stryke cautioned.

'What we don't understand,' Coilla said, 'is what happened to Bhose.'

'Yeah, how the hell did the goblin manage a shot like that?' Jup wanted to know.

'Shadow-wing,' Mallas Sahro replied.

'What?' Stryke asked.

'The bow Gleaton-Rouk used. Its name is Shadow-wing. At least, that's one of its names. It has many.'

'And it's enchanted.'

'Of course. No ordinary bow could perform that way.'

'How does it work? I mean, why did it single out Bhose in particular?'

'Shadow-wing is subject to a very specific type of magic. The shafts it looses have to be daubed with blood from the intended victim. Once so anointed the arrow will always find its target. *Always*. It has nothing to do with the skill of the archer.'

'That explains something we saw when the goblins were retreating,' Coilla recalled. 'One of them risked himself to pick up a weapon.'

'It must have been the weapon that wounded your comrade during the battle. The blood on it would have guided Shadow-wing's arrow. In all probability the goblin retrieved the weapon knowing only that it had wounded an orc. It happened to be your comrade Bhose. It could have been any member of your band who sustained an injury that bled.'

'Why didn't you warn us about this bow?' Jup said.

He shrugged his shoulders. 'We simply didn't have the chance.'

'What do you know about the bow?' Stryke said. 'Where did it come from?'

'It was long thought to be a myth. Like all such fables, there are many stories attached to it, most contradictory. But the prevailing legend is that it was made by the goblins' gods, long, long ago. They have strange gods, as you know, and not a few of them dark.'

'How did these gods come to be parted from it?'

'Again, there are different stories. Some say it was stolen from them by a celebrated goblin hero, who himself has many names. Others hold that the gods gifted it to a goblin in gratitude for a task he performed. Or that it was used by one god to kill another, a rival, and the bow was flung from the clouds in disgust, and landed on earth to vex the world of mortals. The tales are legion. As are those surrounding Shadow-wing's passage through history. What the stories have in common is that corruption, treachery and death always attend the bow. Gleaton-Rouk is a master of those black arts, so I suppose it comes as no surprise that he has gained it. As I say, we thought the bow was just a story. I wish it could have stayed that way.'

'Well, we're heading away from here. Chances are we'll not see Gleaton-Rouk again, much as we'd like to have a reckoning with him. Likely it's you that'll have to face that damn weapon again.'

'If so, we shall be extra cautious about any of our blood that's spilt.'

'I wouldn't count on having seen the last of Gleaton-Rouk, Stryke,' Coilla suggested. 'He has a grudge to settle with us.'

'We're not going looking for him. Thirzarr comes first.'

'I thought this band believed in avenging its own,' Haskeer rumbled.

'We'll go after him once we've settled our score with Jennesta.'

'If we're still alive.'

'If we're able, I vow we'll cross paths with Gleaton-Rouk again.'

'And be careful not to bleed anywhere near him,' Jup added.

Spurral gave him a sharp elbow to the ribs.

'When must you leave?' Mallas Sahro asked. 'Can you stay and take refreshments, or rest?'

'We're moving on soon as we can,' Stryke said. 'Besides . . .' He looked at the elf corpses. '. . . this is your time for grief, not feasting with strangers.'

'At least let us supply you with food and fresh water for your journey.'

'That would help. Thank you.'

'And this,' the chief said, slipping a hand into a pocket in his robe. He brought out a bracelet. Made of a silvery, semi-rigid material, it was about as wide as an orc's finger was long, and was studded with blue stones of various sizes. There was a hinged clasp, indicating that it opened. 'This is a charm to ward off magical attacks. It, too, is old, though not as ancient as the bow. It won't repel the strongest magic, but might buy you a brief respite. Take it.'

'You're sure?'

'I know orcs have no innate talent for magic, as elves do, and we have other charms. I think that you might need this more than us.'

'We'll take any help we can get.'

'Be aware that once the bracelet is on your wrist it will be impossible to remove until either its protection is no longer needed or its power is spent.'

'I suppose it'll stop me losing it,' Stryke reasoned. 'But how long does its power last? And how will it *know* it isn't needed any-more?'

'If unused, its magical energy could last centuries. In the event

626

of it having to counter really potent sorcery, it might be less than a day. As to how it will know when to release itself . . . it will know.' He stared hard at Stryke. 'So, your arm?'

Stryke obliged and Mallas Sahro clamped the bracelet on his wrist. Once the clasp clicked into place the bracelet visibly contracted and tightened. Stryke felt it gently fasten snugly against his flesh.

'By the end of the day you won't even be aware of it,' the chief assured him.

Stryke looked it over, turning his wrist. 'I'm obliged.' His gaze went to the sea. 'We've got to be moving now.'

'I'll have the supplies brought out right away.' He nodded at one of his aides, who hurried off. 'And I have a suggestion. When they left, the goblins abandoned one of their ships; the one they used to try to board yours. It's not quite as big as the one you arrived in, but it's faster. Why not take it?'

'Good idea, we'll do that.'

'Go in peace then, and be assured that you will always have a welcome here.'

Not long after, the Wolverines were back at sea and the elves' island was out of sight. The wind was strong. With Pepperdyne in his usual place at the wheel, and a sleeker vessel, they made good progress.

Stryke was at the stern, sitting on the deck with his back to the rail, studying the bracelet. The chart was spread out on his lap. He had grown more morose since they set sail, and Coilla approached with care.

'Suits you,' she said, nodding at the armlet.

He smiled thinly. 'I was wondering if it protected just me, or all of us. Stupid of me not to ask.'

'Let's hope we don't have to find out.' She glanced up at the ship's black, billowing sails. 'They were right about this ship being faster.'

'I could wish for the magical speed it had when we first saw it.'

'Jode reckons we'll be there soon. Maybe as soon as late tomorrow. Hang on.'

'I've no choice.'

She crouched next to him. 'Stryke . . . about Bhose. I—'

'You're not going to sound off about that too, are you? It's bad enough listening to Haskeer grousing.'

'I'm not about to blame you for anything. I'm more worried that you might be blaming yourself for Bhose's death.'

'No more than when anybody in the band gets themselves killed.'

'So quite a lot then.'

'We're born to kill, and to flirt with our own deaths. It's the orcs' creed. But when you're in command you can't help thinking that some choice you made, an order you issued, might have been wrong and put the band in peril.'

'And Thirzarr?'

'Thirzarr as well. I've put her and the hatchlings in danger. I don't even know if they're still alive.'

'We all signed up for this mission. All right, Thirzarr and the hatchlings didn't, but they're orcs too. My point is: they know the odds.'

'Corb and Janch don't, not yet. They're too young.'

'The clan in Ceragan do. They'll be looking after them, the way we all watch each other's backs in the band.'

'If Jennesta left anybody alive.'

'You've got to have hope, Stryke. Why else go on?'

He pondered that for a moment, then said, 'You seem to be living on hope yourself.'

She was puzzled. 'What d'you mean?'

'You and Pepperdyne.'

'*What?*'

'You hope it'll work out. But you could be storing trouble for yourself, Coilla. Orcs and humans come from different worlds, and you know how much bad feeling there's been between them. The chances are you'll—'

'Oh, you're good, Stryke. You've managed to turn it from you to me. As usual.'

'I mean it. I just don't want to see you get hurt.' His words were not said unkindly.

Because of that, and the strain he was under, she bit back her anger. 'You found contentment,' she replied coolly, 'don't deny it to me.'

'I might have lost it.'

'For your sake, I hope not. But whatever passes between Jode and me is our concern, nobody else's.'

'Just think about what you're doing.'

'Yeah, right,' she said, getting to her feet. 'I'll catch you later.' As she left, Stryke went back to studying the bracelet.

She was fuming as she headed towards the prow.

'Coilla.'

'*Yes?*' she snapped, spinning to face whoever had spoken. 'Oh, Wheam. Sorry.'

'That's all right. It's been a tough day, what with Bhose and everything.'

'You're not wrong. I've been meaning to say: you did well helping defend the ship. We're all proud of you.'

The youth looked both pleased and embarrassed. 'Thanks, Coilla.' Then the cheer went out of his face. 'I wish everybody felt that way.'

'Who doesn't?'

For answer, he nodded. She followed his gaze. Further along the deck, Dallog and Pirrak stood close together. They were deep in conversation.

'Like I told you before,' Coilla said, 'Dallog has charge of all you tyros. You can't expect him to play favourites.'

'He doesn't seem to have any time for me these days. Only Pirrak.'

'Who probably needs special attention. You should be pleased you don't.'

Wheam brightened a little. 'I hadn't thought of it like that.'

'There's usually more than one way to look at things. Don't pick the worst.'

Haskeer arrived, his expression flinty, and would have passed them without a word had Wheam not spoken.

'Sergeant!' Haskeer stopped and stared at him. 'We've all been saddened by the loss of our comrade Bhose,' Wheam said, reaching for the goblin lute he habitually had slung on his back, 'and I've been honouring him in verse. Can I offer you a lament?'

'Only if I can offer you a kick up the arse,' Haskeer growled. He stomped off, scowling.

'Happy ship,' Coilla remarked. 'Don't mind him, Wheam. Why

don't you get some sleep? There might not be much chance after we make landfall.'

'Yes, I suppose I should. But . . .'

'What now?'

'Some of the band have been talking about the Krake, and how it can pull a ship under and—'

'They should know better. Don't worry about it; we've more pressing concerns. Now get yourself to your bunk. And if we get attacked by sea monsters I'll give you a call.'

They sailed on through the night and much of the next day. Late in the afternoon they spotted a landmass.

'That has to be it,' Pepperdyne said, perusing the map.

Stryke nodded. 'So let's land.'

'We need to take care. This chart's not the clearest I've ever seen, but it looks like there could be hidden rocks off those shores.' He pointed. 'Here, see? We'll need to take soundings.'

'Do what you have to.'

They approached the island with caution, and Pepperdyne got one of the privates to measure the water's depth with a length of rope and a lead weight. It proved unusually deep, but there was no problem finding a path through any submerged rocks. Eventually they dropped anchor just off the main beach. A skeleton crew was left to guard the ship, along with Standeven, while the rest of the band waded ashore. They saw no signs of life.

'As islands go,' Coilla said, 'this one's not very big.'

'Big enough for a settlement,' Stryke replied. 'We'll head inland.'

The island's interior was swathed in dense jungle and at first they had to hack their way through. They would have expected to disturb birds or the myriad small animals that lived in the undergrowth, but there was only silence. Soon they came to an area where trees had been felled and the scrub cleared to form an open space. They found the settlement.

It was in ruins. There were perhaps a score of lodges and huts, and not one was undamaged. Something like half were burnt out. They saw the mutilated bodies of a few dogs, but no corpses of any other kind, and certainly nothing living.

'We're too late,' Coilla whispered.

'So what do we do now, Stryke?' Spurral asked.

He gazed about, a look of utter despondency on his face.

'Stryke?' Coilla urged.

'I don't know,' he said.

11

The elves' dealings with the outside world didn't end with the orcs' departure. The day after the Wolverines left, the Gateway Corps ship arrived.

Wary given recent events, the elves flung up their magical barriers. The strange, multi-species group of visitors dismissed these obstacles with almost casual contempt. There was alarm when the goblin Weevan-Jirst appeared; and bemusement at the sight of the elf, Pelli Madayar. Her presence, and her oath that they came in peace, gained a measure of the elves' trust. For their part, they told the strangers what had happened with the goblins, while casting edgy glances Weevan-Jirst's way; and they were honest about the Wolverines having been there. But they stayed loyal to the warband and refused to say where they were headed.

Pelli didn't linger. She took ship immediately and ordered their former course resumed.

Weevan-Jirst was displeased, and showed his irritation when they stood together at the helm.

'We should have *made* them tell us.'

'What are we,' she retorted, 'marauders? Anyway, we don't need a steer from them; we have our sorcery to help us follow the orcs.'

'So why did we waste time stopping there?'

'To gather intelligence.'

'We gained precious little in that respect.'

'I disagree. We confirmed that we were on the right trail, and learned about the Wolverines' tangle with . . .' She shot him a glance. '. . . members of your race.'

If her aide found the reference objectionable in any way he didn't show it. 'You could have pushed them harder. We might have learnt more.'

'Did you see the graves back there? And the number of them? It wasn't the right time for an interrogation.'

'It was exactly the right time, while they were weakened by grief.'

'I thought otherwise.'

'Because they're elves? Your own kind?'

'No. I give no more weight to my own race than any other,' she replied steadfastly. 'Any more than I would hold you to account for the wrongdoings of some goblins.'

He made a kind of low clucking with his bony jaw, the goblin equivalent of tutting or an exasperated sigh. 'The fact remains,' he hissed, 'that we are conducting ourselves with less than single-minded purpose.'

'I think you mean ruthlessness. As I said, I don't see that as an honourable way for the Corps to behave, and I wouldn't want to be part of it if it did.'

'Then perhaps you should consider your position as commander of this mission.'

'The one best placed to determine that is our leader.'

'Unless I, as second-in-command, judge you incompetent.'

'You've already made that point. I prefer Karrell Revers' counsel.'

'As you please.'

'And I'm overdue reporting to him. So if you'll excuse me . . .' Without waiting for an answer she turned on her heel and walked away.

When Pelli got to her cabin she locked the door, something she didn't normally bother with. Then she took out the crystal she commonly used to contact Karrell Revers. In moments, following the appropriate incantations, it was glowing in the palm of her hand.

The image of a mature human's face appeared on the crystal's surface. He spoke without preamble. *'It's been too long since your last report. What's happening?'*

'Events move apace here. Reporting hasn't been my first priority.' She wasn't in the mood to apologise.

Revers looked as though he was going to rebuke her for that. He contented himself with, *'So tell me now.'*

'We're in hot pursuit of the Wolverines. And I'm sure the sorceress can't be far away.'

'Have you actually engaged with either yet?'

'Not since our confrontation on the dwarfs' isle.'

'Which you could have won if you'd used the full potential of your weaponry.'

'I didn't feel it was appropriate. There were innocents present.'

'And orcs.'

'Yes, but—'

'And perhaps your sympathies for them could have stayed your hand?'

'No. I mean, you know I'm in favour of giving them the benefit of the doubt. My belief is that they're being manipulated. But that doesn't in any way compromise my—'

'We seem to have this conversation endlessly. Your one and only aim should be to retrieve the instrumentalities, both the original and duplicate sets. Any other consideration is secondary. Compassion for orcs certainly is.'

The crystal's magic was such that his words were audible both in her mind and, less loudly, in the cabin. It was something she always found a little disconcerting. 'I can get the instrumentalities back,' she replied, 'and if things are handled properly, without too much blood being spilt. Surely that's a better outcome for the Corps?'

'The only outcome that counts is gaining the artefacts. I think you're close to failing in that.'

'So why did you give me this job in the first place?'

'Because I believed you were capable of it, or at least that you'd grow into it.'

'My chances would be greater if my leadership wasn't being undermined.'

'What do you mean?'

'Weevan-Jirst. Did you order him to scrutinise my actions? And to relieve me of my command if he saw fit?'

'Pelli, you must understand that—'

'Did you?'

'There has to be a contingency plan for every mission. You are unproven. I needed to know our objective would be achieved, whatever the cost.'

'So you instructed my second-in-command to spy on me.'

'To keep a watchful eye on you. Just that.'

'And to take over this mission if he didn't like what he saw.'

'The Corps and our calling are bigger than any individual, Pelli. I make no apology for trying to ensure the success of this venture.'

'I gave my loyalty to you, and to the Corps. Is this how you repay me?'

'There would be no threat to your command if you acted decisively.'

'By which you mean taking no heed of casualties among the blameless.'

'Civilian losses are regrettable, but they're trivial in light of the havoc the instrumentalities can cause in the wrong hands.'

'I can't regard the death of innocents as unimportant. That's not what I thought the Corps was about.'

'If you don't know our sole purpose by now perhaps there is a basis for questioning your judgement.'

'It seems you're determined to believe that.'

'No, I think I've given you more than enough chances to prove yourself. But we've got to the stage where there's nothing more to say. I want to talk with Weevan-Jirst.'

Seeing no point in arguing further, Pelli simply replied, 'All right.'

She left the cabin, slipping the crystal into her pocket. But she didn't seek out her second-in-command. Instead she made for a quiet part of the ship and went to the rail.

She took out the crystal, holding it in her clenched fist and not looking at it. It was true there were other ways of communicating with Karrell Revers, but they involved invocations only she knew, and there was no way she was going to divulge them. The crystal was the simplest, most direct channel.

There was a moment of hesitation then, a realisation of the gravity of what she was about to do.

She looked around to see if anyone was watching. Then she dropped the crystal overboard.

The band was worried about Stryke.

He was in a frame of mind that mixed despair with flashes of belligerence. They left him to brood in the ruins of the deserted village.

At Coilla's instigation several scouting parties were sent out to comb the island. No one thought anything would come of it, but it was better than doing nothing. As it was comparatively small, the island didn't take long to search, and the scouts were soon back. They had nothing significant to report.

Calthmon had led one of the parties to explore the opposite side of the island. He had an observation. 'There are other islands, just off this one. Three or four of 'em.'

Pepperdyne had the map, loaned to him without protest by Stryke. He consulted it. 'Yes, we knew that. They're here on the chart. A way off, according to this.'

Calthmon shook his head. 'Nah. You could hit the nearest with an arrow. Water between's shallow, too. I reckon we could walk it.'

'I was worried that this map might not be very accurate. What's over there? Could you see?'

'Nothing. They're just rocky. Barren.'

'Doesn't help us much, does it?' Jup said.

'So what do we do?' Haskeer asked. 'We can't just sit on our arses waiting for Stryke to pull himself together.'

'Damned if I know.'

'Couldn't we go back to the elves' island?' Spurral suggested.

'Can't see that they'd be much help,' Coilla told her. 'Any other ideas? Anybody?'

'I suppose we could sail these waters in the hope of picking up a clue about where Jennesta's gone,' Pepperdyne said. 'Though I'm pretty sure that'd be fruitless.'

'Great,' Coilla sighed. 'Anybody else? No? All right. I think all we can do is hone our blades, check our kit and wait for Stryke to snap out of it. He'll know what to do.'

'Will he?' Haskeer said.

She ignored that. 'Anybody comes up with a better plan, sing it out.'

'If we're waiting, I'm doing it on the beach,' Spurral decided. 'There's more cheer there than in this place.'

Coilla looked at the ruined settlement. 'I'm with you on that.'

'What about Stryke?' Jup said.

'He'll be fine.'

Spurral headed off, and the rest of the band drifted along behind her. If Stryke noticed, he gave no sign.

On the beach most of the band settled down together. They proceeded to overhaul their weaponry, and to discuss the situation in low tones. There was a general air of despondency.

Coilla and Pepperdyne sat apart from the others. Coilla spent the time cleaning the throwing knives she had retrieved after battling the goblins.

'What do you reckon?' Pepperdyne said. 'Can you see a way out of this?'

'Offhand, no.'

'What about Stryke?'

'What about him?'

'*Is* he going to snap out of it?'

'Course he is. I've seen him like this before, though not as bad. He just needs some time. '

'And what you said about him knowing what to do. Will he?'

'No idea. But if anybody can come up with something, it's Stryke.'

'So we wait.'

Coilla shrugged. 'What else can we do?' She glanced at the rest of the band. Like her and Pepperdyne, two others had chosen to sit to one side. 'I want to talk to somebody, Jode. Hang on here.'

He nodded. She stood and moved off.

Almost as soon as she left, Standeven arrived.

'What is it?' Pepperdyne snapped tetchily.

Standeven affected a hurt look. 'Do I have to have a reason for talking to my long-serving helper?'

'There's a motive behind everything you do. And *helper* isn't exactly the word I'd choose to describe our connection.'

'Words, words, words.' Standeven waved a dismissive hand. 'We put too much weight on them.'

'Words like *slave*, you mean? That one's light as a feather. Except to anybody it's applied to.'

'*Connection*. That's the only word you've used that's of any importance.'

'What the hell are you talking about, Standeven?'

'Whatever you want to call it, we do have a bond. We've been through a lot together, and we've always overcome anything and anybody who stood in our way.'

'*I* have, you mean.'

637

'Now we're in another fix.'

'That's a statement of the damned obvious. What's your point?'

'The instrumentalities.'

'Oh, for the gods' sake! Not *that* again. Don't you ever—'

'Hear me out. You think I want to get my hands on them.'

'I wonder what gave me that idea.'

'But all I really want is to get back to our world.'

'You haven't exactly hidden that ambition.'

'Be serious,' he returned sternly. 'I've got a plan.'

'And you're going to tell me about it.' Pepperdyne's tone was one of resignation.

Standeven leaned into him, too close for Pepperdyne's liking, and monopolised his ear. 'Stryke won't be parted from the instrumentalities, quite rightly, so he has to be persuaded to use them to take me back. And you too, of course,' he added as an afterthought.

'Persuaded.'

'Yes.'

'By you.'

'Well, given the way he thinks about me, it'd be better coming from you.'

'Me. And what am I supposed to say to him?'

'It's simple. All he's got to do is take me . . . take *us* home, then return here. We're out of his hair, he's still got the instrumentalities.'

'He's going to do this in the middle of searching for his mate, while his band are going down like flies and a weird bunch of sorcerers are stalking us. Not to mention a revenge-crazed goblin with an awesome bow.'

'It's not asking *that* much, seeing all we've been through with this gang of freaks.'

'This is *insane*. As I told you before, there's no way Stryke would agree to a harebrained idea like that. Get that through your thick head. And even if he did agree, by some miracle, you're forgetting something: there's no guarantee you'd get home. The instrumentalities aren't working properly.'

'So he says.'

'What?'

'We've only got his word for it. How do we know he isn't lying?'

'Why the hell would Stryke do that?'

'Who knows how these creatures' minds work?'

'Yours is more of a mystery. Look, if you want to try getting Stryke to take you back, go ahead and ask him. I think I can guess his answer. But don't involve me in your ridiculous schemes.'

'What about you? Surely you want to get back to our own world.'

'No. At least, not now.'

Standeven adopted a knowing expression. 'Oh, right. The female.' He gave a grotesque, leering wink. 'Prefer to go native with her for a while first, do you? Wouldn't appeal to me, I must say, but each to his own, and—'

'Say another word,' Pepperdyne informed him coldly, 'and I'll break your nose.'

One look at his face convinced Standeven that lingering there wasn't a smart idea. Muttering under his breath, he shambled away.

Further along the beach, Coilla approached Dallog and Pirrak. They sat together a little way from the others, engrossed in conversation, but stopped when they saw her.

Dallog nodded in greeting. 'Coilla.'

'All well?'

'Far as it can be, given where we are.'

'How about you, Pirrak?'

'Me, Corporal? I'm . . . fine.'

'You did well in the battle with the goblins. All you new recruits did.'

'Er . . . thanks.'

She turned to Dallog. 'Can we talk?'

'Sure.' He looked to Pirrak, who got up and left.

'He seems a little jumpy,' Coilla said, watching the tyro walk away.

'Aren't we all?'

'Yeah, I guess so.'

'What did you want to talk to me about?'

'No need to look so serious. I only wanted to ask about Wheam.'

'What's he done?'

'Nothing. It's just that he feels you've been a bit . . . distant from him lately.'

'Did he ask you to bring this up with me?'

'No. He doesn't know I'm talking to you about it. And I think we should keep it that way.'

'Well, it's true. Though I wouldn't call it distant.'

'What would you call it?'

'I'm trying to help him grow, Coilla. You know his story.' He counted off on his calloused fingers. 'He's got a powerful sire who's always on his back. His belief in himself's low. He's got no inborn talent for fighting, despite his orc nature. He's wet behind the ears and—'

'He's getting better.'

'Granted. He's come on a lot since this mission started. But he won't rise much further as long as he's leaning on somebody. I reckoned the time was right to cut him loose.'

'So it's about getting him to stand on his own feet.'

'And he won't do that as long as the props are there.'

Coilla nodded reflectively. 'I can see that. One other thing. It seems to bother him that you're spending so much time with Pirrak.'

'He's bound to resent being replaced by one of the other tyros, as he looks at it.'

'Why are you so interested in Pirrak?'

'Unlike Wheam, he still needs his props.'

'Why?'

'In his way, he's as uncertain of himself as Wheam. Only he's better at hiding it. Mostly. You said yourself he was jumpy.'

'So you don't believe in the tough approach in every case.'

'They're different orcs. Wheam's had his nurturing. Pirrak's isn't over just yet.'

'Can we rely on him? In a fight, I mean.'

'As surely as any other in the band. He's already proving himself. Like Wheam.'

She weighed his words. 'All right. I'm obliged, Dallog.'

'You're welcome, Corporal.'

Coilla left thinking he was a wise judge of character. She was impressed.

Heading back towards Pepperdyne, she saw Standeven shuffling away from him. Halfway there, Spurral joined her.

'Know what I'm thinking?' she said.

'Nope,' Coilla replied. 'Mind-reading's not one of my talents.'

'I'm thinking how much Stryke's search for Thirzarr mirrors what happened to me and Jup.'

'When the Gatherers took you, you mean. S'pose it does. It was a hard time for you both.'

'Yes, but that ended happily.'

'You think this won't?'

'I don't know. I hope it will, of course. But the difference between my situation and Thirzarr's was that you had some idea of where I was being taken.'

'Yeah, it's tough knowing what to do next.'

'Coilla, do you ever wonder . . .'

'What?'

'Do you ever wonder what you'd do if the same thing happened to you and Jode? If you were parted and—'

'It hadn't occurred to me. Go a bit nuts, I expect.'

'You feel that strongly about him, then.'

'That's a sneaky way of getting me to open up about it, Spurral.'

'Sorry.'

Coilla grinned. 'I don't mind.'

'Does anybody else?'

'What do you mean?'

'You must know there are some in the band who frown on what you're doing.'

'You one of them?'

'Me? Come on, Coilla, you know me better than that, I hope.'

'Well, I don't give a damn what any of the others think.'

'Nor should you. And Jode feels the same way?'

'I guess so. Why do you ask?'

'To give you a little support, if you need it, and to say I know how Jode might feel as an outsider. Like me, a dwarf in an orc warband.'

'Do we make you feel like an outsider? Or Jup?'

'No, far from it; and I wouldn't expect it from orcs. If anybody knows what it's like to be outcasts it's your race. But when all's said and done you've got your ways and we've got ours. We can't help our differences. Though it has to be said that dwarfs are more acceptable to orcs than humans, given your history.'

'I can't argue with that.'

'Mind you, Jode doesn't seem typical of his kind.'

'No, that's Standeven.'

They shared a low, conspiratorial chuckle over that, and both of them glanced at Standeven, picking his way through surly groups of Wolverines lounging on the sand.

'I just wanted you to know somebody in the band backs you,' Spurral said, 'and I suspect Jup and me aren't the only ones.'

'Thanks, Spurral.'

'Hey, look, here comes Stryke.' She nodded in the direction of the jungle's fringe.

'Let's hope he's bearable.'

As he drew nearer, Coilla's impression was that Stryke seemed a jot restored. There was a hint of purpose in his gait that had been missing earlier.

He acknowledged them with a slight bob of the head. 'What's happening?'

'We were hoping you'd tell us,' Coilla replied. 'Got a plan?'

'An issue of brandy tots to buck up the band. They look as though they could use it.'

'That's not much of a plan, Stryke.'

'For where we go next, no, it isn't. That I don't know. What I do know is that this fighting unit works best, and figures things out best, when it's in good order. Let's get 'em up and busy.'

'Then what?'

'We'll see.'

Spurral felt a little superfluous. She wandered away, just a few paces, and stared at their ship, gently swaying at anchor offshore.

She noticed splashes of foam on the otherwise calm surface. As she watched, the splashing became more of a commotion. Others saw it, too. Orcs were standing, and some were calling out.

Stryke and Coilla joined her.

There was a great disturbance in the water now.

'What the hell's going on?' Stryke wanted to know.

A large area of the sea was churning. Through the misty spray they caught a flash of glistening, leathery skin.

Spurral whispered, 'My gods . . .'

'What is it?' Coilla said.

Something very big and bulky was rising out of the water.

Spurral tried to speak, but nothing came.

'*What is it?*' Coilla repeated.

Turning to her, Spurral managed, 'The . . . Krake.'

12

For what seemed an eternity the band was rooted, staring at the spectacle.

The mass of grey, rubbery flesh rose ever higher, streaming cascades of seawater. Thick as mature tree trunks, a dozen tendrils emerged and swayed menacingly.

Stryke was the first to come alive. *'It's moving this way!'* he yelled. *'To arms!'*

The band took up their weapons. Coilla and Pepperdyne found each other, as did Jup and Spurral. The tyros gathered around Dallog. Standeven backed away, stumbling in the direction of the jungle, hands shaking.

With amazing swiftness the creature came towards the beach. Its progress threw up a vaporous haze, but beyond it was the impression of multiple eyes as big as hay-cart wheels and rows of fangs the size of gravestones. The forest of tentacles wriggled horribly and gigantically like independent organisms. Water displaced by the leviathan's bulk rushed towards the island and lapped its shore.

At Stryke's order seven or eight members of the band fired their bows. They used bodkin arrows, the meanest they had. All struck, but at least half simply bounced off the toughened skin. Others lodged but didn't seem to have any effect. The archers kept firing.

'We have to do better than this,' Jup said.

'We can't fight the thing,' Spurral insisted.

'If it lives it can be killed.'

'I dunno about that.'

'Oh, come on, Spurral!'

'I've seen what it can do. We have to retreat!'

But retreating was the last thing on the band's mind. Several of the heaving, sucker-encrusted limbs were towering over the beach.

Others began to probe it, sliding in like enormous, bloated snakes. A group of orcs ran to the nearest with axes drawn. It lashed out, swiping them with enough force to bowl most of them over. Scrambling to their feet, they set to hacking at the appendage and succeeded in severing it, releasing a dark green, foul-smelling fluid. The remainder of the writhing limb was quickly withdrawn, leaving a trail of the glutinous liquid to soak into the sand.

The whole band pitched in, attacking the advancing tentacles with swords, spears and hatchets. It was Reafdaw's misfortune to get too close to one particular limb. Quick as fury it whipped around him. Trapped in a crushing embrace, and bellowing, the grunt was dragged seaward. His sword was lost, but he held on to a dagger. He slashed at the tentacle, and what passed for the creature's blood flowed copiously. But it didn't weaken its grip.

A bunch of his comrades gave chase, Stryke in the lead. Catching up, they cut, stabbed and pummelled the limb. Its hold on Reafdaw stayed firm. Then it began to rise, hoisting the struggling grunt off the ground. Its destination was obvious: the creature's cavernous maw.

Stryke leapt, caught hold of the tentacle and scrambled astride it, as though riding a horse. Its upward motion stalled a fraction. The other orcs got the idea. They followed their captain's example, jumping to the raised limb and hanging there until their combined weight brought it down again. A frenzied onslaught saw the limb hacked off, freeing Reafdaw. There were vivid red sucker marks wherever his flesh was bare. He stumbled to snatch up his dropped sword and rejoined the fray.

Haskeer's approach was direct. Scaling a large rock embedded in the sand, he threw himself at one of the questing tentacles. The spear he was holding, tip down, penetrated the thick hide and passed clean through. Temporarily pinned, the squirming limb was chopped to pieces by a swarm of grunts.

Emboldened, Haskeer tried it again. Launching himself from another rock, clutching his spear, he fell towards a snaking tentacle. The spear struck, and snapped in two. He was propelled sideways by the awkward impact, landing heavily on the beach. For a moment he lay there, the wind knocked out of him, his head swimming. Until he felt something nasty brushing against his leg.

The tentacle darted at him. Thicker than he would have been

able to hug, had he wanted to, it moved with shocking speed. Haskeer rolled clear, narrowly avoiding its embrace. He kept moving, backing off, hands pushing at the sand, feet kicking; scuttling like a crab, the need to move outweighing his inability to get up. The tentacle came after him. He took a chance and scrambled to his feet, a whisker shy of getting caught. Still retreating, engaged in a grotesque dance to avoid being seized, he tried staving off the thing with a hastily drawn dagger.

Wheam arrived, along with a couple of the other tyros, Keick and Chuss, the latter still game despite nursing his wounded arm. They laid into the tentacle.

'What kept you?' Haskeer barked.

They were too busy to reply. He added a hatchet to his knife and joined in.

Pepperdyne and Coilla battled a rearing tentacle. Their blades slashed it in a dozen places, yet still it came on. After much dodging and swerving they managed to get either side of it. Their determined, coordinated hacking separated a goodly length of flesh, releasing its foul odour. The rest of the tentacle pulled away. But there was a legion of replacements

'This is hard work,' Pepperdyne said. He was panting.

'It's gonna get harder,' she told him, pointing.

The Krake had got a lot nearer. It was not far off the shore now, a mountain of quivering grey flesh, uncurling more of its tentacle emissaries.

'Can it come on land, d'you think?'

She shook her head. 'I don't know.'

'We have to pull back!'

'Too right.' She looked around, spotted Stryke. 'Stryke! *Stryke!* Look!'

He saw, and began bellowing orders.

The Wolverines disengaged, leaving the beach to the fleshy invaders, and headed his way.

'Inland!' he cried, urging them on. *'To the trees!'*

Haskeer was the last to retreat. Passing a hunting tentacle on his way, he gave it a mighty kick, which proved ineffective but satisfying.

As the band ran for cover the shadow of the Krake fell across the beach. They crashed into the jungle, and kept going until Stryke judged they had penetrated far enough and called a halt. A movement in the undergrowth had them raising their weapons. Hoisting out the source, not too gently, few were surprised to find it was a cowering Standeven.

'What now, Stryke?' Jup wanted to know.

'I guess we wait it out.'

'That's it, is it?' Haskeer said. 'We hide in here and hope that thing goes away.'

'Got a better plan?'

'Fight it.'

'You go ahead.'

'It's what we *do*, Stryke. We don't run from a fight like frightened hatchlings.'

'And we don't waste lives going against something we *can't* fight. Maybe we'd stand a chance if we were an army and not just a warband. But we're not.'

'Well, I reckon—'

There was a sound from the direction of the beach. A rustling, splintering noise. Something was moving their way.

'*Look!*' Coilla exclaimed.

A tentacle ploughed through the jungle. It came to a particularly large tree, wrapped itself around it, uprooted it with ease and tossed it aside. Hardly slowed, it continued towards them. Some way to their left a second tentacle appeared, destroying all in its path.

'Back!' Stryke ordered. 'Everybody back!'

They needed no urging. As they retreated deeper into the jungle the sounds of destruction kept pace, from behind and on either side. The vegetation was much thicker here, and the air was fetid with the sickly sweet smell of rotting things and stagnant water. A reminder that living places were also dying places.

A little further on, the commotion of the pursuing tentacles still plainly heard, they passed a small clearing. At its centre stood a modest-sized altar, made of stone and simple in its design. Four icons were carved on its face. To most in the band there was a familiar look about it.

They pushed on, everyone alert. The band were using swords to hack through the foliage; Jup and Spurral preferred to beat obstructions aside with their staffs. As usual the tyros stuck together, with Dallog to the fore. Wheam plodded grimly, his precious lute strapped to his back. Standeven shadowed Coilla and Pepperdyne, as though the latter was still his beholden protector. In the event, any rescuing Pepperdyne did was confined to hauling up Standeven every time he tripped over a root.

The next attack came with little warning, save a rustling in the green canopy overhead. Suddenly, a tentacle jabbed down like an angry giant's finger, hit the ground and surged in their direction. The band lobbed spears, and peppered it with arrows. Coilla tugged out one of her throwing knives and tossed it with sufficient force to penetrate the tough flesh. The limb withdrew. Not completely, but enough for them to continue their flight.

'Looks like we slowed it down a bit,' Pepperdyne remarked to Coilla as they battled through the jungle.

'All I've done is lost a good knife,' she complained.

'Those tentacles are blind. Obviously, they've no eyes. So how do you think they home in on us the way they do?'

'Who knows? Instinct?'

'Maybe they can detect movement. You know, vibrations or—'

'Does it matter? Getting clear of the things is more important, isn't it?'

'Yeah, course.'

They kept going, and the sounds behind them grew more distant.

'Reckon it's given up, Stryke?' Jup asked.

'Don't know. Could be.'

'How far do you think those limbs can reach?' Coilla wondered.

'An incredibly long way,' Spurral told her.

'More good news,' Haskeer grumbled.

Stryke looked doubtful. 'Not this far, surely?'

'I wouldn't count on it,' Spurral said.

'This isn't that big an island,' Jup reminded them, 'and it's much longer than it's wide. So wherever we go we could be within its reach.'

'Perhaps not,' Pepperdyne replied.

'What do you mean?'

'A creature the size of the Krake would live in deep water. It might not even be able to come on land, the same way a fish can't. Which is why it uses its tentacles to snare prey.'

'How does this help us?' Stryke wanted to know.

'Those islands not far from the shore we're heading towards. The scouts said the water's shallow enough for us to wade across.'

'There's nothing but rock over there.'

'The important thing is the depth of the water around the islands. It wouldn't be deep enough for something as large as the Krake.'

'You're guessing that. Like you're guessing those tentacles couldn't stretch as far as the islands.'

'If they can,' Jup said, 'with no shelter over there we'd be ripe for the plucking.'

'You're right,' Pepperdyne said, 'I'm guessing. But has anybody got a better idea?'

The ensuing silence was broken by a fresh upheaval behind them. Two or three tentacles were coming their way.

'We'll do it,' Stryke decided. 'Let's move.'

They had to travel faster, whatever the obstructions; the limbs were noisily closing the gap. After what seemed an age the jungle began to thin. The trees were sparser and they had glimpses of a much brighter, open space beyond.

Shortly after, they burst out of the jungle. They were on a beach, meaner and more pebbly than the one they had started from. Not far offshore, perhaps a decent arrow shot away, was the nearest of the adjacent islands. It was much smaller than the one they were on, and completely stark.

Snatching a spear from one of the grunts, Haskeer hurled it high and arcing, so that it came down about a third of the distance to the island. It landed almost upright, less than half its length submerged.

'If it's the same all the way across,' Coilla said, 'we shouldn't be more than waist deep.'

Haskeer jabbed a thumb at the dwarfs. 'Except for these two short-arses. It'll be up to their necks.'

'We'll manage just fine,' Spurral told him coldly.

'Even if it is too deep to wade,' Standeven said, making a rare contribution, 'couldn't you swim?'

'With all our weapons, all our kit?' Pepperdyne retorted.

'All right, all right. I only asked. It's not as though I can swim anyway.'

That drew a chorus of groans.

Pepperdyne glared at him. 'Just . . . shut up.'

Ominous sounds were still coming from the jungle, faint but distinct.

'Are we going to get on and do this, Stryke?' Coilla asked, eyeing the barren island.

'Yeah.'

'Suppose those tentacles *can* reach this far,' Haskeer said. 'If we get caught out there we're done for. '

'Then don't linger,' Pepperdyne told him.

'If you're wrong, human . . .'

'Do we have a choice?'

'Let's go,' Stryke ordered.

They moved forward and entered the water, many of them holding their weapons above their heads.

About a third of the way across, one of the grunts cried out and pointed. Everybody looked back. A couple of tentacles were rummaging around the beach they'd just left. As the band watched, several more appeared, twisting high above the trees.

'They're not following,' Coilla said. 'Maybe they've come to their limit.'

'Maybe,' Stryke replied. 'Let's not hang around to find out.'

They carried on, casting anxious glances over their shoulders. The Krake's arms stayed where they were, exploring the terrain like snuffling hounds, and a couple more emerged from the jungle to join them.

At length the Wolverines reached the desolate island and dragged themselves onto its rocky shore. They climbed to its highest point, actually a very modest elevation, and kept watch.

'Suppose it doesn't go away?' Wheam said.

'If it's like any other animal,' Stryke replied, 'it'll tire or get hungry and look for easier prey.'

'How long's that likely to be?' Jup wondered.

'We'll see.'

They settled down, their damp clothes steaming in the heat of the sun.

Enough time passed for their clothing to dry, and tempers to start growing thin, before anything happened.

'Heads up!' Jup shouted.

As one, all the tentacles were rapidly withdrawing.

'It's gone,' Dallog said.

'Hold your horses,' Stryke cautioned, 'it's not over yet. Now we wait and see if the water really is shallow enough to keep that thing away from this side.'

'Yeah,' Haskeer said, casting a hostile glance Pepperdyne's way.

Again they waited. And Stryke made it a long wait, to be sure. The shadows were lengthening when he judged the time right for a move. Cautiously, the band waded back to the main island. They did it in silence, save for Haskeer's muttered grumbling about getting soaked again. Once there, Stryke sent Nep, Eldo and Seafe ahead as scouts.

Before the band got to the beach where their ship was anchored, the scouts were back.

'It's left,' Seafe reported.

'You sure?' Stryke said.

'We couldn't see it. And it's too big to miss.'

'Good.'

'We don't get off that light though, Captain. Our ship's been damaged.'

'Shit. Bad?'

'Well, it's still floating. But it's messed up. Reckon the Krake gave it a slap before it went.'

Stryke sent a party out, including Pepperdyne, to assess the damage.

'It looks grim, but I think most of it can be repaired,' the human explained a little later. 'It's taking on some water, and the main mast took a whack. They're the most important things to take care of.'

'How long?'

'Couple of days.'

'Too long.'

'Might get it down to one if we all sweat.'

'What do you need?'

'Timber, mainly. There's wood in the jungle here that'd do. Not ideal, but—'

'Let's get started.'

'It's not far off night. You want us to work in the dark?'

'Needs must.'

651

'Stryke, once the ship's righted, then what?'

'We'll get to that.'

'We don't know where to go. Not to mention we could be braving the Krake again once we leave here.'

'I said we'd get to it.' There was enough of an edge in his voice to put Pepperdyne off taking it further.

Stryke sent most of the grunts into the jungle to look for suitable wood, both for repairs and for fires to work by. The privates had been gone no time when Breggin came running back.

'What is it?' Stryke demanded.

'We're not alone!' The grunt was breathing hard.

'Who? How many?'

'Dunno. One. Maybe. Couldn't make out what. Just saw something moving in the undergrowth, that way.' He pointed. 'It gave me the slip.'

Drawing his sword, Stryke headed for the jungle at a dash. The rest followed; even Standeven, though he kept well to the rear. In the rapidly darkening interior a number of the scouting grunts joined them. Stryke had them spread out and comb the area. He pushed on, the other officers, the dwarfs and Pepperdyne flanking him.

They didn't have to go very far.

It was dark enough that, at first, Stryke wasn't sure what he was seeing. Then he realised there really was a figure standing in the shadows. He approached warily, and as he got nearer he saw that it had its back to him. It stood completely still, though by now whoever it was, unless deaf, must have heard him and the others approaching.

'No sudden moves!' Stryke barked at it. 'Turn round. And keep your hands in sight.'

The figure remained as immobile as a statue.

Stryke took a couple more steps. 'Show yourself!'

Slowly, the figure turned.

Nearer now, Stryke was sufficiently close to see its face. What he saw made him doubt his sanity.

He was looking at himself.

13

Stryke was too stunned to speak.

He stared at the being he faced. It was like gazing into a mirror. The features were his, identical in every detail. Only the slightly ill-fitting, nondescript clothes his double wore were different: a cloth jerkin over a cotton shirt, thick russet-coloured trews tucked into knee-high leather boots. No weapon of any kind; at least, none that could be seen.

Stryke's reverie was broken by Haskeer yelling, *'Sorcery! Kill it!'*

Blades drawn, he and the others began to advance. Stryke himself stayed rooted.

The stranger who looked exactly like him held up his hands and, in a calm, melodious voice quite unlike Stryke's, said, 'You can lower your weapons. I'm not a threat.'

'We're supposed to take your word for it, are we?' Jup replied, keeping his staff at the ready.

Stryke gestured for them to stay their hands, and he found his voice. 'Who . . . what are you?'

'Forgive me,' his likeness told him. 'It's a little artifice on my part. Now hold, and don't be fearful of what you see.'

Haskeer's wasn't the only chin that jutted in indignation at the remark.

'Watch out!' Coilla warned. 'It's doing something!'

The stranger began to change. Its features became oddly indistinct. The flesh seemed to melt, to run and refashion itself. There was the sound of what could have been cracking bones as the body twisted, contracted, expanded. In a moment the figure was transformed.

What stood before them now was more slender and taller than the imitation Stryke it had just been. Its face was much nearer human than orc, though not entirely so. But there was an androgynous look about the creature that made its gender indistinct. The eyes, green as emeralds, had a distinct slant; the nose was small and a little upturned. Auburn hair had emerged, abundant and collar length. It was a well proportioned face, with finely drawn features, and could be called either handsome or beautiful if its owner's sex was defined.

'What in hell are you?' Stryke said.

'A friend.' The creature's voice remained the same.

'So you say,' Jup muttered.

'My name is Dynahla.'

'You're a fetch, aren't you?' Coilla ventured. 'A shape-changer.'

'I have the ability to assume other appearances, yes.'

'Why make yourself look like me?' Stryke asked.

'Self-defence. In my experience most beings are reluctant to attack someone who looks like themselves.'

'You a he or a she?' Haskeer said. 'Or can you change that too?'

Dynahla smiled. 'I can see you'd be more comfortable dealing with a masculine being.' As it spoke, another change occurred, though it was minor compared to what they had just seen. The flesh ran more subtly, altering features in small ways. The chin, cheekbones and brow all hardened somewhat; the body grew modest muscles and the hips reduced. The result was more obviously male, while retaining a measure of ambiguity.

'I hope you're not going to keep on doing that,' Spurral remarked.

'What're you doing here?' Stryke demanded.

'I was sent,' Dynahla replied.

'By that bunch of sorcerers tailing us?' Haskeer wanted to know.

'The Gateway Corps? No, I'm not with them.'

Stryke was puzzled. 'The what?'

'You have a lot to learn, Stryke, and if you bear with me there'll be explanations.'

'How do you know my name?'

'I know all your names.' Dynahla pointed a trim finger at one after another of the band. 'Coilla, Haskeer, Jup. You must be Spurral. Dallog. That is Jode Pepperdyne, and—'

'How come you know so much about us?'

'It *is* sorcery,' Haskeer declared. 'There's magic at work here and I don't like it.' He half raised his blade.

'No,' Dynahla said. 'Or yes, rather. But not in the way you mean. Benign magic. And it isn't mine. I'm talking about the one who sent me here.'

'You haven't said who that was yet,' Stryke reminded him. He had decided that thinking of this being as male was less confusing.

'Someone you're familiar with, and who means you no harm. I was sent by Tentarr Arngrim, the one you know as Serapheim.'

'*He* sent you?'

'To aid you.'

'What are you to him?'

'Interesting question. An . . . acolyte.'

'A claim like yours is all the better for proof,' Jup said.

'I can prove it. To everyone, Stryke, or do you wish us to be alone?'

'No. We're all in this together.' He gave Pepperdyne a fleeting glance, and Standeven, skulking some way back. 'Whatever you've got to say is for everybody.'

'Then perhaps you would like to gather them.'

He nodded. 'But not here. Let's get back to what's left of the light.' At his order, Dallog gave two blasts on his horn to summon the scouts home. 'You're going under armed guard,' Stryke told Dynahla. 'I don't trust you. Whether I do depends on your so-called proof.'

'I understand.'

'If you start to change—'

'I won't.'

They headed back to the beach.

Sword at the ready, Coilla was one of those flanking Dynahla. Turning to him, she said, 'Fetches are very rare, aren't they? Least they were on Maras-Dantia.'

'So I'm told.'

'They say that seeing a fetch in your likeness, the way Stryke just did, foretells your death.'

'And they say that you orcs can't tolerate daylight.'

'Bullshit.'

'Precisely.'

No more was said until they reached the shore. As the last of the scouts started to return, Stryke asked some more questions.

'Are you of this world?'

'No.'

'How did you get here?'

'The same way you did.'

'You have stars?'

'Serapheim transported me, as he did my predecessor, Parnol.'

'Who?'

'Another acolyte. You knew him only in death. He was the messenger Serapheim sent to you in Ceragan.'

'The human with the knife in his back.'

'Yes. Jennesta was responsible for that.'

'No surprise there then,' Haskeer said.

Stryke's hand went to his throat. 'I've got his amulet.'

'Good,' Dynahla said. 'That was enterprising of you.'

'But it's no use. The stars don't work properly.'

'You still have them?'

'Yes.'

'Have they had any . . . effect on you? You can be truthful. I know that they have affected you in the past, and Haskeer.' He looked at the sergeant. He returned a scowl.

'No,' Stryke replied. 'I've felt nothing.'

'That's good too. Hopefully you've become attuned to them.'

'What does that mean?'

'Each set of instrumentalities has its own signature, what some call its song. A being spending any amount of time in their presence either suffers or harmonises with them, as perhaps you are doing. Do you understand?'

'I think so.'

'But it's not wise to be within their range of influence for too long, even if their effect seems to be benevolent.'

'Why not?'

'Because the instrumentalities embody an unimaginable power. A power that even the most adept of sorcerers do not fully comprehend.'

'I'm not surrendering them,' he insisted, sensing the way things were going.

'I'm not asking you to.'

'Anyway, as I said, they don't work. Not the way they should. Do you know why?'

656

'Yeah,' Jup added, 'and does Jennesta have anything to do with it?'

'What about this Gateway Corps?' Coilla pitched in. 'Who are they? What do they want?'

'And where's Thirzarr?' Stryke demanded.

Dynahla raised a hand to still the clamour. 'These matters are best addressed by the proof I have to offer. Is this all your band, Stryke?'

He looked around. The last couple of stragglers were jogging their way. 'Yes.'

'Then you're about to have some answers. But don't expect everything to be resolved immediately.'

'That doesn't sound too promising,' Coilla remarked darkly.

'Trust me,' Dynahla said.

As they watched intently, hands on weapons, the fetch took a small silken pouch from his pocket and poured the contents into the palm of his hand. As far as they could see it was sand, identical to that on the beach. He threw it into the air. It didn't fall, but hung there in a cloud. Then it rearranged itself, forming a kind of flat canvas, no thicker than an individual grain, suspended just above their heads.

Suddenly it was no longer sand, at least in appearance. It became a rectangle of gently pulsing white light, which in turn gave way to a succession of primary colours, flashing through the spectrum. When it calmed, an image came into focus, raising gasps and exclamations from some in the band.

The human Tentarr Arngrim, Serapheim to the fraternity of wizards and seers, gazed down at them.

Wheam looked terrified. Dallog, the other tyros, Spurral, and Pepperdyne and Standeven, none of whom had much if any knowledge of the sorcerer, were almost as awed.

'This image is recorded in the grains of sand,' Dynahla explained. 'You cannot converse with him.'

'Like back on Ceragan the last time,' Haskeer whispered.

Stryke shushed him.

Serapheim spoke, his voice loud, almost booming, and all could hear. '*Greetings, Stryke; and Wolverines, I salute you. You are to be congratulated on your efforts in Acurial. Your actions there played a not insignificant part in freeing your kind from the shackles of oppression.*'

657

'Didn't get us Jennesta though,' Jup muttered under his breath.

As though responding, Serapheim's likeness went on, *'It's regrettable that you had less success in your dealings with my daughter. But do not reproach yourselves for it, and take heart from knowing that aspect of your mission is far from over.'* The sorcerer paused briefly. When he resumed, his tone was less formal, and betrayed a degree of weariness. *'I've much to tell you, although I fear not all your curiosity's going to be satisfied. Not yet.'* He grew more matter-of-fact. *'First, let me commend Dynahla to you. You've a faithful, dependable ally in this adherent, who has my complete trust, and deserves yours. Dynahla's powers can be of great help to you. All I ask is that you don't allow my most steadfast servant to come to harm. I'd be devastated should Dynahla suffer an end as miserable as Parnol's, whose fate you have doubtless now learnt.'* There was something that could have been a sigh before he carried on. *'As with so much that is corrupt, Jennesta was behind Parnol's death. Just one more casual murder to her, but a grievous blow to me, and to our cause.'*

'We have a cause?' Coilla mumbled.

'I know that, for a time, Jennesta had possession of the instrumentalities you hold,' Serapheim continued, *'and since you regained them they've failed to work properly. Didn't you wonder at the ease with which you got them back? I mean no slur on your abilities, but had she been determined to keep them you would have had a much harder fight on your hands. The fact is that Jennesta wanted you to recover the instrumentalities. For two reasons. First, she has mastered an ancient magical process that allowed her to copy them. Second, she placed an enchantment on the original set she allowed you to take back. A spell which accounts for their erratic behaviour, and may even let her track your movements.'*

There were some knowing nods at that. It was more or less what smarter members of the band already suspected.

'As far as I can tell, the fake instrumentalities Jennesta possesses have as much power as the genuine ones. I don't have to tell you that this makes her even more dangerous. As far as the influence she exercises over your instrumentalities is concerned, Dynahla has the skill to counter it, though in a limited way. I expect to fare better, but only if you bring the instrumentalities to me.'

'Why didn't you come here yourself?' Haskeer said.

'He can't hear you,' Dynahla reminded him.

'Oh, yeah.'

Several of the others glared and waved him quiet.

'As you know by now,' Serapheim's image said, *'we are not the only ones with an interest in the artefacts. The group hunting you are members of a fraternity called the Gateway Corps. They are an incredibly ancient order, active for perhaps as long as there have been instrumentalities. Their sole purpose is to locate and seize the artefacts. This they do from the best of intentions, and given the power of the instrumentalities their concern is understandable, but they pursue their goal with utter dedication, akin to fanaticism. They, too, are danger-ous. Their magic is very potent and they command advanced weap-onry.'*

'You're telling us,' Coilla remarked.

'Again, Dynahla may be able to provide some measure of protection as far as the Corps is concerned. Though your best strategy would be to give them as wide a berth as possible. Let me repeat that you can trust my acolyte, in this and all other matters. Allow yourselves to be guided by Dynahla, who will lead you to me. Be of good heart, and keep faith that your path will lead you to victory.'

Serapheim's image vanished. The shimmer went out of the grains of sand and they fell, a tiny gritty shower pattering down to the beach.

'What about Thirzarr?' Stryke demanded angrily. 'He didn't say anything about her. Where is she?'

'Serapheim warned you that not all your questions would be answered immediately,' Dynahla said.

'Lot of good that does me.'

'But it doesn't mean those answers can't be found. That's one of the reasons he sent me to you; to help you find the truth.'

'The only truth I want is the whereabouts of Thirzarr and our hatchlings.'

'If it's any comfort, we believe your hatchlings are safe.'

'How can you know that?'

'Serapheim has his ways of knowing.'

'But he can't tell me where Thirzarr is?'

'Your mate is within the influence of Jennesta's magic. It cloaks her, and makes her harder to trace. But Serapheim's working hard to penetrate that barrier.'

'What was that about us going to Serapheim?' Coilla asked. 'Why should we want to do that?'

'Because apart from me, he's the only ally you can rely on,' Dynahla replied, 'and the most powerful.'

'So why didn't he come here himself?'

'There are good reasons. You'll see.'

'Where is Serapheim?' Stryke said.

'Our way to him is on this world.'

'What does *that* mean?'

'It isn't far. But first we need to take to sea. And your ship must be repaired for that.'

'Tell me something I don't know. But where are we going?' Stryke repeated.

'West.'

Pepperdyne still had Stryke's map. He got it out and consulted it. 'Where exactly in the west?'

Dynahla looked, then pointed. 'There.'

'There's nothing in that region. It's just open sea.'

'Only according to your map.'

'I know this chart's a bit vague in places, but—'

'There is much it doesn't show. Trust me.'

Stryke wasn't alone in wondering if they could. 'What if we decide not to go with you?'

'You're wiser than that. You know you have no other option.'

He had to concede that. But he didn't say so.

'What about that Gateway Corps outfit?' Jup said.

'Yeah, what about 'em?' Haskeer put in. 'They gonna cause us any more trouble?'

'They'll never stop hounding you until they gain the instrumentalities,' Dynahla explained, 'or you kill every last one of them. Given how powerful they are, that's unlikely, even for a warband of orcs. Of course, that assumes you can avoid the clutches of the Krake. Then you can steel yourselves to face Jennesta.'

'Sounds like a piece of piss,' Coilla remarked sarcastically.

Dynahla smiled mirthlessly. 'Nobody said it would be easy.'

14

The Wolverines worked hard repairing their ship, labouring through the night and well into the next day, with Stryke driving them mercilessly. Shortly after noon they were close to having the vessel seaworthy.

As the only really experienced sailor present, Pepperdyne was given the task of overseeing the work. Anxious to be under way, Stryke had him come ashore to report on progress.

'How much longer?'

'We're all but done,' the human told him. 'Just a few minor chores left, and we need to get supplies of fresh water over there, along with any food we can scavenge from the jungle.'

'I've got the band working on that. You sure the ship's up to the voyage?'

'It's not a perfect job, but it should serve.'

'That's all we need.'

'Some of the repairs are only temporary, mind, and they're not likely to last too long. I'd like to carry them out properly first chance we get.'

'I don't know when that'd be. For now we make do.'

'And . . . the band.'

'What about 'em?'

'They've been working like dogs all night. They could do with rest.'

'No time.'

'They're dead on their feet. If they don't get—'

'You take care of the ship,' Stryke emphasised his words with a finger jab to Pepperdyne's chest, 'and I'll worry about my band. They're used to hard work. Anything else?'

'Nope.'

'Then get back to it.' He turned on his heel and left the human.

As he walked away, Stryke caught a glimpse of Dynahla, standing further along the beach and staring out to sea. Having no appetite or time for any more riddles he let the creature be.

Then he spotted Haskeer, returning at the head of one of the foraging parties. They were rolling barrels towards the shore, and some carried sacks. He went their way.

'Done yet?'

His sergeant nodded. 'Just about. There's plenty of water, but lean pickings far as food goes.'

'We'll get by.' He looked to the group Haskeer had just been leading. 'Thought I told you to take along some of the tyros.'

'Yeah, well, I didn't.'

'That was an *order*, Haskeer. I want the new recruits mixing in more with the band; they're not learning fast enough. Where do you get off ignoring me?'

'You can't rely on 'em. They're greenhorns.'

'What d'you expect if we don't teach them?'

'I'm a fighter, not a wet nurse. Let Dallog suckle his own brood.'

'What is it with you and him? Why're you so down on the tyros?'

'Well, he ain't no Alfray for a start.'

'Shit, not *that* again. It's time you got your head round Alfray being dead and gone.'

'More's the pity. And who we got instead? A puffed up, self-satisfied—'

'Dallog's not trying to replace Alfray. Nobody could.'

'You're telling me.'

'You're being too hard on him. On all of them. The tyros have paid in blood on this mission. Ignar, Harglo, Yunst. All dead.'

'And we lost Liffin, and now Bhose. Either of which were worth a dozen of those rookies. If you wanna talk about dying, Stryke, maybe you should look at the band.'

'Meaning?'

'As if it's not bad enough having a bunch of learners to shepherd, we've a pair of *humans* tagging along.' He all but spat the word. 'And one of 'em an orc killer back in Acurial.'

'We don't know that for sure.'

'Yeah, right,' Haskeer sneered. 'You gonna defend the other one, too, and what he's up to with Coilla?'

'Whatever Coilla and Pepperdyne do is no business of ours, long as it doesn't endanger the band.'

'You sure it won't? This is a human we're talking about.'

'He's done nothing to make me distrust him. The opposite, if anything.'

'What he's doing with Coilla's enough for me. It ain't natural, Stryke. It's . . . *sick*. Now, on top of all that, we've got this fetch, or whatever it is, telling us what to do. Seems to me that all adds up to a pig's ear far as this band goes.'

Stryke was about to reply, or possibly end his sergeant's rant by knocking his teeth out, when Haskeer stared past him and glowered. Turning his head, Stryke saw that Dynahla had silently arrived.

'Am I interrupting anything?' the shape-changer asked.

'Not for me,' Haskeer said. He shoved past them and strode away.

Watching him leave, Dynahla said, 'He has a lot of anger.'

'We all do. What did you want?'

'It looks as though the ship's nearly ready.'

'Almost.'

'And we'll leave shortly?'

'Soon as we can.'

'There could be a problem. I sense that the Krake is still nearby.'

'That's another of your talents, is it, sensing things?'

'I have some ability to do that, yes. Not unlike the farsight dwarfs possess, though somewhat different in nature. But how I know doesn't matter. What's important is what you're going to do about the Krake.'

'Any suggestions?'

'Only that you'd do well to think of a strategy before setting sail. The creature might not bother us, but if it does—'

'Yeah, I get it. That all you've got to offer?'

'I might be able to cloud what passes for the beast's mind, and slow it a little. But not much more.'

Stryke remembered something. 'I've got this.' He showed the bracelet Mallas Sahro had given him. 'Could it help?'

Dynahla studied the bracelet, then bent and sniffed. 'Elf magic.'

'You can tell by *smelling* it?'

The fetch nodded. 'Different classes of sorcery have distinct aromas, if you know how to detect them. As to the efficacy of this totem; it could ward off minor magical attacks. Though you shouldn't expect it to offer any protection against Jennesta.'

Stryke pulled down his sleeve. 'And against the Krake?'

'A creature like that operates on pure instinct. We need a more physical method of hampering it. Perhaps your band can come up with ideas.'

'More time wasted,' he grumbled.

'Better that than facing the monster unprepared.'

Stryke had to agree.

Ordering most of the band to keep at work provisioning the ship, he hastily got together a conclave of his officers. Naturally that included Dallog, despite Haskeer's silent though palpable disapproval. He wasn't keen on Pepperdyne and Dynahla being present either, but knowing Stryke wouldn't tolerate any more arguments, he curbed his tongue.

'We're ready to leave,' Stryke told them. 'Only we've got a problem. The Krake's still out there.'

'What makes you think that?' Jup asked.

'Dynahla here can *sense* it.'

'Really?' Coilla said. 'You can do that?'

'Yes,' Dynahla confirmed.

'So how do we get clear of the Krake?' Stryke wanted to know. 'Any ideas?'

'We don't,' Haskeer offered. 'We kill the fucking thing.'

'Any *useful* ideas?' Stryke restated, ignoring the sergeant's offended glare.

'Can't we outrun it?' Dallog suggested, further stoking Haskeer's annoyance.

Pepperdyne said, 'Unlikely. Not from a standing start, even with a strong wind. Which we don't have off these shores. Though with a good enough diversion I reckon we'd stand a chance of getting away.'

'Such as?' Stryke prompted.

'Remember what the resistance used against the Peczan forces? Acurialian fire they called it, didn't they? Perhaps we could use that.'

'How?'

'Same way the resistance did; as a barrage, and maybe we could tip spears with it, and arrows.'

'That ain't gonna kill the brute,' Haskeer objected.

'But it might slow it down.'

'Do we know how to make the stuff?' Stryke said.

Pepperdyne nodded. 'It's similar to a weapon we had back on Trougath. Mostly it's oil. The other part's something mixed in to make the burning oil stick to its target. We used various things: tree sap, soap shavings, honey, certain gummy berries. Though I guess we'd need quite a quantity for something the size of the Krake.'

'There are plenty of barrels of lantern oil on the ship,' Jup recalled, 'along with pots and other containers to hold it.'

'And lots more scattered around the settlement back there,' Coilla said, jabbing a thumb at the jungle.

'All right,' Stryke decided, 'we'll try it. Let's get that oil ashore.'

'Why bother hauling it over here? We could do the making on the ship.'

'And what happens if the Krake pops up before we're finished? No, Coilla, I want us fully armed and ready when we set sail. So one party to bring the oil. Another to search out the tacky stuff to go with it. You seem to know about that, Pepperdyne, so go with 'em. A third party scours the settlement for pots and the like. The rest get making more arrows and spears. We need lots. And cloth or something, to wrap them with. Now move yourselves.'

Jup and Haskeer gathered the rest of the band and got them into groups. Everybody had a task, including Standeven and Dynahla. The human scavenged for rags; the fetch helped mix the brew.

Barrels were used to blend the oil and a variety of viscous fluids, some more successfully than others. Once they got the mixture right it was ladled into as many suitable vessels as they could find; pots, bottles, flasks, pitchers and jugs. Anything that would shatter on impact. Oil-soaked cloths, jammed into the containers' mouths, served as fuses.

Arrows and spears were made in prodigious numbers. This should have been straightforward, but proved tricky because the wood yielded by the jungle was of variable quality. Once hewed, their sharpened tips were hardened over flame. Nor were the band's usual weapons ignored. Swords, hatchets and throwing axes were whetted, and bow strings tightened.

All that remained was to test the Acurialian fire. Selecting a charged pot at random, Stryke positioned himself about fifty paces from one of the large, half buried rocks that dotted the beach. Fuse lit, he lobbed the bombard. It struck the rock near its crown and instantly exploded. The sticky, blazing oil covered a good two-thirds of the rock's surface, its intense orange flame billowing black smoke. It carried on burning a lot longer than they expected.

'They'll do,' Stryke announced. He turned to Pepperdyne. 'Is the weather right?'

'Tide's up and there should be wind enough. But if we don't go right now it'll have to be tomorrow. I wouldn't relish steering through those straits in the dark.'

Stryke bellowed the order and embarkation got under way.

Once everybody was on board he had the containers lined-up ready on deck. Braziers were stoked, for igniting the fuses. Archers and spear-carriers lined the rails. Jad was dispatched to the crow's nest, and other grunts swarmed on the rigging. The sails dropped and the goblin ship's peculiarly embellished anchor was raised.

Pepperdyne had taken the wheel. Coilla was at his side, clutching a bow. Stryke roamed the decks, scolding, encouraging, swearing. Dynahla stood alone at the prow, crimson hair flowing in the clement breeze.

They set off.

The band fell into a tense silence as the craft gradually started to move. Any exhaustion they had from working all night fell away as they scanned the waters, alert for the slightest sign of anything amiss.

At length, and painfully slowly, the ship nosed its way into the open sea.

'So far, so good,' Pepperdyne half whispered.

Coilla dragged her gaze from the ocean. 'Maybe all that work was for nothing.'

The sails were swelling. They started to pick up a little speed.

'At least we've got an addition to our armoury,' he said. 'This Acurialian fire could be useful if—'

They saw Dynahla's head turn their way. The shape-changer was shouting something, but they couldn't get the sense. A heartbeat later Jad was crying out from the crow's nest and pointing. It was the prelude to a general uproar from those on deck.

Ahead of them, and off to starboard, the water was troubled. A leathery dome broke the surface, larger than any they had ever seen on a temple or a tyrant's folly. It rose inexorably, growing bigger, shedding water and glistening repellently in the light. Several tentacles appeared, thicker than a main-mast and garlanded with seaweed.

Pepperdyne frantically spun the wheel. Sluggishly, the ship began turning to port.

Dynahla was heading their way. Thundering up the stairs to the helm, Stryke got there first.

'Can we lose it?'

Pepperdyne shook his head. 'Don't know. Maybe if we'd been under way a bit longer . . .'

The Krake was still rising, water cascading from its coarse hide. The ship rocked in the swell.

Dynahla arrived.

Before the fetch could speak, Stryke barked, 'What was it you said about clouding that thing's mind?'

'How do you think we got this far? I've bought us a little time. Use it!'

Pepperdyne applied all his skill to manoeuvring the craft. The Krake was still ahead and a lot nearer. It wasn't in their path, but close to it. As the ship swerved to its new course, away from the creature, the Krake surged forward, as though to cut them off. It was hard to tell whose speed was the greater.

They avoided a collision, but found themselves uncomfortably close to the beast. They were still veering. It continued to advance. The gap was closing fast, and the Krake's tentacles stretched their way.

'We've no choice now,' Coilla said, glancing at Stryke.

'So we take the bastard.'

Even though he was coming to know the orcs better than most other humans had, Pepperdyne was taken aback at the wild, almost crazed smiles Coilla and Stryke exchanged. The orcs' hunger for a fight, whatever the odds, was as deeply ingrained in them as cruelty was in his own race.

'Try to keep us clear of it!' Stryke bellowed.

Pepperdyne nodded and bore down on the wheel. Coilla nocked a cloth-headed arrow. Dynahla clutched the rail and stared intently at the looming monster.

Stryke made for the stairs and the deck below. The Krake was a writhing mountain now, blocking out the light. The air had a fishy stink to it.

'*Steady!*' Stryke yelled at the band. '*On my order!*'

Spears and arrows were poised over the braziers. Torches were held ready for the bombards to be lit.

A tentacle brushed the side of the ship. To the Krake, it was no more than a tap, like a hatchling's gentle nudging of a toy boat. It felt like a small earthquake to the Wolverines. The ship listed violently. Several band members lost their balance and fell. Unsecured objects slid across the deck, and the port side took a drenching.

'*Now!*' Stryke bellowed.

The archers were first. A swarm of burning arrows streaked towards the groping tentacles. All struck. The range was close enough that many penetrated, sizzling as they delivered their blazing cargo. Those that didn't pierce still left a stamp of fire on the creature's moist flesh. The nearest tentacle, peppered with glowing, fizzling bolts, dropped back underwater. Another immediately replaced it, and a second cloud of radiant arrows soared its way.

The main bulk of the Krake, its ravenous eyes and gaping maw, could be seen clearly now beyond a growing forest of waving limbs. Arrows like darting fireflies sprayed them. Once the tentacles were running with flame they fell back, but the Krake was only slowed, not deterred.

Stryke was fearful that if it got into range the creature would dispatch tentacles under the ship to upend or crush it. And it was almost near enough to do that. His dilemma was that the Krake was still too far away for the bombards or spears to reach it. The point at which it would be near enough, yet not threaten the ship, was a fine judgement. All Stryke could do was urge on the archers and bide his time.

On the bridge, Pepperdyne and Coilla watched as the fiery rainbow of arrows arced towards the encroaching beast.

'The arrows can't last much longer, surely?' Pepperdyne said, spinning the wheel.

Coilla had an arrow nocked herself. She applied flame, aimed and sent it winging to the Krake. 'No,' she replied, plucking another shaft from her quiver. 'I'm surprised they've lasted this long, the rate we're using them.'

He looked to the mass of living flesh bearing down on them, then back at her. 'I don't know that we can get away from this thing.'

'If anybody can do it, you can.'

'I'm flattered, but your faith might be misplaced. The Krake's moving nearly as fast as we are, despite what we're throwing at it.'

'We haven't thrown everything yet.'

He gave the wheel another hard tug. 'Maybe we'd better start.'

Coilla unleashed her arrow.

A wave of displaced water swept in, rocking the ship again, and more violently than before. The orcs in the rigging had their work cut out hanging on.

Stryke judged the time right to strengthen the assault; the Krake seemed near enough. He just hoped his estimate of the gap separating them was accurate.

At his command, the band began lighting bombards' fuses. A moment later they were flinging them hard, adding their power to the volley of arrows. The distance was a challenge, and took all the throwers' strength, but most of the missiles found their target. On contact with the Krake they exploded with much greater force than the arrows. Some burst reddish when they struck, others yellow-blue or orange, depending on the glutinous liquid mixed with the oil.

'Best you can do?' Haskeer taunted.

Jup glared at him. 'I might be throwing less than you, but at least I'm hitting the bastard.'

'Yeah? Beat this.' He lit a fuse, drew back his arm and took aim. With a grunt he lobbed the flame-tipped pot.

They watched it streak against the darkening sky. It briefly disappeared from sight in the confusion of explosions, flaming arrows, smoke and thrashing limbs. It showed itself again when a reddish-orange bloom erupted on the side of the creature's gigantic head. Tendrils of fire rippled out from the blast, marbling the Krake's leathery hide.

Haskeer shot the dwarf a superior smirk.

'Stand back,' Jup said, hefting a bomb.

He launched it like a discus, spinning round for momentum and letting go with a roar. The projectile soared high and fast. It, too, impacted on the monster's glistening dome; a blood-red blossom, sending out rivulets of lava.

'Right,' Haskeer grated. He rolled up his sleeves and reached for a bomb.

Another wave hit the ship, sending a fierce tremor through it. The roll that followed was the most acute yet. Much of the clutter that was unsecured had already shifted to the port side. This bigger blow shifted some of the heavier objects, including the brazier Jup and Haskeer were standing beside. It toppled, spilling its red hot coals. As the deck was wet that wouldn't have mattered. Except that the jolt caused Haskeer to drop the bomb he was about to light. The pot shattered and its content instantly burst into flames. Leaping back, they were lucky to avoid being splashed by liquid as tenacious as a limpet and as scathing as acid. But they were confronted by a spreading wall of fire. They set about beating at it, Haskeer using his jerkin, Jup a piece of sacking.

Several of the grunts had been given the additional task of firewatcher. For Standeven it was his only job, and one it was thought even he couldn't make a mess of. As the nearest fire-watcher he had to respond, and arrived clutching two buckets, one slopping water, the other filled with sand.

He took one look at the fire and froze.

Jup and Haskeer were on the other side of it, feeling the heat and unable to get to him. They had to content themselves with shouting curses. Standeven was oblivious.

Then Dallog was there with Wheam and Pirrak, and Spurral bringing up the rear. The buckets were snatched from Standeven and he was pushed aside, roughly enough that he went down and sprawled on the deck. They attacked the flames, thrashing it with clothing and sacks. Water was no good; pails of sand had to be chained over, until at last they were able to trample what remained of the fire and kill it.

Standeven was still on the deck, propped on his elbow, staring dazedly at the scene.

Haskeer dashed to him, grabbed him by the scruff and drew back his fist. 'You bloody useless little—'

Stryke arrived, panting. *'Leave it.'*

'This stupid bastard would've let us burn,' Haskeer protested.

'We've more important things to worry about. Get to your station.'

'But—'

'Do it!'

Haskeer gave Standeven a murderous glare, then let him go. The cowering, ashen-faced human slumped. Haskeer returned to the fight.

Casting Standeven a disgusted look of his own, Stryke ordered everyone back to their duties. He also had the spears brought into play.

The bombardment of the Krake carried on. What was left of the band's hoard of arrows continued soaring its way. The bombs exploded incessantly, joined by a cloud of blazing spears.

The creature was on fire. Not in patches, as before, but totally. A fetid smell of charred flesh hung in the air. Punctured by numerous spears and arrows, the Krake slowed its advance, and stopped.

To cheers from the band it began to sink below the waves. When it was completely submerged the fire could still be seen, permeating the water with a ghostly glow.

Stryke raced up to the bridge. Dynahla was still there, surveying the scene.

'Is it finished?' Coilla asked.

'Don't know,' Stryke replied, glancing at the turbulent water where the Krake had gone down. 'But we're not sticking around to find out.' He turned to Pepperdyne. 'It's up to you now, human. Get us out of here.'

Pepperdyne nodded and spun the wheel.

They headed west.

15

Not every landmass in the world of islands was populated. But one such, nondescript like so many others, was hosting surreptitious visitors.

Jennesta didn't want for comforts, whatever her followers had to cope with. While they bivouacked as best they could, her tented quarters offered a haven, and even a measure of luxury. But it was the privacy that she valued most when undertaking certain magical practices, as now.

She stood by a small table. On it sat a representation of the Krake; a miniature, crudely fashioned model. It was on fire. Flames played across its entire surface, but they would never harm the Receptive Matter Jennesta had used to fashion the creature's likeness.

For a moment she was spellbound, literally. She willed the enchantment to unravel, until the link between her mock-up and the real beast was broken, and her control gone. She had been gazing at the flames. With a slight movement of her hand she extinguished them.

She didn't see the encounter between the Wolverines and the sea creature as a defeat. She had harassed the orcs, as she had with the fauns, which caused them trouble and delay. It was an agreeable pastime. A satisfaction.

The Receptive Matter cooled instantly. If it had ever been hot. She picked it up, squeezed it in her palm and returned it to its usual shapeless, colourless state. It was displeasing to her touch, but had a sweet odour that was almost heady. She returned it to her precious stockpile, in its plain silver casket, then put the casket out of sight.

The effort of maintaining the spell had tired her. There would have to be sustenance soon. Preferably fresh, warm and still beating. But that would have to wait.

She wasn't alone, although she could have been for all the awareness her captive had. Thirzarr was seated at the far end of the quarters. She was stiffly motionless, her gaze vacant.

Jennesta moved to the tent's entrance, stopped just short of it and clapped twice, sharply. Shortly after, there was a scrabbling at the canvas flaps. A pair of her undead menials came through awkwardly, and awaited her pleasure, their expressions as vacuous as Thirzarr's.

'Take her back to the others in their cage,' Jennesta ordered, pointing at the orc.

One of the zombies obeyed, and began to shuffle in Thirzarr's direction. The other was Hacher, who remained immobile. Sluggishly, he turned his head towards Jennesta and fixed her with a dull but even stare. She repeated the order, more firmly, but still Hacher hesitated.

'What's wrong with you?' Jennesta snapped. 'Do as you're told!'

He slowly moved. Not towards Thirzarr, but Jennesta. She flicked a jolt of energy at him, as a herdsman might chastise livestock with a whip. The impact half spun Hacher, and he would have fallen if some buried instinct hadn't surfaced and made him reach out to the table for support. His hand came down hard on its edge, causing one of his desiccated fingers to snap off. It dropped to the heavily carpeted floor.

Jennesta laughed scornfully. 'Not much of an iron hand now, are you, General?' Her expression returned to harsh and she added coldly, 'Obey my order.'

Hacher had been staring dumbly at his disfigurement. He looked up when she spoke, and after a moment's wavering began to shamble in Thirzarr's direction.

Jennesta told Thirzarr to rise. In her almost catatonic state she meekly complied, and flanked by Hacher and the other undead was escorted from the tent, the trio moving at a languid pace.

Almost immediately a human officer entered, bowed his head and begged Jennesta's pardon for intruding.

'What is it?'

'Your . . . guest has arrived, my lady. Along with something of a retinue.'

'Send him in. Alone.'

'Ma'am.'

'And take that with you.' She indicated Hacher's severed finger.

Doing his best to hide his distaste, the officer gingerly picked it up with his thumb and forefinger. He left holding it out in front of him, as though he were a nervous scullery maid ordered to dispose of a drowned rat found in a pot of soup.

Jennesta didn't have long to wait for her next visitor. He strode in, his black bow slung over one bony shoulder, a quiver of arrows at his hip.

'I am Gleaton-Rouk,' the goblin declared sibilantly.

'Welcome,' Jennesta replied, a syrupy, artificial sincerity in her tone. 'I'm obliged to you for accepting my invitation.'

'It wasn't your words that brought me.'

'You found the gems and coin I sent spoke more eloquently. I understand. But that was a trifling gift compared to what you could gain.'

Avarice flashed in his dark eyes, along with suspicion. 'What do you want of me?'

'Two things. First, I need an additional ship.'

'Why?'

Jennesta fought down the impulse to tell this creature to mind his business. 'I'm recruiting a certain number of . . . *helpers* on my travels. I need another ship to transport them, and I understand you're best placed to supply one.'

'It could be possible. If you make it worth my while.'

'I've no shortage of funds.'

'I will see what I can do. You said there were two things.'

'I take it that's your famous bow,' she said, eyeing it and seeming to ignore his question. 'It's a handsome weapon.'

'It's not for sale,' Gleaton-Rouk hissed.

She laughed. 'I didn't intend making an offer.'

'Nor can it be taken from me,' he added charily.

'Really? Don't worry; I've no need of it.'

'Then why speak of it?'

'Partly out of what you might call a professional interest, as a practitioner of the ancient art myself.'

He gave a derisive snort. 'Any power you might command would be no match for Shadow-wing's.'

'Be that as it may, I didn't ask you here to debate the efficacy of magic. The bow touches on the second reason I wanted to meet with you.'

'How so?'

'I know you used it recently to kill an orc.'

'What is that to you?'

'I commend you for it. I, too, have a blood feud with the Wolverines, and particularly with its leader. Working together, you and I could bring about a reckoning.'

'I've no taste for being recruited.'

'I said working together. What I'm proposing is an alliance.'

'You have a small army, and you claim magical powers. Why do you need me?'

'Because you have something greater than mere magic. You have a passion for vengeance. As do I.'

'Yet you seek an ally.'

'I need one I can trust. I'm surrounded by fools.'

'And what would we achieve?'

'We could pour pressure on the warband, and bring about the death of its damnable captain, Stryke.'

'What's in it for me?'

'I should hope that the sweetness of revenge would be reward enough.' She noted his expression and added, 'Though of course I would also show my appreciation in the form of further riches.'

Gleaton-Rouk thought about it, and at length hissed, 'I agree. Subject to the details being to my liking.'

'Of course,' Jennesta replied smoothly, reflecting on how best to betray this new partner. She had no doubt he was thinking the same. 'And as a token of my good faith I would like to present you with a further pecuniary offering. As a down-payment, let's call it.' Having looted the treasury before fleeing Acurial, her apparent generosity was of no consequence. Besides, she could always get more, one way or another.

The goblin gave her the tiniest nod by way of acceptance. 'And for my part I shall make arrangements concerning the ship you require.'

'How long will that take?'

'It will be settled before the day's end.'

'Then I suggest you return here to continue our discussion.'

675

Gleaton-Rouk nodded, and together they left the tent.

There was a lot of activity outside. Her troops were going about their chores, along with a few of the zombies. The latter were watched with suspicion and not a little bewilderment by Gleaton-Rouk's entourage. They numbered about a dozen, and stood together not far from Jennesta's tent, clutching their tridents.

As Gleaton-Rouk headed their way, Jennesta stopped him with, 'There's one more small matter to clear up.'

'What might that be?' he said, turning to her.

'When my delegation approached you to arrange this meeting, one of them was killed.'

'A regrettable occurrence. We had no idea who this group of humans were, or whether they were hostile. We thought to defend ourselves.'

'I see.'

'It was no more than you would have done yourself, I expect.'

'Your feud with the Wolverines is over them having killed some of your kin, is that right?'

He was puzzled by the turn the conversation had taken, but replied, 'You know it is.'

Jennesta looked at his retinue. 'These are your kin?'

'Some are, some aren't. All are my clan.'

She pointed at a goblin. 'Is he kin?'

'Yes.'

'What about him?' She indicated another.

'Him? No, we do not share blood.'

Without a further word, Jennesta raised her open hand, palm up, and placed its heel against her chin. Like a child dispersing dandelion heads, she gently blew. A jet of black vapour streamed from her hand. As it flowed it solidified into something resembling a cluster of catapult shot. Faster than the eye could follow, the cloud of shot flashed towards the goblin she had singled out. It struck with tremendous force, riddling his body with a myriad of tiny crimson explosions. Many passed clean through him. Instantly he was rendered little more than pulp, collapsing in a gory heap.

Such was the precision of Jennesta's spell that the dead goblin's companions, although standing with him, were completely untouched, except by their comrade's blood. For an instant they froze, then they began brandishing their weapons, their faces

676

twisted with outrage. Jennesta's followers tensed and reached for their own blades.

'You took one of mine, I've taken one of yours,' she told Gleaton-Rouk, her voice strident enough to be heard by his retinue.

For the first time since he arrived the goblin leader wore an expression that betrayed his true feelings. It was disbelief and awe. But as the realisation of what he was dealing with dawned on him it gave way to the kind of grudging respect one bully feels for another. The whole thing was fleeting, and he quickly returned to seeming passivity, but Jennesta saw.

'I understand the need for . . . compensation,' he said, signing his bodyguards to stand down with a flick of his bony hand. They did so uneasily. 'Let us regard this as a debt paid.'

'And I'll levy no interest,' she replied, giving him a smile designed to be charming without quite achieving it.

'Until later then.' He bobbed his head. Glancing at the lightly steaming remains of his dead follower, he added in a softer tone, 'You must teach me that sometime.'

'I might just do that,' she said.

They left, and she returned to her quarters.

Killing the goblin had fatigued her further. Not seriously, just enough to be annoying. But there was one more thing to do before she could take nourishment.

She ordered complete privacy, and in the cool of her tent enacted a ritual. One that forged a mental link with another party. Someone not too far away, and approaching.

Dynahla leaned against the rail on a quiet part of the orcs' ship, head in hands, crimson locks flowing in the breeze.

'*Hey.*'

There was no response.

'*Hey.* Dynahla!'

The shape-changer stirred and slowly turned.

'You all right?' Stryke asked. He was accompanied by Jup.

'Yes. I'm . . . fine. I didn't know you were—'

'What were you doing?' Jup said.

'Communing.'

Stryke frowned. 'You better explain that.'

'I was in touch with someone. Mentally, that is.'

'Who?'

'Serapheim.'

He was nonplussed. 'You can do that?'

'Under certain circumstances. Though it's not easy.'

'How do you do it?'

'We have a psychic link, you might say. It's hard to explain.'

'You said Serapheim couldn't talk to us directly,' Jup recalled. 'That's why you brought his message.'

'He can't communicate directly with any of *you*. There has to be the link, and even with it, it's difficult. But none of that's important. What he told me is.'

'So spit it out,' Stryke demanded.

'He has an idea where Jennesta is, and it's not far. We have to change course.'

'An idea?'

'More than that. A . . . sense.'

He slowly shook his head. 'I don't know . . .'

'I thought you wanted to find your mate more than anything.'

'I do. But I don't know if I want a wild-goose chase based on a hunch.'

'Trust me, Stryke, this is more likely to be right than wrong. Besides, what other option do you have?'

'You said that about us going to Serapheim,' Jup reminded him. 'And you said we needed him to help fight Jennesta.'

'Ideally, he'd be there. But she's nearer than he is, and we need to seize this opportunity before she's on the move again. What do you say, Stryke?'

'I thought we needed Serapheim's magic to stand a chance against her.'

'We'll have to make do with mine, and your band's undoubted martial skills.'

He thought about it. 'All right. But this better not be a waste of time. I'll get Pepperdyne to alter course.'

'I was just on my way up to take a turn at the wheel,' Jup said. 'I'll tell him.'

'All right, go ahead.'

'*What* am I telling Pepperdyne? About the new course, I mean.'

Stryke looked to the shape-changer. 'Go with him, Dynahla. I'll brief the band.'

Jup and the shape-changer made their way to the bridge in silence. As usual, Coilla was there alongside Pepperdyne. They were told of the change of direction and why it came about.

'Where exactly are we going?' Pepperdyne asked as he took out the well-thumbed chart.

'We need a southward bearing,' Dynahla explained, tracing a line with his finger. 'In this direction.'

'There's nothing there. Just like the last time we looked at this map, before setting our present course. You have a thing about invisible islands?'

'I don't think anybody's ever fully mapped out this world. There's a lot more to it than this chart shows. Believe me, our objective lies there.'

Pepperdyne shrugged. 'If that's what Stryke wants.' He began spinning the wheel.

'I'm supposed to have a turn at steering, remember,' the dwarf said. He glanced at Coilla. 'And yes, I can reach it.'

'I wasn't going to say a thing!' she protested. 'You're confusing me with Haskeer.'

Jup smiled. 'Yeah, I guess he's the one who'd offer me a box to stand on, the irritating bastard.'

'I don't think this is a good time for your lesson,' Pepperdyne said, 'given the change of course. Sorry.'

'It's all right. The prospect of a fight appeals to me more than playing sailors, to be honest.'

'I need to leave you,' Dynahla stated, as though their permission was needed. Nobody blinked, so he added, 'See you soon.'

They nodded and the shape-changer left.

'What do you think, Jode?' Coilla asked in a low tone. 'Is he on the level?'

'Dynahla? I don't know.'

'This new course seems rum,' Jup said.

'And again we're heading for somewhere the map says doesn't exist. Though I can't see what he'd get out of lying. We'd find out soon enough if there really isn't anything there.'

'Might do to keep an eye on him though,' Coilla suggested.

'I'm already doing that,' Jup told her.

'Good idea,' Pepperdyne said. 'There's always a chance that—'

Coilla shushed him, finger to lips. She flicked her head to indicate the stairs. Someone with a heavy tread was coming up them.

Haskeer clambered into view. When he saw Jup his features lit up with something it took them a moment to recognise. It was a smile.

'Jup!' he boomed. 'I've been looking for you.'

'If it's a scrap you're after,' Jup said, instinctively balling his fists, 'forget it. I'm not in the mood.'

'*A scrap*? You wound me, old friend. Why would I want to hurt you?'

'*Old friend*?' Coilla mouthed.

'You couldn't hurt me if I was a nail and you had a hammer,' Jup assured him. 'What's the game, Haskeer?'

'Is it a game to want the best for a friend?'

'You appear in an unusually good mood,' Pepperdyne commented dryly.

'And why not?' Haskeer boomed. 'I'm surrounded by good companions, not least our human comrades.' He lifted a hand. Pepperdyne tensed. But instead of the expected blow he was rocked by a hearty slap to his shoulder that made him stagger.

'I thought you hated humans,' Coilla said.

'How'd you get *that* idea? Aren't we all brothers in arms under the skin, ready to lay down our lives for each other?'

'You been drinking sea water?' Jup asked.

'Ever the joker, aren't you, old pal? My Jup. My little Juppy Wuppy.'

'That does it,' the dwarf decided. 'He's gone insane.'

'If I'm insane,' Haskeer intoned gravely, 'it's with the passion of the fondness I feel for you.' He broke into a broad grin and lurched forward, arms outstretched. 'Come on, gimme a hug!'

'Keep him off me!'

Haskeer stopped and began to chuckle.

'Just a minute,' Coilla said. 'There's something fishy about all this.'

Haskeer nodded. 'Caught me.'

A change came over his features. They softened, shifted and reformed themselves. An instant later, Dynahla stood before them.

'Sorry,' he said. 'I couldn't resist that.'

As their astonishment wore off, the others laughed.

'That was . . . impressive,' Pepperdyne admitted.

'You're telling me,' Coilla agreed. 'I could have sworn it was him. Except for the bullshit, that is.'

'How do you do it, Dynahla?' Jup wanted to know.

'How do you do farsight?'

'I was born with it. Like all my race.'

'But it improves with practice?'

'Well, yes.'

'Most beings are born with at least the potential for magic. True, it's stronger in some races than others. It's much more latent in orcs, for example, but it's there. The trick is to develop it.'

'That takes willpower, right?'

'The dominance of the will is the least important factor.'

'I don't understand.'

'Imagination is much more important.'

'Is it?'

'What's your favourite food, Jup?'

'Huh?'

'Let's say . . . venison. You're fond of it?'

'Yeah. Who isn't?'

'Do you feel hungry?'

'Now that you mention it—'

'I reckon we all are,' Coilla said. 'We've had no chance to eat.'

Dynahla smiled. 'Good. So picture a haunch of venison, turning on a spit, running with juices. See it in your mind. Smell that delicious aroma.'

'You're making my mouth water,' Jup confessed.

'Sink your teeth into the succulent flesh. Think of how good it tastes.'

'Hmmm.'

'Now let's suppose that you can't allow yourself to eat the venison. It's very important that you don't. Let's say your life depends on not eating it. You must use your will to resist wanting to eat that meat.'

'Easier said than done when I'm this hungry.'

'Use the power of your will. Really concentrate. Refuse it. Close your eyes if it helps.'

He did, and they all watched in silence for a moment.

'How did you do?' Dynahla asked.

'Well . . .'

'Not too good?'

'You put a pretty tempting image into my head. It's hard not to want it.'

'All right. Picture that hunk of meat again.'

Once more, Jup closed his eyes.

'Look at how delicious it is,' Dynahla went on. 'It's golden brown. Succulent. Smell that delicious tang of cooking meat. But hang on! What's this? Look closely. The venison's lying in a latrine. It's covered in filth, and swarming with maggots and beetles.'

'Yuck!' Jup made a face. Coilla and Pepperdyne didn't look too cheerful either.

'How easy did you find it to resist that time?' Dynahla said.

'No problem.' He looked a little queasy. 'I don't feel quite so hungry now. But what does it prove?'

'That sorcery is only partially about exercising the will. Much more important is imagining the improbable with enough intensity that you make it real. The imagination is *stronger* than the will. When you understand that, you're some way towards understanding magic.'

Jup found that intriguing, and began questioning Dynahla about it. Engrossed, the dwarf and the fetch waved vaguely at Coilla and Pepperdyne as they left the bridge together.

'Quite a character,' Pepperdyne said.

'Impressive though,' Coilla replied. 'It was the dead spit of Haskeer.' She grinned. 'And you've got to admit it *was* funny.'

'Yes. But one thing worries me, just a bit.'

'What's that?'

'Dynahla can impersonate any of us, perfectly. How comfortable are you about having someone like that in the band?'

16

The veil between the worlds is thin as gauze, unbridgeable as an ocean. It separates an incalculable number of realities, an infinite array of glittering pinpoints hanging in the velvet firmament. Seen closer, if that were possible, they reveal themselves as globes. Some are barren rocks, or beset with volcanic activity, or icebound. A few are fertile.

Two species lived beneath the blue skies and pure white clouds of one such world. The race of humans had carved out a far-flung domain, the Peczan empire, now suffering its first setback despite its great military strength and possession of magic. The newly liberated race of orcs, cause of that humiliation, occupied a more remote, much smaller segment of the planet. Bolstered by their reawakened martial spirit, they were resolved never to fall under human dominance again.

The orcs' land was Acurial. Taress, its largest city by far and the capital, had borne the brunt of the recent occupation. Free at last, the populace determined to erase all trace of Peczan's regime. Buildings that had been commandeered were returned to their original purpose. Structures built by the empire were being torn down, with detention camps, torture facilities and execution blocks the objects of particular fury. Guard stations, billets, signposts and anything else pertaining to the overthrown were demolished and consigned to bonfires, along with portraits of Peczan bureaucrats and military chiefs. Marble busts were pounded to smithereens.

At the same time, Taress was rebuilding itself. Invasion and rebellion had devastated many parts of the city, and legions toiled on reconstruction.

The main square had been one of the first areas to be reclaimed. Work there took a commemorative form. Statues had been erected. The tallest, although in many ways the simplest, honoured the late Principal Sylandya. Acurial's ruler before Peczan's occupation, and leader of the resistance, her martyrdom was the spark that gave fire to the revolution. She was shown seated, but didn't give the impression of being enthroned, as would be expected of a head of state. Her attire and demeanour were humble, her expression mild. The sculptor had made no effort to flatter her memory by disguising her advancing years, as might have been the case with a more vain subject. Her frame was slight, even frail. Yet she exuded an unmistakable authority.

Two orcs stood at the monument's base, looking up at the figure. They were twins, male and female, and less than thirty summers old.

'What would she have thought of this?' Chillder wondered.

'Not much, I reckon,' her brother replied. 'Our mother had little time for the conceits of power. It was one of her many virtues.'

'So was dealing with the mountain of parchmentwork that plagues us now.'

'Not as exciting as fighting as rebels, is it?'

'No, Brelan, it's not.'

'But it's what running a state's all about. It has to be done.'

'You're more like mother than I am in that way. I think you *like* shuffling paper.'

He smiled. 'Like I said; it has to be done. Taking care of the formalities is a price we pay for getting our freedom back.'

'I wish she was here to guide us through it,' Chillder said, nodding at the statue.

'Me too.'

'And if it hadn't been for that bitch Jennesta,' she added bitterly, 'she would be.'

'I know. But our mother's death wasn't in vain. If she hadn't perished as she did the revolution might never have happened. '

'I'm not sure about that. Either way, Jennesta went unpunished, and that sticks in my craw.'

He gave her a moment, then, 'Come on,' he urged gently, 'we ought to be moving.'

They headed across the square.

'Of course, she might have been,' Brelan said.

'Who might have been what?'

'Jennesta. Punished. For all we know, the warband reckoned with her.'

'Or they might have suffered the same fate as our mother. The frustrating thing is we'll probably never know.'

They arrived at the shadow of another monument, and slowed to a halt despite the pressing nature of their business. It was larger than Sylandya's, though squat rather than tall, and housed on a pedestal no more than waist height from the ground. Five life-sized figures were depicted; four orcs, one of them female, and a dwarf. They were in heroic poses, weapons drawn. To the rear of the group was a low stone wall that acted as a backdrop. This bore a carving along its entire length, showing a further twenty or more of the principals' comrades. Controversially for many in Taress, it also showed a human.

The front of the monument was strewn with necklaces of fangs, pots of wine, embellished weapons, sketches of the heroes, not all of them crudely executed, and other offerings. In a not very orc-like gesture, there were even some bunches of flowers. The monument's base carried a plain inscription reading '*The Wolverines*'.

'And what do you suppose *they* would think about *this*?' Brelan asked, echoing his sister's earlier question.

'Haskeer would have liked it. Not sure the others would care much.' She turned to him. 'Where could they have gone, Brelan? Do you think they're still alive?'

'Well, you can bet they didn't return to their so-called northern lands. I never did buy that. As to whether they're still alive . . .' He shrugged. 'Who knows? I'm just grateful they came here when they did.'

'Except for the human. The slimy one.'

'Standeven.'

She nodded. 'Orc killer.'

'Maybe.'

'How can you doubt it?'

'You're probably right. But I can't help thinking even he wouldn't have been stupid enough to murder one of us in our own land.'

'The pity is we let him get away with it.'

'There was no proof.'

'How much did you *need*?'

'That's all water under the bridge, Chillder, and something else we can't do anything about. Now can we get a move on? We've a problem to deal with, remember.'

They resumed their journey.

The streets leading off the square were bustling. Extensive rebuilding work was going on and laden carts jammed the thoroughfares. Passers-by stared as Brelan and Chillder passed, and some waved. They were public figures now.

As they walked, Chillder said, 'I sometimes wonder whether we should be doing all this work.'

'Why wouldn't we?'

'Peczan's pride took a battering. How do we know they won't invade again, if only to save face?'

'We've got as many hands putting up defences as rebuilding. More. If the humans come back we'll know it, and this time they'd face a population ready to fight.'

'Would they? Grilan-Zeat's gone now. What worries me is that our warlike spirit's going to fade along with the comet's memory.'

'I don't think so. Our folk have had a taste of the freedom that fighting brought them. They won't easily forget that.'

'I hope you're right.'

'Trust me. We've more important things to worry about, not least trying to replenish our plundered treasury, thanks to Jennesta.'

'And now this . . . strangeness. What the hell's happening, Brelan?'

'Damned if I know. Maybe we'll learn something from this new event.'

They pushed on, moving away from the centre and entering less crowded streets. The further they went the more they saw of the defensive measures Brelan referred to. In piazzas, or open spaces where buildings had burnt down during the uprising, citizens were being drilled. Mobile road blocks, consisting of hay wagons loaded with rocks, stood at the side of major avenues. Rooftops were utilised as lookout points, and in some places purpose-built watchtowers were under construction. The threat of re-invasion was being taken seriously.

At last the twins reached a district previously given over to cattle yards and storehouses. Now a contingent of Acurial's newly-created regular militia were stationed there. In addition to an armed populace, a standing army was thought desirable, and former resistance fighters made up its nucleus. It was early days for the force; their uniforms were makeshift and their weapons ill-assorted. Their quarters were at a rudimentary stage too, and in common with the rest of Taress the area was a building site.

Waved through the compound's gates by saluting guards, Chillder and Brelan made their way to a recently erected barracks block. They were met outside by an officer, a comrade from the resistance days, who unlocked the barracks' door and ushered them in.

'Not that there's much to see,' he said.

There were only minor signs of disorder in the deserted interior. A couple of the cots were askew, a chair was upended and a few items of kit were scattered across the floor.

'This has been left exactly as it was?' Brelan asked.

The officer nodded. 'Just as you see it.'

'How many?'

'Eleven.'

'When?'

'Some time during the night. We only knew when they didn't show up at reveille.'

'You've searched the camp?'

'Of course.'

'Were any of them . . . dissatisfied in any way?' Chillder said.

'These weren't troublemakers. They were as solid and as loyal as any we've got.'

'Their arms went too?' She pointed at an empty weapons rack. 'Yes.'

'You've told no one about this?' Brelan said.

'No,' the officer replied.

'Good. Keep it that way. You can leave us now. And thanks.'

When the officer had gone, Chillder turned to her brother. 'How many times does this make?'

'Seven, I think. Possibly eight. That's just from Taress, mind. There are a few unconfirmed reports from outside the city. With this new lot I reckon we're talking upwards of seventy militia having gone missing, that we're aware of.'

'So what are we dealing with? Desertion? Hostage taking?'

'As far as we know there's no reason for any of them to have deserted. And I can't see abducting armed bands of warriors being that easy a task, particularly from inside a compound like this.'

'Did all the others go in similar ways?'

'Some did. From their quarters, just like whatever happened here. One group went out on a patrol and never came back. There were a couple of cases of disappearances on guard duty, and one where four, I think it was, vanished from a weapons dump. There's no real pattern. Except nobody saw anything.'

'Could Peczan be behind this? Might they have got agents in and—'

'Humans trying to hide among a nation of orcs? I don't think so, Chillder.'

'Or could it be our own kind? Traitors doing the humans' bidding.'

'It'd take a lot of them, not to mention a pretty big conspiracy. I don't want to think there could be that many traitors. I don't believe there are. There might be one or two turncoats, for some twisted reason, but not on this scale.'

'There's another possibility. Have you noticed the smell in here?'

A faint sulphurous aroma hung in the air, mingled with the scent of the barracks' new wood.

'I'm not sure.'

'Oh, come on, Brelan; you know what it is.'

'Magic?'

'*Yes.* Couldn't that be it?'

'I can't see how. Humans have mastery of magic, not orcs, and like I said; where would humans hide in Acurial?'

'Jennesta's not human. This could be her doing.'

'The same thing applies. I mean, she'd stick out, wouldn't she? Anyway, I don't believe she's still hanging around. The mob would tear her to pieces, never mind her sorcery. That's not a risk she'd take.'

'*What* then? Who's doing this?'

'Whoever or whatever's responsible, we're going to have to brace ourselves for more of the same.'

'You reckon?'

'We've no reason to think it might stop. Whatever *it* is.'

'How do we protect ourselves?'

'Short of gathering the entire army together and watching each other's backs, I've no idea. And who can say if even that would work?'

'There must be *something* we can do, Brelan.'

'We don't know what we're trying to protect ourselves against. All we do know—'

'Is that our comrades have disappeared as surely as the Wolverines,' she finished for him.

He nodded, looking grim.

17

Long after the sun disappeared, and the crisp night sky was speckled with stars, the Wolverines' ship ploughed on.

They used hooded lamps for such light as they needed and conversed in hushed tones. Dynahla was the only real guide to their destination, and as they were uncertain about how close they were, or whether there might be other craft abroad, they ran dark and silent.

Stryke gathered his officers in what had been the master's cabin, or whatever the ship's former, goblin owners called it. Its windows were kept firmly shuttered.

'What do we do when we get there?' Haskeer demanded before they all finished seating themselves.

'That's what we're here to figure out,' Stryke told him. 'Now sit down and shut up.'

Sullenly, his sergeant did as he was told.

'We don't know what we'll be up against,' Stryke said. 'So we need a plan. You're our strategist, Coilla; talk to me.'

'We *do* know what we'll be up against: Jennesta. Question is how best to overcome her and pull off our mission. And not get killed doing it.'

'Isn't that always the way it is when we tangle with her?' Jup asked.

'Yeah,' Haskeer chimed in, 'since when did we worry about odds when it comes to a fight? I say we go in with blades out and give no quarter, Stryke, like we usually do.'

'This is different. I want Thirzarr out of there and safe. That's what Coilla meant by the mission. This isn't just about killing Jennesta.'

'You don't want to fight?' Haskeer looked incredulous.

'*Course* I do. But I want to fight smart.'

'Could be we'll run straight into opposition,' Coilla said, 'in which case it'll be an all-out scrap. But if we can get ashore unseen, maybe a snatch squad's the best option to bring out Thirzarr.'

'What about Jennesta?' Jup wanted to know.

'Once we get Thirzarr clear we can tackle her force head-on.'

'Only trouble with that,' Stryke judged, 'is that it spreads us thin.'

'Yeah,' Coilla agreed. 'Three groups. Snatch squad, main body holding back 'til they get the word to attack, and a group defending the ship.'

'That could be us,' Dallog suggested. 'Me and the rest of the Ceragans. We could guard the ship.'

Haskeer sneered. 'Quick getting in with that bid, ain't you? Frightened of a fight?'

'*No.* It's just that we work well together. We've proved that.'

'You did a good job holding it last time,' Stryke conceded. 'That's your detail then.'

'We're better off without 'em,' Haskeer muttered.

'But I can't spare all of you,' Stryke added. 'Take Chuss, Pirrak and Keick. Wheam can come with us.'

Haskeer loudly groaned. 'As if we didn't have enough trouble.'

Stryke showed him a clenched fist. 'I won't be telling you again. We need all the bodies we can get. He's included.'

'Not in the snatch squad?' Jup said, faintly alarmed.

'No. He'll be part of the main force.'

'Who *is* in the snatch squad?' Coilla wondered.

'Me, you, Jup and a couple of the grunts. I'm thinking Eldo and Reafdaw. Dynahla should be in it, too.'

'Why?'

'He says he's got magic. We might need that. And before you say it; yes, we don't really know anything about him. I'll take that risk.' He looked to Haskeer. 'You'll head the main force.'

'So I get the pleasure of Wheam's company. Lucky me. Pepperdyne, too?'

'Yes.'

'What about the other one?'

'Standeven stays on the ship. You'll keep an eye on him, Dallog.'

Somebody rapped on the door and barged in. It was Finje, breathing hard from a dash.

'We can see it,' he reported. 'The island. It's in sight.'

'It's big,' Stryke said, peering at the long black slab of the island, outlined on the horizon by the spreading dawn. 'Funny it's not on the map.' He shot Dynahla a searching look, coloured with a hint of suspicion.

'There are lots of maps. I doubt there's one that charts this world accurately. Anyway, what's the worry? There it is.'

'You're *sure* Jennesta's there, and Thirzarr?'

'Yes.'

'Because Serapheim told you so.'

'Not just that. Now we're close I can sense the presence myself.'

'*You* can? How?'

'As with so much to do with the craft, it's hard to explain to the uninitiated. Let's just say that living things give out a certain . . . cadence, and some of us can detect it.'

'I can't pretend to understand that.'

'You'll have to take my word for it then. But be certain that Jennesta, and your mate, are on that island.'

They were at the ship's prow, and Stryke carried on staring at the island for a moment before speaking again. 'The plan's to send in a snatch squad to get Thirzarr out before we launch a full attack. Will you be part of the squad?'

'I think I ought to be. Though you should be aware that Jennesta's sorcery is stronger than you know, and quite possibly greater than anything I can summon.'

'That's better than nothing. But here's something *you* should be aware of. All I know about you is what you've told us. On the strength of that I'm trusting you. Betray that trust, or do anything that might harm Thirzarr, and you won't be coming back from this mission, whatever happens to the rest of us. Got it?'

'I understand. You can rely on me, Stryke. Now unless there's anything else, I'd like to prepare.'

'What does that involve?'

'Nothing too drastic. I just need to find a quiet corner for contemplation, to centre myself.'

'I need to do some preparing myself. I'll send for you when it's time.'

From the bridge, Coilla and Pepperdyne watched Stryke and the shape-changer part.

'Think we can trust him?' Pepperdyne said.

'Stryke seems to. Not that he has much choice. Though it'll go badly for Dynahla if this is some kind of trick.'

'It'd go pretty badly for us as well.'

'The band's used to being in tight spots.'

'It's not the band I'm worried about. It's you.'

'You're worried about an orc going into a fight.' She had to smile. 'That's like worrying about a bird flying or whether a fish can swim.'

'Hunters bring down birds and fish lose out to hooks.'

'I'm not a fish or a bird, so I've nothing to worry about, have I?'

'You know what I mean.'

'Look, Jode; my race lives for combat. It's what we do. Or hadn't you noticed? I'd have thought you'd understand, being a fighter yourself.'

'Only out of necessity.'

'And you get no pleasure from winning a fight? No rush of joy when you down an opponent?'

'Well . . . maybe. A bit. But I don't relish putting my life on the line every day the way you do.'

'It's in our nature. We fight, and we fight to kill. If death takes us, that's the price we pay. Though we do our best to make damn sure it's who we're up against that does the paying. We trust to our skill, and to luck and to the Tetrad. If you want an orcs' creed, that's as near as I can get to it in words.'

'I'm not arguing about your nature, Coilla. That's part of what I love about you, and I'd never change it. I only want you to be careful.'

'Why didn't you just say that in the first place?'

Pepperdyne slapped his forehead with the heel of his palm in a gesture of mock exasperation, and they laughed.

'So what's the plan?' he said. 'How are we going about this raid?'

'Stryke'll be briefing us shortly, but the idea's to anchor well

693

offshore and go over in boats. If we get there without being spotted we split into our two groups and the game's on.'

'And if we are spotted?'

'Then it gets messy.'

It happened as Coilla said. All lights extinguished, the ship was anchored as far from the island as practicable. Dallog's unit was left in charge. The rest of the band cautiously lowered the boats, and likewise in darkness, made for the shore using muffled oars.

The sea was obligingly calm. It did little to reduce the tension of the crossing. Eyes and ears sharp, silence imposed, they expected the alarm to be raised at any moment. But they reached the shore apparently unseen. There was no sign of Jennesta's ships; the band assumed they were anchored on another side of the island.

The point at which they met the shore was rocky and too steep for a landing. So they moved along the coastline, keeping close, until they found a sandy beach. Clambering ashore, they headed for the shelter of trees, dragging the boats behind them.

To face Jennesta, they had to find her. Stryke sent out as many scouts as he could spare. Zoda, Prooq, Nep, Breggin and Orbon got the job. Treading lightly, they fanned out into the jungle. The rest of the Wolverines kept low and quiet, and waited.

It wasn't a long vigil. The island was large, but Jennesta had seen no point in penetrating its interior to set up a temporary camp. Her force was located a short distance inland, and to the west. There were guards, of course; and Breggin and Zoda, who got nearest, thought Jennesta's army might have grown. Stryke gave no time to wondering how that could be.

He ordered the band into its two groups. The larger, main force, lead by Haskeer, would follow the snatch squad but at a slower pace. At a prearranged spot it would stop and wait for its signal to attack. If the signal didn't come, no one doubted they would go in anyway.

It was full night when Stryke headed off, with Jup, Coilla, Dynahla, Eldo and Reafdaw in tow, the latter pair carrying bows. Dynahla refused any kind of weapon beyond a small decorative dagger he always wore.

Coilla shot Pepperdyne a quick smile as they left. He returned a wink, braving Haskeer's scowl.

The snatch squad travelled with measured speed, careful not to give themselves away. Soon they were out of sight of the main force at their rear. Following the scouts' directions, they forged on through semi-jungle conditions, aggravating but far from impenetrable, until they came to clearer land. Moon and star shine were more plentiful here, and the band moved sure-footedly. At last they arrived at a grassy rise. Going up it on their bellies, they peeked over its crest at the vale below. They saw a cluster of tents, tethered horses, and figures outlined in the glow of cooking fires and armourers' braziers.

Anticipating a possible refusal, Stryke left Dynahla out of dealing with guards. There seemed to be four, but they weren't fixed. Their patrolling took them across the orcs' path to the camp. Stryke thought to let Eldo's and Reafdaw's bows take care of them. The guards patrolled in pairs, which made the task easier. The trick was to eliminate one pair without the other knowing. That meant waiting until they were out of each other's sight.

The four guards, having completed their rounds, were bunched together. Any attempt to drop them by Stryke's two archers ran the risk of their targets raising the alarm before they could reload and re-aim. But finally the guards parted, each pair moving away in opposite directions. Stryke sent Reafdaw and Eldo to the right, to shadow the duo walking that way. Hunters and prey soon disappeared from view. The other pair of guards, heading left, had also gone beyond seeing.

'How good are your archers?' Dynahla asked in a hushed tone.

'Good enough,' Stryke said. 'It's why I picked 'em.'

'What we have to be wary of,' Coilla explained, 'is the guards going the other way.' She nodded to the left. 'When they come back and don't see the others—'

'It could be yelling time,' Jup finished for her.

Dynahla nodded.

They kept watching.

The wait was long enough that they were beginning to suspect something had gone wrong. Then Eldo and Reafdaw reappeared, giving the thumbs-up. At exactly the same time the two remaining guards returned. With frantic gestures Stryke and the others indicated this, and urged the grunts on. Doubled over, resembling loping apes, Eldo and Reafdaw started to run towards them.

The pair of guards returning from the left were in plain sight now. They were talking to each other, animatedly, and slowing. The absence of their comrades had been noted.

Eldo and Reafdaw arrived, breathing hard and scrabbling for arrows.

'Move it!' Stryke hissed. *'They know something's wrong!'*

The grunts had to rise above the crest of the hill to discharge their bows. As they did, one of the guards glanced their way and saw them. His mouth formed an 'O'. It was too late. The arrows winged towards them, hitting true, and they went down without a sound.

'Come on!' Stryke ordered.

The squad scrambled over the rise and down into the vale.

They checked that the guards were dead, retrieved the arrows and hid the bodies in the undergrowth. That done, they pushed on to Jennesta's camp, moving stealthily.

Using the shelter of a small copse, they had their first close look. They weren't in a good place. There was well lit, exposed ground ahead of them, and at least a dozen troopers were working or lounging in it. Further back, in the shadows, Stryke thought he caught a glimpse of what might have been goblins, and perhaps other non-human creatures. The others saw them too.

'Looks like Jennesta *has* been beefing up her little army,' Coilla said.

Stryke nodded. He turned to Dynahla. 'Feel anything? I mean, is she here? And where is she?'

'She's here all right. Down that way.' He pointed to the westward end of the camp. 'In one of those tents.'

'Doesn't take a wizard to figure that out,' Jup said.

Dynahla ignored him and added, 'We might be facing stronger opposition than we bargained for.'

'Maybe a few goblins and whatnot,' Stryke replied dismissively. 'We can deal with it.'

'I didn't mean them. There's more than one kind of magic here.'

'You sure?'

'Quite. They're of different orders, mind you, and different disciplines. Two unrelated races, probably. What Jennesta radiates is like a great black, angry ocean. This other source . . . I can't identify. But by comparison it's a lake. Filled with blood.'

'Sounds fun,' Coilla offered, deadpan.

'Facing Jennesta's dangerous enough. Going against *two* wielders of magic . . . well, that's asking a lot.'

'You wanna leave?' Stryke said. ''Cos if you're not behind this you can get out right now.'

Dynahla's gaze darted back to the camp, then returned to Stryke. 'No. No, I'm in. And I'll do what I can. I just wanted to warn you about what might be in store.'

'You've done that. Now let's get going.'

He led them in the direction of the cluster of tents. Having to keep hidden, their progress was slower than he would have liked, but eventually they arrived opposite the tents. There was less obvious activity here, save the occasional trooper wandering through. The area was dimly lit, being some distance from the cooking fires, though there were one or two braziers.

'I guess that must be Jennesta's tent,' Jup said, indicating the biggest and most ornate one.

'Has to be,' Stryke agreed. 'Doesn't mean Thirzarr's there though. Any idea where she might be, Dynahla?'

The shape-changer shook his head. 'It's much harder locating a being who hasn't any magical powers. What I can tell you is that Jennesta's in this part of the camp, but she isn't in that tent.'

'Can you tell *where* she is?'

'Not precisely. Except that she's close.'

Stryke sighed. 'All right. Then I guess her tent's where we start.'

'All we have to do is get to it without being seen,' Coilla said dryly.

'I'd like to do that without having to tackle any of the soldiers and causing an uproar. So we stay put until it gets clearer over there.'

'What if it doesn't?'

'We'll think again.'

Once more they waited, keeping well out of sight and never taking their eyes off the camp. As the night wore on, comings and goings grew less, apart from occasional guards making their rounds. There were no lights in the large tent they assumed was Jennesta's. Nor did anybody leave it or go in.

'This is as good as it's likely to get,' Stryke decided, eyeing the now deserted area between them and their goal. 'We'll get into the tent by the back.'

'What if it's empty?'

'You're full of questions tonight, Coilla. If it's empty, we keep looking. Jup, got the horn handy?'

The dwarf patted the satchel at his waist. 'You bet.'

'Be ready to use it when I give the word.' He scanned the camp again. No one was about. 'We go in pairs. You and Coilla first. *Move.*'

They scurried for the tent, making the most of shadows, and reached it without incident. Then they circled to its rear and were lost to view.

'Reafdaw, Eldo; you're next,' Stryke said. 'I want you taking care of the entrance. Can do?'

'No problem,' Eldo grated.

'*Go!*'

The grunts also reached the tent without trouble. Their position, at the front, was more risky, but they did a good job of melting into the gloom on either side of the entry.

'Now us?' Dynahla asked.

'*Wait!*' Stryke hissed, grabbing the shape-changer's sleeve. He pointed.

A sentry had appeared from the far side of the camp, and he was walking towards Jennesta's tent.

They held their breath as he approached. His pace was infuriatingly slow, but it looked as though he might bypass the big tent. That proved deceptive. When he was parallel to it, he turned and headed for the entrance. Stryke knew that at any moment Eldo and Reafdaw would be spotted. He tensed, ready to break cover and tackle the man.

'*What do we do?*' Dynahla whispered.

'*Stay put. I'll deal with it.*'

The sentry was almost at Jennesta's tent. Stryke half rose, hand on his sword hilt.

Eldo stepped into view, hands held up in apparent surrender. Startled, the sentinel drew his sword. But he didn't raise the alarm. Eldo walked slowly towards him, and he was saying something Stryke and Dynahla couldn't hear. Talking, holding the guard's attention, the grunt kept moving, describing a sly circle that had the man turning until his back was to the tent. At which point Eldo stopped.

Reafdaw sneaked out of his hiding place, a knife glinting in his fist. Swiftly, silently, he crept up behind the guard. In one fluid movement he clamped a hand over the man's mouth as he sunk the blade into the small of his back. The guard slumped to the ground. Eldo and Reafdaw quickly dragged his body away, dumping it amongst dense vegetation at the camp's edge.

'Right,' Stryke said, satisfying himself that there were no more guards about. 'Let's get over there.'

He and the shape-changer rushed to the tent. Reafdaw and Eldo, returning to their positions beside its entrance, gave them a wave as they passed. Stryke and Dynahla went round to the back, and found Coilla and Jup waiting there.

'What kept you?' Coilla said, mildly irritated.

'We were writing poetry,' Stryke told her. 'Now let's do this.' He drew a knife. 'Ready?'

The others nodded, and braced themselves for whatever might be inside.

Stryke jabbed the blade into the fabric and cut a long slash. He prised the two sides apart, making an opening big enough for them to look through. The interior was gloomy; only a faint illumination from the camp fires penetrated the tent cloth. Detecting no sound or movement, he slipped inside. The others followed.

Various items of plush furniture were scattered about, causing some stumbling in the dark, but it looked as though no one was there. Then Stryke spotted something.

At one end of the tent, in almost complete darkness, there was a shape. He padded towards it, and realised it was someone seated. For a moment he couldn't make out who or what it was. Once his vision adjusted to the murk, he rushed forward.

'Thirzarr? Thirzarr!' He clutched her hand. It felt cold. '*Thirzarr!*' He got no response. 'It's so damned dark in here!' he cursed.

'This might help,' Dynahla said.

He cupped his hands, and for the first time Coilla noticed how elegant and almost feminine they were. When he opened them again there was a purple fireball nestling between his palms, about the size of a hen's egg. It bathed the scene in a soft, eerie glow. It showed them that Thirzarr was sitting rigidly, and her eyes were open, though they were glazed and unfocused.

'*Thirzarr!*' Stryke mouthed anxiously.

'Jennesta's got her in a . . . kind of trance,' the fetch explained.

'Like the last time we saw her,' Coilla recalled.

'Can you bring her out of it, Dynahla?' Stryke asked.

'Possibly. But not here. We need to get her somewhere safe first.'

'What do we do?' Jup said, 'Carry her?'

'We might not have to. Tell her to stand, Stryke.'

'Will she?'

'She's in a highly suggestible state. The spell binding her should be answerable only to Jennesta's voice. But a familiar voice, one she knows intimately, might be as effective. Try it.'

'Stand up, Thirzarr,' Stryke said.

Nothing happened.

'Maybe we *should* carry her,' Coilla muttered.

'Try again, Stryke,' Dynahla suggested. 'A little more firmly. Order her this time.'

Stryke looked doubtful, but did it. '*Stand up! On your feet, Thirzarr. Now!*'

She stood.

'As long as you don't ask her to do anything complicated,' Dynahla added, ' she should do as you say.'

Coilla snickered. 'That'll be a first.' She sobered when she saw Stryke's face.

He addressed his mate, firmly but not unkindly. 'Thirzarr, come with me.' He took a few steps, watching her over his shoulder. She moved too, albeit stiffly, and began to follow him. 'It'll be easier if we go out the front way,' he decided. 'Check that it's clear, Jup.'

The dwarf went to the entrance and gave a low whistle. Reafdaw poked his head in.

'All clear out there?' Jup said.

Reafdaw nodded and pulled aside the flap for them.

Stryke took Thirzarr's arm and guided her. The others followed. Dynahla came last, closing his fist on the radiant fireball, snuffing it out.

Everything seemed quiet outside. Even the noises from the other end of the camp had died down.

'Now we get Thirzarr away and hidden,' Stryke told them. 'Then we call the main force in. Come on.'

He headed for the perimeter as briskly as he could while still holding Thirzarr's arm.

They were hardly under way when there was movement in the darkness at the camp's edges. Figures emerged. A large number, toting weapons. They approached from three sides, and Stryke didn't doubt more were coming in from the rear. The figures brought light with them, thrown out by blazing torches scattered about their ranks. It grew bright enough to reveal Jennesta in the forefront.

She halted ten paces short of Stryke's party. Her followers took her cue and also held back.

'You're full of surprises, Stryke,' Jennesta said. 'I didn't think you had the wits to find me. You're certainly witless in believing you could walk in here without me knowing.'

'You would have known it.'

'Ah. This is a *raid*, is it? An attack with . . . six of you. Or are you counting on your mate bringing it up to the dizzy heights of seven?'

'What have you done to Thirzarr?'

'I find it so touching that beasts like you can display actual feelings for each other. Or what passes for them in your part of the food chain.'

'I'm taking her out of here.'

'I don't think so. Thirzarr? Here. To me.' Jennesta pointed to the ground next to her.

Thirzarr lurched forward. Stryke tried to hold her back, but she shook loose violently. With a quicker pace than she had previously shown, she made for Jennesta.

'Thirzarr!' Stryke yelled. 'Don't! Stay here!'

Oblivious, she carried on to the enemy ranks and arrived at Jennesta's side, then spun to face Stryke's squad, her eyes still opaque.

'So nice to have you back, my love,' the sorceress purred.

Thirzarr had been obscuring Jennesta's view of Dynahla. Now she saw him properly, and something like a flicker of doubt passed over her face.

Staring intently, she said, 'The Wolverines become more motley by the day. Do I know you?'

'Do you?' the shape-changer replied levelly.

'I expect an answer, not a riddle.'

'It was an answer. Here's a question for you. Do you know yourself?'

What might have been a troubled expression briefly visited Jennesta's features. 'Correction, Stryke: you've brought five fighters and one deranged human. She looked to Dynahla. 'You *are* human?'

The shape-changer said nothing.

'No matter.' She turned to Stryke. 'Your best option is to surrender, here and now. Any other course won't go well for you.'

Stryke tore his eyes from Thirzarr. 'You think so?'

'Oh, I don't doubt the rest of your band's not far behind. But you'll not prevail.'

He scanned her followers. Though they certainly outnumbered his band, he replied, 'You sure about that?'

'That's one thing I like about you orcs; you're not shy of a fight. So let's make it a little more interesting for you, shall we?' She raised an arm above her head, then let it drop, indolently.

More figures came out of the dark. Gleaton-Rouk led his goblin crew, numbering about a dozen. Behind them were the vague outlines of what the orcs still thought of as elder races; an assembly of diverse creatures of the sort they knew, and often fought, back on Maras-Dantia. Their number looked equal to that of the band.

Gleaton-Rouk carried his bow, Shadow-wing, with an arrow ready nocked. 'I'm gratified to meet you again, Captain Stryke,' he hissed.

'You can go and fuck yourself.'

Jennesta laughed. 'That's *it*, you see? Always ready for a brawl. Very . . . *orcish*.' Her tone hardened. 'But this isn't a time to fight. Your only option is to surrender.'

'What I told him,' Stryke said, nodding at the goblin.

'You can be tiresomely stubborn.'

'We going to talk or fight?' From the corner of his eye he noticed Jup slyly edging a hand towards his satchel.

'You seem absurdly confident, given the odds.'

'We judge our enemies by their quality, not their number.'

'In that case,' she replied, smiling, 'let me provide you with opponents worthy of your arrogance.' Again, she raised her arm.

The murk disgorged another group of creatures. Copiously armed, and warband-sized in number, they wore the same dead look in their eyes that Thirzarr had. They were muscular, flinty-faced and savage in appearance.

They were orcs.

18

The Wolverines' main force, lead by Haskeer, were cooling their heels at the designated stop point. Too far away from Jennesta's camp to see it, they were near enough to hear the signal.

The band passed time quietly checking or sharpening their weapons. Some took the chance to gnaw at the hard rations they'd missed out on earlier, and water pouches were passed round. A few stretched out on the sward, helmets pulled down to cover their eyes, and might even have been snoozing.

Unconsciously, Pepperdyne and Spurral conceded their status as outsiders and drifted together. They had marched side by side, and now they perched on a boulder a little apart from the others. Nearby, Haskeer was balling out Wheam for some minor infraction, but the necessity of keeping his voice down meant he got no pleasure out of it.

'You look grim, Jode,' Spurral observed.

'You don't seem too joyful yourself.'

'Well, we've both got somebody to worry about, haven't we?'

'True. Though maybe we shouldn't.'

'What'd you mean? Oh, yeah. Jup and Coilla aren't exactly novices when it comes to a fight, are they?'

'Exactly. Least, that's what I'm telling myself.'

'Me too. But it's Jennesta they're up against, not some common foe.'

'We'll *all* be going against her soon enough.'

'At least we've got Dynahla. He could help in that respect.'

'Hmm.'

'You're doubtful?'

'We know he's got magical powers, but are they a match for hers? In fact, we don't really know anything about him beyond what he's told us. Doesn't that worry you?'

'The way I look at it, if Stryke trusts him—'

'Yeah, that's what Coilla says. I hope you're both right.'

Done with harassing Wheam, Haskeer wandered in their direction. He looked grim, too. Though in his case it was more or less normal.

'We were just talking about Dynahla,' Spurral told him. 'What do you think about him?'

'He's not one of the band. I don't like outsiders.'

'That's us told.'

Haskeer cast a contemptuous eye Wheam's way. 'At least you two can fight.'

'Rare praise indeed,' Pepperdyne said, 'coming from you.'

'Yeah, well, I ain't wooing you, so don't let it go to your head.'

'I think you're being unfair on Wheam,' Spurral declared. 'He's not doing too badly.'

'How long do we have to live before he does *well*? If I had my way—'

A horn blast cut through the night air.

'Here we go,' Pepperdyne said.

The band came to life. Scrambling to their feet, they snatched up their weapons and shields.

'Move it, you bastards!' Haskeer bellowed.

The horn sounded again, its note longer and shriller than before.

They began running towards the camp.

Jup was lucky to get off a couple of blasts of the horn. He was too occupied to manage more.

Paradoxically, a small group confronted by a much larger one isn't necessarily at an immediate disadvantage because, by necessity, the number of combatants who can engage at one time is limited. Not that that meant Stryke's party was in any less peril.

Jennesta must have known Jup's signal would summon the rest of the Wolverines, but seemed confident in her greater force. With a snap of her fingers she had sent a faction of her human troops forward, so that Stryke and his companions were faced by at least two opponents each. She herself held back, content to let her servants undertake the initial assault. Gleaton-Rouk was also still, a bow being a less than ideal weapon for close combat. In any event

Shadow-wing's enchanted arrows hadn't been anointed with the blood of a foe.

Jup discarded the horn and brought up his staff, whirling it with enough speed and skill to befuddle an advancing trooper. Quick as thought he brought it down hard on the man's head, cracking his skull. A second opponent instantly took over. Wary of the same fate, he kept his distance, swiping and jabbing at the dwarf whenever he could get near enough. They began to circle each other, looking for an advantage.

Silently thanking the gods that she always retrieved her throwing knives whenever possible, Coilla tried keeping her adversaries at bay with them. She struck true with her first throw, piercing a man's neck, but her second went wide as her target dodged. Quickly grabbing another blade she set about making a better job of it. In the end, his evasion wasn't up to her skill and the knife found his eye.

Eldo and Reafdaw fought in typical orc fashion by engaging in a slogging match. They battered at their opponents' shields, steel ringing on steel, and drank up the returning blows. Initially, brute force quickly won out over finesse. One of the humans, his guard breached, went down with a gaping wound to his chest.

Stryke faced the most opposition, with three or four of the sorceress' minions homing in on him. They were variously armed, but the most dangerous wielded a barbed pike, giving him more reach than Stryke's sword. Feigning a move towards one of the other attackers, Stryke spun at the last moment and with a vicious swipe parted the pike-man's hand from his wrist. Then he laid into the others.

His real fear was that Thirzarr would be sent against him again. But Jennesta hadn't committed her to the fight. At least, not yet.

As her underlings went down, dead or wounded, Jennesta ordered replacements in, keeping up the pressure. Not the zombie orcs, however, who stood and watched with vacant, implacable expressions. Next to fending off Thirzarr, Stryke's biggest concern was facing them. He didn't know how the Wolverines would deal with having to square up to fellow orcs. He didn't know how he would handle it himself. All he could do was battle on and hope his reinforcements weren't much longer coming.

Stryke, Coilla, Jup, Reafdaw and Eldo were at full stretch,

slugging it out with a succession of troopers and a few of Jennesta's human zombie slaves for good measure.

There was a single exception. Dynahla. He remained still as the mayhem churned all around. A couple of troopers were confronting him, but from at least a sword's length away, and seemed uncertain of their next move, thinking perhaps that someone apparently unarmed had to be dangerous. He took no notice of them, and had his eyes locked on Jennesta. She caught his gaze and returned it, an unknowable look on her face.

As he fought off a succession of challengers, Stryke weighed the option of getting to Thirzarr and dragging her clear, however hard that might prove. He glimpsed Jup from the corner of his eye and thought the dwarf could be considering the same move, and might aid him. Cutting down one of Jennesta's shambling, once human zombies, its flesh rending like ancient parchment, Stryke edged towards his mate.

Then the balance tilted.

The Wolverines' main force arrived, streaming out of the dark, bellowing war cries.

Jennesta reacted immediately. She unleashed her entire complement, including the magically enslaved orcs. All but Thirzarr, whom she kept at her side.

What had been a conflict became a battle.

With the only illumination coming from camp fires, and the brands carried by Jennesta's followers, the light was poor. So it took the incoming Wolverines a moment to realise that those they were confronting included members of their own race. Some hesitated, albeit for a split second. Haskeer wasn't among them. When his blood was up he was hell-bent on fighting anything.

The momentum of the reinforcements' charge had them crashing into the enemies' ranks. Haskeer was to the fore, laying about him with an axe in one hand, a long-blade knife in the other. The less nimble human zombies were the first to catch his wrath. He sliced into their limbs with his blade and used the axe to pound their heads, which in some cases exploded under the impact.

Spurral and Pepperdyne's alliance continued as they entered the fray. He relied on his accustomed sword, and as usual abstained from carrying a shield, preferring to rely on speed and agility. She also kept to a familiar weapon, her staff, and used it to good effect.

In a strategy she had developed with Jup, and which Pepperdyne had seen and admired, they worked together. So that when a chance arose, Spurral tumbled foes and Pepperdyne delivered the killing blow.

But for all their concentration on fighting, both still tried to keep an eye on Wheam. Although he wasn't altogether in need of nannies any more. His fighting skills had developed and his confidence had increased. In any event he was part of a wedge driving into the enemy line, surrounded by comrades who were veterans. As he disappeared into the scrum, his beloved lute incongruously strapped to his back, Pepperdyne and Spurral saw the tyro ramming his sword the way of a trooper's guts.

The battle fragmented as ripples of chaos ran through the warring mob. Jup and Coilla took advantage of it to fight to their mates' sides. And Stryke got himself a little closer to Thirzarr, who remained immobile beside Jennesta. But the toughest opposition, the zombie orcs, were beginning to act. They moved forward a little unsteadily, but without compromise. Any who got in their way, even if they were allies, were ploughed through, or even felled. Some of Jennesta's human zombies, slower to shift, were simply cut down. Gripped by the sorceress' enchantment, the orcs recognised no barrier in obeying their mistress' will.

Gleaton-Rouk and his goblin crew were also beginning to join the fight. But he was unable to use his bow, the second source of magic Dynahla had detected, both because of the crush and the fact that it hadn't been daubed with blood. Stryke worried that it soon would be.

Outnumbered as they were, the Wolverines had one thing going for them. Unlike Jennesta's widely diverse followers and collaborators, they were a unified force, accustomed to fighting as an entity. It gave them a slight edge in the mayhem. Not that it meant they would prevail against such odds. So far, the band had been lucky. But Stryke knew it was just a matter of time before they started taking casualties.

He wrenched his blade from a goblin's chest and let the creature topple. Then he looked to Thirzarr. She was unmoved, physically and apparently emotionally. But it was Jennesta, at her side, who drew his attention. She was staring fixedly at something beyond Stryke. He turned, and saw Dynahla returning her gaze.

In that instant there was a blinding flash of light. It was so intense that everybody stilled, and the fighting halted. Even the enchanted orcs slowed to a shuffling crawl. When Stryke's vision cleared he made out what was happening.

Jennesta and Dynahla were engaged in a duel of sorcery. They were battering each other with shafts of energy. Both had hands raised, palms outward, their faces rigid masks of concentration. The beams of magical vigour they generated pulsed with coloured light; primarily scarlet in Jennesta's case, green in Dynahla's, though other, subtler hues swirled within them. A sulphurous aroma began to fill the air, and the beams gave off blasts of heat.

One of the sorceress' human zombie slaves, a Wolverine axe buried in his back, staggered into range of the alluring stream. Lurching forward, he came into contact with it. He immediately ignited, a sheet of orange flame quickly spreading to cover his entire body. Blazing head to foot, moaning pathetically, the creature was consumed, collapsing into a heap of ash and yellowed bones.

Dynahla was sweating freely. Jennesta wore an expression of extreme attentiveness. The rich tints of the energy they threw at each other grew more vivid and the heat given off increased. All those looking on remained mesmerised.

Still maintaining her magical defence, Jennesta raised a hand and made a gesture. Some of her followers started to move, sluggishly. She repeated the signal with an angry insistence. This time they all responded. Stryke thought they were about to resume the fight, and readied himself. Instead they disengaged and swiftly pulled back. Wary of what might happen next, he motioned his band to do likewise. They obeyed and came to him.

The two sides were soon apart, the space between littered with Jennesta's dead and wounded. Stryke's glance flicked left and right, checking the Wolverines. They were all panting from the exertion of combat. Several had injuries, a couple of them harsh, but none seemed dire.

As if by unspoken agreement, Jennesta and Dynahla simultaneously ceased their clash. The beams snapped out of existence, leaving trace-lines on the eyes of all those watching. Jennesta let out a sigh and looked drained. Dynahla was exhausted. For a second or two his features blurred and flickered, before settling back to their familiar form. He swayed, and might have fallen if Jup and Noskaa hadn't taken hold of his arms and steadied him.

There was movement in Jennesta's ranks. Gleaton-Rouk and his clan were withdrawing to the rear. The human zombies lumbered after them, along with the enchanted orcs and the smattering of other races from her diverse horde who were still standing. They kept going, and were lost to the night.

Stryke suspected a ploy, reasoning that they might be circling to attack from another direction. But moments passed and it seemed they had retreated altogether.

Jennesta and her human troopers remained, with Thirzarr fixed at the sorceress' side. Stryke resolved to order a charge, seize his mate and put an end to the charade.

He noticed that Jennesta was holding something. At first, it was hard to tell what it was in the poor light. Then he realised she was slotting together the duplicate set of instrumentalities.

Their eyes met. Jennesta smiled.

Stryke cried out Thirzarr's name and lunged forward.

The last star clicked into place.

Jennesta and her force disappeared.

19

Pelli Madayar's intuitive sense, a natural receptiveness sharpened by years of training, detected a certain disturbance in the ether. She had no doubt what it meant.

The Gateway Corps unit was at sea, pursuing its objective. Pelli left her cabin and sought out her second-in-command, the goblin Weevan-Jirst. She found him amidships, alone at the rail, standing stiffly. He wore a severe expression.

'There's been a transition,' she told him.

'Really,' he replied without turning to look at her.

'Yes, and by all indications it's Jennesta, using her counterfeit set of instrumentalities.'

'And what would you have us do about it?'

'Do? Follow her, of course.'

'What about the orcs, and retrieving the artefacts *they* have? Wasn't that supposed to be our mission?'

'There's a difference. The Wolverines' possession of instrumentalities is dangerous, I don't deny that. But there's no sign that they're using them maliciously. Jennesta, on the other hand, has evil intent. I judge her the greater threat. We can deal with the orcs after we settle with her.'

Now he did tear his eyes from the star-speckled night sky and looked at her. 'What does Karrell Revers have to say about all this?'

That was something she had hoped he wouldn't ask. 'I haven't communicated with him about it.'

'Why?'

'There were practical problems.'

'Ah, yes. The loss of the crystal.' He was referring to the most direct and reliable method of contacting headquarters.

Pelli had told him, after flinging the crystal overboard in a moment of anger, that it had been lost. Which was true in a way. 'Yes,' she answered, holding his gaze.

'But there are other means of communicating with our commander.'

'Yes,' she repeated.

'Means which you alone can exercise, as possessor of the highest magical skills among those of us present.'

There was something about Weevan-Jirst's tone that made Pelli wonder, for the first time, if he could be envious of her. In reply, she simply nodded.

'Since you . . . mislaid the crystal,' the goblin went on, 'it would seem we must fall back on your talents to contact Revers.'

'If we *were* to commune with him, yes we would.'

'What do you mean?' the goblin hissed.

'I see no need to seek his guidance in this matter.'

'*I* do. Moreover I demand my right as second-in-command to speak with him myself, as laid out in the Corps' constitution.'

'Those same rules state that the commander of a unit such as this has complete discretion when it comes to operational decisions.'

'So you are denying my rights.'

'Only your right to constantly question my leadership,' Pelli came back irritably. 'And we won't achieve our goal if we keep pulling in different directions.' She took a breath, softened and went for conciliatory. 'Look, we have our disagreements, but we both want this mission to succeed. Can't we put aside our differences and go forward in that spirit?'

'It seems I have little choice.' Reading a goblin's mood was hard at the best of times, but it didn't take an expert to tell Weevan-Jirst was disgruntled. 'Though I want to record my misgivings about the course you are set upon,' he added.

'Officially noted. For my part, I pledge that we'll turn our full attention to the orcs just as soon as we've sorted out the Jennesta situation.'

'I will have to abide by that decision,' he replied sniffily. 'My only wish is to end this fiasco.'

'Believe me, the sorceress poses a far greater threat than anything the Wolverines might do.'

'I hope you are right, for all our sakes.'

The Wolverines stared at the place where Jennesta and her follow-ers had been.

Jup broke the silence. 'What do we do now?'

'We go after her,' Dynahla replied.

'Can we?' Stryke said, snapping out of his daze. 'You know where they've gone?'

'Not specifically. But I can follow the trail.'

'So let's do it!' Coilla chimed in.

There was a murmur of agreement from the band.

'All right,' Stryke said. 'What does it take, Dynahla?'

'Hold on. If we pursue Jennesta there's no saying where we might end up. What about Dallog and the others on the ship?'

'We could always leave 'em there,' Haskeer muttered.

Wheam appeared shocked.

Stryke gave his sergeant a hard look. 'We'll get back to the ship. That means a delay. Will this trail you spoke about go cold, Dynahla?'

'We should be all right for a little while. Though of course the longer we leave it the further away Jennesta could be from the spot where she fetched up.'

'Or she could have moved on to another world altogether,' Spurral offered.

The shape-changer shrugged. 'Quite possible.'

'Could you still track her if she did that?' Stryke said.

'Maybe. Providing we don't delay too long.'

'Let's move it then. We'll make for the ship at the double.'

The journey back to the shore was punishing. But they made it in good time, and as they dragged their boats from the under-growth, dawn was breaking.

Back on board the ship, Stryke briefed Dallog, the other tyros and Standeven about what had happened. He got Dallog to bind the wounded. Then he ordered the grunts to gather all the weapons and provisions they could carry, and to be quick about it.

As they were finishing the chore, one of the privates cried out and pointed. Three ships were moving away from the far end of the island and heading out to sea. They were unmistakably goblin vessels.

'That has to be Gleaton-Rouk and his crew,' Coilla said.

'And no doubt Jennesta's collection of zombies,' Pepperdyne added.

'Do we go after them?'

'No, Coilla,' Stryke replied. 'It's Jennesta I want, and Thirzarr.'

'Jennesta's force was bigger, wasn't it?'

'Yeah,' Pepperdyne agreed. 'Apart from making common cause with the goblin, she seems to be recruiting. There were all sorts in that camp.'

'Why would anybody want to serve her?' Jup wondered.

'The promise of power, a chance for riches, or just for the hell of it,' Stryke said. 'Maybe they're even under an enchantment, like her zombies. Who knows?'

'Those zombie orcs were less than . . . right, weren't they? I mean, they wouldn't be, given they were under a hex, but even so they lacked some vital spark.'

'You can bet she's working on that.'

'We're wasting time here, Stryke,' Dynahla said.

'You're right.' He beckoned the band and they drew together. 'Let's do it.'

'I'll need your set of instrumentalities.'

Stryke cast the shape-shifter a wary look. 'I'm happier holding onto them.'

'Haven't I proved myself yet?

'Well . . .'

'I can see that I haven't.

'It's not that I don't trust you, it's just—'

'I understand. But it's going to be really hard manipulating them through you, especially if it has to be done fast. You've *got* to trust me or this won't work.'

Stryke struggled with that for a moment. Then he reached into his belt pouch, took out the stars, and after a second's hesitation, handed them over.

'Thank you,' Dynahla said. He began slotting them together with impressive dexterity.

At the edge of the group, Standeven watched with covetous eyes.

'What's to stop Jennesta messing with where we land?' Coilla asked. 'The way she did before.'

Dynahla paused. '*I* am. I can counter that. At least to some extent.' He carried on readying the instrumentalities, until just one remained to be fitted. 'Brace yourselves.'

The band moved closer. Wheam put on a brave face. Spurral reached for Jup's calloused hand. Standeven looked terrified.

'We don't know what we're letting ourselves in for,' Stryke told them. 'So no matter how bad the crossing is we've got to be ready to fight the instant we arrive . . . wherever.' He nodded at Dynahla.

The fetch clipped the last star into place.

No matter how often they made a crossing, and for all their indifference to fear, they found the experience profoundly disturbing.

Having endured what felt like an endless, dizzying drop down a well made of multicoloured lights, they met hard solidity.

Most of the band were shaken but ready to fight. Some, principally Standeven, Wheam and a couple of the tyros, were less composed. But even they, ashen-faced and nauseous, were quickly if unsteadily on their feet.

They stood on a flat, bleak plain. A sharp wind blew, stirring up a grey substance, more like ash than soil or sand, that covered the ground. Here and there, great slabs of black rock jutted out of it. The rocks seemed to be vitrified, as though some unimaginable heat had melted them, making them flow like liquid before cooling.

Above, the sky had a dour, greenish tint. The sun, a sickly red, looked no bigger than a coin held at arm's length. It was cold, and the air was bad, not unlike the way it stank when a thousand funeral pyres had been lit after a battle.

There was no sign of Jennesta's force, or any other living thing, including trees, vegetation or animals.

On the horizon there was something that looked like a city. Even in the weak sunlight it appeared to be crystalline. But it was wrong. Many of its numerous towers were truncated, resembling broken teeth, or leaned at crazy angles.

The band gaped at it.

It took Haskeer to mouth what they were all thinking. 'Where the *fuck* are we?'

'Somewhere pretty damn grim,' Coilla said, buttoning her jerkin against the chill.

'It doesn't matter where we are,' Stryke told them. 'The point is, where's Jennesta? Dynahla, you sure you haven't brought us to the wrong place?'

'No. She's here.'

'Any idea where, exactly?'

'From my own abilities, no. The psychic charge here is too . . . *murky* to be specific. But that seems the obvious place.' He nodded towards the city.

Stryke gave the order and they headed its way.

It was a much longer march than it first appeared, making them realise how large the city really was, and the ashen terrain was hard going underfoot. But the powdery blanket turned out to have one advantage. When they were about halfway to their destination, as far as they could judge, they spotted tracks in it. They led in the direction of the city.

'Human,' Jup announced, kneeling by them, 'and more than one set. Has to be her.'

Stryke nodded. 'Let's keep moving. And eyes peeled.'

They trudged on, warily.

Before they reached the city the tracks petered out, erased by the wind. But they had no doubt of their destination.

Shortly after, they arrived at the outskirts. Even before it fell into ruin it would have been like no place of habitation they had ever seen. Much of its architecture was inexplicable to them. There were sleek structures lacking doors or windows, buildings in the shape of spirals or cubes, or crowned with pyramids. The remains of one edifice was smothered in strange decorative symbols. Another took the form of a cone, its angles so acute that nobody could possibly have lived in it. They saw the remnants of signs in a completely incomprehensible language, if it was a language, and toppled objects that might have been statues, except they were insanely abstract. And when they looked closer, and ran their fingers over walls and pillars and fallen cornices, they discovered they were fashioned from no materials they knew.

For as far as they could see, the city was deserted, and in ruins. The evidence of decay was everywhere, with crumbling walls, cracks spider-webbing buildings and fissures disfiguring the avenues. But there were signs of more violent destruction, too, in the form of ragged apertures, sheered spires and pockmarks that looked as though they had been made by incredibly powerful projectiles. Charred debris and unmistakable traces of smoke damage in some areas showed that flames had played their part.

'This place makes no sense,' Spurral said. 'What kind of creatures could have lived here?'

'And what put an end to them?' Jup wondered.

'A war?' Dallog speculated. 'Or nature rising up and turning on them with an earthquake, or—'

'Could have been the gods,' Gleadeg reckoned darkly, 'upset in some way.'

'No point trying to figure it,' Stryke said. 'Let's keep to why we're here.'

Coilla cupped her eyes and scanned the scene. 'It's vast. Where do we go?'

Stryke turned to Jup. 'How do you feel about trying farsight?'

'Sure.' He got down on his knees and wormed his hand into the ash. Eyes closed, he stayed that way for a moment. 'Bugger that!' He leapt up, waving his hand about as though it had been burnt.

'What is it?' Spurral asked anxiously.

'The energy's fouled. It's even worse than Maras-Dantia.'

'You all right?'

'Yeah.' He took a breath, calming himself. 'Yeah, I think so.'

'Whatever happened here, the magic or weapons used, has tainted this place,' Dynahla said.

'Don't suppose you got a hint of anything, did you, Jup?' Stryke wondered.

'Not a thing. Sorry, chief.'

Haskeer elbowed his way to the front. 'So what now, Stryke?'

'We'll form squads and start searching.'

'That'll take for ever.'

'You got a better idea?'

'*Stryke,*' Coilla said.

'What?'

She pointed at a jumble of half-collapsed buildings. 'I saw something move.'

'Sure?'

'Yeah.'

'I think I did too,' Pepperdyne added.

'Weapons,' Stryke ordered. They all drew their blades and he led them towards the sighting.

Moving guardedly, they reached the spot. There was nothing to be seen except devastation. They rooted around a bit in the rubble, but fruitlessly.

'You two are imagining things,' Haskeer grumbled, glaring at Coilla and Pepperdyne.

'I don't think so,' Coilla replied evenly.

'*Ssshhh!*' Jup waved them into silence and nodded at an area a little farther along, where heaps of clutter were shrouded in darkness.

Faint noises were coming from it. Scratching and rustling, and the sound of rubble being dislodged.

Stryke at their head, the band quietly moved forward. Again, they found nothing, and the sounds had stopped. But they noticed a narrow passageway, formed by the sides of two adjacent buildings, and at its end there was a faint light. They entered it. As they walked the passage the light grew stronger. When they emerged at its far end, they saw its source.

They came out to an open space that might originally have been some kind of public square. It was strewn with junk, and the scene was illuminated by a number of fires scattered about the place. The flames threw shadows on the walls of the surrounding buildings left standing.

'Where the hell's Jennesta?' Coilla complained.

'She's here somewhere,' Dynahla assured her. 'You can count on it.'

'What I don't get,' Pepperdyne said, 'is why these fires haven't burnt out long since. What's to feed them?'

'I'm more concerned with whatever *that* is,' Stryke told him. He was staring straight ahead.

A shape crept out of the dark at the far end of the wrecked plaza. As it moved into the flickering light they got a better look. It wasn't Jennesta or one of her followers, as they half expected. It was a beast. But of a kind they had never encountered before.

At first sight, some thought it was feline, others canine. In fact, the creature seemed to be a blend of both, and in several respects it was almost insectoid. Standing about waist-high to an orc, it had six legs, ending in lengthy, horn-like talons. Its pelt was a yellowish-brown. The brute's head resembled a lion's, except it lacked a mane and had a much more extended snout. There was a wide, fang-filled mouth, and instead of two eyes there were six, ruby red.

The band remained stock still, watching the thing, braced for an attack. But although it seemed aware of them, its interest was elsewhere. Letting out a throaty snort, it made its way to the biggest of the fires. Then, to the orcs' astonishment, it thrust its head into the flames and began lapping at them.

'My gods,' Coilla exclaimed, 'it's drinking the fire.'

'How can that be?' Jup said.

'Anything's possible in an infinite number of worlds,' Dynahla told them.

Two more of the animals came out of the shadows. Joining the first, they too gulped the flames, the trio snapping and snarling at each other as though squabbling over a kill.

Haskeer looked on in stupefaction. 'They must have hides tough as steel.'

'Let's hope not,' Pepperdyne said.

His wish was pertinent. Having supped their fill, the creatures turned their attention to the band. Their multiple crimson eyes held a malignant intensity.

Coilla went 'Uh-uh'.

The fire-eaters charged.

One of them, in the lead, opened its massive jaws and belched a plume of flame. The orcs in its path scattered, narrowly avoiding a roasting.

'Now we know what keeps the fires going,' Coilla said. 'They do!'

She and Pepperdyne leapt aside to avoid another creature that singled them out. It swerved and, spitting fire, galloped after the fleeing pair. They made for one of the ruined buildings bordering the square.

Stryke and Haskeer barely dodged incineration from the beast targeting them. The flame it spewed flew over their ducked heads and seared a nearby wall. They set to weaving about the creature and harassing it as best they could. Jup and Spurral joined them, along with Hystykk and Gleadeg.

The rest of the band was tackling the third fire-breather, their greater number allowing them to surround it. They were attacking from a distance, employing arrows and spears, though many of their projectiles bounced off its hardened skin, and they had to retreat periodically as it spat gouts of flame.

To no one's great surprise, Standeven didn't get involved. He scurried off to cower behind a pile of masonry slabs.

Adding to the confusion, a fourth creature turned up and darted towards the fray. Dallog spotted it and shouted an order. He and the tyros, Wheam, Chuss, Keick and Pirrak, peeled off and ran to meet it.

Stryke and his crew were making progress in frustrating their opponent if not actually overcoming it. When it turned away from them and loped off they thought it had been beaten. But it stopped at the nearest fire, supped there, and came back at them.

'The fire doesn't last!' Stryke yelled. 'They have to renew it!'

They knew what to do. Jup, Spurral and the two grunts moved to block the creature's access to the replenishing fires. After that it was a case of staying out of its way and landing blows when they could. Before long, the beast exhausted its flame. Its fangs and claws meant it was still a formidable challenge, but a less dangerous one. They moved in on it, hacking with their blades. A swing from Stryke sliced across the brawny chest, causing the head to dip, and Haskeer brought his axe down on its skull, cracking it open. The creature collapsed and lay twitching, tiny puffs of flame huffing from its nostrils.

'The bastards can stick their faces in fire but they ain't unkill-able,' Haskeer announced triumphantly.

The band members fighting the second beast had also noticed that it needed to refresh its flame and followed the example of Stryke's group. They were busy parting its head from its writhing body with a series of brutal strokes.

As they all rushed to aid Dallog and the tyros with their kill, Stryke looked around. 'Anybody see where Coilla and Pepperdyne went?'

Jup shook his head.

Running full pelt, the heat from the fire-breather practically scorching their backs, Coilla and Pepperdyne found an open door-way. Open but two-thirds blocked. Urgency sharpening their agility, they managed to wriggle through. The bulky creature got its head and part of its upper body in but struggled furiously to get any further. It vented its fury with blasts of flame. They quickly retreated into the building and only just avoided them.

The interior was a complete shambles. But there was some light other than that coming from the fire-breather. It came from a small opening, possibly a window, set about halfway up the far wall. A sloping mound of rubble that had probably come in through the aperture made a natural ramp leading to it.

'Think we could get through that?' Pepperdyne asked.

Coilla nodded. 'It'd be tight, but yeah, I think so.'

The creature gave another blast that lit up the room. It afforded a brief glimpse of the chaos and some of the strange objects strewn about, which could have been the remains of curiously designed furniture.

'So let's get out of here,' she urged.

'Hang on.'

Above the door, and over the probing creature's head, was a large quantity of wreckage, including blocks of something like stone. All that supported it was a couple of uprights. To Pepperdyne, the whole thing looked tenuous.

Coilla followed his gaze and guessed what was on his mind. 'If you're thinking what I *think* you're thinking that could bring the whole place down on us.'

'I reckon we could get away with it.'

'Why bother when we can just get out through that?' She jabbed a thumb at the window.

'It wouldn't solve the problem. What's to stop this monster circling round and waiting for us outside?'

Coilla weighed the odds. 'All right. Let's do it.'

'Good. You climb up to the window and I'll take care of it.'

'No way. We're doing this together.'

'It won't take two of us. Look at the state of those uprights. One good kick and—'

'I'm not some helpless female, Jode, and don't you *dare* treat me like one!'

Regardless of their plight he almost laughed. 'I'd never make the mistake of seeing you *that* way, Coilla. It's just practical. If something goes wrong we'd both be in trouble. Better one of us is clear to help if needed.'

The creature at the door grew more frantic. It sent in another sheet of flame.

She nodded. 'You take care, mind.' Then she edged her way to the pile of rubble and started scrabbling up it.

Pepperdyne waited until she reached the window and called, 'Can we get through?'

'Yeah,' she replied, 'I'm pretty sure we can.'

He turned back to the door. To reach the uprights he had to get nearer to the furious creature than he liked. He considered pelting them with chunks of debris, but knew that wouldn't do the job. So he started sliding towards them on his back, legs first. When he got as close as he dared, he gave one of the supports a hefty kick. It let out a loud snap and fell away. Crab-like, Pepperdyne hastily retreated. But nothing happened. It was obvious that the other upright was the only thing holding up the tremendous weight above the door.

The frenzied creature was still trying to force itself into the too small opening, and let out a further gush of flame. It didn't reach Pepperdyne, but he felt the heat through the soles of his boots. He shuffled forward again, aiming for the remaining prop. A powerful kick had no effect on it, so he pounded at it with his foot. The repeated impacts started to tell. A creaking sound came every time he hit it, and the post started to shake.

The upright suddenly gave with a resounding crack. Pepperdyne rolled aside, his hands instinctively covering his face. The debris collapsed with a thunderous roar. Tons of wreckage came down on the creature's head and upper body, instantly crushing it to pulp and disgorging its sticky, green life fluid.

The whole structure didn't cave in, as they feared it might, but a cloud of dust filled the room.

'You all right, Jode?' Coilla shouted anxiously.

He didn't answer right away, and when he did it was only after a coughing fit and having to spit the muck out of his mouth. 'I'm . . . fine.'

Getting to his feet, he climbed up the rubble slope, taking Coilla's outstretched hand. She pulled him the last few steps and they squeezed out of the window. There was just a short drop to the ground.

They found their way back to the square without much trouble.

The rest of the band was there, along with the bloody corpses of the fire-breathers. Standeven had come out of hiding and looked on pasty-faced.

'Been off for a spot of canoodling?' Haskeer taunted, raising a ragged laugh from some of the grunts.

Coilla and Pepperdyne ignored him.

'I was about to send a search party for you two,' Stryke said.

'We're all right,' Coilla told him. 'Any sign of Jennesta?'

'No.' He shot a critical glance Dynahla's way. 'I'm starting to think—'

Right on cue, one of the privates yelled, *'Over there!'*

They all turned. At the far end of the square, near the point where the creatures had emerged, stood a group of figures. Jennesta was at the forefront, and Thirzarr could be made out beside her.

Stryke began running towards them, the band close behind. He called out to Thirzarr.

Jennesta's hands moved. She and her force vanished.

'I think we saw that coming,' Coilla remarked, arriving at Stryke's side.

'Dynahla!' he bellowed.

The shape-changer had the instrumentalities out and was manipulating them. Swiftly, the band gathered together.

'Here we go again,' Jup said.

Dynahla slapped the final star into place and their surroundings disappeared.

They came to a place quite unlike the one they had just left.

It was pleasantly mild. The air was clear, the sky blue, the terrain green and abundant.

They were on high ground. A pastoral scene was spread out before them. Rolling hills, lush grassland, copses, forests, a placid lake, and the distant sparkle of a meandering river. Meadows and hedged fields were evidence of cultivation, but there was no sign of buildings. However, there was a well-made road, surfaced with compacted earth. In one direction it ran straight and open for as far as they could see. In the other it soon came to a bend at woodland and disappeared.

'Where's the bitch got to now?' Haskeer grumbled as he surveyed the landscape. Pointedly, he didn't ask the question of Dynahla.

'Out there somewhere, I guess.' Stryke swept a hand at the panorama.

'Not that I can see,' Jup said, 'and her group should be big enough to spot.'

'The logical thing for her to have done was take the road,' Pepperdyne suggested. 'That way, towards the bend.'

Coilla nodded. 'And a good place for an ambush.'

'Then we'll round it with care,' Stryke said. 'Come on.'

The march wasn't welcomed by everybody. Many of them were still drained and aching from the fight with the fire-breathers, in a world that seemed impossibly far away. Which, of course, it was.

Standeven wasn't pleased either, though his discomfort came from a lifetime of indolence rather than anything as strenuous as fighting, or as dangerous. Abandoning his usual place near the rear of the group, he wormed his way to Pepperdyne who walked alone, Coilla being occupied with Stryke at the front.

'Oh,' Pepperdyne said on seeing him, 'it's you.'

'Yes, me. Your master and title-holder, though you seem to have forgotten it.'

'You just can't get it through your head, can you? None of that means anything anymore. It's a whole different game now.'

'It might be to you. I happen to think a pledge still means something.'

'Do you have any idea how ridiculous your blend of conceit and acting pitiable makes you look?'

'There was a time when you wouldn't have dared to say a thing like that.'

Pepperdyne's patience was running out. 'Why are we talking? What do you want, Standeven?'

'I want to know how much longer this . . . *charade*'s going to last.'

'Charade?'

'This leaping from one stinking place to another, of course.'

'This world doesn't look too bad to me. If you're so tired of what's going on why don't you settle here?'

'Oh, you'd like that, wouldn't you? Anyway, unless we're careful we might all end up being left somewhere we don't want to be.'

'Meaning?'

Standeven nodded at Dynahla, walking at the head of the column with Stryke and Coilla. 'You really think that freak can be trusted?'

That echoed Pepperdyne's own doubts, but there was no way he was going to admit it to this man. 'Seems to me Dynahla's done more for this band than you ever did.'

'Enough to be handed the instrumentalities?'

'It always comes back to that with you, doesn't it? Stryke knows what he's doing.'

'Does he? Whatever you think about me, Jode, I'm not insane. I want to get out of this mess alive as much as you do. If you think Stryke's going the right way about that, it's on your own head.' He said no more, and let Pepperdyne walk on.

They were approaching the bend in the road. Stryke halted the column and sent four scouts ahead. He told four more to cut through the lip of the wood, in case there were any unpleasant surprises lurking in there. They soon returned with word that the way was clear. The band resumed its march.

The road took several other turns, although none were blind, until it curved round the base of a hill, obscuring whatever lay beyond. Taking no chances, they left the road and climbed to the hill's summit. Looking down to the far side, they saw a lone building in the middle distance.

It wasn't a farmhouse, as they might have expected. Seemingly made of stone, it more closely resembled a chateau or small castle. There was a low, round tower at each corner, and a large entrance with its doors wide open. Given its rustic setting it looked strangely incongruous.

Some figures could just about be seen moving around in front of the building. Beyond the fact that they walked upright and appeared to be dressed in white, they were too far away for any more details to be made out.

'Signs of life at last,' Coilla said.

'Yeah,' Stryke replied. 'I wonder what kind.'

They moved down the hill, crossed the road bordering its foot and headed over the grassland.

'Sheathe your weapons but keep them handy,' Stryke ordered. 'We don't want to scare them off if they're not hostile.'

'They look peaceable enough,' Spurral reckoned.

'If they are, maybe they'll be able to tell us where Jennesta is.'

'You think she could be there, and Thirzarr?'

He shrugged.

'Keep your resolve, Stryke. We'll find your mate.'

'Maybe.'

As the band approached, they were spotted by the white-clad beings, who simply stopped whatever they were doing and stared. They didn't seem perturbed by the sight of an orc warband, a couple of dwarfs and several humans arriving out of nowhere.

When the Wolverines were close enough they finally got a good look at the creatures.

'They're human.' The way Coilla said it expressed the surprise most of the band was feeling.

'Why shouldn't they be?' Dynahla asked. 'In an infinite number of worlds—'

'Yeah, I know. Anything's possible. I just wasn't expecting it.'

There were five of them, and the striking thing was how alike they were. All were male, if slightly androgynous in appearance, tall, slim and blond. They were ivory skinned and beardless. Their attire was identical, consisting of a white, smock-like garment covering them from neck to ankles. But their arms, and oddly their feet, were bare. By human standards they were handsome. Some would have said beautiful. From the expressions on their smiling faces their dispositions might have been called sunny.

'Humans grinning like fucking idiots,' Haskeer grated dourly, 'that's all we need.'

'Something's not right here,' Pepperdyne said.

'Your race smiles,' Coilla told him. 'I'm sure I saw you doing it once.'

'What I mean is not all humans look exactly the same.'

'You do to most orcs.'

'I'm serious, Coilla. This bunch are peas in a pod. It's not natural.'

Standeven had gravitated to Pepperdyne's side again. He was looking troubled as well.

Coilla noticed it. 'What's the matter with you two? Jode?'

'There's something about them. I don't know. Something . . . familiar.'

Standeven nodded in agreement, his gaze fixed on the supposed humans.

Stryke went ahead of the others, hand raised in a conciliatory gesture, and addressed the nearest being in Mutual. 'We've come to you in peace.'

'Peace,' the creature repeated, his smile unfaltering.

'Yes. We don't want anything of you.'

'You want nothing,' one of the others said.

Stryke looked to him. 'Right. Except to ask a question.'

'A question?' That came from the third of the creatures.

Before Stryke could reply, the fourth said, 'What question?'

'Er . . . we want to know if another group's passed this way.'

'Another group, you say,' the fifth remarked.

Stryke was getting perplexed, but he was determined to persist. 'A party led by a female who looks kind of . . . odd.'

'Odd?' the second, or possibly the third, echoed.

'You would have noticed her,' Stryke persisted.

'Would we?' the first asked.

'This is *weird*,' Jup muttered.

The irritating exchange continued, with Stryke trying to get some sense out of the creatures and not knowing which one would answer next.

Finally his patience snapped and he bellowed, *'Look! It's simple! Have you or have you not seen any other strangers today?'*

The reply came from all of them sequentially, their smiles never wavering.

'Strangers . . .'

'. . . are . . .'

'. . . never . . .'

'. . . welcome . . .'

'. . . here.'

Then something startling happened. As one, they all unfolded a massive set of wings, hidden until now. The wings were pure white and seemed to be constituted of downy feathers.

'An angelic host,' Standeven whispered, awestruck.

Coilla looked at him, then noticed that Pepperdyne appeared nearly as beguiled. 'What?' she said.

He tore his eyes from the sight. 'They mean something to my race. Particularly to Unis and the like.'

'Good or bad?'

'Oh, good,' Standeven said. 'The *epitome* of goodness, we're told.'

'Well, I think you've been told wrong. Or these things are something different. Look again.'

The comely, benevolent faces of the winged beings were twisting into snarling, hate-filled grimaces. Their jaws dropped, revealing mouths full of razor-sharp incisors. Their eyes, soft and as blue as the sky an instant before, turned into inky black orbs set in scarlet. And as their faces turned nasty, so did they.

They shot into the air in unison, their powerful wings flapping mightily. For a moment they circled overhead, and the band saw that they had produced concealed weapons; gold-coloured maces studded with barbs. Then they dived.

The orcs with shields held them above their heads. They swiped at the tormenting creatures with their blades and axes, but couldn't connect. Arrows were loosed and proved no match for the flyers' agility. Again and again they swooped down, menacing the Wolverines with their maces.

Stryke knew that if the band didn't find cover they were certain to lose the fight. He waited until the flying things were at their highest point preparatory to diving again. *'To the house!'* he yelled. *'To the house!'*

They made for the doors at full pelt, desperately trying to outrun creatures that were potentially much faster. Coilla and Pepperdyne, through some act of instinctive charity, grabbed Standeven's arms from either side and dragged the wheezing human along. For all the band knew there were more of the things inside, but it was a chance they had to take. There was no other shelter.

Getting to the house a heartbeat ahead of the flyers they hurled themselves through. They flung their weight behind the doors and slammed them shut. There was the satisfying sound of at least one flying creature crashing into the woodwork on the other side.

Panting from the effort, and with Standeven fit to have a seizure, the band took a moment to catch their breath.

Recovering, they looked around. They were in a long, high, stone-clad corridor, with several doors on either side and a set of much larger ones at its end. The side doors led to windowless rooms or dead-end passages, so they made for the double doors. Kicking them open they found a spacious chamber, perhaps a banqueting room, wood panelled and hung with weighty candelabra. At its far end, and to the right, there was a further, wide corridor running off at an angle.

'Now what do we do?' Dallog wanted to know.

'I guess we start by seeing if there's another way out,' Stryke replied.

'And if there ain't?' Haskeer said.

'There will be. Or we'll make one.'

'Stryke,' Dynahla said, urgency in his voice.

'What is it?'

'I feel a presence.'

'Her?'

'Has to be.' The shape-changer pointed to the corridor. 'That way.'

They rushed to it.

It was ill-lit, and long, but some way down it there was a crowd of figures. Jennesta was among them. She saw the band. Fiddling with the objects in her hands, she and her pack blinked out of existence.

Dynahla dug out the instrumentalities, and at a nod from Stryke, slapped them together.

The Wolverines materialised in a swamp, knee deep in warm, stinking water. Waist deep in the case of the dwarfs. The air was humid and uncomfortable. There were countless flies, causing the orcs to slap at their exposed flesh. Small, unidentified creatures zigzagged through the water. All about them was a green gloom, thanks to a canopy of vegetation high above their heads.

Haskeer smacked the side of his neck, crushing an insect. 'This is not an improvement.'

'So where in damnations is Jennesta now?' Coilla complained.

'Yeah, there's no trace of her,' Wheam said. 'How come she isn't right where we land every time?'

'We don't always arrive in exactly the same place as someone else who's made a transition,' Dynahla explained. 'That's partly down to me, because it's hard to be accurate. But it's mostly a function of the instrumentalities.'

'So she could be anywhere,' Coilla said.

Dynahla shook his head. 'No. We always arrive within a certain radius. She's here, and not far.' He looked around. 'The question is where.'

'You seem to know an awful lot about the stars.'

'Serapheim was a good teacher. He taught me that—'

'Can we talk about this some other time?' Stryke interrupted.

'So where to, chief?' Jup said.

'There's a patch of drier ground over there. That's where we'll start.'

They waded to it, and found it was the tail end of a much longer strip of land, muddy and tangled with roots, but preferable to the foul water. The band was glad to haul themselves onto it.

'*Now* what?' Coilla wanted to know.

'We could follow this spit of land and see where it takes us,' Stryke said.

'Bit hit or miss, isn't it?'

'Yeah.' He turned to Dynahla. 'Can you feel anything?'

'What I'm getting is confused,' the fetch confessed. 'It's not clear enough to pinpoint her.'

Stryke sighed. 'Great.'

'But there's another way I might be able to help.'

'Do it, whatever it is.'

'All right. Here.' He took out the instrumentalities and handed them to him. 'Best you take care of these until I get back.'

'Get back?'

'I'm going to use my shape-changing ability to scout the area. Any objections?'

'Er . . . no.'

'Then give me some room.'

The band stepped back.

Dynahla got down on the ground and stretched out. He began to change. His writhing body compressed and elongated simultaneously. The arms and legs drew in and disappeared. The flesh turned black as it redistributed itself and stretched into a long, cylindrical shape, a tapering tail at one end, a smooth, hairless head at the other. Shiny scales appeared along its whole length.

Seconds later an enormous water snake regarded them with unblinking, golden eyes, a forked tongue flicking from its lipless mouth. It turned, slid into the water and disappeared.

The silence that followed was finally broken when Jup said, 'That was . . . bizarre.'

They waited, exchanging whispered thoughts about what Dynahla had just done, looking out for an ambush and swatting flies.

Before long there was a disturbance in the water. The snake surfaced and slithered ashore. Immediately, the reversion to Dynahla's original form took place. At its completion he was on his hands and knees, head down, wet hair hanging lankly. He shook off droplets of water, not unlike a dog, and stood.

'That way,' he stated simply, pointing out across the water. 'Not far. On another plot of dry land. Well, drier.'

'You all right? Coilla asked.

He nodded. 'Transformation can drain me, particularly the more extreme ones. I'm fine.'

'Up to moving again?' Stryke said.

'Yes.'

'Then you'd better have these.' He held out the instrumentalities.

Dynahla seemed taken aback. He accepted them and half whispered, 'Thank you.'

Everyone collected their gear and they set off, with the shapeshifter and Stryke in the lead.

When they neared their destination, as signalled by the fetch, they tried to move as quietly as they could given they were practically swimming. Even so, when rounding a vast outcrop of foliage they came upon Jennesta's party almost unexpectedly.

The two sides spotted each other at the same time. A couple of arrows winged the band's way. Taking cover in the thick vegetation, they returned fire. The exchange grew heavier, the enemy's arrows zinging through the greenery all around the Wolverines, and theirs flying back.

One of Jennesta's archers was bold enough, or foolish enough, to let himself be seen as he made to loose a shot. An orc arrow smacked square to his chest and he toppled into the water. It stirred, rippled and churned as the scavengers living in it were drawn to blood and set to devouring his corpse.

Jennesta herself took a hand, lobbing a searing fireball the warband's way. Dynahla deflected it and sent her one of his own. Jennesta swept it aside.

The duel was short-lived. Jennesta employed the stars and her force was gone.

Dynahla quickly checked that everybody was together and did what was necessary to follow.

'She is taking the piss!' Haskeer raged.

They were on a tundra, an immense, glassy plain covered in ice. The only feature to be made out was a black mountain range straddling the horizon.

Snow was falling, a bitter wind blew, and the band, still wet through from the swamp, felt the cold to their bones.

'There!' a grunt yelled, his breath jetting like steam.

Jennesta and her henchmen could just be seen, actually not too far away but almost obscured by the driving snow. Stryke thought he caught a glimpse of Thirzarr.

'*After 'em!*' he shouted over the storm. '*Before they—*'

The sorceress and her followers became one with nothingness.

'*Shit!*' Jup cursed.

'*Dynahla!*' Stryke bellowed.

'I'm on it!'

The band took a leap to somewhere other.

They were in semi-darkness.

It took a moment for them to realise they were underground, what little light there was coming from a myriad of tiny crystals embedded in the walls of a large cavern.

Pepperdyne knew Coilla was less than keen on confined spaces, and he gave her hand a supportive squeeze.

A number of tunnels ran off from the chamber they were in.

'What the fuck way do we go?' Haskeer demanded.

'*Ssshhh!*' Spurral held a finger to her lips.

He was about to badmouth her when he realised what the others had already heard. Echoing sounds, like footfalls.

'*That* way!' Keick bawled.

They ran for a tunnel with a larger entrance than the others.

It was long, and twisting, and the clatter of their boots bounced off the walls like a hailstorm.

They came out in another, even bigger cave, resembling a scaled-down canyon. A subterranean river ran through, with a wall-hugging ledge running round it. Where it reached the far side it widened to a natural platform, a great slab of yellowish rock. Jennesta and her horde stood there. But not for long.

'Not *again!*' Spurral exclaimed.

Dynahla applied the remedy.

At first they thought they were back in the world of the malicious angels.

It was temperate and their surroundings were not unpleasant, but it was a scrubbier, less verdant scene. There was grass, though it was patchy, and trees that could have been fuller. They could see modest, whitish-grey cliffs in the distance.

The band stood on a road, more accurately a trail, wide and well trod. Their prey was nowhere to be seen.

'Listen,' Coilla said. 'What's that sound?'

21

'Drums,' Jup said, tilting his head to one side and listening intently. 'And getting nearer.'

'Not just drums,' Pepperdyne added. 'Can anybody else hear horn blasts?'

They could. And Jup was right; the noise was growing louder. Soon, they could make out rhythmic chanting and the tramp of marching feet mixed into the din.

'An army?' Dallog wondered.

'It's an undisciplined one if it is, making that much of a racket,' Stryke said. 'But whatever it is there's a lot of them. Best to get out of sight.'

At the side of the road there was a row of substantial boulders. The band concealed themselves behind them as the sounds increased.

'Can anybody understand what they're chanting?' Coilla asked.

'There's more than one language in it,' Spurral said. 'A hell of a lot more.'

'Damned if I can make sense of it,' Jup admitted.

'Watch out!' Dallog warned. 'Here they come!'

There was a bend a little way along the road. A number of figures were rounding it. The band recognised them immediately.

'Elves?' Coilla said. 'It's not like them to raise such a clamour, is it?'

'It's not just elves,' Pepperdyne told her, nodding at the road.

The elves, twenty or thirty strong, may have been leading the mob but they were by no means representative of it. Right behind them came a herd of centaurs, trotting in pairs, many of them holding long silver trumpets to their lips. An ogre followed, wearing a harness. It was acting as a guide to a line of trolls, their eyes bound against the hated light, who clasped two thick ropes extending from the harness. Next came a company of swaggering goblins. After that, the races were more or less mixed together. Gnomes walked with satyrs, dwarfs with kobolds. Humans strode alongside bands of dancing, tambourine-twirling pixies. Brownies accompanied gremlins and leprechauns. There were howlers, hob-goblins, harpies, fauns, chimeras and giggling nymphs. Swarms of fairies, mouth-watering to the orcs, fluttered above the horde. There were many other species the Wolverines didn't recognise, mammalian, insectoid, reptilian and unclassifiable.

While most walked, slithered, hopped or flew, some rode, on carts, horses, lizards and giant fowl. Wagons bobbed along in the mass carrying tanks that housed water-going creatures such as merz and river sprites. Flags and banners were waved. Musical instruments were blown, pounded and plucked over the babble of a hundred tongues. The throng was many thousands strong and the noise was deafening.

'There are races down there who never get along,' Coilla said, 'at least on Maras-Dantia.'

'This isn't Maras-Dantia,' Dynahla reminded her.

'Could have sworn I saw orcs,' Haskeer blurted, shocked at the notion.

'Why not? Anything's possible—'

'In an infinite number of worlds,' Coilla finished for him. 'Yeah, we get it.'

The shape-changer didn't take offence. In fact he smiled.

More and more creatures flowed past, over-spilling the road.

'What the hell's going on here?' Jup wondered. He had a thought. 'Could this be something to do with that bunch who were following us? That Gateway Corps?'

'No, this is something else,' Dynahla assured him. 'And if the Corps were following you, they still will be.'

'Oh good, something else to worry about.' He turned to Stryke. 'We haven't a hope of finding Jennesta in this lot. Where do you think they're going?'

'There's one way to find out. Join 'em.'

'Why not? We'd hardly stand out in a mob like this.'

Stryke had to shout so they could all hear over the tumult. 'If we have to get out of here fast, with the stars I mean, we need to keep together! So stay close or risk being left behind in this madhouse!'

He noticed his sergeant eyeing a cloud of fairies. 'And Haskeer! Don't eat anything.'

They left their hiding place and, staying close, elbowed their way into the procession. The crowd was good natured about it. They looked passionate but apparently they weren't hostile. For the band that made a change.

The flow of bodies swept them along. The movement, the noise, the swirl of colours and the smell, of incense and excrement, was near overwhelming. What they could see of the terrain beyond the press of flesh was unremarkable and more or less unvarying. It didn't look cultivated, or even inhabited, consisting mostly of scrubland, a scattering of trees and the road. Always the road.

Some of the band, principally Coilla and Jup, tried to engage fellow marchers in conversation. But they got little out of them beyond grunts, and what sounded like exaltations, as far as they could tell above the uproar.

Dynahla, walking beside Stryke, shouted into his ear. 'I think this is a crossroads world!'

'A what?'

'*A crossroads world.* Not all travel between worlds is purposeful, using the instrumentalities,' he explained, articulating as clearly as he could. 'Sometimes there are worlds that have wormholes that beings fall through from all over. By chance, I mean.'

'I remember Serapheim saying something about Maras-Dantia once being like that. Which is why there were so many races there.'

The shape-changer nodded. 'And I think these —' he indicated the throng they were part of '—may be pilgrims, and this is some kind of religious festival.'

'Could be,' Stryke conceded.

'The question is, what could have united such a mixture of beings?'

The road was on the rise, and they were starting to climb, but it was still impossible to see what their destination might be. Stryke looked back, and with the advantage of the extra height caught a glimpse of the multitude of beings following behind. They seemed endless.

He wondered how the hell he came to be here.

Dynahla touched his arm and pointed. The road had taken a turn, and now they could see a tall hill, or possibly a mountain. On its summit stood a building. It looked like a fortress. On second thought, it might have been a temple. Then again, it wasn't like that at all.

Pelli Madayar stood amongst the ruins of the crystal city. Weevan-Jirst was at her side, the rest of the Corps unit spread about them. The never-ending wind blew in from the plain, bringing a constant swirl of grey ash like fine snow. It all but obscured the feeble light of the ailing red sun.

'She was here,' Pelli asserted. 'The traces leave no doubt.'

'And not just her,' the goblin replied. 'It seems the warband was here too.'

'Yes, it does.'

'We abandon our search for the orcs to follow Jennesta and find ourselves back on the orcs' trail after all. Is that not ironic?' There was an element of smugness in his manner.

At least he didn't say *I told you so*, she thought. But she was damned if she was going to apologise. 'You could say it was an example of unintended consequences having a positive outcome. As the two set of instrumentalities chase each other, we are on the trail of both. I call that an economic use of our resources. Anyway, I've said all along that if we found one group we'd find the other.'

'How very fortunate for you that blind luck should be so obliging.'

She ignored the jibe. 'We've learnt something else. The Wolverines aren't just world-hopping at random. They're moving with a purpose. So either they've suddenly taught themselves mastery of the instrumentalities, which is unlikely to say the least, or somebody or something is aiding them. Not just that. We know Jennesta tampered with the orcs' set and had a measure of control over them. That appears to no longer be the case. Whatever help they have is countering her influence, at least to some extent.'

'Yet another player. This is getting complicated. I would have said that if you were willing to contact Karrell Revers, now would be the time to request that another unit be put into the field. We could obviously use some help.'

'We're quite capable of dealing with this ourselves. *I'm* competent to deal with it.' She hoped that came across with more confidence than she was feeling.

'If you say so.'

There was a stirring in the ruins. A bulky shape came out of the darkness. When it moved into the watery light it was revealed as one of the six-legged, multi-eyed fire-breathers. It came towards them, snorting orange flame.

Casually, Pelli raised a hand, palm outwards, and sent an energy pulse its way. The purple beam struck the beast and converted it into a cloud of minute fragments. They were instantly scattered by the persistent wind.

She felt a little ashamed of herself for slaying the creature. It was an act of pique, and in any event it couldn't have harmed them as they were wrapped in a protective shield of enchantment.

'What do you think happened here, Weevan-Jirst?' she asked, as much to cool the mood between them as anything else.

'Who can say? I assume a conflict of some kind, given that all life forms seem intent on destruction.'

'That's a pessimistic view.'

'It is one I have formed through experience and observation. Wherever there is life, it courts death.'

'What about the Corps? We use force only when we have to, and for the good.'

'As you just did?' He nodded towards the spot the disintegrated fire-breather had occupied a moment before.

She had no answer to that, but granted, 'Perhaps we do all have a primitive brute lurking below the surface, no matter how civilised our veneer. But surely that's an argument for the Corps and anybody else that tries to bring some order and justice to bear?'

'How does that square with your sympathy for the orcs? They can hardly be called a constructive force.'

'It's in their nature to be combative.'

'The same could be said of the creature you just killed.'

'I've no more affection for the orcs than any other sentient race, and no more hostility either. As I said, my interest is in justice, and my gut feeling is that they're somebody's pawns in all this.'

'How can you cast a species that lives for war on the same level as those that strive for tolerance?'

'I thought you said all life forms were capable of death-dealing? Aren't you contradicting yourself?'

'Some try to control their impulses more than others.'

'I've never met a race yet, no matter how savage, that wasn't ultimately capable of some degree of compassion. Why should orcs be an exception?'

'Their actions speak for them.'

'With respect, the goblin folk don't exactly have an untarnished reputation themselves. No doubt you'd argue that it's unjustified, and your membership of the Corps is testament to that. But that's my point. Everything isn't black and white, as you seem to believe. Life's messy. We do our best.'

Weevan-Jirst didn't answer. He just maintained the inscrutable expression common to his kind.

She looked around, saw the broken towers, the mountains of wreckage and the desolation of a wasted world. 'You know what I think? Suppose what happened here came about through an inter-world conflict, because somebody who shouldn't have got hold of a set of instrumentalities. I'm not saying it did, but it's possible, isn't it? In any case it can stand as an example of the kind of thing that can happen if we fail. I think that makes it a fitting reminder of our purpose. So let's do our job, shall we?'

'I've never wanted anything else.'

'Then it's time to continue the hunt.'

22

The nearer the Wolverines were carried up to the structure on the hilltop the larger they realised it was.

It had the look of having been refashioned and expanded over generations, each leaving their own mark by adding whatever architectural mode happened to be favoured at the time. The result was a curious hybrid of styles. Much of it was white stone. But there were sections coloured red or black, and extensions made of timber. It had a central needle-shaped spire, and onion domes embellished with gold decorations. There were a number of towers of various heights and different contours. An assortment of windows studded the many walls, some with tinted glass, jostling for space with balconies. Flying buttresses helped hold the whole affair together.

As the crowd climbed, so did their excitement. The chanting reached a new pitch, the drums beat louder, the horns grew more shrill.

When the band finally reached the massive plateau that stretched out in front of the building they found a scrum of beings.

'What do we do now that we're up here, Stryke?' Coilla asked.

'Go in, I guess.' He looked over his shoulder at the mass pressing in from behind. 'We've no choice.'

'Yeah, but take a look at the entrance. They're only letting in small numbers at a time.'

She was right. At the great curved doorway stood a group of brown-robed figures. Their cowls were up and their features obscured, so it was impossible to see what kind of beings they were, beyond basically humanoid. They were strictly marshalling the flow. One of them, in distinctive blue robes, seemed to be a superior of some kind, issuing orders. From time to time he disappeared inside, presumably to gauge the situation.

'Not much chance of us all staying together while they're doing that,' Jup said.

'Why don't we rush 'em and blag our way in?' Haskeer suggested with typical forthrightness.

'I think we need something a bit more subtle,' Stryke decided.

'I can help,' Dynahla said.

'How?'

He explained.

Stryke nodded. 'It's worth a try.'

'We need to get closer then.'

The Wolverines barged their way to near the front of the queue. That strained the otherwise good-natured spirit of the crowd somewhat, but nobody made too much of a fuss. Once in place, close to the entrance, they waited until the supervisor entered the building.

'Now, quickly!' Dynahla said.

The band gathered round and hid him from view. Seconds later they parted, revealing a duplicate of the blue-robed official. Then they elbowed their way to the door with him.

Their worry was that, not knowing the language the custodians of the entrance were using, the ruse would be exposed. In that event Stryke was considering doing what Haskeer suggested and forcing their way in, and damn the consequences. He'd gamble on the crowd being pacifistic enough not to put up too much opposition.

When the band got to the entrance, several of the brown-robed beings looked askance at their elder appearing from the crowd when he had apparently just entered the building behind them. Dynahla countered that, and the communication problem, by employing some robust sign language whose meaning was universal. After a bout of arm-waving, pointing and fist-making the cowed doorkeepers stepped aside to let the Wolverines in.

Once inside, the band surrounded the shape-shifter again and he emerged in his normal guise.

'That's a really handy skill,' Jup said admiringly.

'Thanks,' Dynahla replied, stretching after the transformation. 'It seemed almost too easy.'

'And it could have been,' Stryke warned. 'So stay alert.'

They took in their surroundings. There were plenty of beings

741

present, but given that entry was strictly controlled it wasn't jam-packed.

The interior was opulent. Everything was white, pink and black marble, highly polished. The walls were lavishly decorated with frescos, tapestries and velvet hangings. Way above, the ceiling was likewise ornate, and tall columns soared on every side. Light streamed in through elaborate stained-glass windows.

They saw that there was a similarly large door at the far end of the great hall they were standing in, with lines of pilgrims filing out.

'That explains something,' Coilla said. 'I was wondering why we didn't see anybody coming *down* the mountain. That must exit to a road on the other side.'

'Looks like we're supposed to go this way,' Jup told them.

Silken ropes threaded between stanchions channelled the faithful into a corridor that proved as splendid as the hall they had just left. It was lined with friezes depicting what they assumed were fables of some kind. In truth they didn't take much notice. Their attention was on the chamber the corridor led to, at the heart of the building.

Again, it was marble, although compared to the entrance hall it was austere. Yet somehow that made it more impressive. There were no windows; the light came from a profusion of candles, and from several massive chandeliers. Nor was there any furniture or ornamentation of any kind. The air was heavy with incense, issuing from a pair of heavy brass burners suspended by silver chains.

In the centre of the room was a large sarcophagus, also of marble, set on a podium. A dozen or so beings of diverse race were clustered about it, some on their knees. The tomb itself was topped by a life-sized statue. They approached it.

'A human?' Haskeer exclaimed, causing heads to turn. 'All this in aid of a bloody *human*?'

So it seemed. The statue was the likeness of a human in his prime, a male of perhaps thirty summers. He was tall, and lean rather than muscular. Dressed simply in trews, high buckled boots and a shirt slashed open to the waist, he cut a dashing figure. He wore a form of headgear, something between a helm and a cap, and he held a sword in his raised right hand.

'There's an inscription,' Coilla said, bending to it.

They crowded round.

'"The Liberator",' she read out. 'And there's a name ...
"Tomhunter."'

'Tomhunter-tomhunter-tomhunter,' Spurral recited. '*That's*
what the crowd was chanting.'

'They've got some really stupid names, those humans,' Prooq
sniggered.

Hystykk grinned. 'You said it.'

Gleadeg, Nep and Chuss agreed. They elbowed each other's ribs
and snorted in derision.

Pepperdyne and Standeven had a slightly different view. The
former was mildly amused, the latter looked indignant.

'What the fuck did this Tomhunter do to deserve all this?'
Haskeer thundered.

'Let's find out,' Stryke said. He spotted a young elf standing
alone nearby, gazing respectfully at the statue, and collared him.
'So what's the story behind this Tomhunter then?'

The elf looked bewildered, and not a little shocked. 'What?'

'This place.' Stryke indicated their surroundings with a sweep of
his arm. 'What's it about?'

'You don't know?'

'No.'

'*Really?*'

'No. We're ... er ... new converts.'

'You don't know about the Selarompian wars or the revolution
in Gimff?'

'No.'

'The Rectarus Settlement or the battle of the Last Pass?'

'Not really.'

'Or the—'

'Just imagine we don't know anything, all right?'

'So why are you here?'

'To learn.' He jabbed a thumb at the statue. 'Tell us about this
Tomhunter.'

'The Liberator? The all-conquering redeemer? The most revered being in the history of civilisation?'

'Yeah, him.'

'If you truly don't know the fabled story of Tomhunter, blessed
be his name, then I envy you. To hear the tale of his exploits for

the first time is an experience that will transform your lives and stay with you for ever.'

'So tell us,' Stryke said through gritted teeth.

'There was a solitary incident that, once you know it, will illuminate the character of this martyr, this saint, this paragon of all that is noble and benevolent.'

'*Which was . . . ?*'

'The single most magnificent, heroic, selfless act he performed, the one feat that enshrined his memory in the hearts of everybody for all time was—'

An arrow zipped between them, narrowly missing both their heads. It struck the tomb, bounced off and clattered on the marble floor.

'*Attack!*' Haskeer bellowed.

A bunch of Jennesta's thugs had entered the chamber, five or six of them, and two were aiming their bows.

'*Take cover!*' Stryke yelled, shoving the terrified elf to the ground.

The band scampered to the other side of the tomb, using it as a shield. Several more arrows clanged against it. The band began returning fire.

There was panic among the pilgrims. Those who weren't hugging the floor were running for the exit. Shouts and screams rang out, appeals to the Liberator filled the air. The mayhem could be heard spreading with the fleeing believers, to the corridor outside and into the grand entrance hall.

When Jennesta's group had spent their arrows, Stryke led a charge against them. The enemy turned and fled, the Wolverines on their heels. They dashed along the passageway and into the entrance hall, then headed across it, bowling over any adherents too slow to get out of the way.

Coilla pointed. 'They're making for the exit!'

'*Move it!*' Stryke urged the band.

They put on a spurt, Standeven plodding along at the rear, panting heavily. Their quarry, knocking aside all in their path, got to the back door and scooted out. At the forefront of the band, Stryke, Coilla and Pepperdyne were the next through. A brace of arrows came near to parting their hair and they ducked back in.

'Did you see her out there?' Pepperdyne asked. 'Jennesta?'

Stryke nodded. 'I thought I saw Thirzarr, too. Ready to try again?'

They were.

Moving fast and low, they tumbled out, weapons drawn. There was a paved area there, similar to the one at the front of the mausoleum, and scores of pilgrims were stretched out on it, hands and paws covering their heads, prostrate with dread. To the right, near the downward path and no more than a dagger's lob away, stood Jennesta and her clique, Stryke's mate amongst them.

But even as the band dashed to them, they were gone.

'*Shit!*' Stryke raged.

As Dynahla made ready to transport the Wolverines yet again, Coilla muttered, 'It was never like this in Ceragan.'

Things had never been quite like this in Ceragan.

As mere hatchlings, Janch and Corb hadn't been told what was going on. But they knew something wasn't right.

They couldn't help but be aware that certain of the adults were no longer to be seen in the settlement, but nobody would tell them where they had gone. Corb, the eldest, suspected that no one knew; and his sibling had picked up the general mood of unease even if he couldn't articulate it. As their own parents had departed to they-knew-not-where, their father willingly, their mother taken, they found this new development particularly unsettling.

Quoll, the clan's chieftain, seemed to find it hard to deal with too. Not that he would have let on, especially to a pair as young as Corb and Janch. What he couldn't hide was that he, along with the elders and soothsayers who advised him, seemed at a loss, despite their many congresses and evocations of the gods.

Now Quoll was trying another tack. In an admission that the mystery had become a threat, he dispensed with counsel and summoned the tribe's remaining able warriors. In effect that meant all barring the very old and the lame, and youngsters yet to wield a sword in anger. Corb and Janch, consigned to the care of this group, had slipped away and were loitering near the longhouse where the parley was due to take place.

They seated themselves on a stack of firewood and watched as everyone went in. Barrels of ale and flagons of wine were brought to oil the proceedings, and several whole game, steaming from the spit, to keep bellies from rumbling. Never lacking a sense of the theatrical, Quoll arrived last, accompanied by his closest attendants. He appeared drawn and uncharacteristically deflated.

He noticed the hatchlings and slowed, and for a moment they thought they were going to get a dressing-down. But he just looked, an expression on his face they weren't worldly-wise enough to read. Then he carried on and entered the hut.

The brothers stayed where they were, despite evening drawing in and the air cooling. Perhaps they hoped the adults would come out and miraculously have some kind of answer about what had happened to their sire and their mother.

They could hear the murmur of voices from the longhouse, and occasionally they were raised. With the distorted time sense peculiar to the very young, it seemed to them that they sat there for a very long time. Janch began to grow fractious. Corb was getting bored and thinking of their beds.

There was a commotion inside. It was different to the usual sounds of dispute they were used to when orcs got together to discuss anything. This was an uproar directed at a common object, rather than a disagreement among themselves. The furore was attended by thumps and crashes, as though furniture was being flung about. It reached a pitch and stopped dead. The silence that followed was more disturbing.

It didn't occur to them to run and hide. Even in ones so young that wasn't the orcs' way. Nevertheless, Corb hesitated for long moments. Finally he stood, and Janch did too. Puffing out his chest, he walked towards the hut, his perplexed brother beside him.

There was another brief wavering at the longhouse's only door. Corb took out the scaled-down axe Haskeer had given him, and Janch produced his own, which stiffened their resolve. Corb went on tip-toe to reach the handle, turned it and gave the door a shove. It swung open and they peered inside.

The interior was empty. A long, solid table was askew. Chairs were overturned. Scraps of food and tankards littered the floor. The windows were still shuttered.

An odour hung in the air, which if they could have named it they would have called sulphurous.

These were strange days in Acurial.

Nobody really knew what was responsible, despite a glut of theories, and the not knowing was breeding mistrust and something close to fear. It was a toxic combination for the new, still fragile order.

Brelan and Chillder, twin rulers, were coming away from the latest occurrence. They'd tried to keep it a secret, like all the others, but rumour and hearsay were more fleet than any clampdown they could hope to impose. The incidents had increased to the point where concealment was not only near impossible but probably counterproductive, given the twins' espousal of openness. But whether the truth was preferable to speculation was a moot point.

This time it had happened near the outskirts of Taress, the capital city. Twenty-three orcs of all ranks had gone, from a mess hall in an army camp originally built by the Peczan occupiers. It had followed the now familiar pattern. No warning. No hint as to how the victims could be spirited away from a confined space in a supposedly secure area. No obvious similarities as to who had been taken, except that they were militia. No real signs of violence, beyond a small amount of disorder. No one left to tell the tale.

To give themselves space to think, away from eavesdroppers and questioning gazes, the twins had taken a walk along the semi-rural roads.

'We'll have to announce a state of emergency,' Brelan said. 'Impose martial law.'

'You know I've got doubts about that,' his sister argued. 'It'd only cause alarm, and maybe start a panic.'

'The citizens have a right to protect themselves.'

'How? We can't do that now. The *military* can't protect themselves. What chance would the ordinary orc on the street have? I say we inform them rather than do anything draconian.'

'And you think *that* wouldn't cause a panic? Let them know what's going on, yes, but back it with troops on the streets, a curfew, checkpoints and—'

'That smacks of the occupation days.'

'It's for their own good.'

'Which sounds like the kind of language Peczan used to justify their oppression.'

'We're not Peczan.'

'Of course we're not. But it's a matter of how we're *seen*. Don't forget that our race has finally regained its combative spirit. Give the wrong impression and we could risk another uprising, against us this time. You're overlooking the political dimension to this.'

'Gods, Chillder, is that what we've come to? Thinking like damn politicians?'

'Like it or not, it's what we are. All we can hope to do is be a different kind. The sort that puts the citizens before self-interest.'

'I wonder if that's how all politicians start out. You know, with good intentions that get corrupted by power and expediency.'

'Our mother didn't go that way. And we're not going to.'

'I can't wait for us to set up the citizens' committees. Give the ordinary folk a say, spread the load and the decision-making.'

'Yes, well, that's going to have problems of its own no doubt, though I'm with you on it. But there's no benefit in going over that now. We've a more pressing concern.'

'Which we're no nearer solving.'

'Look, it's the militia that's taking the brunt of . . . whatever it is that's happening. I'm right in saying that, aren't I? There have been no civilian disappearances?'

'As far as we know. It's difficult to be sure, mind.'

'Let's assume that's the case and beef up security for the military even more.'

'How?'

'Some kind of buddy system maybe, with one unit keeping an eye on another unit.'

'And who keeps an eye on *them*?'

'Or we get all military personnel to check in at really short, regular intervals. Or have them all eat and sleep in the open, in plain sight. Or . . . whatever. My point is that it shouldn't be beyond our wit to come up with safeguards.'

'Measures like that would cripple the army. How effective a fighting force would they be, if we needed them, under those sort of restraints? Not to mention we'd be a laughing stock, and that's hardly going to reassure the populace.'

'What, then?'

'A state of emergency is all I can think of. Even though you're right: it's not the ideal solution.'

'It's not a solution at all, Brelan.' She let her frustration show and added irately, 'If only we knew *what* was doing this!'

'You mean who. It still seems to me that Peczan's behind it, somehow.'

'We've been through that. How could they be? And I don't buy the idea that they have agents among our own kind.'

He sighed. 'Neither do I. Look, I need to think. Would you mind making your own way back? I'd like to linger here for just a while.'

'If you say so. You'll be all right?'

''Course I will. I'll see you later.'

They had walked quite a way as they talked, and were now on what was essentially a country road. There were hardly any houses to be seen, and the nearest was almost out of sight. Open fields stretched from both sides of the road. There wasn't much else except a sluggish stream and the occasional stand of trees. Brelan took himself to the edge of one of the fields and stood looking out across it. Chillder gave him a last glance and set off towards where they'd come from, lost in her own thoughts.

She didn't know what it was that made her stop, just a short way along the road. It wasn't a sound, it was a feeling. She turned.

Brelan was nowhere to be seen. Chillder stayed where she was for a moment, expecting to see him reappear. He didn't, and she began walking back. Then she broke into a run.

When she arrived at the spot where she had left her brother, there was no sign. She scanned the fields on either side of the road, but saw nothing. There was no shelter of any kind, certainly nothing near enough for him to have reached in so short a time. It occurred to her that he might have set off across the field for some reason and fallen into the long grass. But she knew how unlikely that was. She called his name, and got no reply. Again she yelled, louder, with her hands on either side of her mouth, and kept on calling.

A chill was creeping up her spine. And she noticed something in the air, an odour both familiar and forbidding.

The feeling she had experienced as she was walking away returned. She couldn't put in words what it was, but it was no less tangible for that. An awful oppression fell upon her, and her head was starting to swim. She felt faint and slightly nauseous. Her surroundings seemed to blur and she was unsteady on her feet. She tried to fight it.

It was no use.

Darkness took her.

23

The Wolverines landed with a splash.

They were in water, a great deal of it, and it was salty in their mouths.

'We're in a damn ocean!' Jup yelled.

'There's the shore!' Pepperdyne pointed to a sandy beach a short distance away.

Stryke looked around at the bobbing heads of the band and did a quick count. 'Where's Standeven?'

'Shit!' Pepperdyne exclaimed. 'He can't swim.'

'The gods are being kind to us at last,' Haskeer said.

'I can't let him drown.'

'Why not?'

Pepperdyne took a gulp of air and disappeared beneath the waves. The rest of them trod water.

He seemed an awfully long time reappearing and Coilla was getting worried. She was about to dive herself when two heads broke the surface a little way off. Pepperdyne had hold of Standeven, who was blue in the face and gasping for breath. Jode hauled him to the band, where others lent a hand, most reluctantly. They all made for the shore.

'*There's something in the water!*' somebody shouted.

Behind them, but moving in their direction fast, was the blur of a large and scaly creature, its spiked head and a sail-like fin dimly visible through the mist. The band increased their speed, and soon their feet touched bottom.

They staggered onto the beach and moved as far up it as they could, dragging Standeven with them until they dumped him. But the creature didn't come ashore, perhaps couldn't, and stayed out in deeper water, cruising back and forth.

'I thought you said the stars couldn't land us somewhere that might kill us, Dynahla,' Stryke complained angrily.

'No, I didn't. I said they couldn't take us somewhere that *would* kill us. If they eliminated all possibility of danger they wouldn't take us anywhere.'

Stryke snorted. 'Yeah, well . . .' He looked about the place. They had jogged almost to a white cliff-face that backed the beach. Apart from a few patches of dull vegetation, there wasn't much else to see. 'Where do you think we are?'

'Could we be back on the world of islands?' Spurral wondered.

'No,' Coilla told her. 'That had two moons. This has two suns.'

She was right, but they had to look hard to see the pair of dim globes through the milky white cloud that dominated the sky.

'So where's Jennesta this time?' Wheam asked, tipping water from the innards of his precious lute. They were all surprised it had survived intact this long.

'She's close,' Dynahla replied, 'as always.'

'Any clue where?' Stryke said.

'Not exactly, no. But does it matter?'

'Does it matter? *Of course* it matters!'

'No, you don't get my meaning. We don't need to know precisely where she is because she'll soon pop up where we can see her. She's playing with us.'

'I think we worked that out,' Haskeer remarked sourly.

'Yeah, it's all a game to her,' Spurral added.

'Maybe,' the shape-shifter conceded. 'Though her motives could be more than just mischievous.'

Stryke eyed him quizzically. 'Such as?'

'Who knows? Perhaps this *is* all for the hell of it. Even I find her hard to fathom.'

'Even you? What makes you such an expert on Jennesta?'

Dynahla hesitated for just a second before answering. 'I've spent a lot of time with her father, remember, and Serapheim's . . . very informative.'

'Heads up!' Jup yelled. 'There she is, right on cue.' He indicated the headland at the end of the beach, a decent arrow shot away.

A group of figures were there. They stayed long enough to be seen, then vanished.

'Do we have to follow her, Stryke?' Dallog said. 'I mean, if this is some kind of crazy game, do we have to play along with it?'

'What choice do we have? And what about Thirzarr? You want me to abandon her?' He glared at him.

'No . . .' The elderly corporal looked abashed. 'No, of course not, chief.'

'Do what you have to, shape-changer,' Stryke ordered.

Dynahla worked on the instrumentalities.

'If I could just get my hands on that bitch . . .' Haskeer muttered, staring at the spot where Jennesta had been a moment before.

'You'd have to stand in line,' Coilla said.

They materialised in night-time, which would have been a lot blacker if it wasn't for a big, full moon and a sky crammed with stars.

There was nothing special about the landscape as far as they could make out. Underfoot was rough grass, there were some ghostly trees in the middle distance and what could have been a mountain range at the limit of their vision. The temperature was balmy and the air dry, with no wind to speak of. Which was fortunate as they were all wringing wet.

Standeven, still huffing and wheezing after his dip, had plonked down on the ground. They let him be.

'So where is she?' Haskeer said, anticipating Jennesta's appearance with his sword drawn.

'Hard to see anything,' Coilla replied.

Breggin pointed into the gloom. 'What's that?'

They all strained to see. A cluster of shapes, darker than the night, appeared to be coming their way.

'Right,' Haskeer declared. 'This time we don't wait for her to call the shots.' He began to run in that direction.

'Wait!' Stryke called after him. 'There's no point! She'll only . . . Oh, what the hell.'

The others seemed to share Stryke's opinion, or else they were tired enough by now not to give a damn. None of them followed Haskeer.

As they watched him dashing nearer to his goal they expected the group of shapes to flick out of existence. Given the distance and bad light, it was near impossible to make out what did happen, but it wasn't that. The figures remained, and he seemed to engage with them.

'Do you think she's actually staying for a fight this time?' Coilla said.

Jup raised his staff. 'If she is, let's get over there!'

The band was all for it, and they were about to rush into the fray.

'*Hold it!*' Stryke barked. 'Looks like Haskeer's coming back.'

He was, at speed, and the figures were right behind him. As they got nearer, the band noticed something odd.

Spurral blinked at the scene. 'Are they running on all fours?'

'And they look bigger than humans,' Pepperdyne added.

'Ah,' Jup said.

Haskeer arrived, arms pumping, breathing hard. Half a dozen fully grown brown bears were chasing him.

It was one of those times when the band instinctively fell back on their training and experience, and they'd dealt with plenty of wild animals in their time. They immediately formed a defensive ring. Blades and spears thrust out, they began shouting and beating their shields. The bears' charge slowed right down, and they took to circling the band from a distance, looking for a weakness in their defence.

'Toche! Vobe! Your bows!' Stryke instructed.

They nocked arrows and he pointed to the biggest of the brutes, which was rearing up on its hind legs. Both arrows struck true. The shafts jutting from its chest, the bear fell, rolled on its side and was still. Its companions let out howls and quickly withdrew. But not completely. They resumed their circling from afar, dimly visible in the dark, still hoping for a chance to attack.

'Must be hungry,' Noskaa observed.

'Lucky they didn't bite a chunk out of Haskeer's fat arse,' Jup said. That raised a laugh. 'They would have spat it out, mind.' The grunts roared.

Most of them stopped when they saw Haskeer's face.

Stryke wasn't overjoyed himself. 'Eyes front! They're still out there.'

'*Something*'s out there, Captain,' Gant said, nodding at the gloom.

He was right, and it wasn't the bears, which by some means, quite probably magical, had been scared off. What was in the dark now came as no surprise to any of them. They knew the sound of her mocking laughter well enough.

Dynahla got to work on the instrumentalities.

Rain pounded down on them. A bitter wind was blowing. Thunder rumbled and lightning flashed.

'Oh, great,' Coilla grumbled. 'Another soaking.'

It was difficult to see what kind of place they were in through the downpour. Wherever it was, it was awash, with flowing water ankle deep. The ground seemed to be bedrock, in all probability any topsoil and vegetation having been washed away.

A chunk of tree and a couple of dead fish floated past.

Stryke wondered if it always rained here. As if in reply, the furious black sky opened up and dumped even more rain on them.

He got the band to search the immediate area for shelter, but there was nothing, so they huddled together miserably for a while, uncertain what to do next and getting wetter.

Then they became aware of a purplish glow in the deluge. It grew stronger, until they saw that it was Jennesta, dry inside a bubble of ethereal energy. A protection she hadn't extended to her soaked retinue, including the comatose Thirzarr. It was an act of casual meanness that enraged Stryke almost more than anything else the sorceress had done. Even though he knew it was futile, he snatched a bow from one of the grunts and sent an arrow Jennesta's way. The force field vaporised it.

As he thrust the bow back into the grunt's hand, she and her followers vanished.

The Wolverines followed.

They were somewhere high. Dizzyingly high.

It was the top of a building that seemed to be impossibly tall, and the view it afforded was startling. As far as they could see in all directions the landscape was completely urbanised. There were other towers just as tall, and a number even taller than the one they stood on. Looking down, they saw nothing but buildings, jam-packed together, of every conceivable shape and design, and many with an appearance they couldn't have imagined.

Highways sliced through the gigantic metropolis, and wove over and under each other, like strands of ribbon dropped at random by a wayward giant. The roads were host to numerous vehicles of a kind they couldn't identify, and they seemed to move without the aid of horses or oxen. The whole place was in motion and resembled nothing less than a gigantic ants' nest. Even from their great height the band could hear the distant, discordant sounds of it all.

More astonishing were the things that inhabited the sky. They weren't dragons, griffins, hippogryphs or any of the other airborne creatures a sensible being might expect. Some didn't even have wings, and they reflected glints of sunlight as they flew, as though, unfeasibly, they were made of metal or glass.

'This must be the billet of mighty wizards,' Wheam reckoned, awestruck.

'If it is they've built themselves a hellish place,' Stryke said, expressing the sentiment of them all. 'Who'd want to live so cut off from natural things? Where are the trees, the rivers, the blades of grass?'

'And where's Jennesta?' Coilla pitched in.

'I think she'd feel right at home in a hive like this. It's vileness would appeal to her.'

'But not enough, apparently,' Dynahla announced. 'She's left.'

'I won't be sorry to follow her this time.'

The place they turned up in would normally have struck them as either lacklustre or potentially hostile. Compared to where they had just been it felt welcoming.

It was a desert. Sand from horizon to horizon, broken only by occasional dunes. It was hot, but not unbearable, and there was even a gentle breath of wind. There didn't appear to be anything immediate that might threaten them.

'Everybody all right?' Stryke asked.

'I feel sick,' Wheam said.

'You would,' Haskeer came back.

Standeven didn't look too bright either, but he knew better than to complain.

Although they didn't know how fleeting their stay would be, the

756

band took the chance to rest, and most sat or lay down on the fine sand. Stryke was content to let them.

Coilla found herself beside Dynahla, both of them a little apart from the others. It was an opportunity to ask him something she had been pondering.

'Tell me, does carrying the stars have any kind of effect on you?'

'What do you mean?'

'Well, they certainly did something to Stryke's mind once, and to Haskeer when he was close to them for a while.'

'Objects as powerful as these can have an influence on those exposed to them, particularly for long periods. They're not playthings, you know.'

'What kind of . . . influence?'

'Good or bad, depending on the nature and preparedness of the individual. I'm guessing that with Stryke and Haskeer it wasn't good.'

'Maybe strange would be a better word.'

'Each set of instrumentalities has its own signature. And because every set is unique, its effect will differ. But whoever possesses them will feel it strongly nevertheless.'

'But not you?'

'I'm trained to resist their negative power *and* to utilise the positive. And remember that Serapheim created this set.' He patted the pocket containing them. 'What better teacher can there be than their maker?'

'So they'd affect Jennesta too?'

'Oh yes. That's one of the reasons why her having a set is so dangerous. She would certainly prosper from their negative emanations. Although she has an ersatz set, of course, copied from these. I don't know if that would make a difference. It's almost unprecedented.'

'Thanks for telling me that. Though I can't say I understood it all.'

Dynahla smiled. 'The greatest adepts have never got to the bottom of all the instrumentalities' secrets, even Serapheim, and I certainly haven't.' He paused, and briefly closed his eyes. 'She's on the move again.'

'It amazes me that you can tell.'

'As I said, I've been trained.' He turned and called out, 'Stryke! Time to go!'

Stryke came over. 'Already?'

'Yes. I think things are going to take a slightly different turn now.'

'How would you know that?' he replied suspiciously.

'I'll explain later. Meanwhile—'

'Trust you. Yeah.'

He shouted an order and the band gathered round.

The crossing was the longest and most disquieting they had yet experienced.

They opened their eyes to a place like no other.

They were on an enormous, totally flat plain, devoid of any features. Above them, the sky was unvaryingly scarlet, with no clue as to where the light that bathed the scene came from. The ground they stood on was a uniform grey and of some unnatural substance. It was spongy underfoot. The only landmark was a distant, pure-white, box-shaped structure. It was hard to judge the scale of things, but the building looked vast. A tangy, sulphurous odour perfumed the air.

There was no one else in sight, least of all Jennesta and her minions.

'Where the *hell* are we?' Coilla whispered.

'What do you know about this, Dynahla?' Stryke demanded.

'Only that there was a good chance we'd end up here.'

'You *knew*? And you didn't think to tell us?'

'Only a chance, I said. It was by no means certain and—'

Stryke grabbed the shape-changer by the throat and thrust his face close. 'You'd better start telling us what you know about this place.'

'I can tell you that not everything here is real, but all of it can harm. And that nothing you've faced up to now compares with what you're about to be confronted with.'

24

'What the hell are you talking about?' Stryke demanded. 'Where are we?'

'It'd be easier to explain,' Dynahla rasped, 'if you let me draw a breath.'

Stryke had the shape-changer's collar bunched so tight it was crushing his windpipe. He grunted and let go.

'Thank you,' Dynahla said evenly, massaging his throat.

'So what *is* this place?'

'It has lots of names. The Barred Sector, the Proscribed Zone, the Perpetual Discontinuity . . .'

'Bugger what it's called,' Haskeer interjected. 'What's it *for*?'

'A long time ago, a *very* long time ago, it was . . . fashioned. A quartet of great adepts worked together to create it.'

'Why?' Stryke pressed.

'Its purpose isn't completely understood. But the story goes that the four fell out, and they built this environment as a place in which to settle their differences.'

'Like some kind of arena?' Pepperdyne said.

'Sort of, though it's more complex than that. We don't know the outcome of the battle the sorcerers fought here. They've long gone, but this zone remains, and it's potentially very dangerous. That's why it's off limits to those few capable of entering it.'

'Why are *we* here?' Stryke wanted to know.

'Serapheim brought us.'

'What for?'

'Because this is where he is.'

Stryke cast an eye over the strange terrain. 'I don't see him.'

'Well, it's . . . almost where he is.'

'You taking us for fools?' Haskeer growled menacingly. 'He's either here or he ain't.'

'Explain yourself, Dynahla,' Stryke said, 'in a way we'll understand.'

'Serapheim's done something similar to what the four wizards of old achieved here. He's built himself a pocket universe.'

'I said in a way we'd understand,' Stryke warned him.

'He used magic to create a private world, a secret retreat outside of time and space.'

'Why?'

'It keeps him alive. He's old, older than you'd believe, probably, and even he can't hold back the effects of ageing for ever. The world he's made cocoons him from the worst of growing old. It slows down the process.'

'How can that be?' Dallog interrupted, showing especial interest.

'As I said, his world exists apart from space and *time*. He can reduce the rate at which time passes. So although the conditions there can't make him immortal, they can help preserve his life.'

'I still don't get where he is,' Jup confessed. 'How can he be *almost* here?'

'It's more accurate to say we're almost where he is. Though, to be honest, it's a big almost.' Dynahla saw the looks on their faces and tried again. 'Serapheim piggybacked on this place when he built his pocket universe. He fused his magic with the magic here to attach his sphere to this one. Think of it as like putting a new wing on a house, or adding a tower to a fortress. The entrance to his domain is here, in this world. We just have to get to it.'

'How do we do that?'

'By always travelling north.'

Stryke took in their bizarre surroundings again. 'How do we know where north is?'

The shape-changer pointed to a spot just above the horizon. A speck of light hung there, brilliant as a diamond. 'The northern star. Not that north here is the same as north on Maras-Dantia, Ceragan or any other world.'

'My head's starting to hurt,' Coilla said. 'Is anything about this place normal?'

'You can die here.'

'That sounds like the kind of normal we know. What does the killing?'

760

'Almost anything; it's unpredictable. Things happen at random here. That's one of its properties, and why travel is so dangerous.'

'Why do we have to?' Pepperdyne wondered. 'Travel, I mean. Couldn't Serapheim have just taken us straight there, to this pocket universe of his?'

'No. Even with all his great powers he couldn't transport us directly to his world.'

'What's stopping him?'

'If it was easy to enter his world it wouldn't offer him much in the way of protection. We have to make our own way to its entrance.'

'Why should we?' Stryke said.

'Because Serapheim's your only salvation. If you want a chance to have a reckoning with Jennesta, and to help prevent the catastrophe she could bring down on all our heads, you need his aid. In any event we have no choice. The instrumentalities have been nullified. They won't work in this world.'

'We can't leave?'

'No. Even if we could, that wouldn't help you find Thirzarr, who's here somewhere, along with Jennesta.'

'I'll have them back then.' Stryke held out his hand.

Dynahla produced the stars and gave them to him.

Stryke put them into his belt pouch and made sure it was secure. 'Any other pearls of wisdom before we get going?'

'Only that whatever this world throws at us I'll do my best to help counter it. I know Serapheim will too, as much as he can.'

'We fend for ourselves. We don't lean on outsiders.'

'Of course. But try to have some faith in Serapheim.'

'Trust in a human. Yeah, right.'

'There's no question about it,' Pelli Madayar said, gazing at the endless expanse of desert, 'they were here, not long since. And now they've entered a prohibited sector: the Sphere of the Four.'

'*All* of them have gone there?' Weevan-Jirst replied.

'The Wolverines and Jennesta certainly have. There are indications others are migrating there too.'

'Others?'

'I think the sorceress is importing the rest of her army, and the recruits she gathered on the world of islands.'

'I had no idea she possessed the power to do that.'

'Her magic is extraordinarily potent, the more so when coupled with the strength of even a duplicate set of instrumentalities. But I don't think she's the only one bringing lifeforms in. There are signs of another force at work.'

'The situation is descending into chaos,' the goblin hissed. 'Unauthorised beings in a forbidden zone, armed with two sets of artefacts. Think of the havoc they could cause. This has become a crisis of the highest order.'

'It always was,' Pelli said. 'It just got messier.'

'It's more than we bargained for. Have you ever entered a prohibited sector?'

'No more than you have.'

'But like me you must be aware of the peril such a place holds.'

'Of course.'

'And the Sphere has a particularly unpleasant reputation.'

'I know.'

'Surely now is the time to consult Karrell Revers.'

'Later.'

'When? You *must* report this to him.'

'I will. But we're going to the Sphere first.'

25

The grey substance that passed for ground had a slight spring to it, and the crimson sky was unwavering.

The Wolverines found it difficult to judge their progress. There was too much uniformity in their surroundings, and no landmarks except for the white structure they were heading towards and the star hanging above it. The place was bright and uniformly lit, but they couldn't see where the light was coming from. They marched in silence.

Stryke turned to Coilla, walking beside him, and spoke in an undertone. 'Think we're doing right?'

'Do we have a choice?'

He shook his head. 'What about Dynahla?' The shape-changer was forging ahead, and out of earshot.

'Don't know. There always seems to be another twist to him.'

'Looks to me like we're being led a merry dance. You know I'd go to the end of this or any other world for Thirzarr, but . . .'

'But is following Dynahla the right way to go about it?'

'Yeah.'

'Again, what choice is there?'

Stryke sighed. He looked back at the column marching behind. 'I've been neglecting the tyros. I'll check on them.'

Coilla nodded, and he headed down the line.

Dallog and Pirrak were at the end of the column, several paces to the rear of Wheam, Chuss and Keick, and Stryke came to the trio first.

'All well?' he asked.

'We're fine, Captain,' Keick replied.

'Though we never dreamed we'd see anything like this when we signed up,' Chuss added.

'Always bet on the unexpected,' Stryke advised.

'It's incredible,' Wheam said, sweeping an arm at the bizarre expanse they were moving through. 'I can't wait to include it in my epic ballad.'

'Still working on that, eh?'

'When I can. In my head, mostly.' He pointed at the item in question. 'I composed some more today.' He reached for his lute. 'Perhaps you'd like to—'

'No. We're in enough trouble.'

He left Wheam looking bereft.

Stryke found Dallog and Pirrak in whispered conversation, which they broke off when they saw him.

'Corporal.'

'Captain,' Dallog returned.

Pirrak gave an edgy nod and said nothing.

'You're still bunching,' Stryke announced.

'Captain?'

'I wanted the Ceragans mixed in with the band, Dallog, but that hasn't happened.'

'Aren't we all Ceragans? Whether native or adopted?'

Stryke wondered if that was a dig. 'New recruits, then. They won't learn the band's ways from each other.'

'With respect, Captain, you've seen how well we work as a unit. It made sense to keep us tight.'

'What doesn't make sense is disobeying one of my orders.' He cut off the corporal's response with a flick of his hand. 'But I'm not minded to make an issue of it now. We'll sort this later.' He looked to Pirrak. 'You're not saying much, Private.'

Pirrak fumbled for a reply.

'He's . . . shy,' Dallog offered.

'*Shy?*' Stryke said. 'I've heard orcs called a lot of things, but never shy.'

'These new recruits are young. They're far from home. All this is unsettling for them, and it takes them in different ways. That's another reason I've kept us as a unit.'

'The best way to toughen 'em is in the field, with combat.'

'You can't say we haven't had plenty of that. And maybe there's more to come.' He indicated what lay ahead with a nod.

Stryke looked up. The white structure was suddenly and inexplicably nearer, no more than a modest arrow shot away. He couldn't work out whether the peculiar geography of this place had made it seem further off than it really was, or whether magic played a part in drawing it, or them, closer.

Stryke made his way along the column, passed its head and joined Dynahla.

'What is that thing?' he asked, gazing at the white slab.

'An entrance, to this world proper,' the fetch replied.

'You mean this isn't it?'

'This is no more than a vestibule. Our real journey begins in there.'

The building, if building was the right word, was an enormous, pure white block, not unlike a giant brick. It was as wide, deep and tall as any fortress they had ever seen, but bore no other resemblance.

Stryke approached it and laid a palm against its surface. It was as sleek as glass and slightly warm. He had no idea what it was made of.

The rest of the band arrived and began their own investigations.

'It's completely smooth,' Coilla said, running a hand over it. 'No sign of joins or seams or—'

'You won't find any,' Dynahla assured her, 'or a door. It's designed to be impenetrable.'

'If that means it's supposed to keep us out,' Haskeer declared, 'it's bullshit. This'll do the job.' He lifted his axe.

'I wouldn't do that,' the shape-changer cautioned.

Haskeer ignored him, took a swing and struck the wall a hefty blow. The axe rebounded and flew out of his grasp, causing several Wolverines to duck as it soared over their heads. At the same time Haskeer was thrown back, as though hit with a mighty punch. He landed heavily on his rump.

'Meet it with force and it returns that force,' Dynahla explained. 'Increase the force and it repays with interest.'

'Now he tells me,' Haskeer grumbled as he got to his feet. His glare wiped the grins off the watching grunts' faces.

'So how *do* we get in?' Stryke said.

'I'll need the instrumentalities for that.'

'You said they don't work here.'

'They don't in the sense of taking us somewhere else. But they have other uses.'

Stryke shrugged, got out the stars and handed them to him.

Dynahla slotted them together with such speed and dexterity that the others couldn't follow. Then he held the assembly of instrumentalities against the wall for an instant before stepping back.

A pair of parallel grooves appeared, working their way up from ground level, about as wide apart as an orc with his arms stretched out. When they got to above the height of the tallest band member they turned left and right, and kept moving until they met, forming an oblong. It had the shape of a door, but no visible means of being opened. Stryke was about to comment on that when it began to change colour. The white turned to grey, and the grey to black. In seconds it came to look like an entrance, albeit to an interior in total darkness.

Dynahla returned the instrumentalities to Stryke and said, 'Do you want to go first?'

'How we gonna see in there?'

'That won't be a problem.'

'You go first then.'

Dynahla nodded. Without hesitation he strode through the door and disappeared from sight.

Stryke hesitated for a moment, decided to draw his sword, just in case, and followed.

He stepped, not into darkness, but full light. That was something he would normally find remarkable, but he was coming to expect the extraordinary.

Dynahla was waiting for him, in a huge square chamber whose floor, walls and ceiling were dazzling white, like the exterior.

'This is big, but not as big as it looked from the outside,' Stryke said.

'No. This is merely a segment of the interior, but it's the only part that concerns us.'

The rest of the band started coming through, led by Coilla and Pepperdyne. When they were all in, the door returned to white and its outline vanished. Even under the closest scrutiny there was no sign of it ever having been there.

They looked around, not that there was a lot to see. The room was completely empty and unadorned. At its opposite end was another, more conventional looking door. Dynahla made for it, and they all trailed after him.

The door, when they came to it, seemed incongruous. It was made of wood, or something approximating it, and it had a chunky brass handle. Dynahla opened it. Beyond was a tunnel, again white, again brightly lit by an unseen source.

'Now what?' Jup said.

'Not much further,' the shape-changer told him.

He entered the tunnel, Stryke and the rest close behind. As they started to walk, Spurral glanced back. She wasn't surprised to see that the door they had just used was no longer there.

The tunnel ran straight and level for a distance none of them could estimate. In terms of time, they could have sung perhaps ten verses of one of their marching songs before they came to its end.

'Oh look,' Haskeer mouthed sarcastically, '*another* door.'

This one could have been made of iron. It was stout and set with studs, and had a latch with a thick metal ring. Dynahla reached out and turned it. Hands hovered over sword hilts as the door swung open.

A different kind of light greeted them. It was natural, compared to what they had come from, and was accompanied by a mild, fragrant breeze. They filed out.

It was what they thought of as a normal landscape. There was greenery and trees. The sky was a proper colour, and a big yellow, summer sun beat down from it. Yet the northern star was somehow still visible, twinkling above emerald hills. They heard what might have been soft birdsong.

'Don't be complacent,' Dynahla warned them. 'What appears ordinary may not be what it seems.'

'We keep going north?' Stryke asked.

'Yes.'

'How far?'

'Who can say? It could be a short journey or a lengthy march.'

'Can't we speed things up?'

'We could find mounts.'

'In this place?'

'Like I said, there's life here.'

'You've been here before, haven't you?'

'Yes,' the shape-changer confessed. 'Just once, when I first came

767

to Serapheim's private universe. That was a long time ago, and I stayed there until I was sent to you.'

'So you came out this way?'

'No. Serapheim used the power of the instrumentalities to transport me directly to your location.'

'But you've been here once before, so you know what to expect.'

'Only in the broadest sense. Like I said, this place has a random element. I very much doubt it would be the same as it was on my only previous visit.'

Stryke chewed that over as they continued walking.

Eventually they came to a river.

'This is a likely place to find our ride,' Dynahla told them in a low tone, while signalling them to quieten down.

It was softly agreed that Dynahla, Stryke, Coilla and Jup would scout for mounts. They moved stealthily towards the riverbank, leaving the rest of the band sheltering on the edge of a copse.

Luck was with them. They found what they were looking for near the water's edge. Four or five creatures, each as large as three war-horses, with elongated, ribbed bodies of whitish-brown, and a forest of legs. The millipedes' rudimentary faces were dominated by a ravening mouth and a pair of unblinking, black button eyes.

'Dangerous?' Stryke said, peering round the rock they were hiding behind.

'Troublesome, more like,' Dynahla replied. 'But they can be made to carry us.'

'How?'

The shape-changer explained.

Stryke went to fill in the rest of the band and got them down to the riverbank for a look. They took the sight of gigantic multi-legged insects in their stride, even if Wheam went a little pale. Standeven, who didn't know whether to be appalled or disgusted, swore he wouldn't go near the things. A threatening fist shut him up.

When they were set, Stryke said, 'Ready, Dynahla?'

'Yes.'

'Sure you can fake something that big?'

'Just about. It's takes a lot of stamina to maintain it. But once we get them working I can give it up. Now if you could give me some room . . .'

They moved away and watched as he went to the ground and twisted, contorted and expanded. They saw the sprouting of a myriad legs, the emergence of coal-black eyes and rapacious mouth.

Finally he was done. He rose up as a creature identical to the ones scooping water on the riverbank. The question was whether they would accept him as their own. Moving sinuously, numerous limbs working in unison, the bogus millipede scuttled towards them. He brushed Standeven's leg as he passed. The human shuddered, eyes closed.

They need not have worried. After some snuffling, twittering and a winding insectoid dance, Dynahla's counterfeit was accepted. Shortly after, he led them to the band.

The millipedes turned out to be surprisingly docile. They did prove hard to mount, however, and harder to stay on. For Standeven, getting aboard was an ordeal, and he got a lot of unwanted help. The creatures were big enough to take the whole band between them, with six or seven sitting astride each extensive back. The orcs wove vines for reins and to lash themselves in place.

Dynahla's millipede carried no riders. His job was to lead the genuine creatures, a task made possible by assuming a female form. The real ones were all male.

They set off at a fast crawl, the band trying to adapt themselves to the left-to-right, right-to-left meandering gait of their mounts.

The terrain they passed through was basically unvarying. It was all rural, as far as they could see, and they came across no cottages, farms or any other signs of habitation. There was an abundance of animal life, mostly evidenced by rustlings in the undergrowth as they scampered past, or the briefest glimpse of fur or hide as something darted for cover. At one point they saw a herd of beasts, gathered in a field on sloping ground. But they were too far away to make out what they were.

Their journey stretched on, and as time passed they became aware that the day had not matured since they arrived. The sun was in exactly the same place in the sky.

'Dynahla told me that it's always the peak of the day here,' Stryke explained.

'Is it ever night?' Coilla said over his shoulder.

'I asked him about that. He said we wouldn't want to be here when it happened.'

Shortly after, the landscape began to change. It grew sparser, and rocky. A clump of pallid cliffs loomed ahead, with a narrow canyon punched through it.

The Dynahla millipede, in the lead, came to a halt, causing the procession to slow and then stop. He transformed, contracting, writhing and thrashing until he assumed his usual form. The true millipedes seemed unfazed by the loss of their amour.

He was dusting himself off when Stryke slid down and went to him.

'What's up?'

'That.' He pointed towards the cliff.

Stryke had to strain to see what it was. Even so, he could only make out a dark shape against the lighter background of rock. 'What is it?'

'Something you have to take. Assuming you can get away with it alive.'

26

'*What* do we have to take?' Stryke said. 'What's so important?'

'I believe that what lies over there is going to be vital to us. But we need more information. Will you let me take a look?'

'Go ahead.'

The shape-changer transformed himself into a bird. It was difficult to say what kind. A large seagull, perhaps, although it was black. He took off at speed.

'Why does he always seem to know more than he's telling?' Jup wondered.

'That'd crossed my mind,' Haskeer said.

'A short journey, then.'

Dynahla was soon back. Once he changed form he stated, simply, 'It's a weapon.'

'What kind?' Stryke asked.

'A kind you're unlikely to have seen before. You should go and look at it.'

'Why?'

'As I said, it'll be useful for what follows.'

'And what's that?'

'I don't know.'

'Fat lot of use you are,' Haskeer muttered.

'I don't know *specifically*,' Dynahla said, 'but I know there'll be challenges. What I *do* know is you need that device to be able to advance further.'

'*How* do you know that?'

'Serapheim told me.'

'Why didn't you tell us until now?'

'I didn't know I had to until we got here. And all Serapheim told me was that in this place gift horses shouldn't be ignored.

That weapon's here for a reason. Everything is here for a reason. You have to take it.'

'Well . . .'

'At least have a look. Would that hurt?'

'All right. But it better be worth it.'

'I think you'll find it is.'

The band headed for the cliffs.

When they got to the object it proved extraordinary. It was essentially a long dark metal tube or pipe, with the circumference of a hogshead, mounted on wheels. From its arrangement of gears and handles it looked as though the tube's angle could be adjusted. On one side at its blunt end was a large wheel, on the other a lever. The top of the tube had a sight, in the form of a raised ring with an inset cross. There were wide grooves on both sides of the chassis that bore the weapon. They each held around a dozen sizeable black globes, possibly of iron.

'How does it work?' Coilla said.

'I think I know,' Dynahla replied.

Haskeer looked to him. 'Weapons expert now, are you?'

'No. But when I was here before I changed myself into something that could get inside this thing. Well, not that small, but an appendage with an eye attached did the job.'

'And you figured it out?' Stryke asked.

'I think so. Inside that tube there's a very powerful coil, made of some sort of tough, flexible metal. You drop one of these balls down the tube, then turn that wheel at the end. That draws back the coil, taking the ball with it. When it's in place, the lever releases the coil. It comes free with enough energy to launch the ball. And with a lot of force, I imagine.'

'Clever,' Jup declared admiringly.

'They're a size,' Haskeer said, pointing at the weighty metal balls.

'Nearly as big as your head. Though less dense.'

Haskeer contented himself with giving the dwarf a murderous look.

'This thing must weigh a ton,' Stryke said.

'We can couple the millipedes to it,' Dynahla suggested. 'They're strong. And maybe there'll be a bit of hauling where necessary. But believe me, Stryke, we should take it.'

'All right, I believe you. I hope this isn't wasted effort, for your sake.'

Wheam was staring at the weapon. 'How come it's just sitting here? Doesn't it belong to somebody?'

'Quite possibly,' the shape-changer replied. 'In which case you might have to fight for it.'

Wheam looked around. 'Fight who?'

'If we're lucky, nobody. But we should stay alert.'

'That we can do,' Stryke told him.

Using rope the band carried, along with some pleated vines, they fashioned crude harnesses. They found that two millipedes were capable of pulling the load, as well as carrying riders.

When they were finally ready, Stryke said, 'We have to skirt these cliffs. Which means going away from north and then turning back to it once we're round 'em.'

'What about that canyon?' Coilla suggested. 'Isn't that heading north?'

The peculiar daytime star hung directly above it.

'I guess it does. If it's not a dead end.'

Dynahla offered to find out. He changed to his black bird guise and took off. Before long he was back to confirm that the canyon did indeed go clean through the cliffs.

'What's it like on the other side?' Stryke wanted to know.

'More or less like this, though rockier. There are some caves.'

'All right, let's move.'

They set off, unsteadily at first, hauling the weapon.

The canyon was narrow and high-sided. Its floor was stony, with occasional clumps of miserable vegetation. It didn't run straight; there were bends.

As one of these came into sight they saw a shadow cast by something moving their way. Something very large. Stryke halted the convoy. No sooner had they stopped than a creature rounded the bend.

It could have passed for vaguely human, apart from its size. High as a fully grown oak, and looking as hardy, it was male. The creature was naked save for a loincloth of pelts. He was an extremely hirsute specimen, with a bushy head of hair, a full beard and a mane on his chest, all rust-coloured. There was a belt at his waist, and tucked through it a club as big as a young tree. His piggy eyes held a malevolent glint.

When he saw them he gave a furious roar.

'Shit, an ogre,' Jup said. 'That's all we need.'

'I think we can guess who the weapon belonged to,' Spurral added.

'Why didn't you see this when you scouted, Dynahla?' Stryke demanded.

Before the fetch could answer somebody yelled *'Watch out!'*

The ogre had lifted a sizeable rock and was getting ready to throw it at them.

'Back!' Stryke ordered. *'Pull back!'*

'You tried getting these things to back up?' Haskeer shouted, pulling hard on a millipede's reins.

Those hauling the weapon had an even harder time trying to turn in the confined space. But they managed to retreat a short distance, albeit ending up in something of a shambles.

The rock came down with a thunderous crash, short of the band but too close for ease. His simple face twisted with fury, the ogre scrabbled for another one.

'Archers!' Stryke bellowed.

The bows came out and defensive fire was unleashed. Arrows soared towards their bemused target, and many hit. More than anything, the ogre seemed surprised. The shafts may have stung him but they were doing no real harm. Adjusting their aim, the archers tried for more sensitive areas, around the face and neck.

The ogre lobbed his second rock. It was short again but a lot nearer, throwing up a cloud of shale and dust that pelted the band. Immediately, the creature started to advance, hampered a little by the irritation of arrows. Then one penetrated his cheek, drawing an angry bellow. He plucked it out, stared stupidly at it and flung it away. A trickle of blood flowed down the side of his face. He drew the vicious-looking club, and tried batting at the incoming arrows with it.

'This could be the time to put our weapon to the test, Stryke,' Coilla suggested.

'Just what I was thinking.'

'If we can get it working in time,' Jup added, sliding from the millipede's back.

The archers had only a limited supply of arrows but they kept firing. Stryke ordered everybody else to uncouple the weapon, a task complicated by the fact that the ogre's approach was causing the millipedes to become skittish.

To buy them time, Dynahla changed himself into an eagle and flew off to harass the ogre with wickedly sharp talons. Down below, the band struggled to disengage the weapon and turn it.

The ogre took to swiping at Dynahla with his club. Successfully turned, the weapon was being primed. A couple of grunts heaved one of the metal balls into the tube's mouth. Several more privates, along with a bellowing Haskeer, were straining to turn the wheel that drew back the coil.

Dynahla narrowly avoided being struck by the club. He circled, swooped again and was almost caught by it a second time. The shape-changer called it quits and flew down to the band. He landed, and transformed in one fluid motion, as the weapon was being tilted upwards. Nep and Seafe were bouncing up and down on its non-business end to encourage progress.

Finally they were set. The ogre, frantic with rage, was bearing down on them. Stryke had his hand on the firing lever and was peering through the sight.

'What you waiting for?' Haskeer said.

'We only get one chance. I want him nearer.'

The ogre was obliging. He began jogging towards them, the club raised, his footfalls like thunder.

'For the gods' sake, Stryke!' Coilla exclaimed.

Still he hesitated.

The ogre was close enough for them to be in his shadow.

Stryke pulled the lever. The weapon bucked. The ball shot from the cylinder.

It reached its target in a blink, striking the ogre full in the chest with a sickening thump. He expelled a huge breath, face contorted in pain. Then he fell, crashing to the ground and making it shake. He was still.

The band gave it a moment before cautiously approaching.

'Dead as a doorknob,' Jup declared.

'Well, at least we know this thing works,' Coilla said.

'Let's hope he was the only one.'

The killing ball was retrieved. Then Stryke got the band to roll the monstrous corpse to one side of the track so they could get by. Next they had to re-couple the weapon and sort out their mounts. After that they took a short breather and passed round the water bottles. Stryke judged that a small alcohol ration was deserved, too, and let them break out the rough brandy. Wheam had a coughing fit when he took his tot. Standeven drained his in one go and asked for more, but was ignored. A drunk crazy human was an additional burden Stryke could do without.

They set off again, steering past the gargantuan cadaver.

A while later, riding across the scrubby land on the other side of the canyon, Coilla observed, 'This never-ending high noon is putting everybody out, Stryke.'

'It feels strange, yeah.'

'But mostly they need sleep. We all do. We didn't have that much before we came here. And the band needs feeding.'

'I want to push on.'

'They'll be good for nothing if we do.'

He sighed. 'Right. But it won't be for long. Organise the shifts.'

They found a defensible spot by a heap of boulders. The weapon was secured, the mounts fussed over a bit, and sentries posted. Stryke didn't want to waste time hunting for game, if there was any, and got the band to dip into their iron rations. Sleep proved difficult in the unrelenting sunlight, but they were tired enough that most managed at least some.

Far too soon for everybody, Stryke ordered them to break camp, and they resumed their journey rested if not refreshed.

They rode for a long time, heading straight for the northern star. The land became more verdant, and they found themselves moving across a grassy expanse. Fortunately the vegetation wasn't full enough to hamper them. Whether that was because something grazed here, or because the magic of the old sorcerers had willed it so, they didn't know.

Pepperdyne was the first to spot something out of the ordinary. In the distance, running to right and left as far as they could see, was an unbroken, yellowish-brown line. Dynahla once more volunteered to check on it. He chose the form of a dove. The band took the chance to stretch their legs.

'You have to admit he's handy to have around,' Coilla said as she watched Dynahla flap away.

'Still gives me the creeps though,' Haskeer said.

She glanced at the millipedes. 'Do these need feeding or watering? They haven't taken anything since we got them.'

'Suppose so. Don't know what though.'

'They seem content nibbling the grass,' Spurral told them.

'Yeah,' Jup said. 'Dynahla reckons they're not meat-eaters, despite looking the way they do.'

'I think they're kind of cute.'

Jup made a face.

'Ugly bastards,' Haskeer muttered.

'That's the kind of thing that gets said about us,' Coilla reminded him.

'Not to my face it ain't.'

'They can't bear looking at it,' Jup suggested with a smirk.

'How'd you like your own rearranged, pipsqueak?'

'Any time you've got the strength to try, horse breath.'

Stryke was about to slap them down when someone shouted, 'He's coming back!'

The dove fluttered in and became Dynahla.

'Well?' Stryke said.

'It's a wall, and well defended.'

'By what?'

'Werebeasts, as far as I could see.'

'We've tangled with them before. What kind are they?'

'The kind that can switch from basically human to something like a bear.'

'That kind we haven't seen before. Any chance we could parley with them?'

'You could try, but I doubt it. Though I suppose if you had something of value to offer as tribute—'

'We've nothing.'

'I thought not. And it's in the nature of this place that obstacles have to be fought through not talked through. I think you can see now why we've had to haul the weapon with us.'

'There's no way round this wall?'

'No. Well, maybe if we travelled a much longer way we might find that it ends. But I wouldn't count on it.'

'Let's get closer to it.'

'There's at least one gate. I'll show you where.'

When they were near enough to make it out, they saw that the wall looked ancient, but no less solid for that. They could make out figures on its high ramparts and, as Dynahla said, a massive pair of gates, made of timber, with iron straps.

Stryke decided to try talking after all. Thirzarr was on his mind, as always, and some kind of pact would be quicker than having a battle.

'I wouldn't get your hopes too high,' Dynahla cautioned, 'and approach with care. They didn't look particularly welcoming to me.'

Stryke took one of the millipedes, along with Haskeer, Jup, and Calthmon, who was in charge of the beast. They made a white flag, the universal sign of truce, or so they hoped. Haskeer hated white flags. In his detestation of the idea of a token of surrender, or even reasonableness, he was fairly representative of the band as a whole. He refused to hold it, and that fell to Jup.

They made for the wall.

Figures on the battlements watched as they approached. They looked like humans, which gave Haskeer little confidence in the outcome of any talks.

Stopping a short distance away, Stryke cupped his hands and called out in Mutual. *'We come in peace! Can we talk?'*

Several of the werecreatures conferred, but there was no answer.

Stryke called again. *'We're here peaceably! We want to parley!'*

The figures seemed to grow darker and bulkier.

'Looks like they're changing,' Jup said.

'Is that good?' Haskeer asked.

A swarm of arrows came down on them.

'No,' Jup said.

They were lucky not to be hit. But one arrow had struck the millipede, causing it to squirm. Stryke leaned forward and pulled the shaft out.

More arrows came, and several spears. They fell short.

'Get us out of here, Calthmon!' Stryke yelled.

They retreated to the sound of something like cheers from the battlements.

'The weapon?' Jup asked as they headed back.

'Yeah,' Stryke confirmed.

They dragged it to a point where they thought they could hit the wall but far enough away for the werebeasts' arrows to be ineffective. The ritual of loading and priming the weapon was undertaken.

Gleadeg and Prooq were steady, dependable hands. Stryke let them take care of the firing.

'First shot, Captain?' Prooq said. 'The doors?'

'Let's try for the battlements.'

They adjusted the angle.

'Ready?' Gleadeg asked.

Stryke nodded.

The lever went back and the weapon bucked. With a hearty *thomp* the ball shot out and flew almost too fast to be seen.

It struck the battlements. There was a crash of masonry and a cloud of dust. When it cleared there was a hole in the battlements and the werebeasts weren't to be seen.

'Now the doors,' Stryke said.

They were already realigning the tube, and a ball was being lifted. That done, Stryke made sure the rest of the band was mounted and ready.

The weapon went off. The doors exploded in a shower of timber chips and iron fragments.

'Move! Move! Move!' Stryke bellowed.

Most of the band tore towards the doors, with Stryke on the lead mount. The remainder worked frantically to hitch up the weapon and follow them.

For a moment they thought the doors hadn't been completely downed. But as they got nearer they could see daylight through the aperture, and a glimpse of the land beyond. The plan was simple. Clear the battlement. Take down the doors. Get through them, fast. The first two had been achieved, the third was going to be tricky.

They raced to their goal. The pair of millipedes pulling the weapon were at the back. As the wall loomed, Stryke wasn't alone in wondering if the entrance was wide enough to take them.

More werebeasts appeared on the battlements, running in from outposts. They loosed arrows. The Wolverines brought shields up. That, and their speed, got them through the first spate of arrows untouched. The second came just as they reached the gate. Shafts and spears clattered against their upraised shields. Then they were scampering over the ruined doors and through the opening. Another shower of arrows met them on the other side, and proved as ineffective, although two of the mounts took minor wounds.

The rest of the band shot through, braving the deluge from above, which now included rocks and the contents of buckets. Last in was the tubular weapon, its mounts scuttling like fury, a dozen orcs clinging to their backs. The weapon bounced over the debris from the destroyed doors, and at one point looked close to flipping, but it kept steady and escaped.

The Wolverines didn't slacken their speed until they were well away.

27

It took all the skills of Pelli Madayar and her Gateway Corps unit to gain entry to the Sphere of the Four.

Now they stood under a scarlet sky, with a malleable, grey material serving as the ground beneath their feet. The plain spread out all around them, featureless except for the vast white building in the distance. It was a unique experience for the multi-species members of the unit and they were busily examining the terrain.

Weevan-Jirst sniffed the air. 'The energy level seems extraordinarily high.'

'It *stinks* of magic,' Pelli agreed, more pithily. 'I'm not sure that even our weapons could be entirely relied on here.'

'To find out we need to know which direction will take us to our quarry.'

'We have clues. There must be a reason why the only landmark is that structure over there. And I would say the star, or whatever it is that hangs above it, confirms our path. I can see no other signs. Do you agree?'

'Would it matter if I didn't?'

'Of course it would. Unless you think me a tyrant.'

The goblin sidestepped her tacit challenge and merely said, 'I concur with your deduction. We should be guided by the star.'

'Good. Now let's move, and fast. If we've been led to a place like this, events must be coming to a head.'

'Then let us hope we're in time,' Weevan-Jirst replied grimly. 'Because if we're not, the consequences will be dire.' He fixed her with his beady gaze. 'For all of us.'

When they were far enough from the wall that they could no longer see it, and Stryke was satisfied nobody was chasing them, the Wolverines stopped to regroup.

Once the weapon had been checked and secured, the millipedes tended and minor injuries seen to, the band was allowed a brief period to stretch their legs.

Most just squatted or sprawled on the grass. But several drifted a short distance, including Coilla and Pepperdyne, who were deep in conversation. Stryke noticed that Dallog had also wandered off. He was standing farther away than any of the others, with his back to the band, and for once he didn't have Pirrak with him. That individual, Stryke saw, was sitting by himself at the edge of the group. He decided to talk to him.

The new recruit looked uncomfortable when he saw Stryke coming, and stood, awkwardly.

'At ease,' Stryke told him.

'Sir.' He didn't noticeably relax.

'Everything all right with you, Pirrak?'

'Yes, sir. Shouldn't it be, sir?'

'Well, it *should* be, but I get the feeling it isn't.'

'I'm fine.' The response was a little too quick and a little too edgy.

Stryke tried another tack. 'The band's treating you well? They're comradely?'

'Yes, sir.'

'And Dallog?'

There was a pause before he got an answer. 'What do you mean, Captain?'

'He's taking care of you?'

'Yes.'

'Look, Pirrak, maybe I've not been as easy to talk to as I should have been. But you know things have been frantic since we left Acurial.'

The private's expression visibly stiffened. He said, 'Yes, sir,' his voice taut.

Stryke put that down to the youngster's callow nature. 'My mind's been on the mission, and on other things, and maybe I've been forgetting my duties to the band. But I want you to know that if you ever need to talk to me about anything, you can. Or any of the other officers. Though you might not want to make Sergeant Haskeer your first choice.' If Pirrak saw the intended humour in that, he didn't react. 'If Dallog's not around, that is,' Stryke quickly tagged on.

'I understand.' As an apparent afterthought he added, 'Thank you, sir.' There was a more genuine quality in that, and perhaps even a little warmth, than anything else he had said.

'All right. Just bear it in mind. And get a shake on, we'll be moving soon.'

'Sir.'

Stryke turned and left him standing there, looking graceless.

Almost immediately he crossed paths with Coilla and Pepperdyne, on the way back from their tryst.

'See you were having a natter with Pirrak,' Coilla said. 'Pep talk?'

'Kind of. Don't know how much sunk in.'

'Does seem kind of woolly most of the time, doesn't he?'

'He's not the easiest of the new recruits to talk to,' Pepperdyne said, 'but they're all a bit green, aren't they, Stryke?'

'I'd hoped they'd be a little more ripe by now. But I guess that's what comes from letting Dallog keep them apart from the rest.'

'We carrying on now?' Coilla asked.

'Yes,' Stryke replied, 'start rousing 'em.'

Coilla headed off for a bout of shouting, Pepperdyne in tow.

On impulse, Stryke decided to go over to Dallog.

When he came to him he saw that he had his eyes shut, and seemed to be muttering to himself.

'Dallog?'

The corporal came to himself with a start, and for just an instant appeared sheepish. But his crisp 'Captain!' had its usual ebullience.

'What were you doing?'

'Praying.'

'Praying?'

'Asking the Tetrad to look favourably on our mission.'

Stryke knew it was something many in the band did. He did it himself occasionally when things looked rough, and he had turned to the gods more than once since Thirzarr was taken. But it wasn't the sort of thing anyone talked about much. He tended to think of it as a personal matter and none of his business. So he simply said, 'Sorry to disturb you, then.'

'No problem, Captain. What can I do for you?'

'I've been talking to Pirrak.'

Dallog's gaze flicked to the grunt in question, who was gathering up his gear. 'Have you?'

'Yeah. And I'm still wondering if he's fitting in.'

'Oh, *that*. Like I told you, he's a little on the quiet side. Bit of a thinker, if you know what I mean. Not that it makes him any less dependable in combat.'

'Maybe not. But he'll fight better if he mixes with the band more. All the tyros will.'

'You've already made that point, Captain.'

'Just so you know I mean it. There are going to be some changes in future.'

'If there is a future for us.'

'*What?*'

'I mean, I sort of figured this mission was a one-off. I don't know if you have any plans for the band after that, or whether we'd be part of it.'

'I don't know myself. And you could be right: maybe there's no future for any of us. Who knows how this thing will pan out?'

'That's a glum way of looking at it, Captain. I'm sure that under your command—'

'Yeah. We'll see. Meantime, keep an eye on Pirrak.'

'You can count on it.'

'And get 'em ready; we're moving out.'

They rode on for what could have been a quarter of a day, if they had any means of judging it accurately. The constant sun sat high in the sky, as it always did, and their sense of time was shot.

The landscape stayed the same, not quite lush and not quite scrub, until a change loomed. Ahead of them was the edge of a forest. It spread a long, long way to the west and east. Stryke halted the convoy.

'Through or round?' he asked Dynahla.

'Round is going to delay us a lot, and would probably be as perilous.'

'Forests are too good for ambushes. I don't like 'em. Unless I'm doing the ambushing.'

'I could scout it for us. But if there's no obvious trap in there—'

'You might not see it. I know. That's why I don't like forests.'

'Well, shall I?'

Stryke nodded.

The shape-changer took on a bird guise again, a small one this time, presumably to make it easier to negotiate the forest. They watched as it flew towards the tree-line, but lost sight of it before it got there.

There was such a long wait that they were starting to think they'd seen the last of the fetch. Then the bird reappeared, travelling at speed.

Back in his familiar form, Dynahla reported. 'It's big. Took me a while to get all the way over. I didn't see anything that looked threatening, but that might not mean much. It's pretty dense in parts, and dark.'

'We going to be able to get that through?' Stryke stabbed a thumb at the curious weapon.

'I think so. Though I expect there'll be a certain amount of weaving about.'

'I suppose we'll have to do it then.'

'Like I said, everything in this place has a purpose. The forest's there because we're supposed to enter it.'

'That's another way of saying we *will* run into something.'

'Not necessarily. It could be just a forest. But it pays to expect trouble.'

'What the fuck,' Haskeer said. 'We *love* trouble.'

'You're unlikely to be disappointed,' Dynahla told him.

Stryke made sure everybody had at least one weapon close to hand, and got the archers to nock their bows.

They resumed their journey.

The nearer they got to the forest the more it came to dominate, and it became obvious that many of the trees were enormously tall. Entering it was like being swallowed by some gigantic beast composed of timber rather than flesh.

Mulch from untold numbers of rotting leaves carpeted the ground. That made for soft going, but slowed rather than totally hindered them. Generally, the trees were spaced sufficiently far apart to allow them to get through, although there were exceptions. Most obstructions could be steered round, but several times they had to backtrack and look for another way. Even so, they made reasonably good progress.

That came to an end when, by Dynahla's estimate, they were about halfway. The area they were passing through was boggy, but deceptive because a covering of recently fallen leaves disguised the threat. The millipedes bearing only riders partially sank but scrabbled on. Seeing the danger, Stryke bellowed for the mounts pulling the weapon to be stopped. But it was too late. Under the weight of both the weapon and riders, the mounts floundered in the mire. The load they were pulling began to sink, and the band had to cut the millipedes free. By the time that was done, the weapon was stubbornly bogged down.

They tried hauling. But even the combined strength of the band couldn't free the weapon's carriage.

'We need something to lever it out with,' Haskeer said.

'We're in a forest,' Coilla reminded him. 'Take your pick.'

'That one should do it.' Stryke pointed at a nearby tree. 'Get it down.'

Haskeer was first there. He swung his axe and whacked it into the trunk.

There was a distant wailing sound that stopped them all in their tracks. It was doleful. In its terrible despair it was almost beautiful. Others joined it, but they were angered, and soon the eerie chorus was one of fury.

'That sounds familiar,' Jup said.

'Yeah,' Coilla agreed. 'Nyadds.'

'What are they?' Wheam asked. He looked spooked.

'Spirits of the forest. Or that's what some called them back in Maras-Dantia. They're forest fauns, and they're all female. At least, nobody I know ever saw a male. They're usually so bashful you wouldn't know it if you walked right by them.'

'Except when you mess with their trees,' Stryke added.

'Is that so bad a crime?' Pepperdyne said.

'Each nyadd is bound in spirit to a certain tree. If it dies, the nyadd dies. When a tree's hurt, like this one, they all feel the pain.'

'And they get very pissed off,' Coilla explained. 'Jennesta's said to be part nyadd, which should give you some idea.'

'What do we do, Stryke?' Spurral wanted to know.

'They sounded a way off, and we've still got to dig the wagon out. Let's gamble on them taking a while to get here. Haskeer, the tree.'

'Seems almost cruel after what you said about the nyaads,' Spurral mildly protested.

'Got a better idea?'

'Hell, no.'

Haskeer's axe bit into the tree. Several of the grunts joined in, and made short work felling it. Then they set to cutting the wood they needed. Soon they had a couple of stout levers, and a lengthy pair of planks to give the wheels traction.

Even with these aids it was a struggle freeing the weapon. Only once it was out and re-hitched, and the racket they had made had died down, did they realise that the wailing had stopped. The forest was silent.

Not for long. A crowd of figures emerged from the trees all around. They were tall, lean and olive-skinned, and their nakedness was partially hidden by ankle-length auburn hair. Their handsome faces were contorted with fury, revealing unusually white, and unusually sharp, teeth. They were armed; mostly with curved daggers, though some had snub swords.

A keening version of the wail went up and they raced at the band.

The nyadds had their fury. The wolverines had weapons with a longer reach. On Stryke's order these were deployed. Nine or ten nyadds fell with arrows in their chests. It didn't deter the others, and while the archers were reloading, the first of the attackers reached the band.

Stryke put down two with a single wide stroke. Coilla caught another with a throwing knife, and Jup leapt up to crack a skull with his staff. The dagger-wielding nyadds couldn't get close enough to inflict much damage, but they threatened to overrun the band. More and more of them were streaming from the trees.

By a cowering Standeven, Pepperdyne lunged and ran-through an advancing nyadd. Nearby, Haskeer laid about them with his axe. Dallog's unofficial unit were hacking in unison. But for all that it was like spearing fish in a barrel, the tide was relentless, with fresh attackers stumbling over the bodies of their fellows to get to the band.

'We're not going to hold this for ever,' Coilla said as she slashed at a nyadd's probing dagger.

Stryke parried a nyadd's thrust, wrong-footed her and took off her head. Golden blood spattered his tunic. 'Then we'll go for their heart. *Archers! Burnables! The trees!*'

They understood, and drew their flammable arrows. Flint sparks ignited the tar-soaked cloth and flame blossomed. The burning arrows streaked out and hit a dozen trees. Most took fire immediately.

An even greater wail went up from the nyadds. They backed off and stared in horror at the burning trees. As they watched, the orc archers loosed a second round, spreading the flame.

The nyadds weren't simply routed; they forgot about the fight. Now many of them were showing signs of distress, and even pain. Some shook violently, some sank to their knees, some just collapsed. A cruel malady swept through them, and as the fires grew stronger their torment grew as well.

Here and there, nyadds were bursting into flames. In some cases they fell and burned, with a kind of sad resignation. In others, the fire-swathed nyadds lurched and stumbled, and shrieked as they blazed. Some ran into the forest, illuminating its depths. The smell of charred flesh filled the air.

The Wolverines waded in and helped the process along with their blades. But what was happening to the trees was a more effective weapon. Shortly, only a handful of nyadds were left standing, and those not for long.

Stryke scanned the carnage. 'Let's get out of here!'

'What about this fire?' Spurral said, nodding at the burning trees. 'We can't just leave it to spread.'

'We've no time for fire-fighting.'

'You'd destroy an entire forest?'

'Look at it. I doubt we could put it out now if we tried.'

'And you're not going to?'

'I wouldn't worry too much,' Dynahla interrupted. 'You're forgetting the magical nature of the world we're in. This place takes care of itself. Only I think we should get out while we still can. The fire's going to surround us soon.'

They left before it did. The fire burned on at their rear, throwing its light after them so that they cast long shadows. But before long it faded, then died as the forest overwhelmed all but its memory.

The band met no more hostility, and eventually came to the forest's end.

They emerged on the top of a gentle slope running down to a green expanse. Crossing this was a dead straight artificial waterway. They couldn't see far enough to say where it came from or went to.

There were several barges on the water, and one very large one tied-up next to a small cottage. This was weathered red brick with an unkempt thatched roof. Figures moved around it.

Coilla cupped her eyes. 'Looks like . . . gnomes.'

'Miserable bastards,' Haskeer said.

'That canal runs north,' Stryke realised. 'And they've got a barge.'

Coilla nodded. 'Think it'd take all of us and the weapon?'

'I reckon. But we'd have to let the millipedes go.'

'Shame.'

'Let's see if we can parley.'

They headed down to the waterway. The panic started before they reached it. Seeing an orcs warband charging towards them, mounted on giant multi-legged insects and towing a black tube, was enough to unnerve the gnomes. It sparked an exodus. They scrambled into wagons and headed off along the towpath at speed.

'Rude buggers!' Haskeer exclaimed. 'They could have given us a hearing.'

Jup shrugged. 'Saves us having to negotiate.'

Stryke didn't waste time. They got the weapon onto the barge, which proved a tough task. Then the band embarked and they cast off, using the barge's oars. There was a small sail too, and Stryke had it unfurled, despite little wind.

As they moved away they saw the liberated millipedes undulating towards the forest. Everybody was sorry to see them go. Except Standeven.

28

The waterway took them through terrain that was mostly flat and lacking in any particular landmarks. All they saw was an expanse of green, dotted with the odd tree or rock. An occasional low hill, glimpsed in the distance, became an event to be remarked on. Taking advantage of their stately progression, the band rested, fed themselves and maintained their weapons. Curiously, they met no other boats.

As best as they could estimate it, more than a day went by as they slowly glided towards their unknown destination. Some in the band wondered if there *was* a destination, and whether the canal might not go on for ever. Those who thought there must be a destination speculated on how they would know it. The only certainty was the north star, and they were still heading straight for that.

Into the second day they saw the peaks of a mountain range ahead, and also noticed something strange about the star above it.

'It's definitely getting bigger,' Coilla decided.

'I think you're right,' Stryke agreed. He turned to the shape-changer. 'Dynahla?'

'It's to be expected the nearer we get to our goal.'

'You mean we are, at last?'

'It's in the air. Can't you feel it?'

Haskeer gave a prolonged, noisy sniff. 'I can't.'

'Take my word for it, Sergeant; our destination's imminent. Though we shouldn't get too excited. It may be closer only in distance.'

After that, the star and the mountains it crowned rapidly grew larger.

Eventually the problem of where their destination would lie was solved: the canal came to an end. It terminated in a modest dock, which had the benefit of a winch that proved sturdy enough to unload the barge. But that was the end of their luck as far as the weapon was concerned. Without beasts to help with the burden, it had to be moved bodily. The band was hardly keen on the idea, but they had experience of hauling siege engines over long distances. Once roped up, they found it took about half the band to pull it, which meant they could labour in shifts.

Now as big as a harvest moon, and rivalling the sun, the star was suspended above whatever lay behind the mountains. Fortunately there was a wide pass cutting through them. They made for it.

Halfway along, the pebbly stone floor of the vale began to be covered in patches of fine sand. By the time they got to the end of the pass there was nothing but sand underfoot, and it was quite thick. They had to work even harder to negotiate it. The temperature was also noticeably hotter.

Ahead of them was a low ridge of granite. Leaving the weapon at its base, they climbed the gentle incline to see what was beyond. Lying on their bellies, they looked out at the beginning of a vast desert. More arresting was what stood on it in the near distance. It was a pyramid, the largest any of them had seen, and it seemed to be made of milky glass. At its apex was what looked like a massive, multifaceted gem. Sunlight glinted on it.

'What in hell is that?' Coilla said.

'Something legendary,' Dynahla explained. 'If I'm right, it's the Prism of Sina-Cholm.'

'Which is?'

'An artefact created by the wizards who built this world.'

'What does it do?' Stryke asked.

'It kills.'

'How?'

'Can you get one of the archers to send an arrow its way?'

'Sure. It's in range. But I don't think an arrow's going to hurt it.'

'That's not the point.'

Stryke shrugged and ordered one of the grunts to string-up.

'It might be an idea if we all kept our heads down,' Dynahla suggested.

The archer loosed his bolt and it soared towards the pyramid. It had almost reached it when an intense white beam shot from the gem at the apex, striking the arrow and obliterating it.

'It targets anything that approaches,' Dynahla said.

'Is there somebody in there operating that thing?' Pepperdyne wanted to know.

'No, it functions entirely by itself. It works by drawing energy from what passes for the sun here, concentrating it and using it to defend itself.'

'Do we have to tackle it?' Stryke said.

'You know the nature of this place by now. It's there because it's the next thing we have to overcome. Maybe the last thing. Fortunately, we have a chance because of that.' He nodded at the weapon parked below them.

'Won't the pyramid just destroy what we fire at it?'

'What if we were to fire more than one thing at the same time?' Coilla suggested.

'That's not a bad idea. Think it might work, Dynahla?'

'Your faith in my knowledge about this place is touching, Stryke. Frankly, I don't know. But it's worth a try, isn't it?'

They needed a spot where they could get the weapon to see its target, and where there was some kind of shelter for the band. Scouts found such a place not far from the incline they climbed. It was a ground-level slab of stone big enough to accommodate the weapon, and with a perfect view of the pyramid. There were enough sizeable boulders strewn around it to give the Wolverines cover. They set about hauling the weapon to it.

'All right,' Stryke said when they were installed, 'let's get the thing loaded and lined-up.'

While that was going on he picked six archers.

There was a lot of fussing with the weapon's alignment, and when he was finally satisfied, Stryke stood ready at the lever. The archers nocked their arrows and drew back the strings.

'*Now!*' he yelled, pulling hard on the lever.

The weapon coughed its missile as six arrows were loosed.

The arrows travelled faster than the ball, which described an arcing path. A flash came from the gem and one of the arrows vaporised. There was another dazzling streak and a second arrow disappeared. Then it was the ball's turn. A beam sought it out, shattering it to fragments. The remaining arrows got through and clattered feebly against the pyramid's face.

'Fuck it!' Haskeer cursed.

'We proved it can't handle several things at once,' Stryke said.

'But it got the important one, didn't it?'

'We'll do it again, with more archers this time.'

Ten archers lined-up as the weapon was reloaded and its angle slightly adjusted.

Again the launch was simultaneous. The beam from the gem got two, three and then four arrows, and they were picked off before they had travelled as far as the first volley. But the ball got through. It struck the pyramid low down, near its base, and did some damage, although nothing terminal. A cheer went up from the band.

The weapon was primed once more and its angle altered on the basis of the previous shot. Arrows were readied.

'*Now!*' Stryke bellowed. He pulled the lever and rushed forward to see the result.

The beam singled out no less than five arrows this time, and intercepted them much nearer their firing point than before. Tumbling through the air on a high trajectory, the ball travelled unscathed.

There was a blinding flash and a roar. Stryke found himself on the ground, along with the others, not knowing what had just happened. As they looked up, they saw the ball hit the pyramid at the point where the gem was fixed to its peak. The sound of the impact was tremendous. Swaying for a second, the gem tumbled, and as it fell the pyramid itself rippled with numerous cracks and began to fall apart. Great shards of the glassy material plunged to the ground to shatter into thousands of pieces. In a brace of heartbeats the entire structure gave way, the remains shrouded in a cloud of dust from the debris.

The band cheered. It took them a moment to hear Coilla shouting at them and to realise something was wrong. Stryke turned and saw what it was. The weapon was on its side, the tube broken into several pieces, the woodwork blackened with charring. Its ammunition, the iron spheres, were scattered all around. Some were split in two.

Coilla was on her knees next to something half under the toppled weapon. Stryke and the others dashed to it.

'The pyramid fired at us just before the ball hit,' she explained. 'Vobe was standing next to the weapon.'

Stryke looked. Their comrade was crushed, bloodied and unmistakably dead.

They would have liked to give Vobe the send-off he deserved, but they knew that wasn't always possible in the field. So Stryke and Coilla said a few words about one of their longest-serving brothers-in-arms, and Dallog commended his spirit to the Tetrad with Haskeer looking on disdainfully. Then they buried the body as deep as they could in the desert sand.

'Strange to think we've buried him in a place that doesn't actually exist,' Coilla said as they moved away.

'Nothing that happens these days surprises me,' Stryke replied. 'But I wish we could have seen him off on a pyre on Ceragan, where he belongs, with feasting and drinking in his honour. He deserved at least that much.'

'We'll raise a tankard to him when we get out of this.'

'Think we will get out?'

'Of course we will. And you don't want to let the others hear you talking like that.'

'No, you're right. But what with Thirzarr, and now Vobe—'

'I know. But the best way we serve them is to complete this mission, the way we set out to do.'

'That feels like a long time ago, and it seemed so much simpler then.'

'Tell me about it.'

Dynahla approached them. 'I don't want to intrude on your grief,' he said, 'but we should be thinking about moving on.'

'Yes,' Stryke agreed soberly. 'But which way?'

'To what Sina-Cholm was guarding. Now the prism's gone we should be able to get through.'

Heavy-hearted, the band set off over the sand towards the ruins of the pyramid. They realised how big the thing had been when they had to negotiate a vast quantity of debris, much of it viciously keen shards of the glass-like material it had been constructed from. But they struggled onto its base, and after rooting through the chaos uncovered an aperture in the floor with a flight of stone steps that descended into darkness. They filed down, weapons in hand.

At the bottom of the stairwell they found that their way was lit, just as other areas had been on their travels in this world, from an unknown source. They were in a wide, tall tunnel, seemingly constructed without blocks, bricks or any evidence of joins. There was only one way to go and they took it.

'This I do know something about,' Dynahla told them. 'I was in this labyrinth when I first came to Serapheim's pocket universe. Take heart. We're very near our destination now.'

They trudged along the tunnel for what seemed like an eternity, their surroundings never changing and the light staying at the same uniform level. More than one of them noticed the sulphurous whiff in the air that indicated a magical charge. And it was getting stronger.

There was a brighter radiance somewhere far ahead, and it shone more and more strongly as they approached it. When they arrived at its source they found that the tunnel ended at a waterfall of multicoloured light.

'We're here,' Dynahla announced. 'All we have to do is step through this curtain of energy and into Serapheim's world.'

'Is it safe?' Spurral asked.

'Perfectly. Stryke, I think you should have the honour of going through first.'

'I reckon this . . . entrance or whatever it is should be big enough for us all to go through together.'

'Good idea,' the shape-changer said. 'Shall we?'

The band lined up in front of the dazzling cascade, not quite believing it could be an entrance of any kind. Standeven, as usual, hovered a few steps to the rear of the others, looking fearful.

On Stryke's word they moved forward and stepped into the luminous whirlpool.

The sensation was not unlike world-hopping with the instrumentalities. It felt as though they were falling from a great height through a madness of churning colours and exploding stars.

They opened their eyes on something like paradise.

The sun beat down on a verdant scene of grassy pastures, soft rolling hills, trees in full leaf and silvered lakes. So blue it almost made their eyes hurt, the sky was host to a few fluffy white clouds.

The air was fresh and a gentle breeze blew, fragrant from a thousand wholesome, growing things. There was no sign of the vibrant curtain they had walked through.

'This is quite something,' Pepperdyne said admiringly.

Spurral nodded. 'It's . . . beautiful.'

'It's based on Maras-Dantia before it fell into corruption,' a voice boomed from behind.

They spun round. Serapheim stood before them, a broad smile on his face. 'Congratulations on getting here,' he said, 'and welcome to my world.'

29

Tentarr Arngrim, or Serapheim as the world of sorcery knew him, looked very much as the band remembered from their first meeting on Maras-Dantia, albeit he showed the signs of ageing. But he had at least the appearance of vigour, despite what Dynahla had said about his failing health. His back was still straight, his build lean. He had shoulder-length auburn hair and a tidily trimmed beard. There were lively blue eyes above a slightly hawkish nose, and his mouth was well shaped. He was dressed in a blue silken robe and shiny black leather boots. The shape-changer was at his side.

'Greetings, Wolverines,' he said. 'It's good to see you again, and a pleasure to welcome some new faces.' He looked to the Ceragan recruits, Spurral, and Pepperdyne and Standeven. Then he took on a more solemn tone. 'Allow me to commiserate with you on those who fell on the way here. I know the loss of your comrades must be a grievous burden.'

'I think you've got some explaining to do,' Stryke told him.

'Yes, I have. You deserve no less. But come, let's do it in more comfort than standing here.'

He led them to a white marble villa. It was elegantly fashioned and tastefully furnished, and it was hard to credit it all as a product of magic. In a room the size of a banqueting hall he invited the Wolverines to rest themselves and take refreshments. Several young male and female humans, similarly dressed in blue robes, appeared with trays of water, juice and ale, and platters of bread, cheese, fruits and freshly roasted meat and fowl. It was hard to believe that the food and drink, like the villa and the world in which it stood, literally didn't exist.

Serapheim let them pick at the food and take some of the drink before moving on to weightier matters, despite the obvious impatience of Stryke and several others.

At last he said, 'I can understand your frustration and your puzzlement at the turn events have taken.'

'Can you?' Stryke replied frostily. 'We signed on for this mission to get our revenge on Jennesta. But it all got a lot more complicated than that, didn't it?'

'Not really.' He raised a hand to gently forestall Stryke's objection. 'You signed on with two objectives in mind. One was helping to liberate the orcs of Acurial, and you achieved it. You should be proud of that. It again gives the lie to the slander that orcs are selfish, purely destructive creatures. As to the second prong of your mission, settling with my daughter, that was and remains the prime purpose of the assignment.'

'There's still hope that we can do that?'

'Every hope. It's why you're here. And let me add, Stryke, that I'm fully aware of the situation your mate, Thirzarr, is in. Her wellbeing is as important as defeating Jennesta, and I give you my word that every effort will be made to reunite you.'

'Maybe she wouldn't be in this mess in the first place if I hadn't agreed to this crazy scheme.'

'If anything I've done has been responsible for putting Thirzarr in danger then I apologise. That was never my intention. But you have to understand that she would have been in danger anyway, sooner or later. From Jennesta. We are all in peril because of my daughter. You know of her scheme to create an army of obedient zombie orcs?'

'Course I do,' Stryke replied angrily, 'Thirzarr's one of them.'

'No, she's not. She's being held in a state between normality and mindless servitude. It suited Jennesta to have it that way, so she could more easily manipulate you. Or so she thought. Her demise would see an end to the hold she has over Thirzarr, and all the others who have fallen under her influence.'

'We kill her—'

'And they live, yes.' He looked around at the others in the room, all of whom were intent on what was being said. 'Some of you, particularly those new to this warband, might find it difficult to understand how I can talk so calmly about the death of my own flesh and blood. But Jennesta is no longer my daughter. It's as if I had never fathered her. I renounced her long ago, and my heart is heavier about that than you can imagine. The fact is that I helped bring evil into being when she was born. My only wish is to put that right.'

'You tried once before,' Stryke reminded him.

'Yes, and somehow, by some fluke, she survived the vortex. This time my thought is to serve her a fate from which there is no escape.' He fell into a kind of reverie for a moment, undisguised sorrow in his eyes. Then he roused himself. 'But about her plan for a slave army. Do you know who inspired that idea in her?'

'No. Should I?'

'In a way, you already do. I'm afraid we've been a little deceptive with you, Dynahla and I, and for that, too, I offer my apologies.'

'What do you mean?' Coilla asked, finding her voice.

Serapheim turned to Dynahla and said, 'Shall we show them?'

The shape-changer smiled and nodded. He stood, and immediately began to transform.

The band watched in awe as the process twisted and contorted Dynahla's body. At the end of it they were looking at a handsome, some would say beautiful, woman. Only her crimson hair was retained, tumbling to her milky white shoulders. It was hard to estimate her age, but she appeared to be in the prime of life for a human.

'Allow me to introduce Vermegram,' Serapheim said. 'My mate, my partner, my bride. And Jennesta's mother. She is as old as me, which is to say very old . . . I hope you'll forgive my indiscretion, my dear . . . and as high an adept in the ways of sorcery as I am.'

'Why?' Stryke said. 'Why the deception?'

'To protect her, and your band. If Jennesta knew that you were consorting with her mother, whom she despises, she wouldn't just have toyed with you, or with Thirzarr. The likelihood is that you'd all be dead by now.'

'I'm sorry,' Vermegram said. 'We weren't trying to trick you. It just seemed the safest way to offer you some protection and guide you through this world.' The band found it hard to get used to the soft, almost melodic voice of someone they had thought of up to now as a male. 'As to my inspiring our daughter's obsession with raising her slave army, I think at least some of you know a little about that from Serapheim. Basically it was because I tried to do something similar myself, a long time ago, when Maras-Dantia was still as fair as this artificial world. Unlike Jennesta my intentions were benign. I wanted to do good. But as the old saying goes, the road to Hades is paved with the tarnished gold of noble intentions. I was damned for that and I've been trying to rectify the error ever since.' She glanced affectionately at Serapheim. 'We both have.'

The silence that followed was broken by Haskeer asking bluntly, 'Are you a real fetch or what?'

Vermegram smiled. 'I'm human. Basically. I wasn't born with shape-changing abilities; I acquired them as a result of my magical studies.'

'Your kids—'

'Why do they vary so much in appearance? Why does Jennesta look the way she does? Why did her late sister, Adpar, turn out a hybrid? And she was another bad lot, I'm ashamed to say. It was because of tampering with myself, altering the very core of my being, when I took on the power to shape-shift. There were unanticipated consequences. One of which was that I passed on certain unusual traits to my offspring. Only my youngest daughter, Sanara, has a normal human appearance. Fortunately, her path has always been one of good, unlike her siblings.'

'Which reminds me,' Serapheim said. He reached out a hand. A velvet bell cord appeared from thin air. He gave it two tugs and it disappeared.

'Nice trick,' Coilla muttered.

A door opened and Sanara entered. She was wearing a similar set of blue robes to her father's. When she saw Jup she made straight for him, throwing her arms around him and giving him a kiss on the cheek. Spurral looked on flint-faced. Jup was blushing. Then Sanara waved a greeting to the other band members who remembered her and took a seat by her parents.

'Vermegram and I cannot confront Jennesta's forces alone, for all our powers, because hers have grown at least as strong,' Serapheim explained. 'My own, I confess, are wavering. As this pocket universe is kept in existence by the force of my will, I find I need the additional mental strength of my apprentices, the young people who served you the food, and the support of what's left of my family.' He exchanged smiles with Vermegram and his daughter. 'Sanara is one of our allies in this fight. Would you like to meet some others?'

He led them through a door and along an airy passage. Another door took them out into the open air and a large area resembling a parade ground, except it was grassed over. It was crowded.

Quoll, Ceragan orc chieftain and Wheam's father, was there, along with what looked like all the able-bodied males of the clan. So were Brelan and Chillder, formerly of the Acurial resistance, and several hundred of their troops.

There were greetings, warriors' hand clasps and hugs.

'This is amazing,' Coilla said.

'We were only too pleased to help,' Chillder said, 'after what you did for us.'

'Though we could have done with a gentler way of getting here,' Brelan added. 'Serapheim's method of transport was kind of disconcerting.'

Wheam approached his father, looking anxious.

'There's no need for timidity,' Quoll assured him. He clapped a meaty hand on the youth's shoulder. 'From what I've heard you've much to be proud of, and I know you'll make me proud in the scrap to come.'

Wheam smiled.

Stryke made his way to the chieftain. 'Quoll,' he said, almost afraid to ask the question. 'Janch and Corb. Are they—'

'They're fine, Stryke. Safe and well, and under the clan's protection. How could it be otherwise? Though they're missing their sire and mother, of course.'

He felt a wave of relief. 'Thank you.'

'But I regret we weren't able to stop Thirzarr being taken. I'm sorry about that.'

'No need. Few are a match for Jennesta.'

'The bitch. She took the lives of some of our best, and devastated our lodges. I can't wait to make her pay for that.' He slapped the broadsword he wore.

'Do you know what you've let yourselves in for here? Do any of you?'

'Yes,' Brelan offered. 'Serapheim explained everything.'

'That's more than he's done with us.'

'And that's remiss of me,' the magician said, appearing at Stryke's side. 'You need to hear the plan. Come with me and I'll tell you.'

He took Stryke back indoors and to what looked very much like a sorcerer's study, complete with shelves of massive, leather-bound grimoires, vials of potions and powders, and assorted skeletons of unidentifiable small creatures of bizarre appearance.

'It will come as no surprise to you that Jennesta is here,' Serapheim announced when they were settled. 'She's gained entry to the Sphere of the Four, to which this world is adjunct. And she's used her fake instrumentalities to import the followers she left behind. From a world of islands, I'm given to believe. It's only a matter of time before she gets in here.'

'Can't you stop her?'

'Stop her? I *want* her here. That's part of the plan.'

'Why?'

'Several reasons. First, if there's to be a battle between her forces and ours, better it should be here where only combatants and not the innocent are affected. Second, the set of instrumentalities she has doesn't function here, although I don't think she knows it and I want to keep it that way. That takes away her option to flee if she has to. Third, the plan we have in mind must be executed by Vermegram, Sanara and myself, and as I can't conveniently leave this world I contrived to lure Jennesta here.'

'What is your plan for dealing with her?'

'No disrespect, Stryke, but I'm keeping that to myself. Only because what you don't know can't be got out of you. Oh, I know you're tough and not given to betraying confidences, but this is Jennesta we're talking about.'

'Fair enough. So what do you want us to do?'

'I want the Wolverines to be part of our little army and engage her forces. But I want you to pick two or three members of your band to help you carry out a special task.'

'Not fight, you mean?'

'I expect they'll be fighting all right, it's just that I don't want you in the battle proper. I've something else in mind, though it's more dangerous. If you're willing.'

'If it gets at Jennesta, I'm willing.'

'There will be a point in our run-in with her when it's vitally important that she be distracted. Have more coming at her than she can cope with and still think straight, in other words. That's where you come in.'

Stryke nodded.

'I'll let you know when the time is right,' Serapheim added, 'and make sure you can get to her. You might like to go and select your helpers now.'

'Hold your horses. I want to ask you something. We've been dogged by an outfit called the Gateway Corps. What do you know about them?'

'It's said they've been around almost as long as instrumentalities themselves have existed. The Corps' self-appointed mission is to track down the artefacts and limit the damage they can do. An ambition I don't altogether disapprove of.'

'They're a problem I didn't need.'

'Understandably. They're tenacious, and have allegiance only to their cause. But we can deal with it.'

'From what I've seen, they're powerful.'

'So are we. But I believe the Corps to be basically virtuous, and potentially useful allies. They are not our first concern, however. Put them from your mind.'

Stryke shrugged and made to leave.

Serapheim waved him back into his seat. 'There's one more thing. It has no real bearing on the task in hand, but you might find it . . . interesting. You know that the world you've just travelled through was created by a group of high adepts called the Four. But do you know what their names were?'

'No, why should I?'

'They were Aik, Zeenoth, Neaphetar and Wystendel.'

'The Tetrad?' Stryke was shocked, despite believing he was beyond being affected by any revelation at this point.

'I tell you this not to undermine your beliefs. I think they *were* gods, in a way. They are certainly seen as that not only by you orcs but a number of other races too. You only have to look at what they created to see their god-like qualities. I tell you this as a lesson. The lesson being that you shouldn't always rely on what you think you know or think you see. That could be valuable in what's to come.'

'I think I understand.'

'Keep it in mind. Now you'd better—'

The door flew open and Sanara came in. 'Father! Jennesta's

here. She and her followers have just breached the western membrane.'

'That was to be expected. Indeed, hoped for. Take your position, Sanara. Stryke, brief your band and wait on my word.'

The Gateway Corps unit had also penetrated Serapheim's hideaway, though with immense difficulty.

'This place is glorious,' Pelli remarked as she surveyed the scene.

'Looks can be deceiving,' Weevan-Jirst reminded her.

'Still, it's hard to believe anything nefarious could be going on in this kind of setting.'

'Yet we know it is.'

She gave up on his obduracy and held her peace.

They had wandered away from the body of their unit to explore the options and decide which way to go. There were no roads that they could see or any signs of habitation. Pelli thought the place was like an enormous garden.

'What's that?' Weevan-Jirst said. He pointed to a nearby hill.

There were figures on it.

Pelli strained to see. 'They look like . . . goblins.'

'So they do.'

'I wonder how they fit into this.'

'We could ask them.'

'Is that wise?'

He gave her the goblin equivalent of a condescending look. 'They're my own kind. I'm sure I can converse with them in a civilised manner.'

'All right. We'll go up and—'

'I think it would be best if I did this alone. My folk don't always react well to other races.'

'As you wish. But take care. I'll either be here or back with the others.'

He set off and she watched him go. But she didn't leave. She was curious to see how he would handle it.

As he walked by a cluster of bushes a figure leapt out and began to struggle with him. Shocked, Pelli called out and rushed to help. As she approached the figure ran off.

She arrived at her second-in-command panting. *'What . . . happened?'*

He showed her his arm. It had a gash across it and the blood was flowing freely. 'He attacked me.'

'Who did?'

'A goblin.'

'Was he trying to kill you?'

Weevan-Jirst was binding his arm with a field bandage he'd produced from his belt pouch. 'I don't know. I don't think so. It was senseless. He leapt out, slashed my arm and made to run off. I tried to stop him but he got away.'

She noticed movement on the hill. One figure was running up it, towards the others. 'Is that him?'

He looked. 'I suppose it could be. I've a mind to go up there and—'

'I think it would be wise not to.'

'They're *goblins*. My kind. Why would he do that?'

'There are good and bad in all races. And I'm beginning to suspect who they are and their relationship with Jennesta.'

Before she could go on he said, 'Does one of them have a bow?'

She looked. 'I think he might. We should either get out of here or be prepared to defend ourselves magically. He seems to be aiming this way.'

'Then he's a fool. No archer on any world could achieve a shot like that. The distance is too far and the angle's wrong.' There was the sound of something cutting through the air. 'Why does he think—' A spasm shook him and he let out a strangled gasp. A black arrow jutted from his chest.

'Weevan-Jirst,' Pelli said, stunned. *'Weevan-Jirst!'*

He fell. She went down on her knees to him, felt for a heartbeat, not the easiest task through a goblin's carapace, then tried the vein in his neck. He was dead.

She looked up to the hill again. The archer and the others had gone. Her thought was that anybody who could use a bow like that, over such a distance, commanded a strong form of magic and was best avoided. Keeping low, and still numb from what had just happened, she hurried back to the others.

The area Serapheim occupied buzzed with activity as the diverse force readied itself for battle. Serapheim's apprentices, perhaps a dozen in number, had joined its ranks with the intention of using their magic in aid of the cause.

Stryke stood apart from all that with three others. The band had been dismayed when he told them he wouldn't be fighting along-side them. But once they knew why, they were approving.

He had decided to take Gleadeg, Coilla and Pepperdyne with him on the mission Serapheim had allotted. The human he might not have chosen, good a fighter as he was, but Coilla insisted that they stay together, and Stryke wanted her along. None of them had any idea where Standeven was, or particularly cared.

There was a commotion. A chorus of *'They're here! They're here!'* went up. Stryke and the others rushed to see what was happen-ing.

On the plain that stretched out not far from Serapheim's villa, a force was advancing. They recognised Jennesta at its head. Her human troopers from Acurial were with her, along with shuffling human zombies and the more sprightly orc kind. There was a mass of flotsam and jetsam of various races she had recruited from the world of islands, including what looked like the remnants of the Gatherers. Racing to join them at the rear was the goblin Gleaton-Rouk and his piratical gang.

Stryke knew Thirzarr was somewhere in the horde but couldn't spot her. At least he hoped she was there. He didn't like to think about what had happened if she wasn't.

Jennesta's army was even more ragtag than the one Stryke was a part of. But hers outnumbered his by at least two to one.

'Stryke!'

He turned and saw Serapheim approaching, and he wasn't alone. Pelli Madayar was with him, along with her multi-species Gateway Corps comrades.

'I have granted admission to a group I think you know,' Sera-pheim explained.

'Hello again, Captain,' Pelli said.

'What are you doing here?' Stryke asked suspiciously.

'I've long felt that your band has been a mere pawn in this game. The Corps' principles, and my training, have prevented me from acting on that impulse. But recent events have made me question my impartiality. There comes a time when a side has to be chosen and to hell with the consequences. I've decided . . . we've *all* decided that yours is the one to offer our services to.'

Stryke thought about that for a moment, then said, 'Glad to have you aboard.'

30

The two armies faced each other.

For Jennesta it was the culmination of the revenge she sought to inflict on her father and the hated Wolverines. For the defenders it was a matter of survival.

Hostilities started from a distance, using a combination of magic and arrows, the former blocking most of the latter. Streaks of energy, yellow, white and red were exchanged, resembling a hatchling's coloured streamer caught by the wind. Shimmering defensive bubbles were up, cast by Jennesta on one side, the Gateway Corps on the other. The difference being that Jennesta's was to protect her and a small coterie, while the Corps was trying to shield everyone.

When the sides finally began to advance it wasn't at a charge. The pace was more deliberate, almost stately, save for the taunts and foul curses each side rained on the other. But ultimately they had to meet, and when they did it was bloodily.

The roof of Serapheim's villa was an excellent vantage point. From it, Stryke, Coilla, Pepperdyne and Gleadeg had the best view of the battle. All of them would have liked to be there.

Serapheim came to them. 'There,' he said, pointing. 'You can just see Jennesta over on the far side. Having set the fighting in motion she's retired to a safer distance.'

Stryke looked, but had to strain his eyes. He could make out Jennesta. There were others with her, and he thought one of them might be Thirzarr, but he couldn't be sure.

'You must get to her,' Serapheim continued. 'You can either go round the field of battle—'

'Too long,' Stryke told him.

'Or through it, I'm afraid. Shall I assign you some extra bodies to help?'

They looked at each other and Stryke answered for all of them. 'No. We can manage.'

'I hoped you'd say that. We can't really spare anybody.'

Coilla gave a gentle dig. 'Some army.'

'Valiant as they are, it isn't them we're relying on. It's you. Take care.'

Stryke and the others set off.

When they got to the plain, the battle was hotting up and there was a great roar coming from it. Stryke had hoped to cross by moving through their own ranks, but things had got mixed. It was still the case that most of Jennesta's force was on the right and Stryke's was on the left, but both armies had been contaminated with each other's fighters.

They drew their weapons. Stryke tried to pick a spot with more friends than enemies, and they plunged in.

The Wolverines were where they always liked to be, in the heart of the battle.

For Haskeer it was all the excuse he needed to crack skulls and sever limbs with his axe. He preferred the living opponents. The zombies were basically dusty demolition jobs with little fight in them. The orc zombies were livelier but still lacked a spark. Haskeer had no qualms about fighting them.

Jup and Spurral were side by side, as usual, working in unison with staffs and knives. They made a point of seeking out goblins, and were duelling with a pair of them, staffs against tridents. Nearby, the Ceragans fought together, with Dallog leading them. Wheam stood with his father, and he had made the supreme gesture of leaving his lute back at the villa.

Gateway Corps members were all over the battle, discharging magical punches that downed men and caused the human zombies to explode in clouds of dust. Pelli Madayar was fighting conventionally, something the Corps was required to be proficient at. She finished off a Gatherer with a sword thrust and, spinning, bumped into Wheam. They exchanged nods and turned to their fresh respective opponents.

Shortly after, in a rare lull, they both happened to catch sight of Weevan-Jirst, skulking at the battle's ragged edge, looking for prey.

'Do you know him?' Pelli said.

Wheam nodded. 'His name's Weevan-Jirst. He killed one of our band.'

'With an arrow?'

'Yes. His bow's enchanted. Didn't you know?'

'I guessed as much.'

'An arrow smeared with his victim's blood always finds its target. *Always.*'

'That explains something.'

'What?'

A uniformed human came too close. Pelli fended him off and he was caught up in the swirl. 'Doesn't matter.'

'I've got an idea about Weevan-Jirst,' Wheam confided. 'Something that could hurt him.'

'Can I help you with it?'

As they battled their way through the melee, so did Dallog and Pirrak, but moving in a different direction.

Initially, Stryke and his tiny crew made good progress. They were well into the crush before they hit a foe, then trouble came thick and furious.

But now, sweating and breathing hard, they were in sight of Jennesta. She had Thirzarr with her, rod straight and blank-eyed. There was also one of her once human zombies and a handful of troopers.

'So how are we going to do this, Stryke?' Pepperdyne said as they worked their way closer.

'I'm thinking just straight in, fell the guards.'

'What about the biggest threat?'

'I'm counting on Jennesta still wanting me and the band serving her. Why else would she keep Thirzarr alive?'

'You better be sure about that,' Coilla said. 'She might be keeping her as a pet.'

'If you can think of another way in the time we've got—'

'No, let's do it. I've come to trust your hunches.'

They fought their way to the battle's rim, lingered in the crowd for an opportune moment then charged across the open ground. The guards were their first target. There were five of them, all human, so the odds were no problem. Gleadeg got the first with a single blow and surprise. Pepperdyne had as easy a time with his mark, felling him with a brace of strokes. Stryke and Coilla had a bit more of a slog. Their opponents had some fire and it took a moment to put them down.

There was a human zombie present, but for some reason Jennesta hadn't set him on them. He stood immobile, and they recognised him as what was left of Kapple Hacher.

The sorceress had a jewelled dagger at Thirzarr's throat.

'Give it up,' Stryke advised.

'You dare to speak to *me* like that, you snivelling animal? And while I'm holding a blade to your bitch?'

'I was never much of a one for niceties.' He wished Serapheim and the others would turn up. Equally, he hoped none of Jennesta's supporters in the battle would notice what was going on and come to her aid.

'If anyone should give up,' Jennesta announced haughtily, 'it's you.' She pressed the dagger closer to Thirzarr's throat. The crease in her flesh was plainly visible.

'I think if you were going to kill Thirzarr you would have done it by now.' He prayed she wouldn't call his bluff. And thought of the Tetrad and what Serapheim had told him.

'You think I wouldn't?'

It was sliding into a stalemate. Stryke was wondering how far to push it when they were all distracted by movement and noise.

A couple of Jennesta's troopers had detached themselves from the battlefield, as Stryke had feared, and were rushing to save her. But as they neared and Stryke fought to bring up his sword, another figure ran into their path and viciously engaged them. It was Pirrak. He felled one man in quick order. The other put his sword through Pirrak's guts. In his turn, the attacker was felled by a Wolverine's blade.

Dallog came out of the scrum and joined the others around Pirrak.

The youth was mortally wounded and they all knew it. He was losing blood fast and could hardly talk, but he tried. '*Sorry . . . sorry about . . . Acurial.*'

'What was that?' Stryke said.

'*Acurial . . . didn't want . . . he . . .*'

'I can't make it out,' Coilla said. 'What do you mean?'

'No . . . choice . . . in Acurial . . . sp— Uhh.'

Pirrak had a dagger in his heart, with Dallog's hand on it. The deed was quick and smooth.

'*What the hell?*' Stryke exploded.

'What are you *doing?*' Coilla exclaimed.

'He was suffering and I put an end to his misery. It was a kindness.'

'Are you insane? He would have been dead in a heartbeat anyway.'

'Or was it something he was about to say that you wanted to put a stop to?' Stryke ventured.

'Ah,' Dallog said, and rose from the corpse.

In the turmoil they had almost forgotten about Jennesta. Now Dallog crossed to her. When he reached her side he turned and faced them. 'Yes, it would have been embarrassing if Pirrak had talked. Not that it matters now that my allegiance is no longer a secret.'

'Your *what?*' Coilla said.

'I serve the Lady Jennesta. At least this once.'

'You serve me whenever I want you to,' she informed him coolly.

'This started in Acurial, didn't it?' Stryke hazarded. 'It was you.'

'Who?' Coilla said. 'What happened in Acurial, Stryke?'

'We know what happened. We just didn't know who did it. When that orc was found dead in the resistance safe house.'

'You think *he* did that?' She pointed at Dallog.

'I'm not denying it,' Dallog told her.

'And we've been blaming Standeven,' Pepperdyne said, 'the poor bastard.'

'How did you do it, Dallog?' Stryke wanted to know.

'I got the youngster to help me. We were passing information about the resistance to the Peczan forces, and to my lady here. Something I've done more recently about the band.' He flicked a finger at his head, then indicated Jennesta's with it. 'We have a way of talking. I called it praying, you'll remember, Captain.' He smiled. 'The dead orc back in Acurial was a cohort, strictly for coin. He got greedy and said he'd expose me. It suited me to let Standeven take the blame.'

'You said you *got* Pirrak to help you. How did you do that?'

'He was no saint. He fell in with my scheme easily enough.'

'You mean he was young and green, and easily swayed. Or bullied. You slur Pirrak's name. He died an honourable death.'

'Saving *you*,' Dallog sneered.

'Why did you do it?' Coilla wanted to know. 'What did she promise you?'

'Something you could never offer. Something that's wasted on Pirrak and Wheam and all the other whey-faced hatchlings I've had to wipe the arses of. She's promised me my youth back. I'll be young again, now and for ever.'

'You're a fool,' Stryke told him.

'This is all very interesting,' Jennesta said, 'but I was about to cut your mate's throat.'

'Reward me now, my lady,' Dallog said.

She gave him a look usually reserved for dog shit. 'What?'

'I've done all you asked, and more. We had a pact. I've fulfilled my part.'

'You don't have a great sense of timing, do you? It may have escaped your notice but I'm a little busy at the moment, what with a war and everything.'

'My true loyalty's in the open now; there's no point in delaying. And with my youth restored I can serve you so much better. You can do it easily, I know you can.'

'*Enough.*' She extended her free hand. 'Come then, claim your reward.'

Stryke and the others looked on impotently as Dallog, beaming, took a step closer and bowed slightly so that Jennesta could lightly touch his forehead.

'As age is your problem,' she said, 'let this put an end to it.'

A change came over him, but not necessarily the one he was expecting. More wrinkles appeared on his face, not less, and his skin began to grey. Blue veins started to stand out on his neck, arms and the backs of his hands. His fingernails were turning yellow. The smile had vanished now and there was terror in his fading eyes. He tried to struggle, but whatever enchantment she was using prevented him from breaking free.

The others watched in horror as flakes of skin fell away and his face sagged. His body shrank, the bones showing through rice paper flesh. His rotting teeth dislodged as his mouth gaped in a silent scream. He shrivelled, his flesh turning to dust until his skeleton could plainly be seen. Then that crumbled too, falling like poured sand. In seconds he had been rendered to a scattering of ashes.

Jennesta was still holding a portion of his skull with discoloured skin attached. She casually tossed it aside and it shattered when it met the ground. 'The old are such a trial, don't you think?' she said.

'We're taking a hell of a risk,' Pelli said as they got themselves nearer to their target.

'We can do it if we're quick,' Wheam assured her.

'Are you sure you're right about this?'

'Yes.' He pointed. 'That goblin over there is some kind of healer, I reckon, and he seems to be looking after only Weevan-Jirst. I've been watching him. And that bucket by him has got bloody bandages in it.'

'Doesn't mean it's Weevan-Jirst's blood.'

'No. But I think there's a good chance. When we saw Weevan-Jirst before I noticed that he had two bound wounds, on his upper and lower arm. But even if it isn't his blood on those bandages it'll be from some other goblin and that's got to be a result, hasn't it?'

'I guess so.'

'Are you ready?'

'Yes. But remember to close your eyes when I tell you to. You'll be all right when you open them again. But if you don't close them when I say—'

'Yes, I know. Let's get going.'

The healer was off the battlefield and to the side, some way from his master though in sight of him. He was alone, and rummaging through a bag of kit. They got as close to him as they dared.

'Now!' Pelli ordered. 'Close them!'

She closed her own eyes too, and cast what was basically a simple spell but a very effective one. It generated a burst of incredibly intense light that briefly blinded everybody in range. That meant more than just the healer, but they thought that was justifiable as it gave nobody a real advantage, except in the unlikely event of someone who happened to be fighting with their eyes closed.

The potency of the flash did its job. When Pelli and Wheam looked, the healer was rubbing at his eyes and blundering about. He wasn't the only one.

'Quickly!' Pelli urged. 'It doesn't last long!'

Wheam darted towards the medic, dodging several of the temporarily sightless. He reached the bucket, grabbed a bandage and raced back. Then they lost themselves in the confusion.

Finding a corner of the field away from the still churning battle, Wheam got out the distinctive black arrow he'd found on the battlefield earlier. They smeared it with blood from the bandage.

'The next bit's even trickier,' Pelli said.

'You can do it.'

'Let's see.'

They made their way to where they had last seen Weevan-Jirst. He was still there, and aiming his bow, seemingly at random over the heads of the combatants. The arrow flew, circled a couple of times and came down to strike someone in the crowd.

'That's one more on our side he's claimed,' Wheam remarked angrily.

'Come on, let's get nearer.'

They approached the goblin as closely as they dared, and saw that the arrow sheath he wore was almost empty. But another, full one, stood on the ground beside him, presumably containing a store of arrows tainted with blood collected by his gang.

Pelli took their arrow from Wheam. 'Guard my back, will you? This takes some concentration.' She added under her breath, 'I hope nobody sees it.'

She laid the shaft across her outstretched palms and stared at it. Nothing happened for a second, then it twitched. The twitch became a more animated judder. Suddenly the arrow soared from her hands, and under her direction headed straight for the quiver. It did a neat flip and fell inside. It was all so swift that no one appeared to notice, least of all Weevan-Jirst.

'Well done,' Wheam congratulated.

'We don't know when he'll fire it, or even if he will.'

'We've done our best. Now let's get away from here.'

They rejoined the battle. But whenever there was a rare moment of stillness they glanced the goblin's way. Twice they saw him loose arrows that seemed to hunt their targets like a living thing, and both times found them. Wheam and Pelli began to think their plan wasn't going to work.

A bit later, in another brief pause that starved them of anyone to fight, Wheam nudged Pelli and nodded towards the goblin. He was drawing his bow again. They watched with no great expectation.

The arrow Weevan-Jirst fired went way over the battlefield, made a couple of circuits and headed back in his general direction. He looked on, presumably to see who the latest casualty would be. But the shaft was coming towards him. When it was close enough for there to be no doubt of its goal the goblin's expression turned to dread and he tried to run. The arrow took him square in the back. He went down heavily. Other goblins ran to him, but what they found looked pretty conclusive even from a distance.

Wheam and Pelli slapped their right hands together and let out a whoop. It was joined by a cheer from pleased onlookers.

Stryke was thinking of rushing Jennesta and overpowering her. It was a sign of his desperation that he would consider such an unwise move. The chances were that Thirzarr would suffer for it, and likely they'd all die. But Serapheim and his kin still hadn't turned up and the situation was even more edgy after what Jennesta had done to Dallog.

He got the impression that Gleadeg, Coilla and Pepperdyne might also be thinking about attacking Jennesta. Catching their eye, he tried to convey through facial expressions how reckless a move that would be. He hoped they got the message.

'I'm getting bored with this,' Jennesta said, her knife still at Thirzarr's throat.

'That must be tough for you,' Coilla told her.

'How shall I relieve it? By killing this one?' She twisted the dagger a touch. 'By killing you four? Maybe both.'

'You're big on talk,' Stryke said. 'Why don't you let Thirzarr go, and face me, one to one?'

She laughed. 'And you think you'd stand a chance?'

'Try me, then,' Pepperdyne offered. 'I'd take you on.'

Jennesta looked him over. 'Hmmm. Not bad. For a human. Perhaps I should let you *take me on*, pretty boy.'

Coilla stared daggers at her.

At that moment there was what could only be called a shift in the air. It was rapidly followed by a burst of light. When everybody blinked back to normality there were three more beings present. Serapheim, Vermegram and Sanara had finally arrived.

'Ah,' Jennesta cooed. 'What a pleasant surprise. A family gathering.'

'Let the female go, Jennesta,' Serapheim said. 'She's nothing to do with this.'

'I don't think so.'

'Don't make me make you.'

'You're so melodramatic, Father.'

'That's rich coming from you,' Vermegram said.

'And you have no sense of melodrama, Mother? There's no attention-seeking when you take the form of some mangy animal?'

'I don't hold knives to innocent beings' necks.'

'You should try it, it might brighten up your dull, sanctimonious little life.'

'That's enough,' Sanara said.

'Oh, *please*, little sister. You're nothing but an even more prissy version of our mother. I couldn't care less for your condemnation.'

'Put the knife down,' Serapheim demanded, his tone like ice.

'Go to *hell*.'

He made a swift movement with his hands. The dagger Jennesta was holding became malleable, then melted like an icicle in a heatwave. It ended as a metallic coloured puddle at her feet.

At the same time, Vermegram wove her own spell. Thirzarr started, staggered and seemed to come to herself.

'Stryke!' Serapheim cried urgently.

Stryke dashed to his bewildered mate, took hold of her and dragged her away.

Alarmed at the speed of events, Jennesta's perplexity turned to anger. Lifting her own hands, lips moving through some incantation, she prepared to retaliate.

'*Get clear!*' Serapheim shouted.

Stryke and the others didn't need telling twice. They withdrew from the line of fire.

Jennesta hurled energy at her kin. They repelled it by instantly throwing up a glossy protective bubble, and answered with fiery bolts. These Jennesta batted aside as though they were no more harmful than a swipe from a kitten.

'What in hell is going on, Stryke?' Thirzarr asked. She looked exhausted as well as baffled.

'I'll tell you later,' he promised, pulling her closer.

The duel built in intensity, so that even those fighting a short distance away took a step back from their opponents to watch.

Then there was a development from an unexpected quarter. The zombie Hacher, who had stood to one side, forgotten through all this, now stirred himself. Perhaps there was just enough humanity left in what remained of his senses, or enough unforgiving malice. Lurching towards her from behind, he grabbed hold of Jennesta, encircling her in a death-like grip.

'Get off me, you scum!' she shrieked, struggling to free herself.

When she failed to break his hold she resorted to a more extreme measure. A small hand gesture was all it took. What had once been Hacher let out a moan of agony and began to writhe. He let go of her and his hands went to his head. They weren't enough to hold it together. It erupted as surely as a melon hit with a mallet. A sticky black liquid seeped through his fingers and down his chest. He collapsed, truly dead.

Serapheim and the others were still mounting their magical attack. It was all becoming too much for Jennesta. She reached into her gown and took out her ersatz set of instrumentalities. Four were already in place. Grinning triumphantly at her enemies, she quickly slotted the fifth into place and disappeared.

'I thought you said they didn't work here,' Stryke complained. 'You've let her get away!'

Jennesta's parents and her sibling looked truly mournful. Vermegram and Sanara might even have had moist eyes, as was the way with humans.

It was Serapheim who spoke, his tone weighed down. 'No, they don't work here, and she hasn't got away. That was our plan.'

'I don't understand.'

'Working together, because that's what it took, even with a counterfeit set of instrumentalities, we managed to alter them from afar. Jennesta thought she could use them to get away, and no doubt had the coordinates for a safe location. We changed those coordinates.'

'Where's she gone?' Coilla asked.

Serapheim looked up at the sky. 'I'll explain.'

The world Serapheim created was in every respect artifice, fuelled and maintained by magic and the force of his will. But for all practical purposes it was real. The food it produced could be eaten, the rain that fell was wet, the perfume of flowers was just as sweet. Pleasure could be experienced there, and pain and death. The reality extended to its sun. It was no less the giver of warmth and light than any that existed in the so-called natural universe.

And so it was that as Serapheim explained what had happened to his depraved daughter, on the surface of the sun he had brought into existence there was the tiniest blip. A minute, incredibly short-lasting flare of energy as a foreign body, newly arrived, was instantly consumed by that terrible inferno.

Jennesta's going had a number of effects on the battlefield. Her human zombies simply stopped functioning, and fell to dust. The entranced orcs had the chains binding their minds severed, and came to their senses. Others, of many races, also felt her influence seep away, and they threw down their arms. Yet others, those far gone in depravity who followed the sorceress willingly, fought on. As the battle descended into part dazed chaos, part fight to the death, it was one of the latter who was responsible for what happened next.

Stryke and Thirzarr stood with Coilla and Pepperdyne, a little apart from the others, watching the turn of events when a fighter on the battlefield took aim and unleashed an arrow.

Given the unpredictability of a conventional longbow, it could have struck any of them. It chose Pepperdyne. The arrow plunged deep into his chest, passing through the side of his heart as it travelled. He fell without a sound.

The cold hand of horror clutched at Coilla's own heart. She went down on her knees to him, and if confirmation of what had just happened was needed, she saw his white singlet rapidly turning scarlet.

On the battlefield, the archer who sent the bolt, a Gatherer perhaps or some other form of lowlife, was cut to pieces by an avenging pack of Wolverines.

Stryke got hold of the arrow jutting from Pepperdyne's chest, thinking to remove it. Pepperdyne winced and groaned. Stryke let go. Spurral caught his eye, and almost imperceptibly, shook her head.

Coilla took her lover's hand. Pepperdyne's eyes flickered and half opened. He stared up at her face.

'Take it easy,' she whispered. 'We'll patch you up and—'

'No . . . my love,' he replied almost too softly to be heard. 'I'm . . . beyond . . . patching up.'

'Don't leave me, Jode.'

'I'll . . . never . . . leave you.'

Coilla squeezed his hand tighter. 'How can I go on? How can I live without you?' She turned to Serapheim and his kin. 'Can't you do something?' she pleaded. 'With your great powers, surely—'

Serapheim shook his head sadly. 'There are limits to even our abilities. Some things must take their course. I'm sorry.'

Desolate, she returned her gaze to Pepperdyne. He tried to speak again, and Coilla had to put her ear to his mouth to catch what he said. Whatever it was, it brought the flicker of a smile to her face before grief replaced it.

Epilogue I

Stryke, Jup, Spurral, Pelli Madayar and Standeven stood in the semi-arid wastes of a drought-ridden slice of Maras-Dantia. The sun beat down without mercy, the air was verging on foul.

'This isn't fair,' Standeven whined. 'You could at least have brought me somewhere other than Kantor Hammrik's fiefdom.'

Stryke pointed across the desert. 'I reckon if you walk for about three days in that direction you'll be out of it.'

'I've no supplies, no proper clothing, no—'

'Here's a bottle of water. You better make it last.'

Standeven snatched it. 'I was as upset about what happened to Jode as any of you, you know.'

'Yeah, right.'

He was still whining and muttering curses when the others vanished and left him to it.

Stryke, Jup, Spurral and Pelli looked out at a considerably more pleasant world. It was blessed with fecundity and almost entirely unspoilt. In the valley below was a small village of round huts and longhouses. Smoke lazily climbed from cooking stoves, and in an adjacent field cattle were grazing.

'A world comprised solely of dwarfs,' Pelli said, sweeping an arm at the scene. 'The Corps has had contact with the inhabitants before, and we're on good terms. They're expecting you down there. Just mention my name.'

Jup and Spurral thanked her, then turned to Stryke. Pelli moved off to a discreet distance.

'Well, we've already had our goodbyes,' Jup said, 'and you know I'm not one for emotional gestures, so I'm offering you my hand, Stryke.'

Stryke took it in a warriors' grasp and squeezed hard.

'You and your *I'm not one for emotional gestures*,' Spurral teased as she shoved past Jup. 'Well, I am.' She gave Stryke a powerful hug, her head not quite up to the level of his chest. 'Thank you, Captain. For everything.'

'And you,' he returned.

Spurral had tears in her eyes. Jup pretended there was a speck of dirt in his.

They didn't linger, but set off down the hill to their new life.

Stryke and Pelli watched them go.

'Is Coilla going to be all right?' she asked.

He sighed. 'I hope so. There's a great sadness weighing on her now. But just before we came here she told me about something that I think is going to keep her mind off it for a while.'

'I trust time will heal her. Oh, there's just one more thing, Stryke.' She held out her hand.

He dug into his belt bag and produced the instrumentalities. For a moment he studied them, then handed them over.

'Sorry to part with them?' she asked as she slipped them into her tunic.

'No.' He thought about it. 'Well, yes *and* no.'

She smiled. 'They do have an enticing quality. But the Corps is right. They shouldn't be abroad.'

'I'll drink to that.'

'Come on, let's get you all home.'

Epilogue II

In the months that followed, the destruction Jennesta had brought to the orcs' settlement on Ceragan was cleared up. New long-houses were built and corrals repaired.

The more personal hurts took longer to fade.

Stryke wandered through a fine summer's day. The sky was blue, the birds were singing, there was abundant game in the vales, forests and rivers.

He passed Thirzarr, sitting at a wooden bench outside their lodge, chopping a carcass with a razor-keen hatchet. They exchanged a smile. Nearby, Haskeer was fooling on the grass with Corb and Janch, the hatchlings fit to burst with laughter. Stryke increased his pace a little at that point, lest Haskeer collar him to say, once more, how right he'd been about Dallog.

Wheam and his father, Quoll, were sitting on the steps of the chieftain's longhouse. Wheam was plinking on his battered goblin lute. Quoll was acting as if he enjoyed it.

Farther along, in a quieter corner, he spotted Coilla sitting on the ground by Pepperdyne's grave, a spot she still came to fre-quently. He went to her.

When she saw him she said, 'What do you think Jode would have thought of it here?'

'I reckon he would have liked it. Might have been a bit of a change from what he was used to though.'

'I don't think he minded change. None of us should. Didn't somebody say the only thing that stays constant is change?'

'Probably. And it's just as well you feel that way.' He reached out and gave her greatly swollen stomach an affectionate pat. 'Because nothing's going to be the same again.'